THE

FREDERICK

MANFRED

READER

Frederick Manfred's Works

THROUGH 1951, Manfred used the name Feike Feikema. All works listed here represent first publication; some have appeared in later editions by other publishers. Stories, essays, and other individual items published in periodicals but uncollected are not included here. An full annotated bibliography of Manfred's works through 1980 may be found in *Frederick Manfred: A Bibliography and Publishing History*, by Rodney J. Mulder and John H. Timmerman, published by Augustana College's Center for Western Studies in 1981.

The Golden Bowl, St. Paul, Webb Publishing Company, 1944.

Boy Almighty, St. Paul, Itasca Press, 1945.

This Is the Year, Garden City, Doubleday, 1947.

The Chokecherry Tree , Garden City, Doubleday, 1948.

The Primitive, Garden City, Doubleday, 1949.

The Brother, Garden City, Doubleday, 1950.

The Giant, Garden City, Doubleday, 1951.

Lord Grizzly, New York, McGraw-Hill, 1954.

Morning Red, Denver, Alan Swallow, 1956.

Riders of Judgment, New York, Random House, 1957.

Conquering Horse, New York, McDowell, Obolensky, 1959.

Arrow of Love, Denver, Alan Swallow, 1961 (stories).

Wanderlust, Denver, Alan Swallow, 1962 (Trilogy: *The Primitive, The Brother, The Giant,* revised and published in one volume).

Scarlet Plume, New York, Trident Press, 1964.

The Man Who Looked Like the Prince of Wales, New York, Trident Press, 1965 (published in paperback as *The Secret Place*, New York, Pocket Books, 1967).

Winter Count, Minneapolis, James D. Thueson, 1966 (poems).

King of Spades, New York, Trident Press, 1966.

Apples of Paradise and Other Stories, New York, Trident Press, 1968.

Eden Prairie, New York, Trident Press, 1968.

Conversations with Frederick Manfred, moderated by John R. Milton, Salt Lake City, University of Utah Press, 1974.

Writing in the West, Deland, Florida, Everett/Edwards, 1974 (recorded lecture).

The Manly-Hearted Woman, New York, Crown, 1975.

Milk of Wolves, Boston, Avenue Victor Hugo, 1976.

Green Earth, New York, Crown, 1977.

The Wind Blows Free: A Reminiscence , Sioux Falls, Augustana College Center for Western Studies, 1979.

Sons of Adam, New York, Crown, 1980.

American Grizzly, Minneapolis, CIE, 1983 (video portrait).

Dinkytown, Minneapolis, Dinkytown Antiquarian Bookstore, 1984.

Winter Count II, Minneapolis, James D. Thueson, 1987 (poems).

Prime Fathers, Salt Lake City, Howe, 1988 (essays).

The Selected Letters of Frederick Manfred, 1932–1954 , edited by Arthur R. Huseboe and Nancy Owen Nelson, Lincoln, University of Nebraska Press, 1989.

Flowers of Desire, Salt Lake City, Dancing Badger, 1989.

No Fun on Sunday, Norman, University of Oklahoma Press, 1990.

Of Lizards and Angels, Norman, University of Oklahoma Press, 1992.

Portrait, St. Paul, KTCA-TV, 1992 (video interview by Freya Manfred)

Duke's Mixture, Sioux Falls, Augustana College Center for Western Studies, 1993 (miscellany).

The Wrath of Love (unpublished).

Black Earth (unpublished).

THE
Frederick
Manfred
Reader

Edited by
John Calvin Rezmerski

HOLY COW! PRESS
Duluth, Minnesota
1996

We gratefully acknowledge permission to reprint excerpts from the following sources:
From *No Fun on Sunday: A Novel*, by Frederick Manfred. Copyright © 1990 by Freder-
ick Feikema Manfred. Published by the University of Oklahoma Press. From *Of Lizards
and Angels: A Saga of Siouxland*, by Frederick Manfred. Copyright © 1992 by Frederick
Feikema Manfred. Published by the University of Oklahoma Press. From *The Chokecherry
Tree*, "Brother Can You Spare a Dime," Copyright © 1932 by Harems, Inc., lines from
"Who's Afraid of the Big Bad Wolf," Copyright © 1933 by Bourne, Inc., lines from "And
It Comes Out Here," Copyright © 1935 by Saintly-Joy, Inc., New York, New York, "Danc-
ing Cheek to Cheek," is used by permission of Irving Berlin Music Corporation. From
The Golden Bowl, Golden Anniversary Edition, Copyright © 1992 by Frederick Manfred.
Published by the South Dakota Humanities Foundation. From *Prime Fathers*, Copyright
© 1988 by Frederick Manfred. Published by Howe Brothers.

Library of Congress Cataloging-in-Publication Data

Manfred, Frederick Feikema, 1912–1994.
    (Selections, 1996)
    The Frederick Manfred reader / edited by John Calvin Rezmerski.
        p. cm.
    Includes bibliographical references.
    ISBN 0-930100-67-0
    1. West (U.S.)—Literary collections. 2. Western stories.
    I. Rezmerski, John Calvin. II. Title.
    PS3525.A52233A6 1996
    813'.54—dc20   95-25872
                                                                  CIP

This project is supported, in part, by grants from the Literature Program of the National
Endowment for the Arts in Washington, D.C., The Arrowhead Regional Arts Council
through an appropriation from the Minnesota State Legislature, The Estate of Frederick Feikema Manfred, The Council for Arts & Humanities (Rock County, Minnesota),
Elmer L. Andersen, Mara Kirk Hart, and by other generous individuals.

In memory of
the Fathers,
Lefty and Sam

Acknowledgments

GREAT THANKS first of all to Fred, the cause of it all, and godfather to so many of us writers of Greater Siouxland.

And gratitude, too, to the Estate of Frederick Manfred, for permission to use the works that make up the body of this volume. Grateful acknowledgement is made to the University of Oklahoma Press for permission to use selections from *Of Lizards and Angels* and *No Fun on Sunday*; and to Lynn Milton and the estate of the late John Milton for permission to use selections from *Conversations with Frederick Manfred,* an indispensable book for anyone who wants to understand Manfred's world-view. John Milton's contributions to our understanding of the West, and to literature generally are inestimable. Thanks also to the Center for Western Studies at Augustana College for photographs.

The editor wishes especially to thank Joe Paddock, who first conceived the idea for *The Frederick Manfred Reader*, who summoned together the editorial committee, and who continued to offer advice, ideas, and encouragement throughout the time the project was underway. Gratitude is due also to the other committee members for their efforts and encouragement: Bill Holm, Nancy Paddock, Chuck Woodard, and Freya Manfred. Freya's assistance with photographs, permissions, and information was especially generous. Arthur Huseboe also offered encouragement and assistance.

Lynn Fellerman and Beth Luwandi made great contributions to the editing effort, not only by doing most of the filing, copying, and library work, but also by reading, note-taking, evaluating, interviewing, transcribing interviews, and compiling databases. The editor is deeply grateful for their competence, diligence, and enthusiasm for Fred Manfred's work and for the work of this project. Jane Devlin and Gretchen Michlitsch are due special thanks for their assistance above and beyond the call of duty in scanning and typing seemingly endless pages. Jeanine Genelin gave invaluable assistance in transcribing tapes.

This project was supported in large part by a grant from the Minnesota Private College Research Foundation with funds provided by the Blandin Foundation of Grand Rapids, Minnesota. The editor especially thanks Dr. Chandra Mehrotra, Program Evaluator for the Foundation, for his kind encouragement and advice.

Contents

WORK

SECTION FOUR
Leaves

Introduction

THIS BOOK IS A SAMPLER of Manfred's work and an introduction to the world he depicts, presenting in a single volume an overview of his vision of Siouxland and some of the major themes associated with it, entirely (except for this introduction) in his own words. *The Frederick Manfred Reader* is intended to expose and explore the varied textures of his writing. The first-time reader is offered an opportunity to sample the magnitude, range and vitality of his achievement. The reader already acquainted with some of his novels is offered opportunities to develop insights about the stories' relationships to one another in the context of Manfred's personalized vision of Siouxland history.

Manfred: Man and Writer

FREDERICK FEIKEMA MANFRED was born Frederick Feikema at Doon, Iowa, in 1912, the son of farmers of Frisian descent. Raised in the Christian Reformed Church, he graduated from Calvin College, Grand Rapids, Michigan, in 1934. After graduating, he hitchhiked both east and west, working at various jobs, and lived for a while in New Jersey. In 1937 he became a sports reporter for the Minneapolis Journal and the next year helped to organize the American Newspaper Guild. Tuberculosis put him in Glen Lake Sanatorium in 1940. After his release two years later, he married fellow patient Maryanna Shorba (from whom he was later divorced). They have three children, Freya, Marya, and Frederick. Manfred began his full-time writing career in 1943. His first novel, *The Golden Bowl*, was published under the name Feike Feikema, a name he used until 1951, when he legally changed it to its present form. Beginning with *Lord Grizzly*, his books appeared under the name Frederick Manfred. He lived in Minneapolis, Bloomington, and finally Luverne, Minnesota. He taught for a brief time at Macalester College, and served as Writer in Residence at the University of South Dakota. He was six feet nine inches tall. He died on September 7, 1994.

Manfred was a writer. He was not a farmer who wrote, not a teacher who did some writing on the side. From the time he was in college, he wanted to be a writer. From his earliest childhood, he thought about being a writer. When, as an adult, he became a newspaper reporter, he recognized that he did not want to be a reporter, he wanted to be a writer of fiction. Then he did what few people who want to be writers do. He stopped working at other things and started writing. For fifty years, he wrote. That was his job, and he did it every day five days a week, and thought about it on the other two days. When he built a house, he built a room specially designed to be a writing studio. When he built another house, he did the same thing, only better. Besides that, he had a little shack where he also wrote. Above the desk in the shack, he kept a chart planning the books he intended to write. He was not the kind of writer who shut the world out of his life while he was working on a book; he put in a certain number of hours each day at the typewriter, and devoted the rest of the day to the world around him. Nearly all the way around his "tipi," the turret-like room that was his study, were windows that let him look out over the broad sweep of prairies and bluffs, the fields, the roads, and the river.

He had a good-sized personal library both in the tipi and in the living area of the house. In the tipi were editions of the books he had written, some of them in translation, and his special favorites: Chaucer in Skeat's edition, Shakespeare in both English and Frisian, Robert Penn Warren's novels, Thoreau, Melville, Whitman, Steinbeck, Smollett, Fielding, Boswell, Faulkner, Hemingway, Emily Dickinson, Twain, Edmund Wilson, James Agee, Walker Percy, Raymond Chandler, along with several versions of *The Odyssey*, *The Iliad*, and Greek drama, three versions of Don Quixote, and Charles Montagu Doughty's works.

This room also housed the books he used for research. There were the volumes that might be expected in anyone's library: dictionaries, encyclopedias, an almanac, the Bible. But Manfred's reference collection also included Bergen and Cornelia Evans' *A Dictionary of Americanisms*, Johnson's dictionary, an encyclopedia of Friesland, a book of Frisian fairy tales, a *Phonology and Grammar of Modern West Frisian*, several critical books on Chaucer, Mencken's *American Language* with supplements, Adams' *Western Words*, Fowler, Jespersen, and dozens of other books on language, etymology, and specialized vocabularies. Some of these glossaries included Fred's marginal notations: which words he planned to use, which characters might use them in which books, which words he had already used. And there were the books he used for reference in connection with the various project on which he was working: medical books, the 1902 Sears-Roebuck catalog, county histories from Minnesota, Iowa, and South Dakota, *The British in Iowa*, *Pioneer Women*, *The Red Lamp of Incest*, and dozens of books on sex, both scholarly and popular. Lots of books on the West.

When Manfred started planning a book, he researched it thoroughly. His papers, preserved in the University of Minnesota archives, include the notebooks he used in preparing to write his novels. They show his exhaustive research and planning. The notebook for *Sons of Adam*, for example, includes a list of over a hundred terms used for various jobs in meat-packing plants. Fred made sure he knew the difference between a butt puller, a crotch breaker, and a rumper, between a stenciler and a tagger. The notebooks are full of lists of possible character names, sometimes dozens of possibilities for a single character. Each character is sketched out in detail, often including phrases that the character uses, and personal habits. Plots are also laid out carefully, and details of setting, and notes about the real persons on whom characters were based, and

where more information about them might be obtained. And he would specu-
late on the psychology of his characters. As he said:

> I try to let them run their own life in the book. And set up a tableau
> where people are moving around. And if possible I like to have them speak
> their own lines. Every character has the right to his or her own paragraph.
> And so on. That way instead of telling the story you show it. Then you
> don't have to worry about point of view. You just let them talk and it
> isn't important where the author sits, because pretty soon I'm gone and
> you can't sit in my brain, either literally or figuratively . . . Before I start a
> story, all the characters are clear in my brain. I know what they look like
> and I know where it's going to be. I know what the weather is like.

Sometimes these notebooks run over a hundred pages. Sometimes they were
completed over a very long time. For example, his earliest notes for *Of Lizards
and Angels* and *The Wrath of Love* were recorded in 1943, before his first book
was published.

This is not to portray Manfred as a bookworm, or to imply that he has merely
constructed his books out of bits and pieces from other books. If one reads *The
Wind Blows Free* or *Prime Fathers,* or the letters or conversations, it becomes
clear exactly to what extent Manfred is an autobiographical writer. It is not only
that the specifics of his life are represented (with or without alteration) in his
stories; it is also that the concerns of his life find their way into his fiction. His
ongoing disagreement with Christianity and its institutions, for instance, is not
just continuance of an adolescent conflict; he describes himself as being concerned to maintain in his books a kind of open-endedness that his Calvinistic
church would not allow. "I was accused one time of being a man filled with
free will," he said in an interview. "Free will is right."

Philosophical concerns often drive his fiction. When Manfred revisited Calvin
College, he sought out his old philosophy teacher, Dr. Jellema:

> I was told I could only see him for a half-hour or hour because he was very
> old. But once I arrived in his house, he kept waving his nephew away and
> he said, leave him alone, I want to keep him here. So I was with him from
> about 9:00 until 5:00, all day long. And I brought it up to him, I said,
> "Remember, you only gave me B's because I arrived at [my conclusions]
> intuitively."
>
> "Yes, I have to tell you this," he said, "Now philosophers know that
> the intuitive method is a legitimate form of inquiry philosophically."
>
> "In other words," I said, "I would now get A's."
>
> He said, "Yes."
>
> And I said to him, "I have something else I want to throw at you . . .
> A very good epic poet or a very good novelist, say Tolstoy or Robert

Penn Warren, isn't what they do when they write also a legitimate form of philosophical inquiry?"

He sat back a little while. He started to smile. "I know why you asked that—because in a sense you want to have some vindication or validation in what you're doing—but you're right."

That's what you get for asking a question.

There is also a spontaneous, physical, sensual dimension to Manfred's writing. He has the ability to physically feel what his characters feel, to imagine himself in a character's body, that comes from his own keen senses and appreciation of them. In 1945, he wrote to Van Wyck Brooks:

> I am sitting here in the sunlight right now, looking through an enormous plate glass window, facing our valley—the Minnesota River—and looking down it for twenty miles. All afternoon the shadows have been changing. The valley varies from minute to minute. The windmills on the horizon seem to walk across the hills. The farms, below, and above on the hills, spread out like vast sheets of linen white. And I am eating a red apple, snapping the bites into my mouth, tasting the running juices, suckling it and thoroughly enjoying it, exciting my taste bulbs, and enjoying the moment to the full. For I am writing a friend, someone who knows exactly what I mean when I write about the wind brushing back the green grass from the forehead of the hills.

That clarity of sensory experience was always important to Manfred's writing—as important as the philosophical inquiry. One of the indicators of his achievement as a writer is the way in which the two modes go along with each other, neither disrupting or contradicting the other, and both of them integrated seamlessly (usually) into the material that has come from his life and the research he did. For all their surface simplicity, there is always a great deal going on at several levels (and not hidden) in the straightforward narratives he delivers. In Jungian terms, Manfred took steps to make sure he was using all four mental faculties when he wrote: thinking, feeling, sensation, and intuition. That carefulness contributes heavily to the feeling of integrity, of wholeness, in his work; I think that is one reason why even people who disagree with his views nevertheless do not stop reading him. Another reason (as his daughter Freya Manfred told me in a letter) is that "With Fred Manfred, you want a story, you get a story! Even if you don't agree with the writer's philosophy. . . or don't like a character, you can't stop reading because it's a bang-up story, pulling you along. You wanna know what happens!"

Wallace Stegner and others have noted that Manfred has "made a fictional country, and peopled it, and given it a history." But there is an aspect of Manfred's creation of a "fictional country" that has been rarely noted. He has created not merely a fictive region (a kind of alternate world in which there is a town called Bonnie where our world has a town named Doon, in which Savage has been replaced by Brokenhoe and Luverne is named Whitebone, and in which nevertheless, Sioux Falls is still Sioux Falls and Minneapolis and St. Paul are still the Twin Cities) but also fictive characters with fictive families who have (it must be said) a fictive immigrant background (Manfred's view of Friesland and Frisians owes perhaps as much to his appetite for a good story as to documented history), and several fictive versions of himself, even in the non-fiction writings. And all these characters speak a fictive language. What seems not to have been noticed is the core philosophical principle at work in his creation: a strong strain of solipsism in his work, evident in many ways, starting (for convenience) with his desire to turn his B's in college philosophy courses into A's by legitimizing his fictional investigations of the world as philosophical inquiry. It may be that fiction is an avenue for legitimate philosophical inquiry, but the significant point here is that Manfred felt obligated to redefine his experience and the consensus that emerged from it. We can also see his solipsistic bent at work in his stated rationale for writing the Buckskin Man stories: "I wanted to be my own progenitor." It appears again in his accounts of his reading experience, and his abiding goal of making the public see that Doughty is a writer who ranks with Chaucer, above Shakespeare.

This ranking shows us something important about Manfred's literary values. Manfred thought Shakespeare too contrived, too much infused with the values of the nobility, too Latinate in his language, too devoted to verbal cleverness for its own sake. He liked better Chaucer's earthiness, unaffectedness, and sympathy with people of all classes. He thought Chaucer understood humanity better than Shakespeare, and tried to follow Chaucer in his devotion to depicting both the workings of the broader society and the most ordinary motives, emotions, and activities of individual characters.

This is true in both the serious and comic works. Hugh Glass, while of heroic stature, achieves his heroism not from abstract notions of honor and nobility, but from his anger at being abandoned, his simple desire to stay alive, to fill his belly, and finally, to see from his experience that others are like him in their needs. Elof Lofbloom is no Lysander or Demetrius, much less an Oberon or Puck, but neither is he a Bottom or a Flute; he is neither wit, nor trickster, nor buffoon. He is what he is—your neighbor, or even yourself—a person who bumbles through life trying to do right, trying to be happy, trying to make something of himself and to experience, however inexpertly, some romance along the way.

Manfred not only preferred Chaucer to Shakespeare, but also elevated Doughty above Shakespeare as a manipulator of language and as a depictor of the physical world, and took Doughty as his role-model: "When a man can so write about an experience that you, the reader, feel lonesome for his life, like a grownup longing for the good old days of youth, that sir is writing." Like Doughty, Manfred had a strong urge to reconstitute the language, Manfred doing so because

he wanted to make it more strongly American, in addition to restoring it to its
historical Anglo-Frisian vigor. Whatever Doughty's merits, and in spite of his
salubrious effects on Manfred's aspirations, it clearly took a great leap of solipsistic faith to assign him a star higher than Shakespeare's.

By Manfred's own account, this solipsism, this desire, intention, and discipline of redefining the world in one's own terms was present even in his youth-
ful baseball fantasies:

> Somehow I got to Catalina Island and I had a picture of myself taking the
> boat over, because that's when the Cubs trained over there. . . . And I would
> picture what the boat looked like and then I would show up and the man-
> ager would take a look at me and say, "My God, we don't got a uniform
> big enough to fit him. But we'll find one for him." I just visualized the
> whole business . . . So pretty soon my arm is limbered up . . . And I started
> throwing to those tough batters in there . . . And I'd get up on the mound.
> See, this is all in my imagination: how I would wind up and I'd see where
> the batter was standing and I'd start the ball down and I'd start seeing it
> going. And I'd think, "Oh, my God, it's the wrong pitch!" And I'd pull it
> back. In my head, see. That's as real as it was to me. That's what I mean
> by seeing it. You really see it. And then you describe what you see.

The most telling part of this account is that he was able to call back a pitch when
he felt he had thrown the wrong one. This is not simple fantasizing, but a fully
developed solipsistic exercise.

Stegner seems to have caught on to Manfred's solipsism (though he does not
precisely label it) when he tells us, "Reality is too small for him."

To call Manfred a solipsist, moreover, is not to disparage him or his talent.
His solipsism may be the source of his talent for fiction, may be the glue that
held together his philosophical, intuitive, autobiographical, historical, and sensory impulses and made of them a disciplined fiction, and allowed him to create the coherent fictive world in which he could crusade against the tyranny of
religion while loving his pious mother, his prudish aunt, and his steadfastly
Christian philosophy professor. It may also be what allowed him to present such
a comprehensive picture of Siouxland, allowed him to harmonize the virtues
of wilderness and American Indian attitudes toward the land with an agricultural vision in which Pier Frixen could be a hero even while ruining his land and
helping to create the Dust Bowl, and in which farming could be seen as the model
of cultural virtue even while the theocratic farmers practice a way of life that
creates riches for a few and misery and poverty for others. If Manfred had not
been a solipsist, he could never have made so much of his life. We should be
grateful for the many transformations he worked upon it in loving detail and
great variety.

Solipsism is one of the cornerstones of American literature. Much of what
has been called visionary or utopian in our literature is really not utopian in any

traditional Platonic or Howellsian sense. It springs not from abstract ideals of justice or political and economic theories, but from our urges to continually redefine ourselves and to make the world into whatever we need it to be. "Go West, Young Man, and Make Something of Yourself." Thoreau was a solipsist. Whitman was a solipsist. Ahab was a solipsist. Jay Gatsby was a solipsist who couldn't cut it. Manfred was a solipsist, but an uncommonly disciplined one, and as a result he has created in Siouxland a Midwest that is both better and more liberally principled than the Midwest that the rest of us have created.

For the Midwest, Frederick Manfred's work epitomizes the literature of place. He coined the name "Siouxland" to refer to the region in which most of his work is set: Minnesota, South Dakota, Iowa, and Nebraska, and especially the region where those states meet near the confluence of the Big Sioux and Missouri rivers. The name "Siouxland" has entered the vernacular and is now used by both scholars and business people to describe the region once ranged by the tribes called Sioux, an area with its own characteristic pattern of social, economic, and cultural evolution.

Manfred details that pattern for us in his works. The books tell of the ways of the Dakota before the coming of the whites, the early intrusions of the fur traders and "mountain men," the encroachments of settlers and soldiers, the hardships of pioneer life, the growth of farming communities, and the contemporary lifeways which developed from this history. His books deal with all the strata of society, vividly depicting the situations and roles in which men, women, and children discover themselves within these cultural contexts. In down-to-earth fashion, he incarnates the myths people of the region have lived by, and documents details of life at an earlier time that have mostly been missed by historians and collectors of artifacts. His mythography of the frontier is not like the Hollywood version—it is rooted in human frailty, a sense of kinship, and an appreciation of the work people do. For example, he not only tells us about the economic importance of the horse in early twentieth-century agriculture, and not only describes for us the equipment used in farming, but shows us what it felt like to be a boy plowing behind a horse. He has the true novelist's eye for detail, instinct for incorporation of others' reported memories, and ear for the language of the people.

He has done for Siouxland what Faulkner did for the South, and like Faulkner he is not simply a regionalist (though the Eastern literary establishment has often treated him like one—by ignoring him, to his chronic disadvantage, both artistically and financially). The late poet William Stafford wrote: "All art is local, somewhere." And Charles Woodard reminds us that when Faulkner turned to his own home county for his chief subject matter, "Because his novels were so specifically, energetically, passionately about his place, they were also about everywhere else." Woodard could as well have been talking about Manfred.

As with Faulkner, and as with Sinclair Lewis, Manfred's work is unified by a vision, a sense of universal conflicts being played out and resolved. These aspects of Manfred's work have been examined and praised by scholars and by such fellow novelists as Wallace Stegner and Robert Penn Warren, but there has been no comprehensive reprinting of Manfred's works, and no single collection of Manfred's work that lays out the scope and detail of his vision—that does for Manfred's work what Malcolm Cowley's *The Portable Faulkner* did for Faulkner. Ironically, Manfred credits Cowley's collection with enabling him to appreciate Faulkner after having been ready to give up on reading him. Since many of Manfred's works are either out of print or not easily available, there is a whole new generation of readers mostly unfamiliar with his perceptive depictions of the roots from which so many of them sprang, and of his mighty wrestling with the same conflicts inherent in rural life with which so many of them now struggle.

This is not to say that the only appropriate audience for Manfred's books is a primarily rural audience. There is no more reason to consider *This Is the Year* a book that only farmers can appreciate than to consider *Catcher in the Rye* a book for prep-school students or to think of Chinua Achebe's *Things Fall Apart* as a book that only Nigerian villagers can appreciate. Manfred immersed himself in the best of what European and American culture have to offer, and a good deal more besides. He was insatiably literate, inquisitive about physics, astronomy, linguistics, archaeology, anthropology, music, painting, architecture, botany, local gossip, the literary politics of New York, the give-and-take of political campaigning at the state and national level. . . . And that literacy and curiosity made him stick his nose and his fingers into the corners and crannies of American culture, and let him write of his beloved Siouxland in full consciousness of the whole America and the whole universe he revered with full Whitmaniac earnestness and energy.

I have mentioned Manfred's "vision," without describing it in detail. It has several components. One of them is historical, including the relationship between Indians and the land, the conflict between the white takers of the land and the Indians, the formation (or failure to form) new attachments to the land on the part of whites, the abuse of the land that led to the Dust Bowl, followed by new prosperity and a flight to the cities. A second component is cultural, including the manifold mutual artistic, religious, social, and linguistic influences and conflicts among Indians, native Anglo-Americans, and immigrants. A third is a thoroughgoing materialism, not in the cliched and debased sense in which the term is most commonly used, but in a sense that finds expression in love of physical detail, devotion to manual labor, awareness of our animal nature, and skepticism about religious and spiritual claims; for Manfred, "spirituality" appears to be a blend of relatedness, empathy, creativity and sensitivity to nature. The fourth component of his vision is sexual, an awareness of the ways in which the sexual drive motivates behavior while the "authorities" (especially the Church) try to use sexual guilt to control people's lives; Manfred has been accused of being obsessed with sex, but careful reading of his works will show that his writing is remarkably free of the hysteria and shame-boundness that characterize so much of our public discourse about sex.

The unifying element in "the Manfred vision" is best introduced through Manfred's notion that we carry inside us the "Old Lizard," not exactly the Id, not quite the "old Adam" or "Old Eve," not precisely an archetype, but an actual physical entity, the brain-stem that is an anatomical relic of our reptile ancestors. The Old Lizard both links us with the dinosaur and tells us that what the preacher is saying is contrary to our interests. The Old Lizard gives us our instinct for self-preservation. The Old Lizard wants to reproduce. And the Old Lizard is held in check by our neocortex, which allows us to imagine, to create, to aspire to the stars, and to love. Because we are beings in which the neocortex and the Old Lizard maneuver around each other, we are both believers and freethinkers, lovers and rapists, workers and thieves, stewards of the land and despoilers of it. We have made a world in our image, and we cannot live in it successfully without taking account of both the cool lizard and the warm mammal. From that relationship between the parts of our own brain, we project our relationships to each other, to other cultures, and to the land we occupy. We see this thematic complex working itself out over and over in Manfred's chronicles of Siouxland.

In creating Siouxland, Manfred provided a template against which we can measure "the real world." Manfred felt not only a sense of mission, to seek his truth and to say it (and not a single, monolithic truth), but also to make it work in life. He developed this sense quite early in his career. In 1944, he wrote to Paul Hillestad:

> I believe we are much more animal than we think we are, and also much more "lighted" than we think we are. And this belief or hypothesis (for that is what it is since Reality is always eluding me or eluding the scientists, though the more we find out about it, the more impersonal we discover it to be) has given me less headache and less heartache than any other, and has given me more fun, has given me the outlines of a greater challenge to do something. In fact, the greater the universe and the more insignificant I become in it, the greater is my urge to cut my mark on the stone of eternity (which in time will also wear away). I've had more ambition to do things since I've discovered this hypothesis than ever before. It has given me enough dignity . . . to accept my wife's true nature and to want to live with her, to forgive or to live with my mother-in-law, to keep my eyes relatively free of wild patriotic fervor about this War (for I still think that wanton killing is terrible in the sense that we are robbing ourself of a little victory).

In October, 1946, he wrote a long letter to President Truman, concerning the atomic bomb. In the letter he says he has developed the feeling that Truman is not paying attention to "advice from the most society-minded brains of our time." He says:

> Mr. President, let us put this on a personal basis. Should the Atomic War detonate over us, it will mean your death. No longer will you be able to play your piano, and take your brisk walks, and attend family picnics, and play poker with your jokesters.
> It will mean the death of your daughter, Margaret. No longer will there be a dear daughter getting a diploma, a dear child with an arch smile, and pictures in the society sections of the nation.
> It will mean the death of your wife . . .
> It will mean the death of your aged mother.
>
> Imagine a family taking a ride in the cool of a green evening. Suppose too, by some twist of fate, or accident, that the irresponsible member of the family somehow got behind the wheel, and that the other members out of a sense of politeness, and even fairness, decided to tolerate the driver for this one ride. Can you, however, imagine the family restraining itself when the driver suddenly heads the car straight for the edge of a precipice?

Manfred used essentially this same letter as one of the chapter epigraphs for *The Chokecherry Tree*. The story was clearly intended to carry this message to his readers (along with a good many other messages in that uproariously melancholy book).

He had only a few years before gone through the experience of having some of his Christian Reformed relatives and religious friends write to him implying that his long struggle with tuberculosis was a well-deserved comeuppance from an angry God tired of his trifling skepticism.

"Christianity is supposed to offer a haven and a comfort for the weak & weary in the struggle of life," he wrote to John DeBie. "To offer love. . . . I still . . . write kindly and frankly to my relatives. To explain. My wife thinks I am a fool for doing it. But I cannot forget that once I too was ignorant and humble . . . and that, if you listen closely to my footsteps on the walk, you can still hear the footfall of the farmer."

Indeed, as Manfred has acknowledged, even though he did not become a domeny as his family had wished, he became something more of a preacher by going his own way and speaking his own sense of the way things are and could be. His goal was always to show us that the world can be better if we undertake to make it so, if we change our thinking, if we practice forgiveness and reconciliation.

Manfred's innate appreciation of practicality and the way the world really works makes it clear that *action* is required of good citizens. We must not passively stand by while the irresponsible among us try to send us over a precipice.

Standing together does not require running together like proverbial lemmings; on the other hand, that we are urged to act like lemmings should make us fear neither standing together nor standing alone. We are invited to participate in a project for solipsists; by so doing, we may improve our world and make Siouxland, the Midwest, the World, the Universe, a fit place for intelligent and sensitive beings. The solipsist may be solitary, but because he is intellectually and emotionally engaged in creating and sustaining the world and its society, he has an enormous stake in justice, peace, and mutual understanding. His notions of peace and justice are not abstractly derived, but are constructed out of the particular acts and motives of individuals, beginning with himself. For the solipsist, universal truths are not created at the world's inception, but are made by individuals studying individuals and reacting to them. That makes them no less universal and no less valuable.

Robert Wright, one of Manfred's most insightful critics, used similar terms, speaking specifically of *Scarlet Plume* and *Conquering Horse*: "Because these fictions do get at universal truths and move people's hearts toward reconciliation, Manfred's books are to be cherished as instruments of peace." Manfred read that quotation to me one time; nothing pleased him more than to recognize that it was true.

Manfred, the Readers, and the Critics

WHEN I FIRST VISITED Minnesota years ago in the company of Bill Holm, Bill's mother, a vigorous and outspoken farm woman with no advanced education, but an avid reader, was telling him about some of Fred Manfred's legal problems, which were reaching the pages of newspapers.

"Who's Frederick Manfred?" I said.

"You mean you're an English major and you don't even know who Manfred is?" she asked, genuinely appalled.

That's the way Manfred's regular readers are. Either they take his greatness for granted and think everyone else does too, or they directly bypass conventional notions of greatness and think of him simply as someone who is important to *them*, as if to say, "It might not be great literature, but I know what I like."

Recently, another friend told me that all my talk about Manfred had moved him to go to his local public library and see what all the fuss was about. What he discovered was that Manfred's books were always *out*; he had to put his name on a waiting list.

Whatever Manfred's critical reputation—and I believe it is secure and bound to grow—it is clear that he has readers, eager readers, loyal readers.

But there's that disturbing phrase: "Whatever his critical reputation." Critical esteem for his work has not been universal. Nor have all of his readers become loyal fans. Reviewers have often commented stupidly about his books. That old bugaboo of Midwestern writers, The Awful Eastern Literary Establishment, was rarely kind to him, and often patronizing. Bluestockings and bluenoses have taken him to task. Some citizens of Doon once put up a sign proclaiming it home of the famous novelist, and another group, not wanting their town to be sullied by the reputation of the prodigal son, defaced the sign, which was eventually removed. (Doon newspaper editor Harold Aardema said, "Manfred won in the end, for he was gracious and forgiving.") Even members of his family attacked him for the things he wrote.

Some literary lights have been ambivalent about Manfred's work. Wallace Stegner has said, "He is not a writer in the usual sense. He is a natural force, related to hurricanes, deluges, volcanic eruptions, and the ponderous formation of continents." This extravagant comment does not entirely constitute praise. In the same essay, he speaks of what he takes to be Manfred's shortcomings:

> On reading and rereading Manfred I have sometimes wished that he were not as regional as he rather belligerently is. The very concentration on Siouxland that gives him is strength is also, it seems to me, a limitation in that he has nothing to compare it with, he does not see it from outside. To try to create a province, I believe, is a good thing, but not so good a thing as to try to create a world.

This objection makes me wonder whether Stegner had taken into account *Wanderlust*, Manfred's major interlude away from Siouxland and the West, a trilogy of novels about Thurs Wraldson's education in Michigan, his experiences in the East, and his encounter with Marxism. These stories wear their philosophical hearts on their somewhat tattered sleeves, and provide a clear view of where Siouxland fits into Manfred's known universe.

Manfred's view of Siouxland is almost always a view from outside, in the sense that he had felt himself so much an outsider both in the East and in Siouxland (though he continued through his life to have great affection for Doon, which he called his "social laboratory"). He was not an angry rebel, Harold Aardema recalls, but one who felt the tension between calls to the two worlds perceived by the children of immigrants: the world of home and church, and the world "out there." Free Alfredson, Hugh Glass, Elof Lofbloom, Manly Heart, Juhl Melander, No Name, Judith Raveling, and Thurs Wraldson are outsiders in their communities, heroes who either want to be (or are forced to be) "out there." Manfred himself has frequently talked about feeling like a freak. In both fiction and autobiography, he persistently tries to imagine himself (or his viewpoint characters) outside the context of home, school, town, region, time. The long sweep of American, Frisian, European, world history; the Old Lizard that keeps us linked to the time of the dinosaurs; the possibility of life on other worlds; all this is part of a universe which to Manfred is alive in imagination—which he takes to be the core of personality—not merely alive in books, but alive in his intimate awareness that neither he nor anyone else is bound or fixed at a certain point in Iowa or Minnesota, or in Calvinism or Marxism, but is traversing a continuum in which neither current position nor momentum can be determined except by pausing to observe one's interactions with others.

As I have explained in the previous section of this introduction, Manfred's bent is solipsistic. He is continually involved in the creation of a fictive world. It happens that within that world, there is a province called Siouxland, and he gives most of his attention to that province not because he is unconscious of a wider world, but because the fictive Siouxland is the place that overlaps most precisely with the familiar, where the details of interaction can be seen most precisely. But those physical details constitute no restriction of the ideas, the issues, the experiences, the ideals that Manfred pursues and attempts to enlist us in the pursuit of.

I do not mean to suggest, by the way, that Stegner is at all hostile to Manfred's work, only that conventional notions about regionalism have clouded his perception of it.

His assessment of Manfred is on the whole generous and affectionate. He sees himself as Manfred's ally:

> Writers ought to stick together against the arrogance of critics, whose function is too often to whittle a writer down to the critic's size. I have no desire to whittle Fred Manfred down. I like him the size he is, or even bigger, and I would like to see him judged, not by devotees who admire everything he does simply because it *is* regional, and not by provincials from New York who haven't the slightest notion of what he is talking about, but by fellow writers and fellow Westerners who do understand what he is doing and do feel the pull of his materials.

The conflict between New York Provincials and Plains Writers is a very real one, and has a good deal to do with why Manfred's audience has been mostly (though by no means entirely) Midwestern. The "Buckskin Man" stories (*Lord Grizzly, Conquering Horse, Riders of Judgment, Scarlet Plume, King of Spades*) have their own wider audience because they are classifiable (by publishers and bookstores) as westerns. But Manfred's other books have suffered somewhat in popularity because they have been pigeonholed as "regional."

The problem, of course, is not simply Eastern Establishment prejudice against regional *writers*. The problem is that the Easterners are most interested in their own region, and that the many Midwesterners, Southerners, and Westerners who go to the East are eager to put their roots behind them; and since the Easterners (natives and immigrants) are at the seat of power, the Other (or Outer) Provinces are not seriously considered as potential sources of anything meritorious. The Great Sneer is not directed particularly against Midwestern writers, but against the Midwest itself. And it is not entirely from the East; it has infested academia and commercial publishing in the United States generally. We can see it in its baldest form in James B. Hall's 1976 critical comments on Manfred in *Contemporary Novelists*: "On balance, possibly because of his unswerving commitment to a midwestern, American region 'Siouxland' *where the literary audience is notoriously few and unfit,* Manfred's work remains not much appreciated at the present time." [italics mine] Hall follows his sneer with a little sniff: "Presently this sub-genre of American literature is insufficiently explored possibly because it represents an old-fashioned, limited concept of the novel form." In other words, Manfred isn't "with it."

In general, *The Golden Bowl* was well received by reviewers. *Boy Almighty* was, too, although some criticized it for its "too realistic" accounts of blood and hospital life.

This Is the Year got some praise, and was even a Pulitzer contender but the book was rebuffed by elements of the Eastern Establishment, sometimes for its language, sometimes for its plot and characters. Mark Schorer called it "a long midwest farm chronicle" which displays "a near total failure to differentiate subject from experience [*a critical hobbyhorse of the time*—JCR] and a total failure to extract theme from subject." Schorer added that it seems to be "about everything and nothing." One wonders what kind of critical blinders or impoverished range of experience could prevent a reader from seeing exactly the plainly presented themes of the book. The critical establishment also chewed Manfred up over the World's Wanderer trilogy, and sometimes seems to have missed the point of *The Chokecherry Tree.*

All those books had been published under the Feike Feikema name; with the publication of *Lord Grizzly* under the Manfred name, his reputation got a boost, and it stayed quite high during the Fifties and Sixties, a period during which his books were reviewed in newspapers nationwide, though somewhat predictably. A certain percentage of the reviews could always be counted upon to say that his sex scenes (mostly pretty tame by post-Lady Chatterley standards) were too explicit, and that his language was unnecessarily crude. But almost everyone agreed that he was a first-rate storyteller.

After the publication of *Eden Prairie,* Manfred was increasingly finding it difficult to place his books with the commercial publishing houses. His most loyal audience was aging, and younger audiences were not discovering his books, or were not finding them "relevant" when they did discover them. (Again, the "Buckskin Man" stories were exceptions). Often, Manfred's novels were not discovered because they were not available widely enough. I believe that one of the greatest misfortunes in twentieth-century American literature is that *Green Earth* did not achieve greater distribution, reach a wider audience, and gain more critical attention. It is a book whose like we have not seen, and may never see.

Green Earth is perhaps the finest example of what Manfred called the "rume." In an essay titled "A Modest Proposal Concerning the 'Rume,'" originally published as an appendix to *The Brother,* he made a useful distinction between novels, tales, and what he calls "rumes," which are long fictional ruminations on autobiographical materials. Unlike novels, rumes do not have tight plots, and they focus on the experiences of the central character rather than on events external to him. The term has not caught on, and I make no brief for it; I simply believe that Manfred has made a useful distinction, and while it is particularly useful in examining his own work, I think it also describes a genre in American literature that includes most of the novels of writers like Jack Kerouac and Henry Miller, as well as individual works like Mari Sandoz's *Old Jules*, and that is still going strong in the work of writers like Tobias Wolff.

To return to Manfred's career and critical reception, I think it is fair to say that (except for the "Buckskin Man" tales) lack of promotion by big commercial publishers, the aging of his old audience, and snobbery have combined to make his work less accessible than it ought to be, and could be. The University of Oklahoma Press is to be commended for publishing two of his most recent novels, and University of Nebraska Press and University of New Mexico for reissuing other books, as well as the Center for Western Studies for republishing *The Golden Bowl*. The "Buckskin Man" stories and *The Manly-Hearted Woman* stay in print in mass market paperbacks, and continue to sell well. Nevertheless, some of his best work is not currently available, and ought to be. We should all be thankful once again for the libraries that keep older work accessible, and for small presses like Dancing Badger and Holy Cow! which somehow find the resources to publish books like *Flowers of Desire* and *The Frederick Manfred Reader*.

Not all of Manfred's work is equally effective. But most of it is of very high quality and I think that continued critical attention will cause his reputation to grow. Many aspects of his writing have been essentially unexplored by critics—his well-researched, meticulous, and innovative use of language, for example. Some reviewers have taken him to task for using neologisms (and he does, though some of the terms that have been cited as neologisms are actually archaisms or dialect terms; reviewers and critics who rely on a desk dictionary to deal with Manfred's language are arming themselves for a sword-fight with a pocket knife). Some (with tin ears) have thought his use of certain words and names foreign to the way people actually speak; others, conversely, have considered his use of the vernacular to be too-slavish copying of colloquial speech. No fiction writer with whose work I am familiar has been as thoroughly attentive to his language as Manfred (I am not forgetting about Twain, Faulkner, or Robert Penn Warren), and if he is occasionally guilty of inaccuracy or infelicity, it is because he has failed to adequately convey a nuance he perceived, or because he attempted more than others did, but never recklessly. Attention to his language only deepens appreciation of his erudition and imagination.

It should not be presumed from any of the foregoing that Manfred has been without defenders. Quite the contrary. Among those thoroughly familiar with his work, he has been revered. His supporters have included the likes of Robert Penn Warren, William Carlos Williams, Meridel LeSueur, Thomas McGrath, and Robert Bly. As Manfred liked to tell anyone who would listen, he was nominated a few times for the Nobel Prize. He was also nominated for other prestigious awards he never received. But he never allowed himself to feel like an also-ran. For him, literature was not a race, but a baseball game.

The important principles were to train yourself, play your best, play for the right team, and stay loyal to your team. Winning was gravy. Even if you lost, you still had a pretty good time. And you kept hoping to make it to the World Series, not for the pungency of triumph, but because you liked playing ball in company of that caliber.

This Book and How It Came to Be

PLEASE DO NOT look here for a "Best of Frederick Manfred," nor for a systematic survey of the body of his work, nor for a rigorously representative selection. Nor should you expect to find the editor's personal favorites, nor Manfred's own favorites, nor favorites according to any poll of his fans, admirers, or critics. I have tried instead to provide an overview of what I think of as "the Manfred vision," a selection that displays the major constituents of Manfred's complex depiction of Siouxland during two centuries, historically, thematically, and by genre.

Constraints of space have made it necessary to exclude much that I would have liked to include. At the last stage before making the final choices, the table of contents was more than fifty percent longer. At the stage before that, I had forced myself to reduce my selections by half. When the project was just beginning, I had hoped to include something from every Manfred book, and as the advisory committee began to submit their nominations, it became clear that the task of culling would not be easy. One committee member submitted nearly four hundred pages to consider for inclusion. My own nominations from the books I had assigned myself for special attention amounted to more than four hundred additional pages. There was so much to choose from!

During his half-century professional writing career, Frederick Manfred published 22 novels (23 if we count *Wanderlust*, his combination and revision of three earlier novels into a single book). Most of those novels are of substantial length; some of them are of formidable length. He published nine other books of stories, poems, essays, memoirs and letters. At the time of his death, he had one novel (*The Wrath of Love*) seeking a publisher, had completed a draft of another (*Black Earth*). Years earlier, he had completed at least one more novel, for which he had essentially given up on finding a publisher. Additional reviews and interviews were still uncollected, and a second volume of his correspondence was being prepared for publication.

In 1990, much of Manfred's work was not in print, and much was not available in local libraries. That summer, at the instigation of Joe Paddock, a small group of area writers and scholars (Joe and Nancy Paddock, poets, oral historians, and experts on land stewardship and the literature of place; Charles Woodard of South Dakota State University, editor of *As Far as I Can See: Contemporary Writing of the Middle Plains*; Bill Holm, poet, essayist, and teacher of rural literature and immigrant literature; Freya Manfred, poet, fiction writer, and daughter of Fred Manfred; and I) met with Manfred to discuss a plan for a book that would make Fred's work readily available to new and old audiences.

We first thought in terms of a collection of samples of Fred's best prose. But as the members dug into the books they had been assigned, most found themselves unwilling to confine themselves to stylistic criteria. That was inevitable. Manfred is above all a storyteller, a compulsive and irresistible storyteller, and it was (or should have been) unthinkable for us to conceive a book that did not focus on the playing out of complete stories (though not necessarily complete novels). So almost right away, the conception of the book changed.

The book would collect a selection of stories, poems, excerpts from novels, and letters written by Manfred, along with introductions. As we discussed it, we decided that the book would provide selections of the very best of his work, while showing the breadth and depth of its development. We all agreed to carefully reread assigned Manfred books (often overlapping assignments), and to nominate selections for inclusion in the reader. I was named editor, and was assigned responsibility for coordinating the project, negotiating for publication, and writing the introductory matter. Manfred offered his full cooperation, as well as his own nominations for passages to be included. He insisted from the beginning that his nominations were not to be given special preference.

Because of other demands on the time of committee members, the process of reading and nominating selections took more than a year. There seemed no point in hurrying the process, because I had set myself the task of reading or rereading all of Manfred's books before making any decisions about what to include or exclude. In the meantime, that August I taped eight hours of interviews with Manfred at his home in Luverne, was given liberty to explore his personal library, and had begun to struggle with the problem of organizing the book: chronological in order of composition? chronological within the fictive history of Siouxland? thematic? topical? Nothing seemed quite right. In April 1991 I received a grant from the Minnesota Private College Research Foundation that enabled me to employ two student assistants for three months to work on the book. By that time, I had completed about half of my reading, had visited with Fred several times to discuss the project , and had received most of the nominations.

I recruited Lynn Fellerman and Beth Luwandi to assist me and in June began working full-time at editing the book. The summer's work included finishing my reading of Manfred's works, enlisting my assistants to read several of his books and make their own nominations, charting possible selections, coordinating my list with the suggestions received from the committee members and with Manfred's own suggestions, and gathering material for possible use in the introductions to the various selections. With such capable assistance, I was able to make much progress.

After a month, we altered the fundamental conception of the book. I freely admit that for a while we were seduced by the dark side of the Force. Bigger and better. Prompted by the amount of material that had been suggested and by our enthusiasm, we began to imagine a large-format coffee-table book. By this time, I had read the published correspondence and *The Wind Blows Free*, and had gathered much material from the University of Minnesota archives, where Manfred's papers are kept. Lynn had transcribed the taped interviews. Examining all that material led me to think of using extracts from it as annotations to the text of the stories. Then I struck the idea of having all of the introductory material be in Manfred's own words. Lynn and I had been discussing the ways in which Manfred sometimes uses the same material or similar material (often autobiographically based) in different ways in different books, and I was taken with the possibility of setting at least some parts of the book up in the form of parallel texts. Each selection could be accompanied by a column at the outside edge of the page, in which Manfred would comment on the stories' sources, their publishing history, or their critical reception. In some cases, he could provide a bit of autobiographical or historical background. In other cases, two treatments of the same subject could be juxtaposed (the initial example that occurred to me was the two descriptions of the Badlands found in *The Golden Bowl* and *The Wind Blows Free*).

That became the plan for the book, but it meant a much more thorough search for articles and interviews in which Manfred had made comments about his work. As I continued working on my reading and making selections, Lynn and Beth went to the library and began searching out articles, books, and bibliographical information. We started a set of files, each Manfred book having its own file. Each file included the passages committee members had nominated, copies of related pages chosen from the interview transcripts, letters, and essays, and notes that I had taken. We had made considerable progress—in fact, we had accumulated so much ancillary material on some books that it seemed some passages would have introductions nearly as long as the passages themselves.

Fred was enthusiastic about the idea, so we spent July 5–7 at Roundwind, Fred's home on a bluff overlooking Luverne, Minnesota, taping eight more hours of interviews and talking about the plan for the book. Fred conducted a tour of his former house (now the interpretive center of Blue Mound State Park), where he had written many of his books, and of Lyon County, Iowa, where he showed us the several houses and farmsteads where he had spent his youth, as well as the schools, churches, baseball fields, roads and towns that appear in his stories, all along the way providing a stream of commentary about the characters in his stories, where he got the ideas for plots of particular stories, and the changes that had taken place during his lifetime. Manfred is a very physical writer, and the sensory detail of his books was accentuated by our experience of the tour.

One problem persisted: how to organize *The Frederick Manfred Reader*. The amount of material to be considered was forbidding. The addition of all that supporting text made the problem even more difficult to deal with than it had been at the beginning. Obviously, I was going to have to carefully sift through likely selections and weigh the alternatives as I approached a final round of choices.

As I committed myself to selections, I found myself more and more sure that none of the chronological, thematic or topical approaches would work. I was afraid I would have to mix and match, as awkward as that would make the book. But I still held out some hope that an organic plan of organization would present itself. The "Buckskin Man" tales seemed to be a clearly definable unit, and so did the rural stories set in the early twentieth century, as did the "World's Wanderer" trilogy. But there were other stories that did not fit any groups, and I had no idea how to arrange the groups in relation to each other.

Then Lynn handed me a copy of Russell Roth's article "The Inception of a Saga: Frederick Manfred's 'Buckskin Man,'" from the Winter 1969–70 issue of *South Dakota Review*. In that article, Roth places the "Buckskin Man" tales within the context of Manfred's other books. He identifies *This Is the Year* as the logical transition between the world of the Buckskin Man and the world of the prairie farming communities. And, he says, *The Golden Bowl* "stands as something of an epigraph for the entire body of his work. . . ." Roth quotes Malcolm Cowley on Faulkner's saga of Yoknapatawpha County: "All the separate works . . . are like wooden planks that were cut not from a log, but from a still living tree [which] continues to grow." Then Roth says of Manfred's work: "His books are not so much planks cut from a still-living tree as they are the tree itself. . . . *The Golden Bowl* is the root, far more substantial than its physical dimensions would imply; the Buckskin Man Tales, the trunk; and *This Is the Year*, the beginning of the branchings into the novels, the short stories, the poems, and what Manfred calls the 'rumes.'" Roth adds, "In other words, there is an historical and social critique implicit in Manfred that has its basis in the progression from green earth to dust bowl. It is announced in *The Golden Bowl*, delineated in the tales, and exploded in final portentous cataclysm in *This Is the Year*."

Roth's insights struck me at once as perfect responses (years ahead of time!) to the problem I was facing. Here was both a concise statement of the substance of "the Manfred vision" and the organic plan I had been looking for! I've had to amend it to include the many works Manfred published after 1969, but I think it works.

First, the great taproot of the Manfred tree includes *The Golden Bowl*, announcing Manfred's "historical and social critique," along with *The Wind Blows Free* and the early episodes of *The Primitive* (in this *Reader* taken from the text in *Wanderlust*) as indicators of some of other thematic concerns that have occupied him throughout his career.

Second, excerpts from the "Buckskin Man" tales, along with *The Manly-Hearted Woman*, begin to define a historical and cultural agenda, a relationship between settlers and the land, a particular slant on humanity, and a characteristically American set of virtues, ideals, and failings.

In the third section, I chose thematic "branches" rather than the generic branches that Roth suggests, selecting eight themes or motifs that recur in Manfred's work. Others of equal importance could have been selected. "Paired Personalities" is one that I had planned to use and eventually excluded because the selections would have had to be too long; but there are many examples in his stories of pairs of persons who are individually like halves of a single personality. Many of the themes that are not given their own sections here will nonetheless be apparent to readers as they recur throughout the selections in the *Reader*. "The Idea of the Hero," "Masculine/Feminine" and "The Land" are especially prominent. Within the thematic sections presented in the *Reader*, I have tried to make selections that allow free exhibition of as many of these other themes and motifs as possible, a task made somewhat easier by the extent to which many of them pervade all or most of Manfred's stories.

At the end of August, we made another trip to Manfred's house, to interview Fred about some additional questions we had developed, and to discuss with him and members of the committee the plan for the book. That weekend Fred was hosting Cornstock, an open-stage poetry reading (punctuated by a little music), that has been held four times a year for more than a decade. Organized by former state senator Gary DeCramer, it is most often held in Ghent, Minnesota, but sometimes at other places. Fred had been a Cornstock regular since its early days, and beginning sometime in the late eighties, he began hosting the gathering at Roundwind. The Paddocks, Bill Holm, and I were also Cornstock regulars, and Chuck Woodard and Freya Manfred were occasional visitors. It seemed like a good time to have a little meeting to discuss progress on the book. Fred liked the idea of organizing the book around Roth's analogy. "I give you an A," he said.

His grade was premature. The summer had come to an end, the grant had run out, Fred was deeply immersed in writing *The Wrath of Love*, and for the next two years I had to turn most of my energies to other book projects to which I was committed. I continued reading and taking notes, continued checking with Fred occasionally to ask questions, to get reactions, but the process had slowed.

The Roth analogy no longer seemed like a panacea for organizing all that material. If the scheme were to be followed through, it seemed, it would not be possible just to whittle down the list of nominated inclusions; it would be necessary to work out possible patterns and to round them out by selecting still more passages. It became very clear that, if we were to take the tree analogy seriously, the book needed to be based on Manfred's total vision of Siouxland; it needed some kind of integrity, needed to be not merely a collection of pieces. That meant seeking more thematic and stylistic overlap between the selections; it meant incorporating some demonstrations of how Manfred often uses the same autobiographical or thematic material in several places; it meant selecting passages that show how his use of language is adapted to different circumstances or characters in different books. The job of making selections had become more than a matter of making hard choices; it had become subtle. And slow.

It was very clear that the book would not be ready by Fred's 80th birthday, as we had hoped. I was somewhat discouraged. I regretted having made the project more elaborate than the original plan called for, I regretted having let other projects interrupt our progress. I was frustrated by the press of other duties that left too little time for work on *The Frederick Manfred Reader*. Manfred, too, was discouraged. We had hoped that the book would be already be out, would attract new attention to his work, and that the attention would result in an easier time finding a publisher for *The Wrath of Love* and *Black Earth*. In the meantime, we had talked some more about the plan of the book, and while we still thought that the organizational scheme was the best we were likely to find, and that having the introductory matter be entirely in Fred's own words would give the book a unique character, there were difficulties presented by the format and length of the volume. In a conversation with Fred, I discovered that we had each independently come to the same conclusion: that the book needed to be in a "normal" size volume as opposed to the large format two-column page we had been thinking about; we wanted a book that would be convenient for readers, not a reference book, not a coffee-table book, not a library tome. In short, it had to be shorter.

By June 1994, I had the book whittled down to what I expected would be about 800 pages. It had to be shorter. However, there was good news. Holy Cow! Press had expressed an interest in doing the book. But it would have to be reduced to about 500 pages if it were to be a single volume. Jim Perlman of Holy Cow! generously suggested that perhaps we could do 800 pages if we did it in two volumes. I sounded out several members of the committee, and Fred himself. We were all agreed that keeping it to one volume was essential. I had been away from home for three weeks during late June and early July, and had planned to get together with Fred in mid-July to interview him again to fill in some gaps I perceived in the introductory materials. It had already been clear that much of the introductory material would have to be drastically shortened to meet the new length requirements for the book. I was committed to keeping the introductions completely in Fred's own words, so I did not feel I could paraphrase to achieve brevity. There were some things I needed to have him say succinctly, and another interview session would take care of the problem very nicely.

Then some bad news. I called Fred's house to confirm an interview time, and got no answer. A short while later, I got a call from Freya telling me about his illness. It was important that he get as much rest as possible while undergoing radiation therapy for his brain tumor. The prognosis was grim. Freya told me the doctor had said the longest anyone ever survived after therapy was eleven months. "So I have eleven months?" Fred had said, characteristically optimistic. The doctor told him, no, that's what's possible for someone in his forties, that he could expect most optimistically about six months. If the therapy worked, he would have two months of total exhaustion, but then a few months of revitalization, during which he could expect to be physically and mentally nearly back to normal. Then the cancer would begin to grow again and his condition would rapidly decline.

During his hospitalization, visitors were restricted, but Fred had indicated that I was welcome. Bill Holm and I visited and found Fred weak but upbeat. We talked about completing the interview when he got out of the hospital, and we planned to talk about how to reduce the size of the book. At my next visit, a couple of weeks later, his condition had drastically worsened. An infection had taken hold. Freya and Fred's son, Frederick Manfred, Jr., had told me exactly how bad his condition had become. He was occasionally hallucinating, and even when he was lucid it was difficult for him to speak clearly. But he wanted to talk. We talked about the old days when we had done reading tours in small towns together with other writers. "We should get that going again," he said. We talked about old friends. We talked a bit about his work. All this in about fifteen minutes. He was exhausted. Before I left, I helped him with a glass of juice. I told him I'd drive down to see him again the following week.

"It's good to have friends come," he said.

"Goodbye, old friend," I said, aware that it might be the last time I'd see him. I took his hand, and he seemed to brighten a little, to have a little more energy drawn from somewhere deep inside him. His hand tightened on mine, and the gesture turned into a real handshake.

"I've still got the old grip," he said.

He died the day I was supposed to visit him again.

Under congenial pressure from Jim Perlman, I set about putting the book into its final shape. Finally, I got ruthless about cutting things out. I had never intended to include something from every single book, but I had to eliminate more than I liked. For example, I drastically edited a selection from *Flowers of Desire* and I particularly regretted that in condensing it I had to refocus the point of view the book. I desperately wanted to keep that book's particular slant on sexual desire. Finally, I had to give it up, but I hope readers will seek the book out. It's a story that links the prehistoric with the modern, and which simultaneously shows how drastically sexual attitudes can change in a generation or two.

Sometimes, trying to reduce the total number of pages yielded unexpected dividends. I removed some selections from *Scarlet Plume* that I had originally included, and replaced them with other sections more easily subject to condensation. In making this change, I saw an opportunity to parallel Judith's escape with Hugh's crawl in *Lord Grizzly*. The parallels are surprisingly specific, right down to the way they both say, "Meat's meat."

For the sake of balance, I also decided to prune away some sections of *Green Earth* that I had selected (regretfully, because *Green Earth* is my personal favorite); however, I kept "New Pa" even though it tells a story that is told in shorter form in "Ninety Is Enough," because I wanted to incorporate as much as I could of that feeling of familiarity that comes from revisiting various incidents in different retellings as one reads through a number of Manfred's books.

I decided to use "Lew and Luanne" in spite of its length, because it seems to me a quintessential Manfred story with a structure that is simultaneously loose and tight depending on how you look at it, because I wanted to have at least two complete stories, because *Arrow of Love* is the hardest one of Manfred's books to find, and finally, just because I like the story so much.

The difficulty of selecting excerpts for this book revealed to me something significant about Manfred's craft: his stories do not easily lend themselves to excerpting. On first reading, his books often seem episodic, but on closer examination, it can be seen that single episodes most often do not contain clearly definable segments of the plot. There are few definite closures; instead, scenes offhandedly introduce elements that will figure prominently in later scenes, and the later scenes are not fully intelligible without the elements previously introduced. Manfred is weaving together a unified story, not connecting anecdotes. That is why some of his books are not represented in this compendium; they really need to be read whole.

The introductory passages and postscripts (the passages in italics) are drawn from Manfred's letters (in the edition edited by Arthur R. Huseboe and Nancy Owen Nelson, a wonderful collection that fully displays Fred's warmth, humanity, and erudition; it also displays the breadth of his stylistic abilities), from various published interviews (especially the indispensable *Conversations with Frederick Manfred*, moderated and edited by John R. Milton), and from unpublished interviews which I conducted. It should be noted that the sources of the comments are not noted within those introductions. That is because the various passages are often conflated from different sources, and I did not want to introduce any apparatus that would interfere with the job they are supposed to do, which is to give some sense of Fred's voice, and the way he talked about his own work. However, I have restricted the length of most of the passages, even though Fred liked to comment at considerable length about things. At whatever length, I never found him boring. Nor did anyone who was mentally really alive. But readers should be aware that the shorter comments are somewhat atypical.

Because there were things I wanted to include that did not fit comfortably within the remaining thematic sections, I created a fourth section called "Leaves" to foliate Roth's tree. This section is a miscellany of set pieces. I felt the book needed some baseball to really reflect Fred's interests, so I included a chapter from *No Fun on Sunday*. I included the section "Kisses" from *Green Earth* mostly as a personal bow to Fred. He used to read that selection when we toured together. "The Carnival at No Place" is extracted from a chapter in *The Chokecherry Tree*, which is one of Fred's finest accomplishments. It shows off his not inconsiderable talents as a satirist. "The Land Sermon" demonstrate off his skill as a rhetorician and homilist.

Finally, I had intended from very early on to make the eulogy for Sinclair Lewis the concluding piece in the book, ending as it does with a challenge to a new generation of writers and readers. It seems even more appropriate now that Fred has died—substitute the names Manfred for Lewis, Fred for Red, and the piece is still 95 percent accurate in describing its subject.

Many of the titles for the individual selections presented in this reader are not Manfred's titles. Wherever I have used a selection that Manfred had titled himself, I have used his title; but wherever a selection consists of an untitled chapter, or a part of a chapter, or overlaps two chapters or sections, I have taken the liberty of assigning a title, for the sake of consistency and for the sake of giving the reader a handy reference.

I hope that *The Frederick Manfred Reader* provides a satisfactory abstract of Manfred's complete works, and that all or most of the significant features of his writing have been preserved in it. Reading through the complete works of Frederick Manfred in preparation for editing this book has given me a great deal of pleasure. I hope readers will be able to sit down with the *Reader* and read it straight through with the same degree of pleasure and the sense that it has a structural integrity of its own that coincides with the structure of Manfred's vision, and with an understanding of how the various elements of life in Siouxland are all related parts of a single tree, as described in the works of Frederick Feikema Manfred.

There is one more thing I should add about the goals of this anthology: Partly it is intended to shamelessly shill for Fred's work. I have taken some pains to try to avoid "spoiling the story" for anyone who wants to read any of the novels in full, and I encourage you to read them all. While I have tried to make each selection be as self-contained as possible in terms of telling a complete story or at least a complete episode, and have tried to edit them in a way that will not leave the reader mystified about any essential detail, I have left some things hanging, unexplained, as "teasers." To find out more about the rattlesnake, for instance, you'll have to read *The Wind Blows Free* and *The Golden Bowl*.

I want people to read Manfred. I want Fred to live forever. He will if you read and buy his books and urge others to do the same.

—*John Calvin Rezmerski*
September 1995

Frederick Manfred's parents, Frank and Alice Feikema, wedding portrait.

Farm near Doon, Iowa, that was Manfred's adolescent home.

The Feikema family. Rear—left to right: Frederick (Manfred), Alice (mother), Edward, Frank (father), Floyd. Front—Abben (baby), John. Not shown: Henry.

The 1928 Gild Edge church team, Doon, Iowa. Manfred was the pitcher (with baseball).

Manfred at Calvin College (Summer, 1933).

Manfred outside his house at Blue Mound, Minnesota, 1970s.

Manfred with stuffed grizzly bear (Science Museum, Saint Paul, Minnesota, 1973).

Frederick Manfred signs books at Southwestern State University Bookstore, 1967.

Lynn Fellerman and Beth Luwandi interviewing Manfred at his Roundwind home, east of Luverne, Minnesota, 1991.

Manfred's Blue Mound house, front view.

Manfred at work in the "tipi," the study of his Roundwind home.

Frederick Manfred at
Blue Mound, August 1991.

SECTION ONE
Growing Roots

The Wind Blows Free

Foreword

I'VE OFTEN BEEN ASKED how I got started as a writer.

In my boyhood I didn't have a single friend interested in writing. I didn't study creative writing in college. And I didn't meet a well-known author until sometime after I was published.

At the age of five, though, even before I started the primary grade in a country school in northwest Iowa, I already had the dream of becoming a writer. I had seen in our farm home a slim green volume of privately printed verse written by my father's sister, Kathryn Feikema. Aunt Kathryn lived with us and was one of my very first teachers. She loved me and taught me to read before I started school. She and my mother used to play rhyming games with me while my mother made supper. And once I began school I soon developed into a good reader. My father and my mother used to say of me that they could always find me in one of two places: either exploring the hummocks along the creek in the pasture or sitting on the screen porch with my head in a book.

What really put the heat into my private burning bush was a hitchhiking trip I took in August of 1934, a few months after graduating from Calvin College in Grand Rapids, Michigan. I went to see the Shining Mountains of the Far West. That trip released my soul.

Three years after that trip, on a Saturday, I was invited out to a party at my friend Jim's house. I had by that time, after much wandering, found a job with the Minneapolis *Journal*. Saturday was always a tough day at the plant, from eight in the morning until almost midnight when the final edition of the Sunday paper was put to bed.

As I stepped across the street in the dark to get my car out of the *Journal* parking lot, I wasn't too sure I cared to go to the party any more that night. I was pooped.

But my old Dodge fired on the first revolution and soon I was driving across the Washington Avenue bridge over the twinkling Mississippi River. I took a right and followed the East River Road around to Franklin Avenue. The streetlights burned a bright citrine under the black green oaks.

The deep gorge of the Mississippi and all the wonderful trees and the lovely greens along the boulevard made me wish I had a date for Jim's party. It was time I fell in love again. I'd pretty well gotten over a college love and was ripe

3

for a new romance. I wondered if maybe there might not be a new shining girl at Jim's house.

It was quarter past twelve when I eased the Dodge up Prospect Hill. When I got near the top I saw that the lights were still on in Jim's house. Good. The party was still going. I parked my car on a side street and walked around the side of the house and entered by the back door into the kitchen. Two strangers, a man and a woman, were talking politics by the sink. They'd each just opened a fresh bottle of beer. I pushed through the swinging doors into the living room. It was full, some twenty people, all talking at once about the President. I knew only five people there, Jim and his wife, Laura, a widow social worker, Mac, a man from the Department of Education, and Starke, a psychologist from the University of Minnesota. I settled on the floor near Jim.

The argument about the President was pretty well divided. Some thought the President's liberal program was going to win out and lick the Depression; some thought he was going too slow and should be more radical. Looking around I noted no one was drinking hard liquor. Just beers or cokes. There never were orgies at Jim's house; just wonderful good talks by people dedicated to do some kind of social good. High class people. All college graduates at least. I liked them. And I always learned something just sitting around listening to them.

Pretty soon Jim noticed me. "Where's your beer?"

I lifted a shoulder. "There an extra bottle for me?"

"Of course. In the icebox. Help yourself."

I gathered myself up on my legs and wandered out into the kitchen. The couple there had quit talking about politics and were busy smooching by the door. They broke apart and smiled sheepishly. I wondered a little about them. They were probably only sneaking a kiss in the kitchen while their spouses were arguing politics in the living room. I helped myself to a Jordan beer and returned to the living room. Jim in the meantime had found an empty chair for me and I sat down.

Talk got around to vacation trips some of the people there had taken that summer.

Jim broke in. "You should hear Fred tell you about the trip he once took through the dust bowl in the Dakotas."

"Oh, it wasn't much, really," I said. "I was just hitchhiking through it."

"No, go on and tell them." Jim gave everybody a warm smile. "Fred really saw some pretty raw stuff."

I still demurred. I was quite aware that even when I told a dirty story I had trouble holding people's attention, especially if there were a lot of people around. Two people, maybe; more, no. I was still too ill-at-ease, too shy, in crowds. In college I'd had trouble reciting in large classes. Also, when I finally did get started, I had a tendency to tell too much, get sidetracked on some juicy detail.

"Go on. Tell about the hobo and the snake. And oh yes, especially about that old maid."

"Well, all right."

So I started at the beginning. Within a few minutes I noticed that everybody in Jim's living room had fallen silent. Encouraged, I began to go into more detail, to dramatize what had happened to me. Here and there I embroidered the tale some. When I finished there were wide smiles, a few belly laughs, and many questions.

Later, on the way home around two o'clock, having completely forgotten about looking for a girl at Jim's house, I was in a glow. For once in my life I'd finally told a story well enough to hold everybody's attention.

For months, ever since I'd started work on the *Journal* and had brought myself a portable typewriter, I'd also been trying to write stories. I'd read Hemingway for a while and then try to write like him. Result: an overly mannered Ernie. Then I'd read Steinbeck for a while and try to write like him. Result: an overly sentimental John. And then I'd read Dos Passos and try to write like him, especially Dos's poetic biographies of Veblen and La Follette and Hearst. Result: things that sounded like *Daily Worker* sob stories. Imitations, apings, all of them.

Sitting behind my steering wheel, it came to me what I should do: write the way I'd told that dust bowl story that night. Somehow I'd done something right there. I hadn't told the tale as a Hemingway might tell it, but had told it according to *the way I saw it in my head. I* wasn't seeing the tale through someone else's eyes or out of someone else's vision, but through my own eyes and out of my vision. With my kind of hesitations in it, and my way of breathing, and my way of talking. Even my way of walking behind the cows bringing them up from the pasture. Me. Therefore *my* style.

When I got to my room, instead of going to bed, I went directly to my typewriter, got out a wad of paper, and completely forgetting that earlier I'd been pooped, started in, retelling that tale of the Dirty Thirties. I knew that if I waited until morning the mood and the method would be gone.

I wrote through the rest of that night and all the next morning and well into the afternoon. As I went along, it delighted me to see my imagination go to work on that wonderful tour of the Dust Bowl. I filled some fifty plus pages.

Then I went down the street and had myself a lake trout dinner at the Bridge Cafe. And at last went to bed.

The next night after work, Monday evening, I got out the fifty plus pages and read them.

When I finished reading them, I slowly got up out of my chair and ran a hand through my hair. "You know," I said to myself, "by God, I can write. I've found out who I am as a writer. I've found my tone, my pacing, my angle of vision. This is the way I've got to do it. The hell with Hemingway and Steinbeck and Dos Passos."

In the next months I completely rewrote that first draft, singling out in particular the part having to do with the hobo and the snake and building it into a novel. That novel, after seven different tries at it, was later published in 1944 as *The Golden Bowl*.

What follows then in this book is the story, a reminiscence, I told that magic night at Jim's house. The reminiscence is written in the third person. The Frederick Feikema of those days is forty-five years back there in time. He's enough of a stranger to me today to write about him as though he were a Hugh Glass. Also, by putting it in the third person, it helped me to see myself as others see me, as well as helped me dredge up from memory many facts and incidents I didn't get around to telling that night at Jim's house.

Thus do not be too startled when you see that the first name of the hero is also the first name of the writer.

Setting out from Sioux Falls

FRED WALKED OVER to a Standard Oil station down the street.

An old gentleman with brush-stiff gray hair and freshly ironed blue trousers was sitting inside with feet up on a battered desk. The place was oily neat.

The old gentleman gave Fred a sour look. "Another bum looking for a hand-out, I see."

Fred quick checked his own clothes. His burgundy trousers hung in a straight crease all the way to his tan oxfords. His red tie was still snugged up neat into his shirt collar. Fred smiled. "I see you got out of bed on the wrong side this morning."

"What do you want?"

"I could use a couple of maps. South Dakota. Wyoming."

"Do you drink gas?"

"Homebrew beer, yes. Gas, no."

"Then you can't have any."

"Suppose I bought a candy bar?"

The old gentleman swung his feet down and popped upright out of his swivel chair. Four quick strides and he was standing behind an open candy case. "What would you like? O'Henry? Baby Ruth?"

It made Fred smile some more. He set down his suitcase and ambled over. The O'Henry was bigger than the Baby Ruth. "I think I'll take the short story over the homerun."

"Come again?" The old gentleman's hair ridged up under his blue attendant's cap. "You threw me a curve there, son, when I'm a fastball hitter."

"You played ball?"

"With the old Sioux Falls Canaries."

"Hey, I always wanted to pitch against them."

"Who'd you pitch for?" the old gentleman asked.

"Doon."

"I've heard about 'em. Got a long-legged kid pitchin' there . . . Naw. That can't be you, can it?"

"Your guess is as good as mine."

"Hell. Take all the maps you want."

Fred asked, "What did you play?"

"Shortstop."

"Then you were part of that doubleplay combination with Swede Risberg."

"The same. And was he good."

Risberg had been kicked out of the American League for throwing games while playing for the White Sox in a World Series with the Cincinnati Reds. Fred was curious to know what Risberg was like in real life but decided the old gentleman might not like to talk about Risberg's shady past. There'd been some talk that Swede Risberg had too many friends in the underworld of Chicago. "I better have a candy bar anyway. For later on when I'm down the road a ways. I'll take the O'Henry."

The old gentleman handed him the candy bar. "What was that about taking the short story over the homerun?"

Fred dug a nickel out of his collection of loose change and handed it over. "A fellow named O'Henry wrote short stories."

"I didn't know that."

Fred stepped over to the Standard Oil map rack and took a map for both South Dakota and Wyoming. Both covers showed a pair of gray geese winging their way across a deep blue sky with a red car below zooming along a blue road. Both goose and car were headed east, not west. The land was shown in purple with a white halo along the horizon. "Thanks."

"Don't mention it. And the next time you throw me an O'Henry curve, telegraph it a little, will you? I'm only a .241 hitter."

Fred laughed. "Them I always had the most trouble with."

Out on the street again, Fred looked east up 16. No cars in sight. After a little thought, Fred decided he'd better walk out to the west end of town. There he'd be sure to catch any Sioux Falls traffic heading west.

He walked under more huge elms. Some of the underbranches were dead. The lawns and porches were mostly neat.

Fred kept glancing over his shoulder on the watch for rides. A drayman came by. Too short a ride. A block farther along a jitney full of yelling young toughs, all of high school age, roared by, out open. "Hey, long gears, how's the weather up there?"

"Why don't you grow up and find out?" Fred yelled back with a smile.

Highway 16 jogged left several blocks, then speared straight west. The houses slowly turned drab and the lawns became more littered.

A freshly painted combination filling station and cafe glinted near the last stoplight. Two trucks waited to one side of it. The drivers were inside having a cup of coffee. A good place to hook rides. Fred set down his suitcase. He checked his necktie and fly and got out his smile. He was ready.

Across the street stood the last house. The lawn around it had been watered just enough to keep it a fresh green. It was almost an eyesore it was so lovely.

Looking closer, Fred spotted a private well. The fellow had been lucky enough to hit a good vein of water.

A Truckload of America

THE SUN WAS ALMOST OVERHEAD. Fine particles of dust riding very high gave the atmosphere a strange platinum sheen. Close up, though, the air appeared to be clear.

∽

The stoplight in the middle of the highway clicked from red to yellow to green.

A cattle truck with a South Dakota license plate pulled up in the combination filling station and cafe. Instead of cattle it was full of people. A dozen of them. They stared out with glazed eyes.

The driver and another man got out of the truck's red cab and entered the cafe. They didn't look back at the load of people up in the rack.

The stoplight in the middle of the road clicked from green to yellow to red.

Presently the driver and his friend came out picking their teeth. They strolled along in an easy loafing manner. The friend got in on his side of the red cab and the driver came around on the near side kicking rubber and then climbed in.

Fred bet the truck was going a long ways.

The driver caught Fred's look. He fiddled with the knob on the shift. He looked back through the rear window at the people behind him and then looked back at Fred.

Fred picked up his suitcase and stepped over. "'Got room for one more?"

The driver smiled easy. He was heavily freckled. His cap was tipped back and his forehead was so sunburned the skin had begun to scale off. "Steer or bull?"

"How about a maphrodite?"

"Can't start up a new country with them."

"Oh, I dunno now. Plato thought so."

"You mean, in Plato, South Dakota, they do?"

Fred laughed. "No. How far you going?"

"I turn off at Kennebec."

"Say, that's quite a ways."

"West River Country."

"Can I?"

"At your service." The driver noticed Fred's neat clothes. "Just take it easy leaning against the rack. I took some cattle out east first to greener pastures before I picked up these people on the way back."

Fred nodded.

"What was that about Plato again?"

"Oh, a guy named Plato once wrote about a race of people who had two faces and a double set of arms and legs." Fred had loved being a member of the Plato Club back in Calvin College. He'd gotten more out of that club than he had out of any class. "Round and fat like an apple dumpling."

The driver let go with a good laugh. He had a two-day growth of red beard and his eyes and teeth flashed white. "That's them guys from Plato all right. Round and fat. And about as two-faced as you can get."

Fred went around in back, and setting his suitcase inside, leaped aboard. The first step he took he almost slipped and fell. The trucker had thrown some straw on the floor of the truck to cover fresh cow dung and Fred had the tough luck of stepping where a fresh pile of it lay hidden. Fred quick steadied himself by grabbing a sideboard.

The driver hit the starter and after a second muffled explosions shook the truck. There was a smooth meshing of gears expertly done and with an easy lurch they were off.

Before the wind got too strong Fred quick had a peek at his South Dakota map. Kennebec. Kennebec. There it was, some forty miles beyond the Missouri River. By nightfall he should be halfway to the Black Hills.

When he looked around for a clean spot along the rack sideboards he found that all the good places were taken. He'd have to ride standing up, knees slightly bent, balancing himself, ready for any roll of the truck. He placed his suitcase between his feet.

There were exactly a dozen people aboard. A family of five, father, mother, three young boys, had the best place. They were lined up against the back of the red cab. They wore wash-faded clothes. Five grain hands stood along the right side of the truck rack, each with well-beaten duffel bag. It was always easy to spot a grain hand working his way north with the ripening wheat. He invariably carried a pair of pliers in the plier pocket on the right trouser leg, a can of tobacco in the left rear pocket, makin's in the bib pocket, and a big red bandanna round his neck. His duffel bag was usually packed tight with an extra set of underwear, a half dozen pair of extra brown work socks, handkerchiefs, and a fresh set of overalls and shirt for Saturday nights.

A young couple stood on the left side of the rack. The two had apparently got on last; their side was the most crapped on. Going east, the cattle had stood facing the wind out of the south and had crapped north.

The couple looked at Fred with interest, a wondering smile on their lips. The man appeared to be about thirty, dark-skinned with curly black hair, wise crinkles at the corners of his black eyes, with the air of an actor. He wore New York-cut clothes, blue jacket and blue trousers, light-blue shirt open at the collar, and two-tone shoes. The girl was much younger, about twenty, a vivid gold blond with very light-blue eyes. She wore a rather tight yellow dress, quite short for the day, revealing pair of marvelous legs. It was even more obvious she was an actress and more than likely one who would lap up flattery.

The truck hit a deep dip in the road and Fred almost lost his balance. He had to throw out his arms to keep from falling.

"Whoops," the girl said.

"Yeh," Fred said, turning pink.

The man shook his head in sympathy.

Fred took another look at the dung-spattered south side of the truck rack, finally decided he'd try a spot right of the couple where it was relatively free of cow manure. He shagged his suitcase over between his legs. Luckily the straw underfoot was free of suspicious-looking mounds. Gingerly Fred caught hold of one of the rack uprights.

The couple on his left rode the dips and swoops in the road with an easy grace. They were probably used to standing up in streetcars and subways. Fred envied them. He longed to see New York and its shimmering skyscrapers someday.

Exhaust fumes from the truck mingled with the smell of urine-soaked straw.

The couple watched the countryside go by with lively interest. They kept pointing things out to each other: a windmill beside a water tank, a red barn with white trim, a binder standing idle at the end of a field, cows and horses scattered across a pasture, chickens working the roadside ditches. They had the air of visitors at a zoo.

The truck picked up speed and the wind got worse. Because Fred stuck out a good foot above everybody he really got a blasting. His ears boomed with it sometimes. Fred liked to go bareheaded but the way the wind was whipping his hair around, sometimes in his eyes so that it was like looking through a brown veil, he wondered if maybe he shouldn't dig out his blue cap from his suitcase.

The red truck bumped on the pavement cracks one after another. Heads bobbed on loose necks. The road speared straight west, its gray cement slowly turning white in the distance until it finally vanished into what looked like a little hole. The bronze haze along the horizon began to deepen.

"It's all so flat," the girl said to Fred.

In the bruising wind Fred wasn't sure he'd caught what she'd said. "Flat? Wait a while. This country is full of surprises."

"Never having seen anything like it before, I find it all fascinating."

The fellow beside her slipped his arm around her.

"What I don't understand is how people can make a living here." The fellow had a suave mellow voice. "I mean, what do people do during drought times?"

Fred laughed. "I wonder about the same thing when I ride past all those endless blocks of houses in Chicago."

"I don't get you."

"Well, what can they be doing for work when they aren't raising some kind of produce? Who pays them for doing what?"

It was the fellow's turn to laugh. "Yes, I guess it's all in how you look at it, all right." He glanced at Fred's "I'm Sam Rivers. And this is my wife Joan."

"Glad to meet you. And I'm"—Fred held up a label on one side of his red college sweater on which his name had been sewn—"I'm Frederick Feikema.

See?" With strangers Fred was always hesitant to give his last name. People rarely caught it right the first time and almost always mispronounced it. Pronunciations ranged all the way from Fee-ke-ma, with the accent on either the first or second syllable, to Frycake, with a sneer in the voice. It hurt to hear one's family name mangled. There were even several dirty variations, and that really got him. But it helped if the stranger could see the name in print.

Rivers gave the name a second glance. ""Feikema. What nationality is that?"

"Frisian."

Rivers' dark eyes lit up. "Oh yes. I've run into that in my dictionary. The Frisians were related to the Angles and Saxons and once helped settle England."

Fred began to feel better about the couple.

"Do you speak Frisian?"

"I heard it around me as a boy. My father and his uncles. So I understand most of it. In fact, when I went to college I was surprised to learn I could read Chaucer."

"Holy mud."

"I wasn't just a member of a minority group within a minority group. A stiff-necked Frisian despised by a dumb Dutchman who in turn was laughed at by Americans. But about as English as one could be. Old English even. Suddenly I was a charter member of the English-speaking world."

Rivers' eye fell on the single gold stripe on the left arm of Fred's sweater. "I bet you played center."

"Yeh."

"I bet you could just reach up and drop 'em in."

Joan looked up at Fred's height and then glanced down at the front of his trousers. She slipped her arm around Rivers.

Rivers said, "You from around here?"

"Just left my home town Doon about an hour ago. Back over in Iowa there."

"How come you're riding west instead of east?"

"I'm out to see the mountains. I've already seen the east a little. Lived four years in Grand Rapids where I went to college."

"But you haven't seen New York?"

"Nope."

"That's the place to go."

"That's where you're from, aren't you? You both look like actors."

Rivers and Joan glanced at each other. "What makes you say that?"

"You both look like you've been sanded off a little."

Rivers crooked his head to one side.

"I'll be damned. But you're right, Frederick. I was an actor. But now I'm a writer. I just had a play of mine put on in an off-Broadway theatre. It ran for about two months, and made me some money, and when it closed down, we decided to see the country." Rivers gave his wife a little pull against his side. "Joan here had one of the lead roles in it."

Fred narrowed his eyes at Rivers.

A playwright. Fred wondered if he dare tell Rivers that he wanted to be a writer too someday.

∼

They rolled on mile after mile. Bump-a-bump-a-bump. The thudding tires and the creaking side of the rack worked into bones and brains. The sun burned straight down.

Joan pointed ahead.

Fred craned his head to look past the edge of the rack. Ahead a valley opened, and in a moment the red truck began to drop into it. The driver let up on the footfeed and the engine fell to a murmur. Only the gears, dragging, ground a little. The valley turned out to be an enchanting sight. A little stream meandered down the center of it. Willows and cottonwoods with shiny leaves grew along its banks. A herd of cattle and some dozen horses cropped grass in a narrow meadow. One horse, a gray stallion, looked up at the rolling truck. The truck dropped, down and down; it was like taking a deep dip in a rollercoaster.

Rivers whispered, "Lovely."

Fred said, "Yes, just when you're about to give up on this country, it always comes through with a surprise. A little green valley."

"Look," Joan said. "What's that gray horse got under him there?"

"That's what's known as an erection," Rivers said.

"Is that what it is," Joan said. "Great. Now I've seen that."

Fred played it with a straight face. "Kind of a misnomer though to call that an erection when it's aimed down not up, wouldn't you say?"

Rivers had to laugh.

"You!" Joan said.

The wheels of the red truck drummed over a wooden bridge. A sign read: *East Fork, Vermillion River.*

Joan continued to examine the stallion. "Kind of weird. Like a rolling pin."

Again Rivers had to laugh. "More like the handle of a tennis racket."

As the truck rolled up the hill the engine took hold again. Gears ground. When the driver had to shift to second the gears began to howl and the engine kicked out a little cloud of smoke. The driver shifted to low. The engine began to pound.

Joan tugged at her ear. Presently she picked a hairpin out of the bun in her hair and very carefully pried the curved end of it around in her earhole. She gingerly lifted out a ball of wax the size of a pea.

Up on the table land once more the country again turned sere and dry. Corn stood half-burnt, not having quite eared out. There'd been some grain, but it was so short the farmer'd had to cut it with a mower instead of a binder.

Pastures resembled badly worn rugs.

Tumbleweeds hung caught in the fences. Sometimes they were piled so high the four barbwire strands looked more like thick hedges than fences.

Some of the farmers had plowed their stubblefields. The raw earth lay a pulverized light brown with no hint of moisture. Here and there in it were hard slick chunks of earth resembling well-troweled cement blocks.

Rivers pointed at the roadside ditch. "Isn't that blowing dust?"

Fred nodded. The wind was just strong enough to pick up the loose dust from the plowed field and carry it into the ditch. New dust banks were slowly forming across the ditch.

The truck picked up speed. The regular cracks in the cement paving clicked faster and faster. Bellies hardened against it. Kidneys hurt after a time.

Hard wind tugged at Fred's hair. It kept making new partings, first on the left, then on the right.

The sun moved directly overhead. Back home Pa and family would be eating a big dinner. Fred wet his lips several times, discovered they were coated with a thin film of finest dust, acrid and slightly salty. Alkaline.

Joan licked her lips too, revealing a fleshy tongue.

"We could all do with a drink of water," Fred said.

Rivers said, "We probably should have stopped back there and had us all a drink at that stream."

Fred hooked a finger over his nose. "Come to think of it, it's a miracle it had running water. Back home the river's stopped running. Just a series of scummy pools."

They watched the barren farms pass by. The bronze cloud along the far west horizon slowly rose. Fred worried about that bronze cloud. If it was a dust storm they were in for hell riding up on that open truck.

The woman sitting with her back against the red cab opened a voluminous gunny sack and came up with a thick paper bag. She peered into it, and then deftly began to pluck out some sandwiches. She handed one each to her three little boys, one to her husband, and last took one herself. She closed the paper bag. She did it all without apology. It was a duty and needed no explanation. The husband, however, threw a look at the others on the truck, especially at the five grain hands, as if to say he was sorry he couldn't share his bread with them. All five of the family ate slowly, thoroughly, as though they'd got used to making sure they got every last bit of nutrition out of their food.

Fred remembered the candy bar he'd bought. Like the husband he wasn't sure it was good manners to be eating when others couldn't. After jouncing along another mile, Fred finally couldn't resist stealthily sliding his hand into his pocket and teasing open one end of the candy bar. He broke off a chunk, and when the truck hit a particularly sharp bump, making everybody grab for support, he quick slid the chunk into his cheek. It didn't take long for the chunk of chocolate and nuts and caramel to melt and disappear.

Joan saw him swallow. She looked down at his pocket. "Taste good?"

Fred reddened. Peripheral vision was hard to beat. With a self-conscious smile he pulled out the rest of the candy bar and offered both Joan and Rivers each a bite. Both smiled, and declined.

Out of the corner of his eye Fred could feel the five grain hands eying his candy bar too. One of them licked his lips. After a moment Fred decided it would be ridiculous to offer all five a bite from just one candy bar. It'd be better to put it away for later. He quietly folded over the open end and dropped the candy bar back into his pocket. The one bite he'd taken would have to be enough until the truck stopped somewhere up the line.

Again the flat table land dropped over into a little surprise valley. The sign by the little bridge read: *West Fork, Vermillion River.* But the West Fork was dry; not even scattered pools of water in the sharper deep turns. There were no trees. Only a few patches of buckbrush. And no cattle or horses. The narrow meadow on both sides of the stream had long ago been grazed off close to the ground.

Stanley Corners came up, where 81 crossed 16. There were two filling stations, one Standard and one Shell, and a general grocery store with a post office. Tumbleweeds were caught in the fence surrounding three setback houses. Someone had forgotten to hook the door to one of the privies and it whanged, whanged. It was as though someone inside the privy was vainly trying to kick it closed against the slowly pushing south wind.

The trucker slowed to second gear as the truck jerked across 81; then picked up speed again.

The bronze cloud in the west continued to rise in the sky. It slowly turned lighter in color.

Five miles more and Bridgewater came up with its cylinder-shaped water tower, black and glossy in the sunlight. There were some fifty homes and a main street two blocks long. It had trees but most were dead. The curbs along the west side of every street were fringed with dust drifts, all the result of black blizzards earlier in the year. Here and there a tumbleweed bounced down the north-south avenues. There wasn't a building that didn't need paint.

The road crossed a railroad track and abruptly became a gravel road. The difference was dramatic. The road was mostly a series of ribbed bumps, worse than a washboard. Everybody up in the truck got an awful shaking. A fellow had to either close his mouth, teeth tight, or let his jaw hang loose. The breasts of the two women, the mother sitting against the red cab and Joan Rivers, jiggled as though the two women were caught up in beaters of a threshing machine. Dust stived up behind the truck. Sometimes the dust whirled back up into the truck.

Dead trees at the ends of pastures were stunted. Dwarfs. The plowed earth changed color, brown and gray and ochreous yellow.

The truck slipped down into yet another valley, this time a shallow one. The sign on the small bridge read: *Wolf Creek.*

The highway turned north. Immediately the dust behind the truck, pushed by the south wind, caught up with them and made everybody cough.

In the distance hung a black water tower.

Fred dug out his map of South Dakota. "That has to be Emery."

"Another little town," Joan said. "Och! They all look so awfully lonesome. It must be dreadful to live in them. So forsaken."

Fred put away his map. "Depends. It's all there if you know how to look for it. Births. Loves. Deaths. Myself, I kind of like little towns."

Rivers said, "But how can anyone be inspired to write in them? No theatre, no symphonies."

Fred licked dust off his lips. "Well now, take Emery coming up here. It used to be a great place for music."

"Oh come now."

"Really. Where I went to high school, Hull, Iowa, they had a glee club and everybody went to hear it."

From Emery the road zigzagged west, then north, to Alexandria. The gravel highway gradually narrowed. Meeting oncoming cars the truck had to take to the shoulder of the road. The ditches were filled level with fine drifted dust and sometimes the wheels on the right side slewed as though caught in syrup.

The road got rougher; the yellow dust thicker. Everybody rode with lips closed tight. It was hard to daydream.

Fred kept picking up different scents as they rumbled along. Dry rot in fence posts. Sun-roasted buffalo grass. Crushed sunflowers. Cracked meadows. He could smell the too early fall of a late dry spring.

The road veered west. The sun rode over the red cab at three o'clock high. It burned into the eyes. The land was utterly flat with the horizons slightly curled up at the edges.

They passed one abandoned farm after another. The doors to the houses and the barns hung open, some of them on one hinge. Windmills clanged aimlessly. The horseballs in the barnyards were old and the manure piles by the hog houses resembled doormats.

The land tipped down and ahead lay a valley several miles wide. A river wriggled down the center of it fringed with trees. For once most of the trees had a few green leaves. A sign on a black suspension bridge read: *James River*. The river was still running, narrow trickles connecting stagnant opalescent pools. To either side of the trickles lay a cracked earth. Some of the cracks were several inches wide, forming a multitude of irregularly shaped clay cakes. Dead fish, carp and minnow, lay bleaching on the hard clay cakes.

Across the river on the next rise a mile away loomed a silver water tower and the considerable spread of a little city.

"That's got to be Mitchell." Fred consulted his map. "Yep. The Corn Palace town."

"Corn? Palace?" Joan said.

"Every fall they cover a frame building with ears of corn. About three thousand bushels worth."

Rivers gave him a sliding smile. "I suppose with turrets and towers."

"Sure. They have a six-day festival every fall and everybody for miles around comes to town. Whites. Indians. Grain hands passing through."

"Did you ever go to one?"

"No. Heard about it though on the Yankton radio." Fred pursed his lips.

"This fall there won't be much to celebrate. The birds'll have eaten much of the corn up on those walls."

It was hard talking and they fell silent again. The road became smoother beyond the bridge. A maintenance man had just passed through with a road grader.

The truck lifted up with the road into Mitchell. The houses on the edges of town were as sandblasted as those of the towns they had passed through. Most of the city lay to the north, and there the houses, sheltered by trees, had a better look about them. The paint on them was still in good shape. They rolled into a truck stop. The driver pulled beside a gas tank, brakes squeaking. The motor, relieved of its load, murmured quietly; then, the key being turned, whuskered off into silence.

The driver got out. He looked up at the riders in the truck rack with a cracked smile. He stretched his arms and rose on his toes several times. "Time for coffee and cream for the engine and gas and oil for the stomach."

He looked at Fred, and then at Rivers and Joan. "Privies are around in back there."

"Thanks."

Everybody got down. The two women headed for the door marked Women and the father and the three boys headed for the door marked Men. The five grain hands headed for the cafe for something to eat.

Fred found himself lingering behind with Rivers. Fred had to go too but thought he'd wait until everybody had finished.

Rivers shivered. "Lord, have I got high water."

Fred eased into a smile. "Well, maybe we should turn you loose on the landscape. Relieve the drought."

"Yeah. Uhh." Rivers shivered again and slid a hand into a pocket to pinch himself back.

"Like Pantagruel flushing out the streets of Paris."

"You've read Rabelais then."

"In college. Laughed my head off for weeks."

Rivers looked up at Fred with a quirked serious expression. "You like books."

"Yes."

"What's your ambition?"

"They tried to make a teacher out of me, but I didn't like it. Then I thought a little about baseball, but I hurt my arm when I was seventeen. Pitched three games in two days. While also pitching bundles."

"You'd probably make a good first baseman."

"I thought about that too. And I can hit. But."

"Yes?"

"Well, it's hard to imagine Lou Gehrig writing books after he retires from baseball. *Leaves of Grass* by Lou Gehrig. *Much Ado About Nothing* by Lou Gehrig."

Rivers laughed at the same time that he looked nervously at the privy marked Men. "Yeh, or *The Comedy of Errors*."

"Ha."

"So you want to write too."

Fred regretted he'd let it slip out. "Yeh."

"Plays?"

"No. I was a member of the Thespian Club in college but plays weren't for me."

"Why not?"

"I'm never convinced it's real up there on the stage. I can't get taken in. Like I do in movies. Or in a good novel."

Rivers hopped around on one leg while holding himself back. "Novels then?"

"I started one once but when I let a girl in college read it, she hooted at the way I described women."

"Why?"

"They weren't real, she said. Too many petticoats."

"Don't tell me you're still a virgin."

Fred blushed. "Mostly it's that I had no sisters."

"About time for you then to dunk your doughnut."

"There's more to it than that."

"Well sure. But . . ."

Fred shivered. He had to go bad too. "Mostly I've written poems."

"There's no money in that."

"I know."

Rivers kept looking at the men's privy. "Tell you. Go to New York. You'll meet other writers there. The excitement of meeting other creative minds will be good for you. And meet women. Women of talent you can go to bed with."

Fred had a little smile. "Your wife Joan hasn't got a sister, has she?"

Rivers gave him a strangled look.

Just then the father and the three boys emerged from the men's privy.

"Good!" Rivers exclaimed, and with a skip and a jump headed for it. "C'mon."

"No. You go ahead." Fred was shy about going to a bathroom with strangers.

The father and his three boys headed for the outdoor pump. The father began working the pump handle while his boys took turns drinking from a tin cup.

Rivers soon emerged from the men's privy. "Okay. She's all yours now."

Fred took his turn next. He closed the door after him. It was dusky inside, light coming from the cracks in the wall and the quarter-moon cut in the door. Shyly he held his hand over his private parts as though someone might be present.

The south wind gave the door a hard shove. With his free hand Fred shoved it closed again.

The truck driver blew his horn, twice, sharp. "Time to get rolling," he called out.

"Wow. I better hurry," Fred murmured to himself. "I guess I waited too long."

Fred thought it a kind of cosmic irony that while one part of a man could be dreaming of writing poems another part of him could be busy eliminating waste.

There were footsteps outside and then a rap on the privy door. "You still in there?" It was the truck driver.

"Yep."

"Better come now. I've got to get back to the ranch before dark."

"Okay. I'll be right out."

Fred buttoned up. Then outside again, as he passed the pump, he quick had himself a cup of water.

When he got into the truck he was surprised to discover that a newcomer, a young hobo, had taken over his spot beside the Rivers couple. Fred considered the fellow a moment, then said, "I'm sorry but you're standing in my place." He was about to point to his suitcase standing against the rack, when he discovered it had been set in the middle of the truck.

The hobo sneered at him. "Too bad, bud."

Fred made a move as though to push in anyway.

The young hobo instantly flashed fierce gray teeth at him, at the same time that his right fist, clenched white, popped into view, not an inch away from Fred's nose. "Back off, bud."

Fred retreated a step. "Some people's kids sure got manners."

"Make something of it. Go ahead."

Rivers and Joan, and all the others aboard the truck, watched to see what Fred would do about it.

Well, Gramma would say he should be the bigger man. Fred smiled a little to himself. Of course if it came to a fight he could easily beat the tar out of the fellow. The bum could never be a match for one who knew how to box and who'd once lifted a thousand pounds of shelled corn off the ground. Fred decided to let it go for the moment.

The trucker stepped on the starter. The engine fired instantly and in a moment, with a lurch and a grinding of gears, they were off.

Fred straddled himself over his suitcase, legs wide apart to keep his balance.

Joan pointed back down the highway. "Is that the corn palace you talked about?"

Fred glanced around. A round mosque-like tower showed over the trees. It had a sun-darkened yellow color. "That's it, I guess."

Rivers said, "Strange to be seeing such a tower in this kind of country. Alien, really."

Fred nodded. "Not native, you mean. Autochthonous, as my favorite prof would say."

The young hobo kept giving Fred the eye. He had the hard look of a much older man. The livid light in his grey eyes went on and off as if a kaleidoscope were slowly spinning inside his skull. His gaunt hollow cheeks had the look of weathered bacon. His lips resembled the just healed edges of a light knife cut. He had a loose Adam's apple. As the truck clattered down the ribbed gravel road his head bobbed like a turkey's. There was a sandblasted look about his overalls and shirt. In contrast he had on good workshoes, well-oiled, with thick soles, and the laces were still without knots.

They passed a farm where there'd once been a considerable mudhole around a water tank. South winds had so dried out the mud that cracks a half-foot wide zigzagged all through it. The skeletons of two cows lay bleaching near the tank. They'd been picked white by vultures.

"You see that?" Joan cried, horrified.

"Yeh," Rivers said.

"It's like looking into Dante's Inferno."

"People are fools to live out here."

Fred said nothing. It was sobering to see those glistening white bones.

"Truly, a land of savages."

The hard-eyed hobo let go with a loud snort.

At Mt. Vernon they were suddenly back on smooth paving again. The terrible jolting gave way to a ride as smooth as a dream. Everybody smiled in relief. Joan adjusted her underclothes through her yellow dress. The woman sitting with her back to the red cab did the same.

The young hobo leaned over the side of the rack a while, looking down at the passing tar road. Then, as if he'd come to some kind of conclusion, he turned to Fred. "Hell, come on, I'll move over a little. You can stand here too."

Fred wasn't too sure he wanted to accept the offer. Anyone subject to such abrupt shifts in mood wasn't the best kind of riding partner, especially close up.

The young hobo moved over a good full step. "Come on."

"Oh, all right." Fred picked up his suitcase and advanced to the side of the rack. What a relief to be able to hold on to something.

Fred could feel both Rivers and Joan quietly studying the hardmouth fellow. They too had their private thoughts.

The hobo looked down at Fred's red sweater. "You one of them college bums?"

"Yes. Sorry."

"Well, my cousin went to college too and he managed to turn out all right."

"Where you from?"

"Oklahoma." The fellow more threw his words over his shoulder than spoke directly at Fred. "That's where they really had a black blizzard."

"So I heard."

"Man! Down there we had human skeletons laying around water tanks. Like a necklace of white pearls. Yeh, it was a roughty all right."

Fred saw the young fellow had his good side too.

"My mother and father died from it. Christ."

"Sorry to hear that."

"Nothing one could do about it though. It's time to get out when even the wild animals leave a country."

They rolled through Plankinton.

Fred began to feel very hungry. He pulled out the rest of the candy bar and opened the folded over end of it. Before taking a bite, he offered the young man a piece of it.

The hardmouth stared at the bit-off end; then, wetting his lips, took the candy bar, opened the wrapper at the other end, broke off a bite, almost a third of it, and handed it back. "Thanks."

Fred finished the rest of the bar.

Cracks in the earth began to show up everywhere, not just in the mudholes. Sometimes the fissures were deep, and angled in every possible direction across the passing fields. The earth had the odd look of a huge apple that had dried too fast.

Near White Lake, on the edge of town, they passed what had once been a huge pond. The old pond bed was so scorched that its cracked cakes of dried mud were frosted over with a sugarlike icing. Several of the cracks had fissured out across the road. In two places the tar paving had separated a good four inches. The trucker had to slow down for them. The several cracks in the earth jolted the riders.

The bronze haze in the west continued to thin out as they approached it. What had once looked like a distant dust storm now appeared to be a holy ambience of a rawgold texture. Dreamlike. Otherworldly.

The black water tower of Kimball came into view just as the tar road changed back to roughboard gravel. The ribbed road worked on bonejoints once more.

"Where you headed?" the hardmouth fellow asked.

"West. Nowhere in particular. Just see the sights."

"That's me. I've already been through here a couple of times looking for work. I just ramble back and forth like a tumbleweed."

"Say, my name is Fred."

"Mine's Beeford."

"That a first name?"

"Hell, no. I don't give out my first name. My ma gave me one but I never liked it. So I dropped it." Beeford stared at the label on Fred's sweater and tried to read the lettering. "Frederick Feek . . . what the hell kind of name is that?"

There it was again. Always the damned problem of the American tongue not being able to pronounce Feikema. "I suppose you could say it's Dutch. Though it's really Frisian."

"Christ, and here I always thought Beeford was a funny last name. But yours. Course Fred is all right. But Feek-e-ma?"

Fred gave Beeford a sheepish grin. It was best to laugh such things off. He couldn't blame people. Though he himself never felt alien. He felt American. In the country school he'd gone to the first five grades there'd never been any question that he belonged to the local earth north of Doon. "It's Fy´-ke-ma."

"Hm. Well, that way it don't sound too bad."

The road veered toward Pukwana, place where there'd once been a good smoke with a peacepipe. They entered the goldbrown ambience. Fine bits of brown dust floated in the air, just barely perceptible. It had an odor like stale old chocolate cake and a taste like rusting cast-iron.

Fred asked, "How do you pay your way?"

"Catch jobs where I can. Steal a chicken when I have to. And so long's it's summer I sleep outdoors. Never rains, you know."

Fred wasn't exactly flush with money himself, what with only eight dollars plus on him, seven of them in his shoe, but the thought of not knowing where one's next meal was going to come from, that was going pretty far.

The horizon began to change again. There was a rumpled look about it. And then, shortly, the edge of the earth ahead appeared to drop out of sight, away and down into a vast valley. In a moment, as the truck turned north a short distance, a broad running belt of water shimmered into view.

"The Missouri River," Fred whispered.

"Really?" Joan cried.

"My God," Rivers said, "that's wider than the Hudson."

Beeford snorted.

The lowering sun made the river look like a vast sheet of burning silver. It was hard on the eye even as the eye kept circling back toward it.

"I never dreamed it'd be that big," Fred whispered.

The humpshouldered bluffs on both sides of the river were of a kind with the great stream. The bluffs were covered with tan grass and resembled two long windrows of huge sleeping mountain lions.

The truck turned left and they began to roll downhill, the engine murmuring, the tires whistling on smooth cement paving. The first homes of Chamberlain drifted by. Then came the edge of the downtown section and the rising approach to the silver suspension bridge.

As they rumbled across the river, Fred stared down at the vast sheet of moving water. It was tan in color, with small drifting whirlpools, bobbing logs, occasional halfsoaked tumbleweeds, upboilings of ochreous sands. There was even a hugh live cottonwood bobbing along with its green leather leaves still cliddering in the breeze. The Missouri was the gathered up sum total of all flowing streams above. The Cheyenne. The Grand. The Yellowstone.

With a bump they left the long bridge. The truck picked up speed to climb the long road ahead as it snaked up through the folded bluffs. While they climbed everybody looked back. The vast river changed colors, subtly, tan turning to gray then to lightblue then to darkblue. Irregularly coursing ripples broke the flowing mirror.

Fred had the feeling that he'd passed through the lower reaches of a tremendous church, with far walls of browngold, with lofty ceilings of light floating gold, all of it suffused by the tawny music of a primitive stone organ.

They reached the top of the bluff line. A cinnamon sun lay almost level with their eyes. Darkbrown shadows reached across all the falling draws.

Rivers asked, "Where did he say he was going to turn off?"

"Kennebec," Fred said.

"Let's see that map of yours."

Fred got the map out and in the falling umber light they studied it together. "Let's see. Twenty-two miles to Reliance. Then fifteen miles to Kennebec. Thirty-seven more miles."

Rivers studied the sun. "It'll be about dusk then. Wonder if there's some kind of hotel there. Joan and I have just about had enough for today."

Fred studied the map some more. Despite the jiggling truck he made out that the name Kennebec was printed in darker letters than the names of the other towns around. "Looks to me like it's the county seat of Lyman County."

"Good. There's bound to be a hotel of some kind then. County commissioners'll certainly make sure of that."

Beeford broke in. "Not to forget the cowboys."

"Oh? Is this cowboy land?" Joan asked. She got excited all over again.

Beeford waved his hand at the long flowing land. "Take a look for yourself. Don't see many farmsteads around here. It's pretty much all ranchland."

Joan placed a slender hand on Rivers' arm. "Maybe we can have dinner with a cowboy this evening, dear." Rivers nodded. "That would be lovely."

Beeford snorted. "Dinner? Only city hicks call it that in the evening."

There were very few dust drifts. The roadside ditches were clearly defined. The old unplowed prairie sod held the soil in place.

In Reliance the buildings had a curious architecture. Most homes appeared to be made of several shacks stuck together. The whole town had a ramshackle look. Apparently the first pioneers had tried farming in the area and then, after repeated crop failures, had quit and moved their shacks to town.

The bumpy gravel road became smooth tar paving with several miles yet to go to Kennebec.

"That's better," Fred said, sighing. His belly hurt and he was tired of all the beating his bones had taken.

Rivers allowed himself a smile. "County commissioners probably also saw to that. Making sure the county seat would have good roads leading to it."

The black cylinder water tower of Kennebec hung in the sky directly above a round red sun.

The trucker slowed at the Kennebec corner, turned right, and headed up the main street. He pulled up in front of some gas tanks outside a garage. The motor fell to a mumble, backfired and coughed, and fell silent.

The trucker swung out on the runningboard. "Well, folks, this is as far as I go on 16. I live north of here."

Everybody got down, the five harvest hands, the family of five, Rivers and his wife Joan, and last Fred and Beeford. The family of five and the five grain hands headed for a bean palace called Min's Cafe across the street.

Rivers looked at Fred. "Care to join us for dinner at the hotel?"

"I think I'll just have me a bite to eat in that cafe across there."

"Aren't you going to stay over in the hotel?"

"No, I think I'm going to try for some more rides yet before dark."

"Oh." Joan more than Rivers appeared to be disappointed. "Well, suit yourself."

"Sorry."

"Remember now. Go to New York the first chance you get. You're ready for it."

"Okay."

Rivers and Joan trudged up the street.

Beeford tugged at Fred's elbow. "You really gonna eat in that cafe?"

"Yeh. Just a hamburger."

"You got the velvet?"

"I got me a roll as big as a wagon hub."

"So long." Beeford turned and headed back for Highway 16.

Fred watched him go a few steps. The fellow didn't even have a bindle he was so hard up. Sometime during the evening some chicken coop down the road would be minus a rooster. "Hey, wait up."

Beeford kept striding away.

"Wait up. I'll buy you a hamburger."

"I ain't takin' charity." Beeford snapped the words over his shoulder. "The hell with that."

"C'mon."

"No." Beeford hurried on, looking east to see if there might not be a car or truck coming.

Fred finally shrugged, then picked up his suitcase and headed across the street.

Min's Cafe wasn't much of a place. There was a smell about it as if it had once been a produce house, of eggs and sour cream.

The five grain hands sat lined up at the counter while the family sat around a table in back. They were the only customers. A fat dumpling of a woman, the Min of the place, wasn't really happy at all the sudden business. There was a pinched grimace at the corners of her lips.

Fred mounted the end chair at the counter.

"Something for you?" Min asked.

"I'll have a hamburger and a malted."

Fred tried not to look at Min's bulging fat. He thought it funny that so fat a woman should live in so lean a country. Even her big greyblue eyes rolled in fat.

The hamburger turned out be a surprise. The paddy of meat was a half-inch thick and a good four inches across. The bun was also thick, with a good chunk of homemade butter smeared on both halves. It came with a large slice of dill pickle. And the malted was so rich it stood up almost like freshly made ice cream. Fred relished it all.

"Anything else?"

"Yes. How about a nice glass of water?"

"That'll be another dime."

"What!"

The other ten customers looked up. They weren't so much surprised by Fred's exclamation as they were by the fact that a glass of water in Kennebec cost a dime.

"You're charging for water?" Fred went on.

"Got to. It costs us to have it hauled in from the Missouri River."

"My God."

"Sorry. But that's the way it is." Min licked her thick lips. "We're all but dusted out of here, you know."

"I'll go without the water then." Fred stood up. He checked the loose change in his pocket and saw he didn't have quite enough. He dug out his billfold and handed her the single dollar bill in it.

Min took the bill and looked at it a moment.

"It ain't counterfeit," Fred said, lips twisting a little.

"I ain't worried about that. It's that I maybe don't have the change." She rang up the amount, 25¢, on the cash register. The drawer banged open with an empty sound. She fingered through the several little compartments, finally came up with a handful of nickels and pennies. She counted them out. The broad calloused pad of her forefinger was larger than the pennies she pushed toward Fred. " . . . eighty, eighty-five, ninety, ninety-five, one dollar."

Fred stared at the pile of copper and nickel-silver.

One of the nearby hands allowed himself an interested smile. "Looks like you're about ready to open a bank with all that cash on hand."

"Yeh. I'm going to have to get me a cart to haul all that around with me," Fred said.

"That's the way it is," Min said flatly.

Fred cupped up the copper and nickel coins and dropped them into his trouser pocket. The money lay on his thigh like a warm brick. Then he picked up his suitcase and stepped outside.

The sun was down. The whole west horizon was streaked with a series of rising cathedrals of color, most of them a brilliant transparent citron. Main street had the look of the promised golden streets of heaven.

Fred walked toward the highway. He saw that Beeford still hadn't caught a ride.

Beeford greeted him with a little curl of lips. He first looked at Fred's belly, then his eyes.

Fred set down his suitcase on the shoulder of the tar road beside Beeford. "No cars I see."

"Not even a cowboy on a horse."

"Getting pretty late in the day, actually."

"There still might be an empty cattle truck coming back from Iowa."

Fred watched the citron cathedrals in the west change to a whole shining range of fantasy mountains leaning off to the north. Very high winds were at work shaping different atmospheres of fine dust.

Beeford had a further sneer. "Ain't you gonna sleep with that New York pair in the hotel tonight?"

"Where are you going to sleep tonight?"

"Where else but on the ground. That's been my only bed the past year."

"That should be good enough for me then too."

Beeford liked what he heard. "Listen, bo. I got a plan. Care to join me?"

Fred was afraid of what was coming next. "Yeh?"

"The last time I was through here I found out that from Chamberlain on they close down the passenger trains on one side. All the depots are on the same side of the tracks from here to the Hills. We can ride all the way sitting on those steps on the blind side. Train comes through here around four in the morning."

Fred considered the idea. What with the dust already flying plus the black soot from the engine, it was going to make for a pretty gritty ride. "You sure?"

"I did it before." Beeford stood with one hand in pocket scratching his thigh through cloth. "Course we got to be careful how we hop aboard. We don't want the local station master to see us standing alongside the tracks waiting for the train or he'll call the railroad dick. When it gets pitch dark, we'll walk over and go tuckybed a couple blocks from the tracks. When the train stops we'll sneak up in the dark and hop on."

Fred glanced down at his neatly pressed pants.

"This'll get pretty grimy."

"Well, it's your butt."

The fantasy mountain range faded away. In a few minutes darkness out of the east rushed west to shut down the whole world.

Lights came on in the town behind them. Most were the weak lights of kerosene lamps. The only electric lights on were those in the windows downtown.

"Well," Beeford said, shoving both hands into his pockets and making bulges of them, "about time we hunted us up our featherbeds."

"Yeh, I suppose there's no use waiting here."

Beeford led the way. He took a circuitous route around the west side of town, well out of range of the lamps of the houses. Presently they hit the railroad tracks. The tracks lay flat on the prairie without an embankment.

Fred almost fell down carrying his suitcase. "Cripes, what a guy won't do to save a buck."

Beeford pushed his toes carefully across the windblasted sod. "I was hoping that somewhere along here we'd find a little depression we could hide in. But no such luck. Well, we'll just walk out a little farther to make sure the big eye don't pick us out."

"Big eye?"

"Yeh, you know. The headlight on the steam engine."

Fred followed blindly after. He'd once heard there were rattlers on the west side of the Missouri. He hoped that the occasional soft lumps he felt with the toes of his oxfords were horseballs, not sleeping rattlesnakes.

"This is far enough," Beeford said. His face, a gray oval in the brown darkness, was barely visible. He made a little scurrying circle like a dog looking for the right place to light in, then knelt down and with a groan stretched himself out on the ground. "Ah, in bed at last. After a hard day's work."

Fred considered getting out his beautiful maroon blanket and spreading that out on the bare earth, but then remembered that the week before he'd had that cleaned.

"Can't you find your spot?"

Fred stooped and felt around with his fingers. "I'm okay." A couple of steps on the other side of Beeford his fingertips found a small plot of dried grass. The grassy plot didn't feel too dusty. It would have to do. He lay down. Using his suitcase as a pillow, he stretched out. "Ah, bed at last."

"Sweet dreams."

"Yeh."

There was just enough dust riding to blot out the Milky Way.

"I could do with a woman," Beeford said, more to himself than to Fred.

Fred said nothing. He wondered what Rivers and Joan were doing. Rivers was probably right at that moment making love to voluptuous Joan. But Fred didn't envy Rivers. He'd much rather spend a platonic evening with That Special Face back in Grand Rapids. He and Special Face would be soft as violets touching each other. Reciting poems to each other. Making up their own poems for each other.

"When's the last time you had it?" Beeford asked in the dark.

Fred had never done it. But he could hardly admit it to hardnose Beeford. Beeford wouldn't believe him. Unless Beeford meant masturbation. Or even worse, unless Beeford was a queer. The last thought made Fred stiffen. He'd run into one such fellow while hitchhiking from Calvin College to Chicago. Fred had been so shocked at the time that for a while he'd had trouble getting his breath and his heart had skipped occasional beats.

"It's been a month of Sundays for me." A rustling noise came from Beeford as though he were playing pocket pool. "But God, was that last one a good one. Man man. The way I put the blocks to her . . . och!" Beeford bounced up and down several times in memory. "I can hardly stand to think about it."

Fred stared up at the few stars. He couldn't imagine what kind of memory Beeford was having. It certainly had to be a whole lot more satisfying than that time he himself and the hired girl had tried fumblingly to make connection, first on the horsechair sofa and later that same night on the kitchen floor. It was a memory he didn't particularly care to dwell on. Too furtive. Too guilt-ridden. Too sad all around.

"You got a sweetie back home?" Beeford asked.

Fred said nothing.

Beeford sighed. Sighed twice. "Well, I had one once. I learned with her. And she learned with me. The first time we did it, why, it was like our brains fell out. Man."

"Was she a neighbor girl?"

"Yeh. How'd you know?"

"Just wondering."

"Yeh. She lived across the road from us. We always walked a mile and a half to school together. It's a long ways to go to school in Oklahoma. We were into everything together. You see, we were only kids and so had nobody else to play with."

"What happened? Where's she now?"

There was a sound in the dark of Beeford stretching his arms.

"Sorry. Didn't mean to pry."

"It's okay, bo." Beeford made a noise as though he were licking dry lips. "Haven't thought about Ellen in quite a while. Had so many women since she's almost washed out of my mind." Beeford coughed, once, softly. "We was about to get married when the big dust storms came. She commenced to cough about then. She coughed and coughed. Like to coughed her gizzard out. Come winter she died of pneumonia. About then my folks lost their farm to a mortgage company. No crops, no money. My folks went to town and lived on relief, and me, I went on the bum. The next time I came by, my paw and maw had died. I think they just up and quit. From a broken heart, you might say."

"Cripes," Fred said. Fred didn't know which was worse, having a dead lost sweetie or a live lost sweetie. After some further thought Fred decided maybe the bum had it the worst. The bum had lost a sweetie with whom he'd made love, while he'd only lost a sweetie with whom he'd exchanged a dry good-bye kiss.

"Yeh, it was roughty."

Fred asked, "There wasn't a baby on the way, was there?"

"Not that I know of."

"That last one you had, where did you run into her?"

"She was a small town teacher. She told me she was just out tooling around in her Chevy. About thirty. Just hadn't quite run into the right man yet. She pulled up where I was standing, looked at me fer about a minute sizin' me up, and then asked where I was going. Well, I knew right away what was troubling her. So I told her it was just to the next town. So she nodded for me to get in." Beeford sucked in his lips.

"Then what?"

"Well, we tooled on down the road. Pretty soon she said, 'I wonder, would you mind if we'd first go have a look to see if the plums are ripe along the river?' And I said, 'Not at all.' She said, 'You like plums, don't you?' And I said, 'I sure do.' So we stopped by the river. Then as we got out of the car and started for the plum trees, we bumped into each other, and then, for a fact, in about two minutes it was over."

"God."

"Yeh. It was sweet. We did it twice. The second time was the best. Because it lasted an hour."

"Then what?"

"Nothing. She took me to the next town and then she went back home."

"You mean, she did it like an animal might? No regrets?"

"Yep. It's best to do it with a stranger, you know. That way no one will ever find out about it. I didn't ask her name and she didn't mine. Besides, it's best when you do it like an animal."

Fred lay picturing the scene.

"Well," Beeford said, "for now I guess all I can do is cross my legs and pinch off the brain."

"If you could get a job, would you settle down?"

"Too late. I've been ruined for work."

"Don't you want to get ahead?"

"Ahead to what?"

"Well, you know, make a success of yourself?"

"Listen, bo, I'm pretty good at what I'm doing right now."

"But that's not what a man would call work."

Beeford sighed. "Bo, it's too late for me. I've gotten used to being free as the wind."

"Oh."

"I guess you think I'm pretty low."

"I didn't say that."

"Yeh, I can just feel myself getting worse every day. And one of these days I'll be lower than whaleshit on the bottom of the ocean."

Fred almost laughed. He thought that remark quite a conceit.

"Well, time to turn in. Night."

"Good-night."

The wind died down completely. Fred could feel an occasional large particle of dust settle on his face. He licked his lips now and then.

The patch of grass felt pretty good. Gradually Fred slipped off into sleep.

He awakened feeling cold. He listened in the night. Beeford was breathing slowly and heavily a little ways off. An involuntary shiver coursed up Fred's body. At last, with a sigh, hating to stir, Fred sat up, and opening his suitcase, got out his maroon blanket. Closing the suitcase again, and lying down, he spread the blanket carefully over himself.

That was better. The blanket instantly lay warm over him.

He dreamed up at the dark night for a while. He felt something in the corner of his right eye. With a finger he pried it out. Dust dingle. He gave it a pinch. It was gritty with the finest of sands. Sand so fine it could float on air.

Presently he heard a sound under him. He listened closely. Why! the whole earth under him was humming a single organ note. Continuous and alto. He'd never heard that before. But it was there all right. He wasn't going nuts. Everything had quieted down, the wind, animals moving, cars moving, people moving, everything, and with his ear against the earth he was really hearing it.

It thrilled him. He wished Special Face or John were there so he could share the marvelous discovery with them.

It made him wonder after a while if he himself didn't have a sound. Personal and his own. He lay even quieter, stiller, almost stiffening, straining to hear the better. But all he could hear was that low powerful pervasive alto sound of a turning brown earth.

Too bad he'd never taken music. It would be wonderful to get that sound into a piece of music. Build a symphony out of it. He'd call it The Found Chord.

He became aware that the wind had changed. He pushed out the tip of his tongue. It was coming out of the northwest. He snuggled under his maroon blanket. And doing so, he lost the alto sound of the earth. And slept.

Travels with Miss Minerva Baxter

THE PIERIAN CLUB, of which he'd been miraculously elected president, was having its annual picnic on a sandy beach along Lake Michigan, near Muskegon. As president, he'd finally talked her into a date. They rode with Red Hekman, a rich man's son. Young Hekman had suggested they double-date in his dad's Cadillac. Fred wasn't sure if Special Face went along with him because she liked riding in style in a Cadillac or because he'd begged her so hard for the date.

On the way home, sitting together in the back seat, zooming along as though in dream, she touched him on the hand. "Feike," she whispered, "if you want to you may."

His brain lit up like a telephone switchboard after a tornado. "You mean?"

"Yes. You've been telling me to give you a chance, that if we were to touch, something magical might happen between us."

"Oh, yes. That." For a second he'd thought she meant they should do it, copulate, on the back seat of the Cadillac, and he hadn't thought she'd ever have such thoughts, and it stunned him to think it.

She touched him again. "Feike?" She had a way of saying his nickname that hinted of another word, the one lying submerged just beneath it. "Feike?"

"Yes?"

"If you want to?"

He groaned, and with yet another moan all the way out of his bones, turned ever so slightly and slipped his arms around her, and held her up off the seat, a little light slim bunny, not quite crushing her, holding her so that he took the bumps of the pavement for her by making a swing of his arms. But he was too paralyzed with love to make love to her.

After the long long ride back to Grand Rapids, it was soon all too apparent that she'd lost interest in him. He hadn't taken advantage of her the one time she was willing, press in and make ardent love. . . .

~

"You do go to church Sundays, don't you?"

Fred almost jumped out of his skin. His soul snapped back from Grand Rapids to Miss Minerva Baxter's Super Six Essex. Ye gods, it was as if the forty-five year old spinster sitting next to him had picked his brain for those two words "church Sundays."

"Or aren't you really much of a church-goer?"

"Oh, I go to my father's church all right."

"You mentioned you were Frisian-Dutch. Do you go to the Dutch Reformed Church?"

"Dutch Christian Reformed."

"Oh," she said, pleased. "They're strict!"

"They sure are."

"Don't you like your church?"

Fred pursed his lips. "Oh, there are a lot of fine people in it. But the church and I don't see eye to eye on some things."

"Such as?"

Fred resented the question. She'd burst in on some choice private rememberings. The impulse to be a bit cruel with her took him over for the moment. "Well, the church is dead wrong about sex. God would never have given us a powerful sex drive and made it so pleasurable if he didn't think it was all right. I don't think He ever intended that we should think of sex as sinful."

Miss Minerva gave herself a violent hunching motion beside him. Her face remained, composed, however, and her voice quietly pedagogical. "What about the Seventh Commandment?"

"That's about adultery. I'm talking about sex between two people who love each other. Between a man and a wife who love each other very much."

"Sex! Sex! All you young people think of nowadays is sex. You're sex-besotted." Her whole mouth fell back into a set expression, as though she were about to yell out of an old agony. They'd hit on the one subject on which she was extremely touchy.

"Don't you believe in touching at all then?"

"Heavens, no. My father never touched me. Nor my mother, as far as that goes. Nor did my brother in Boise. We just never did that."

"Well, my family was a family of touchers. My mother was always touching us boys. And Pa was too. Somebody's hand was always on us. Loving and kind."

"Och! how awful. I just can't stand to have anybody touch me."

Stamford drifted by. One building housed all the business places: general store, post office, filling station. A single red gas pump stood out front. There were two houses in back. The walk to the best house was lined with collapsed geraniums.

Miss Minerva gave herself another hunching motion, moving away from him as far as she could. "Now I am glad I made that filling station boy draw an outline of you on his wall. Because I can already see that you have it in you to be a potential sex fiend."

"Oh, come now, Miss Minerva."

"It's true!"

"Really, now. I haven't even remotely made the slightest move toward you. Not even one fingertip."

"Ohh but I know your kind."

Fred decided she'd probably been rushed by some brute of a fellow. "Listen, Miss Minerva, a lot of us fellows are still idealistic, still considerate. I know that I for one am one of those. I couldn't rape you anymore than the man in the moon could."

"I don't believe you."

"Well, Miss Minerva, it goes like this. And now I'm going to have to say something you won't like. To rape a woman you have to have an erection."

Miss Minerva almost shot up through the roof of her Super Six Essex. "Erection! Why . . .!" She began to gasp like a fish thrown up on shore. "Why Mister Feikema! I forbid you to use such dirty words in my car."

"Nevertheless, there has to be an erection for there to be intromission. And I know. I'm one of those guys who'd go impotent if he'd try rushing a girl who didn't like him. It just isn't in me to be that kind of brute."

"Och! I can hardly believe you. You're just as bad as the rest of them. Because where did you learn all such talk? Disgusting."

"On the farm, Miss Minerva. Chickens, pigs, cows, horses. You see it all around you every day. Especially in the spring."

"But I don't believe that about some men not being able to."

"Why, Miss Minerva, you even see impotence, or disinterest, in the animal kingdom."

"Ho, ho."

It happened that off on their right a black bull stood alone on a knoll. The bull appeared to be dejected, head lowered as if he were the last of his kind in all of that dry country.

Fred pointed. "There's probably one of them right now. A bachelor bull."

"You mean gentleman cow."

Fred stared at her. The old Essex motor purred underfoot. "Ha. That's what my Aunt Kathryn calls 'em."

"You mean the lady who wrote the letter I read?"

"Exactly."

Miss Minerva was somewhat mollified. "Well, I can see where despite your being a man, you come of good people."

"Oh for godsakes. Listen, Pa often used to . . . We once had an old bull named Tom. Pa thought him the best he ever had. Active? Man! But yet there'd always be one cow he'd never cover. As if he didn't care for her."

"I don't believe it. I just don't believe it."

"True though. In fact, Pa usually got rid of the cow that Tom wouldn't cover. Pa said she had to be no good if Tom didn't care for her. Tom knew."

"Thomas the gentleman cow, you mean."

Fred threw up his hands in exasperation; quickly resettled them on the steering wheel.

Belvidere with its few scattered buildings up on an airy slope came toward them like an apparition. A woman in the last house on the west end of town was hanging out her wash.

The road turned to washboard gravel again. Miss Minerva, deep in thought, had more to say.

"Well, maybe there are those kind of men. Jesus was like that."

"You mean Jesus was a gentleman cow?"

"No no!" she snapped. "Don't be sacrilegious. I mean, he was the kind of man who would be most considerate of a woman."

Fred nodded with a little smile. "Jesus could hardly be accused of rape."

Miss Minerva fronted him with a hard brown look.

"You know, there's a cynical air about you that I don't like."

"Can't you take a joke?"

"Not when it comes to my Savior Jesus Christ."

"Now now, I'm sure that the Good Lord has a sense of humor."

"As a Methodist I don't like it."

"All right."

"You know, really, you're a bit uppity for one who's getting a free ride. I should ask you to get out. And let you walk the rest of the way to Kadoka."

~

He decided to tell her a little how it felt, really, to be a hitchhiker. "Actually, you know, a hitchhiker is kind of an old time minnesinger. He entertains the travelers he catches rides with. A car comes along and stops and gives him a lift. The hitchhiker repays the kind driver with the tale of his life. He sings for his ride so to speak. I caught a lot of rides going to Calvin for four years and I noticed after a while that I got better and better at telling my life story. Hitchhikers get to be excellent story tellers. They're constantly redoing their story to suit the audience's taste."

Miss Minerva sniffed. "Weren't the minnesingers really gay troubadors who went from town to town singing love songs to the maidens to win them over to their hedonistic way of life?"

Fred crooked his head. She had a point there.

~

He dug out his Standard Oil map of South Dakota. He traced the road for her with a long forefinger. "See? Instead of sticking to 16 and going north here, we could go straight south a ways down to Interior, and then once again head west and follow the north rim of the Badlands almost all the way to Wall."

Grudgingly she looked at the map. "Suppose my car breaks down in there?"

"This Super Six Essex? Never."

"Well, I had planned on seeing some of the sights."

Fred did some calculating. "It shouldn't be more than about fifteen miles out of the way."

"And I suppose it is educational."

"My friend Don took it once and he says the U.S. Government has built a nice road through it."

Miss Minerva finally nodded. "All right, we shall see it. Drive on, young man."

Fred craved a smoke. It had been hours since his last one back in Vivian.

"Something the matter?"

"Nope." Fred put the car in gear. "Here goes nothing." They crossed the corner and headed west. They were about to see a great thing.

The gravel road was rough. Five miles farther along the land dropped away on their left, and a whole valley full of rampant tyrannosaurs opened to view.

Fred slowed down. "Look at that. It's hard to believe."

Miss Minerva wasn't sure she liked it.

Then the opening in the land closed and once again they rode on flat burnt land.

"Wasn't that something."

She frowned to herself. "It's hard to figure out what the Good Lord had in mind creating such desolation. But He must've had a purpose in mind."

"His purpose was probably to show us that sometimes He can be an artist too."

"God is a God of justice, not of art."

"That's where I differ with you again. Besides, true full justice includes art."

The road turned left, zigzagged several times, then once again the land on their left dropped away. Before them lay a confusion of weird beautiful shapes, natural pyramids, ghostly peaks, tottering pinnacles. Delicate pink and cream and rose and chalk-white colors set off the various strata. The road wound down through it all, first right and then left, at last headed for a one-story government building.

Fred stopped the car beside a sign. Both he and Miss Minerva stared up through the windshield to read the legend. It told how an ancient stream had once flowed through that very spot some 23 million years ago. The stream had left gravel and coarse sand behind. Some of the gravel later formed into a conglomerate called sandstone. The upper third of most cliffs and most of the taller spires were partly volcanic ash. It accounted for the strange luminescent purple tinting.

Someone had tacked a notice on the bottom of the sign warning that there might be an occasional prairie rattlesnake sunning itself on the sand. "Stay on the trail and stay alert."

Fred could still feel the chill of that rattler sleeping against him under his red blanket. "Great country, but I sure don't like rattlers."

Miss Minerva didn't much like rattlers either. "Let's move on. I'd like to get to Rapid before dark."

Fred swung the old Essex over onto the road. The gravel road went south a ways, then swung west. They passed one sharp-edged yellowgold gully after another. The road wound through a magic land of natural minarets and castles and fortress walls. Pink and ochre and yellow lay in level parallels in all directions.

Miss Minerva couldn't stand it after a while. She lowered her eyes and picked at a thread in her skirt.

Fred drove slowly through the scenery. The different angles and serrated projections hit him like sharply struck notes on a piano. The oranges and yellows and ochres kept blending off into each other in the most delicate of shadings, reminding him of Fritz Kreisler playing *Liebestraum* on the violin. He had to fight off the impulse to get out of the car and jump up and down.

Fred finally spotted a parking area ahead and made up his mind. He drove into the parking lot and stopped the car and turned to Miss Minerva. "I don't know about you, lady, but I've just got to get out and see this close up. Okay?"

Miss Minerva continued to pick at a thread over her knee.

"It's wrong to rush past such marvels. I've got to walk into it a ways. Touch it."

She sat like a hen that'd spotted a hawk overhead and was making herself as small as possible.

"I'll be back in a jiff." He slipped out and closed the door behind him.

There were several other cars in the parking area, with license plates from distant states: New York, Massachusetts, Oregon, California. The cars were empty, everybody having scattered out along the winding path into the canyon.

The sandy clay path crackled under his oxfords. The sound of it was like walking on kernels of corn left scattered on a cement feeding platform. The path curved left down through a patch of juniper. Dusty purplish berries studded every branch. The sweetish odor rising from the juniper reminded him of a shaving lotion.

Clusters of stunted cottonwoods grew in the moist turns. The cottonwood leaves had brilliant red stems. Dark green rubber rabbitbush grew in the deeper reaches of the canyon. Tiny birds cast flitting shadows in the thicker bushes.

Fred spotted red berries in some bushes with silver leaves. That had to be the buffalo berry Grampa Feike used to talk about. It made a delicious clear jelly.

There were voices up ahead, excited children clambering up the slopes of the various downslumps, and nervous parents warning them to be careful. Mingled with it all were the raucous complaints of several black-and-white magpies. The magpie was a daring bird and didn't move until one was almost upon it. Then it jumped up, squawking loudly, appearing to use its long black drooping tail to give itself a pushoff.

The path wound around an immense monument-like pillar. The pillar thinned as it rose upward, until at its very tip it fluted out to a flat crest. Hundreds of strata hung outlined in the pillar, all the shadings possible between pink and gold.

Around yet another corner Fred came upon a perfectly sculptured candelabrum. It was so delicately balanced on a slender stem that but a touch of a finger would send it crashing to earth.

He smelled something dead. Rabbit? He moved into a side arroyo and the smell became stronger. A few steps more he saw it. A dead coyote. Someone had shot it. Two small-headed black turkey vultures were tugging away at its burst bowels. Shadows touched Fred and looking up he spotted two more vultures circling overhead, tiny heads peering down.

Fred glanced at his wristwatch. Four bells. He'd better get back.

Just as he turned the corner past the delicately balanced candelabrum, he noticed a bone sticking out of a yellow-pink wall at about eye level. The bone was huge, as big as a stovepipe. That had to be the thighbone of a dinosaur. He reached out and touched it. It felt dry and very old. It looked like the bone he'd once seen in the Field Museum in Chicago. With a fingernail Fred scratched the surface of the bone. It broke open easily, exposing a honeycomb structure.

Fred's heart beat big and slow and hard. His vision was jarred with each pulse. He had the feeling that the top of his head had opened up like a huge coneflower, that his brain had become a great eye looking straight up into angel country. His nostrils felt as big as barrels.

Ecstasy. He was having the brain explosion of a Chaucer or a Van Gogh. It was how they felt when they were at the top of their bent.

Vaguely a voice penetrated his euphoria. Miss Minerva.

"Mister Feikema? Mister Feikema?" There was a note of concern in her voice. Ah. She was beginning to like having him around.

He trudged back, slowly. He hated to leave the yellow wound. The falling sunlight fell bright on the golden erosion. The serrated knife edges of the buttes shimmered like they might be the saffron flames of a burning strawpile.

Miss Minerva was standing outside the car when he turned up the last winding curve. She was upset. Her fingers twitched. "I was sure you'd gone and hurt yourself. Slipped and fell somewhere."

Fred let himself down reluctantly. "No."

"You were gone so long."

"You should have come with me."

"Well, perhaps I should have. But I'm not much for the marvels of nature."

～

They eased into Buffalo. . . .

Miss Minerva pointed. "Let's stop at that Standard station ahead there. I see a hamburger stand across the street from it. . . ."

Several sun-wizened cowboys strolled by, boots clicking on the concrete sidewalks. They'd just ridden into town and had tied their saddle horses to a telephone pole. Farther down on a low bridge over a creek a dozen men stood talking. One of the men, a very white old-timer, was holding a fishing pole. Further on the creek curved through an expanse of thick pasture grass right in the middle of town. The scent of the fresh grass amongst the buildings was especially sweet.

"Here's your burgers and cream soda."

"Thanks." Fred placed the dollar bill on the counter and got back seventy cents in change.

Miss Minerva was waiting for him, a hungry look in her eye. She set her pop on the hood of the car and then carefully unfolded the wax paper from the hamburger. She took a deep sniff of the meat between the bread, then looked at Fred with an apologetic smile. "Just making sure the meat wasn't spoiled."

Fred smiled back. "Around here you don't have to worry. They're all fresh meat people."

Miss Minerva nodded. She took a good healthy bite, followed it with a good sip of cream soda.

It was the first time Fred had seen Miss Minerva do something hearty.

~

"I was just thinking now would be a good time for me to learn how to drive in the mountains. I have a good driver with me to teach me how."

Fred thought: "Oh, Lord. Now watch my stomach get tighter than a freighter's knot."

Miss Minerva gave Fred a great smile. "Don't you think?"

Fred hitched himself up, first on one side, then the other. "Well, it's your car. . . ."

Following the typed instructions on the windshield, pedaling and shifting gears, Miss Minerva soon had them rolling. She got the car up to thirty miles an hour and then held to it. They cruised out into open ranch country. The tar road changed to ruggly gravel.

For a dozen miles on level land Miss Minerva didn't do too badly. She'd picked up a few of Fred's driving mannerisms by just watching. She no longer kept working the wheel back and forth as she drove but held it steady. She drove with her hands positioned on the bottom of the steering wheel instead of at the top. Fred had to admire her. She might not have a wild hair, but she at least dared to take a chance.

They followed Clear Creek up a winding canyon and then climbed up through heavily wooded slopes. The old Super Six Essex had the power, and Miss Minerva didn't have to shift down.

Miss Minerva allowed herself a quiet smile of satisfaction. "Just you watch the sights now, you hear?" Fred nodded.

They mounted a wide sweeping plateau. Long slopes of beautiful standing pine, broken by occasional meadows of the greenest grass, opened ahead of them in a vast V. The V slowly but imperceptibly lifted up into dark hilltops. There were lovely trickling streams of very clear water everywhere. Cattle grazed in scattered groups as far as the eye could see.

"South Dakota could sure use some of this."

"What?" Miss Minerva kept her eye on the speedometer to make sure she had the right speed for the gear she was in.

Muddy Ranger Station came into view on their right. Two green pickups stood outside.

Fred said, "Maybe we should stop and ask how the road is up above." Fred was secretly hoping that after they got out he could somehow maneuver himself behind the wheel again.

"We're going all right, aren't we?"

"I guess so."

Mountain jays flew up off the road ahead. They'd been feeding on some horse droppings. "Clack-ak! clack-ak!" they squalled, black crests stiffly erect. Fred noted that their markings were different from the jays he'd known on the prairies. The mountain jay blue was an intense cobalt.

"Aren't we doing all right?"

"Sure. Steady as you go." Fred had the feeling that his whole left side, cheek, shoulder, thigh, had become a separate being with an extra set of eyes concentrated on her driving. "You're doing fine."

The road made a turn left and began to climb. Soon their ears began to crack.

Around a second turn, to the right, they came upon road graders at work. The Wyoming Highway Department was widening the road. The gravel became loose red dirt.

Miss Minerva, eyes on the speedometer, noted they'd fallen below twenty-five miles an hour, and immediately shifted down to second. The road graders saw the car coming and got out of the way. The begrimed men watched them go by with a shake of the head. The smell of raw red mountain earth was like the sweet fresh manure of colts. Two miles farther on the new grading ended and they once again rattled along on ribbed gravel. Miss Minerva shifted back to high. Muddy Creek tumbled rough and brownish alongside the road.

On the next bend in the road the climb stiffened very sharply. Before Miss Minerva could shift down the car began to miss and to chug. But the moment she got the car into second it took hold even and powerful again. A quarter of a mile later the climb became even steeper and again the motor began to miss and to chug. Miss Minerva shifted down into low.

Fred tried not to watch her driving. At the same time he was absolutely sure that in a couple of minutes things were going to get wild. He tried to concentrate on the landscape, noting that the timber had opened up and become sparse, that the grass was once more pale and dry like it was back on the dry plains. Many little springs trickled out of the roadside cut, some of them piling up behind self-made dirt dams and spilling palely across the gravel road.

"I think I'd speed up a little," Fred said. Miss Minerva glanced at the card of instructions on the windshield:

WHEN SPEEDOMETER SHOWS 15 MILES AN HOUR SHIFT
TO INTERMEDIATE. SAME PROCEDURE AS ABOVE.
WHEN SPEEDOMETER SHOWS 25 MILES AN HOUR SHIFT
TO HIGH. INCREASE SPEED AS NEEDED.

"But I'm almost doing fifteen miles an hour."

"Well?"

"But if I go over fifteen I'll have to shift up into second and then she'll start to chug on us again."

"It won't hurt to go over fifteen miles an hour in low. Then you'll have more power in low. And you may need it up ahead."

"But the instructions say—"

"—the heck with the instructions. Just listen to me. I know."

"But—"

"—didn't you just say back in Buffalo that you were glad to have me with you because I was a good driver who could teach you?"

"Yes, I think I did."

"Well then, speed up a little or the first thing you know the motor'll miss even in low. The air up here is very thin."

But Miss Minerva didn't speed up. Her chin came down grimly and her brown eyes turned stubborn.

With an effort Fred turned his head away and again tried to look at the scenery. The scape became even more barren. Enormous jagged granite peaks shoved up around them. Fred thought it hostile cold-hearted country. Yet it was also very beautiful. In some of the steep high north valleys lay great drifts of old yellow snow. There were tiny dots of color everywhere, white, blue, yellow, even orange, and when Fred looked more closely he saw that the varied dots were tiny flowers growing in moss-covered tundra.

His ears cracked. He swallowed to clear them. The smell of old snow reminded him of a frozen piece of chocolate cake he'd once eaten in grade school.

The highway veered around to the right; became extremely steep. Off on their left a sheer dropoff thousands of feet deep wheeled into view. The sensation was as if the continent were dropping away from them and they were left on the only remaining high ground.

The old Essex began to cough. As Fred had feared it was having trouble firing in the rarefied air.

"Give her some gas!" Fred cried. "Step down on that footfeed."

"Nevermind now. I'm doing the driving."

"That's just the trouble. Step on the gas, woman!"

Miss Minerva stubbornly refused to step on it.

Fred's belly became as tight as a snare drum.

The view beyond the left front fender of the Essex became sensational. Vaguely, far down, a little town could be made out in the light blue mist of a great distance. The blue atmosphere shaded off into varied tossing landscapes of brown and red and orange. The blue atmosphere made the colors work in lovely harmony. In the midst of it all a single bald eagle hung on air perfectly poised, unmoving, as if stuck into the atmosphere with a taxidermist pin.

Fred could see they were near the top of the climb. Several hundred more yards and they'd make it. Ahead, on the right, was a large signboard. Squinting, Fred made out the legend:

MUDDY PASS

ELEVATION 9666 FEET

The Super Six engine coughed again; choked; coughed; quit. The car chugged to a stop.

"Oh dear."

Fred's brain began to prickle like a limb having fallen asleep.

Miss Minerva studied the typed instructions on the windshield, began following them to the letter. She first put the gear in neutral. Then she touched the starter. The starter whirred; whirred. Nothing. There was only the desperately sucking sound of the carburetor.

The car began to roll backward.

Fred glanced over his shoulder. Because of the curve in the road he could see that if the car rolled a couple of dozen feet straight back it would sail off into space, falling God only knew how far. Something had to be done.

Fred lunged across in front of Miss Minerva, his left elbow catching her in the belly, and jerked back the handbrake by the door, while with his right hand he grabbed the steering wheel and turned it to make the rear wheels stay on the road.

Miss Minerva gasped. He'd hit her so hard in the belly he'd knocked her breath out. "Uh . . .uh . . ."

Next with his left hand he shoved the shift into high gear. The gears under the floorboard crashed.

"The-uh . . . nerve-uh . . ."

Both the handbrake and the dead engine began to take hold. Chug . . . chugg . . . chuggg . . .

Again Fred glanced over his shoulder. The car was rolling dangerously close to the loose gravel along the edge of the road. Beyond the edge he caught a glimpse of a depth he had trouble believing. The dropoff at that point was tremendous. It had to be a precipice of at least a thousand feet. God.

Chug-ugg. And the car stopped dead.

"Get out!" Fred commanded.

Miss Minerva got her breath back. "Uch." Instantly she flew at him like some old brood hen robbed of her eggs. "Why, you terrible man, hitting me in the stomach like that! Why, I have half a mind—"

"Get out of the car!"

"—to ask you to get out of the car and make you walk the rest of the . . . what?"

"Get out of the car so I can slide over under the wheel. Because I'm driving from here on in."

"Swearing at me?"

"Woman, you damned near killed us with your damnable dilatory reading of those silly instructions."

"Dilatory? What's that mean? Why, you—"

"Will you get out from under that wheel? Because so help me God if you don't, I'll jump out and let you roll off the mountain by yourself."

"—ruffian you!"

"Take a look for yourself back there then."

With an outraged look she slowly twisted around in the seat and looked back. "Oh!"

"Yes!"

"Oh dear."

"Yes. And now will you please for Sweet Jesus' sake get out from under that wheel? There'll be just enough room for you to walk around in front of the car and get in on my side here."

"Oh dear."

When she still didn't move, but sat there exclaiming mildly, Fred gave her another punch in the belly with his left elbow, lighter though than before, and then gave her thigh a good pinch.

The pinch did it. "Oh dear," and she got out deftly.

"Just hang onto the side of the car and you'll be all right."

"Yes yes."

The moment she was out Fred carefully slid over under the wheel and got control of the old car. He waited until she'd got in on the passenger side. Then, half-twisting in the seat and looking back, he carefully let out the brake a little and then pushed in the clutch a bit and let the Essex start rolling again. He let it roll until the right rear bumper caught on a projecting rock in the cut on the right side of the road. Then, safe, Fred let out a great breath. "Wow."

The two of them sat very still for a moment. There was only the loud cracking of the sinuses inside the head.

Fred said, "I'm going to set that a carburetor a little richer so we can get out of here. The next thing you know another wild-eyed tourist will be on our tail." He got out and opened the hood to see what tools he needed. "Do you have a screwdriver in the car?"

"Yes." Miss Minerva moved in jerks. "In here." She pawed through the glove compartment and came up with a brown-handled screwdriver.

Fred reset the screw on the choke. Then he closed the hood and got in behind the wheel. He handed back the screwdriver. "Now." He turned the key and pushed the starter. The starter whirred several times, and then, miracles of miracles, the engine fired. It coughed a few times; then leveled into an even purr. Presently it ran merrily. "Good."

In a moment he had the car in gear and they proceeded to the top of the pass. "May our merciful God be thanked," Miss Minerva whispered.

The road down the other side of the mountain was even steeper. At times the hairpin turns were so tight Fred had to put her in low, with the brakes on, and wheel her hard left and hard right, elbows swinging back and forth. There were great gaping canyons off the edge of the road, first on the left, then on the right. The turns were so tight it sometimes looked as though the road were going straight off into space.

Miss Minerva had to look and yet hated to look. She couldn't believe she was where she was. When the dropoffs became even more pronounced, she finally couldn't take it any longer and leaned forward, hiding her face in her hands on her knees.

Fred was still angry. About halfway down they came to a curve he was sure was meant to shoot them off into space. There was no way the highway engineers could have completed the curve around the sheer rock on the left.

Miss Minerva asked, voice muffled, "Is the road getting any better?"

Fred smiled. She'd given him such a scare she deserved one good jolt in turn. "Yep. In a minute we'll be in heaven."

Very gradually she raised her head. When her eyes came up level with the bottom of the windshield and she saw what there was to see, that the road speared off into nothing, space, she gulped; dropped her face down on her knees. "Mercy sakes!"

Fred laughed. At the same time it surprised him that he sometimes could be mean to people.

"You fooled me!" she cried muffled into her knees.

In the late afternoon sun the rock walls of the canyon had a smooth satiny red color. It struck Fred that here would have been the perfect place to stick Devil's Tower.

Fred let the motor drag as much as he could, braked hard, gritted his teeth, wheeled her over a hard careful left. And made the deadly curve.

Fred drove carefully around two more curves. And then the road leveled and at last straightened out. All around them towered great granite rocks. The shadows off the staggered mountains enveloped them in deep purple dusk.

Fred turned on the lights.

Miss Minerva heard the click. "Is it all right now?"

Fred let down. "Yes, Miss Minerva. You can look up now. We've finally made it to the bottom."

Again she raised her head, cautiously. When she saw that, yes, truly the canyons were gone and the land was leveling off, she let go with a vast sigh. "Merciful Father in heaven." She took a deep breath, and then said, softly, "That was a dirty trick, Frederick." It was the first time she'd called him by his given name.

"I know."

"It was very mean of you."

"Yes. And I apologize."

She sniffled back a few tears.

Fred said, "And I must admit I also should have had my wits about me in the first place. I should have had that carburetor set richer back there in Buffalo. I just wasn't thinking, I guess."

The lights of Tensleep swung into view around a curve. A filling station, a grain elevator, several stores and saddleshops lined both sides of a wide graveled street, all of them false-front frame buildings. A dance pavilion stood set back on a lot by itself. Across the street from the pavilion stretched a row of gray tourist cabins. A bright light burned over the door of a nearby cafe. Miss Minerva cleared her throat. "I think we should stop here. We've had enough for today."

∼

The next morning they gassed up, checked the oil, kicked rubber, and with Fred at the wheel were off down the curving gravel highway.

∼

"Greetings," the ranger said, leaning down into the car on Fred's side. "Welcome to Yellowstone National Park." The ranger was a slim vigorous looking fellow, with a pinkish-brown face and lively brown eyes. His brown eyes seemed to look everywhere at once both in the front and the back seats. He spotted the food. "Be careful you do not feed the bears. It may seem cute to see a bear eat an apple or a doughnut, but if he should happen to demand more, he can be very dangerous."

∼

The sun was almost down. The top of the mountain ridge to west hurled long purple-green shadows at them. The bracing smell of crushed needles entered the car.

Fred pulled up in front of the information center. . . . "You want me to find us a cabin?"

Miss Minerva quickly got hold of herself. She clutched her purse. "No, I'll make the arrangements. You just stay near the car. And watch out for the bears." She got out and went over to talk to the ranger in the information center. . . .

"A cabin is really that much," Miss Minerva said, biting on her lips. "Well then, how much are the tents?"

"One dollar a night."

"Are they safe from animals?"

"Just be sure to leave your food in the car. And make sure the car is locked."

. . . Miss Minerva finally made up her mind. "Well, I'll just have to take it." She looked at the number over the canvas flap door. "Twenty-two. I've already spent more here than I planned on. That entrance fee I hadn't expected. Now I've got to save that back."

"A dollar a tent isn't much. I'll pay for my own."

"No, no, I don't want you to spend any money so long as you're working for me. No, what we'll do is I'll sleep in the tent and you sleep in the car. Every dollar adds up, you know."

~

He was just drifting off to sleep when he heard it. A cautious padding of heavy feet. A slow deep sniffing of the air. A twig cracked. Yes, a brain was sending out its feelers to see where everybody was sleeping. After a second Fred felt those alien brain feelers within a foot of his head. If it wasn't a camp thief it had to be big Black Bimbo. Probably checking out the car for the smoked bacon.

The ranger from the information center had said, "He likes to come around about this time of the day and throw a scare into people. He's one of the few bears around who likes his steaks well-done. About the only raw meat he cares for is smoked bacon . . . They can smell it through a cement wall."

The hair all over Fred's back ruffed up. There were several slowly drawn snuffs immediately behind Fred's head. Apparently satisfied the smoked bacon wasn't in the Essex, the searching brain backed away from the car.

Fred relaxed a little.

There was some more cautious rustling nearby. The black brain was sniffing over the ashes. Then the black brain retreated into the woods and there were no more sounds.

Gradually Fred nodded off to sleep. He dreamt he was sitting in a big wooden swing and that Pa was trying to give him a push but no matter how hard Pa tried he couldn't budge the swing. It had the brakes on and the two ropes just would not bend. Pa gave the whole thing another look, the stiff swing and the big cottonwood tree it was tied to, and made up his mind. He put his arms around the huge cottonwood and with a mighty wrenching heave tore the tree out of the earth, roots and all, and then, with another mighty wrenching motion, threw everything, with Fred still in the swing, into an enormous canyon. Fred hung onto the swing for dear life. But when Fred saw where he was going to land, in the great red mouth of Black Bimbo the bear, he—

There was a terrified shriek.

Fred jerked upright, cracking his head against the roof of the car.

There was another shriek, this time even louder, of both terror and outrage.

Miss Minerva. Something had happened to her. Fred already knew what it was. He lifted his legs off the steering wheel and bounced out of the car. He was just in time to see, in the vague light under the trees coming from the parking area, the huge burly hairy form of something black galloping off into the dark with an odd-looking object in its teeth.

Miss Minerva continued to shriek, shrill on quavering shrill. The shriek radiated out of her tent like the whistle of a siren.

Everybody came rushing out of their tent doors, halfdressed, hair wild, mouths open. "What happened?"

The park ranger on duty in the Information Center came on the dead run carrying a rifle, "What's going on out here?"

Fred pointed at Miss Minerva's tent. One side of it appeared to have been deftly rolled up in a couple of feet while the other side had been blasted out with the staked ends flipped back over on its log roof.

"My God." The ranger jerked a long flashlight off a hook on his belt and flicked it on and aimed its beam of light through the blasted tent.

There on her back lay Miss Minerva in her nightgown on the floor, bare legs up in the air and pumping like she was in a furious bicycle race. Her eyes were tight shut and her mouth was wide open. Her shrieks continued to fracture the night air. The ranger worked his flashlight quickly through the tent, but not finding any culprits next flashed it all around outside, far out under the pines and then up and down the line of tents.

Fred said, "I think it was that big black bear we saw earlier in the evening. The other ranger called him Black Bimbo."

"Yeh," the night duty ranger said. "There was a note on my desk about that. Miss Baxter never did bring in her smoked bacon."

"I was afraid of that." Fred settled on his heels and called into the tent. "Miss Minerva?"

Miss Minerva continued to shriek and pedal the air.

The ranger said, "She's hysterical."

"Yeh." Fred noticed the double ring of faces that had gathered around them, staring, mouths agape. "Get back, you people. This is private."

"Not if a bear did that, it ain't," an older man said.

Fred crawled inside the tent. He placed his hand firmly on Miss Minerva's belly. "Now now. Quiet down here. It ain't all that bad."

She paused, gathered breath, eyes opening very wide and white. She saw his silhouette; promptly pinched shut her eyes again and cried out. "I knew it, I knew it!"

"Oh shut up, Miss Minerva." Fred gave her a rough shake. "Everything's all right. You're still alive and that's all that matters."

Again she fell silent. "Frederick?"

"Yes, Miss Minerva, it's me, your driver. Come, get yourself up off that floor." She jerked erect. "Where's my bathrobe?"

The light from the ranger's flashlight fell on a chair over which she'd draped her clothes. The cot she'd slept on was tumbled over on its side, partially collapsed, with one of the blankets pulled partway outside. Fred spotted a red-and-black robe. "Here you are."

Stiffly she got to her feet and slipped into her bathrobe. Then she opened her tent from the inside and stepped outside. When she spotted all the gaping faces in the wavering light she turned sideways to them.

"Mercy me."

The ranger aimed his flashlight around at all the faces. "Okay, you can all go back to bed. Everything's under control here." He had the alert face and erect stance of an athlete.

Not one face left.

The ranger took Miss Minerva by the arm. "Are you all right?"

"Of course I'm all right. Though I didn't think so a minute ago when that monster almost raped me."

"What happened?"

"Well, I was sound asleep, dreaming about my brother and how nice it would be to see him again, when all of a sudden I awoke feeling myself being lifted up in the air as if an earthquake were erupting under me. When I threw out my hands to save myself, I felt all this hair. I thought sure Frederick my driver here had come to rape me. Och!"

"My God, Miss Baxter," Fred cried.

"Well, I did. And considering everything, how was I to know? I know nothing about what makes you men such animals."

"Me, of all people?"

The ranger broke, in. "Then what happened?"

"Well, then the next thing I knew this hairy beast got his nose between the mattress and the cot and proceeded to pass between the two."

The ranger gave her a sideways look. "You put some food under your mattress, didn't you?"

Miss Minerva went on the attack. "What kind of a park do you people run here, letting wild animals get in among civilized people." Miss Minerva flexed herself up on her toes. "And so what if I did decide to hide my bacon under my mattress? Isn't that my privilege in America? It's a free country, isn't it, where I keep my bacon?"

The ranger almost smiled. He said politely, "Weren't you warned about the bears when you drove into the park?"

"Well, I certainly wasn't told about bears wanting to get into bed with one."

"And wasn't it suggested that you should place your bacon in our icebox for safekeeping?"

"Well, I thought my bacon would be perfectly safe where I put it. And anyway, I tied my tent shut and that should have been safe enough, and if it wasn't, then you shouldn't be allowed to rent people tents around bears, but should have only secure log cabins with steel locks."

Fred smiled. "Well, anyway, Miss Minerva, everything's turned out all right in the end, hasn't it? What's important is that you're safe. So why don't we all go to bed and get in some sleep. Okay?"

"But my bacon? What'll we have for breakfast?" Fred took her firmly by the arm. "I'll buy us a breakfast in the cafeteria in the morning. Come, let's go to bed. I'll help you tie down the sides of your tent."

The young ranger thought that was a good idea. He waved his flashlight at the other campers again. "All right, everything's under control. You can go back to bed now."

There was some muttering about the danger of wild bears, and several of the men campers stood talking a moment, but soon everybody went to bed.

Fred and the ranger put Miss Minerva's cot back together again, and restaked the sides of her tent, and comforted her with joshing small talk until, with several clucking sighs, Miss Minerva got back on her cot.

Fred was wide awake and he walked with the ranger part way back to the Information Center. "Thanks a lot."

"All part of a night's work."

"She's sure some dame."

"She relation of yours?"

"No. We just met a couple of days ago. I was hitchhiking in South Dakota and she picked me up. She needed a driver."

The young ranger became alert. "She doesn't know you very well then?"

"No, nor I her. And I'll be glad when our ways part."

"Well, aren't you free to leave her any time you want to?"

"I suppose I am." Fred scuffed at the gravel in the path. "But you see, sir, she's a lousy driver. Until a week ago she'd never driven a car and then all of sudden she bought that Essex in Chicago and started driving west to see her brother in Boise. Man, I don't know if you noticed it or not, but she's got driving instructions pasted up on her windshield and she doesn't make a move without referring to it—even in the middle of traffic. Or, as she once did up in the Big Horns, on a curving turn near Muddy Pass! I thought for sure we were goners until I took the wheel away from her."

"Oh."

"So, even though I'm getting awfully sick of her being so bossy, I thought I'd stick with her until I got her safely into Idaho."

"Where you going?"

"I've got a friend living up in Belgrade. That's west of Bozeman there."

"Hmm." The young ranger slowly allowed himself a smile. "Well, I don't envy you. But it's pretty swell of you to take her under your wing like that."

Fred smiled. "All part of a night's work. Especially if you've been raised right."

"Yeh, I suppose. Well, good-night."

"Night."

Fred went back to the old Essex and draped his legs over the steering wheel once more and nuzzled around on the front seat until he found his old position. He laughed a couple of times as he replayed in his mind what had happened. Once he laughed right outloud, merrily, when he recalled Miss Minerva's remark that, upon feeling all that hair, she thought it was her driver Frederick come to rape her. She sure must've had some racy thoughts about him if she thought he'd have that kind of hair on him somewhere.

Fred slept.

The Golden Bowl

*I was hit by [the dust bowl] experience while riding in the back of this truck
through South Dakota. Plus the memory of that boy who to me seemed like
he'd once been a very nice fellow, but who was now empty, hollow, defeated.
I wasn't satisfied with that idea for myself because I personally wasn't defeated. That's why in this book I have Maury return home. That's the part
that's invented.*

*I remembered this boy's voice, and some of his mannerisms, but I filled in
all the rest around that voice from my general knowledge of people and from
the experience of my people who hung on and survived the dust bowl.*

Maury Comes to the Thor Place

MAURY SAID DRYLY, "Well, it's a nice country, but you need water."

"Oh, we'll get some," Pa Thor said hopefully. "I felt my leg actin' up again
this mornin'. An' it's one a the best weather vanes in the country. Never fails.
An' right now it seems to be achin' around fer a change in the weather." He
looked at the sky for a sign of a cloud. "I'm almost sure we'll get a change tonight.
Ache is pretty strong."

Maury grunted as he dried his face on an old towel. "Well, I've been achin'
fer four years now, every bone in me, an' if each ache had meant a cloud the
world would've washed away by now."

Pa Thor stilled. He settled on his heels on the steps.

Kirsten sat down beside him.

Then, presently, Pa Thor stirred again. He coughed, and said, "Well, the dew
always helps a little, though. Freshens up the greens some."

"Yeh, an' helps fry 'em better when the sun gets high."

"Well . . . it'll be all right. Some day, when the rains come again, the land will
turn green an' lift into the hills, an' roll again. I know it will." He looked dream-
ily over the land. "That'll sure be nice, when she cracks over the land. "That'll
sure be nice, when she cracks with growin' things. It sure will. There'll be bright
greens, an' chickens peckin' away under the tall grain. Why! we're liable to
have a bumper any year now!"

Maury murmured disgustedly to himself. He waited for Pa Thor to get up
to wash and then took the old man's place on the steps beside Kirsten. He fumbled with his cigarette makings.

They were silent together. There was only the noise of Pa Thor splashing his face with water. Kirsten sat as still as a watchful creature.

Soon Ma Thor came to the door. "You kin come in now," she said.

They filed in slowly.

Maury looked quickly around. The house reminded him of his home. There, in the back to the north, was the room where the family slept. Its door opened near the wall. Here, in the kitchen, they were assembling about the table against the south wall. A black stove with nickel trimmings stood against the center of the west wall. A window opened on either side of it, and he could see the fields stretching away to the rim of the earth. An old, well-oiled shotgun hung over the stove beneath the worm-elbow of the stovepipe. A dish cabinet and a cooking work-table stood against the east wall. There was a window in the center of the wall. The curtains were gray and frayed and much washed. There was an atmosphere of neatness about. Maury's face lighted a little. When he turned to the table, he saw that Kirsten had been watching him. He smiled briefly.

Ma Thor said, "Mister, you take that chair there, across from Kirsten. Pa, pull up your chair from the winder."

Pa Thor groaned a little as he pulled the chair across the room. "My leg does ache a little harder this mornin'."

"Sure, Pa. Sure. That's good," Ma Thor said, comfortingly.

Pa Thor shifted in his creaking armchair and rubbed his leg.

Ma Thor pushed the plates around with little nervous gestures. "We ain't got much. We just got some tapioca an' some bread an' coffee. Used to have some bacon, but . . ."

"Oh, that's all right," Maury said, sliding a portion of tapioca onto his plate. "This looks plenty good to me."

There was a brisk smell of coffee in the room. After a moment, Maury felt comfortable. He expanded a little. "Sure nice a you folks. Takin' in a stranger like me. Pretty nice. Very." then he added hastily, "'Course, I know how farm folks is. They're all friendly. My folks was too."

Ma Thor asked, "How long since you left the farm?"

"Four years ago. Four years." He looked at his plate. "Golly, that's a long time to be nowheres at all! Golly! An' I ain't done nothin' since. If this keeps up I won't have nothin' to look forward to, or nothin' to look backward at."

Pa Thor hitched his chair closer. "Son, are you pretty broke?"

"Yeh." Then after a few ticks of silence, he added, "Yes. Pretty broke."

Pa Thor went on, craftily, "You know, you act like you think it ain't gonna rain in this country again."

Maury looked at him directly. "Well, to tell you the truth, I don't think it is."

Pa Thor nodded. "Well, 'course my leg could just be kickin' up a little. Anyway, that crick a mine is still runnin' with water. And all of it is slippin' away an' doin' no good. I was thinkin' it over yestiddy, an' figgered that if it wasn't gonna rain no more it might not be such a bad idea to build a little dam down there where she turns by the willers. Nice little spot there fer a dam. It'd soak up the ground on the lower forty, an' if a man took some time an'd run the water along little ditches, why! a man might get a few bushels a grain and corn."

Maury rolled a lump of food over in his mouth. He visualized the idea, then said, "Well, now, that sounds pretty good." He chewed the food and swallowed it. "You know, it's a cinch it won't rain any more. Danged if that ain't a hell of an idea."

Pa Thor pulled his chair closer. "Well, that's what I thought. An' my two hay-burners, Becky and Beaut, they've been eatin' pretty good these last few weeks, an' they kin stand a little work now. An' I got an old scraper. One a the handles ain't so good, but there's spare branches around that won't do no more growin'. But you see, I'm too old to hold down the danged scraper. The ground's too goldurn hard. It's like cement. An' Kirsten . . . by golly, I don't want my daughter to rip up her belly doin' it either. So you see how it is, son."

Ma Thor poured out some more coffee for Maury. She held the lid on the coffee pot with the corner of her apron spread over her fingers. She said, "If we had Tollef, but . . ." A few tears came into her eyes.

Maury knew what was coming. He felt uncomfortable. "Well, I dunno now."

Ma Thor went on, "This boy looks somewhat like him too, don't he?" she asked Kirsten wistfully.

Kirsten nodded.

Maury said suddenly, "Now look here. Damn it, I'm in a hurry to get back to the Hills. Just gotta hurry to get out there. Just gotta. I've been wanderin' aroun' fer four years, four years a my best life. An' there's a chance, just a chance I kin lay up a little dough diggin' in the gold mines, an' then set out fer myself. An' if I stay here to help you, well, hell, probably the jobs will be all filled up."

Pa Thor reflected, "But if you've been out in the open so long, on the road an' on the farm do you think you'll like the gold mines? Do you think you could live inside a dark, wet hole?"

Maury was stubborn. "Anyway, I can't stay here. I've been talkin' a workin' in the gold mines fer days now, an' ain't never got to it yit. Now that there's jobs there, I ought to go. I just gotta go on."

Pa Thor considered. "Well, we can sell a little of the cream. Maybe . . . do you think, Ma, Kirsten, do you think we kin pay him a little somethin' besides keep?"

Ma Thor said, "I dunno now. We got to get you a new overall. An' there's bakin' stuff to buy. Gotta think a that, too."

"I know."

Ma Thor said, and Maury could feel her looking at his shoulders and his grim mouth, "I think we can give him something, Pa."

Pa Thor studied the streaks of tapioca in his plate. "Well, son, supposed we give you a dollar fer three days' work. That'll just do it. We kin do the dam in three days, if there ain't no rain. An' if there's rain . . . why! then we'll pay more."

"No."

There was a silence in the room. Maury sat awkwardly at the table.

Ma Thor said, "Well, if the young feller don' wanna . . . why, Pa, I s'pect you ought to let him go. He knows his own mind."

Maury said, feeling easier, "Well, I would help you, but you know, I gotta get started. I feel like I've been wastin' a lot a good time these last four years."

Pa Thor stood up tiredly. "Guess I better get to movin' on the yard. Kirsten, you gonna help me get the horses?"

Kirsten stood up and nodded. She looked at Maury silently, then followed Pa Thor through the door.

Maury stood up to go.

Ma Thor began to pile up the plates. "Pa feels bad about your not helpin' him. He's been trying to get some one out here fer a couple a weeks. But there just ain't nobody. Some a them bums in Sweet Grass got the time an' need the money, but they think the dam's a fool stunt. No, Pa's gonna feel bad, and Kirsten too."

"But you see how it is, Mrs. Thor."

Ma Thor nodded. "If the dam works, you could stay all year round, you know. Pa's thataway."

Maury said weakly, "I'd stay a couple a days. But . . . well, trouble is, you people'd figger I'd stay all year round. An' . . . Mrs. . . . Ma, I'd go nuts if I had to work here knowin' there was nothin' ahead 'cept starvin' and chokin' in the dust."

Ma Thor looked at him sharply. "What about us? An' Kirsten?"

Maury looked at his feet He was standing in the open door and he could hear Pa Thor and Kirsten calling the horses. "I know it," he grumbled. He thought a moment, scratched his backsides, and then said, "Okay then. But the only way I'll help is knowin' that at any minute I kin quit . . . that I'm doin' it as a lark."

"Sure, son."

Maury scuffed his shoe on the doorsill. "Guess I better bring in my things then."

Ma Thor said, "I got a cot upstairs in the attic. It's Tollef's. I'll get it down and set it by the stove, there by the winder. An' you kin set your things there fer the time bein'."

Maury brought in his bundles and then went outside. He walked across the yard and then, hesitant, entered the barn.

Pa Thor, harnessing the horses, held his hands still and stared at him.

Kirsten straightened quickly.

Maury's eyes shifted to the ground. Then he said, "Well, c'mon. Get the harnesses on. The sun's et a big hole in the day already."

Pa Thor swallowed twice.

Kirsten brightened.

Maury looked at the harness, and then reached for the crupper. He slipped it under the tail. "Which one is Becky?" he asked.

Pa Thor said hastily, "This one. This spotted gray one. The straight gray is Beaut."

"Good horses," Maury commented, slapping Beaut's rump. "But they's a bit weak yit."

"Well, we'll work 'em easy, son."

Maury nodded. He slipped off the halter from Becky's head and replaced it with bridle. Then he led her outdoors.

Kirsten had gone ahead. She was already pumping water into a cracked, wooden tank.

Looking at her, Maury asked, "Water 'em?"

Pa Thor nodded. "Know how to hitch horses?"

"Sure."

"Well, I have to get an axe an' some nails an' a hammer. May have to do a little buildin' to brace up the dirt."

The Crazy Wind

NEAR MORNING Maury was awakened by a drumming sound. He lay quietly for a few minutes, not knowing, at first, where he was. When it became clear to him, he looked up, to see Ma Thor's gray face sad in the lamplight as she worked on her darning.

"What time is it, Ma?"

"About four."

Maury raised himself to a sitting position. "What you doin' up so early?"

She nodded in the direction of the door. "Lissen."

He listened to the noise a moment. "Oh. The wind."

She didn't move for a moment. She stared at him. She said, "Yes, a big wind."

Maury listened for a time. There was dust on the sheets. His mouth and fingers felt gritty with fine sand. "How long's it been blowing up, Ma?"

"A long time."

"Funny it started in the night."

"Yes."

"It usually starts about noon, when it starts. Funny." He shook his head. Something more than a big wind was up, he felt. He was wide awake now. "What you doin' up, Ma?"

"Waitin' fer Pa. He's gone to put the animals in the barn. An' get sacks ready to put dust mufflers on 'em."

Maury remembered. One night in Oklahoma when he and Pa had gone outdoors to mask the cows, the black wind had been so strong that it had extinguished the flame in a kitchen lamp his mother had been carrying. And she had stumbled in the dark house and had broken her leg. When they had come back, they had found her, tumbled on the floor by the table. He ground his teeth now as he remembered that ancient anguish. And, suddenly stubborn again, he growled, "Ma, wake me when it's five. I gotta get started today."

"I will, son."

Maury turned his back to her and lay like a stone.

The wind tore at the shingled roof and sprayed sand over his face. The house shook when the wind bore directly down upon it. Sometimes there was a steady banging sound, as if a door were slapping somewhere in the wind. The sound of the creaking gate outside was like the scratch of a spoon on a pan.

He snuggled deeper beneath his blankets. And, pressing his knees against his chest and his heels against his bottom, he dropped off to sleep again. He dreamed of Kirsten. He dreamed of hunger in a black, dry land.

When Ma Thor called him at five o'clock, Maury got up heavily. He spat dust out of his mouth.

Ma Thor set out a basin of water for him on the kitchen table, and beside it she laid out a plate and a fork and a knife and a spoon. Then she set out a cup of steaming coffee.

Just as he finished washing, Kirsten stumbled out of the back room, her hair straggling over her cheeks, her eyes thick with sleep.

Maury, excited, and full of tolerance now that he was going on, stooped to a little flattery, and said, "Well, here's one woman who looks pretty in the mornin'."

Ma Thor smiled briefly and rubbed her hand over Kirsten's brow. "Yes, Kirsten is a good girl."

Kirsten murmured something unintelligible.

Ma Thor said, "Now, now. You better go wash your face. It'll make you feel better." She pushed Kirsten toward the sink and then went to the stove for the cooker of tapioca and poured some out in Maury's plate on the table.

As he ate the hot gruel, he watched Kirsten bending over the sink. Her dress lifted a little. He saw the soft flesh of her thigh. Catching himself scheming again, he looked quickly down at his plate.

For the first time, he noticed that the food was gritty with fine sand. He shivered each time his teeth bit on a grain of it.

By the time he had finished his breakfast and lighted a cigarette, Kirsten had finished her washing and had combed her hair. She looked bright again. He watched her peering through the window to the east, where it had begun to lighten.

Kirsten turned. "You're goin'?"

Maury nodded.

She hesitated, looked once more at him, and then quietly went over and began to roll up his bundles for him.

He watched her a moment, startled by the meaning of her gesture. Abruptly, he jammed his cigarette into his plate and went over and pushed her away to pack the bundles himself.

Finished, he turned, looking off to one side toward the floor, "Well, so long. I'm gonna try it." He glanced briefly at Ma Thor, then at Kirsten, and, turning, quickly picked up his bundles and stepped outdoors into the black wind.

He was glad that Pa Thor had not been in the kitchen. He would have found it hard to bid the old man good-bye.

After a struggle, he came upon the edge of the gully and dropped quickly into it. But the ditch beside the road gave him little protection. The dust fell thickly on him, filling his mouth and his eyes. He spat fiercely and blinked as he fought his way to the corner.

He stood there a little while. It became light enough to see objects vaguely. He looked up the road and waited. There was a real dust storm roaring in, all right. He could not see more than twenty feet in any direction. His clothes became heavy and clogged with the dust and sand. He worried about his guitar, that it would fill with dust and lose its tone.

His lips drew back into a bitter, wrinkling grin. He blew his nose. He coughed and spat with the wind. He cleared his throat. He could feel his lungs become sore. He leaned into the wind. But no car came.

He endured it for an hour before giving up.

And when, finally, he did turn to go back to the Thors, he felt broken inside. He went to the door despondently. Without knocking, he opened it and entered.

Kirsten jumped up from her chair. He saw her repress a quick smile.

Ma Thor calmly walked to the stove and picked up the coffee pot. She refilled his cup.

The hours went by slowly.

Maury sat in Pa Thor's chair by the window. He felt guilty about not going to help the old man, who was still in the barn, but he could not find it in himself to fight the storm.

It was Kirsten who went out to help.

The hours lifted the morning into noon. The wind continued to raise the surface of the earth into the sky. The grass in the pasture and the hay land, and the young corn, lay bent against the ground. They became brown and riddled, and black-edged holes opened in the stems and the leaves.

They were in the house. Pa Thor had come in again. He sat in his armchair near the window, looking dolefully out into the bruising storm. Kirsten worked over a dress. Now and then she stood up, put her hand on Pa Thor's shoulder and looked with him into the darkness outside. Maury tried to read an old magazine by the light of the fluttering kerosene lamp on the table. Ma Thor patched on a pair of overalls.

Once, Maury, watching the wind shake out its long black arm at him from the south, tried to ease the feeling in the room. "You know, Pa, the way the wind's been blowin' from the south, I expect any day now to see my Pa's Oklahoma farm come flyin' by on its way to North Dakota."

But no one said anything. No one shrugged in answer.

Quite without warning, Ma Thor began to make a weird sound, like a whistle rattling before it breaks into a scream.

Maury jumped up and stared at her.

Ma Thor was staring out of the window, her eyes opened very wide, her nostrils flaring, and her face very white except for a red patch over her right eye which seemed to throb like a heartbeat.

For a second, Maury had the fleeting impression that Ma Thor was acting a little. Her actions, coming on so suddenly, seemed to have an unreal quality about them. But it was her voice that convinced him that there was something really wrong.

Pa Thor had jumped up too, as had Kirsten. Pa Thor leaned over her. "What ails y'u, woman?"

She continued her strange gurgling, her staring. Her face began to work a little.

Maury was sure she was having an epileptic fit. He had once seen a hoboing buddy of his have one.

Pa Thor shook her. He was very frightened. "Hey, woman, cut it out! Are you goin' nuts, woman?" He shook her. "Come now. Use some sense!"

"Don't Pa," Kirsten was saying, "don't hurt her. You old fool."

"Damn it, I'm not hurtin' her. I'm only tryin' to find out what's the matter."

Then Maury understood. It wasn't epilepsy. He came around. He took Ma Thor's face in his big hands and looked into her eyes. Suddenly, he slapped her violently on the cheek. And, when she did not respond, he hit her again. A third time. Then she came up out of darkness. And her eyes rolled, and she sighed.

When her eyes had cleared, and she seemed to be with them again, Pa Thor sucked in a long nervous breath and then let it out with a great blast. "Httth! By God, woman, you had me goin' there fer a minute. What the hell was ailin' y'u?"

"Don't bawl her out, Pa," Kirsten begged.

"Bawl her out? Bawl her out? Who the hell wouldn't bawl out his wife if she started to act like a crazy one. Huh?"

"Well," she growled, "well . . . she didn't mean to do it."

Pa Thor snorted.

Maury was surprised by the old man's vigor. He hadn't expected him to react to danger violently as he had. But he said nothing. It was their affair, not his. He went back to chair, after making sure that Ma Thor had come back to her senses.

Pa Thor slowly went back to his chair, too, eyeing his wife with misgivings. As he settled down, he rubbed his leg slowly, muttering to himself.

Ma Thor sighed. She shook her head. "I sure felt funny," she murmured. "I sure felt funny. So funny." She looked at the floor. Her eyes seemed to be contemplating a great catastrophe. She had the vague eyes of a person who has almost died through heart failure.

But Pa Thor was not satisfied. His existence had been shaken. He demanded an explanation for it. "What ails y'u, Ma? Tell us."

"I dunno. Dunno. I . . . it was so funny." Then, "Maybe I was worryin' too much. All this dust. It'd make anybody go crazy."

Pa Thor cleared his throat a little angrily and spat into the fuel box near the stove. "Take it easy, Ma. It ain't half as bad as you make it out to be. It'll be all right." Then a smile wrinkled the crow's-feet around his eyes into sharp lines. "My old leg's been achin' like blazes all morning. I ain't said nothin' because nobody believes me. But, really, it's never ached like this in a dust storm before. Somethin's up."

"Well, I hope so," Ma Thor whispered.

Pa Thor slapped his leg. "Sure, you just set down now an' quiet yourself." He rubbed his leg vigorously. "You know, this leg is really achin' now!"

Moved by the old man's affection and by his instinctively optimistic response to any danger, Maury observed then, "You know, my old blood-poison cut, down in my foot here, it's achin' up for the first time in years, too. Maybe there is somethin' in the air!"

"Sure," said Pa Thor. "Why sure. Just set tight here, everybody, an' it'll be all right." He filled and lighted his corncob pipe.

Maury felt a little torn inside. He hadn't believed all he had said, but he felt deep pity for Ma Thor. He talked on. "Why sure. This ain't bad. Wait'll it gets as bad as it did down in Oklahoma a couple a years ago. Why, shucks, one time the Big Wind kept blowin' night and day fer forty days, kept right on blowin'. Got so bad down there that there was about three foot of solid dust layin' all over the land. An' the people got pretty worried about that time, an' they started to hold prayer meetin's. They invited over a lot of prayin' ministers, this one and that one, tryin' 'em all out. But none of 'em worked. An' so then one day, they heard of a rain-prayin', rain-makin' itinerunt preacher over in Missouri. An' they called him. An' he came. An' he looked at the land, an' at the people, an' offered a prayer. An' he'd hardly started when the raindrops began to fall. The itinerunt preacher give one more blast a prayin', then blessed the people, an' left fer home. "Well," Maury paused for breath, pleased that the gift of invention had not deserted him in this moment, "well, it rained. It rained an' rained. It rained so hard so long so fast, that the water stood all over. An' the three foot a dust turned into three foot a mud. An' everybody got stuck in it. The cattle an' horses, everybody. An' so, finally they had to send a delegation to that preacher, to ask him to come back an' ask God to call it off. An' the preacher came. An' he looked at the swampy fields and the washed-out roads. And it looked so hopeless, he said, 'God, I did ask fer rain, but, Christ, this is ridiculous!'"

Pa Thor laughed and slapped his leg. He rolled in his chair. His pipe almost fell from his mouth. "That's a good one! A good one!" he roared. Then he narrowed his eyes. "I can just see him standing there, I kin. Just see him." He laughed again. "God, I did ask fer rain, but, Christ, this is ridiculous!" He slapped and rubbed his leg.

The womenfolk looked down, vainly trying to restrain their smiles.

"Reminds me," ruminated Pa Thor aloud, as if he hadn't noticed either Ma Thor or Kirsten, "Reminds me. Neighbor Grayson down the road a piece, had a wife ready to give with child. He was worried about her, worried more than most farmers are. Because, you see, she was awful small. So he took her to Sioux Falls. That's where all them rich an' high monkey-monks live. An' while he was waitin' fer the kid to come, another feller came out, an' sat down to wait too. He was a fat rich feller, had all the sugar in the coffee he wanted. An' they set there waitin'. Pretty soon a nurse come out. 'Mr. Jones?' That was the rich feller, an' he sings out, 'Here. Yes?' 'Mr. Jones, you're the father of a nice, fat, eight-pound baby boy.' 'Great guns!' he roars. 'That's wonderful!' He jumps up and down, an' kisses the nurse and offers my neighbor a cigar. 'Here. Take two. Celebrate with me. It's wonderful, having babies! You're waiting too, I suppose?' My neighbor nods a little, nervous, you know. The rich feller says, 'Say, just to show you what kind of a good sport I am I'll wait an' keep you company till you hear from your wife.' So they set there, an' pretty soon the nurse comes out, an' she says, 'Mr. Grayson?' 'Yes.' The nurse was a little nervous an' she acted kinda funny, an' then she said, 'Well, you had a boy.' 'Oh,' he said. 'Oh. An' how much did it weigh?' The nurse wasn't gonna answer him at first, but finally she said, 'Well, it was about a pound.' Grayson thanked her an' started up to go out. 'Great guns!' yells the rich feller, 'only a pound? That's tough luck, feller. Tough!' 'Hell no,' says Grayson. 'That's not tough. Livin' out where I do, in the dust bowl, why hell! we're lucky to git our seed back.'"

Maury laughed, and, unconsciously imitating Pa Thor, slapped his leg too.

"That's enough," Ma Thor said sharply. "That's enough. No need to get funny. Stories is all right, but none a that kind. Pa, you've been around Ol' Gust too long fer you own good."

Pa Thor then played up a whine, cunningly. "Why, Ma, that story wasn't bad. I tol' you that one last year an' you laughed about it then."

"Oh, shut up," she said, getting up from her chair and hustling toward the pantry. "It ain't fittin' fer a person to hear such stories. Not at all. It's very degradin'. What kind a uplift is there in them fer the soul?"

Pa Thor laughed. "Why, Ma, I didn't know you was such a high class woman! Why, Ma!"

Ma Thor turned her face to hide a smile.

It was Kirsten who first noticed it. She jumped up, went to the window, and exclaimed, "Say, I believe it's quittin'. Sure. Look." She ran to the door and opened it.

And it had quieted. Sinisterly so. It was as if they had all been pulling mightily on a rope and now, as the rope gave away, felt themselves falling without support. They rubbed their ears and listened.

Then they all got up and went to the door to stand beside Kirsten. They looked over the land. They looked at the sky.

Maury pointed. "Look! Look up there. There's a hole in the sky . . . an' there's a cloud . . . a great one!"

Above them towered an immense thunderhead, creamy in its richness, and towering like a mountain peak. they could see the cloud moving in from the northwest. Great palisades of dust partly obscured the white, fluffy tops of the heaven-high cloud, and hid the dark blue bottom of its belly. The wind had been coming in from the south all day, but now, with the wind abating, an invisible wall moving ahead of the cloud pushed the dust back into the south. Lightning suddenly cut down through the middle of the cloud and speared the earth. The thunder blasted, rattled, and died away.

They stepped outdoors together and waited tensely beneath the war in the sky.

Then Maury pointed again. "See. Look! The two winds are comin' together. Look at them pieces a clouds sluggin' around! Just like somebody's beatin' them with a great big whip." As he yelled, he felt like a little boy at play again.

Small fragments of mist fluttered wildly in the opening between the dust cloud and the rain cloud.

"It's gonna rain at last," Pa Thor breathed. "I told you people my leg had a special ache today. By God, if there ain't a powerful rain storm brewin'!"

And even as he spoke, they heard a gradually increasing roar, its drone swollen with rumbles of thunder.

Maury shadowed his eyes with his right hand and looked along the horizon.

Just then the setting sun pierced the underside of the thunderhead with a long shaft of brilliant red light. There was a long dark column beside it.

"Tornado!" he whispered.

"No!" Ma Thor whispered.

"No!" exclaimed Kirsten.

"Aw, no. Not now," Pa Thor cried.

They stood stiffly, awestruck at the coming disaster.

Then Maury moved. "It's comin' all right. And right this way. C'mon. Where shall . . . down in the gully! Quick!"

But Kirsten broke away from them, running fleetly toward the barn.

"Where you goin'?" Maury shouted.

"The little pigs! The little pigs!"

"To hell with the little pigs!"

Kirsten shook her head and ran on.

Maury bounded after her. He caught her halfway across the yard. "You god-damn fool you. You goddamn fool. You're worth more than all the pigs in the world!" He grabbed her roughly, threw her over his shoulder like a sack, and ran back to the house with her. "Hurry," he shouted to Pa and Ma Thor. They still stood stupefied, fascinated into immobility, starting at the snarling hose-like snake writhing toward them with an ever-increasing whining roar.

With his free hand, Maury grabbed Ma Thor's arm. Pa Thor shuffled after

them, running backwards, facing the tornado. Maury pushed Kirsten down
the bank of the gully. Ma and Pa Thor scrambled after her. Then he tumbled
down, too. "Lay down as flat as you can! Flat!" he commanded.

Then the crazy, dancing, ripping roar of dust was on them.

Then, abruptly, there was a great quiet.

They sat huddled against the side of the gully's wall.

They waited.

Presently, Maury crawled slowly up the side of the gully. He looked carefully
to the northwest, to the southeast. He sighed. "Well, it missed us. And," he added
casually, "if you'll stick out your hand, you'll find it's rainin'."

"By God, if it ain't!" Pa Thor exclaimed. "Christ! This ain't ridiculous atall!"

Maury and Kirsten

AFTER A TAPIOCA SUPPER, they went out to sit on the stoop.

The ten-minute rain had cleared the sky of dust and sand. The sun was setting with a luminous red. Long shafts of purple and orange pierced the bowels
of the retreating clouds. Their creamy folds and rising towers of gold spread
against the blue. A wind came softly from the west, carrying the scent of green
corn and soaked grain. The ground itself had a new smell.

Kirsten, sitting beneath Maury on the lower step, her bare feet in the soft
mud, her overall pantlegs rolled up, turned suddenly and said, "Maury, why
don't you play us a little something on your guitar?"

"Naw."

"Please do. It . . . this is sort of a holiday."

"No." He remembered he had once sworn not to, and he was stubborn
enough to hang onto a foolish pledge.

Pa Thor nudged him then. "Go ahead, son. We ain't got no radio or no
phonograph. We ain't heard music since goodness knows when. Go along now,
an' get your guitar."

"But I ain't much of a player. I only play fer myself an' ain't much good."

"Well . . ." Pa Thor shrugged. "Well . . ."

Maury stood up suddenly. "Aw . . . All right."

And soon he began his tuning. They watched him intently, craving the sound
of the twanging chord. He was embarrassed at first. He fingered the strings. He
sought a haphazard tune in his memory. But it would not come. The only tune
he could think of had a special meaning. Presently he sang it—

> *I'm lookin' pretty seedy now while holdin' down my claim,*
> *An' my vittles are always too much the same.*
> *The mice play slyly 'round me as I nestle down to rest*
> *In my little old sod shanty in the west.*

The hinges are of leather and the windows got no glass,
I hear the hungry coyote slink in the grass,
The old board roof is warping, the blizzards try the frame
Of my little old sod shanty on my claim.
My claim . . .

His strong chords drummed on the still, dusk air. A rapture lifted his face. And theirs.

Oh! bury me not on the lone prairie,
Where the coyotes howl and the wind blows free.
Blows free . . .

Oh! bury me not on the lone prairie,
Where the rattlers hiss and the grass runs free.
Runs free . . .

Ma Thor sat upright for a while. And then slowly she relaxed. Once, when Maury looked at her, he saw that her eyes had closed and that she was resting her head on Pa Thor's shoulder, and that Pa Thor's arm was firm around her. Immediately, the low chords deepened and the light chords became more tender.

And then Kirsten began to sing, softly at first, as if her voice were not sure of the tune—

I've reached the land of desert sweet
Where nothing grows for man to eat.
We have no wheat, we have no oats,
We have no corn to feed our shoats.

O Dakota land, sweet Dakota land,
As on thy fiery soil I stand,
I look across the plains
And wonder why it never rains,
Till Gabriel blows his trumpet sound
And says the rain's just gone around.

I've reached the land of hills and stones
Where all is strewn with buffalo bones.
O buffalo bones, bleached buffalo bones,
I hear your moans, I hear your groans.

Maury softened his strumming. He pulled the deep chords easily, lifting her voice sometimes, shading it again and then pulling it down. The lemon voice rolled around on the yard and echoed off the barn and ran over the prairie.

As suddenly as it had begun, the voice stopped. Maury's guitar went on alone, and then, hesitant, like a little boy without the hand of his elder sister, the guitar trembled. The notes fell from it like the sound of water dropping on dust.

Then, the mood changing, he sang, "Hallelujah, I'm a Bum," and in a moment Kirsten, laughing, joined him.

A long time later, they stopped, tired.

Pa Thor said, "That's fine good music, children."

"Play some more," Ma Thor whispered. "Play some."

"Yes," said Pa Thor, tightening his arm over Ma Thor, "yes. Play some more. Play that one about the 'dreary Black Hills'."

Maury looked at him quickly, wondering what the old man had in mind. He searched out the tune in his memory—

> *Kind friend, to conclude, my advice I'll unfold,*
> *Don't go to the Black Hills to hunt for your gold;*
> *The gamblers will fleece you of your new dollar bills*
> *If you take the trip to those dreary Black Hills.*
> *Black Hills . . .*

Maury smiled a little, and then searched for other tunes. He became inventive. The fresh earth talked. He spilled fresh notes around, soft chords that rose and fell, that swelled and quivered like grass filling with rain and then bursting into seeds and then withering beneath the hot sun. He composed new words and new notes as he went along, told them about his aches as he waited along the corners of lonely roads, told them of watching the sky for clouds, told them of his hunger for thunder and lightning, told them of his fear of death, told them of his life in Oklahoma—

> *Gone from the land, dead is my Pa.*
> *Gone from the shack, dead is my Ma.*
> *Gone from the plow, gone from the cart,*
> *Gone is this bum, dead is his heart.*
> *His heart . . .*

Abruptly, tune and words became light-hearted—

> *Oh! he was smiles and sweet wiles*
> *When they met by the fire.*
> *Oh! she was wise to the lies*
> *Of that dirty black liar.*
> *Liar!*

Oh, he was slick, he was quick
When they set by the fire.
Oh! she was turned, she was burned
By that dirty black liar.
Liar!

Then, suddenly, he stopped.

Kirsten turned. "Play some more," she whispered.

"No," said Maury. "No, no more. That's all."

Kirsten looked at him.

In the half-pink light, Maury was stirred by her face. "You look like you've been somewhere," he said.

"I have," she answered.

Maury looked down. He carefully covered the guitar and then shut the case.

" 'S matter, son, tired?" Pa Thor asked.

"No."

"Play some more then."

"No. No more."

Ma Thor stirred. "It was nice. Real nice."

Maury set the case behind him and then leaned forward, resting his chin on his knee.

Pa Thor asked, "Why don't you play some more, son? We don't hear anythin' like that. Not out here."

Maury had been looking west toward the creek. "I wonder," he began, "I wonder... say, you know, we never thought a lookin' to see if that tornado ripped up our dam."

Pa Thor jerked upright, jolting Ma Thor and almost upsetting her. "I never thought of it either. We better look."

Kirsten jumped up too.

Maury looked at her. "Let's just you an' I go look," he said meaningfully.

A shrewd gleam appeared in her eyes. Then she nodded coolly. "All right."

They started together.

Pa Thor exclaimed. "Hey! What's the idea! I'm goin' too. Wait up."

Ma Thor came out of her dream. "Pa! Pa. Set here. You set here by me. Let the young ones go."

Pa Thor blinked, then understood. He relaxed a little, but not until he had rolled out a little growl to satisfy a sense of injured pride.

Maury and Kirsten went slowly across the yard, slipping in the mud. Kirsten opened the gate near the barn and then closed it after them.

Maury pointed to her feet. "Your shoes?"

"What about 'em? I like to walk in the mud. Don't often get the chance."

"Say! I think you got something there. I ain't done it fer a long time either. Wait a spell." And he leaned over and unloosened his shoes and hung them on the fence near by. The mud was cool and soft to his feet.

They walked along together. There was only a faint glow in the west now. It was dark, and the stars were bright and sharp above them.

Maury looked up and smelled deeply. "You know," he observed, "that sky-ful of stars there now. It's just like a blue-black dress I've seen."

"Polka dots?"

"Yeh. Yeh. That's it. Polka dots." He took another deep breath. He looked down. He sloughed his feet through the mud. "Rain didn't go very deep. Just tied down the mud a little an' soaked the top."

"Won't this rain help none?"

"Depends on the kind a weather we get tomorrow. If it's hot, it won't do much good. Fry the stuff. If there's a mist, an' clouds, it'll do some good."

Kirsten remained silent.

He reached for her hand in the twilight.

She permitted him to hold it for a way and then released it.

Maury became uneasy. He tried to think of something to say.

Then they were near the dam.

"Tornado missed it all right," he said.

Kirsten nodded.

He looked at the narrow, shining fold of water. Star reflections were knitted together on the undulating surface. "Say," he exclaimed. "Say, I'm gonna wash my feet." And he sat down on the edge of the dam and rolled up his pantlegs. He thrust his feet into the water. "Jeez!" he exploded, suddenly jerking them out again, "Jeez, it's cold!"

"Sure, you silly! Water's always cold after a rain."

Maury dropped his feet in again.

Kirsten looked at him a moment and then settled beside him. She pulled her overall pantlegs up high over her knees. Her flesh gleamed in the dusk.

Maury could dimly see her firm limbs, her arched back. He said, "I see you wear an overall right along."

"I don't like dresses. They clutter up so."

They splashed their feet in the water. He looked upward, watching a few streaks of clouds thicken and thin beneath the stars. As he fumbled for cigarette makings, he saw something move along the other bank. He studied it sharply for a moment and then laughed. "Danged tumbleweed had me scared fer a minute. Must be a li'l wind out."

Kirsten slapped water over her knee and then lifted a handful to her nose. "Smells good," she said.

But Maury had begun meditating. "You know," he said, "I'm not any smarter than that tumbleweed there. I'm driftin' back an' forth over the country, not getting any place. The wind blows west and I roll west. The wind blows east, and I roll east."

Kirsten said matter-of-factly, "Well, if it bothers you so much why don't you stay put here?"

"No," he said. "No, I couldn't do that. 'Course you got a little rain today, an' you got a dam started, but . . ."

Kirsten waited.

Maury said, puffing slowly on his cigarette and breaking a stick he had found into small bits with his fingers, "I remember one time when I was thumbing my way through Pennsylvania. The long hills there was like the shanks of a woman. They were good hills, they were. Soft hills. Not hard." Maury moved his feet slightly and slapped them in the water. He studied the eddies and then went on. "Well, I was tired one day an' I lay down in the grass, an' I saw a thin green worm crawlin' on the end of a blade of grass. I watched it, reachin' and lookin' an' reachin' fer some place to go. It reached an' reached, an' finally . . . I pushed another blade a grass so the worm could reach it. Then it crawled down an' hid in the deep roots."

Kirsten rubbed her legs, looking at him wonderingly.

"Sometimes I gotta feelin' that you people are pushing a blade a grass fer me."

"Maybe we are," she said.

"I thought so."

"Anything wrong in that?"

Maury made a gesture toward her and then became deeply interested in his cigarette. He puffed at it a few times and then snapped it through the air. It made an arc of yellow fire and hissed as it hit the water.

"Naw," Maury said finally. "No. I couldn't do it. Couldn't live here. I can't fergit how my Pa an' Ma suffered. I don't wanna see it again. A man shouldn't have a brain, shouldn't have a memory." He rubbed his chin. "A memory is an awful thing," he said fiercely. "An awful thing. I once knew a guy down in Kansas. Swell fella, too. Met a gal. Married her and when the little kid came along, she died. He couldn't get no doctor. An' then the guy went on livin' on the ranch anyway, jus' tryin' to get on alone. But he couldn't fergit. Saw her dancin' in front of his eyes all the time. So he took to whiskey, an' then he croaked hisself one night."

Kirsten pulled her feet out of the water and rolled over on her stomach, holding her head in her cupped hands. She watched him.

Maury went on. "Yeh, knew another guy too. Swell guy. Met him in a bindlestiff camp in Omaha. A fella could tell he had class. White hair. Back as straight as a broomstick. Full a guts. Nobody knew him well. Knew nothin' about him, 'cept that he had class. An' when he passed out, they found he was a big shot, a count from over in the Old Country. Sure he was. This guy came to America to fergit somethin'. Tried to make some money, too, to keep his title polished. Took his wife an' kid with him. Lost all his dough, an' then his wife and kid got some kind a sickness. I think it was milk fever. Then he couldn't get work. An' there he was, a count in a bum's stall. Kirsten, stuff like that is awful. Never will fergit him standin' one day on the edge of a hill. I came up to him and called out the time a day. But he didn't hear me. I called two or three times, but he didn't hear me. Finally, I poked him. Then he woke up. Shoulda seen his face. God, it was awful! The fella jus' couldn't fergit, is all."

Kirsten said slowly, "You've seen a lot of bad things, haven't you?"

Maury went on, deliberately trying to shock her. "Yeh. Well, yeh, guess I have. Never will forget that guy who had cancer in his backsides. Blllll! God, it was awful!" Maury shook his head involuntarily as the image came back to him. "When I asked him how he felt, he'd say, 'Okay, I'll be okay tomorrow.'"

"Didn't he know?"

Maury withered her with a sharp glance. "Why sure, he knew!" Maury pulled up his leg and ran his fingers between his toes. "Sure. He just had guts. An' I couldn't eat fer a week, an' everytime I pulled out my handkerchief, I could smell the guy."

Kirsten remembered a story now. "Our family's pretty tough, too. Take Uncle Holger once. He really looked like a kind man, all smiles, like he couldn't move a speck a dust fer fear he'd hurt it. An' yet, way inside, he was made a rock. We was there once fer Sunday dinner. An' he was prayin' along with a long prayer. All of a sudden he stopped. Everybody looked up, wonderin' what next. Uncle Holger jus' got up an' pulled out a tooth with a pair of pliers and then went right on prayin' an' thankin' God."

Maury said sarcastically, "Yeh, that's the one thing your family ain't short on. Guts. Huh! Too much guts. Blind fool guts."

Kirsten was silent.

Maury looked at her and then rolled another cigarette. He heard the water slapping against the bank beneath them. "Look," he said, describing a semi-circle with his arm. "Jus' lissen now. What do you hear out there? Nothin'. Nothin'. Why! a man should be hearin' frogs croakin' after a good rain like that! There should be crickets. Peepers. Why! even them dumb bunny little cotton-tails, them dumb little bunnies has pulled out. Then little animals got more sense than you people have. They knew it was no use, an' gave up an' croaked."

Kirsten stiffened. She did not answer.

Maury puffed reflectively on his cigarette. He thought to himself for a time and then added, sadly, "A man hates to see his work go fer nothin'. A man hates to see his work go up in smoke. He hates to sin against his own soul." He paused and puffed on his cigarette again. He rubbed his hands together. The callouses in his hands squeaked.

Kirsten sat up. She said quietly, "Them's long words, mister."

Maury shrugged. He watched the rippling stars on the sleek surface of the water and then looked up at the sky. He straightened suddenly. "Hey! Look! There's a bat flyin' around!"

She followed his pointing finger.

He watched its irregular flight above them. He saw it disappear into the willows. Then he said, "Now, how do you suppose that bat makes a livin'?"

Kirsten looked down.

"Can't figger it out," he said, still musing. "It sure is funny. I ain't seen a bird fer so long I get all hepped up just seein' a bat." He puffed on his cigarette and then tossed it into the water. "It's just like when you're standin' along the road, waitin' fer a shiny new car and instead, a dirty cattle truck shows up. But you get all hepped up because you're sure you're gonna get a ride. Your heart pounds. Your fingers tingle. And then you wave. You actually smile. The fella comin' along is Christ comin'. He's gonna save you. Pick you up an' give you a chance."

"That's terrible! exclaimed Kirsten suddenly. "Terrible!" Her voice was full of commiseration. "Terrible that a good man like you has to get thinkin' things like that!"

He studied her words in silence. He was pleased by the warmth in them.

They sat quietly for a time.

"Well, maybe you're right." He put his arm about her.

She drew away.

"Aw, c'mon. Don't act as if you ain't been kissed before."

She stood up abruptly.

Maury said, squinting at her, "You know, I think I got you figgered out. You'll come if I'll stay. Huh?" He waited for a reaction, then added, "Well, if that's the case you kin go to hell."

"Maybe I better go back to the house. They're waitin'."

Maury looked down at the water, and in the faint light could dimly see his white feet in the water. "Go ahead. I think I'll take a bath."

Kirsten began to move toward the end of the dam.

But Maury could not let her go. He stood up, too, and followed her. He caught her by the willows. He asked, suddenly daring, very urgently holding her close, "Kirsten, why don't you take a bath with me?"

"What?" She jumped away.

Again he placed his hand on her. "Aw, now, don't snap off my ears."

Kirsten shook him off angrily.

"Well, okay, sister, okay. But I'm gonna take a bath right here in front a the dam." He began to loosen his overall suspenders.

"It'll be awful muddy there," she said abruptly, curtly.

"Well, at least it'll be deep enough to cover my ankles."

Kirsten pointed south. "There's a better place half a mile down."

"How deep?"

"'Bout two feet. I used to go wading there with Tollef."

"Sand?"

Kirsten nodded.

"Come, show me."

She hesitated.

"Come."

Kirsten turned then, and together they walked along the stream below the dam.

The sound of the water trickling beside them was the sound of tiny stones falling on taut wires. The short grain whispered near them. The bare limbs of the willows were as white as flour. The few leafy branches were purple dark against the sky. The headlights of a passing car on the highway a mile away pierced the night with long, weaving, slanting shafts of yellow. A thin film of blue outlined the entire horizon.

Kirsten pointed to a bend in the stream. "There," she said. "Water digs in a little there, and right below it the sand's piled up."

"Comin'?" Maury asked again, his voice persuasive. He had felt her trembling near him.

Kirsten held her breath. "All right," she said, finally. But she waited for him to undress first.

Maury, pulling off his shirt and loosening the side buttons of his overalls, quickly saw her intent. "I think I'll have a smoke first," he said slowly. He felt a few tufts of grass beneath his feet. "Here's a good place to sit. Come." He drew her down, holding her shoulders as she sank with him. "There." Then he took out his cigarette makings and rolled a tube of tobacco with meticulous care. He lighted it. In the glare of the match lame, he glanced at her eyes. "Go ahead," he said. "Go ahead. Don't wait fer me."

Kirsten shook her head.

Maury laid his cigarette carefully on the ground. He loosened one of her suspenders, and then, slipping the other down, loosened her blouse and drew it off. Nervous suddenly, he muttered, "Why! you don't wear one a them breast halters, do you?"

Kirsten pushed his hands away and finished undressing herself.

Maury trembled as he picked up his cigarette again. Seeing her body silhouetted against the stars, he felt a sudden, great craving for cigarette smoke. He puffed deeply, staring at her.

Kirsten moved toward the water slowly and then dipped her feet in it. She played her toes in the water a moment and then went in. She looked upward and then stretched, her breasts lifting.

Maury threw his cigarette quickly into the water then, and tore off his overalls. In a moment he was beside her. He reached out to touch her. He ran his fingers over her smooth skin lightly, hardly touching her, as if he were touching something holy.

Kirsten drew away from him. She settled slowly into the water. She gasped when the water filled in beneath her armpits and came up over her breasts.

Maury stood looking at her and then settled beside her. He put his arm over her shoulder.

She permitted it to rest there for a moment and then drew away from him again.

He followed.

She took his hand then and held it in her hands. She pressed it nervously.

He reached for her.

But once more she drew away.

Giving up the chase, Maury settled back into the water. He stretched out his feet and let the water run over his body.

Presently he rubbed his body energetically, splashing his face and snorting a little. He dipped his head under. Then he turned and splashed her face, trying to touch her breasts with the same motion.

Kirsten laughed and then she shot water into his face by skimming the flat of her hand sideways over the surface of the water.

Maury fought back.

The water sparkled between them.

Then Maury raised his arm, pointing. "Look," he said. "Look. There's the moon. Just coming up."

Kirsten turned.

An enormous blood-gold saucer was slowly being shoved up over the rim of the earth by an invisible force. Silhouettes of distant trees were etched against it thinly, like the scrawls of a child. The northeast heavens became yellow and bright. Stars faded above. The saucer expanded. It swelled. Raised. When the disc was almost free of the earth, the lower part clung to the dark horizon for a moment like a drop of water clinging to an object before it parts. Then the moon drew the reluctant part into itself and the yellow-red orb rose slowly.

He sat watching it, breathlessly. Slowly the prairie lighted. The willow thrust up in distinct dark strokes against the sky. He turned to see what effect this prairie glory might have on Kirsten.

Kirsten was playing. She had lifted a palmful of water and was now slowly pouring it, watching the thin silver stream thicken into a deep gold.

Maury took her in his arms.

"No," she whispered.

"Please. My bunny. My bunny little cottontail. It's all right. I won't hurt . . ."

"No!"

Maury pushed his nose into her hair and breathed deeply. He whispered her name. "Kirsten. Kirsten. My bunny little cottontail."

Kirsten trembled. "If I knew . . ."

"Knew what?"

"If I knew you'd stay."

Maury hesitated.

She went on. "If I knew you'd stay. I don't like to have a baby alone by myself. I'd like to have him see his pa."

Maury drew a sudden breath. For a moment he had the feeling that he was about to fall into a chasm. He steeled himself, hardened himself against her.

She looked down, as if she were blushing. "You don't have to marry me. Just so you'd stay."

Suddenly Maury leaped to his feet and carried her to the sand below.

Some time later, when his mind cleared, he swore. He drew away from her with a sudden distaste. He went over to where he had thrown his clothes and fumbled in the dark for them. He muttered to himself. "I'll be a bastard, I will. I'll be a bastard. I'm just the guy to pull a stunt like this! I'm always forgettin' myself. I'm such a goddamn fool!"

Kirsten sat on the ground, looking at him imploringly. "Wait! Wait!"

Maury jerked on his clothes roughly. He swore under his breath. It had come to him. If he stayed another moment, he would be trapped for the rest of his life, trapped in a land of slow death. Dust and death. And loneliness more pervasive than any he had ever experienced on the road as a bindlestiff. Trapped, and possessed by an utterly helpless feeling of being unable to stop the unraveling of life and of the earth beneath it. He started hurriedly toward the farmyard.

"Maury!" Kirsten called.

Maury ran on.

Kirsten stood up, naked, and ran a few steps after him. "Maury! Maury! Wait!"

But Maury went on. When he came to a rise in the land, he turned, and saw that she had fallen to the ground, a white mound in the moonlight.

Maury ran swiftly over the half-burnt grainfield. He remembered he had hung his shoes on the lane fence and ran back to get them. He leaped swiftly over the barnyard gate and then, as he came toward the house, saw Pa and Ma Thor still sitting on the steps.

He stopped, breathing hard. He stared at them. The gold light of the moon brightened their gray hair into silver. He hesitated. They had so few moments of happiness. He stared at them, and suddenly realized that here was the future picture of himself and Kirsten.

Then he walked up to them, and Ma Thor stirred and asked, "Why! where's Kirsten?"

"She's comin'."

Pa Thor blinked, remembered, and then asked, "Say! that dam still there?"

Maury growled, "Yeh, it's still there, al right." He went inside the house. Both Ma and Pa Thor came after him.

"What's happened, son?" Ma Thor asked. "Where's Kirsten?"

Maury picked up his bundles and started for the door.

Ma Thor ran before him. She blocked his way. "Son, there's something wrong!"

Maury cried, "I didn't hurt your girl none. I just wanna go. Let me go."

"Son!"

The word cut like a whip. "I can't help it! I only know I got to get out of here. Right away. I'm . . . I'm . . . let me go!" He pushed Ma Thor roughly aside.

Pa Thor called. "Son? Son?" His voice echoed over the hard.

Maury ran swiftly, and gathering himself into a short, mincing run, sprang from the edge of the gully. He reached half way up the other side. His guitar twanged in his arm. He crawled up the remaining distance and gained the road. He strode south, then west.

His footsteps beat hard on the gravel road. He tried to keep from thinking.

The moon rose steadily. As it lifted into the heavens, its gold steadily faded to silver. It shrank. The stars faded near it. A meteor cut a wide, irregular gash across the southern sky.

Maury stumbled on. His feet slipped sometimes in the rough gravel. Occasionally, when his foot dropped into an unexpected dip in the road, he felt his belly muscles jerk.

He walked a mile before he heard a motor drumming on the soft air of the prairie night. The sound came sweetly to him. He stopped to listen. His grim face brightened. He adjusted his suspenders and brushed his clothes. He pulled his cap around to give himself a happy-go-lucky appearance. He remembered to smile.

But the car went by.

And others went by. The old days had come again, the old days of waiting and waiting, of building up artificial smiles every little while.

After the sixth car had passed him without slowing at all, Maury knew he would not catch a car that night. Cursing a little, he hurried his steps, lengthening them over the gravel road, following the turn in the road toward the west, hurrying on toward Long Hope where the night freight would run a two in the morning, and go chortling and rattling west to the Black Hills.

Several hours later, a train whistled north of him. He ran hard to the summit of the next long swelling rise. Reaching it, he stood looking north, his breath short, afraid that the train he would see would be the night freight.

And then, there, at last, he saw it. There was a shaft of light creeping swiftly over the land. An orange glare exploded directly behind the source of the light where the fireman coaled the engine. White smoke curled through the brief, orange illumination. He looked along the train. There were no lighted coaches. It was the night freight, all right.

Disgusted, Maury swore and dropped his bundles on the edge of the road. He sat down, hung his feet over the shoulder of the highway and rolled a cigarette. He lighted it and puffed until his fingers, trembling from the exertion of hard running, quieted.

Soon his thumping heart quieted too, and he looked out over the land.

In the moonlight, the land was lifeless. It was as endless as endless silence. The prairie stretched mile on mile to the horizon. No insect life stirred in the night. The slight knolls lay like stones. The earth was dead. It did not breathe. Its nostrils, the plants and the animals, were dead, choked by the dust.

Maury crunched his teeth. He rubbed his hand roughly through his hair. He cracked his foot roughly against the hard ground. The dust bowl was hell.

And, as always happened when he took off a little time from his wandering to muse a bit, his mind teemed with images and memories. He was haunted by old faces and old times. He had never been able to forget his father's last despairing days on earth. Or his mother's wretched life of slavery, which, like her body, had gone up in dust. It was always bitter to think of them.

But more so now. For there had come a new Pa and a new Ma into his life. Looking at the other side of the ditch, as if it were a frame for a picture, he saw Pa Thor and Ma Thor, saw their faces of just a few hours ago when they'd questioned him, round-eyed, about his going. "What happened, son? Where's Kirsten?" and Pa Thor's wretched, wailing, "Son? Son?"

He shook his head. But the ghosts were vivid. They were persistent. There they were, across the ditch, caught pictured in those tufts of weeds. How very much like Ma was Ma Thor! How very much like Pa was Pa Thor!

They were such good people. Such stubborn, lovable, childish people. They had given him board and room. Room they had plenty of, but the food must have been worth heaps of gold to them. He had taken their food, had eaten it. And then he had taken their daughter and thrown her onto the earth and taken her like a wild bull. Compared to them, what an animal he was!

He jumped to his feet. He grabbed up his bundles and started a few steps westward again.

Then he hesitated. He thought. Then, abruptly, he wheeled about and started back toward the Thor home.

He stumbled on through the early morning hours. It had begun to lighten a little in the east. He hurried. The gravel crunched beneath his rapid feet. Sometimes a sharp stone dented the sole of his shoe, bruised his foot.

He waved an arm as he went along. He began to mutter. "Yeah, it was a dirty trick, all right. A dirty trick. A helluva thing for a guy by the name of Grant to do."

The gravel squinched beneath his hard beating legs. "Well, I missed the goddamn train anyway. I'd a had to wait a whole day anyway."

He sniffed the night air. He coughed, cleared his throat, and spat to the side of the road. "It was a dirty trick, all right. Ruining a nice girl like that. Poor kid." He sniffed, and spat again. "But if I'm stayin' a while, I'm ignorin' her. I'm not laying my hands on her. I don't want to get tied down to this. Wimmen are worse than glue." He muttered along to himself. "I'll stay a couple a weeks, that's what I'll do. A couple a weeks. Two weeks won't make or break me. If there's a job for me in the mines, it'll be there when I get there two weeks from now too. An' in the meantime, I'll give the family a little lift."

He strode on, nearing the farm again.

"But by God, now that I'm stayin' they gotta listen to me, too. I got some ideas about that farm. An' old Pa Thor's gotta listen to me, or else. I got a plan."

When he came to the house, it was still dark, though the gray in the east had risen a little.

Ma Thor was up. When he entered the door, she looked up questioningly. He snorted a little, embarrassed, and then, laying his bundles beside the cot, muttered, "I . . . I been out fer a kind of a long walk." He rubbed his nose. "Well, it's late. I better get some shut-eye afore the roosters crow."

Ma Thor nodded her head, and then got up and went to the back room where the family slept. As she opened the door, he caught a glimpse of Kirsten standing in her nightgown. But before he could turn his head away from her, she had turned away. It was Kirsten who began the ignoring.

Wanderlust

*I remember that I really was Republican [up to] that point, but the student
body had an election in 1932 . . . Hoover got one vote. Roosevelt got ten, and
everybody voted for Norman Thomas, the preacher who was a socialist.
And there was a scandal. The church had a special meeting. All the synod
members from all over America came to Grand Rapids, Michigan, to discuss this phenomenon of these goddam socialists on the campus of Calvin
College. . . In '32 times were really tough. . . There were 17,000 heads of families out of work. . . Long lines of relief everywhere you went in '32. So the
students were reflecting that, you see. Then, I didn't vote for Hoover. I voted
for Norman Thomas but not until I ran into that whole thing, the discussions
at noon hour at the dormitory tables and in the hallways.*

A Change of Intellectual Climate

WILLEM AND THURS AND CHRIS got in back, Ben got behind the wheel,
Happy spun Siouxland Susie's tail, and away they went again, the left rear wheel
ratcheting, ratcheting.

Thurs had a question to ask. "What's Christian like, Chris?"

"Well, it's the usual kind of denominational college. Has an enrollment of
around five hundred, with another hundred in the seminary. Some of the students
come from little towns like yours, from all over America. But most actually come
from Zion itself. All Christian. No movies, no cards, no dancing allowed. Offi-
cially, that is. Ha. And perhaps with good reason. After all, our parents foot the
bill, and for their dough they have a right to expect a certain brand of religious
instruction."

"What's Zion like?"

"Oh, it's a city of about a hundred thousand. Mostly of our denomination."

"Not really an American city then, is it?"

Chris laughed. "No, I guess most of them still think they're living in the
Old Country."

"What's dis?" Willem cried. "You say Zion ain't American?"

"Skip it."

The talk drifted to other things, to affairs of the day.

"I saw in a paper back there," Ben said over his shoulder, "that there's over
eight million unemployed in the country."

"That's propaganda!" Happy cried, turning in his seat, "communistic
propaganda."

"Well, now, it all depends on how you look at it," Chris said, affecting the
objective manner, "how you break down the figures. We all know that some of
the unemployed will never work. Take—"

"—the no-good bums," Happy broke in, "the lazy bastards who won't work and who've never done anything worthwhile in their lives."

Chris smiled. "Well, I was thinking more of the cripples and the blind. And the aged."

"Well," Happy said, "there are those too of course. But I tell you nothing gets me madder than to see a bum on the street begging for a dime so he can buy himself some more beer."

Ben threw Happy a quick searching look. "Tell me something, Happy, have you ever held down a job? A real job?"

Happy waved the question aside. "Nuts. What this country needs is faith. Good old red-blooded American faith."

At that Willem woke up. "Faith. You bet-h. D' worst sabatoors we got are d' sinners who stay away from church. How can our people become a great nation if nobody goes to church?"

"Well, now, gentlemen," Chris said, like an old sage let loose among primitive freshmen, "to return to Ben's original remark—the '29 collapse and the current recession were the result of certain profound forces at work in our economy, forces which for the most part have escaped the scrutiny of our politicians. In a way, Happy is right. We do need faith. Faith in American capitalism. It was the lack of such faith that caused the stock market crash, that slough of despond, that absolute nadir of supply and demand, into which the American economy fell last fall."

"Hey, Chris." Willem said, leaning across, ramming an elbow into Thurs's belly, "Hey, can't you talk plain?"

Chris laughed.

"All them big words—why don't you use d' plain ordinary common American words that God gave us?"

Chris laughed some more.

"Well, and I say it was more mismanagement," Ben said. "Plain ordinary mismanagement."

"Crep!" Willem roared. Let me tell you what I tink it was. I tink it was a punishment God's for all our sins. And you boys know that too."

It became dark outdoors. Each man became a blurred hump in the car. Sometimes a face glowed up behind a pipe or cigarette. Sometimes a hand made a sharp silhouette against the mirroring windows. Smells of heated oil and rubber from the motor seeped through the floorboards. The headlights up front moved palely from pole to pole. Looking back out of the rear window, Thurs saw that the planet of love was out, bobbing in the west, lighting up the Siouxland he had left.

Thurs's back began to ache. He said to Chris beside him, "Mrs. Brothers mentioned something about driving all night."

"That's right."

Thurs stirred his feet. He felt wrenches on the floor and a wad of softness that he took to be an oil rag. "What about sleep?"

"Sleep is a waste of time."

∼

They entered the older portion of the city, a section built for the rich two generations before. A house on the left had white pillars. Its front, Howard remarked, reminded him of the stage setting for O'Neill's *Mourning Becomes Electra*. A stone mansion on the right was almost hidden by climbing English ivy. Thurs said it reminded him of a picture he had seen of Tennyson's house.

They topped a hill. Below lay downtown Zion, bustling, a blue haze rising from it, sunmotes glinting in the afternoon brilliance. Immediately on the left, beneath some empurpled oaks, stood a white colonial art gallery: on the right, a tall Masonic temple. Beyond these were factories, department stores, hotels, apartment houses, all of brick and stone, all handsomely done and clean.

Howard said, "I have to admit that despite the narrow-mindedness of its citizens, Zion is a beautiful city."

Thurs had a question. "Howard, if you dislike the Christians so much, how come you're at Christian?"

Howard walked a half a block before answering. Then he said, "My mother wanted me to go here. She belongs to the Christian Church in St. Paul. And since she contributes to the support of our college she felt I had to go."

"Your father?"

"He didn't care one way or the other."

Thurs envied Howard his parents, Christian or not. He asked, "What does your mother think you'll get out of Christian?"

"God only knows."

"Really now."

"I think she'd like me to become a teacher. Somewhere in the Christian educational system."

"Ahh."

"So I've decided that if I have to, it'll be in political science or history." Howard spoke with impatience, snapping his fingers against his gray gabardine trousers.

"Just like Mrs. Brothers," Thurs said. "She wants me to become a teacher too. In fact, she's all hepped up about me becoming a preacher."

"Are you?"

"Preacher? Never."

"But teacher?"

"Maybe."

"What field?"

"I don't know. Maybe English."

"Then you've got the wrong guy in Freshman English. That Meeth fellow is enough to make a man run for the Wild West."

"I know."

"Apply for a change. Mr. Whiting is at least human. And he knows his fiction."

"Well, I don't want to make a fuss."

"Fuss? Man, I'd never tolerate that fish of a Meeth if I were you. Heh. He's so limp at the wrists he could put on panties and go as Miss Meeth."

"Like the dean of women could put on pants and go as Mr. Drake?"

"Ha. Exactly."

The light on the next corner was green and they strolled through parted traffic. A woman in a blue car goggled up at Thurs as they went by. Howard said, "Yes, as covenant children we're doomed to walk the straight and narrow for the rest of our lives."

Down a side street off Monroe they found a second hand furniture store. Thurs picked out a Morris chair, a red-fringed reading lamp, a green bed lamp, a table model radio, a colorful Sioux rug, and two framed pictures, one a print of Eakins' *Max Schmitt in a Single Scull* and the other a print of Homer's *The Thinker*. Thurs paid for the items and arranged to have them delivered to his room the next afternoon.

Walking past a linen shop, Thurs spotted some marked-down pillows in a showcase. One of the smaller pillows was advertised as being filled with eider down. "Just what I need," Thurs said.

Howard laughed. "What for? You won't even know you got it under your head it's so fluffy."

"It's to cover my head. That damned Calvin Batts wiggles in his bunk below all night long. Like a skunk in leaves."

Howard gave him a look.

"Besides, back in the orphanage I got used to sleeping with a pillow over my ear. There was always so much noise around."

They found a bookstore and browsed around. Howard, acquainted with such establishments back in St. Paul and knowing where to find things, pointed out some of the masters he had read and liked: Melville, Rabelais, Tolstoi, Omar Khayyam.

Thurs was stunned by the number of books Howard had read. Howard's high school life had been ever so much richer than his own. Howard already knew as a freshman what Thurs hoped to know someday as a senior.

Howard picked up one of the latest best sellers. "Here's something you should look into, Thurs. *Elmer Gantry* by Sinclair Lewis. This will help clinch your decision not to go into the ministry."

Thurs paged through it. "Really haven't got the money to buy it."

"Tell you what. When we finish here we'll get one at the city library."

"Good." They fumbled through the poetry stacks, looking for Whitman.

Off to one side Thurs spotted the elfin blond who took history with him in Mr. Pick's class. She was paging through a magazine. Again she was wearing blue, this time a suit with a white-frilled blouse. He could just barely catch a glimpse of the pink upper slopes of her bosom. Perched on her head was a tiny cuplike hat, also blue.

Howard had to bump Thurs to get his attention.

Remembering Howard's deflating remark about her and her two other friends, Thurs behaved as if he hadn't seen anyone they knew, and looked at the volume that Howard held up for his inspection. Thurs hoped that the rustling of a half-dozen other shoppers would keep Howard from noticing her.

From time to time, as they browsed deeper into the back of the store Thurs glanced back at her. She reminded him of Solomon's psalm to loveliness. "Behold, thou are fair, my love, behold thou art fair. Thy lips are like a thread of scarlet. Thy two breasts are like two young roes that are twins which feed among the lilies. Who is she that looketh forth as the morning fair as the moon, clear as the sun, and terrible as an army with banners? Thou are all fair, my love. There is no spot in thee."

At last Howard found a *Leaves of Grass*. "Here's a beautiful volume. Wonderbar." The book was bound in brown buckram, with gold lettering on the spine, and had large print. The title of each poem was set in exquisite brown type and the pages were wide and of a rippled texture.

"But the price," Thurs said. "Six dollars!"

"But you're buying Whitman, man. A friend who'll be with you for the rest of your life."

"He wouldn't like these fancy clothes."

"What? Aren't you a lover of beautiful books?"

"It's still too expensive."

Howard's eyes narrowed until only the blacks of his pupils were visible.

"Look. Do you really want Walt, or do you just think you want him?"

Thurs angered, and showed it.

Howard said, "All right. Okay. Tell you what. I'll make you a present of him."

"No. No. That's not necessary."

Howard pushed him aside and started for the cashier, getting out his bill fold. "Don't insult me. Except for the gifts I've bought my family, this is the first real gift I've ever bought anybody."

Thurs took it.

Going out of the door, pillow and book under an arm, Thurs took one last look at the elfin blond. She was still paging through a magazine, standing serene and in blue amongst the other shoppers.

Howard took him to the city library where Thurs got a card and the book *Elmer Gantry*. "Better keep it out of sight when you get back to the Dorm," Howard advised. "It's classified as seditious literature at Christian, you know."

In the original trilogy, the World's Wanderer Trilogy [later shortened and rewritten as Wanderlust*], I wrote an essay concerning the rume. That's a word I invented, a word that goes back to "rue" and "ruminate." Originally the word "ru" meant to rue from your soul, to burst forth out of your pain and anguish. I felt that was a legitimate form of literature, that you could take autobiographical material and build a novel out of it. In fact, it was tougher to build a novel out of autobiographical material than, say, some his-*

torical lint you ran into. Because you had so much to overcome and so much to set in such a way that if they knew nothing about you, it seemingly was a creation out of history rather than out of your own life . . . My only regret is that I couldn't make these autobiographical novels better. I would have liked to make them even more objective, seemingly more objective as if it occurred to other people.

SECTION TWO

Buckskin Man, Buckskin Woman

The Manly-Hearted Woman

An English professor at Vermillion handed me twenty pages in David Lavender's Bent's Fort. There was the story of Flat Warclub, the Arapaho. The only dreams he could have were about picking up clams in the river, and those are women's dreams, not male dreams. But it didn't particularly catch my eye. I took it home with me and then I read the whole book. Then later on he handed me some more stuff, that among the Plains Indians, and especially the Crow, the women also had their societies, like the American Legion— there's a Legion and the Auxiliary Legion that the women have. And they had the same thing in the Indian world. And one of them that they had was the Manly-Hearted Women. . . . And I got to thinking, I wonder what would happen if I could work up a character that could only have dreams about getting clams in the river—that was his vision—would meet a manly-hearted woman, who could hunt with the men and shoot as well and so on. What would happen if those two met? What sort of relationship? Wow. Everything started exploding in my head. I was weaving all up and down the freeway all the way home. And by the time I got home I had about six pages of scribbling, maybe more than that. And I was typing up the final draft of Green Earth, and I stopped, and walked around for a couple days thinking it all over. And it popped into my head, how to do that book. And I wrote it all in about a month's time, the first draft.

In The Youth of Manly Heart

MANLY HEART LIKED the stylish young man. One good look at him and she knew he was fated to do something remarkable. She herself knew what it meant to become someone remarkable.

As a little girl she was already different from her friends. At the age of five her mother Clean Woman had difficulty getting her to quit playing with her brother Stalk. When Clean Woman urged her to stay in the tepee and help her with the household duties, so that she might learn how to become a good wife as well as a good mother, Manly Heart would have none of it. She ran outside instead and looked for Stalk to play with.

Stalk, who was a year older, soon began to avoid her. Their father Spear Carrier told him that it was not a good thing for a boy of six or more to be playing with his sister. At six it was time for the boy to learn how to become a good husband as well as a good provider.

When Manly Heart finally realized that neither her brother nor any of the other boys her age would play with her, she bowed her head for the time being and, sullen lipped, attended her mother and helped her with tepee work.

But while she worked with her mother, Manly Heart watched with envy as her brother joined the other boys in games of hunting and fighting and riding. It galled her that her brother should be taught to be bold in the pursuit of game and of the enemy, while she had to learn to sew and smoke meat. She saw her brother Stalk grow away from her as grown-up men taught him how to go about hunting and fighting with a cool manly air. Manly Heart was sure that she could do as well in the manly arts.

She begged her uncle Happy One to teach her how to shoot the arrow, how to mount a horse on the run, how to achieve a vision. Happy One did not know what to do. Since she was his only niece he found it hard to deny her. He had always favored her, and abashedly, almost in a shamed way, did show her how to shoot the arrow and how to mount a horse. Though he refused to tell her how to achieve a vision. Only men had visions.

At the age of twelve she finally found one boy who would play with her. When they were alone together she often led in sex play. It was taboo for a girl to suggest they look at each other's naked bodies and the boy was at first shocked by her behavior. But he told no one and presently began to look forward to those times when they could be alone. It was then that Manly Heart began to understand a little why her brother should be called Stalk. His name had a double meaning.

Soon all the young boys began to speak of her in derision. They said they would make sure that when she became a fully grown maiden she would never be given the chance to help carry the sundance pole. Only virgins were permitted to cut and get the sapling cottonwood for that great occasion. How could she be considered a virgin so long as she persisted in playing with the lout Hollow Horn? Hollow Horn like to brag to his friends that he could make milkweed juice a dozen times a day. For shame. And the young boys made the sign of ultimate disgust, first pointing the right hand downwards over the heart with fingers tight together, and then holding out both forefingers and letting them fall inward toward the belly.

Manly Heart endured their sneers until the day she learned that play with Hollow Horn might lead to babies. She was horrified. For her to have a baby before marriage would be the final shame. Abruptly she began to shun him. Hollow Horn didn't like being rebuffed and for some time thereafter told foul stories about her.

When she turned fourteen, her father and mother decided it was time she got married. It would help settle her into her true role as woman. It happened that a very old chief known as He Is Empty wanted a sit-beside wife for his last days. He no longer was interested in the joys of the flesh. Instead he had taken an intense liking to gossip. He loved young people and thought it would be instructive and pleasant to talk with a young woman.

Again Manly Heart was horrified. Marry that old dried-up parfleche? When she was avid to play with her brother Stalk if it could only be permitted? Never.

But the old chief He Is Empty employed a nephew of his to bring two ponies to the door of her father's tepee, and when that did not prove to be enough, brought two more ponies, as well as all of the fine earthenware of his deceased wife.

The beautiful earthenware settled it. Clean Woman had for years coveted the black-orange-brown pots. She instructed Manly Heart to get married to old He Is Empty. She said that the old man would not live long and then Manly Heart would be a wealthy widow and could have her choice of any of the young men still available. Sullen-faced, Manly Heart finally agreed. She could see that her name, because of her playing around with Hollow Horn, was not a good one and that she would have trouble finding a good man.

Life with He Is Empty turned out to be much more lively than she expected. At first she did serve only as his sit-beside wife, handy for gossip and raillery, as well as for making him special manly perfumes which he liked very much. And then about two months after they were married, as they slept together one night warm and cozy in a buffalo sleeping robe, he woke up with a considerable stalk in bed. Hiyelo. Before it could become limp, he mounted her. Despite all the bad that had been said about her, it actually was the first time for her. She was both delighted and shocked, delighted that it was so pleasurable and shocked that old men could still do such things.

From that point on He Is Empty gradually awakened more and more as a man. At first he took pleasure with her once every two weeks, then once every week, and finally twice every week. Also he appeared to grow younger, both as to the skin around the eyes as well as to the vigor of his strolls about camp. It turned out that the whole encampment was pleased with the marriage. The marriage had erased the chance that they might have raised a bad girl in their midst. Also it had restored what had once been a wise man to his rightful place in the council.

About three years after they were married, when she was seventeen winters old, in The Moon Of The Flowering Puccoons, old He Is Empty took pleasure with his young wife twice during the night and once again in the morning. He was exultant. For a little while he resembled a very young man. He sat glowing by the little stick fire in their hearth while sipping at a bowl of soup. He bragged that, after the past night, he was sure to become a father. Not even the best stallion in the village, Plum Eyes, had ever mounted as many mares in the space of one day. He finished his soup and held his bowl out for more. "Wife," he said, "it is a good day to die and you have given me much pleasure. I desire more soup."

Smiling, for she had come to love the old man in her way, she picked up the buffalo horn spoon and refilled his bowl.

He sniffed with pleasure at the rising steam from the soup. He relaxed against his lazyback. "Wife," he said, "I look upon you with much pleasure. It warms my heart to see how firmly you twist your hair into two long braids. It delights me to see how neatly you keep your doeskin dress. And I am well pleased with thee also for taking the daily bath and anointing your skin with the perfume of the wild rose. Would that I could take you with me into the next world."

"It would make me glad to go with you," she said.

"It is good to be a man again."

"It is good to see you so happy."

"No longer are you my sit-beside wife. You are now my lie-beside wife."

She put the spoon to one side. She smiled down at her lap.

Then, as he reached out a hand to touch her and let her know that she pleased him beyond all saying, he pitched toward her, and fell dead out of his lazyback.

Manly Heart missed her old man husband very much. She scarified her legs and breasts in mourning. Weeping she helped her brother Stalk and her father Spear Carrier put up a scaffold upon which to place her old husband's body. Her husband had no kin, thus every evening when the sun went down she found herself weeping alone at the foot of his scaffold. Finally, when the wind and sun, and the gobblehead vultures, had consumed his skin and flesh, so that there was nothing left but dried bones, she and her father and her brother buried the old bones at the edge of one of the burial mounds across the river.

After a decent interval, she had many suitors.

At first she rejected them all. She wasn't sure she wanted to get married again. Her old husband He Is Empty had been very gentle with her. She knew that some husbands beat their wives. She had heard the wives yelling in pain inside their tepees. To those wives the beatings came as a great shock since parents never chastised their children.

She often took walks alone. She did so despite the warning of their camp crier Wide Mouth. Wide Mouth told her it was dangerous for anyone to be wandering alone along The River Of The Red Rock. Pumas had lately been seen. And of course there were the Omaha.

She found a little pond near the big river. She studied her reflection in the water where it reached out from the red rock she sat on. After all that had happened to her she was not one to be vain. She could see that she was not as comely as many of the other maidens in camp. She had good large breasts and they at least could be said to be womanly. But she had the bold eyes of a man as well as the strong chin. Her black hair was coarse and did not grow as fast as a woman's. And lately she knew she had several times caught herself walking like a man, a slow rolling gait, open-legged. Yankton women tended to walk with a close tight walk with their knees brushing each other.

She stared a long time at her image floating on the still water. There were a few wrinkles at the corners of her eyes. There was even a wrinkle on her high forehead.

"Ae, I am not a Yankton beauty. Thus he who next marries will do so for my old husband's horses."

Her black eyes looked back at her with milky despondency. Her life was not worth keeping. It was better to throw it away.

On the way back to camp she decided to hold a giveaway. It was a custom among the Yanktons for the bereaved to give away all their possessions, both their own as well as those of the deceased, after the bones had been buried. She had been slow to hold such a giveaway because she was not sure she truly believed the custom was a good one. She decided she would do it to put to the test how much her own people liked her and if now they had truly come to respect her.

She wept in the customary manner as she carried all her goods and possessions out of her tepee and set them on the grass in the middle of the camp. She wailed loudly as she dismantled her tepee and laid out the lodgepoles and the buffalo hide covering. Everyone in the camp watched in silence. A few of the older women gathered near. Nothing was said.

When she had finished placing everything she owned in the middle of the camp, she settled down on the grass and covered her head with a fox skin shawl. And waited.

After a decent interval of silence, medicine man Person In The Moon emerged from his lodge and approached her. He surveyed the dismantlement of what had once been the home of He Is Empty. He had not approved of the marriage between He Is Empty and Manly Heart but at the time had said nothing. Person In The Moon was a very slender man, almost as if he'd been made out of willow withes rather than out of oak branches, and he had odd purple shadows under his eyes. Also both his lower eyelids sagged a little so that one could see a fat yellow tear trembling in them. Not everyone liked him. When he was a little boy he had dreamt of The Person In The Moon and after that everyone knew of course that he would never marry a woman. He was one of those who couldn't stand to have a woman touch him. Many of his kind, when they appeared in a band, sought out another man to live with, usually a young boy. But Person In The Moon did not care much for men either. He liked only his old mother Wise Crow and lived with her. Soon visions and prophesies began to come to him and the village accepted him as their shaman.

The whole camp waited for what Person In The Moon might have to say.

At last he clasped his hands in front of his stomach, with the back of his left hand down. "Peace, woman. We do not wish for your possessions. You have suffered enough. You have shown the proper respect for the deceased husband. If the others in this camp care to listen to what I have to say, they will hear what my helper has told me. Listen. I say this to you. Keep the household goods and the tepee and the horses. I have said." Person In The Moon turned slowly and in an hieratic manner returned to his lodge. His old mother Wise Crow, standing beside his lodge, held the leather doorflap open for him and then both disappeared inside.

After a moment Clean Woman appeared at Manly Heart's side and helped her daughter to her feet. Together the two women set up the tepee again and carried all the goods inside.

About two months later, Manly Heart married a widower named Red Daybreak. He'd come around visiting her with his lover talk and letting her know that he was a good provider and a bold brave in war. She knew he was all these things but she was also aware that there had been something dark about his first marriage. And it wasn't either that he'd beat his first wife, because in a leather village such things were always heard.

She found out what the darks with him were the fourth night of their marriage. The first three nights he slept beside her as a sister might. Even the fourth night began in felicity. They crept into their sleeping robe, and chatted, and laughed a little about the strange antics of a pet dog, Four Eyes, he'd brought to their marriage, and then, turning their heads away from each other, fell asleep. Of a sudden at dawn she'd felt clutching fingers at her throat; and then the next thing she knew he was upon her trying to thrust his stalk into her. She fought him. She was very strong and almost managed to free herself from the gripping hand on her throat, but in the loose-limbed way she writhed and wrestled she at last happened to open her thighs and he was into her. Sweat had also helped him. To her considerable surprise she discovered that it was somewhat pleasurable. And then, when he had finished, he let go of her throat and began to sob upon her breasts.

It was strange behavior. It was so strange in fact that she didn't tell anyone, not even her mother. Who would believe it? But she was sure of one thing. The same thing had no doubt happened to his first wife. And on one of those nights, in one of his more violent fits of passion, he had accidentally choked his wife to death.

Manly Heart considered what to do. She knew she was much stronger than his first wife. She could fight him off.

She considered divorcing him. But that way lay shame. No one had shunned her for marrying the very old man He Is Empty, but if she declared she was divorcing Red Daybreak because of the strange way he took pleasure with her the whole camp would laugh at her.

She lay awake most of the next night getting ready for his attack at dawn. Somewhat to her disappointment, he didn't bother her. He slept like a lazy dog beside her.

The second night she was so sleepy she couldn't stay awake. Thus it happened that he was at her throat and then at her thighs before she knew it. Once more her powerful muscular body saved her.

It disturbed her that the deadly wrestle with Red Daybreak was also pleasurable. It wasn't quite the pleasure her mother Clean Woman said a woman should expect from a husband, a crazy kind of fainting away as though a vision were about to come upon one, but still it was enough to cause the corner of one's mouth to smile in a twisted way.

The next day she caught him looking at her with grudging respect. It was the kind of look one brave would give another after a show of prowess. Deep back in his black eyes a recognition was growing that she was a match for him. Her sturdy squarish body was proving to be as powerful as his.

As time went on he attacked her less and less often. Where her first husband, ancient He Is Empty, began slowly with her and then gradually worked himself up to mounting her more and more, her second husband, dark Red Daybreak, began wildly with her and then gradually fell off to less and less.

Manly Heart was greatly puzzled by the behavior of the two men. Several times she found herself a lonely red rock to sit on to ponder on the ways of men. Now that she had married twice she began to understand that many of her women acquaintances in the village were living strange private lives with their husbands.

Six months after they were married Red Daybreak no longer touched her. While he was friendly during the day when around her and would talk with her about the various events of the day at supper, at night he was a stranger to her. Once it got dark he would not talk to her. It was as though he in turn was afraid she would attack him.

She became ever more lonesome. She took to humming, and then to singing, to herself as she worked around the tepee.

The singing made him angry, especially when she did not sing the words clearly. He accused her of singing love songs meant for another man.

She couldn't resist tormenting him a little. "Perhaps."

"A woman who sings to herself surely is singing to a secret love."

"Perhaps."

"Are you singing a song for some other man?"

"Are there not wife-stealers in our camp?"

"Who?"

"Eii. Perhaps I am only singing to the ghost of He Is Empty."

"Houw. He was but a shell."

"I am only sorry that we did not have children."

"With him?"

"Even with him."

He fell silent. He was so crestfallen that even his single war feather appeared to hang limp.

She got sick of having him around. He wasn't much of a man. She thought she preferred him more during those days when he had tried to strangle her.

When one day the Soldier Society got up a hunting party, she asked if she could go along. She said that both she and her husband Red Daybreak had good hunting horses and that if he could go she could go because she could ride and shoot as well as he.

Her husband was ashamed of her and looked the other way.

Turning Horse, who had been selected to lead the hunting party, had seen her run and shoot. He'd several times had target practice with her and had been beaten by her. He respected her prowess and was known to say that it was too bad she wasn't born a man. Also he was inclined to be gentle with the strange ones in camp. He had once pointed out Crazy Leg, the bachelor, as one who spoke better medicine than Person In The Moon.

"You know that my old husband He Is Empty prided himself on his horses," Manly Heart said. "It was because of the four beauties he brought to my father's tepee that my father said I should marry him."

"I know this."

"Thus I too have a good hunting horse," Manly Heart said. "Besides the horse my new husband rides."

"Houw."

"Do you not want the best hunters to go with you?"

"Get your horse and get your bow. Hiyelo. We shall try it this once." Turning Horse glared around at the half-dozen hunters sitting on their horses ready to go. "Let there be no lewd remarks." Then he turned a baleful eye on Red Daybreak. "Nor will I hear any backbiting from you. Unless you wish to stay home and breed dogs."

Red Daybreak sat angry on his red horse, glaring down at its black mane. He was proud of his male dog Four Eyes. He'd found Four Eyes lost by the river one day and had recognized it instantly as one of those of an ancient breed. It was said that the Old Ones had the breed when they came across a pond that was as endless as the sky. Four Eyes was black over its back and over the top of its head, and tan below. It had two tan spots just above its eyes, giving it the appearance of four eyes. It was a small dog but it could carry good-sized loads strapped onto its back without tiring. It tended to stay home more than the mongrel dogs did. Finally the flesh of that breed was said to taste better than the flesh of other dogs. All the women of the camp knew this and they were eager to have their bitches bred by Four Eyes.

Many Heart watched her husband with contempt. Ae, that was all he was good for now, to peddle dog seed. Himself he had none. It came to her that that was why she had not had a child by him. Not once that she could remember had their been any sign after his attacks that he had discharged seed as a buffalo bull might upon a buffalo cow. While curiously enough, with old He Is Empty, toward the end of his life, there had been some little sign after each time they'd taken pleasure that he might just possibly become a father.

Red Daybreak was no good.

"Have you got your horse and your bow?" Turning Horse asked kindly.

Manly Heart ran swiftly to her tepee. She took off her woman's clothes. She dug through an old parfleche where she had stored mementos of her first husband. There was a breechclout she'd made for He Is Empty which he'd never worn. She'd decorated the front of it with porcupine quills in the shape of an arrow. Smiling, she slipped it on and found that it fit her perfectly. She next got out his favorite hunting shirt and slipped it on. It too fit perfectly. She selected He Is Empty's favorite bow and a quiver of arrows. She picked up a bridle and then went out and got up on her old husband's hunting pony White Hooves.

When she came riding up to the hunting party, her new husband Red Daybreak took one look at her clothes and again looked the other way in shame.

The other braves did the same. Only Turning Horse looked upon her gravely and asked if she was ready.

There were no buffalo near or on the Blue Mounds plateau, and they had to hunt for stragglers along the sloughs of The River of The Red Rock. They finally found a small herd grazing near a beaver dam an hour from camp. The ground was very soggy and the buffalo had trouble getting started. It took but a moment to turn the leaders, several swift cows, back in on the herd. The herd milled around and around. As they did so, Manly Heart and Turning Horse and Red Daybreak and all the other braves rode in and out of the flying mud and shot them down. Not one buffalo escaped. When they counted the slain animals afterwards, they discovered they'd downed ten young calves, eleven cows, and five bulls.

When the hunting party stopped to catch its breath, they discovered that Manly Heart like the others had shed her hunting shirt upon making their run at the buffalo. The sun glistened on her round sweaty breasts as it did on their own brown chests. After one quick glance all the braves avoided looking her way again.

Red Daybreak threw her a desperate look asking her to go get her shirt.

Manly Heart had shot down three cows, one bull, and two calves and thought she deserved better from her husband. What had a naked bosom to do with anything when she was a great a hunter as anyone in the party? Especially when she was sure her husband had only downed one buffalo, a little red calf?

She plunged in with the rest of the men when they butchered up the carcasses, carefully cutting away the hide, slicing off the precious hump meat, cutting off the quarters. She covered herself with blood from head to foot. Like the others she helped herself to a chunk of raw liver, dipped it in bile, and ate it with relish. The raw liver of a young cow could sometimes taste as sweet as bumblebee honey. It was always a special ritual treat on the spot for the successful hunter. She helped the men hang the meat on the packhorses. Because there was plenty of meat they took only the choice parts.

They washed up in the river. Like the men, she removed her clout and swam naked with them. That time all save Red Daybreak took her for granted. She was a good hunter.

When they arrived at the thick clump of wild plums just east of the camp, Turning Horse decided the hunt had been successful enough for them to make a triumphant entry in through the horns of the camp. Already the little children had spotted them coming and were dancing for joy along the Blue Mounds stream. Turning Horse made the sign to dismount, placing the first and second fingers of his right hand astride his left hand and then lowering the two fingers and pointing at the ground. Everyone leaped happily to earth and began to paint himself.

Manly Heart had taken the precaution of carrying her old husband's decoration kit with her. She knew they would have a successful hunt. She began to paint her face to show how many buffalo she had killed.

Again her new husband tried to dissuade her with covert gestures, telling her she shouldn't act like a man.

Manly Heart burned. Her limp mouse of a husband, who could be a man only when cruel, had gall to be telling her how to behave. With a quick short motion she gestured defiance at him, placing her thumb between the first and second finger of the same hand and pushing it sharply at him.

Turning Horse saw the gesture and had to choke back laughter. He was enjoying the way Manly Heart was carrying on. She'd earned the right that day.

Red Daybreak heard the choked laughter and hid his face from the others. He went off by himself a ways to paint his face.

Manly Heart couldn't help but taunt him. "Be sure to use vermilion for the red calf."

Red Daybreak once more had to hide his face.

Finally they were all ready. Turning Horse mounted his horse grabbing the lead rope to his packhorse. The other Soldier Society members followed him. In a moment they formed a parade line with Turning Horse in the lead. Manly Heart was given the right to ride third in line behind Raincrow for all the buffalo she had killed. Red Daybreak brought up the rear.

Slung chunks of raw meat gleamed on the packhorses. Blood dripped on the grass as they rocked along. The buffalo hides, neatly turned inside out, showed patches of purplish fleece fat.

The little children were given permission to run out and meet them. They came crying like happy yuwipi. They dipped like swallows around and through the parading hunters. From the face paint markings they could tell who the great hunters were. They cried out the names of Turning Horse and Raincrow. They cried out the name of Manly Heart.

"Oo-koo-hoo! The hump meat will taste very good."

Manly Heart rode smiling and looking straight ahead.

"Wana hiyelo! The blood! The blood!"

The women of the camp stood watching with a hand over the eyes. They smiled white at all the food. Not one had a dark look for the way Manly Heart was behaving. It was good in their eyes that she had helped to bring in the meat.

The people of the Blue Mounds sat up all night cooking and eating.

But Red Daybreak sat by his hearth, a downcast brave. He ate listlessly of the broiled flesh buffalo hump.

Manly Heart did not trust the limp manner. She knew he could be a beast. She suspected he was probably thinking of divorcing her. Should a man be unhappy with his wife, he could give her away at the next dance. Any woman given away to the young men at a dance had to give up her tepee and her possessions and go back to her mother. She knew Red Daybreak was capable of being very mean.

When they went to bed, Manly Heart gruffly ordered Red Daybreak to lie beside her in her sleeping robe.

Shocked, Red Daybreak gazed at her with ringed white eyes.

She asked, "After such a great killing, are you not like other men, wanting to take pleasure all night?"

He said nothing. Though he did slide into her sleeping robe beside her. He was afraid not to. He groaned with a kind of whimpering sound.

It was almost dark. She could just make out his abject eyes. "If you wish, you may pull at the wings of where I have been punctured by the gods."

He jerked away from her dumbfounded. He slid out of the sleeping robe and sat apart by himself. "Ae. But surely you would not ask me to do such a thing."

"I have been told it is a custom among the Mandan. The men delight in pleasing their wives and the women cry with joy when their wings are pulled."

He sat as stiff as a piece of red rock.

"I demand it of you."

"Now it is you who are being cruel. Suppose I told the men this at our next council meeting?"

"They would laugh you out through the horns of the camp."

"It is still a cruel thing."

"You have never given me pleasure. And now I demand it."

He sat like a red rock for a long moment.

She made a gesture with her right hand, raising her first and second fingers so that her nose slid between them. "Come, it will be very fragrant for you."

Finally, craven, like a beaten dog come to a bowl of food, he tugged at her wings a little.

She let him touch her twice, and then, in vast contempt, belched disgust and hurled him from her. "Get away. You are no good."

Fury flashed in his eyes for a second, and he showed his teeth. "But it was what you asked me to do?"

"You are no husband."

Several nights later, Raincrow, the brother of Red Daybreak, invited them over for a treat. Raincrow and his soft wife Wren had been awakened one morning to discover a young mud turtle trudging through their leather lodge. They considered it a gift from the gods in answer to a prayer. The evening before Raincrow had expressed the wish that, oh, wouldn't it be a fine thing if they could only have some turtle soup again.

With some reluctance, Manly Heart agreed to come.

As they sat around Raincrow's hearth, sipping noisily of the turtle soup, Red Daybreak after a while managed a sickly smile. The two brothers, though different from each other as flower from weed, loved each other. Red Daybreak had several times said that if his brother Raincrow should ever die in battle he would be from that moment on related to nobody, so much he depended on his brother.

When they'd finished the meal, the men relaxed against a lazyback and the women sat at ease with both knees tucked to one side. Raincrow was a josher and he loved to tease his sister-in-law Manly Heart. He gave his wife Wren a hilarious and exaggerated account of how Manly Heart went at the killing of the buffalo. He said that, wherever Manly Heart rode with her horse White Hooves, blood spouted like cloudbursts upon the ground. Later, he said, when they went to butchering the fallen buffalo, she went at the cutting so savagely, slicing off a hump here and a quarter there, he was afraid she'd finally hack off one of her breasts.

Manly Heart roared with laughter. She thought Raincrow's raillery very funny. Back in her thoughts she had several times decided that Raincrow was perhaps a vigorous husband. His joking confirmed it.

Wren laughed heartily too, in a lesser way.

Red Daybreak looked upon his wife's hilarity with his brother with stoical indifference.

Raincrow ogled her with a wise eye. "My wife Wren boasts that you can make moccasins faster than any woman in our village, and set up tepees faster, and make clothes faster. Tell me, after seeing your bravery in our last hunt and your prowess with your bow, tell me, what is there you cannot do?"

Manly Heart turned serious. "There is one thing I cannot do." Raincrow raised his brows questioningly. Raincrow had very dark skin. There were times when his cheeks had the color of an overripe gooseberry.

"I wish I might learn the song that men sing."

"Why should you want to sing in the manner of men?"

Manly Heart gave him an appealing look. "But some women do."

"Well," Raincrow said, "I suppose that is true. My little wife Wren says there are times when she does."

Manly Heart scowled around at her husband Red Daybreak. "My husband is no good. And I live for nothing. I am not happy with my life and I have several times thought of throwing it away to the vultures."

Raincrow's face blackened over. He did not like to hear bad things about his brother. At the same time he did not like to hear either that his favorite sister-in-law was not happy. He raised himself from his lazyback and picked up a little twig and began to break it into tiny pieces. He threw the pieces one by one into the hearth fire. He pushed out his thick lower lip in torn thought. Finally he said, "You can already do so many things very well. Why must you have everything?"

"The next husband I marry," Manly Heart said stoutly, "shall be a real sport. One who has had an elk vision and so has gotten great power over women through his elk love medicine."

"Ha," Raincrow snorted. "Such a one you will not like either. He will be spending all his time combing his hair, and culling his lice, and perfuming himself, and will have little time for the hunt."

"Does my brother-in-law want me to marry one of those who puts on the dress of a woman and who does embroidery work?"

"Do not speak ill of my brother. We played together in my mother's sleeping robe."

"My new husband is no good. He cannot even peel a wild onion."

Raincrow at last leaped up enraged. He pulled off his leather shirt and dropped his breechclout. He stood totally naked before them. His phallus hung in a little curl. It smiled at them with the tiny smile of a baby mouse. He grabbed up his phallus and his testicles full in his hand and swore by them. "By the power of my seed I declare that my brother is a great man. Houw. You must be one of those women who have a namni with teeth in it, that he does not care to take pleasure with you." He gave his phallus and testicles a final shake. "I have said." With that he sat down.

Manly Heart was enraged in turn. She jumped to her feet too and pulled down her leather skirt. She stood completely naked before them. She grabbed herself under the thigh. "Your brother has nibbled me. Ask him if he has found teeth in my wings."

Wren was so ashamed of all she saw and heard that she picked up a sleeping robe and buried herself in it.

Raincrow stood with his mouth open. He stared so hard his eyes appeared to retreat under his brows. Then he dropped to the ground and lay back on his backrest. He was suddenly exhausted. Manly Heart was too much for him.

Red Daybreak was so ashamed of his wife that he got to his feet and sought to cover her nakedness with her skirt. "Come. Let us go home."

"Why should we go home? What will we do when we get home?"

"Come. Let us return to our lodge. Put on your clothes."

Manly Heart pushed him away. "The only way you will get me to go home is to carry me. Naked as I am. I will not go otherwise."

Greatly embarrassed, while his beloved brother Raincrow sat by helplessly, Red Daybreak carried his naked wife home in a robe.

The moment the doorflap was closed, Manly Heart leaped out of his arms. She stood chubby and strong before her slender husband. She picked up a stick from the edge of the nearly dead fire in the hearth and broke it in half and threw the broken pieces at him. "Listen. I have had you for a husband long enough. Depart."

His mouth fell open.

She saw in his manner that he had been planning on divorce, too. She had beat him to it. He had verily been thinking of turning her over to the youth of the village but he hadn't quite had the courage to do it.

"Must I break another set of sticks at you before you will understand? Take your clothes and your weapons with you." She glared at the single eagle feather hanging sideways at the back of his head. "Perhaps it is time for you to catch another eagle at Eagle Rock up on the Blue Mounds. You need a fresh feather."

Broken, craven, he gathered up his possessions and left her. He went to his mother's tepee.

Manly Heart lived alone in her lodge for a time. She could do as she wished anytime she wished. She could go about clothed or go about naked without having to worry what anyone else might say.

Conquering Horse

> ... I wanted to show how the Indian lived at that time. Why he did what he
> did. His beliefs and his fate came up out of the land. You see, I think people
> ... tend to be the voice of the land. ...
> I was interested in the "no name" business because people do try to find
> their identity. Who they are. In all times, in all languages, in all countries,
> and on all planets. Who they are. In the beginning they are born with no
> name.

Dancing Sun

DURING THE NEXT DAYS, No Name made a close study of Dancing Sun. Packing food, he managed to walk completely around the stallion's range. Hiding in tall trees, he observed him early in the morning, at high noon, and late at night.

One thing soon became apparent. Dancing Sun never galloped. Dancing Sun was a gaited horse. No matter how fast the others in the bunch might run, Dancing Sun never broke out of his pacing gait. Always he ran along easy, serene, head up, legs stroking lightly. He took twice the stride of the best pacing mare in his band. As he ran, his long red tail brushed along the tops of the grass. From a distance he seemed to skim over the ground like a low-flying white eagle.

In all, Dancing Sun had a band of some forty mares and some thirty colts. Rare was the male colt over a year and a half old. Twice No Name saw Dancing Sun drive a two-year-old stud from the band, cutting one of them, the more reluctant of the two, to ribbons with his hooves so that he died. The two young studs had been caught in the act of trying to corner themselves a bunch of mares. Only he, Dancing Sun, was going to be king of the females.

Dancing Sun could be merciless. Once a tall noisy whirlwind came racing toward them. Dancing Sun, ever on the alert, saw it coming. He whistled a warning and set the whole bunch in motion at right angles to the whirlwind. He circled his bunch at full speed, nipping laggards here, charging drifters there. Then a mare dropped back because her freshly born colt had trouble keeping up. Instantly Dancing Sun dashed for the colt, seizing it by the neck with his teeth, and smashing it to the ground. The mare whinnied shrilly in anguish. In a fit of frenzy she lay down beside her broken colt. Ears laid back, Dancing Sun drove at her, bit her cruelly over the back and neck. Finally, when she still would not get up, he ran off a short ways, then whirled and made for her, teeth bared, head so low he resembled an enraged wolf. So fierce was his aspect that the mare leaped to her feet in panic and raced off to join the rest of the flying bunch. Looking back over his shoulder, Dancing Sun saw that the whirlwind had not only gathered in size and speed but had changed direction. He shot swiftly after his band, pacing up one side and racing down the other, ramming his bluff chest into the ribcage of one mare, whirling around in full flight and kicking another, raking still another with his bared teeth, biting into the flesh of still another. Gradually, squealing his commands, he turned them in the direction he wanted them to go, at last drove them out of sight of the whirlwind where all was safe.

One day No Name discovered a male colt more than two years old in the band. The male was brown and quite fat. This surprised No Name and after watching a while he decided it was because the brown one was not much of a stud. The mother of the fat son indulged him much, often neighing him over to where she had found some specially luscious sweetgrass, and letting him get the first drink while the water was still clear, and shielding him from the sharp teeth of jealous mares. Mother and son were always together, often standing side by side, head to tail, switching flies off each other. Sometimes they leaned across each other's necks, nuzzling each other affectionately. Dancing Sun had his eye on them as they roamed and grazed together but did nothing about it. But then one fine morning the brown one found himself a stud at last, and after some nuzzling together with his mother, mounted her and made connection. The white master spotted them almost immediately and with a great scream of jealous rage was upon them. He drove at them so hard he bowled them both over. He sent the mare off galloping for dear life, then leaped for the slow stud. He fastened his teeth into the slow stud's withers and with one great jerk ripped off a piece of hide all the way to the rump. The brown stud rolled over backwards from the force of the jerk and hit the ground so hard his neck broke. He was left alone, gasping in death.

Dancing Sun controlled a range some twenty miles across. To make certain that interloper stallions understood just where his empire lay, Dancing Sun made it a practice to leave cones of droppings at each of the four corners. Every few days he made the circuit, checking his pyramids of dung to see if visitors had left notices around. Occasionally he would find one and then would carefully smell it over. Usually what he found did not disturb his regal calm much.

The great white stallion also had private staling spots along his run. When some of the young male colts tried to approach these hallowed grounds, Dancing Sun chased them off. From these spots No Name saw more evidence that the stallion was wakan. The white one's stalings caused deep green rings to jump up in the grass. It was as if his watering of the earth prompted springs to burst forth, even on high dry ground. His whitish-yellow stream was of Wakantanka himself, a supernatural fluid.

Occasionally Dancing Sun was stand-offish, moody. When a fresh wind came out of the north, bringing with it the cool sweet scent of the snow country, or

when the prairie was all aflower with pink peas, or when the wild clover made
the air thick with its lush aroma, Dancing Sun would run off by himself. He
would take his stance on the highest point of land, head lifted into the wind,
inhaling with great gusto. Sometimes he would point his nose at the blue sky
and grimace as if about to break out into godlike song. And sometimes he would
even whinny to himself, his lonesome cry floating on the wind as pure and
clear as the morning call of the cardinal, full of elation and joy at being alive in
the midst of the flowering plains. The white one reminded No Name of Sounds
The Ground and his lonesome pondering of flowers.

Later, breaking out of the pensive mood, Dancing Sun would round up his
band and bunch them up into a tight knot, so tight there seemed to be nothing
but raised heads and whistling tails. With a fierce and terrible mien he would
pace around and around them, close-herding them harshly, and would keep at
it until he had worn a trail in the grass. Every mare and colt betrayed the greatest fear of him during these times. Not one would dare to stray out so much as
the length of a neck or the breadth of a rump. Then, having kept them standing tight together in fear and trembling for an hour or more, the harsh disci-
plinarian would suddenly lift up on two legs, whirl completely around, then cut
through the middle of them, squealing fearfully, scattering them all over the
prairie.

No Name wondered about the stallion's strange whim of close-herding, until
the morning he witnessed an attack by a pack of lobo wolves. Some forty of them
came streaking out of a ravine, gray sliding shadows. No Name was sitting high
in a tree on the edge of a lookout at the time, so missed being hunted down himself. The moment Dancing Sun spotted the wolves, he let go with a deep full-
chested roar. To No Name he suddenly sounded like a combination mad bull
and raging lion. Without even looking around, or wondering what it was all
about, the mares called in their colts, "Euee! agh-agh-agh," and immediately
formed a circle around them. The mares stood facing out, teeth bared. Meanwhile the white master paced around and around his bunch, mane lifted, teeth
bared too, heels carefully kept away from the wolves to keep from being ham-
strung.

The wolves were somewhat startled to run into a stallion with such a defense,
and they withdrew to a prairie knoll to reconsider. They sat on their haunches,
tails whisking, every now and then glancing over at the dancing stallion and his
tight knot of fierce mares.

After a short wait, two of the wolves approached the stallion in a playful manner, as frolicsome as puppy dogs, rolling on the ground in front of him. They
frisked about as if they had always been his friends and meant him no harm.

Dancing Sun resorted to a stratagem of his own. First whickering a low warning to his band to keep tight, Dancing Sun pretended to be taken in by the
playing wolves. Slowly he grazed toward them, cropping grass one moment,
rearing his head in inquiry the next. Finally, just as the two wolves had maneuvered themselves into position, one at his head and the other at his heels, just

as they were about to spring, Dancing Sun made a great leap for the nearest wolf. With snarling teeth he caught the wolf by its ruffed neck and tossed it high in the air. The moment the wolf hit ground, Dancing Sun leaped on it with both front hooves, crushing its skull. Then, before the other wolf could collect its wits, he seized it too with his teeth and trampled it to death.

Howling at the skies in disgust, the rest of the lobo wolves gave up. Toothy jaws flashing a last time, they drifted off one by one, over the edge of the ravine.

Two mornings later, No Name saw for a second time why Dancing Sun trained his bunch in close-herding. Perched in the same tree on the edge of the lookout, No Name saw Dancing Sun lift his head and look off to the southwest. No Name looked too. Over a rise came a small band of horses, running straight for Dancing Sun and his bunch. What surprised No Name was to see that the small band was all male. They were bachelors who had been driven out when colts. They were of almost every color: blood bays and dark bays, light chestnuts and dark chestnuts, rust roans and strawberry roans. At their head ran a powerful black. His mane and tail glowed like the shine of a black grackle. Bluish streaks kept racing over his coat as he turned and wheeled in the sun. There wasn't a mark on him. He too had the swift gait of the pacer. He and his male chums came on with a rush, manes raised, ears shot forward, tails arched high.

Dancing Sun trumpeted piercingly. The glory of his nostrils was terrible to behold. His neck seemed clothed in thunder. A chill of terror shot through his mares and colts and instantly they bunched up into a tight knot. Head held low like a predator, snarling, Dancing Sun began to circle his herd around and around. His growl was like that of a monster wolf, deep, primordial. Then, sure they understood that he was their mighty king and dominator, that he would permit no dallying with any of the visitor bachelors, he turned and went for the intruders. He had made up his mind to fight them all, to the death. He went straight for their leader, the black one.

The big black had watched Dancing Sun close-herding his bunch, had seen him whistle his mares and colts into submission, had even seen how half of his own bunch of odds and ends had backed off a way. But for himself, the black one was not afraid.

Black One bared his vivid white teeth, laughing scorn both at Dancing Sun and at the craven cowardice of his comrades. He reared, whistled a shrilling challenge. Then he dug his forefeet into the hard ground as far out in front of him as he could reach, waggled his head furiously, stopping only to see what effect his mad antics had on Dancing Sun, then jumped gracefully around in the air, swapping ends like a frisky dog snapping at flies.

Black One's show of haughty defiance enraged Dancing Sun. He raised on his hind legs too. Eyes flashing blue lightning, teeth glinting like a grizzly's, ears laid back tight to his head, he shrilled and shrilled. His gray forefeet cut the air as if he were a dog digging a hole. Rampant, thighs stretched like massive white birches, he closed on the other in towering majesty.

Black One shrilled loud too, came on terrible and black, his blackness making him seem almost taller than Dancing Sun. They squealed at each other
until white foam ran dripping from their jaws. Their started eyes blazed with
primal hate and rage.

Suddenly they lunged for each other, lunged with all their force. They hit
with the sound of colliding cottonwoods. They raked each other with slashing
hooves, from front to rear. Their hooves beat a tattoo on each other's barrels.
Teeth caught hold of skin and ripped until flesh bled black. Sometimes, when
their bite slipped off, their teeth clicked together with the sound of hammers hit
on rocks. They went after each other like mad lions. Once they got a good grip
with their teeth, they hung on until flesh pulled away. They rolled on the ground
like wrestlers, over and over. They screamed. Mouths open, teeth glittering, they
dove for each other's throats. They whirled around as quick as cats. Kicking at
each other, rear to rear, their flint-hard hooves hit together with the sound of
crackling chain lightning.

Raw patches began to show on the Black One's glossy hide, on the rump,
over the shoulder, along the belly. Streaks of blood began to show on Dancing
Sun's immaculate white coat. One moment both puffed exhausted, the next
they went at it again with snarls of rage. Flecks of blood and froth flew in all
directions.

Finally Dancing Sun managed to catch Black One's nose between his jaws.
He bit in and shook him with all his might. He growled. He backed around and
around, shaking and mangling him. Black One suffered it for a few moments
Then, rousing himself with great effort, Black One gave a desperate jerk—and
broke free, with half of his nose gone.

They backed off. They let fly another ear-splitting piercing challenge. Then,
rampant, they flew at each other yet once again, throwing their whole weight
into it. They hit. The ground shuddered under them. Dust puffed up. For a moment they hung balanced against each other. Then, slowly, Black One tottered
over on his back. Dancing Sun pounced on him in a flash, stunning him with
his sharp forefeet, cracking open his skull. Again and again Dancing Sun struck,
cutting him to ribbons with his hammering hooves. With his teeth he stripped
off Black One's ears, flung them across the prairie. He struck until Black One's
brains began to run out.

Sure that Black One was dead at last, Dancing Sun suddenly set out after
the other ambitious lovers, scattering them pell-mell, chasing them until they
were out of sight.

When Dancing Sun came back, head high, he appeared to disdain the loving attention of his mares and colts.

During all this time, Leaf worked like a muskrat mother, preparing her nest.
She made a cradle by weaving a flat platform out of willow withes and covering
it with buckskin. She scraped and tanned hides for a small tepee to be used on
the way home. She dried many cases of meat. She made her husband a dozen

pair of tough moccasins. She also tanned him a new buffalo robe, a new pair of leggings, and a new fetish case.

For herself she made a dress, a loose supple piece of doeskin which she worked until it shone like fresh snow. She covered it with beautiful quillwork, blue and yellow and white and red. Even the lift strings, used to tie up the dress when the grass was wet with dew, were placed in pleasing symmetry all around the bottom. Every now and then she held up the dress against her body, smiling and tittering to herself, as if surrounded by a circle of admiring women friends.

Sometimes No Name caught her sitting silent by herself in the entrance of the cave, her black eyes on him but not seeing him, absorbed in herself. Her look caused him to recall what his mother had once remarked about pregnant women. "Before her child is born, a good Yankton mother always fixes her mind on a certain hero. This is done so that when the child grows up he will desire to do great things and become a great hero himself." He wondered if Leaf had him in mind, or her father Owl Above, or her brother Burnt Thigh. Though tempted, he dared not intrude upon her thoughts and ask her.

For some odd reason, another of his mother's warnings came to him, that a woman should not look too hard at an animal before her child was born. "There was once a woman," Star said, "who found a rabbit hiding in some wild plums. The rabbit was gentle and soft. She took it in her arms and petted it and held it close to her face. When her time came, her child was born with a split nose. This man is still alive." No Name hoped that some evil spirit had not placed the thought in his mind. They of the other world often knew beforehand what was to come to pass.

Eyes averted, yet studying Leaf closely, he soon came to see that he was one of those who had been fortunate in the choice of a wife. Leaf rarely complained about her lot in life. She accepted what came. She did not long for tomorrow that it should bring her some great and wondrous surprise. The great thing was now, it was happening now, and she lived it to the full. When she ate juicy broiled hump, she enjoyed the hump, fully, at that moment. When she sucked marrow from a warm bone, running her tongue deep into it, she lived in the tip of her tongue, for that moment. When she looked into the fire, she enjoyed the warmth and color and the mystery of the flames, fully, at that moment, then. When she crooned a hero song to herself for the coming boy, she lived in her throat, in the song, for the moment even becoming the hero.

One evening No Name came home to wife and cave bonetired, exhausted, dispirited. He hardly noted that Leaf took off his moccasins and rubbed his feet as usual.

He got out his pipe. He lit up with a coal from the fire, much in the manner of his father. He blew up a big puff of smoke. It hit one of the broad leaves of the fallen cottonwoods above, baffled around it, streamed up in finer wisps, and vanished.

He inclined his head to the left, still waiting, as he had waited all week, for his helper to speak to him.

Presently Leaf served him supper. He ate slowly, with little relish. When he finished his first helping of boiled meat, he turned his dish over to signify he no longer had hunger.

Leaf retreated into the shadows. She sat watching him.

Again he lighted his pipe. He brooded. This time the pipe had an unpleasant taste. And he finished his smoke only because it was bad luck not to do so.

"You have not told of today, my husband," Leaf said finally from the shadows.

A frown drew his brows together. He did not like it when she began the talk. "Nothing of importance happened today."

"When will you catch the stallion, my husband?"

He swallowed back a sharp word.

"My husband?"

"It is for the gods to decide."

"This cave is a dark place even in the day. Well, I am afraid for our child. The cave will cast a shadow over its life."

He put his pipe away. "Now you speak as one touched by the moon being." He sat staring at the graying embers along the edge of the fire.

She waited an interval, then said again, "You have not told of today, my husband."

Suddenly he said it all in a rush. "Today I saw Dancing Sun walk along the horizon. I became afraid. He walked, yet he looked like a ghost horse going very swiftly. He walked, yet his mares and colts had to run very swiftly to keep up with him. Ai, sometimes I think it is the same horse that Holy Horse saw. One day this white stallion will take me to the middle-of the-earth too where the demons will overcome me and I will not be heard of again."

"What does your helper say?"

He started. How had she known it had fallen silent? "Ai, woman, I am still waiting for him to speak."

"Have you offended him that he does not speak?"

"I have thought of this. Yet I can not remember anything."

Again, after a silence, she asked, "My husband, this Dancing Sun, is he as all male horses?"

"I do not understand, my wife."

"Does he torment his sons?"

He fell silent. After a moment he shuddered. He remembered what Dancing Sun had done to the slow brown stud. Leaf persisted. "What do the mothers say to this?"

"They submit," he said shortly.

She sighed. "Ae, so it is with the Yanktons also. The fathers permit us to hold the sons for a short time. After that they take them away and send them to a high hill where they must seek a vision."

"I love my father very much and do not wish to hurt him. He has always been very tender with me his son."

"Thus it seems," she said quietly, eyes downcast, hand on her swollen belly. "Yet did not your father require that you torment yourself?"

"My father wished for me to show my bravery that I might be ready to replace him as chief when the time came for him to join those of the other world."

"A mother's heart is always large for her son. She will always weep when it is time for him to leave on his trail."

"It is not the way of all Yankton mothers," he said patiently. "My mother told me a great thing when I was about to depart. 'Son, the thing you seek lives in a far place. It is good. Go to it. Do not turn around after you have gone part way, but go as far as you were going and then come back.'"

Leaf sighed from the depths of her belly. Her breasts stirred under her leather dress. At last she said, "When I am old, may it be given me to say such a great thing to my son."

He had been careful to keep their horses, the sorrel gelding and the dun mare, well hidden from the white stallion, either in the brush under the cottonwoods when the wind was north, or in the back of the cave when it was south.

But one evening the white stallion surprised him by coming alone to the meadow just west of the cliff. The white stallion walked out to where a patch of blue-eyed grass grew deep and lush. After sniffling around at it some, the white one began eating with relish.

"Haho!" No Name exclaimed softly to himself, watching from behind a thick cottonwood. "It is as Sounds The Ground said. He likes to go into the low places and eat the flowering grass. I well remember him saying this."

No Name stole softly out of the brush to get the mare and the sorrel before Dancing Sun got wind of them. The mare, whom they had named Black Stripe because of a thin band of dark hair running down her spine, was in heat. She stalled frequently. Dancing Sun was certain to scent her before very long and come and steal her.

But as luck would have it, the wind changed before he could get Black Stripe into the cave, and in a few moments Dancing Sun's shrill inquiring neigh cut through the evening silence. No Name tried to hurry the mare inside, but the stallion's call had roused her and she hung back on the rope.

Dancing Sun shrilled another high piercing call of desire. This time Black Stripe let up on the rope long enough to whinny loudly in answer.

There was a sudden crashing in the brush and the next moment the green leaves parted and out paced Dancing Sun, noble head high, long mane flowing in two scarlet waves. He came on swiftly, smoothly.

He spotted No Name pulling at the rawhide rope. Instantly his whole demeanor as a lover changed. He became the warrior. His head came down, his teeth flashed, his ears shot forward. His tail pointed straight back like a cat's, jerking spasmodically. Then, with a resounding snort, he made straight for No Name as if he no longer saw the mare, but saw only the man.

No Name dropped the mare's rope and leaped to one side just as Dancing Sun, dazzling and white and huge, lunged for him. Dancing Sun missed him by no more than a hair.

Then, as Dancing Sun stopped short to wheel around for another charge, No Name, on a sudden impulse, born as much out of fear as out of inspiration, leaped astride the great stallion's back. No Name grabbed hold of the flashing scarlet mane with both hands, gripped the horse's belly hard with both legs.

Dancing Sun reacted volcanically. He went straight up on all fours. No name felt him rising under him like a wave on the Great Smoky Water. At the top of his jump, Dancing Sun broke four ways, and when he came down, as each leg hit ground one after another, there were four separate jolts. Then, shrieking outrage at finding something still latched to his back, Dancing Sun began a strange twisting run on the meadow. No Name felt the great muscles of the horse squirming and bulging and undulating powerfully under him. It was like riding an enormous snake which had just had its head chopped off.

Dancing Sun stopped dead. He seemed to reflect to himself a moment. Then, snorting, he turned his head and snapped at No Name. His face was so close, No Name could see red inflamed arteries pulsing furiously in the backs of his blazing eyes. No Name ducked to one side to avoid the terrible snapping teeth. Again Dancing Sun rose wonderfully under him, very high. And at the top of the jump, because of the awkward way he sat on the stallion, No Name lost his hold. He arched into the air in a tumbling somersault and landed on his back.

It took a moment for No Name to collect his wits. Then he sprang to his feet, fully expecting to find the mad stallion on top of him. But to his surprise, the stallion did not come on. The stallion was still snorting and shrilling with rage, but he was being held at bay by Leaf. Leaf had fire and smoke in her hand and was waving it in the stallion's face.

No Name stared. Then he understood. Leaf had heard, then seen, the stallion come for the mare Black Stripe too. When No Name dropped the lead rope, Leaf had quickly secured the mare with the gelding, who was already in the cave, and then had seized a burning brand from the fire and had rushed out to help her man. Instinctively she had known what to do. Fight fire with fire. In the rust-tinted dusk the smoke from the burning brand was almost exactly the color of the stallion's coat.

No Name saw how Leaf strained to be quick despite her heavy oblong belly, saw how ferocious her eyes were. He leaped to help her and took the burning brand from her.

Dancing Sun seemed to understand that the hot brand had changed hands, from female to male, and once again charged mouth and head down like a raging predator lizard. No Name thrust the burning brand into his face. Dancing Sun shrieked, reared, struck out with both forefeet, almost knocking the brand from No Name's hand.

Again Dancing Sun charged. Again No Name jabbed the brand into his face.

The furious action roused No Name, and fear in him changed to anger. He too suddenly became enraged, completely forgetting that he had ever thought the horse wakan. He began to roar. "Back, you white devil! Hehan, so you wish to make my heart hot this day? Good, eat this! Fire you are and fire you shall have!"

Behind him Leaf had become infuriated too. "Kill him, my husband!" she cried. "Burn his eyes! Do not be afraid. Rush him, he is afraid of fire!"

Still the white fury came on. Dancing Sun reared and struck out at them with his glittering gray hooves. He whistled piercingly.

Then, from behind No Name and Leaf, the mare Black Stripe in the back of the cave whinnied, high, wonderingly.

The stallion seemed to go blind at that. He drove so fiercely at No Name and Leaf that both had to retreat under the fallen cottonwood. Teeth bared, froth flying in flakes, Dancing Sun made a final snap at No Name. He caught the burning brand with the side of his mouth and knocked it sailing into the stream at their feet. The brand went out with a quick whistling sizzle.

No Name jumped back, so hard, he knocked himself and Leaf backwards into the cave, falling past the embers of the fire in the entrance. No Name was sure the stallion, gone crazy, was coming into the cave with them.

There was a loud cry behind them, and suddenly the mare in the dark back of the cave lunged and tore loose her rope and made a break for it. She shot past them both, rawhide rope trailing for a second through the fire, and joined the stallion outside.

The stallion reared, suddenly whickered in a very low guttural voice, and then, the fierce heat of desire coming over him again, forgot about the man enemy and his wife. With a great frolicsome leap, and a snort, he ran off with the mare into the dusk over the meadow.

The next afternoon, sitting high in his lookout cottonwood on the north side of the river, No Name watched the horses come down to drink again. The white one and his sister sentinels stood guard as usual on the bluffs.

He spotted the dun mare Black Stripe with the first bunch, submissive, no different from the other wild ones except for what was left of her lead rope trailing in the dust. Dancing Sun paid her no more attention when she went past than he did any of the other mares.

Later, when the second bunch came down, No Name once more saw Dancing Sun run over and nip his favorite, the light-gray mare with the twinkling feet, in love and play. She was leading the second bunch with slow heavy dignity and as before accepted his show of affection placidly.

It was while he was looking at the pregnant mare, and also thinking of his heavy Leaf, that his helper finally told him something. "Take the sorrel gelding and ride slowly after the light-gray mare with the twinkling feet. Go mostly at a walking pace. Twinkling Feet cannot run very fast very long. Pretend to chase no one but her, not the white one. The white one loves Twinkling Feet and will always stay near her. Keep chasing her. The stallion will give the commands to the old buckskin his mother where they are to go. He will keep them circling and have them come back to this watering place. When they return to this place, do not let him or the mares drink, but keep them moving. Chase him until he is very thirsty and very tired. Even four days and four nights. Otherwise he will kill you. After he is very tired, make a loop in your rope and throw it and catch him."

No Name thought to himself, "Four days and four nights without sleep? That is a very long time. Well, I must be brave. The time has come for me to be valiant."

That night he made himself a short heavy whip from a leg bone and some extra thick bullhide. He added a thin piece of buckskin at the tip for the popper. The white one would never again catch him unarmed.

In the morning he told her.

"Today it begins. Listen carefully. The stallion drives his band slowly because the one he loves will soon have a colt. I will trail after them on our sorrel. Because of the one he loves, he will not run very far ahead of me. Well, after a time he will get used to me. Then it will be given me how to catch him."

"But, my husband—"

"Woman, listen carefully. Each day he will try to come to his watering place under the bluffs. But I will not let him. I will chase him on. After he has gone by, I will come quickly to water the sorrel. Woman, have a parfleche of food and a heartskin of fresh water ready for me at that time. I will eat and drink quickly and then go on."

"But, my husband—"

"Today it begins."

"My husband, I am afraid. My time is very near. Perhaps I cannot always have the food ready."

"The birth of our son must wait. The fulfillment of the vision comes first." His black eyes glittered.

She bowed her head. Her hands strayed over her belly. "I hear you, my husband."

"Haho! In four days I will return in triumph with a painted face."

"I will wait."

"Hang the provisions each day in a certain tree that I will show you. Do it before the stallion comes. Do not try to meet me. The stallion will get used to my smell after a time and accept it. But the smell of another will scare him off. Do as I command and it will go well with us. This I know."

"I hear you, my husband."

He ate heartily and drank long and deep. He readied his lariat, his whip, his war bridle with its long rein, his parfleche of dried meat, and his new white buffalo robe. He filled a heartskin with fresh water from their stream. He placed a skin pad stuffed with hair on the sorrel for a saddle. He showed Leaf the tree, a green cedar growing on the near side of the west bluff, where he wanted her to hang fresh provisions each day. He gathered driftwood from the river and piled it on the horse trail where it emerged out of the ravine on top of the bluffs. He scattered sacrificial pinches of tobacco along the trail in the ravine and across the tops of the bluffs. Then, ready, he waited on the middle bluff, sitting on the hard ground, holding the long rein of his sorrel in hand as it grazed.

It was well past noon before he saw them coming. He waited until he could make out individual horses, then went over and set fire to a pile of driftwood. Soon white smoke rose in a high billowing plume, straight up, like an enormous ghost tree. The fire made such a crackling noise he had trouble keeping the sorrel quiet. He jumped on his horse and waited in the shadow of the cedar tree, whip dangling from his wrist. He watched the band come on.

Presently Dancing Sun came pacing from behind, where he usually ran, and took over the lead from the old buckskin mare. Dancing Sun called up his white sister sentinels. It was only then, as he wheeled them all for the bluffs, that he spotted the bonfire and its high floating plume of smoke. He let go a warning snort. Instantly the band stopped dead in its tracks. All stood with raised heads, ears shot forward, wild and roused, looking more like alert deer than horses. Dancing Sun whistled again and they quickly bunched into a tight knot. He approached alone. He came up to within a hundred yards of the fire before he saw No Name on his sorrel under the green cedar. Again Dancing Sun trumpeted a command. The knot of mares and colts tightened even more. Dancing Sun looked from the fire to No Name and back again. He moved around to his left, then around to his right, trying to get No Name's scent. But the wind was northeast and he couldn't quite get around far enough to pick it up. He snuffed. He clapped his tail in irritation. He stamped. The band behind waited in a close profusion of raised heads and whistling tails.

No Name watched him. He sang a song of self-encouragement in a low private voice:

"Friend, you are like the sun. You are a begetter of many fine children. The white mare said you would be fierce. Friend, a Yankton has come to get you. Friend, it has been said. Epelo."

Then, strong in the knowledge that the gods had nothing but good in mind for him, No Name touched heel to flank and he and the sorrel moved out of the shadow of the green cedar.

Dancing Sun snorted. Haughty head up, snuffing loudly, he ran forward a few steps. He sniffed. He pawed the earth like a bull. He took a few more steps. Then, at last getting wind of the man enemy's scent, with a scream of rage, he charged.

No Name waited until Dancing Sun was almost on top of him, until the sorrel under him tried to double away, then suddenly he sat up very straight and with a quick hard sweep of his arm snapped his new whip in the stallion's face. The buckskin popper at the end cracked, loud, directly in front of the stallion's eyes. Astonished, Dancing Sun skated to a stop on all four legs. He reared, staggered backwards. Then, before Dancing Sun could collect himself, No Name raised his big white robe and snapped it vigorously around and around, yelling "Oh-ow-ow-ow!" at the top of his voice. He dug his heels hard into the sorrel's flanks, forcing him toward the stallion. The sorrel bucked, again tried to shy off. No Name brought his whip hard across the sorrel's flanks, both sides, again reined him toward the stallion. Dancing Sun staggered back some more. Then of a sudden, abruptly, he spooked. He raced off toward his band. With a blood-curdling yell, No Name followed them.

Dancing Sun bugled piercingly. Instantly the whole bunch ahead of him wheeled and broke into a wild thundering run, stampeding west. Up front, galloping as wild as the wildest of them, ran Black Stripe, Leaf's dun mare, her dragging line raising a little snake of racing yellow dust.

No Name went after them furiously for a short way, still howling, still snapping his white robe around and around. The white one and his bunch and their following dust were soon out of sight. No Name reined in his sorrel and let them run, content to go along at a slower pace, certain that the stallion would not let Twinkling Feet run very far.

No Name found it easy to track the bunch. Dancing Sun ran his band from the rear, and as a pacer, not as a galloper, left a characteristic track that was always easy to pick out. No Name followed the fresh tracks for an hour, then headed his horse almost straight south, quartering across the stallion's run.

He rode naked except for a clout. The sun sank down a brassy sky. In its raw light his body glowed a blackish brown. The air on the high barrens was so dry it made the nostrils crack. To keep breathing he sometimes had to lick the inside of his mouth. The sorrel's hooves kicked up minute dust storms. The little puffs of light-gray lingered in the air behind them for a long time. Every now and then he checked to see that the long rein of his war bridle was securely tucked in folds under his belt. He had long ago learned that, somehow thrown from his horse, he could always catch hold of the rope as it payed out along the ground. On the prairies a man was no man at all unless he had four feet.

He saw the horses again just as the sun set, far to the south, circling out of the west. They were grazing quietly along. He had cut across at exactly the right angle, and thus had saved his sorrel miles of running. He reined in. He let the sorrel graze quietly toward them. He guided him toward the pregnant Twinkling Feet.

After a while Dancing Sun saw them. He came racing up, snorting a challenge, then checked himself as if remembering the buckskin popper. He wheeled, and with a single high whistle set his band in motion, this time at a good walking pace.

No Name smiled. He urged the sorrel up and followed them.

The sun set. A coppery light slowly suffused all things, the sparse grass, the prickly pear cactus, the occasional tufts of gray-green bunchgrass. The grazing wild horses with their prevailing cream colors resembled rolling balls of pounded copper. The brassy sky changed to gold, then to gold and purple, at last to purple and pink. There was no wind. Raised dust, after hovering a while, fell back into place again.

The moon rose before dark. It came up round and full, a globe mallow, flowering huge and orange out of the horizon. It came up turning, and for a little time it seemed to be rolling toward them. Dancing Sun wondered about its strange rising too, and challenged it with a sharp rolling snort. Then gradually the great globe mallow parted from its stalk, floating free of the earth, and became the moon proper.

No Name pushed the band along at a steady gait. The band sometimes trotted, sometimes galloped, while he kept his sorrel to a good walk. He quartered across the stallion's run at every opportunity. Dancing Sun hated the pushing and often bugled his displeasure. His snorts kept the bunch in a jittery state. Every now and then his imperious neighs sent them dashing ahead, going hard, with thundering sound.

"Are you angry, great white one? I am happy. It is good. You are twice the horse that my sorrel is. Therefore I want you to cover twice the ground. We will tire together. Perhaps after that I will get off and walk. I will be fresh, you will be tired."

The moon lifted. It became smaller, became silver. It cast a smoky ghostly light over the dry barrens. Dust became yellow smoke. The occasional tufts of bunchgrass resembled the gray feelers of a catfish. The white stallion became a silver stallion. His scarlet tail became a pink tail.

After one of their spurts ahead, No Name found the bunch standing in sleep. Even the white one slept. In the silver night they reminded No Name of immobile snowmen.

No Name became sly. He readied his lariat, setting the loop, tying one end to the belly band of his pad saddle. He gave his horse the heel.

One of the white sisters on the flank awoke. She looked around, saw them, whistled sharply in warning. Dancing Sun awoke with a jump. He too looked around, then trumpeted loudly. He gave his head a certain shake to one side and sent his mares and colts crashing away in the soft delicate night.

No Name rewound his lariat. "Wise white ones, I will wait until you are very tired and very thirsty. Also I shall try to keep you from some of your sleep. It will be the worry and loss of sleep that will make you mine."

Horses, both tame and wild, usually napped three times a night: shortly after sunset, at midnight, and just before dawn. The final nap was the soundest, the most refreshing. No Name decided that he might let them have one of the earlier naps, if it meant he himself could get some sleep, but he would never let them have that last nap.

They moved on, gradually circling around to the east, then to the northeast. Dancing Sun ran behind his bunch, keeping himself between them and the man enemy. The old buckskin mother and the two white sisters remained alert to his every command. If he lifted his head higher than usual, they hurried the band along. If he lowered it, they slowed the horses down. If he ran sideways, head to the left, they turned the bunch to the left. If he ran with his head to the right, they turned the bunch right. Occasionally one or another of the mares or colts would drop out of place, on the right, or left, or behind, and Dancing Sun would promptly move up, showing his teeth, bugling, to put them back in place. Occasionally too he would run beside his favorite, Twinkling Feet, and nip her in love, and seem to whisper to her that all was well.

A high white haze began to move across the moon. Soon a bluish circle appeared around it. Later the same kind of haze, a mist, began to slide across the land close to the ground.

No Name nodded. He slept. He awoke. With a start, looking, he saw them still ahead. "Ae, my sorrel has learned the game and now follows them without instruction." He petted his sorrel over the withers. "Friend, you are my helper. After we have caught him, I will take you to my father's meadow beside Falling Water where the grass grows very sweet. I will give you a long rest in reward. I give you the name of One Who Follows."

He nodded. He slept. He awoke. And waking, he saw them all as white shadows, white silences, of the other world. Both he and his sorrel and the white one and his bunch were spirit ghosts. They were all gods together in the night. They had now no need of either life or death. They had need now only of song, of vision, of long white wings.

They drifted on. The bluish mist thickened. He slept again.

Waking, he saw a strange thing. Objects were continually changing before his very eyes. Sometimes Dancing Sun and his band stalked along as tall as a grove of rustling trees. Sometimes they slid along the ground as lowly as a family of mud turtles. Sometimes they walked above the blue mist. Sometimes they walked under it. When the land dipped and the mist lifted a few feet he could see nothing but horse legs, many legs, like walking birches. When the land raised he could see nothing but flowing manes and alert ears. The horses seemed to be swimming across a lake of milk.

He slept. And waking, he saw that the horses had vanished.

Well, he did not care. The night was wakan and he was very tired. Besides, he now trusted One Who Follows.

He slept. And waking, he saw that the horses had reappeared. He smiled. He had known One Who Follows would never lose them. One Who Follows was a wise one and would keep quartering after them.

Two hours before dawn, he suddenly felt rested and wide awake.

"Ha-ho!" he said aloud. "It is good. It is as I planned. And now I must make sure that Dancing Sun and his band do not rest. I will keep them snorty, even a little wild, during their best hour of sleep."

He pushed them hard. After an hour of it, Dancing Sun turned and came snarling at him. The horse resented being kept from his golden nap time.

No Name rose against him. He kicked up his sorrel and went after him in cool fury, cracking his buckskin popper in the stallion's broad white face to remind him that man enemy now had the overhand.

Of a sudden, almost between steps, the moon vanished behind a silky web in the west. Then, the next moment, the sun was up. The sun came up as red as a blood clot from a slain buffalo's lungs. It swelled, became huge. It too seemed to roll straight for them for a time. Then, rising, oscillating, it ascended the skies.

No Name opened his parfleche and gnawed on some dried meat as he jogged along. He washed the meat down with a drink from his heartskin. He also gave his faithful sorrel a drink.

A light wind drifted in from the southeast, touching him on the right cheek. The wind had in it the smell of a robe freshly washed in rain water. Both horse and man snuffed it in pleasure.

No Name studied the western sky. A blue haze hugging the horizon made him wonder if rain was on the way. "Helper, it is not rain we want. Tell it to stay beyond the river. We wish to keep the ground hard and thus give the horses sore feet. Also, a rain will fill the little hollows with water and give the wild ones to drink."

He kept them going, cutting across the inside of the stallion's run, sometimes walking.

At mid-forenoon, Twinkling Feet the pregnant mare began to lag behind. Dancing Sun spotted it. Tail glowing like a down-flowing flame, he ran up and inquired with a wondering whinny. When she didn't respond, he urged her up. Still she lagged. Finally, half in love, half in anger, he nipped her at the root of her tail. She turned heavily and snapped at him. He snorted, then nipped her again, this time hard. At last she gathered her huge belly into a rolling trot and rejoined the bunch, taking her place in the center again with the jolting yearlings.

At noon, hot, the earth shimmering under a white glaring light, No Name happened to throw a look up at the sun. As he did so, one of the rays of the sun broke away and became winged one. Astounded, No Name watched it slowly form into the shape of a hawk.

"Ai!" he whispered, "the sun is sending a messenger. He wishes to tell me something. I will watch the shape closely to see where it will fly."

Slowly, silently, in ever larger ovals, like a maple leaf drifting down, the hawk settled toward him. Presently No Name could see its rust-red tail, then make out the ribs in the individual feathers of its wavering wings. Its claws worked spasmodically. Its eyes blinked down at him. At last it opened its beak and cried, "Kee-er-r-r!"

No Name looked up in awe. "Take care? Will the fierce white one attack me again?"

"Kee-er-r-r!"

Then the hawk, dipping its wings, lifted up, up, finally blended off into the sun, becoming one of its rays again.

He leaned forward and whispered in the hairy earhole of his horse One Who Follows. "Something is coming. Get ready."

One Who Follows twitched his ear, then shook his head, trying to get rid of the tickling words.

"I am ready," No Name said. "My helper is near me." He placed his hand over the charm hidden in his braid. "It is good to know the gods approve and are willing to warn me."

Out of the shimmering heat waves along the northeast horizon a faint line gradually appeared. No Name stared at it a while, then recognized it as the valley of the River of Little Ducks. Presently the tops of the cottonwoods began to show. The stallion's watering place was at hand.

Just as he was beginning to wonder how he should spook the wild ones past the place, Black Stripe the dun mare accidentally helped him out. Tiring the last while, she had taken to jogging along at the rear. All of a sudden her lead rope, still trailing from her neck, got caught on the stump of an old wolfberry bush. It tightened, stretched, abruptly hauled her up short. She reared. There was a loud snap and the rawhide broke, with what was left of it coiling up and lashing after her. The snakelike lashing of the rope scared her. She bolted. The faster she ran the faster the trailing rope raced after her. With a scream of terror she charged straight through the bunch, scattering them in all directions.

Dancing Sun was instantly on the job. Trumpeting loudly, he raced back and forth, up one side and down the other, trying to turn them into a compact unit again. By hard running, and vicious biting, he did manage to get them bunched. But not until they had all run well past the watering place. They headed west, starting around the circle a second time.

No Name waited until they were almost out of sight, then turned his sorrel for the cedar tree on the near side of the first bluff. He found the provisions hanging from a limb just as he had ordered, with Leaf herself nowhere in sight. Using some big leaves from wild hemp as gloves, he transferred the dried meat and fresh spring water to his own parfleche and heartskin, very carefully so as not to pick up her scent.

He headed his sorrel for the river. One Who Follows instantly picked up his head and trotted down the trail between the two bluffs. One Who Follows was so happy at seeing the water again he ran halfway into the river and stuck his head under all the way to the eyes. In his eagerness to drink he almost drowned himself.

No Name laughed. "My brother, you behave like a foolish colt." No Name removed his moccasins and slid off into the water, stumbling stiff. He gave the bridle a jerk and held the sorrel's head out of the water for a few moments. "Friend, patience. Drink little by little or we will never catch the white one."

One Who Follows nuzzled against No Name's belly as if he understood, then lowered his head again and drank slowly and steadily. Soft swallows chased up the underside of his neck one after another. The hollow between his belly and hips slowly filled out again.

No Name was overjoyed at seeing the water too. He bathed his limbs, he splashed his chest, he refreshed his face and neck. He drank long and deep from the ocher waters.

The sun was almost down when he picked up the trail on the barrens again. The white one and his band were completely out of sight, even their dust. No Name set his course straight south, knowing for certain this time that he would run into them again on the far side of the circle.

Long after the round red ball of the sun had halved itself out of sight, a glory of scarlets and golds continued to reach far across the skies. The colors suffused the land, transforming it into a vast plain of rich reddish earth covered by golden grass. The sorrel became a red-gold horse and he himself a red-gold god. For a little while he forgot his quest, and where he was, and where Leaf might be. The scarlet and gold flowed into him and he conceived himself as having a scarlet soul and golden blood. Later, in turn, the moon rose out of the east. In the gradually thickening haze, it came up a deep red, almost like a morning sun. It remained red until halfway up the heavens, then slowly turned into a flying yellow pumpkin.

"The sun is my father. He shines upon me. The moon is my mother. She shines upon me. I am strong when they look upon me in love. I am happy. Hoppo! May this continue for the rest of my life. The earth hears me."

He let the sorrel take its own gait. Hoofbeats falling into the soft dust were the only sounds in the dreamy yellow light. He hooked his foot under the belly band. He looked heavy-eyed at the flat and endless world for a while. Then gradually he drifted off, rocked to sleep by the swaying walk of the sorrel. He dreamed of a white sun with a scarlet mane.

A terrible squealing awoke him. He came to with a start, one hand instinctively seeking his bow and the other an arrow over his shoulder. Directly in front of him, rampant, teeth flashing, stood Dancing Sun. Behind the stallion stood his mares and colts, alert, in the posture of the hunted, ears shot forward. For a moment No Name could not understand it. Hair raised on his scalp. "Is this a nightmare, my helper?" Then the sorrel under him shied, almost unseating him, jerking the leg he had caught under the belly band. "Ai, it is a true thing. Also I have hit upon them again as I planned. But I have done so in my sleep. Well, that Dancing Sun was a smart one to see that his enemy was off guard."

No Name let go his bow, instead grabbed for his bone-handled whip. He swung with all his might. This time, instead of cracking loudly, the buckskin popper hit flesh, cutting the white one over the nostrils. Dancing Sun screamed. He reared higher; struck. His flashing hoof hit the sorrel a glancing blow high on the withers, just missing No Name's thigh. Then No Name raised in wrath himself. Again he lashed out, this time with redoubled might. His whip caught the stallion squarely across the broad forehead, cutting him over the eyes.

Dancing Sun wheeled. Bugling, falling into his ceaseless swinging pace again, he sent his bunch roaring away, their manes flying, tails popping, dust following in a high slow-moving cloud.

No Name watched them go, curving off to the east. He set his course accordingly. He hooked his foot under the belly band again and relaxed.

He slept. He dreamed. He was in a canoe riding across choppy waves. He dreamed a second time. A hawk swooped down to lift him from his horse. He dreamed a third time. His father Redbird came to take a red bull-baby away from Leaf.

Near dawn he awoke. Ahead of him walked the bunch. "My brother," he said to One Who Follows, "twice now you have followed them while I slept. When we return to Falling Water, I shall give you a year without labor on its sweetest meadows."

He ate a little of the dried meat. He refreshed both the sorrel and himself with spring water.

The sun came up an ugly red, resembling a buffalo cow that had not cleaned well after a birthing.

He rubbed dust out of his eyes with a knuckle. He examined the band ahead. It seemed to him they somehow looked different. Most of them hoofed it along dead tired. Somehow too there did not seem to be as many. He counted them. "Ho! a third is missing." He turned sideways in his saddle and looked back. There, against the red horizon, stood some twenty horses, head down, exhausted, motionless. All would soon be wolf bait.

"They lack the water. Soon even the strongest will drop out. Then it will be given me what to do."

It came to him then, like a blow on the head, as he studied the bunch in front of him, that Dancing Sun was not among them. Twinkling Feet the light-gray mare heavy with young was still there but not the white one. Then he understood why the horses had been drifting along in such a hangdog manner. Dancing Sun was not there to keep them bunched up and on the alert.

Again he turned sideways in his saddle and looked back. He could still see those that had dropped out clearly against the horizon, head down, motionless. Some were mares, some were colts. But Dancing Sun was not among them.

"Horse," he cried down at One Who Follows, "what have you done? I trusted you to follow him while I slept. Yet now I awake and find him gone."

The sorrel under him stopped dead, as if in disgust, and began to crop at dry spears of buffalo grass. One Who Follows did not even bother to flick his ears at the words.

No Name's eyes filled with wonder. Was One Who Follows trying to tell him a thing? No Name looked at the grass underfoot. He could not imagine a horse enjoying it, much less eat it. It was thin, as sparse as the solitary hairs on an old dog's nose.

His eye happened to catch sight of some fresh droppings. He saw immediately they were hard and dry, not shiny and ripe as they usually were when a horse had enough to drink. Ha-ho, the hard droppings meant the band was about dried out.

The dry droppings next reminded him that Dancing Sun had his own private places for dunging, four of them, marking the corners of his empire. No Name remembered that one of these corners was nearby, beside a deep washout. He turned his sorrel toward it. To his surprise, the sorrel readily gave up his grazing.

They were almost within sight of the curious pyramids of dung, when of a sudden from behind them came a rolling snort and then the furious oncoming beat of horse hooves. No Name jerked viciously on the reins, wheeling his horse around.

It was the white one, just emerged from a yellow ravine, head held low like a rabid lobo wolf, teeth flashing. He came straight for them.

No Name grabbed his heavy whip, sat high on his horse. When Dancing Sun's head came up below him, he lashed down at him with all his force. Dancing Sun took the blow across his ears just as his teeth sank into the skin over No Name's thigh. Dancing Sun gave a vicious rip and a small slab of flesh came away. No Name was too startled to scream. There was no pain. Only a sudden numbness shot all up and down his leg.

Dancing Sun reared directly in front of him, looming over him. Holding the bloody tatter of skin and flesh between his teeth, snarling, Dancing Sun shook his head, snapping it back and forth like a dog trying to shred a grass doll to pieces.

"Friend," No Name cried, "it is very plain you will breed wakan warhorses. The enemy arrow will never touch them. Friend, you are a great horse. Become my friend. I have said."

Dancing Sun still shook his head like a mad dog. He waggled his head so hard back and forth the flap of flesh at last flew out of his mouth and sailed across the dry land, landing in a patch of prickly pear. Then, still rearing, whirling completely around on two dancing legs, Dancing Sun jumped away. He raced across the plains, tail flowing, head up, looking this way and that.

No Name followed him slowly. He bathed his oozing wound with spring water from the heartskin. He bound it with a piece of rawhide. "Friend," he said, shooting the words after the white one with a pursing of lips, "friend, at last you have tasted the blood of a Yankton warrior. Do you like it? Well, there is much more. Be careful that a Yankton does not taste your blood. I have said."

Dancing Sun flew at his band. With a single loud trumpeting snort, ears laid back, shaking his head vigorously at the old buckskin mare up in the lead and the white sisters on the flanks, he sent them beating across the barrens once more.

There was no wind. The dust they raised lofted high into the blue-gray haze. No Name rode first on one side of his buttocks, then the other.

It was Leaf who spooked them when they approached the watering place the next time. She was standing under the cedar tree. The lead buckskin mare got a whiff of her, shied, popped her tail, and before Dancing Sun could stop them the bunch was off and running.

No Name watched them go, smiling grimly. Yet he could not refrain from scolding Leaf when he rode up to her. "Well, I see now I have a wife who disobeys."

Leaf looked meekly down at her hands. She was trembling. "I heard coughing in the night, my husband."

"Ai-ye!"

"Perhaps it was Rough Arm and his killers."

No Name was instantly all eyes and ears. He flicked a swift fierce look to all sides. "What was the cough, one that could not be helped? Or one done in warning to say that a stranger approached?"

"I was sleeping, my husband, and did not hear it clearly. Yet I heard it."

No Name looked down at her. He recalled that a woman heavy with young often imagined strange things the last days. He decided to indulge her. "Woman, you were wise to come and tell me. After I have given the horse some water and grass, I will look for sign. Return quietly. If I find they have been here, I will come to help you hide in some other place. Otherwise I will go on. The white one is tiring."

"How soon will it be?"

"I can not tell. It has not been given me when to catch him. Have patience. Great things come slowly and after much bravery. I have said."

She saw the bloody bandage on his thigh. "Ai, he has bitten you. He will kill you." She came up to touch him.

He kicked the sorrel in the flank, making it shy away from her. "Woman, have I not told you not to touch me? Go back. The white one knows my smell and has become used to it. If I come with yet another smell he will not let me come close. Return to the cave."

"It will end sadly," she said in a low voice. "Already the wild one has taken a bite from my husband."

"Return, woman."

"The cave is dark, my husband. The place where you sleep is cold. In the night I hear spirit ghosts. The Old Ones who lived in the cave in the old days come and wake me. I am very lonesome."

He pretended not to hear her. He looked at the fresh provisions hanging in the cedar. He noticed she had hung up a new shirt beside them. "Woman," he cried angrily, "have I not told you I cannot even change clothes or he will take fright at the new smell and run away to some other range? I do not wish to begin the circling all over again. Take it with you."

She hid her face. Then she began to cry. Turning heavily, she pulled the new shirt from the tree and started for their cave.

He watched her walk down the face of the bluff, going with heavy falling step, her back stiff, her small buttocks taut, her swollen belly swinging from side to side in front.

Dark face stern, he turned his back on her. He moved the fresh provisions to his own parfleche and heartskin, then rode down to the river to refresh his horse and wash his wound.

He found Dancing Sun just before dusk. The white one and what was left of his bunch, some thirty head, plus the gravid light-gray mare, had given up grazing and instead were slowly dozing along. Only the stallion still showed grace in his carriage.

The sky hazed over. The haze became so thick the sun vanished before it set. At last a bad thing was on the way. Rain.

Then, just after dark, he saw it, a low line of smoldering lights all along the northwest horizon. It resembled an advancing enemy carrying torches. He stopped his horse and watched it with narrowed eyes.

Finally he made it out. Fire. Prairie fire. Ai-ye! so that was what the sun hawk had tried to warn him about. Leaf was perhaps right that Rough Arm had been skulking along their river. Rough Arm, to get revenge, had fired the prairie grass. Rough Arm hoped to spoil his vision of catching the great white stallion. Luckily there was but little wind. It would be a while yet before it overran them.

Dancing Sun also spotted the prairie fire. With a single snort he rounded up the remnant of his band and bunched them into a tight waiting knot, then ran a short distance toward the advancing line of flames, nostrils fluttering loudly, trying to get scent of it. He ran close to where No Name sat on his horse, for the moment ignoring his man enemy.

The fire came on. As it advanced it also slowly spread toward the north.

"Rough Arm has fired the grass all along the River of Little Ducks. He has cut off our retreat. He knows there is no water at all to the south."

As No Name and Dancing Sun watched, a puff of wind, hot and dry, hit them. Then another wafted past, stronger, drier. Again, another. Finally a gale of hot wind began to blow past them.

"Now an evil god is helping Rough Arm. He has sent him a strong wind. The grass is short and thin. Yet it burns as if it were tall and thick. Even the earth is burning."

Dancing Sun abruptly wheeled. He bugled piercingly. He gave a certain vigorous waggling motion of his head and faced his bunch around into the fierce wind.

Then No Name saw a thing that made him marvel. The stallion whistled again and all his mares and colts began to trot straight for the advancing ring of fire. Hehan! What a great chief the stallion was. Such control of the spirit souls of others was of the gods, was wakan.

Yet even so the mares, especially the gravid light-gray one, showed reluctance to buck the fire. They held their heads sideways as they advanced. Some tried to shy off to the left, others tried to dodge around to the right, but Dancing Sun was always there with his fierce teeth, his blunt chest, his striking flashing forefeet, to force them back into place. And as always, swift feet flickering, he glided smoothly along.

"Will he never tire, my helper?"

But Dancing Sun had not reckoned with other wild creatures. Suddenly the barrens were full of streaking fourleggeds, yowling wolves and coyotes, bounding deer and jackrabbits; of flying wingeds, numbed meadowlarks and owls, dumbfounded ducks and quail. Dancing Sun screamed, and wheeled, trying desperately to keep his mares and colts from being stampeded by the terrorized creatures. But finally another band of wild horses, led by a roan stallion, came pounding by, tails and manes whipping like the flames of the prairie fire itself, and he lost control. What had been dead-tired dozing laggards were now suddenly breakneck racers.

Dancing Sun shook his great mane with a final shrug of despair, and let them all go. But one. That one was his favorite, Twinkling Feet. He ran along beside the light-gray gravid mare neighing winningly, commandingly. She wanted desperately to fly along with the rest, but he kept bearing in on her, turned her each time she dodged, nipping her, biting her, bumping her first on one side, then on the other. And finally she gave in. Nose down, she turned and headed into the advancing fire with him.

By that time the wind was howling around No Name and his sorrel. Smoke wafted toward them in enormous streams of gray. No Name coughed. One Who Follows coughed. So did Dancing Sun and his mate immediately up front. The whole sky ahead and the earth beneath raged with mounting manes of fire. No Name found it difficult to make out Dancing Sun and his mare against the flames. They seemed to have become orange flames themselves, dancing, snapping, rushing. In the weird snapping hellish light, No Name's face glowed a stone red, while the sorrel's coat glowed a clay yellow. Heat surged toward them in jumps. The air became so searing hot No Name had to cover his mouth to breathe.

A burning rabbit bounded toward them. With every leap it started up a new little fire. It ran crazed. It screamed. It ran veering from right to left to right. Finally, blind, it circled back into the oncoming fire, and, squeaking, fell dead.

It seemed inconceivable to No Name that so little grass could cause such a raging fire. It could only be that, besides the powerful wind, the earth itself, truly, was burning up.

Head to one side, looking past his hand, coughing, No Name saw the fire dance toward them but a couple of dozen jumps away. The grass immediately ahead of it seemed to ignite of itself, here, then there, then everywhere. Then before the ignited little spots could themselves become racing prairie fires, the main line of the flames was upon them, engulfing them.

A slow-moving badger, running desperately, and yet for all its desperation waddling along hardly faster than a turtle, came straight for them. The sorrel shied, almost unseating No Name. Then, not a dozen yards away, the badger burst into a single searing yellow flame, its fat body exploding with a snap like the crack of a buckskin popper.

Dancing Sun shrilled. Then he bit his heavy stumbling mate one last time, and charged. He leaped high over the line of fire. His leap seemed miraculously high to No Name. And he cleared it. A split second later the mare went up and over too, for all her weight lifting high and graceful. Then with the white one she vanished into the wall of exploding smoke.

No Name was next. He whipped his sorrel, hard, across the flanks. Head to one side, coughing heavily, One Who Follows understood what was wanted of him. At precisely the right moment, just as a bunching of grass underfoot burst into flames, he leaped, high, soaring aloft. The main fire raced under them. It stung the soles of No Name's feet. Instantly a great blast of hot wind hit them, almost doubling them up. Then they landed, hard, stumbling on the other side in smoking darkness.

"Hi-ye!" No Name cried. In a frenzy he whipped his horse, viciously. They galloped. They raced through popping plumes of pink smoke. No Name held his breath. They pounded. At last the smoke cleared some. Then, up ahead, in the weak light reflecting from the fire behind them, he saw Dancing Sun, noble head still up, scarlet tail glowing like a swamp ghost, phosphorescent, pacing gracefully beside his favorite mare.

"He is of the spirit of fire itself, truly," No Name whispered. "Fire can not touch him. He knows this. He will make a great warhorse for the Yanktons."

They walked through a waste of black. Thin columns of smoke twisted off still burning horseballs and thick whorls of grass and seared cactus. Underfoot a half-fried meadowlark craked mournfully. A seared lobo, looking very skinny without its hair, sighed a last rasping breath out of a gaping mouth. A baked rabbit stroked its feet spasmodically, kicking up black soot. The smells of the burning waste shut the nose.

They moved on.

The wind let up, at last died out altogether. Behind them raced the fire, rushing south across the farther prairies, gradually sinking out of sight beyond the curve of the earth.

The heavy mare lagged. The white one lagged with her. Gradually the sorrel caught up with them. Soon they were as one band, the stallion and the mare and the sorrel with the man enemy aboard walking side by side. They headed north, going straight for the watering place.

On the morning of the fourth day, the sun came up a gold ball out of a black horizon. It rose into an orange sky. Ocher smoke and gray haze drifted low in the farther reaches.

No Name touched the piece of horse chestnut in his braid. "Were it not for my helper we would now be in the other world."

They came across occasional, smoldering half-burnt bodies of gophers. They skirted fire-blackened coils of rattlesnakes. They rode past a prairie dog town where surviving inhabitants sat beside their blackened honeycomb of holes discussing the past night's disaster. They turned aside to avoid the burnt gaunt body of a colt from the roan stallion's wild bunch. The smell of fried flesh and burnt hair was nauseating.

Then his helper spoke to him, clearly. "Let the white one drink. Also the mare if she wishes."

"But, helper, the white one still seems fresh. See, he walks with his head high. A drink now and he will be again as he once was."

"He is brave. He is a warrior. He is very tired and sleepy yet he hides his inner torment from the watching eye. Let him drink. He is so thirsty, so crazy for water, he will drink too much. A sudden heavy drink will stiffen his legs and shorten his wind. It will founder him. While he is in the river prepare to meet him on the trail halfway up between the third and second bluff. Have both your loops ready."

"Will he attack?"

"Perhaps. But this time it will be given you to capture him."

"Yelo."

Against the black earth and in the orange sunlight, the whiteness of the white stallion seemed more dazzling than ever. No Name had to shield his eyes to look at him. Dancing Sun seemed to scatter a whiteness like floating snowflakes on the air.

The valley of the River of Little Ducks at last appeared. Except for the taller cottonwoods and the deeper green meadows, everything south of the river was burned off. Only the north side remained strangely green.

No Name reined in his sorrel. He let the stallion and the mare go on by themselves. The white one did not stop to investigate from the height of the middle bluff as he usually did, but walked quietly, stolidly, down the trail into the ravine. The mare followed him. Despite her gravid state, there were wide hunger hollows between her hipbones and her belly. She stumbled along, almost as one blind. Looking at her closely No Name saw that her dugs were waxy and had dropped.

While the two drank below, No Name slipped to the ground and let the sorrel have the last few swallows of spring water in his heartskin. The small amount would not founder the sorrel; if anything would freshen him greatly for the struggle ahead. Having drunk, the sorrel lowered his head and snuffed at the ashen grass on the fire-shaven earth. Every spear of growth had been seared off at the roots. No Name petted the sorrel. For the first time he saw how gaunt his faithful mount had become. He considered taking the sorrel across the river for a few bites of grass. Instead he went over and plucked a handful of green leaves from a dying cottonwood sapling in the ravine. The sorrel ate the dryish green leaves with relish.

No Name looked down at the white stallion below in the river. "Truly, he is wakan. He went without water for four days and yet has remained a lusty one."

He watched Dancing Sun stalk out of the river and enter a small patch of green grass on the north side. Dancing Sun was so ravenously hungry, ate with such fury, that he tore up the grass, roots and all, even chunks of earth, as he grazed along.

No Name glanced west toward the cliff. To his surprise he saw that the fallen cottonwood still showed green where it lay across the opening to their cave. The prairie fire had missed it. "Ho, Leaf still lies hidden in our underground lodge."

No Name rode halfway down the ravine. He got off his horse and spread the loop of his longest and toughest lariat across the narrow part of the trail. He did not bother to hide it. Dancing Sun was now familiar with his smell. He tied the end of the lariat to the sorrel's belly band. He also readied the loop of his second lariat.

While the sorrel chewed the last of the dry cottonwood leaves, No Name sat on his heels in the black dust. In mimicry, a boy again with a small stick-horse and two buckskin thongs, he pretended to be catching a stallion. To his satisfaction, the white one was roped and thrown and tamed.

He looked down at where Dancing Sun still tore angrily at the grass. He sang in a low private voice. "Friend, you are strong. Friend, you are fierce. But a certain Yankton brave has come to get you. Get ready. Something you will see." He looked up at the strange orange morning sun. "Thank you for coming. Thank you. I can do anything when you are shining. I seem to have more power when you my father shine on me." He turned to the southwest where the moon hung almost obscured by a thick haze. "Thank you. I see that it will all happen as the white mare promised. Soon I will tell this to your friend, Moon Dreamer."

His bitten thigh began to throb under the rawhide bandage. He set his face against it. It was not a good thing to look at. It might weaken him for the struggle.

Dancing Sun left off grazing and re-entered the ocher river. He drank long and deep, nose under, bubbles rising. Once he lifted his head and trumpeted a short winning neigh at his wife Twinkling Feet.

No Name waited. He scanned the green horizon to the north, looking out as far as the enveloping purple haze would permit. He saw no sign of Rough Arm and his wild men.

He almost fell asleep. Clopping steps jerked him wide awake. Looking down, he saw Twinkling Feet and Dancing Sun come stepping up the trail. They came heavily, water-logged, stiffened. Quickly No Name positioned the sorrel so the pull on the ground loop would not throw him. He held the rope in hand, ready to jerk.

His pulse beat painfully in his wound. His head came up. He sniffed in anticipation. His fierce black eyes glittered. Red passion glowed in his brain. A cold-blooded green-eyed predator writhed in old darkness in his belly. He licked his lips, once, already wildly happy that he had seized the white one.

The heavy mare stepped over the waiting loop. Her hoof touched the edge of it. She paid no attention to it. She waddled heavily on.

Then the white stallion stepped into it with his forefeet. He also paid it no mind.

In that instant No Name moved. He gave the lariat a flip. The flip undulated down the lariat and lifted the loop off the ground under the stallion. Again No Name moved, this time giving the lariat a powerful jerk at the same time that he quirted the sorrel under him. Just as he had planned in mimicry, the rope jerked high and the loop caught the white one well up on the forefeet. It threw him. The stallion hit the ground with a loud whumpfing grunt. Black dust puffed up. The mare ahead heard the crash of bones behind her and with a startled snort came up out of her self-absorption. She lumbered heavily up the bluff and out of sight.

Dancing Sun lay stunned a moment; then, with a scream of astonishment, of outrage, at the great indignity suffered, tried to rise. His head arched gracefully up, his forefeet came part way up, even his belly rolled.

No Name quirted the sorrel again, viciously. The sorrel leaned until the quivering rawhide threatened to snap.

Once more No Name quirted the sorrel. This time the rope rolled Dancing Sun completely over. The sorrel kept digging, began to drag the white one across the ground.

"Hehan!" No Name leaped to the ground, second lariat in hand. He gave the sorrel another whack on the rump to make sure he understood he was to keep the rope taut, then went hand over hand down the rope. He approached the wild one carefully, going in from the side. He placed his knee on the great arched neck, tried to catch up the stallion's near back leg. Dancing Sun felt the knee, kicked violently, and No Name missed his grab.

"Hold him!" No Name cried back at the sorrel. "Hold him tight!"

One Who Follows understood. He leaned back so far he looked like a great dog sitting down.

Again No Name reached for the back leg. Dancing Sun shuddered. Suddenly he came around at No Name with his head and tried to bite him. His eyes were blazing. Mysterious sounds gurgled in his belly.

"Ho, I have a horse who likes to bite Yanktons! Well, all you shall have for your teeth is empty air."

At last No Name got the other loop around the back leg. He pulled it tight. Then, as the stallion once more tried to bite him, he also caught the lower jaw in a half loop. This too he pulled up tight. Then he flipped another loop around the head and had him bridled as well as lashed down. He pushed the rawhide down the nose until it lay exactly in the right place, so that the slightest pull would put painful pressure on certain nerves.

Dancing Sun tried to move; couldn't. He groaned; lay still. Slowly the look of a trapped eagle came over his bluish eyes.

No Name stood up. "I have you, mighty white one!" he cried, exultant. "Wait until my father hears of this. I shall be known. Hey-hey-hey! I feel the power of it in me all the time."

There was a great clap of thunder behind them, then a cracking echo off the cliff. He looked up and around. There, all along the horizon behind them, from the southwest all the way to the northwest, almost on the ground, lay a low, angry green cloud. He had been so busy catching the wild one he had not noticed the sky suddenly becoming overcast.

Ahead of the low green cloud were still other wild clouds, raggy, boiling, darting. The wild gray shrouds seemed to be rushing toward a common center above him. Listening, he heard a sullen roar descending.

Dancing Sun and One Who Follows heard it too. Both horses whickered strangely, brokenly. They understood some sort of disaster was impending.

"Helper," No Name said in a low voice, "what, are you deserting me at this time? I have the white horse. Let us keep him. He is a good one. Send the storm along some other path."

There was another crackle of lightning. It hit the ground higher up the trail. Pinkish blue light dazzled all around them; stunned them. A tremendous boom of thunder exploded against the earth. The valley seemed to crack apart.

No Name threw another look around behind them. The low green cloud came on, rolling down the valley. Even while he watched, it engulfed the yellow cliff, then the first fat bluff, then his grizzled lookout cottonwood across the river. Meanwhile above them the boiling gray shrouds concentrated into a churning black mass. A great droning roar as of some tremendous spinning top came pressing down upon them. His ears began to hurt with it. He could feel the blood beating in his dogteeth.

A few hailstones the size of robin eggs struck around them. A moment more, then the swirling blast of a great wind whelmed over them. Hailstones and black smut and grayish water churned as one. He covered his head with his free hand against the striking hail. He could feel the sorrel tugging through the white horse. He looked around but could not see the sorrel. Hailstones the size of eagle eggs began to hammer around them. Then a hailstone the size of a baby's skull plunked him squarely on the brow and arm. He saw fire. The arm over his head became numb. He changed arms. It too was hit, became numb. The roaring of the wind deepened. It began to whine hoarsely, like the terrible and continuous and reverberating roar of a lion. Under the pounding balls of hail the stallion beneath him struggled with wild frenzy.

"Ai-ye!" No Name cried, coughing under the pummeling hail, "He will hurt himself."

He took his knife and boldly cut the rope from the white one's forefeet. The sorrel, suddenly released, fell over. No Name next cut the rope from the wild one's rear leg. Then suddenly, before the wild one could realize he was free to rise, No Name jumped on his back, clamping his slim legs tight.

The stallion rose under him like a canoe overcoming two successive waves. No Name could feel the warm muscles gathering under him for a jump. Again he was struck how much it felt like riding a massive writhing snake. Then, risen, ducking his head to one side away from the falling hail, the stallion bolted heavily up the trail for the barren above. Once he slipped. Quickly he regained his step and beat on. Hailstones splattered around them in the mud. Dancing Sun squealed every time a hailstone hit him over the ears.

"Run, great one," No Name cried. "You are my god. I will take care of you."

Slipping, regathering himself, quartering away from the storm, Dancing Sun bounded up the trail.

"Run, let us escape the Thunders who want to kill us. Would that my father Redbird were here. He would appease them with a powerful prayer of supplication."

When they reached the level prairie above, the stallion began to buck, sunfishing, trying to stand on his head. No Name was ready for him at every turn, at every twist. When the stallion dropped to the ground and rolled to get rid of him, No Name stepped to one side. When Dancing Sun got to his feet again, No Name quickly remounted him.

Howling winds pressed down from the skies. Green hail thickened. The big stones raised blood blisters on both man and horse. Sheets of water rose over the ground, first hoof-deep, then ankle-deep. Soon islands of hailstones were floating to all sides.

"A cloud has burst," No Name cried. "My father once spoke of having seen such a thing. There will be a flood in the valley and it will be fearful."

Then, abruptly, hail and wind slackened off. And the stallion quit his pitching.

They drifted with the storm. It rained, rained. No Name did not dare to open his eyes except under a protective palm. The rain came down so sheeting thick he could scarcely make out the stallion's white ears. No Name's head and the backs of his arms felt like one solid bruise.

Presently the rain let up too. Horse and man stopped. Both lifted their heads and looked wonderingly around. Ahead of them a solid gray wall of slanting driving rain moved swiftly on.

There was no land to be seen. Even the black ashes of the prairie fire had vanished. The whole flat top of the hogback was covered with bubbling ice and water, all of it beginning to sheet off toward the low places to either side. It went with a slowly gathering rush. It had rained so hard so fast the water had not had time to run off.

"It is my father's friends, the Thunders. They sent the hailing rain to help me subdue the wild one. Thank you, thank you. I am happy."

He sat at ease.

At that moment Dancing Sun exploded beneath him. Despite the mud, the wild one managed to rise almost twice his height in the air. At the top of the jump, his head and rump went down, his back up.

No Name grabbed desperately for the scarlet mane, hung on.

Dancing Sun hit the muddy ground on a slant, came down with such a jolt No Name's head snapped like the head of a floppy grass doll.

"Helper!" No Name cried, "what is this? He still thinks to be free?"

A new and even stronger voice seemed to speak to him. "Take courage. This is a good day to die. Think of the children and the helpless at home who expect you to be valiant. Do not fear. What is to come has already been foreseen."

In anger No Name gave the bridle rope a hard jerk. The jerk pinched the wild one's nose. He squealed. He rose off the ground like a great fish leaping free of water and standing on its tail. Again they came down, hard, both grunting.

Red rage rose in the dark back of No Name's head. "Cursed one, do you not know the gods have already foreseen what is to happen?" He whipped the stallion across the flanks with the end of his raw-hide rope, hard, on both sides, raising welts.

Dancing Sun screamed. A whipping he had never had before. He lowered his head and bolted straight ahead.

Slops of mud and drifts of gray-green hail still lay everywhere on the hogback. It made heavy going. Yet Dancing Sun sped over the ground as if it were hard and dry. He ran as sure-footed as a bighorn. He paced so smoothly, so swiftly, No Name had a vision of himself riding a white bird flying low along the ground in a gray-green dream. It was the same as having a nightmare while wide awake.

The smoothness of the flight enraged No Name still more. He whipped the stallion again.

Dancing Sun shivered, shuddered, let go a deep rasping roar, broke into a gallop.

"He-han!" No Name cried. "I have won! I have broken you. You have galloped at last. You are now as all other mortal horses. Run, run, run! Ah, that my father could see this great thing! I feel like a man. I can feel the power of it with me all the time."

They leaped about on the hogback. They went in circles. The stallion was a great white crane trying to get rid of a weasel on its back.

Between jumps, catching sight of the land below the three bluffs, No Name was startled to see that the whole valley had filled with a racing sheet of yellow water. Uprooted trees, ripped up bushes, dead bodies of half-burned deer, scuds of loose leaves and sticks, floated swiftly east.

"Ei-ye! another Great Smoky Water has entered the valley."

Then he recalled something. When just thirteen, he had once helped his father tame a balky pinto. They had driven it into the River of The Double Bend at flood time. In deep water the pinto was suddenly helpless. The pinto hated getting its ears wet, had to swim for its life, had no time for fancy curvetting. By the time the pinto reached shore, it was docile. No Name remembered the time very well. What great sport it had been to sit on the pinto's back in the racing water. He had thrilled to the warm feeling of the horse's body between his legs, bunching and humping its big muscles under him, desperate, vigorous, yet always easy to control.

No Name jerked on the bridle rope, pulling the white stallion around. Then, by slapping him over the eyes, first one side, then the other, smartingly, he headed him for the trail.

In his frenzy the wild one did not seem to mind. He galloped in long mud-slopping strides straight for the river. Pellmell they went over the edge of the bluff and down the ravine past the green cedar, and then, with a spring, jumped into the roaring flood. They went completely under. After a moment they popped up, spilling water. And still the stallion wanted to gallop. He humped along in the water like a stumbler in a sticky dream, up and under, down and up. Like the balky pinto, the white stallion also hated getting his ears wet. All the while he humped and galloped in the flood, he somehow managed to keep them above water.

The mad bobbing, the driving current, gradually made No Name lose his grip. Feeling himself sliding off, he decided to take to the water. To keep from getting kicked by Dancing Sun's stroking hooves, No Name grabbed hold of the horse's tail and swam along behind. Dancing Sun took the full shove of the current while No Name swam in gentled waters.

Yet still Dancing Sun wanted to gallop in the water. He could not break out of it.

"Helper!" No Name cried, gulping in the moiling waters, "what must I do? He is as one gone crazy. They of the underworld are stirring his brains with a stick."

Dancing Sun seemed to have heard. He let out a great sigh; sank; came up sputtering. Then, calmer, he began to swim in a horse's usual manner.

No Name let go a great sigh, too. Taking a firm hold of the horse's tail, he began to steer him through the sliding sudsing water. They turned in a slow circle and headed for shore.

They drifted a long way down river before the stallion touched solid ground. It was at a place where the prairies sloped gently into the valley. As they emerged, No Name quickly slipped up on Dancing Sun's back again. Both dripped muddy water. Froth hung from the corners of their mouths. The stallion's dazzling white coat was now a soppy placked-down gray, almost the whitegray look of death; the red flame in his mane and tail was dowsed.

They went slowly up the greasy rise. Standing water had by now mostly run off the plateau. Only irregular drifts of hail still lay over the ground.

No Name guided Dancing Sun toward the bluffs. The horse went meekly, seemingly subdued at last.

When they reached the middle bluff again, where the footing was fairly firm, Dancing Sun groaned and suddenly lay down. No Name had just time to jump to one side to keep from being crushed.

Great head lying stretched out in the mud, worn out, covered with blood-tinged sweat, sobbing convulsively, the stallion lay as if about to die. Drops of blood gathering in the corners of his delicate bluish eyes ran down his long white face. A trickle of blood also ran out of his pink nostrils and stained the hail-studded sod.

No Name's heart melted within him. He let go of the bridle rein and knelt beside him. He caressed him, shushed him tenderly. He ran his hands gently over his ears and nose. He marveled to see the breadth of the great white forehead, that part where the horse knows all, marveled to see the deep arch of the neck, that part which shows the horse to be of noble birth.

He massaged Dancing Sun's neck and shoulders and back, working slowly.

He grunted to him in gruff friendly tones. "Hroh. Hroh. Hroh." He stroked the horse's flanks, his legs. There was not one part of the horse's body he did not touch. He worked into the horse his man smell, his touch, his spirit.

He took the stallion's head in his arms and exchanged breaths with each nostril. He took some of the blood dripping from his own nose and mingled it with the blood in the stallion's nose. He also took some of the stallion's blood and mingled it with the blood in his own nose.

"Horse, now you have my breath and blood and I have yours. We belong to each other. You are now my brother and I am your brother. We are brothers forever. We have lived through a great thing. We will return known to all as great ones. Let us have peace between us."

Dancing Sun suddenly snorted, shooting a spray of blood and froth all over No Name. His eyes blazed red hate. With a last supreme effort, his head came off the ground, then his forefeet.

"Ho, what is this? What does my brother wish now?"

Quickly, just as the horse got up on all fours, No Name leaped aboard again.

Dancing Sun shuddered. Then a mad spirit seized him, and sobbing he ran in a pacing gait west down off the slope of the bluffs. Straight across a meadow he flew, then up to the top of the cliff. No Name hung on, grimly.

A dozen leaps and they passed where the cottonwood lay fallen across the ravine. Looking over the horse's scarlet mane, No Name saw the valley ahead and below approaching with sudden swiftness. No Name's eyes bugged out in horror. He barely had time to realize that the flash flood had subsided some, that should the horse leap off the cliff there would not be enough water to break their long fall. Instead they would splatter onto the hard rock where the spring flowed past Leaf's cave. With each rolling throw of his hooves, Dancing Sun gathered speed. No Name reached ahead and slapped the horse across the eyes, on the right side, again and again, trying to head him off to the left. Dancing Sun ignored the slapping. Obsessed, he drove on.

Seeing it hopeless, that in the next couple of jumps they would both sail over the precipice, No Name let go of the scarlet mane and, sliding, bouncing, fell to the ground. He just had time to look up to see Dancing Sun take a final jump and then go soaring off, noble head up, neck arched, long scarlet mane snapping, lifted tail fluttering. Then, descending like a statue, Dancing Sun passed from view. A moment later there was a shrill scream, triumphant, derisive, and then came the crash of bulk and bones on rock.

No Name hurried down. He arrived in time to see the great mystery slowly die out of the white one's soft delicate bluish eyes.

He looked down at the broken white king, and then, impulsively, knelt beside him and threw his arms around his neck. "I love you, my brother," he cried. "Why must you leave me? You are scarred on my heart forever. I shall never forget you."

He stood up and sang the stallion's death song. His voice, lamenting, echoed clearly, word for word, off the cliff. "My brother, you are gone. Go then. Depart. Tell them of the other world that I loved you. You were my god. But now you are dead. Why did you die? You have broken my dream. You have destroyed my vision. You have confounded my helper. Now I am nothing. I have said."

He wept.

After he had wept a sufficient time, he arose and took his knife and cut off part of the scarlet mane between the ears as the white mare of his vision had commanded him to do. As he cut, he noted that under the coat of white hair a strip of black skin ran down the stallion's back. It reached all the way to his tail.

"Ae, the sign of the First One. Now I see. Now I know. It tells why he was the father of so many spotted ones, perhaps even of brave Black One."

Next he slit open the belly of the stallion and took away the heart. It was still filled with blood and he drank therefrom. Then he cut a few slices off the heart and ate them.

"This I do to bring our spirits together. Now I can die a brave one."

Again he looked down at the broken white one. Slowly a littering white-gray look of death stole up the horse's muzzle. Watching it, a feeling of revulsion passed over No Name. He shuddered.

"Horse, I give you to Wakantanka. I shall let you lie upon the rocks. I do this that the elements may take you back: the spirits your white coat, the air your lungs, the earth your blood, the rocks your bones, the worms your flesh. It was from all these that you were formed and it is to all these that you must return. Life is a circle. The power of the world works always in circles. All things try to be round. Life is all one. It begins in one place, it flows for a time, it returns to one place. The earth is all that lasts. I have said. Yelo."

> One Yankton Indian lady, who helped me with Conquering Horse, told me she didn't like the book. My face fell because I wanted her to like it. And when I finally pinned her down, she said, "Well, you whites think we Sioux women are loose. But the truth is we're stricter than you Dutch Reformed people." It was assumed that all girls would remain virgins until they were married. I said, "Well, apart from that, what did you think of the book?" She said, "Oh, it was fine."

Lord Grizzly

I might say that the reason I wrote Lord Grizzly *. . . was primarily that I began to feel a thinness in my own heroes. No matter how hard I worked, how much I thought about them, somehow they did not have all the dimensions for me. They lacked something; they lacked a . . . "usable past" within themselves; there wasn't enough history or country or culture for me to throw it up to use as a background, for me to throw my characters against . . . And it happened that when I was doing* The Golden Bowl *I ran across a reference to Hugh Glass in the* South Dakota Guide Book *and it instantly caught my eye—this man fighting the bear alone—it struck me that here was the first real contact of the white man with the raw West.*

When I saw what Hugh Glass did—he did a greater thing than Achilles did. Achilles killed Hector then dragged him around Troy. So I thought we've got heroes bigger than the Greeks had. So it's time that we celebrated them.

Encounter

THE PARTY STOPPED FOR A REST at high noon. Hugh and Jim and Fitz unloaded the pack horses; watered them; staked them out to graze in some sweetgrass in a low turn in the river. The men had themselves some dry biscuits, jerked meat, fatback, and coffee. Then came a smoke and a catnap.

A wind came up. It moved in cool from the west and freshened the grazing horses and resting men. It also chased the mosquitoes and lighter flies to cover. Only the swift heavy botflies remained to torment the horses.

Far away, behind a bald hill, a mourning dove called three lonesome, clear, haunting notes: oowhee-oooo-ooo.

But Hugh still seethed inside. He was mad at Major Henry for what he thought was a womanish order. He was mad at the boys Jim and Fitz for having gotten him in the soup by sleeping on their watch. He was mad at himself for good-naturedly having stuck his neck out to save their skin.

By midafternoon, right after Major Henry had sent gaunt Allen and two men ahead to make meat for supper, old Hugh was fit to be tied. The little paired arteries down his big bronze nose ran dark with rage. His gray eyes glittered.

The party defiled through a brushy draw coming down from the left. The party leader for the day, George Yount, had to break a way through the plum and bullberry bushes with a double ax.

In the commotion Old Hugh saw his chance to go hunting off by himself. He was last in line and could slip away unnoticed. With a sulphurous curse, and a low growled, "I don't take orders from a tyrant," Hugh turned Old Blue aside and climbed the rise to the east.

He skirted the brush at the head of the draw until he was well out of sight. Below and ahead, on his right, across the Grand River, he saw Allen and his men dodging along through a grove of cottonwood and willow. Hugh was careful to keep an equal distance between the three hunters ahead and the party behind.

It was sport to be out on one's own again, alone. The new, the old new, just around the turn ahead, was the only remedy for hot blood. Ahead was always either gold or the grave. The gamble of it freshened the blood at the same time that it cleared the eye. What could beat galloping up alone over the brow of a new bluff for that first look beyond?

The wind from the west began to push a little. It dried his damp buckskins, dried Old Blue too.

The valley slowly widened. Shelving slopes on the right mounted into noble skin-smooth tan bluffs, rose toward Wolf Butte. The country on the left, however, suddenly humped up into abrupt enormous bluffs, three of them almost mountains.

After a time Hugh understood why the valley widened. The Grand River forked up ahead, with one branch angling off to the northwest under Wolf Butte, with the other branch wriggling sharply off to the southwest under the three mountainlike tan bluffs.

There was no game. He didn't see a bird. It was siesta time. The eyes and ears of Old Earth were closed in sleep.

A wide gully swept down out of the hollow between the last two bluffs. A spring drained it and its sides were shaggy with brush. Most of the growth was chokecherry, with here and there a prickly plum tree.

Hugh felt hungry. Looking down into the draw he thought he spotted some plums, ripe red ones at that, hanging in the green leaves. Ripe black fruit also peppered the chokecherry trees. Chokecherries, he decided, chokecherries would only raise the thirst and hardly still the hunger. Plums were better. They were filling.

Before dropping down into the draw, Hugh had a last look around. A man alone always had to make sure no red devils were skulking about, behind some cliff or down in the brush. From under old gray brows, eyes narrowed against the pushing wind, Old Hugh studied the rims of the horizon all around. He inspected the riverbed from one end to the other, including each of the forks. He examined all the brushy draws running down from the bald hills on both sides.

He gave Old Blue the eye too. Horses often spotted danger before humans did.

But if there was danger Old Blue was blissfully unaware of it. Old Blue made a few passes at the dry rusty bunch grass underfoot. Old Blue blew out his nostrils at a patch of prickly-pear cactus. Old Blue snorted lightly at a mound of dirt crumbles heaved up by big red ants.

No sign of alarm in Old Blue. It looked safe all right.

Vaguely behind him, a quarter of a mile back, Hugh could hear the party coming along the river, breaking through brush. Allen and his two men were nowhere in sight ahead.

A turtledove moaned nearby: ooh—koooo—kooo—koo.

With a prodding toe and a soft, "Hep-ah," Hugh started Old Blue down the incline into the brush. Grayblue back arched, legs set like stilts, Old Blue worked his way down slowly. The saddle cinches creaked. Stones rattled down ahead of them. Dust rose. Old Blue lashed his blue tail back and forth.

The first few plum trees proved disappointing. The fruit was small; it puckered the mouth and made a ball of Hugh's tongue. Sirupy rosin drops showed where worms had punctured through.

Holding prickly branches away, sometimes ducking, waving at mosquitoes, Hugh preyed through the thicket slowly, testing, spitting. They were all sour. Bah!

The draw leveled. They broke through the shadowy prickly thicket out onto an open creekbed. Spring water ran cool and swift over clean knobs of pink and brown rock.

Old Blue had the same thought Hugh had. A drink. Hugh got off even as Old Blue began sipping.

Holding onto a rein, laying Old Bullthrower on a big dry pink stone, Hugh got down on his knees. He put a hand out to either side on wet cool sand; leaned down until his grizzled beard dipped into the water; began drinking.

Suddenly Old Blue snorted; started up; jerked the rein free and was off in a gallop lickety-split down the creek, heading for the forks of the Grand.

Hugh humped up; grabbed up Old Bullthrower; started running after Old Blue. But Hugh couldn't run much on his wounded game leg, and Old Blue rapidly outdistanced him and disappeared around a turn.

Hugh gave up, cursing. "By the bull barley, what got into him?" Puffing, Hugh took off his wolfskin cap. "Now that does put me in a curious fix. With the major already riled enough to hamshoot me." Hugh waggled his old hoar head. "Wonder what did skeer him off, the old cuss."

Hugh cocked an ear; listened awhile; couldn't make out a thing.

There was an odd smell in the air, a smell of mashed chokecherries mixed in with musky dog. But after sniffing the air a few times, nostrils twitching, he decided it was probably only some coyote he'd flushed.

Hugh stood pondering, scratching his head. "Wal, one thing, Ol' Blue won't run far. In strange country, a horse always comes back to a party. Gets lonesome like the rest of us humans."

Hugh put Old Bullthrower to one side; got down on his knees for another drink. The shadow of a hawk flitted over swiftly, touching the trickling water, touching him. Finished drinking, Hugh picked up Old Bullthrower; automatically checked the priming; cocked an eye at the brush.

Hugh worked down toward the Grand River to meet the line of march of the party.

Halfway down toward the Grand River another creek came angling out of a second draw, the water joining with the first creek and tumbling on toward the river. Hugh looked up the second draw; saw another cluster of plum trees. Ho-ah. Good plums at last. Smaller but blood ripe. Hugh couldn't resist them. He'd give himself a quick treat and then go on to meet the party along the river.

The tiny trickling stream curved away from him, to his left. He broke through low whipping willow branches; came upon a sandy opening.

"Whaugh!" A great belly grunt burped up from the white sands directly in front of him. And with a tremendous tumbler's heave of body, a silvertipped gray she-grizzly, Ursus horribilis, rose up before him on two legs. "Whaugh!" Two little brown grizzly cubs ducked cowering and whimpering behind the old lady.

The massive silvertipped beast came toward him, straddling, huge head dipped down at him from a humped neck, humped to strike him. Her big dog-like mouth and piglike snout were bloody with chokecherry juice. Her long gray claws were bloody with fruit juice too. Her musky smell filled the air. And smelling the musk, Hugh knew then why Old Blue had bolted and run.

Hugh backed in terror, his heart suddenly burning hot and bounding around in his chest. The little arteries down his big Scotch nose wriggled red. His breath caught. The sense of things suddenly unraveling, of the end coming on, of being no longer in control of either things of his life, possessed him.

She was as big as a great bull standing on two legs. She was so huge on her two legs that her incredible speed coming toward him actually seemed slow. Time stiffened, poured like cold molasses.

She roared. She straddled toward him on her two rear legs. She loomed over him, silver neck ruffed and humped, silver head pointed down at him. Her pink dugs stuck out at him. She stunk of dogmusk.

She hung over him, huge furry arms ready to cuff and strike. Her red-stained ivorygray claws, each a lickfinger long, each curved a little like a cripple's iron hook, closed and unclosed.

Hugh's eyes set; stiffened; yet he saw it all clearly. Time poured slow—yet was fast.

Hugh jerked up his rifle.

But the Old Lady's mammoth slowness was faster. She was upon him before he got his gun halfway up. She poured slow—yet was fast. "Whaugh!" She cuffed at the gun in his hands as if she knew what it was for. The gun sprang from his hands. As it whirled into the bushes, it went off in the air, the ball whacking harmlessly into the white sand at their feet.

Hugh next clawed for his horse pistol.

Again she seemed to know what it was for. She cuffed the pistol out of his hand too.

Hugh stumbled over a rock; fell back on his hands and rump; like a tumbler bounded up again.

The cubs whimpered behind her.

The whimpering finally set her off. She struck. "Whaugh!" Her right paw cuffed him on the side of the head, across the ear and along the jaw, sending his wolfskin cap sailing, the claws tipping open his scalp. The blow knocked him completely off his feet, half-somersaulted him in the air before he hit ground.

Again, like a tumbler, Hugh bounded to his feet, ready for more. He felt very puny. The silvertip became a silver blur in his eyes. She became twice, thrice, magnified.

It couldn't be true, he thought. He, Old Hugh Glass, he about to be killed by a monster varmint? Never.

Hugh crouched over. He backed and filled downstream as best he could.

The she-grizzly, still on two legs, both paws ready to cuff, came after him, closed once more. She roared.

Hugh scratched for his skinning knife. There was nothing for it but to close with her. Even as her great claw swiped at him, stiff but swift, he leaped and got inside her reach. Her clubbing paw swung around him instead of catching him. He hugged her for dear life. He pushed his nose deep into her thick dog-musky whitegray fur. He pressed into her so hard one of her dugs squirted milk over his leathers.

She roared about him. She cuffed around him like a heavyweight trying to give a lightweight a going-over in a clinch. She poured slow—yet was fast. She snarled; roared. His ear was tight on the huge barrel of her chest, and the roars reverberated inside her chest like mountain avalanches. He hugged her tight and stayed inside her reach. She clawed at him clumsily. Her ivorygray claws brought up scraps of buckskin shirt and strips of skin from his back.

He hugged her. And hugging her, at last got his knife around and set. He punched. His knife punged through the tough hide and slipped into her belly just below the ribs with an easy slishing motion. He stabbed again. Again and again. The knife punged through the tough furred hide each time and then slid in easy.

Blood spurted over his hands, over his belly, over his legs and her legs both, came in gouts of sparkling scarlet.

He wrestled her; stabbed her.

The great furred she-grizzly roared in an agony of pain and rage. He was still inside her reach and she couldn't get a good swipe at him. She clawed clumsily up and down his back. She brought up strips of leather and skin and red muscle. She pawed and clawed, until at last Hugh's ribs began to show white and clean.

Hugh screamed. He stabbed wildly, frantically, skinning knife sinking in again and again.

Her massive ruffed neck humped up in a striking curve. Then her head dug down at him. She seized his whole head in her red jaws and lifted him off his feet.

Hugh got in one more lunging thrust. His knife sank in all the way up to the haft directly over the heart.

He felt her dogteeth crunch into his skull. She shook him by the head like a dog might shake a doll. His body dangled. His neck cracked.

He screamed. His scream rose into a shrill squeak.

He sank away, half-conscious.

She dropped him.

Raging, blood spouting from a score of wounds, she picked him up again, this time by his game leg, and shook him violently, shook him until his leg popped in its hip socket. She roared while she gnawed. She was a great cat chewing and subduing a struggling mouse. His game leg cracked.

She dropped him.

Snarling, still spouting blood on all sides, coughing blood, she picked him up again, this time by the rump. She tore out a hunk the size of a buffalo boss and tossed it over her shoulder toward the brown cubs.

Hugh lay limp, sinking away. He thought of the boy Jim, of Bending Reed, of a picture-purty she-rip back in Lancaster, of two boy babies.

Time poured slow—yet space was quick.

The next thing he knew she had fallen on him and lay deadheavy over his hips and legs.

He heard a scrambling in the brush. He heard the voices of men. He heard the grizzly cubs whimpering. He heard two shots.

Dark silence.

Ordeal

A COLD NOSE WOKE HIM.

He tried opening his eyes; couldn't; found his eyelids crusted shut.

He blinked hard a few times; still couldn't open them; gave up.

The back of his head ached like a stone cracking in heat. His entire back, from high in his neck and across his shoulder blades and through the small of his back and deep into his buttocks, was a slate of tight pain.

The cracking ache and the tight pain was too much. He drifted off into gray sleep.

The cold nose woke him again.

And again he rose up out of gray into wimmering pink consciousness. He blinked hard, once, twice; still couldn't quite uncrack his crusted eyelids.

A dog licking his face? Dogs never licked bearded faces that he remembered.

The cold nose touched him once more, on the brow. And then he knew he wasn't being licked in love. He was being sniffed over.

Hugh concentrated on his crusted eyes, forced all he had into opening them. And after a supreme effort, the stuck lashes parted with little crust-breaking sounds. Blue instantly flooded into his old gray eyes. There was an unusually clear sky overhead. Yellow light was striking up into blue. That meant it was morning. If rust and pink had been sinking away under blueblack it would have been late afternoon. Also a few birds were chirping a little. That proved it was morning. Birds never chirped in the late afternoon in August. At least not that he knew of.

August? Where in tarnation . . . ?

With a jerk Hugh tried to sit up.

The jerk like to killed him. His whole back and his rump and his right leg all three became raging red monsters. He groaned. "Gawd!" His whole chest rumbled with it.

Out of the corner of his eye he saw a bristling whitegray shape jump back. Sight of the jumping whitegray shape kept him from fainting. That whitegray bristling shape had a cold black nose. It was a wolf.

Then it all came back to him. What had happened and where he was. Major Henry had ordered him to shave off his beard. He had refused. Major Henry had then given the hunting detail to Allen and two other men. He'd got mad and gone off hunting by himself—only to run smack into a she-grizzly.

Miraculously he was still alive then.

Holding himself tight rigid, Hugh opened his eyes as far as he could to size things up. He saw green bottleflies buzzing around him, thousands of them, millions of them. They were like darting spots before the eyes. Every time he rolled his eyes they buzzed up from his beard and wounds and swirled and re-settled. Just above him hung a bush-choked draw: ooah—koooo—kooo—koo.

He had hands. He moved them. The green bottleflies buzzed up; swarmed; resettled. He moved his hands again, first his right, then his left. The right hand seemed slightly bruised; the left felt whole.

He studied the small blue marks over the back of his right hand. That was where the silvertip she-grizzly had struck him when she'd clubbed first his flint-lock and then his horse pistol away from him.

Thinking of his gun, he instinctively reached for it. He couldn't find it. He pawed the sand, the dirt, the edge of a fur, over his belly. Not there. Green flies buzzed up; resettled.

He sighed. Of course. The guns were still in the bushes where the she-grizzly had popped them.

He felt of his body. The green death flies rose; swirled; swarmed around him. He found his head bandaged with a narrow strip of cloth. A huge welt ran from his grizzly cheek back past his swollen red ear and up into his scalp. The welt was a ridged seam. Someone had carefully sewn up his long terrible wound with deer sinews. The ridged welt ran up around his entire head. A few small stitched ridges ran off it. The clotted seam also felt fuzzy. Someone had also carefully webbed the bleeding wound with the fuzz plucked from a beaver pelt. Beaver fuzz was the thing for quick crust building. Many and many was the time he'd put it on cuts himself.

He ran his hand over his chest; over his gaunt belly; found everything in order. The front of him was still all in one piece. Even the leathers, his buckskin hunting shirt and leggings, were whole. Flies buzzed up angry; resettled.

He felt of his right leg; reached down too far; stirred up the red monsters in his back and game leg and rump again. "Gawd!"

The flies began to bite him, on the backs of his hands and the exposed parts of his face and ears and the exposed parts of his shoulders.

He wondered what he was lying on. He felt around with his good left hand; found a bearskin beneath. Lifting his head, brushing away the swirling buzzing flies, looking past a crusted lid and swollen blue nose and clotted beard, he saw it was the skin of the silvertip she-grizzly he'd fought. He let his head fall back.

He felt of it again to make sure. How in tarnation . . . ? Who had skinned the she-grizzly? He couldn't have done it himself. That was impossible. The last thing he remembered was the she-grizzly lying deadheavy across his belly and legs. So he couldn't have.

He remembered hearing voices. He remembered hearing the little grizzly cubs whimpering. He remembered two shots. Ho-ah! The party had spotted runaway Old Blue and had probably heard him screaming. They had come up to help; had shot the cubs. They had pulled the Old Lady off him and had skinned her and had made a bed out of her fur for him. And they had dressed his wounds. Ae, that was it.

He smiled. Ae, real mountain men, they were, to come to comrade's relief. He smiled. Real mountain men. They had a code, they had.

"Ae, lads, this child was almost gone under that time, he was."

No answer. Only the trickling of the brook, the buzzing of the green death flies, the padding of the circling hungry wolf.

Flies? Wolf? Silence? What in tarnation? Quickly he perked up again—and the raging red monsters tore into him.

Somehow he managed to roll over on his side, the grizzly fur sticking to his crusted-over back and lifting up off the sand. The weight of the hide tore away some of the flesh from his ribs. He screamed. Eyes closed, he caught his breath and screamed again.

When he opened his eyes once more, he saw it. His grave. Beside him, not a yard away, someone had dug a shallow grave for him, a grave some three feet deep and seven feet long.

Old gray eyes almost blinded with tears, with extreme pain, green bottleflies buzzing all around, he stared at it.

His grave.

He shook his head; blinked.

His grave.

So that was it. He was done for. His time was up.

His grave. He lay on his right side looking at it, bewildered in a wilderness.

"Ae, I see it now, lads. It's this old coon's turn at last."

Or maybe it was the other way around. Maybe he was the only one alive, with all the others ambushed, killed, and scalped.

Cautiously he rolled his eyes around. He looked at the mound of yellow sifting sand beside the yawning grave. He looked at the bullberries hanging ripe overhead. He looked at the silvertip she-grizzly hide under him. He watched the green death flies hovering and buzzing around him. He looked up at the blue sky.

Not a soul or a dead body in sight on that side.

He looked all around again as far as his eye could see; then, despite terrible blinding pain, he rolled over on his left side.

Cautiously he rolled his eyes around. Nothing there either. No horses. No men. There'd been no ambush on that side either, so far as he could see.

What in tarnation had happened? He'd been sewed up and placed on the she-grizzly's hide. Also someone had dug a grave for him. Yet no one was about.

He studied the open grave some more. To dig that the men must have thought him dead.

But if they thought him dead, why in tarnation hadn't they finished burying him?

It was too much for him to understand. His head cracked with it.

"This child feels mighty queersome," he murmured.

He felt of his skull again. Yes, his topknot was still in place, though it was ridged and seamed all over like an old patched moccasin.

He blinked; fainted. He fell back, body flopping with a thud on the fur-covered sand. Green flies resettled on him.

The wolf approached him a couple of steps; sat down on its haunches. It watched him warily with narrowed yellow eyes. The wolf sniffed, brushtail whirling nervously. Presently the wolf got up; approached a few steps closer; sat down on its haunches again. It waited.

~

A cold nose woke him.

His crusted lids cracked open. Blue sky filled his old gray eyes. He remembered it. He remembered the last time he was up. Red monsters rending him. Green death flies. A padding white wolf. An open grave.

They were all there again. And this time another was waiting. A turkey buzzard. Floating on wavering three-foot wings, coasting, sometimes flopping to gain height, bald snakehead peering down at him, snakehead gaggling in and out on a long neck, it hovered over him, circling, rising, falling, floating.

The turkey buzzard meant if he wasn't dead he should be.

The green death flies puzzled him. They rarely sat on a man until he was dead. The white wolf and the black turkey buzzard had enough sense to wait until he was fully dead. Why not the green flies.

There was dead meat around somewhere then.

Well, it wasn't his because he was still ciphering—unless the Resurrection had come and dead meat had learned to cipher . . . or he was a soul floating around outside his own dead body.

He remembered it. He'd found himself upon the she-grizzly's fur beside an open grave, his back and head sewed up. He remembered he'd fainted away trying to cipher what had happened.

The green flies continued to puzzle him. They usually never went to work until after the wolves and the buzzards had had their fill. What did he have they wanted so bad?

He woke gradually. Hearing came back; sight came back; feeling in his finger tips came back; smell came back.

Something stunk something awful all right. He hoped it wasn't himself. It stunk like a rotting buffalo carcass.

He heard the wolf padding near him. He was in part glad to hear it. As long as it kept padding, that long he was alive.

Through narrowed crusted lids he watched the turkey buzzard circling overhead. Its hooked dull-white beak worked sometimes. Its flesh-colored feet clawed and unclawed. Its reddish-tinged neck became long, became short. Its wings shone greenblack. Its bald head gaggled at him first with one blinking eye then with the other blinking eye. It hung above him seemingly without effort. There was no wind. It waggled a few times and stayed up endlessly.

He sat up; fought the red monsters; survived them; fought a faint; survived it. He brushed the green death flies away. He steadied.

He saw the yawning grave again; saw the whitegray wolf, this time two of them; saw the silvertip fur under him.

Then taste came back. Thirst. Great thirst. "Wadder," he murmured. "Got to have wadder," he murmured. He was dizzy with it. His lips, tongue, roof of his mouth, all were so parched he couldn't get his tongue out of his lips. His lips felt white, felt cracked. They worked under his clotted beard. "Wadder," he murmured, "wadder."

His eyes, his ears, turned him to the sound of water. "Wadder," he murmured. His body settled forward from the hips. He rolled over. The fur hide, still stuck to his back, came up with him. "Gawd!" he undulated slowly toward the trickling stream. The stream was only a few feet away but it took him miles to get there. "Gawd!" he crawled on the sand. He hunched forward. Crawled. "Wadder," he murmured.

His good foot caught in a root. He got a good toe hold; gave himself a tremendous shove; moved half a foot. It brought him to the edge of the water trickling over clean white stones. He dug his good toe in again; gave himself a great shove again. This time his shove got his grizzled face into the water. He let it shove in. He drank like a horse with his head half under. Bubbles escaped his nose and mouth; guggled up through his beard; came out at the top of his clotted, seamed head of hair.

He drank until his stomach hurt, until it raised him a little off the white stones.

"Ahhh. Water." He shook his grizzly head. Drops sprayed off to all sides. "Ah, what is better than water?"

He drew back to a kneeling position. Again the weight of the furskin, still stuck to his crusted back wounds, tore at the flesh over his ribs. He screamed. He fell flat again.

He puffed. He waited for strength. He lay staring at the clear water directly under his nose. He saw a tiny bloodsucker waving black from a pebble. He saw a tendril of green moss waving from a stone. He saw green minnows fleeting upstream.

"Got—to—get," he puffed, "got—to—get—that—skin—off—somehow." He puffed. "Best—soak—it—in—water."

He rolled over slowly, dragging the skin with him. he slapped forward on his back until he lay with his back in the water.

The water felt cool and it felt good and it soothed him.

Presently he felt the minnows tickling him, nibbling at his crusts. He lay in the shallow waters of the stream and let the minnows lip the wounds. "The minnies'll heal me," he murmured. "Water is medicine but the minnies'll leech me. Purify the blood."

The white wolf wriggled its cold black nose at him. It sat on its haunches. It waited. The turkey buzzard gaggled its wrinkled bald head in and out and hung on its wings. It waited. The green death flies buzzed over him. A few of the flies hit the water, floated away downstream, drowning.

Ripe buffalo berries hung above him. He reached up for a cluster; put it all in his mouth, stem, skin, pit, flesh. After the fresh water he thought the bullberries had a fine grape flavor.

"Wonder where everybody is? The lads wouldn't've left me alone here."

It became high noon. And hot. His back, submerged in running water, felt fine, but his face and front sweat where the overhead sun struck him through the bullberry bushes. At the same time he was sure he was almost as hot from a fever as he was from the sun, because his back, which should have been chilled to the bone in the running spring water, actually felt warmish too. The water trickled in through the gaping rents of his leathers, around and over his turtleshell crusts, around and into the grizzly bearskin.

The minnies lipped him.

He murmured to himself. "The fur must be soaked loose by now." He reached a hand around to feel of his back. One of the red monsters awoke. He cried out. "Gawd!"

He reached around a bit further. The crusts had become soggy in the water and the fur was loosened in most places. He could feel ridges, seams, running everywhichway over his back. Someone had sewed up his back with deer sinews too. In some places the buckskin whangs had been tied into hard knots, each knot with a pair of little ears. His back felt like a patched up tepee. It was as uneven and as bumpy as the breaks in the Badlands. And probably as inflamed: burnt red, pus yellow, rotted purple. Blotched over like a case of eczema peppered with boils.

Hugh's hand came away stinking. Then he knew where the bad smell came from and why the green flies and the white gray wolf and the hovering wrinkle-necked turkey buzzard fancied his meat.

He found a patch where the bearskin was still stuck to his back. With a pushing finger moving very cautiously, probing, he pried it off. He grimaced in pain. The beard over his mouth quivered. The pain was so terrible at times that consciousness came and went in waves.

After a rest he pried farther. The bearskin parted with little rips, from the waterlogged crusted wounds, came loose with tiny rending sounds.

He shuddered—and the last of the silvertip bearskin fell away. "Ahh!" he breathed. "Ahh." He shook his head. "Gawd! that was hard doin's! By the bull barley, that was." He sucked breath. "Gawd, I feel queersome. Like a buffler shot in the lights."

He felt better after a while. He sat up. Gray bullberry leaves brushed his brow, touched his matted gray hair. He shook his head; blinked; blinked.

"Whaugh!" he roared suddenly, and the whitegray wolf jumped back a dozen steps and the turkey buzzard overhead flopped its wings and flew in a higher circle. Hugh laughed.

The raucous laugh caught his ear. Ho-ah! His voice seemed to have changed some. Or else his ears had gone on the blink. His voice had always been heavy, a cross between a bear grunt and a deacon's growl. But now it sounded cracked and coarse. The Old Lady must've given his talk box a whack too.

A little way from the golden mound of sand beside the open grave Hugh saw something. Ashes. A heap of them. Gray with white irregular rings. A few half-burnt twigs and branches stuck out all along the edge of the ashes like green lashes around a huge blind-white horse eye. Around the ashes were molds and pudges in the sand where men had sat and lain.

With a grunt, and a groan of pain, Hugh lurched forward on hands and one knee. His bad leg dragged. He crawled past the grave and around the mound of gold sand. The green flies buzzed over his back. The whitegray wolf retreated a step. The greenblack turkey buzzard lifted its wing-wavering orbit above him.

He approached the ashes carefully. He studied the sand for tracks. There were many moccasin prints, most of them faint. But some of them were fresh and all of them were of two kinds: quiet Fitz's small print, the boy Jim's big-footed print. He knew that moccasin print anywhere. The two lads had bought their moccasins from Bending Reed. And there was that new contrary stitch she'd lately taken to using. The Heyoka stitch.

He circled the ash heap carefully, staying well away from it at first, and only gradually working in on it. Yes, all the fresh prints belonged to either the boy Jim or downer Fitz. And all the old prints belonged to the rest of the party: Major Henry, Silas Hammond, George Yount, Allen, Pierre the cook, all the lads.

Ho-ah! He saw it then. Ae. The major had left Fitz and Jim to stand watch over him while the rest of the fur party pressed on, going northwest and on up to Henry's Post on the Yellowstone and Missouri.

The major had probably made up his mind that Old Hugh was going to die and had asked for volunteers to keep the deathwatch and afterwards bury him decent. And the boys, Jim and Fitz, had probably chirped up because they felt they owed it to Old Hugh, after the way he'd covered up for them, covered up that they had fallen asleep while on guard duty.

Hugh looked at the shallow grave. "Decent?" Ha. A half-dozen strokes and the varmints had him dug out of the sand tearing and gorging before he even turned cold. The lads'd sure been lax and lazy digging that grave.

Hugh shivered. He passed a hand over his hot brow.

One leg dragging, still on hands and one knee, grizzled, tattered, crusted over, looking like a he-bear in molting time after a terrible fight, he examined the sand around the ash heap, around the grave, also the spot where he had lain when he first came to. Except for the usual camp litter of broken tins and ripped paper packs and rinds of fruit and slicked bones, there was nothing. Not a thing. Neither gun, nor pistol, nor knife, nor steel and flint, nor food of any kind.

He glanced over toward the bushes where the silvertip she-grizzly had popped his flintlock and pistol. No, nothing there either.

"What in tarnation . . . ?" he muttered again. "Where's the lads? They must be around somewhere."

He called out, hoarse voice more like a bear's growl than a human call, "Jim? Fitz! Hey! Where be ye?"

No answer. Not even an echo.

"Jim! Fitz! Hey!"

No answer.

"Lads! Where be ye? Jim? Fitz?"

Still no answer.

Hugh sagged and lay down on his belly. He couldn't cipher it. They'd dug his grave but hadn't buried him. Why? Indians? Red devils up on the hills? Sign? And the lads hiding in the brush?

He lay puffing on his belly.

Green flies settled on his crusts again. The wolf drew up a step. The turkey buzzard floated lower.

The stink of rotting flesh came strong to him again. It came on a rising breeze, not from his torn back. He sniffed the breeze wonderingly. Ho-ah. Something else was stinking up the gully besides himself.

The breeze felt fine on his back, warmish, and helped blow off the down-burning sun and the burning fever.

He raised on his elbows, eyes following where the nose said.

Ho-ah. Green flies in a cloud to one side of the ash heap, under a chokecherry bush. Meat then.

That same instant he felt hunger. Terrible hunger. "Meat," he murmured, "meat. Gotta have meat."

He crawled on hands and one knee and found the meat: a pile of bear ribs with scraps of rotting meat still on them, the she-grizzly skull grinning horribly at him, and a large hump of shoulder roast. All rotten. Meat the vultures for some reason had left to the green flies.

With his nails he clawed at the hump roast. Ha. Inside there was enough good meat left for a meal, even if it was a little on the prime side. He brushed off the flies.

What he needed now was a fire. Carrying some of the meat in either hand, he crawled to the ash heap. Carefully he brushed off the top ashes; carefully he shoved in a hand. Ahh! Warmth! There just might be a few live coals left. A spark or two.

Hugh scratched about under the bushes and gathered up a handful of wispy dry grass. He coiled it up into a nestlike roll, placed it carefully on the sand, piled a few leaves over it.

He turned back to the ash heap. He brushed layer after layer aside. When he got nearly to the bottom, he blew into the ashes softly.

And found it. A live coal the size of a ruby. Quickly he whisked it into the coil of wispy grass; deftly closed the wisps down over like a jeweler folding velvet lining down over a precious jewel; blew on it between cupped hands, blew on it long and slow and soft.

At last a slow twist of smoke rose out of the nest. Another long soft breath, and a flame licked out the size of a bird's tongue. He blew on it once more, long and slow, and it flashed up in his beard. Breath short, he grabbed up all the half-burnt twigs within reach, laid them on the burning grass in pyramid fashion, green spokes to a red hub. The flames grew. He laid on half-burnt branches and finished it off with bits of log. Presently he had a good fire blazing and crackling.

The flames chased back both the whitegray wolf and the turkey buzzard.

Old gray eyes feverish, Hugh broke off a long twig from a chokecherry bush; with his teeth cut a point on the end of it; jabbed on the strong hump roast; held it in the fire.

The burning sun, his rising fever, the jumping fire made him sweat like a jug in humid weather.

But he held on. Hot or not, rotten or not, he had to eat. "Meat's meat."

Lying on the side of his good leg, he turned the meat slowly in the fire. The burnt-meat smell almost drove him mad. His cracked lips worked, the gray fur over his cheeks and chin stirred.

When he thought some of the meat done, he bit in, burning his lips and nose tip, sucking, lipping up the strong fat dripping into his beard. He gnawed into it. "It's my turn now," he growled, remembering how the she-grizzly had growled and roared and gnawed into him. He chuckled as he thought of it. The old she-rip. Well, and she was flavorsome too, despite the spoilage. Ae, and filling.

He gorged until his belly hurt. The pain in his belly told him he'd probably lain without food for days. The lads must've had a time with him. Couldn't feed a man who was out of his head. Couldn't make a dead man swallow.

His belly hurt powerful. He hoped he wouldn't have to vomit. He remembered he'd always had a strong stomach. Once he got his meat trap shut down, it wasn't too easily opened again. And nature usually took its course. He hoped so.

He belched loudly, the putrid smell expelling through his nostrils. He broke wind.

He lay panting on his belly in the sand. He could feel his stomach jumping around inside. It hopped about like a bad heart.

The fire died down to a suffing glow. Every now and then the breeze coming up the gully peeled off a layer of gray ash and exposed coals as live as flesh.

The wolf drew up a step. The buzzard came down a rung. The flies resettled on his crusts. The sun began to sink toward the west.

It came to him then. Those ashes he'd dug into for that live coal—they were at least a day old. Ho-ah! That meant the lads weren't hiding in the bushes after all waiting for Rees to pass on so they could finish burying him. It meant that for one reason or another the lads hadn't been around for a spell.

What in tarnation? They couldn't've deserted him, could they?

Hugh shook his head. Hardly. Not Jim. Not Fitz. Not mountain men. Especially not after what he'd done for his companyeros, saving them from the major's wrath because they had slept while on guard.

No, not his lads. Certainly not Jim. And practical Fitz, for all his book learning, not him either.

What could have happened? Scalped and killed by Rees? Hardly. The lads would have been laying dead around him then. And the Rees would certainly have counted coup on him, their old enemy, too.

His gun and possibles—who'd taken them? Not the Rees, because they hadn't taken his scalp. The boys? Impossible. Not the lads.

A cracking headache set up in Hugh's head. "I feel queersome," he said.

He felt of his brow. It was slippery with fever's sweat. Ho-ah. Blood poison had set in then. Ae, rot in the blood.

He lifted his head. And wasn't too surprised to see the gully swinging back and forth like a sailor's hammock in a tossing ship. Ae, the putrid rot all right.

Slowly Hugh slipped away into delirium.

～

A cold touch woke him. Something moved against his good side.

Hugh rolled his grizzly head to have a look. The moment he moved, the something suddenly stiffened against him; abruptly set up a loose rattling noise like little dry gourds clattering in a wind.

Rattler. Hugh forced himself to hold still. The least move and he'd have a batch of rattler poison in his blood, besides all the rot he already had in it.

Rattler? Ah! Fresh rattler made good meat.

Ae, but how to catch it.

After a while he could feel the rattler relaxing against him. It made a faint dry slithering sound. Presently he could feel it begin to crawl away. Its pushing touch slowly drew away from him.

He waited until he was sure it had crawled at least a couple of feet away. Then he moved, moved quick. He sat up against the howling red monsters in his back and rump; snatched up a heavy stone; lunged; mashed the snake's head before it could coil and strike.

He watched the snake thresh in the sand. It was a huge devil, some six feet long, and quite fat.

He found another stone, this time a flat one with a rough ragged edge like a crude Digger hatchet. With it he jammed the snake's head off at the neck. He jammed off the skin along one side a ways and skinned it. Then he cut the rattler into a dozen or so separate steaks. Blood welled over his hands.

He brushed through the ash heap, luckily found a couple of hot coals again, built himself a fine roaring fire. He roasted some of the rattler meat thoroughly and filled up. The meat was stringy, but it was fresh and fairly tasty. "Can't shine with painter meat. Or even old bull. But meat's meat when there's hard doin's."

Finished eating, and caching the rest of the rattler meat under dry sand, he crawled to the running water and had himself a long and cooling drink. He also lay in the water for a while, on his back, and let the stream and the minnies wash away the impurities.

He had no idea how long he had slept since eating the putrid bear meat. From the way his stomach felt he could have slept a couple of days. Certain it was that he had slept at least a full night because once again yellow light was striking up into blue, which meant morning.

His fever was down some, of that Old Hugh was sure too. He was still very stiff, very sore all over, and the deer-sinew stitches pulled terribly every time he moved. But the hotness, thank God, was pretty much gone away, and his eyes saw clear again, and taste had returned to his tongue.

He ran a cautious hand over his body, exploring his crusted wounds. His jaw felt much better, and the crust in his beard was already beginning to peel away along the edges. The welt up in his hair felt good too.

He explored his back. Except for one bad spot which he couldn't quite reach, he found that somewhat improved also. The near edge of the bad spot was greasy and very swollen. Green flies were still buzzing around it. He pushed his hand around as far as he could, touched it all gingerly. There was quite a gap. A flap of flesh hung down from it, and he thought he could touch bone, touch the curve of a rib.

He explored his torn rump and was surprised to find that completely crusted over. The old she-rip had taken her biggest bite out of him there. He had expected it to be a horrible mess.

The right leg was different. It was swollen almost twice its size, was discolored blackpurpleblue. He felt of it gingerly; then steeled himself as he dug in to find the line of the bone. Halfway down, directly below where her great teeth had bit in, gnawed in, through the hard swollen flesh, he could feel a crack, a ridge the size of a rim on a stone crock. He looked down the length of the grotesquely fat leg and thought he could see where it bent off a little at a slight angle. That meant trouble. If he let the cracked bone knit as it now lay, he was doomed to become a cripple. Probably never be able to run again. Which meant the end of his prairie days. A down bull had no business in red-devil country.

"Whaugh!" he roared. "Whaugh!" He laughed to see the dozen or more waiting dun-colored coyotes and whitegray wolves jump back. "G'wan, go way. You're gettin' no free bites out a me. G'wan! What ye fancy in this old bull is more than this child can cipher. And I'm not sharin' any of my cache snakemeat with ye."

He squinted up at the dozen or so turkey buzzards floating around above him. He roared up at them too. "Whaugh!" He laughed to see them raised their wavering, gliding, greenblack circles.

It took him two full days to make up his mind to set the leg himself.

Cost him what it might in inhuman pain, it had to be done. It was that or give up forever being a mountain man in the free country.

Once his mind was made up, he went about it doggedly. He crawled over to a sturdy little chokecherry tree with a crotch a foot off the ground. Grimacing, cursing, he lifted the bad leg into it, hooked the heel and toe well down in the crotch, with his hands caught hold of another nearby stubby trunk—then heaved.

Pain filled him from tip to toe. He passed out a few seconds.

When he came to, he rested a while, panting desperately.

The mourning dove souled in the gully: ooah—koooo—kooo—koo.

When he thought he could stand it again, he set himself and once more gave his leg a mighty wrenching pull. There was a crack; something gave; and he passed out again.

He came to gently, easily, up out of black into blue into yellow light.

He rested a little.

A magpie scolded a squirrel in some bullberry bushes across the brook. The squirrel skirled back.

Breath caught, he felt of his leg carefully, finger tips probing through the swollen rawhide flesh. Ho-ah. The bone had popped back into place. Ae. And now to splint it.

Working patiently, doggedly, saving his breath, he broke off a half-dozen straight chokecherry saplings about an inch thick. With his crude stone chisel he jammed off a long strip from the grizzly hide and built a tight splint around his leg. The strap of raw bearhide was still moist. In time it would shrink and make the splint fit snug.

The sun was almost directly overhead when he finished. Heat boiled out of the gully in waves. A dead calm radiated over the land. The vultures lay back waiting, wondering at all the movement of him. They turned slow wheels. It puzzled them that a stinking, filthy, hairy skeleton of a creature could show so much life.

Hugh crawled back to the stream and in the shadow of the bullberry bushes let the water run along his back. He splashed water over his face and chest and belly and legs. The water was wondrous cool, wondrous soothing.

He napped.

He dreamt. And in the dream he heard Jim and Fitz talking about him.

But while the dream was very clear and very real, the talk in it was muttery, unclear. He couldn't make out what they were saying. He could see their mouths going, and could make out it was about him, but he couldn't make out the sense of what they said.

He dreamt. And in the dream he dreamt he had died alone in a gully, his leathers and meat torn to shreds, his bones picked over by green snakenecked buzzards. He cried out in his sleep; awoke in a buzzing stupor.

Afternoon came on. Water washed him. Minnies lipped him. Afternoon waned. Water soaked him. Minnies tickled him.

Toward evening, the air cooling, he revived again. He dug up a few of the rattler steaks he'd stashed in the sand and roasted them. For greens he ate grass tips. For fruit he had some buffalo berries and chokecherries. Ripe plums hung near; they looked very inviting, but he couldn't get himself to touch them. He washed his supper down with cool spring water. The meat and the greens and the fruit and the water strengthened him.

Later, when the sun had set and the stars and the mosquitoes came out and the wolves and coyotes began padding around him on the sand, he recalled his nightmare dreams of the afternoon. Though again he couldn't make out what it was Jim and Fitz had said in the dream.

"Wonder where the lads went to? Can't understand it. There must be some reason for the lads not bein' around. 'Tis a deep puzzle to this old coon."

He rolled it over in his mind. He couldn't wait any longer for the lads to show up. He had to begin thinking about himself.

He nodded. Yes, think of himself. He had to get out of that gully and that part of the wild country soon or he was a gone goose.

He rolled it over in his mind some more. The first thing was to get back to the settlements some way. As the crow flies it was at least some two hundred miles north to Henry's Post on the Yellowstone and Missouri. And Ft. Kiowa was some two hundred miles back the other way. Either way the country was buzzing with Rees as mad as hornets. There were also the rapidly increasing number of Sioux war parties. Even some Mandans.

He thought on it. One thing was certain—he couldn't follow the Grand River back to the Missouri and then follow that back to the fort. Too many mad Rees that way. They were thicker in that direction than in any other. So if he went back to the fort he'd have to cut across the open country to the south.

He puzzled over his broken leg. He wouldn't be able to crawl on that for at least a month, let alone walk on it. He either had to lay around until it knitted or somehow drag it after him. The first alternative meant he might starve to death, if he didn't freeze first; the second meant excruciating pain.

He puzzled over his splinted leg. If he could somehow carry it off the ground he might be able to crawl along on his elbows and one knee.

He puzzled on it. And finally decided to make himself a slape—travois, as the pork-eaters called it—a pair of shafts such as the squaws hooked up to dogs and ponies to dray their possessions. He remembered seeing Bending Reed make one down in Pawnee land along the Platte.

"I feel queersome," he said, and presently fell asleep.

Mosquitoes hummed over him. A light breeze came up and tousled his gray hair.

~

He decided on Bending Reed and Ft. Kiowa two hundred miles away. He had to have the benefit of her cooking, her care, her potent herbs. She'd heal him. She'd put him back on his feet. Good old Reed. What a fine mate she'd made him all these years in the far country.

Calmly he set to work. He built a slape out of two long willow poles. He bound one to each side of his bad leg, starting at the hip socket and extending well out beyond his toes so that the entire leg rode well above the ground and had the benefit of the springy tips to absorb shock.

He knew there'd be a lot of prickly-pear cactus most of the way back. He had to find some protection for his elbows and arms, for his one good knee and leg. Looking around he hit on it. Cut out patches from the old she-rip. With his crude chisel he jammed off a set of patches, with tie-strings, and bound them on tight. He sloughed off what dried fat and meat was still stuck to the rest of the bear hide and cut armholes in it and drew it on over his back.

He also collected the grizzly's four claws. Bending Reed had often lamented that while he might have counted coup on many a brave in battle and had scalps to show for it, he still hadn't counted coup on a grizzly. She wanted to see her brave decked out with a necklace of grizzly claws. Well, he'd at last got his grizzly, and in a hand-to-hand fight at that.

He laughed when he thought of what she'd do with the claws. She'd hold a victory dance around them; then string them on a deer sinew; then drape them around his hoary old neck.

He planned his trip carefully. It would be safest to crawl at night; sleep during the day. Best, too, to take a creek up one gully to the top of a divide; cross on the hogback ridge; take a gully down on the other side, and so on until he crossed the Moreau River and got to the Cheyenne. At the Cheyenne he'd be far enough south and out of range of the Rees to once again head toward the Missouri.

He began the terrible odyssey on the evening of the ninth of September, the ninth day of the Moon of Maize Ripening. The sun had just set and the high bald hills across the Grand River valley glowed like round piles of hot copper slag. Dusk came in out of the east like dark doom.

He followed the South Fork of the Grand. It veered almost directly south. He crept along the sides of the bluffs, halfway up, overlooking the meandering stream. He kept a wary eye on the brush in the draws on either side, on the trees beside the flickering stream, on the horizon rims all around.

He crept along on his elbows and one good knee. His splinted leg slaped behind him in its travois. A pair of whitegray wolves and a lone coyote trailed after him. The green wrinkleneck buzzards had given up.

Silvertip bearskin thrown over his back, bearhide guards on his elbow points and good knee, dried paws dangling from his neck on a deer sinew, he looked more like a wounded grizzly than a wounded human, looked like a bear who'd come off second best with a nest of bear traps.

A herd of antelope spotted him in the evening dusk. Curious, they approached him cautiously. When they finally got a whiff of him, they bolted over a bluff, white tails flagging.

Darkness fell slowly, changed over him like a sea of clear blue water gradually turning to black ink. Stars came out low and sharp.

He crept along cautiously. He felt his way along with his finger tips, foot by foot.

He crawled around boulders. He pushed through clumps of bunch grass. He dragged across barren gravel heads.

He ran into ant mounds, which suddenly became alive with wriggling stings. He ran into beds of prickly-pear cactus, which each time reminded him of a pack of crouching porcupine. He ran into one coiled rattler, which gave him fair warning.

The first quarter mile went fine. But after that it was tough going. His wind gave out, and his elbows stung, and his one good leg tired. Oddly enough, the tiredness in his good leg set up a cramp in his bad leg.

He rested flat on his belly. He sweat. One ear on the bare ground and one ear up, he listened to the night sounds. He heard the stealthy ghostly prowling of the two wolves and the coyote. He heard the itching movement of armored beetles deep in the earth. He heard grasshoppers chawing spears of grass. He heard angleworms squirming up out of their holes and excreting rich crumbles of dirt on the surface of the earth.

The thought of being completely alone in a wild savage country, miles from any white settlement anywhere, sometimes rose in him like personified terror, like a humpnecked striking creature. He fought it, fought it, and swallowed it down.

Rees could be skulking anywhere. The two trailing wolves could at any moment multiply into a pack of wolves and make a rush for him. Another she-grizzly could be on the prowl.

One thing he was thankful for. Halfway up the bluff sides where he crawled along there were no mosquitoes to bother him. And of course in the night no green flies.

Now and then a puff-soft breeze rose out of the gullies and caressed his brow and soothed his warm itching back.

He rested flat on his belly. He thought of silent Fitz and the boy Jim.

Where were the lads? He recalled all their good points. They were fine laddies, they were, and deserved better. Gone under like the other Jim and the lad Augie.

Himself? He'd make it all right. He would play it close to the belt; cipher cautious all the way; save his breath whenever and wherever he could; sail carefully; man the rudder with a steady hand all the way into port, Ft. Kiowa, and come in loaded for bear and killing. Oh, he would all right. Old Hugh had rawhide muscles and a buckskin belly and the stretchingest a-double-s in captivity.

He crawled; rested; crawled.

Once he slept. And woke with a start. How long? How much of the cool black night had he wasted? He couldn't guess. Perhaps an hour. Maybe four. In any case he felt refreshed and rested.

He crawled along briskly again for a quarter mile.

He kept to the sides of the bluffs, in one side gully and out the other, on, on, always quartering south toward Ft. Kiowa, to Bending Reed who'd heal him with her nursing and her herbs and her soups, to the fort where the clerk would re-outfit him with a gun and possibles for the time when he'd be whole again, up on two legs, and ready to join Major Henry and the other lads up in the far sweet-grass country.

When dawn broke pink in the east at last, he was exhausted, gaunt with thirst, gray with fatigue. His fever had come back some. The red monsters had returned in his back and in his leg again.

Looking back along the bluff sides, along the highland, he guessed he'd crawled some four miles, perhaps five. A short way, yes, but for a broken man a great way. Only one hundred ninety-five miles left. Ae, he'd done better than he'd expected. There was still plenty of life left in the old gray mare. Looking back he saw, too, that by sticking to the highland he had saved himself many a weary turn alongside the wriggling meandering stream of the South Fork.

~

The dark thought wouldn't leave him alone. The tougher and grimmer the crawl up the hogback became, the more he became convinced, even possessed, with the idea that his lads Jim and Fitz had deserted him, that Fitz had somehow talked Jim into it.

Deserted. The lads had deserted him. That Irisher Fitz had done it.

Damned Irish. Never was any good for anything except run away from a fix. A fighting Irishman usually meant an Irishman afraid of being called a coward. They could talk forward faster and walk backward faster than any other dummed two-legged creature on earth. He'd sensed it in Fitzgerald from the first. Too practical, too cautious. Hard front and soft back. And the boy Jim, though a

Scotchman like himself, too young to know better. Damned Irish. That's what a man got for learning life out of books.

Deserted.

A wave of hate swept over him. If there was one thing Old Hugh hated, it was cowardly deserters. Amongst mountain men alone in a far wild country full of enemy varmint there just wasn't room for cowards, deserters, or they would all go under. In red-devil country mountain men had to stick together. It was the code. He himself had often risked his topknot to save some comrade left behind in battle. Many a time. He didn't deserve to have this happen to him. Especially not at the hands of his own lads, Jim and Fitz. Not after the way he'd saved their skin from the major's wrath.

How could his own lads have come to it?

He crawled on. Nosed on. Crept on.

But the dark thought was back again the next time he lay flat on his belly to rest.

Could they really have deserted him? His lads?

He couldn't shake the notion. He remembered too well how the lads had let him cover up their sleeping on guard, remembered how they had not talked up like men to say they were guilty of negligence, that they had indirectly caused the death of Augie Neill and Jim Anderson. If they could be cautious once, they could be cautious twice.

Cautious. Ae. Too cautious. "Ae, and you can lay your pile on it that it was Fitz's idee too. He talked Jim into it. Poor lad."

But Jim was a coward to let Fitz talk him into it. The black-hearted bugger. Leaving him to die the hard way.

"If this child ever gets out of this alive, the first thing he's gonna do is track them cowardly cautious devils down and kill 'em. Inch by inch. Slow torture 'em. Skin 'em alive. Fry 'em alive. Punch pine needles and pine slivers in 'em like the Pawnees did to Old Clint and make torches out of 'em. At the same time, so they can watch each other go up in smoke." Hugh ground his teeth; clenched and unclenched his fists.

Another wave of hate passed over him. The cowardly snakes. The cowardly squaws. Leaving him to die the hard way. Alone.

"Oily cowards. Someday this old coon will have a showdown with ee, lads."

Those two devils who called themselves mountain men had a code all right. Deserter code. Ae.

Well, he had a code too. A code which said a man had a right to kill deserters. It was a crime before God and man both to desert a man in a wilderness full of howling red devils, taking his possibles away from him, leaving him without food, with nothing but his naked hands left to fight off the varmints. Leaving him without a last bullet to kill himself with in case of unbearable pain. Or in case of capture by red devils. The lads knew a hunter always saved one last ball for himself in case of a pinch. If he could help it, a hunter did all he could to avoid torture by Indians—like Old Clint suffered at the hands of the Pawnees.

Leaving him with a ripped-up back and a broken leg. Ae, he had a code too, and it said to kill deserters on sight.

Waves of hate flushed over him. He ground sand in his clenching fists.

"Them oily cowards. If it's the last thing I ever do, I'm gonna live long enough to kill the both of 'em. The major is gonna know too. They're maybe laughin' to themselves right now, thinkin' they got away from it, not buryin' me, playin' me for a sucker, and runnin' off with the best rifle this side of the Ohio. But they'll have another think comin' someday."

He got to his hands and knee and crept on. He crept until he couldn't anymore.

~

The bronze quartermoon had just set when he ran into the remains of a Sioux warrior. Sewed up in a skin bundle, lying out full length, some six feet above ground on a scaffold of dry saplings, it swayed slack and lonely on four upright posts, black against the star-pricked sky. The tattered edge of a skin snapped in the slow breeze too.

Looking up at it, Old Hugh found himself suddenly lonesome for Bending Reed and the rites of her tribe, found himself lonesome even for the old days on the Platte with the Pawnees. The decaying leathery remains of the unknown warrior brought tears to his eyes. The white man might sometimes bury his dead kin six feet under, as deep as he made his privies, but the red devil placed his dead six feet above ground for all men to see, out of reach of varmint, as high as he would carry his head in the happy hunting grounds of after-life. Ae, there swayed the honorable end of a free brave's life on Mother Earth, reared up out in the open so that his gross dark ignorant body could be given back to the powers of heaven and to the four quarters of the universe and to all the rains and to the wingeds of the air and to the little people of the earth. Ae, the red devil still knew the old and true religion. He still walked with Grandfather Wakantanka on the bosom of Grandmother Earth.

Looking up at the swaying recumbent reposing body, watching the little memento bags belling in the breeze, and imagining the pennyskinned hawknose face composed in stoic calm and peace, Old Hugh found himself hating cautious Fitz and the boy Jim with redoubled fury. Even in the midst of the most precarious existence, the Sioux tribes had time to give their fallen warrior a decent and an honorable burial. But his two friends had not only deserted him, they had left him unburied.

"If I ever lay hands on those two low-lived snakes, them oily cowards, not even their bitch of a mother is gonna recognize 'em after I get through with 'em. I'll tear 'em limb from limb, and then feed 'em hunk for hunk and rib for rib to the coyotes and turkey buzzards, and then collect their bones and burn 'em and dump the ashes in a whorehouse privy. I will. If it's the last thing I ever do. And may God forget to have mercy on their souls."

Looking up at the peaceful body of the Sioux brave withering away in the slow cool night wind, Hugh vowed he'd at least live long enough to exact his sacred vengeance.

"And when I've finished with 'em, I'm quittin' white-man diggin's. I'll join up with Reed and her tribe, beargrease or no, like I've always had a hankerin' to. I'll make the Ree my true enemy, not just low-lived red varmint like I've always said. The red devil has a code. We ain't."

He nubbed on, hand for hand, one good knee and one bum leg sliding along.

Old Mother

A COLD NOSE WOKE HIM.

Two pairs of furred slanted yellow eyes glittered down at him out of a very bright blue sky. One pair of narrowed eyes glittered very close. Dogs. Indian dogs gone wild. Strays from the Rees who'd passed by the day before. Or the advance guard dogs of a second Ree village on the move.

Hugh snapped up both hands; caught the dog around the furred neck; choked it with a frantic fanatic grip. The other yellowgray dog leaped back. The caught dog struggled, and doubled its neck around to snap at his hands, and dug its claws into his leathers trying to get away, and rasped piteously for breath.

"You devil! So you and your companyero thought you'd make a meal of me, did ee? Well, you've another think a comin' on that. It's me who's gonna eat, not you."

Hugh hung on. Gradually the dog's struggles weakened; ceased altogether; and at last the wild cur fell slack across his belly.

"Fresh meat is good meat," Hugh grunted. "Even if it ain't prime calf meat."

He sat up slowly. His limbs and back cracked like dried rawhide.

In the midst of the dry canebrake he found a heavy white stone the size of a bowling ball. With a quick stroke he crushed in the wild dog's head. He found another stone, this time a flat one with a rough cutting edge, and jammed at the dog's tough furry neck until the jugular began to spout blood. "Nothin' like a bucket of blood to start the day."

He skinned two of the dog's legs and gnawed them down to the bone. The meat was tough and flat. He chewed until the roots of his old teeth hurt him again.

He noticed after a while that the other dog had disappeared. It meant the two dogs probably hadn't been wild after all, that they belonged somewhere.

Grizzly predator head rising slowly out of the canebrake, bright afternoon sunlight silvering his matted gray hair, Hugh surveyed the river valley all around, east, west, north, south. As he'd noted the night before, he had nested down in the midst of a considerable grove of cottonwoods and willows and a few wild fruit trees. The heavy yellow cottonwood leaves clattered briskly in a wind coming out of the west. Some of the cottonwood leaves let go and spun around and around until they hit water or sandy ground. The pink willows were tougher and less noisy. The red plum leaves fluttered softly. From where he crouched Hugh had trouble telling the leaves apart from the drying wrinkly plums.

Less than a dozen yards away the waters of the big creek joined the fanning washing Moreau. Both streams ran clear and clean over gold-sand deltas and occasional beds of pebbles, beds dull orange and speckled with bits of black and flecks of white.

Up from both sides of the Moreau the land rose in thrown slopes of grassed-over clay and gravel. To the north still loomed omnipresent dull-red Thunder Butte. To the south rose the first smooth slopes of the Fox Ridge bluffs. While out of the west and into the east the bottoms of the Moreau swung and angled along.

Hugh was about to settle back in the canebrake when his quick eye spotted the other wild dog. Pink tongue out and puffing it was sitting on its haunches in front of an old ragged patched-up tepee, exactly across from him on the other side of the river and up on a low bench of gravel.

Hugh ducked down and began to sweat. He swore softly to himself. "Right in my eye practically and I missed it. That dummed stomach of mine is gonna get me in trouble yet."

Hugh puffed. "Red devils, no doubt. Ae. And they've probably spotted me too."

He sat crouched and very quiet for a long time. He listened for the sounds of approaching stealth in the whistling tossing canebrake.

When nothing happened, he cautiously and noiselessly wormed his way to the edge of the canebrake and parted the last few stalks and looked out from a spot low near the ground.

A tepee all right. And the wild dog too.

But it was only one tepee, and an odd one at that. It looked Sioux but it wasn't Sioux exactly. It looked like a tepee made by a Sioux and then traded to a Ree who'd made it over to fit his ways of staking and decoration.

For a half hour Hugh studied the tepee and the dog, never once moving from his prone position at the edge of the canebrake. During all that time he saw nothing moving in and out or around the strange tepee. And in all that time too the wild dog sat in front of the tepee doorflap, pink tongue out and calmly puffing.

Hugh couldn't understand it. Had the Rees left some old crone or brave behind to die? They sometimes did when on the move. In hard times, when the old became too weak to travel, tribal custom sometimes said they had to be left behind. In fact, the old often asked for the privilege themselves. Bending Reed had once told him that her own old brave of a father had made such a request. "My children," the old wrinkled pennyskinned sack of bones had said, "my children, our nation is poor and we need meat. Think not of me, but go to the country where there is meat. Go, and leave me to what lies in store for me. My eyes are dim, my legs no longer can carry my body, my arms can no longer bend my bow. I wish to die. Go, my children, go make your hearts brave and forget me.

Go, I am good for nothing and my days are done." With a catch in his throat Hugh remembered Bending Reed's telling of it. After his desertion by the boys such memories were like searing heartburns.

That was it, all right. An old brave left to die. With a few provisions to last out his days. And his favorite dogs left to watch over him, and maybe, gone wild, to eat him if the wolves didn't get him first.

Hugh waited another half hour before venturing out of his hiding place.

The dog in front of the old tepee took one look at Old Hugh's grizzly aspect into the brush behind the tepee. It made Hugh smile. "He ain't forgot about what this grizzly did to his companyero. No siree."

Hugh waded on elbows and knee through the river, bum leg in the slape trailing after like a wetted plew of beaver on a sled, and boldly approached the tepee. Still no one in sight, still no wild warwhoop out of the yellow brush and the yellow grove to indicate the tepee was an ambush.

Hugh lifted the flap and peered in past a dangling medicine bundle.

He was right. An old one left to die alone. An old withered crone. She was lying prone on a fur beside the ashes of a fire in the center of the tepee. A striped blackred woolen blanket covered her. Her eyes were closed. But she was still breathing. She was incredibly old and wrinkled.

Somehow she looked familiar, Hugh thought.

Hugh crawled in for a closer look.

A white weaselskin amulet hanging from a stick thrust in the ground behind her head finally helped him identify her. Hugh sucked in a breath. Ho-ah. It was the old mother of Gray Eyes. Hugh's flinty eyes rolled. When the Rees fled their villages above the Grand on the Missouri, Pilcher's boys had been instructed to set fire to the villages. Just after they'd fired it, they found the old mother left behind in a mud-covered round lodge. Hugh clucked his tongue. The Rees must have snuck back into the burning village to save her from a fiery and ignoble end. And in their subsequent raveling over the country, they had managed to take her along this far.

His quick old eye fastened greedily on the paunches of food left at her side. A small bag of rich pemmican, soft enough so the toothless withered old lady could mouth it down; a cake of cornbread, also soft and easy on the gums; and a bladder of fresh water—all provisions for the rest of her journey here on earth and for the first of her journey into the new spirit world.

Hugh pounced on the pemmican and cake. Human food for his poor old stomach at last.

There was a quiver in the wrinkled oldpenny eyelids. The old woman's eyelids parted and old blackcherry eyes tinged with a deadskin-gray looked up at him.

Hugh held still, eyes furtive in bushy face.

Her old wrinkled leathery lips moved. "——face."

The old word whispered out of an old throat gave Old Hugh a pause. The old word said in Arikaree he readily understood. He knew a little Ree—it was a cousin language to the Pawnee which he knew well. Face. Paleface. She didn't see him then the way the dog saw him. Paleface. Ae, with the long beard he now had he was a paleface sartain sure. Major Henry was right that it stuck out.

The old black eyes brightened and the dead skin on the eye slid to one side like the winking nictitating third eyelid of an old hen. One of the withered bony arms stirred under the striped blackred blanket. Her old leathery voice-box harsed low again. "Meat."

The second old word jolted Hugh. He dropped the bag of pemmican and cake of cornbread.

Once more the old throat harsed the old word. "Water."

Hugh's eyes filmed with tears. He couldn't help it. Poor old soul. He knew what it was to be left alone to die. Ae. He knew.

"So it's water ye want, is it?" Old Hugh's voice cracked. "Well, Old Mother, water it is ye'll have. This child can't begrudge ye that."

He angulated his body and leg over and sat beside her. He cradled her old head in an arm and, with his other hand, held the mouth of the bladder of water to her lips. Her old black braids fell across his soiled leather sleeve.

She drank slowly. Some of the water pulsed down her throat; some of it spilled and ran down the wrinkles cutting her head carefully down on the tan-black buffalo robe again. Hugh had the feeling that if he hadn't been careful, her head could very easily have parted from the spine despite the old tangle of veins and sinews and leather skin holding them together.

She thanked him with filmy eyes; then her eyes closed. She puffed slowly, with long pauses in between. Sometimes the puffed breaths came so far apart Hugh was afraid she'd breathed her last.

"Poor old soul," Hugh said, eyes tearing over again. "No, there's some things this child won't do, no matter how far his stomach's made him backslide. I can't skulp a live red devil, or desert a friend, or take orders from a tyrant, or hurt Indian wimmen. Pa'tic'ly old red-devil grammaws on their last legs."

She heard him. Her old filmy eyes opened and cleared for another slowly brightening live look. "Meat."

"Ae, an' meat ye shall have too, Old Mother." He held up the pemmican. "This suit yer taste?"

She tried to shake her head; roved her eyes back and forth instead. "Meat."

"Ae, so it's live meat ye want. Well, in that case, this child'll have to go back to the canebrake for that dog he killed."

Saying it, it occurred to him. It was one of her dogs he'd killed. Unbeknownst he'd taken meat, and favorite meat at that, from a dying critter. All Indians thought dog meat a great delicacy. Unbeknownst. But yet done. "Ae, Old Mother, meat, live meat, ye'll have."

He heard a noise outside the tepee. He jerked erect, tense, eyes fixed on the doorflap. Rees come back?

It was a sliding noise, a noise of something being dragged, slaped, over the sand. With a quick surging roll of a grizzly he lunged for the doorflap. He peered out.

It was the still-live dog dragging the dead carcass of his companyero dog. The live dog apparently had been trained to retrieve. Good. The live dog had saved him the trouble of getting the carcass himself.

Hugh was careful not to scare the live dog this time. The live dog might come in handy later on. But careful as he was, the live dog again bolted at the sight of him.

Hugh shagged the partly eaten dog into the tepee.

"Now, Old Mother, did your companyeros leave ye any fire-fixin's maybe?"

He searched and found flint and steel in a leather bag near her head under the fur she lay on. He also found an old knife, worn back almost to the haft.

Hugh rubbed his gnarled hands in joy. "Hurrah! Old Mother, good meat it'll be. I hope ye'll allow the cook a taste." Old Hugh winked at her.

The wink wasn't lost on her. Her old leathery lips tried to form a smile; made what looked like a grimace of terrible pain instead. Hugh thought it one of the finest smiles he'd laid eyes on. "Ae, Old Mother, I'll bet ye was a merry lass in your day, wasn't ee? Ae. The pennyskin Rees was always said to be the best on the Old Missouri."

Old Hugh found dry twigs; hustled up firewood; with flint and steel soon had a blazing fire going Indian-style. With the old woman's knife he skinned the dead dog. He impaled it on a slender green willow rod; placed it in the forked ends of two stakes set at either end of the fire; began barbecuing.

When it was finally done, the dog meat tasted wonderful. Hugh fed her first, fed her like he might feed a baby, mashing the flesh with a stone and giving it to her in thin strips. Between feedings he couldn't resist licking his fingers now and then.

Presently she indicated she'd had enough. She thanked him with another flowering of brightness in her old filmy black eyes.

"Don't mention it, Old Mother. I'd do the same for me own mother, God bless her, departed as she is from this valley of trials and tribulations." Again tears popped in Hugh's eyes. He blinked them back, inwardly a little ashamed of his gullishness.

Sure that she had enough, Hugh pitched in himself. The meat had been turned to a fine brown faretheewell. It was crispy on the outside and tender on the inside.

The live dog outside couldn't resist the wonderful smell of singed browned flesh either. It poked its twitching cold black nose in through the doorflap, warily, irresistibly drawn.

Hugh smiled until his whiskers moved up his cheeks. He tore off a piece of meat and tossed it to the cold black nose.

The half-wild yellowgray dog slipped into the tepee and with a single pulsing swallow snapped it down. Its eyes begged for more.

"A friend it is I want ye to be, pooch. Me and the old lady here may have need for ee in time to come. One way or another." Hugh tossed it another strip of well-done flesh. "Dip in, pooch." Hugh winked at the dog.

Again the dog downed the browned meat in a single pulsing swallow.

When Hugh turned to see if the Old Mother was enjoying the humor of it with him, he found her dead. She'd been so far gone that the first stir of her stomach became a stumbling stone for her old heart.

"What? So soon, Old Mother?"

Hugh stared at her for a minute; then burst into tears.

"What? an' we just friends?"

Gently he closed her eyes, first one, then the other.

Eyes streaming, he stared down at her. "Ae, at least ye had the luck to ha' a human around to close your eyes. But who'll close the eyes of this old hoss when he goes? He ain't got nobody back in the States to remember him. My lads'll have long forgot their old man. Ae. The old she-rip'll ha' seen to that."

Scarlet Plume

I wanted to do something about the Sioux Uprising in Minnesota, a piece of our history that had vanished because the Civil War was afoot at the time . . . One day I came upon a letter General Sibley wrote to his wife in which he refers in scathing tones to a young lady they both knew who preferred to go with her Indian lover into the wilds rather than go back to her husband and child who were waiting for her.

Women are far more practical than men. When the chips are down the girls choose the right course for survival. Not the course, say of intellectual truth, but the course of a living truth, survival truth . . . I had to work it that she became so emaciated that all her morality had left her and all that was left was to feed that belly, an alimentary tract.

I was also thinking by this time that why didn't I just put this book in the woman's mind. I had never done that before. And then see what I come out with. That's a real challenge.

Judith's Flight

THE YANKTONS OBEYED Smoky Day's request and removed to a place known as Where Part Of The River Turns Through A Red Cut In The Land. Judith called the place simply Dell Rapids. A fork of the River Of The Double Bend ran through a deep and beautiful red rock gorge. In one turn the red gorge widened out and formed a natural amphitheater. The amphitheater had a sandy floor and made a perfect spot in which to hide a village. The stream ran slow and clear, and formed many pink swimming holes. The looming columnar walls of the amphitheater were covered with grapevines and scarlet sumac. Plums grew in wild profusion both on top and along the bottom. Farther along, where the amphitheater shaped off into a narrow gorge again, the Yanktons sometimes used the west wall for yet another Buffalo Jump.

Judith was out gathering ripe plums when she became aware that "those" had at last come upon her. She let go a big relieving sigh. "Thank God I am not mother again." By her reckoning she had been a good week overdue. She had had the whites quite bad the last few days and these she had heard always preceded conception. It had happened the time she'd had Angela.

"All that awful work done to me must have thrown them off. Well, they're here and thank God for that at least."

She put aside the parfleche of plums and gathered a lapful of cattails from a swampy spot upriver. She would catch the flow with their tender fluff.

When Judith returned to Whitebone's lodge she said nothing about her "those." According to strict Yankton taboo she was required to retire to a retreating lodge or menstruation hut. She made up her mind she was not going to conform to this. She would be obedient to the old chief in some things but not in this. She was from St. Paul, where women knew how to handle "the curse" and still be free like men. The Yankton taboo in this matter belonged back even before the time of the Old Testament. She would cover her "those" with the perfume of juices squeezed from wild flowers. At night she would so arrange it that Whitebone would not find out. Somehow for five nights she would avoid his nosy hands.

She spent the evening getting water, washing out the cooking pot, and mending moccasins. She made a point of presenting a face without guile. The corners of her lips would not give her away. She was the dutiful, seemingly pregnant wife interested in keeping her nest neat and orderly.

Later that evening Walking Voice went about the village handing out invitation sticks to a Virgin's Feast. It would be held the next day. Everyone went to bed looking forward to a day of showy ceremony and much good eating.

Judith got ready for bed only after she was sure Whitebone was sound asleep. She decided she would go to bed with her dress on. This also was not the usual custom with the Yanktons. But Whitebone was snoring so hard she was sure he would not catch her at it. And she would make certain to get up before he did in the morning. Wearing a dress in bed would help hide her difficulty. She scented herself thoroughly with wild perfumes, then carefully slid under the sleeping robe beside him. She was careful not to let cold air touch him. She was also careful to stay well on her side of the fur bed.

She lay still. In between Whitebone's slow snores she could hear the gentle regular breathing of Scarlet Plume and Two Two. Tinkling slept soundless. So did Born By The Way. The stick fire slowly turned to ashes. Stars moved across the smoke hole.

The sand under the fur bed for once gave in just the right places and Judith had just about sunk away into the first fluff of sleep, when Whitebone, snorting, awoke with a start.

Judith stiffened awake. Her heart instantly began to pound, shaking her breasts. "Dear Lord," she breathed to herself, "dear Lord, please let him fall asleep again."

Whitebone spoke suddenly. "What is this I smell?"

Judith lay frozen.

"Woman, what is this I smell?"

"Wh-what?"

"I smell crushed juice of many flowers. Have the mice gotten into the parfleche where the perfumed bear grease is kept?"

"Perhaps." Judith let herself relax a little.

"Where is the dog Long Claws?"

"She sleeps."

"Wake her and let her chase the mice away."

"Ah, she is good for nothing but chasing rabbits. A mouse and a mosquito are all one to her."

"Hrmm." Whitebone continued to sniff the air. "It is pleasing to smell all the perfumes, but is it a good thing to waste it all in one night? Perhaps someone should arise and chase away the mice."

"Yes, my lord."

Whitebone grumped. "What is this 'my lord' you speak of?"

"It is only a manner of speaking among the whites."

"Wagh. Is this because the white husband believes he has the right to knock down his wife like she might be a warrior?"

Judith recalled the fighting Utterbacks. She could feel her lips smile at the corners. "Perhaps."

"Hrmm."

They lay very still, each in his place.

Scarlet Plume and Two Two continued to sleep soundly.

Stars moved across the smoke hole.

Of a sudden, with a grunt, Whitebone rolled over on his side. He reached across and placed a hand on Judith's belly.

Judith stiffened again.

"Woman," Whitebone inquired mildly, "are you chilled that you wear a dress in bed?"

Judith quickly seized on the suggestion. She feigned a shiver. "A down draft strikes me from the smoke hole where I lay."

"Can you not adjust the ears of the lodge to prevent this?"

"It is not a pleasant thought to get up in the cold night."

Whitebone sniffed the air. This time as he did so his hand slowly stiffened.

Judith held her breath.

Whitebone drew in a long, long breath, his big nose carefully going over every atom of it.

Judith waited.

All of a sudden Whitebone let out a terrified scream. He convulsed into a ball and bounded up. He went up like a dog that had accidentally lain down on hot coals. He tumbled to one side of their bed. He groaned a great groan. He flopped up and down four times, then stiffened out like a board.

Scarlet Plume and Two Two came alive like two startled panthers. Born By The Way let go with a loud bawl. Tinkling threw a handful of bear fat on the fire and immediately the pink embers in the hearth exploded into high dancing flames. The sudden light was dazzling.

Judith was struck dumb. She turned and stared at Whitebone.

Whitebone's old eyes slowly turned up into his head. His whole body seemed to be gradually turning to stone.

Scarlet Plume jumped over. He stuck his broad face into Judith's face. "What have you done to offend our father?" Scarlet Plume's cold squared lips were those of a hated male.

Never had she seen such outrage in a man's face. Husband Vince's rages were laughable by comparison. A hot smell radiated from Scarlet Plume. She recalled her father once saying that when a wild boar really got mad one could smell the mad in him a mile off.

"What have you done to offend our father?" Scarlet Plume cried again.

Tinkling knew. She shrank back from Judith as far as she could on the women's side.

"Tell us, what have you done to offend our father?" Scarlet Plume reached out as if to shake Judith.

"Do not touch her!" Tinkling cried to Scarlet Plume. Tinkling covered her mouth and her eyes. She shuddered.

Scarlet Plume drew back. "What is this?"

Tinkling whispered, "The white woman has done an evil thing." Tinkling couldn't resist throwing a spiteful look at Judith through her fingers.

Scarlet Plume stared at Tinkling. "What evil thing do you speak of? Our father dies and we wish to know what it is that we may save him."

Tinkling spoke one word. She more hissed it than spoke it.

Scarlet Plume's eyes opened in terror, and he jumped all the way back to the slanting wall of the tepee. Two Two also jumped back. Both stared at her as if she were some fearsome monster from the other side.

Judith felt horrid. It was her flaunting of a Yankton taboo that had thrown the old man into a seizure. In the eyes of the old chief what she had done was wickedly obscene. For a Yankton man to touch a menstruating woman was to invite some kind of ultimate barbaric curse. In all her life she had never seen grown men show such shock.

Humpneck Tinkling was the first to recover her wits. She ran over and knelt beside Whitebone. She touched his arms, his legs. "He turns cold. Quick, dig a hole under the hearth. The heated sand will restore warmth to his limbs."

Scarlet Plume dropped to his knees, scooped up the fire with his bare hands and set it to one side, then dug out a shallow trench. Sand flew between his legs like he might be a dog digging for a gopher. Then together Tinkling and Scarlet Plume lifted the stiff chief into the trench. They crossed his arms over his chest and covered him with warm sand. Scarlet Plume quickly painted Whitebone's face with vermilion to give him the color of seeming health.

Tinkling next snapped around at Judith. She grabbed a knife and cut a slit up the back of the tepee. She held the edges of the slit apart. "Step through this," she said to Judith. "We cannot let you defile the front door with your going."

Judith did meekly as she was told. She slipped out into the night.

Tinkling hissed at her. "Stand still until I can attend thee. When we have brought the old father back to life, and we have purified the tepee, then I will help thee put up the separation lodge." She added more kindly, "Understand this. The Yanktons consider the woman spirit a powerful thing. If it is not kept in bonds it will destroy the man, perhaps even destroy the woman. When blood flows from that place where the child is born, it is a sign of the terrible power for harm in the woman. Therefore you must stay in the separation lodge until all danger is past."

A picture of home in St. Paul flashed through Judith's mind. She remembered how ardently she and Mavis had once argued in favor of equal rights for women: the right to vote, the right to own property in their own name, the right to appear in public without a hat, the right to nurse the wounded on a battlefield. In fact, both she and Mavis had taken the extreme feminist point of view in these matters.

A wild, hysterical laugh broke from her. "To think that I once got so excited about all that, and now I'm standing here." Then she fainted and fell upon the pink sand.

Later, when she came to, she found herself in a little hut alone.

~

Six days later Judith wandered downstream to take her purification bath. She knew of a lovely beach where the branch made a leisurely turn deep in the Dells. It was private, the pink sand was very fine, and the high red rock walls kept out the wind.

She slipped out of her doeskin tunic and leggings and moccasins. Kneeling naked at the edge of the slowly sliding stream, she scrubbed her clothes clean with pink grit, then draped them in the sun over a large boulder.

A small hollow of water gleamed beside the large boulder. It was a place where birds might come to drink and bathe. It was perfectly smooth and shone like a polished mirror.

She stood looking down at the hollow of water. She saw herself on its surface. Her blue eyes, she saw, had a lost, beaten look. Her hair, done up in two heavy braids, was strangely darkish. Her cheeks and neck were also strangely dark-skinned. She was quite thin, even stringy looking. The rest of herself she could recognize—a pink skin with a faint golden fuzz.

She shuddered. "Thank God I am not mother again."

She undid her braids. With her fingers she combed them out. She looked for lice; found none. Her hands became greasy with tallow.

She toed into the water. It was surprisingly warm for September. The sun was directly overhead. She went in over the ankles, then the knees. The pink bottom shelved downward slowly, deeper. She cupped up water in both hands and let it run down her arms and off her elbows. She cupped water to her face. She cupped water over her pudding belly. She loved it. She waded in deeper. Water welled up her thighs. Water touched the gold tufts of her pudendum.

"Oh! It's so good."

Water lapped around the paired loaves of her buttocks, then up around her hips.

The bottom seemed to shelve off steeper and she decided to swim for it. She slid forward, her breasts going under and then her shoulders. She paddled along gently. She nosed into the shadow under the south wall of the turn. The darkened water seemed a bit forbidding to her. After a moment she turned and paddled back to sunny waters. She swam leisurely, slowly. She luxuriated limb for limb in the warm branch water.

"Oh, it's so good, so good."

Her fingertips touched bottom and she stood up. She stretched to her full height. Her chest lifted, her belly shrank, her seat arched back. She looked around to make sure no one was watching. She saw only a fox squirrel playing in a gnarled oak high on the south wall. She stretched again.

"Wouldn't Angela have loved this. So beautiful here. So by one's self."

A wave of gall-like nostalgia misted up in her. Never again would she sit with Angela and Vince around their once happy table. St. Paul was the dearest spot on earth to her and never would she see it again.

She fell to her knees. Her lips shaped a prayer. She thought this strange. She and Vince had never been much on religion. "Oh, Christ Jesus," she prayed, "thou who art able to save souls from hellfire, come save my body from fiends. I am lost in a far place. Amen."

The fox squirrel chattered at her from the very tip of a twig in the gnarled oak.

Embarrassed by the sudden need to pray, she moved into shallower water and began to scrub herself thoroughly with handfuls of pink grit. She cleaned herself between the thighs. Not only would she purify herself, but she would also rub off all touch and memory of what the Indian studs had done to her. She scoured her face. She filled her hair with pink sand and rinsed it out. Again and again. A frenzy of scrubbing and scouring and washing possessed her.

Gradually the tallow and tannin came out of her hair. Slowly its original color returned. In the sun her hair became a sun-whitened gold again.

She rinsed her hair until it made a squinching sound between her finger tips. She threw her long hair over her shoulders this way, then that way.

She laved her limbs with the warm, clear water. She poured handfuls of water down her shining belly. She felt renewed. She felt clean again.

She ran. She skipped across the pink beach. She pirouetted on her toes. Eyes half-closed, dreamy, she let the sun make love to her skin.

She let her tongue play along the edge of her lips. The tip of her tongue touched four black stubs of hair on her upper lip. Goodness. She had completely forgotten about them. They had grown back. She recalled again how she had always been careful to keep them pulled so Vince wouldn't see them. Well, she had no scissors with her and would have to let them grow.

A pebble fell from high off the south wall, plunked into the dark, deep part of the stream.

She glanced up, wondering what the playing fox squirrel was doing.

She stiffened. Someone had been observing her all along. Whitebone. Old face of the same color as the weathered red rock, he sat in a crevice in the shadow of the gnarled oak. He sat immobile, so fixed that the fox squirrel played unconcernedly just above him in the green leaves of the oak.

Judith dove for the deep water. She stood in water up to her neck. A delicate crimson came and went on her scrubbed cheeks.

Whitebone stood up. He spoke in a low, grave voice, full of awe. "White woman with the white sunned hair, know this. I have seen a great thing today. You are sacred. I see that I have done a bad thing. It was wrong for me to wive a sacred white being. You are wakan. This I did not know. You belong in the company of the spirit of the Buffalo Woman, she who lives behind the braiding waters at Falling Water. From this time on, you shall live in a sacred tepee apart. No man shall touch you again. Wakantanka reveals his presence in all white creatures. Your presence shall make the Yanktons a great people. This is true. This is right. Bathe in peace, white woman with the white sunned hair, this is your sacred bathing place. I have said."

Judith listened to it all with gradually widening high-blue eyes.

With a groan Whitebone got to his feet and stomped back to his camp.

By the next night Judith found herself living the life of a white goddess. She was given a white doeskin tunic, white leggings, and white moccasins, all exquisitely worked and decorated with porcupine quills. The Yankton women set up a new buffalo-hide tepee in the center of the camp circle where she was to live alone. The new tepee was nearly white and translucent. She was given a sacred white buffalo fur for a bed, a white wolf fur for a sleeping robe, and a pair of white weasel mittens for cold mornings. As a special favor, the new medicine man, Center Of The Body, instructed her to wear her hair loose and flowing. The people were to see and to take heart from her sacred sunned hair. She was also instructed to avoid walking or sitting in the sun unless fully clothed so that the skin on her hands and neck might regain its former pristine whiteness. Whitebone himself took his sacred white emblem, the weathered jawbone of a dinosaur, and adorned the top of her lodge with it. Two guards stood outside her door.

Judith liked the privacy. No longer would she have to fend off urgent savage studs. But she saw too that she was now more trapped, more prisoner, than ever. There was no escaping the Yanktons.

~

Once one of the bolder boys came up to her and said, "I see the white woman looks sad. I want to shake hands with her."

Judith let him shake her hand.

Yet it could not go on. She was no goddess.

Her new role was false. She was only too human and soon would once again do something offensive to the savage mind. And the next time something was bound to happen. A certain turning, and there it would be. Death.

"Yes. There's no doubt of it now. I'm going to die out here."

One evening after dark, as she lay alone in her white fur bed, Judith heard many footsteps passing by her tepee. The footsteps were those of men. They all led to the big council lodge nearby.

The night was windless. The least sound came to her magnified. She could hear the braves shift their feet in the sand inside the council lodge. The small stick fire in the center of the lodge burned with a sound as though a continuous breath were being expelled from an open mouth. Light coughs sounded almost as if inside her tepee. A sacred council pipe was being smoked and passed from hand to hand.

At last Whitebone spoke in the quiet. "My son, come straight for the pipe. We wait."

Scarlet Plume spoke. "My father, at last the time has come for me to speak of the new vision that was given me."

"Come straight for the pipe. The single hole in the stem does not lie."

"My father, a white ghost came to me in the night. It woke me in my sleep and it spoke to me."

"What did the white ghost say? We wait."

"The white ghost said to form a new society. The white ghost warned that many of the Yanktons would not like the new society, that perhaps no one would join it, that perhaps I would be the only member in it. The white ghost warned that even my father would be unhappy with it."

"Come straight for the pipe. What did the white ghost say would be the name of this new society?"

"The white ghost said it should be called Return The White Prisoners Society." Silence.

A single pair of moccasins squinched in the sand.

When Whitebone spoke next, his voice was a snarl of just barely controlled fury. "Come straight for the pipe!"

"The white ghost said that the Woman With The Sunned Hair must be returned to the white people." Scarlet Plume's voice resounded strong inside the leather lodge. "If Sunned Hair is not soon returned, all the Yanktons will be destroyed. That is all I have to say."

"But Sunned Hair is wakan. She is white and sacred. She is now a Yankton goddess."

"The white ghost has spoken. I wish to form this society."

Whitebone snorted with ridicule. "This society of yours, it is a crazy fool society."

There was another silence. Even from where Judith lay she could feel blackness gathering on the warrior faces.

"Come straight for the pipe." There was a sound of flaming hate in White-bone's voice. "Speak truly. What did the white ghost say?"

Scarlet Plume continued to talk strong. He believed in a certain thing and it was in complete control of him. "The white ghost says that if we do not return the white woman to her people, the Thunderbirds will strike us. Even the new Contrary, my brother Traveling Hail, will not be able to help us."

"My son, we have spoken of a certain thing before. It is that you turned over in your mother's belly before you were born. It was a great thing. It was a sign. It was told us that you were favored by the gods and would do a great thing for the Yanktons someday. Is this now the great thing you would do?"

"My father, I am helpless. I know only what the white ghost has told me."

"A white ghost? Why was it not a red ghost? Are not the Yanktons red? White. White. You know that one does not climb a hill for water nor listen to a white man for straight talking."

"My father, the white ghost says that if we do not soon return the white woman, some other bullhead warrior will rise in crazy anger and kill her."

"My son, does not the law of the Dakota say: Justice for our red people and death to all the whites? Let my son say if that is not true."

"My father, why should this young innocent woman be killed by a bull-head? Has she not always been kind to us, smiled upon us? Has she not washed your feet as a good wife should? Did she not give her breast to suck to our child Born By The Way? Even when she had no milk to give? Do not all our children love her as a tender sister? Why must a crazed Yankton be permitted to kill her?"

"My son, she is now a sacred person. No one shall touch her. We all worship her, even the new bullhead, Plenty Lice."

"My father, I smoke the pipe and cry to you—let her go free."

"Who will help her return to her people?"

"The white ghost says that certain members of the Return The White Prisoners Society must accompany her until she has safely arrived in the Fort Of The Snelling."

Whitebone snorted. "Who are these certain members?"

"Your son waits for others to join the society."

"Ha. Are there any here present who wish to join this crazy fool society?" Silence.

Judith was suddenly filled with a wild exultation. If Scarlet Plume had his way, she was going home! The mention of Fort Snelling thrilled her so profoundly she shuddered from head to foot. Going home. St. Paul. In her extremity, in the midst of desolation, one man, a savage, had suddenly arisen to plead for her freedom.

She had always admired Scarlet Plume, had even a love dream about him. How right she had been about him. Once in the long, long ago he had thrown a dead white swan at her feet to warn her that she must fly to save her neck.

And he still wished to save her. Yes. Yes. He was more than just a simple red man. He was a great man.

Whitebone spoke tauntingly. "We see then that there is only one crazy fool in your society."

"I wait for others to join this new society."

"My son, why is your mind set on this girl? Can she work moccasins better than others? Can she carry a heavier pack? Can she dress a buffalo skin better?"

"My father, you took her to wife. I did not. Why did you take her to wife? Why this one?"

There was a pause, a long one. When Whitebone finally spoke, it was in a startlingly soft voice. "When I looked upon the Woman With The Sunned Hair for the first time, I knew she was buried in my heart forever and my wife she had to be. It was done to appease the manes of my wife that was."

Scarlet Plume spoke courteously. "This I ask again. Why this white woman? You have now declared her to be wakan. How can this be when she is buried in your heart and she has slept with you skin to skin? I wish to know. It is a strange thing."

Whitebone jumped to his feet. His heels ground into the sand. "The whites, ha. The white man does not deserve this sacred woman, no. The white man does things for gold, for goddung, ha. He tries to sell the earth to his brother, yes. Who can tear our mother into small pieces and sell her?" Whitebone raged in a slow, clear, decisive voice. "The white man knows how to make things but he does not know how to share them. The white man is one of the lower creatures. He is an animal. Look at him carefully. His face is covered with hair. His chest is covered with hair. His legs are covered with hair. Only animals are that way. What can one think of a creature that has short hair on his head and long hair on his face?"

Scarlet Plume continued in a quiet, insistent voice. "This I ask. Must we believe then that Sunned Hair is a daughter of a hairy dog?"

Whitebone snarled, "Ha! We see now that Sunned Hair is also buried in the heart of my son. Does the only member of the crazy fool society wish to lie with her in the grass when he returns her to the Fort Of The Snelling?"

Scarlet Plume bounded to his feet. His heels hit the sand with a thump like that of an angry buck rabbit. "Wagh!"

Judith quivered. The two were sure to come to blows over her. She almost cried aloud in torment at the idea.

Then another thought shot through her. "Scarlet Plume loves me."

A tired voice interposed. It was the new medicine man, Center Of The Body, once known as Bullhead. "Brothers, Dakotas, let the feast-makers serve the meat. Later we shall have a further smoke on the matter of the Woman With The Sunned Hair. I have said."

While the council ate meat, Scarlet Plume stepped outside and walked down to the pink stream.

Judith got to her knees and peeked out of her tepee door. She saw Scarlet Plume in the vague starlight. His head was high, long black hair flowing to his shoulders. Presently he began to pace back and forth. The sound of his footsteps on the strand was firm and crisp in the night. He moved tall and muscularly powerful. The single scarlet feather upthrust at the back of his head quivered at his every step.

"Yes, those two are bound to kill each other," she whispered. "And after that? A hell on earth. The whole band will fall to killing each other in a wild blood bath." It was chilly. She drew her sleeping robe around her body. "I know this much. If I don't get out of here right away, escape right now, I'm dead in any case."

And there was something else. If Scarlet Plume were to touch her, she was dead in another way. She would never be able to resist him. She would have to go savage, eat raw liver.

She made up her mind to go. She had to go.

∾

It was day. The sky was blue. The sun was straight overhead. Crystals of light came glancing down through the leaves of the brush under which she lay snug and warm.

She remembered. Last night she had escaped the Yanktons. She had run and walked, and walked and run, straight south by the stars, toward where she thought the village of Sioux Falls lay. At last, chest burning, with dawn just beginning to show in the east, she had crept into a patch of what she thought were wolfberries.

She yawned, and stretched. Her throat worked, and swallowed. She wet her lips with the tip of her tongue. Time to eat.

She fumbled for the parfleche, and in so doing found herself covered with a thick blanket of loose grass.

Loose grass? She lifted her head. Yes. She was lying under a pile of haylike grass. She stared. She couldn't recall having scratched up long grass the night before. But there it was. She must have done it while half asleep.

She thought again of Whitebone and his Yanktons. By now they would have discovered she had flown the nest. She could almost see them making casts all around the Dell Rapids encampment to find her trail.

She lay very still, listening, so still that not even the loose grass rustled. No, there wasn't a sound. No stealthy footsteps. No neighing ponies. No creaking leathers. The only thing audible was the odd croaking beat of her heart.

Poor Scarlet Plume. He was sure to get the devil from Whitebone for having called a council meeting. It made her smile to think that while the council discussed Scarlet Plume's visit of restoring the white woman to her people, the white woman had escaped. Yet Scarlet Plume was powerful. Whitebone would not dare to punish him. Scarlet Plume was probably at that very moment already searching for her, along with the rest of the braves. She feared Scarlet Plume's hunter eyes more than she did the eyes of the others. Very little ever escaped him.

~

She ran when she could, walked when she had to.

She went back over the days since the massacre at Skywater. There was the night when Whitebone gruntingly took her to wife. Dear Lord in heaven. There was the day when Bullhead murdered Theodosia. Pray God Theodosia might now be safe in the arms of her Lord. There was the evening when Scarlet Plume, sitting alone in swamp willows, caused a wooden effigy of a buffalo to dance on a mound of sand. Such devil's doings. There was the night when Scarlet Plume danced up the buffalo. Sight of him naked had been even wilder than her craziest dreams. After that the days blurred off into each other.

Counting from the last day spent in the separation hut, her best guess was that it was around the twentieth of September. Also there had been only one light frost so far. First frosts were known to come to that part of the country around the twentieth. By hard walking, and some luck in catching Rollo, the mail carrier, she could be in New Ulm in about two weeks. And then in St. Paul by the end of another week.

She made up her mind to keep track of time. Just to make sure she wouldn't forget, she jerked off one of the doeskin fringes of her sleeve and carefully tucked it into her parfleche. It would stand for the twentieth of September. Tomorrow she would jerk off another one for the twenty-first. Not to know the time of the year made one feel more lost than ever.

~

She pushed on. She ran; she walked; she ran.

A side-ache began to stick her under the heart. It cut her breath. She came upon a round boulder and sat down to catch her wind.

What to do. What to do. If there were only a man along to help her. A pair of strong shoulders and keen eyes she could rely on. Show her the way. Even comfort her. Because maybe the river went west for miles in a really big looping bend.

The side-ache gradually throbbed away. Her breath came evenly again. She got to her feet and hurried on.

The bend did turn out to be a big one. Slowly too the footing became squishy. There was little or no sand, mostly caked mud, with the surface stiffish like thin frosting on a spongecake. Her moccasins began to slap on her feet.

Her cheeks itched. Then her neck. Then the backs of her hands. Once it seemed something bit her. She slapped at the itches. On one of her slaps her fingers brushed against something wispy. Spider webs?

Mosquitoes. Dear Lord. There were millions of them. The air was suddenly stuffy with them. She felt tickles in the back of her throat. She coughed. Puffing with her mouth open, she had been breathing them in by the dozens.

Then she saw it. Something was following her. A gray shape.

Coyote? She hoped it was a coyote. A coyote was not as ferocious as a wolf. A coyote was also known to run silently after its prey.

Her heart began to pound. She held her hand to her throat. She had to work to get her breath. It was a wolf, she was sure.

She turned to face it. If it was going to jump her, she would at least meet it head on.

The gray shape, or whatever it was, stopped too.

Or was it a mote in her eye? Because when she turned her head a little to hear the better, the shape seemed to move too.

She listened, all ears, trying to catch the sound of its breathing. Were it a farm dog following her, tongue lolling, it would be breathing with happy, audible puffs.

She waited. She breathed shallow breaths. Her own heart shook her. Soon trembles shook her thighs. She had to let her mouth hang open to keep her teeth from chattering. She almost wished she were back in the safety of her wakan white tepee.

Darkness became heavy. The gray shape stood out even more clearly.

It became very hot out, close. Sweat trickled down her face. Mosquitoes trailed across her cheeks with a thousand tickling legs.

A tremor beginning in the calves of her legs moved up until it made her neck crack. Her breasts shook.

"O Lord, if it be thy will, let this pass from me."

Almost as if in answer, a blast of lemon light exploded above her. She bowed under it. She sank involuntarily to her knees. A split second later, thunder came out of the ground. She steadied herself with a hand to the earth. The sudden stroke of lightning and thunder completely took her breath away. Chest caught, squeezed tight, she sucked and sucked for air.

At last, willing it, working the muscles of her belly, she managed to make a pinched wheezing sound, then take a tiny breath. It took a while before she could resume her shallow, rapid breathing.

Rain dropped from the skies like a bucket overturned on a hot-air register. It hit her like a blow with the flat of a hand. It pushed her down. The mosquitoes vanished.

She cowered under the storm. She tucked the parfleche under her. She sat on her heels, crouched. Huge drops fell on her back like little fat pancakes.

The rain was so cold. Water poured in around her neck and down inside her tunic. She could feel her nipples harden. Goose pimples swept over her like wild measles. Water trickled into her ears. Every now and then she had to hold her head to one side, first this way, then that way, to let the water run out. She shivered. She waited. She worried that the gray shape might jump her. Blood boomed in her temples.

"Enemies and much adversity ring me about."

Rain came down in varying sheets, drenching, with weight.

"A woman sitting upon a scarlet beast."

Another dazzling blast exploded above her. The ground under her shook like a rickety table. She fell on her side, hugging doubled knees to her chest.

"Though my sins be as scarlet, they shall be as white as snow."

Abruptly there was a sound of great rushing high above her. Rain began to hit around her like water being spilled out of a whirling pail.

"Baby Angela a year old and in my arms again. Please, yes."

The wind swooped down and began to move along the ground like a vast broom. It snapped the leather fringes on her sleeves. Rain hit her like the stickles of a scrubbing brush. It was cold, cold.

"Just some little child's body I could hug and hug and hug."

Warm tears mingled with cold rain on her cheeks.

"Something to love up."

The rain stopped. Presently the wind let up too. Thunder and lightning moved slowly into the northeast.

Wonderingly, she opened her eyes in the new silence. Stars were sparkling merrily above her.

She sprang to her feet, ready to fight off the gray shape.

The gray shape was gone.

"Mercy me."

~

She decided to risk going across open country in daylight. It shouldn't take her too long to go a half-dozen miles. And then she'd be safe.

Parfleche tucked under her arm, she hurried up the rest of the hogback. Near the sandy top the grass became prickly. Twice she had to step around prickly-pear cactus.

She hurried.

~

The sun coming out of the cloud bank on the eastern horizon was an eye being gouged out of a skull. Presently it bathed her in a light tinctured with blood.

Judith had to set herself to keep from plunging down a steep bluff. Her hand came up and lightly she held her throat.

Below her, green grass sloped down to a huge bed of exposed red rock, and there, down through the middle of it all, tumbled a full-size river. Water rumpled across zigzag cataracts, then dropped off a stiff fault in the red rock, then in a series of whirlpools chased itself down a tortuous channel. The wild, twisting waters reminded her of a pack of dogs milling about and snapping at their own and each other's tails. Farther on, the river flattened out and flowed serenely across broad shallows of pink sand.

It was a noble waterfall. Even in her extremity, Judith noted the wonderful primitive colors: grass as fresh as lettuce, rocks as red as just-butchered buffalo flesh, water the color of newly brewed green tea. And the year's first frost had turned the leaves of the ash to gold and the grapevines to wine. It was stunning to find such a lovely spot on the lonely prairies. Miles and miles of monotonously rolling flat land, and then suddenly this, a little green paradise beside a waterfall.

A faint mist hovered over the maeling waters at the foot of the falls. The little dancing mist took curious shapes in the light wind. Watching it, she understood why the Yanktons believed a guardian spirit, the Spirit of the Buffalo Woman, lived behind the braiding waters.

She looked upstream. And there they were. A dozen log cabins and sod dugouts surrounding a little cluster of stores, all built on a bench overlooking the cataracts and the falls. Sioux Falls. At last.

She angled down the face of the green bluff toward the village. She hurried, full of expectation, face radiant, heart beating with joy. She was home at last. Soon someone would spot her coming and then they would all come out on their doorsteps to greet her with happy, excited voices, glad for her that she had been saved. There would be white faces and the sweet sound of white tongues.

"Easily might I have been lost, but I was not, for Thou wast beside me. Amen."

She hurried toward the first cabin. Sumac burned scarlet all around the base of it. A gnarled scrub oak flung an oblong shadow on the grass in the yard. The garden beside the house was dug up and littered with dried-up potato stems. She passed through the neat white picket gate, went up a pink gravel path to the log stoop.

She was about to knock when, looking at the doorknob, she saw a heavy bronze lock hanging in the door hasp. The lock was snapped shut. There was no one home.

"Probably out visiting. I'll try the neighbors next door."

She hastened to the next brown cabin. This time she didn't have to go through the white gate to find the front door locked. She could see the closed lock from the street.

She took a few hesitant steps farther down the rutted pink street, and stopped. She stared down the line of dwellings, not wanting to believe, not being able to believe, what she then saw. All the cabins and dugouts, even the stores, were locked tight. Most of the windows were boarded up. The city fathers, everybody, had flown the nest. Deserted. That explained why there were no children or dogs out playing.

"And after all I've gone through."

She sat down on a red rock just off the street. Her pulse beat strangely, so trippingly swift she thought she was going to have heart failure.

Gradually she began to understand what had happened. Of course. Rollo, the mail carrier, would have brought the news to Sioux Falls that the Sioux were on the warpath. And, from the looks of things, with not a single house or store or barn burned down, the whites had all escaped alive. Thank God for their sake at least.

She wondered if one of the storekeepers might not have left a back door open. Methodically she made the rounds. She climbed over a pile of lumber, skirted a mound of stacked empty boxes, stepped across splashes of broken glass, pushed through a patch of head-high ragweed. Everything was locked tight.

She peered through the windows of one of the stores. The shelves and counters were bare. Everything that could be moved had been taken along. That explained why there were no wagons or runabouts around.

Dejected, she trudged back to the first cabin. She stood looking at it.

Need for sleep finally made up her mind. She would get in anyway. There was no point lying on the cold ground as long as there were empty beds around.

She picked up a stone the size of a clam and chinked it against the bronze lock a few times, hoping the spring would let go. But the lock was rusty, and stubborn.

She went around to the window on the south side, then to the window on the east side, to see if she could pry them up. Peering through the dusty glass she saw they were nailed to the sill. She flipped the stone in her hand a few times, weighing the idea of knocking our a windowpane with it. Glass was precious out on the frontier, a real luxury.

She stepped around to the front door again. She studied the door hinges. They were iron, also rusty, and very heavy. The pins in the hinges had heads at either end and couldn't be punched out.

She found herself a heavier stone and chunked it, hard, on the bronze lock. Teeth set, she hit the lock a good dozen times, each time harder than the last. Finally she gave it one big whack, on its flat side.

That did it. The lock clicked, let go, sprang open.

She gasped in relief, and rushed inside as if it were her own home she had at last managed to enter. She closed the door behind her, barring it.

The morning sun streamed through the east window, casting a square shaft of saffron light across a large single room. The light fell on an oak cupboard, revealing shelves full of glistening glasses. On the pantry shelves gleamed blue dishes and a handful of silverware. A black, well-polished cookstove stood near the chimney. A fallen mound of yellowish ashes lay between the andirons in the fireplace. A multicolored hook rug covered most of the puncheon floor.

In a far corner stood a four-poster with a creamy gray wolfskin for a bedspread. She went over and sat on the bed. She almost sank to her waist in a feather tick. She reached under the quilt and found actual sheets, clean and white. There was also a pillow with a white case. She nuzzled her face down in the clean white linens. The smell of lye soap was in them. She stroked the creamy wolfskin.

"Poor woman, whoever she was. After having brought these lovely things all the way out here somehow, prized precious possessions, then she had to run and leave them."

Searching through a wooden bin she found a few measures of flour. In a tin box she discovered a few leaves of black tea. And in a stone crock she found a slab of smoked bacon. Food. White food at last.

She found a tin bucket and got some water. She gathered up an armful of wood and soon had a fire going in the black stove. She put on a kettle of water for tea. She fried herself a mess of bacon, then a round dozen flapjacks. She ate, at first ravenously, then more sedately, chewing all thoroughly to make it go the further. The smoked bacon strips made up for the lack of molasses.

Fatigue moved in her like a fog, engulfing her mind until sight blurred. She undressed, hanging her doeskin tunic and her leggings over a three-legged stool. Naked, she rose on her toes, stretching to her full height, arms out. She held her breasts in the palms of her hands and fondled them. They seemed less full than usual, she thought. She'd been starving them the last while. Well, when she got back to St. Paul she would take care of that. She cast a glance at the sunken mound of her belly, then at the golden brush over her privates. Sighing, allowing herself one last luxurious stretch, she crept into bed. The sheets felt delicious to her skin. The sheets were like sweet ices on a warm tongue. She curled over on her right side. She could feel the creamy wolfskin bedspread slowly embracing her. The sound of the steadily pouring waterfall outdoors made her drowsy.

"A body rests all over when she lies down in a featherbed."

Even before she could straighten out her under leg, she was sound asleep.

~

The light in the cabin was different. She turned on her pillow and looked. A shadow slanted across the south window. It meant the sun was setting beyond the bluffs to the west. Evening shadows were rising out of the earth. A whole day of sunshine had gone by.

"What a sleep that was."

She had slept so long and so deep she only now began to realize how tired she had really been. Yes, and had been since Skywater.

That horror at Slaughter Slough had almost slipped from memory, so long ago it seemed now. And looking back at it, it actually did seem more nightmare than true fact. But the worst was she had taken to dreaming in Sioux, not American.

She scrambled out of bed and moved from window to window, cautiously looking for sign.

~

Stepping outside, she became aware of the river once more. The Big Sioux, sliding golden-green across the red cataracts in a thousand little separate brooks and then over the falls in one huge splash, was a wonder.

The sparkling water looked so inviting in the falling sunlight, she just had to have a quick dip. She skipped down a pink path. Close up, the roar of the waterfall hurt the ear. Humps of water-honed red rock fit the arch of her bare foot exactly. They reminded her of well-licked blocks of pink salt in Pa's cattleyard. She watched the flooding green tea tumble over and around and down the haphazard cataracts. She watched the sliding flood drop over the fault in the rock and splash in the maeling pool below.

She climbed to a shallow pool higher in the cataracts. The bottom of the pool was as smooth as the socket of a just-butchered buffalo's hipbone. She threw her wolfskin aside and knelt in the river and cupped herself a drink. The water was warm. She sat down in the pool. The water rose over her hips to her navel. She splashed herself, cupping water with both hand over the slopes of her pear breasts. She took down her golden hair and unbraided it and rinsed it from side to side in the gently riveting water. She turned over on her belly and doused her face. She lolled in the water from side to side with only the back of her head and her buttocks showing.

She sat up. She combed her hair with trailing fingers. She looked directly into the red eye of the setting sun and sang a song:

> *Aura Lea, Aura Lea,*
> *Maid of golden hair;*
> *Sunshine came along with thee,*
> *And swallows in the air.*

She gathered a handful of reddish sand lying in a curl of the stream and scrubbed herself. She wrung the water out of her hair.

When the sun set she snatched up her wolfskin and scampered naked up the path toward the brown cabin. She felt marvelously refreshed.

It was dark inside the cabin. She gathered more wood and lighted a fire in the hearth.

She decided not to put on her Indian garments again. Instead she searched through the closet to see if the woman of the house hadn't left some clothes behind. To her delight she found a shimmering purple petticoat and a green dress. On the floor beneath them stood a pair of black button shoes. She held the petticoat and the dress up to the light, then held them against her body. A perfect fit. She slipped them on, then sat down on the three-legged stool and slipped on the high black shoes.

She paraded up and down the cabin. The clothes weren't new. But they were civilized. What a joy to be wearing decent white things again. With all her soul she wished she were back, right then, in St. Paul and wearing her own clothes. How moldy they must smell by now in the closet behind the fireplace. With a yearning hotness, she wished she were standing, right then, in the little corner of their bedroom where she always dressed.

~

Well-groomed at last, feeling quite dressed up again, she set about making supper.

She found herself a gay blue apron and tied it on over the green dress. She made herself some unleavened bread with what was left of the flour. She found a jar of wild plums on the top shelf of the cabinet.

She recalled the potato patch in the garden outside. "There's bound to be a couple of spuds left in the ground. Digging with a fork you sometimes over-look a few."

It was as dark as Egypt out. Stooped over at the hips, she scratched through the crumbly humus. Halfway down the third row she found a root still tight in the ground. She probed along it and found four lovely fat tubers. One of them was almost as large as a piglet. Happily she gathered them up in her apron and hurried back into the cabin. She peeled the potatoes and dropped them in boil-ing water. She set the water for tea. In place of steak she cut herself several thick slabs of smoked bacon. She set the table for one, with her chair facing the fire-place. She hummed to herself. It was so good to be at home in a wooden house again.

She ate in a leisurely manner, pretending she was among fashionable people. She spooned her plum dessert in style.

As she sipped her tea, pinkie lifted, she spotted a newspaper in a magazine rack on the wall. Avid for news, she got it. It was an old copy of the St. Paul *Press,* a triweekly, dated September, 1861, at least a year old. As she read, it came to her that she had seen that issue before, beside her own fireplace in St. Paul. Rollo, the mail carrier, must have brought it down long ago on one of his trips to Sioux Falls. The newspaper was worn and much fingered, indicating it had been passed from hand to hand. There was an odor of old straw in its creases. She even read the editorials, which before she had ignored. Finally, finished reading, she put it back where she had found it.

Nostalgia set in. She wept when she thought of her dead Angela. Never, never would the two of them sit down to a good meal again. She wept when she thought of her soldier husband, Vince.

It was night and time to get on. She cleared off the table, washed the dishes, put things away just as she would have done in her own home.

She made the bed, tightening the sheets and fluffing out the pillow and straightening the quilt. She respread the wolfskin cover.

She sat down on the edge of the bed a moment to catch her breath. What a change the furnishings of a white home were compared to those of a tepee. She leaned down to take a last sniff of the pillow. The smell of soap in it was as pre-cious as the aroma of any perfume she'd ever known. The woman of the house was a good housekeeper.

She let her hand trail across the creamy gray wolfskin cover. She settled back against the headboard.

She jerked awake. Her heart beat in her chest like a pounding fist. Red inch-worms galloped across the line of her vision.

She had been dreaming of husband Vince. She had just dodged out of his reaching arms, running to her corner in their bedroom, with Vince following close on her heels. He was angry with her, demanding his rights as a husband. "It is your duty to submit," he said. "It is God's will that you be the good wife."

He reached for her throat with both hands, intending to shake some sense into her. Surprisingly she found his hands warm. She had hoped they would be cold and clammy so she could hate his touch.

She shuddered when she thought of the dream again. The aftereffect of it was like too much smoke in the nose. And the worst of it was that Vince's American tongue had sounded strange to her Sioux ears.

Warmth touched her hand. Looking at where her hand lay on the pillow, she saw why she had dreamed of a warm touch. The sun was just up, and from where it came in through the east window, it had caught her precisely across the throat and the hand.

Her glance went back to the window. What? The sun coming up? It had only gone down a bit ago.

"Stars alive, I've slept around the clock."

It was hard to believe. But there the sun was, rising in the east.

"I better skedaddle. I don't like the idea of traveling in the daytime but I can't stay here forever either. I'll just have to be doubly cautious, is all."

She jumped to her feet. She took off the other woman's clothes, putting them neatly away in the clothes closet, and slipped into her buckskins again. Indian clothes were best for roughing it. She rebraided her hair and pinned it up in a rope around her head.

She snapped off two fringes from her sleeve for the two days idled away in Sioux Falls, and stored them carefully in her parfleche.

$\sim$

Judith stuck close to the Big Sioux River. Somewhere along the line she was bound to come across Rollo the mail carrier's tracks.

Noble hills, like great loaves of brown bread, lay one behind the other on her left. She was careful to make her way along the bottoms, staying to the underbrush as much as possible. When the river ran naked of trees, she walked along the water's very edge, staying well below the crumbling black bank.

She learned to take a quick jerking look around to all sides, furtive, like that of any savage in the wilds.

It was straight up noon when she came to where the Big Sioux angled south. The time had come for her to strike out across the open country, northeast toward Skywater and New Ulm. She took a last drink of water, washed her hands and face, then started up the side of the steep bluff.

A soft wind greeted her when she topped the rise. It breathed out of the east, damp on her cheek. Ahead lay a prairie the color of wolfskin.

As she stood looking, little white mushroom scuds appeared in the sky.

Presently, breath caught, she headed out across the flat land.

The white scuds began to build up into cumulus clouds immediately ahead of her. She watched the clouds merge into towers of cream and gold.

She walked.

The undersides of the highest cloud towers turned black, and shafts of purple shadows began to trail to earth. The clouds moved with slow, massive silence ahead of her into the northeast.

She walked.

The sun shone hot on her neck and back. She stepped through undulating sweeps of gray-green grass. She could feel the soles of her moccasins thinning and wearing through.

She had tramped for perhaps two hours when she came upon a patch of bare, sandy ground. Across the middle of it, like a series of well-wrought brush strokes on yellow canvas, lay innumerable pairs of buggy tracks. And down the middle of each of the paired tracks lay the prints of horseshoes. All of the tracks were old.

Her face lighted up. Rollo's trail at last. Now all she had to do was follow it and she would eventually arrive at New Ulm.

She walked.

Rollo's trail dipped down to the creek and crossed a red gravel ford. Two red rocks straddled the stream like the portals of a gate to a city. The two rocks, once a single rock, had been split down the middle and parted just enough to let the stream through.

She was about to start down the slope, when she spied the purple flowers of wild onions. Beside them grew a tangle of wild roses. She pulled up a dozen of the pencil-slim onions and gathered a handful of rose hips, then sat down on thick grass to eat them. She would save the strips of bacon in the parfleche for supper.

She ate slowly, chewing thoroughly. The wild onions were gently sweet, while the rose hips had the taste of citron. She wondered if the rose hips wouldn't go good in a fruitcake.

She lay back in the grass a moment. She liked the warm spot in the lee of the rosebushes. On the slow wind came the smell of freshly fallen sweet rain. Lightning as swift as fireflies flew through the high escarpment of clouds.

She fell asleep.

A whispering in her ear awoke her.

She looked up into the blue sky. Again she had dreamed of Scarlet Plume. This time Scarlet Plume had led her back across the stepping-stones and up a path toward a white tepee. He whispered urgently to her in the pure Yankton Sioux tongue and she replied in kind. Ahead lay a horror of some sort. The dream left her feeling depressed.

Well, it was hardly surprising. She'd often found herself thinking about Scarlet Plume. Too often. And thoughts bred dreams. What a fool she'd been to let her mind dwell on him at all. He was red; she was white. He was a Stone Age savage; she was a civilized American. Yes. Yes. Therefore it was plainly sin to think of him. He was part of a past she had to forget. Gritting her teeth, determined to do the right thing from then on, she sprang to her feet.

~

She had gone about a mile, when on one of her quick, furtive looks around to all sides, she sensed as much as spotted something following her. It was gray, and large, and it kept to the bushes. A wolf had picked up her trail.

Gasping, trembling, yet somehow managing to find it in herself to be resolute, she turned to face it. Her heart began to beat violently, her knees turned to mush.

The gray something stopped dead still at the edge of a clump of wild roses. As she watched, the gray something gradually vanished from sight. It reminded her of gray mist slimming away under a hot sun. Perhaps it wasn't a wolf after all.

She waited to see if it would reappear out of the wild roses. It didn't. She moved her head slowly from side to side to make sure it wasn't spots before her eyes. It wasn't. All the while the roaring flood in Split Rock Creek kept rising.

Her thoughts were like squirrels with their tails tied together and straining to go in all directions at once. If only she hadn't come to Skywater to visit her sister Theodosia. None of this would then have come to pass. And Angela would have been alive. "Good night, Mama." Those little words, how sweet they were. They were sweeter even than the doxology of the Christian Church.

A meadowlark lighted on a little ash. The top of the little ash had been cropped off by passing buffalo. The meadowlark sang, "I am the bird of fidelity and this I know for a certainty. Relief is near!"

She glanced at the wild roses again. Still no sign of anything gray moving in them.

She looked ahead. The little valley in that direction was bare of all growth. She decided that would be the test. If something really was following her it would have to cross that open space.

She had gone about a mile, when sure enough, there it was crossing the open space. The creature was gray, as she'd first thought, with a touch of cream over the shoulders where the wind ruffed the hair. And it was big.

She cried out, and broke into a stumbling run. As she ran she kept looking back over her shoulder.

After a bit it seemed to her that the creature moved oddly for a wolf. It had more the heavy-footed gait of a bear than the easy lope of a wolf. Somewhat clumsy. Crude even, at times.

The little valley changed. Soft feminine knolls gave way to rocky ground, then to towering palisades of red rock. The palisades took on bizarre forms: blockhouses without windows, foundered arks, fallen pulpits. The sudsing flood whirlpooled down swinging turns. The water took on a winy color from the purplish rock and red gravel. It tumbled along with a low sullen roar.

The meadowlark followed her. It called from a low rock. Its yellow-streaked gray blended perfectly with lichen-covered rock. "I am the bird of fidelity and this I know for a certainty. Relief is near!"

She looked over her shoulder to see if the great wolf still followed her. It did. It seemed to be picking its way, though, with some care across the rough rocks. And it had fallen behind some.

She took hope at that. She was gaining on it. The wolf probably had a sore paw. Maybe she could lose it in the coming darkness.

She ran.

Wild elders appeared on high land. The sun was about to set, and the elders struck dark-purple shadows across the slender valley. The shadows offered refuge.

She glanced back. The gray shape was gone.

She stopped, catching a hand to her throat, suddenly panting. The gray shape had fallen behind or she had outrun it.

When she got her breath back she hurried on.

The valley deepened into a considerable canyon. The riverbanks became red cliffs. Wild cedars grew dark green on the heights and in clumps as thick as little farm groves. She had to pick her way around deep side gulches. The gullies on her side ran bank full. It meant the cloudburst had dropped mostly on the right side of Split Rock Creek.

The sun set in a sky as opaque as a faded robin egg. It cut a hole into the horizon, slipped into it, disappeared. Bland yellow light lingered for a time, then gradually changed to the color of fall grass.

On one of her quick, furtive looks around she saw it. The gray shape was back. It was directly west of her on a rise of land, not more than a hundred yards away.

All of a flutter, suddenly gone almost crazy, she looked wildly around for a place to hide.

The promontory she stood on was part of where the Split Rock canyon made a curving turn to the left. The promontory ended in an abrupt cliff. The cloudburst boiled some hundred feet straight below. No escape that way.

At the foot of one of the wild cedars along the edge, Judith spied a split in the earth. The rock under the mantle of earth had cracked apart, forming an opening. It resembled an irregularly smiling mouth, gums showing. It shot through her mind that this might be an entrance to a cave. If it was, she was safe. Parfleche in hand, she quickly sat down on the edge of the lip, swung her feet into the opening, then let herself down.

Her hands slipped on the wet red edge. Down she dropped. Her head banged against a rock wall. All light vanished.

A tear fell on her cheek. Again. Again.

Gradually she came to. She rose out of darkness, only to find she was still lying in darkness.

Something dropped on her cheek again. It was cold, so it couldn't be tears. It had to be water dripping from somewhere above her. She moved slightly to avoid the drops.

She stared upward, straining, trying to make out where she was. She saw stars, one, two, three, four. She could just vaguely make out a frost-edged patch of black sky. The patch was shaped like a partly opened mouth. Then she knew where she was. Late at dusk she had tried to escape a gray wolf by dropping into a crack in the earth, and had come tumbling down into this place, cracking her head against a rock.

She ran her hands over her body. Nothing seemed broken. Everything felt all right.

She was surprised to find herself lying flat on her back. Nurses in a hospital couldn't have done a better job of putting her to bed. She had been quite lucky after all. It was a miracle she wasn't lying all of a tangle with a broken neck.

She ran a hand under her body and found a matting of cedar twigs, and under that a layer of soft dirt. She could smell the spicy aroma of the twigs. Only in one spot was there a hard lump, under her shoulder. She moved slightly. There. Comfortable again.

The sound of the rushing flood below seemed to have softened some. Most of the cloudburst had probably passed by. In the morning she could cross the creek and then head east to pick up the mail carrier's buggy trail again.

She stared up at the four stars in the mouth of the cave. She could imagine, almost see, the gray wolf lying stretched out on the grass on the edge of the lip, head on its paws, patiently waiting for her to emerge. The wolf would lie as still as a lichen-covered stone. Only its eyes and nostrils would look alive.

She shuddered. "How could I have been such an utter fool as to let myself get into such an awful mess? All because of a silly notion, thinking I had to visit my sister once."

Her buckskin clothes clung warmly to her skin. With both hands she slowly stroked her pear breasts upward. Fleetingly her lips shaped themselves to receive a kiss.

The stars moved.

It occurred to her that for once she had not dreamed of red him. Nor had she dreamed in the Sioux tongue. That was because she had lain unconscious, not asleep.

"I've just got to get him out of my mind. Burn out all memory of him."

In her mind's eye she saw him again as he danced up the buffalo near the Blue Mounds. All man. Magnificent. Shockingly a stud. And plainly a sin.

She slept.

She awoke ravenous. Soft light dreamed down through the mouth of the cave. A clean blue sky blossomed high above.

She remembered there were still a few strips of bacon left in her parfleche. She recalled having the parfleche in hand when she let herself down into the mouth of the cave. Ah, there it was. Of all things. Without knowing it she had been using it as a pillow. No wonder her head had felt comfortable all night. For good luck, she decided to save one strip of bacon for later in the day. "It'll go good with broiled gopher." She smiled wryly to herself.

She jerked off a fringe and tucked it away in the parfleche to mark the passing of another day. She was pleased to find herself calm.

She glanced up every now and then to see if the gray wolf was spying on her over the edge of the crack. Pretty soon the wolf would get tired of waiting for her to come out and then there would be an awful time. He would come down after her.

She decided she had better have some kind of weapon handy. Yet search around as she might, she found nothing, no stick or branch, not even a loose stone.

She recalled the lump under her shoulder in the night. She scratched into the mat of cedar twigs and after a moment unearthed it. A bone. She held it up. It had the look of a human thighbone. It would make a considerable weapon.

Something drew on her eyes to look into the shadow of a water-honed recess.

"Eii! No wonder that was a human bone!"

A chalk-white skeleton sat looking straight at her. There was a wild grin on its face. Fragments of a buckskin shirt still clung to its shoulders and forearms. A war club lay in its lap and war feathers hung adraggle from the base of its skull. Some tribe long ago had buried a beloved chief in the cave with full tribal honors.

"Yii! Dear Lord!"

She looked quickly into each of the dark recesses around her. Thank God. There weren't any other skeletons quietly staring at her.

The cave wasn't large, about as big as a hall in an ordinary house, with several short cul-de-sacs to the right and left. The walls of the cave were flesh red and as smooth as the ventricles of a heart. She could not for the life of her imagine how the walls of the cave could have been formed to be so snake smooth.

"Unless it was scoured by an ocean of grit. Millenniums of it."

She became aware of another source of light behind her. It came from a curving passage. Perhaps it was a second entrance to the cave. It had to be.

"Because this is no place for a Christian."

Scrambling to her feet, she decided to explore it. The passage was narrow, and low, and she had to go on hands and knees to get through it. Once she almost got stuck, but by some adroit wriggling, and keeping calm, she made it. Another time she had to cross a tiny running spring. She stopped for a cool, refreshing drink.

Presently she came out on a ledge. Far below, at the foot of a sheer red cliff, water boiled in a series of reversing whirlpools. Looking across at the sandbar on the other side of the creek, she saw that the flash flood had subsided considerably at that.

With the wolf still waiting for her to emerge above, she wondered if she couldn't work her way down the sheer cliff, find handholds and toeholds in its face somehow, and after that swim for it and land on the sandbar. The other side of the canyon wasn't very steep and she saw she could easily climb it. With luck she could be across and gone before the big wolf became aware of what had happened.

Another passage loomed up on her right. It resembled a huge artery. It occurred to her the passage might lead to yet another outlet, lower down and nearer the level of the creek bed. She decided to try it.

The new passage was pitch dark for a dozen feet, then opened out on a narrow, deep cut. The cut led steeply down toward the boiling creek. Though the cut was but a yard wide, enough sunlight fell into it to encourage a few chokecherry shrubs. Near the bottom dangled a thick grapevine. Here was her chance.

She descended the thin cut with care. Her toes felt the cold of the damp rock through her moccasins. She grabbed at shrubs, sharp projections, narrow cracks for handholds and toeholds.

About halfway, the cut became so steep she had to back down. She maneuvered carefully. She strapped the parfleche around her belly under her doeskin. She slid over a breast of rock. With her toes, blindly, she reached for a red ledge. But stretch as she might, she couldn't quite make it.

She decided to let herself drop. But the red ledge wasn't quite what she had expected it to be. The flat of her moccasins hit the edge of a sloping wet surface and slid off. She lost her balance, began to topple backward. A scream rose in her throat. Remembering the wolf above, at the last second, she gulped the scream back.

She was going to go. Knowing she would hit rock below if she fell straight down, she gave herself a backward kick with both feet, like an expert diver pushing away from a springboard. Her body arched out. As she began her plunge, she sucked in a deep breath and held it. She made a complete somersault in free fall before sudsing water abruptly appeared beneath her nose. She slipped in splashless, a falling human arrow.

She hit water-honed rock bottom with her hands, lightly. The driving stream tipped her, began to carry her off. She righted, got her head up, and opened the surface above. She changed air in one quick breath. She bobbed along. An underwater rock hit her hip a glancing blow.

A whirlpool sucked at her. Before she could do anything about it, the whirlpool began to swing her around in a circle. It reminded her of a merry-go-round she had once ridden as a kid at a carnival. A snort broke from her. This was one merry-go-round ride she didn't want, even if there was no charge for the ride. Furiously she flailed her arms and kicked her legs. But she couldn't quite work free of its grip. She made a complete circle a half-dozen times. It was obscene the way it held onto her, a passionate whirlpool. A short gray log bobbed around and around exactly across from her. She wished she could latch onto it so she could rest a moment and catch her breath. She swam for all she was worth. Still she couldn't escape the whirlpool's tremendous sucking action. Her furious paddling only served to keep her from being drawn immediately into the center of the twisting pit. She thought she could hear, over the splashing gallop of the waves, a weird whining ipping sound. The sound of the centering suction terrified her. The log across from her slowly began to slide into the depth of the twisting pit. It went around faster and faster. On one of its swifter turns the gray log shot past her. It took one more turn, upended, held a moment, ulp! went down. Then she truly was terrified. She flailed and flailed. Her soft doeskins became completely saturated with water. They dragged on her arms and legs like sheets of syrup. "Dear Lord, have mercy." It was like being caught in some awful nightmare. Dark arms from the deeps had grabbed hold of her and were trying to drag her down. And she was going down. She flailed and flailed. Eii! now there was no doubt of it. Like the log she too began to go around faster and faster as he inexorably neared the whistling center of the whirlpool. Why, really! It was as if she were drowning in one of her own nightmares. Frantic, she wondered how she was to wake herself if she wasn't already awake. Somehow she had to get herself out of this mesmeric gyrating whirlpool. "God!" She fought, knowing she was doomed. What a terrible thing it was to have a true-to-life whirlpool turn into a desperate nightmare. "Yii!"

She was hit an awful thump from below smack in the belly. Akk. She was hit so hard she had to let go the swimming and clutch her stomach. Her hands hit a heavy round object, fastened onto it. It was the gray log. After being sucked to the bottom, it had escaped the whirlpool, shot out from under and come thrusting to the surface. The log pushed her clear of the whirlpool, outside the ring of it. It had hit her so hard it almost knocked her out of breath. She groaned. She worked for breath. She groaned. She went under. She rose to the surface. She flailed her arms and legs. She went under. She rose. She went under. Then her chest hit hard-packed gravel. She got both hands under her, then her feet, and to her surprise found she could stand up. She was in water only up to her hips. She had made it to the other side.

She staggered to shore. She managed to stumble up the slow slope of the bank. She turned behind a big red rock, and, out of sight of the wolf, collapsed.

She lay gasping for breath. Her fingers worked spasmodically, digging eight little grooves in the red gravel.

She vomited. Her innards seemed to want to get out of her all at the same time. The vomiting seemed to have a definite mind of its own and shook her like a wolf might shake a cottontail by the neck. Bits of chewed bacon and blood gushed from her.

"Oh, misery me."

She rolled over to get out of her own scarlet vomit.

She lay a long time. She rested. Slowly the crazy jumping of her heart quieted.

She spoke aloud her mind, in outrage. "Of what earthly good is all this wilderness anyway? God must have had a mad on when he made it. Terrible. Crazy. Some of these little valleys might make a cozy location for a town, all right, like Sioux Falls, like here. But for the rest, it's all too crazy lonesome to be good for anything decent and civilized. No boundaries. No fences. No sheltering little hills. Just open to all sides to anything and everything that was to come along. Wolves. Bears. Pumas. I wouldn't take it as a gift even if they were to pay me. I say, this wild country belonged to the Indian, it fit the Indian, the Indian liked it, so let the Indian keep it. Amen."

~

She had to tear off four more fringes from the sleeve of her tunic before she found the mail carrier's trail again. She found the trail at the foot of the Blue Mounds, between the base of the red cliffs and the River Of The Rock, buggy ruts and horse tracks cutting across a short stretch of hard gravel.

She fell to the ground and kissed the tracks. Thank God at last, at last. Ahead lay Fort Ridgely and New Ulm. Then St. Paul.

She had got lost once during those four days. She had to turn south to get around a huge swamp, and when later she swung north again she began to go around in a circle. A morning sun after a cloudy night got her on course once more. Mosquitoes rose from the swamp so thick she breathed them in with every breath. Their stinging was ferocious. To keep from getting all bit up, she made a hood out of her parfleche to cover her head and neck. To see where she was going she had to take a quick peek now and then. She couldn't remember Indians complaining about mosquitoes. She wondered if maybe the Indian way of life, sitting half-smoked all day long in a fumid tepee, accounted for it. There were also terrific dews at night, so heavy that water gushed from her moccasins at every step. The humidity was so heavy she could drink dew by drawing blades of grass through her lips. All she had to eat was that last strip of bacon, and rose hips and grape leaves. She remembered Pa saying his cattle always did well on grape leaves.

She rolled over on her back. Out of the corner of her eye she could see the crest of the Blue Mounds high above her. In what now seemed a long, long time ago she remembered how she had run across the top to help the Yanktons drive buffalo over the Jump. A light south wind ruffled the tan leaves of the oaks at the foot of Buffalo Jump. Scent of drying grass hung sweet and fermentive on the breeze.

Meat. She needed meat. Any kind of meat. She was starved. She was so exhausted she could taste dust. A juicy mouse, raw, would be a treat. A real delight.

She was empty of feelings. What was grief again? Angela, Theodosia—had there actually been such people? She stirred on the hard gravel. It crunched softly under her.

"No matter how I lay myself my bones still burn." She rolled over on her belly.

Directly in front of her, on a small stone the size of an egg, stood a grasshopper flexing its big rear legs. It twigged its nose, sideways, twice. A spit of tobacco juice dripped from its green behind.

Her eyes fixed on the flexing legs. She thought she could detect the workings of muscles in them. Meat. In her gaunted mind the muscles of the grasshopper loomed large. Meat's meat.

Cautiously she moved up a hand, got herself set to strike. She would make a snatch at it, strike as swift as the flick of a frog's tongue. She took a slow, soft breath; and snapped at it. Miracle. She caught it between thumb and forefinger. She was careful not to squash it. It struggled. Its straining reminded her of a safety pin trying to unsnap itself. She gave it a hot, intent look, then downed it in a single gulp. She didn't care to taste it. She just wanted the muscles, the meat.

She noticed green flies buzzing around her. Slowly she sat up. The green flies seemed to be interested in her legs. Looking down, she realized for the first time that she was bleeding. The dipping ripgut grass she had walked through that morning had cut her toes and shins to the bone. Both her moccasins and her leggings had long ago worn away. She had patched one worn pair of moccasins with the other worn pair, yet even the combined pair had been threshed to shreds. The leggings hung in tatters from her knees.

"Put an end to it." Sight of blood gave her an idea. Carefully she selected a rough-edged blade of grass, and sawing it back and forth, managed to open a vein in her arm. She drank a little of her own blood to blunt her hunger. It startled her that blood should taste salty.

When she lay down again she was astonished to see an eagle hovering above her. The eagle lay on the breeze like a pair of brown drapes wavering on a rising column of furnace heat. Its snaky golden-brown head hung down, a brown eye fixed piercingly on her. Her lying down had startled the eagle, causing it to mount the air a few feet. It had been about to strike.

It was the green flies. The eagle thought her carrion. Pa had often remarked that where you find green flies, there you find buzzards.

A snarl gathered in her throat. Her feet and hands came up like a cat's, clawing the air. She showed her teeth, ferocious.

The eagle gave her a startled eye, shook its golden head, then with huge flaps of its paired drapes carried itself off toward the heights of the Blue Mounds. A few moments later it lighted on a red crag. It fluffed its wing feathers, settled down to watch her. It could wait.

She breathed shallow. She waited for the meat of the grasshopper and her own blood to restore her strength.

She napped. She dreamed of a fat, perky gopher. The gopher stood erect beside the entrance of its lair. It whistled at her. Then it spoke to her. "You want me? Guess again." And down the hole it plunged, in.

Something brushed against her. She awoke. Too tired to turn her head, she looked sidewise.

Snakes. Families of them. Hundreds of them. Papa snakes and bigger mama snakes. Baby snakes of all sizes. All had diamond markings and a green-brown hue. Rattlesnakes.

Too spent to be frightened, she watched the wrigglers crawl around and over each other. Some were six feet long; some only two feet. The rattles on their tails were silent. They quivered scarlet tongues at each other as if exchanging lickerish bits of snake gossip. There was an odd air of amiability about them. It took her a while to see this. Her idea had always been that a snake was naturally surly and went around being dangerous most of the time. She watched. Yes, there was no doubt of it, these snakes were having a party, sporting in the sun on warm gravel. They were playing tag with each other. As one family left, another family replaced it. They all seemed to be coming from the river and heading for the stone heights above. Their company was agreeable. She even thought she could understand, a little, why Eve had let herself be beguiled by a snake in the Garden of Eden.

She breathed shallow.

The presence of the snakes explained something to her. With them around, it was hardly a wonder she hadn't seen any gophers or mice the last while. In filmy reverie, smiling bemused to herself, she wondered how all those snakes could have missed that fat gopher in her dream.

She itched at the edges of her hairline. It was time to go on. She staggered to her feet.

Careful of where she walked amongst the snakes, she followed Rollo's trail across the patch of gravel and then through more deep ripgrass.

The eagle saw her go. It fluffed its wings in disgust; then, falling from its perch, it lifted and disappeared into the northern skies.

Her toes and shins bled again. She stopped. She stared at the oozing scarlet. She would have to do something about it.

She emptied her parfleche. To her astonishment she found four strips of dried meat neatly tucked in one corner.

She stared at the dried jerky. How in God's name had it got into her parfleche? She couldn't for the life of her recall having packed the jerky when she escaped the Yanktons. And she certainly hadn't taken it from that cabin in Sioux Falls. She couldn't understand it. Couldn't. Bible times were surely past. Another Elijah miracle was hardly likely. "And the barrel of meal wasted not, neither did the cruse of oil fail."

Well, there the jerky was and she was hungry. She should just simply accept it and eat it without worrying about where it came from.

"So many outlandish things have happened to me lately it really shouldn't surprise me though. Live long enough and a miracle is bound to happen to you sometime."

After a little chewing the jerky became quite savory. The four strips worked down to a little ball of tough tissue. She chewed and chewed the little ball. It retained its savor. It reminded her of one of her childhood dreams, that she could buy a piece of gum that would never lose its sweetness no matter how much she chewed it.

She stumbled down to the edge of the River Of The Rock, between some golden ash, and cupped herself a long drink to wash it down. She washed her face and hands and laved her cut, bleeding feet. The tough, dry jerky and the tepid water restored her.

Up on the riverbank gleamed a flat red rock. It gave her an idea. She spread her parfleche out on it and with a sharpedged stone pounded and cut the parfleche in half. With a pointed stick she punched holes along the edges. She took the fringes she had saved, one for each day since her escape, and fashioned crude shoes for her raw feet. It was clumsy footwear but it would do. As for the fringes she had saved so far, well, what was the use of counting the passing days? She would get to St. Paul when she got there.

She walked on, light-headed.

She came upon a meadow where the grass had been cropped short by passing buffalo. Patches of sunflowers nodded in the soft wind. She loved the flowing wash of the sunned petals. Her brain hazed over with gold. She took one of the riper flowers and ate it. It was all a dream.

"Cannibal at last."

Her hair itched. She was too tired to scratch the itching.

She could feel sweat gather between her shoulder blades. It trickled down her spine and then down along the inside of her legs. Splotches of sweat showed in the armpits of her weathered tunic.

She walked.

Within the hour the gnawing in her belly was back. It came with a scalding thirst in the throat. She drank more water from the warm river. It didn't help. She kneaded the gnawing with her knuckles. She was so gaunt she could feel the buttony knob of her navel through her leather tunic. It slid around under her knuckles like a fifty-cent piece lost in the lining of a coat.

Once, looking down, she was surprised to find herself trudging along pigeon-toed through the prairie grass. It was the way Smoky Day walked. And Tinkling. And all the Yankton women. It was the manner of all women with heavy burdens to bear. She recalled the days when she used to walk with her toes pointed out a little. As in a fresh tintype she could see herself stepping briskly along in black kid button shoes down a boardwalk in St. Paul.

She watched herself walk. Yes. She now definitely walked different. Well, why not. It seemed the sensible way to walk, especially if one was weak. Walking with the toes turned in helped a body keep one's balance. Also, it enabled one to take full advantage of the length of the foot. Walking mile after mile, every inch counted.

She followed the river north. The ridge of the Blue Mounds fell away behind her. Trees became fewer. Except where beavers had built dams, the river ran shallow. She crossed a ford. She gave herself another long drink. She groomed her hair in the mirroring surface, retightening the rope of gold braids about her head.

A meadowlark sang from a nodding sunflower. "I am the bird of fidelity and this I know for a certainty. Relief is near!"

Memory of the gray shape came to her. She hadn't seen it since Split Rock Creek. Casually she looked around to see if it might not have returned. It hadn't.

The itching along her hairline became so fiendish she finally just had to dig into it with her fingernails. A scab, something, caught under a fingernail. It felt like something caught between one's teeth. The something scab seemed to move. She held it close up. Yes, it moved. A louse. Her blue eyes widened. She looked again to make doubly sure. Yes, all its little legs were waving madly at her. Lice had awakened in her hair. The Yanktons had been lousy after all, despite Smoky Day's assurances they were a clean people. Judith cracked the louse carefully between her thumbnails.

She found more lice, using her fingernails as a rake. She killed them too. She recalled having seen Sunflower searching through her husband, Pounce's, hair for lice. When Sunflower found some she carefully bit into them, then ate them. A case of where the eaten turned on the eater.

She trudged on, one big toe after another.

The sun slowly eyed itself down the sky.

A pinkish-brown bird, a ruffed grouse, a hen, fluttered in the grass ahead of her. It flapped along as though one of its wings were broken, crying piteously.

It took Judith a moment to understand it was a ruse. The ruffed grouse was a mother and to protect her chicks she was trying to draw attention to herself.

Tender fowl. Meat. Judith's tongue worked. Somewhere underfoot sat hidden a half-dozen wild pullets. She loved pullets. Mmm. A single suck on a well-done pullet leg and the meat just fell off in one's mouth.

She searched the wind-woven grass very carefully. The pullets had to be somewhere around.

The mother became desperate. She put on an even more elaborate act of being hurt.

Judith decided the wild pullets were immediately underfoot. She knelt. She lifted first one swatch of gray-green grass, then another.

A fingertip touched a prickly fallen rose. Judith sucked at the fingertip, then nipped out a thorn with her nails.

Ah, there they were. Cleverly hidden under a burdock. All six were sitting in a row, very much like six Sioux children sitting in a Bible class, brown eyes bright, waiting for the magic word. Mmm, they looked good. Broiled over a stick fire out in the open, they would be just wonderful. The second on the right was the fattest.

She set herself. Then she pounced. She caught the one she wanted, the second on the right. The grouse pullet squealed. It struggled desperately. The other five pullets immediately fluttered up, and on a cry from the mother, dove into the grass a dozen feet away, disappearing in perfect camouflage. The mother next flew straight for Judith, bristling, beak foremost. The mother came at her with such fury Judith had to throw up an arm to protect her eyes. The mother with her pecking beak and snapping wingtips and scratching toes seemed to be everywhere at once. Judith finally had to put up both arms, and in so doing involuntarily let go of the chick. On that the attack ceased, and by the time Judith's eyes cleared, mother and chick had also vanished in perfect camouflage.

Judith sighed. "Well, I can't say as I really blame her. Poor creature."

Judith tramped on. Presently the mail carrier's trail left the River Of The Rock and went northeast up a creek valley.

Two days later, Judith came upon fresh moccasin tracks. She spotted them as she knelt for a drink in a sandy place along the creek. The moccasin tracks were clearly fresh and they belonged to a grown man. The man's moccasins had been patched and the mark of the seam was the first to fill with water seeping up from below.

Judith snapped a quick jerking look around, so quick her neck cracked. No one was in sight.

Yet the tracks were fresh. Whoever it was had seen her coming and had quickly hidden himself. It was probably some red brute from Mad Bear's band and playfully biding his time to scalp her.

Well, let him scalp her. She was too tired to care. She was ready for the hereafter, as ready as she ever would be.

She knelt. Nose tip touching running water, she sipped herself a slow drink.

As she rose to her feet, she spotted a plum pit lying off to one side of the moccasin tracks. The pit was fresh, still wet. Someone had spit it out only moments before.

Plums? Again she looked around to all sides, this time slowly. There were no plum trees in the little creek valley that she could see. And wasn't it a bit late in the season for plums? In fact, too late. What was going on?

She looked down at the fresh moccasin prints again. In a vague way, forlornly, she wished she were strong again, as she was in the days when she'd helped her father make hay. Let her have that strength again and she would take a club to the Indian and kill him. Yes. Kill him. And, now that she thought of it, maybe even eat him. It certainly was an idea.

In her mind she could see herself skulking after the Indian. If he were fat, all the better. She would overtake him from the rear and bash his head in. She would have one good hearty meal at last. Broil one of his big muscular arms and slowly gnaw away on it, a hand to either end of the bone. Mmm. Good. People were fools not to eat human flesh when they were starving to death. It had to be the best meat, no? since the human being was the true end of creation. The best for the best. Yes. Her mouth watered. Nothing like a well-broiled human arm. Savor it with some sweet wild onion, sprinkle on a little ground-up rose hips, and it would make quite a delicacy.

She blinked. She caught herself standing crouched, ready to pounce, hand up as though about to strike with a club.

A most unhappy thought came to her. She stood very still, considering it, full of patience for herself. Yes. Yes. It was probably true. She knew now. She was slowly losing her mind.

She wavered on. She hardly realized she moved.

The creek ran quietly through seas of deep bluejoint. Sometimes the effect of the wind streaming through the top of the head-high grass was like a pack of bushy-tailed dogs chasing across a meadow. The sides of the valley gradually deepened. Naturally terraced bluffs and ribboned cliffs appeared. Scars of old Indian villages were visible on some of the hills, ocher spots where the green flesh was worn away. One of the bluffs, on which the sun shone just right, had the look of a freshly baked loaf of bread shiny with melted butter. There were plover everywhere and the calls of the curlew were maddening.

Ahead of her, on a slight rise of ground where a side stream came in from the north, a body lay prone in the air bout a dozen feet above ground.

She stopped dead in her tracks. She was at last, truly, seeing things. She had come to the end of her rope. Her brain had snapped.

She fastened all of her attention on it. Her eyes went over the apparition piece by piece. She stood slightly humped over, trying to ride out the blow, the shock, of knowing she had gone insane.

At last, staring hotly, she saw it wasn't an apparition after all, that it was actually an Indian wrapped in a buffalo robe. The Indian lay on some kind of platform. Four posts supported it.

It was an Indian burial out on the plains. An honored chief of some sort lay on a scaffold.

She approached it warily, looking up at it. She wondered if relatives had left food behind to sustain the chief on his long journey down the spirit road. She hoped so. She could use the food better than a dead body could.

Then she began to wonder how fresh the body was. If it was only a day or so old, she could still have herself that broiled arm after all.

She stood under it. She shook the posts supporting it. A gourd made a soft belling noise. She shook the scaffold again. A piece of buffalo fur slipped open on one side, and out rolled a white skull. The skull fell with a light thump at her feet.

She looked at the weathered skull with regret. No meat there.

A voice suddenly sounded behind her, a familiar voice. "I see that the white woman feels sad. I want to shake hands with her. That is all I have to say."

Judith turned slowly, not wanting to see what she knew she was going to see.

Scarlet Plume. He was holding out a hand to her. There was a warm, grave smile on his wide, dark face. The usual yellow dot inside the blue circle lay on his left cheekbone.

She also saw something else. It made her wild inside. He was wearing a creamy wolfskin over his shoulders, the same wolfskin she had left behind in the brown cabin in Sioux Falls. Numbly she realized he had been following her all along. He was the gray shape that had been haunting her.

SECTION THREE

Siouxland
Themes

*I am sure that over half of my work will tie back to my "boy-
hood heaven and hell." It is land adjoining the Sioux River
. . . I've peopled it with many towns, mostly fictions (though
real) and people, and situations, and tragedies.*

*I call it "Siouxland and environs" because some of my peo-
ple wander off, but they take what Siouxland is to wherever they go.*

*Who are the ones that stopped? Did they choose the place,
or did the place choose them? If you look carefully, only
the people stay in a certain place who can make a go of it
there, which means that the place is busy picking whoever
is going to represent it . . . "You're going to be my voice eventually; I'm going to keep 2000 of you here, and among those,
one of you will be a poet or sage or oracle, and I'll get said
what I want to get said."*

Generations

This Is the Year

Every damn spring, no matter how tough it has been the year before and how bad the winter was, the farmer, when the first smell of spring comes up out of the Gulf, the first spring rains and then things turn green, says, "By God, this year we're gonna do her. This is the year that we're going to really do her."

When I wrote This Is the Year *I didn't mean particularly to celebrate the Frisians as Frisians; it just happened that I knew something about them and I thought it would be intriguing to describe such a small embryo settlement which never really will take hold. Eventually it will break up, as it did, and as is happening now. . . I could as well have written about the Norwegians or any other one. I didn't particularly mean to celebrate any one group. I wanted to show that eventually they do intermarry. Even Pier the hero. He marries a Norwegian girl from the north a ways. And the legends that his father had disappear—pieces of them remain and they're transformed. . .*

Glossary of Unusual Words and Phrases
(most of them Frisian) which appear in the text

ÂLD FRYSLÂN: *Old Friesland. Also known in ancient times as Frisia. Located in north Netherlands and in northwest Germany near Denmark, including all the Frisian Islands in the North Sea.*

ÂLD STARUM: *Old Starum. Legendary capital of ancient Frisia, now known as Stavoren, the Netherlands.*

ÂLDE: *Old, or old one*

FAMMEN: *Girls, maidens*

FOSITE: *A pagan god. Frisians worshipped in his temple on the North Sea island of Fositelân. Legend has it that his island could be either the modern-day Helgoland or Ameland.*

193

FREYA: *One of "the most propitious of goddesses. She loves music, spring, and flowers, and is particularly fond of the Elves (fairies). She is very fond of love ditties, and all lovers would do well to invoke her."* Quote taken from Bulfinch's Age of Fable, page 336, Everyman's Library. *The Frisian name for the sixth day of the week is Freed.*

FRISO: *Sometimes known as Frixo. The legendary ancestor of the Frisians. He is supposed to have built dikes, to have constructed terps or high mounds as a place of refuge when the North or Frisian Sea came crashing in over the lowlands, and to have organized societies of druids.*

IT ÂLDE BOEK: *The Old Book. An imaginary book dealing with Frisian legend and history.*

IT REAKLIF: *The Red Cliff, located near Starum, Fryslân's old capital.*

LÂN FAN MYN ÂLDFAERS: *Land of the my old fathers (ancestors)*

MERKE: *A fair or carnival*

SEGUENER: *Gypsy*

THOR (TONGER): *The god of Thunder, the god who presided over all mischievous spirits in the elements. Our Thursday is named after him as well as the Frisian Tongersdei.*

WOASTE FRIEZEN: *Wild, untamed, unchristianized Frisians. "Woaste" means "waste, desolate."*

WODAN: *A god. Father of Thor (Tonger). The furious one. Our Wednesday was named after him, as well as the Frisian Woansdei.*

WRÂLDA: *The ancient of ancients. He was supposed to be the father of all gods. The Frisian "wrâld," the English "world," the Old Norse "veröld," are related to it. The original meaning of the word was "man's life, man's dwelling."*

Two Lands

HE SHUFFLED WEST toward Blood Run Creek. To his left towered Red Bluff.

The hill stirred him. Its rusty gravels and scrubby growth reminded him of the old legends, of the Old Country, of It Âlde Lân.

As an honorable freeholder in Âld Fryslân he hadn't had a chance against the big absentee landlords. They had slowly squeezed him into the servant class. But he had had too much pride to accept the inevitable and had promptly migrated to America. Like Friso of old, who had chased an ancient people out of the marshes of the North Sea and become an Adam to his tribe, he had come to America to drive the Indians out of the prairies of Iowa and set up a line of free Frixens.

Âlde Romke wasn't sure he was glad he had come. Sometimes he wondered whether it might not have been better to have been the servant of a Frisian landlord than to have become lonesome in a free land. In Âld Fryslân it had been possible to have a few dreams and warm friends. People felt safe on their little squares of bogland sod. The very land was sweet with the dust of the brains of fathers and friends.

Âlde Romke looked at the sweep of Iowa land to the east. It was as open as the endless universe. How could a man feel safe in a place where the skin of a home was open on all sides to the wild elements, where the moan of the mourning doves was the echo of eternity blowing across the earth? Ae, It Âlde Lân, with its land walled up against the wild furies of the ocean, with its towering Stone Man to guide the lost and weary at sea, ae, there, there was the land where a man's bones were safe in a storm, where heirlooms and friends were always near to warm the cockles of the heart when things went wrong.

He glanced at Red Bluff again. He remembered how he had chosen, out of all the prairies he had seen, this land because the rusty hill had reminded him of It Reaklif, of its legend—how in the time of Christo a flame of fire had roared out of it, how, four days later, a smoking dragon with a flame for a tongue had hovered in the sky above it for an hour, how the dragon had gone into hiding, how, two hundred years later, the cliff had exploded and vanished, how the dragon had come out once more to terrify the people. From that time on, until 1825, no clouds, no rain, had been able to touch the area. And then the North Sea had come in to flood it and swallow it forever.

He walked on, passing ol' Spit Triggs's sleepy rendering works, turning south with the creek. The creek doubled up to strike through a narrow gully.

The worm stirred in his brain. He waved his hands. He gestured, berating Pier in his mind.

"Pier. Soan. Now that you have been given your head, don't forget the ways of your fatherland. Deny not the blood in your bones. For remember, I ha' put my hands on you, an' upon you has fallen the task of keeping the Frixen line alive. You are 'n stamhâlder."

He mumbled, muttered, gestured. He stumbled across the tangles of dead weeds, upon new seedlings that were trying to get through the dead growth.

"An' don't neglect the breeding of our cattle. The cow is sacred to us Frisians."

He climbed the rise on the northwest corner of Pier's farm. He looked across the valley of Blood Run Creek. Just this side of Old Dreamer Pederson's five-acre place, on a terrace, bubbled the mounds of the Mound Builders. The mounds resembled the old terps in Âlde Fryslân. The mounds, like them, were almost leveled by wind and water. He recalled how in 1869, the first year of his coming, when he was a peppy twenty-three, he had climbed one day to the top of Red Bluff. For hours he had stood gazing at the flowing grasses on the prairies beneath, to the east, to the south, to the west down by the Big Sioux banks. Suddenly he had seen, looking to the north across Blood Run Creek, rows of mounds on the land. The grass on them had been burned by the sun. A cropping of stones and gravel just beneath the surface had fried the growth on them. He had stared at them, fascinated. He counted a hundred forty-three. What strange thing was this? Had a people as ancient as the Free Frisians lived and worshiped here in the olden days? Had there lived in this wilderness a tribe like the lost Israelites? And when? Had they worshiped a golden calf too? And a serpent?

Then he had seen something that made him shiver. The glistening burnt yellow spots lay in seven wriggling rows, like seven long gigantic serpents wriggling toward the Hills of the Lord to the west. Even the mound where the head should be was of proper size, and higher, as if the serpents were lifting their heads to hiss at the hills. He recalled that the children of Israel, swervelings in the desert of Arabia, had worshiped a serpent made of brass by Moses to save themselves from venomous snakes. Ae, it could easily be that an ancient people had worshiped the serpent here too.

Âlde Romke, standing on a level with the mounds, and remembering, wondered and shook his head. It was a strange land, a land of hexes, of pagan ways. Stavo, Wodan, Thor, Fosite, Freya, even Wrâlda, the ancient of ancients, would feel to home here.

Or, could it be that the Free Frisians themselves had built these terplike mounds? Had not the Free Frisians periodically cast lots to see who should leave and colonize new land to relieve the overpopulation in Âlde Fryslân? And hadn't It Âlde Boek talked about a tribe of people who had built barrows all through northern Europe and England and America?

Or could it be that this was It Âlt Lân, or Atlantis, that It Âlde Boek spoke of?

Trembling at these thoughts, Âlde Romke filled his curved pipe. Tobacco grains spilled over his jumpy, veined, gnarled fingers. He lighted a match; and then, a stream of smoke veiling out behind him, strode on.

He imagined that he was a hero again, struggling against the evil ones, against segueners, against the widow witch Kaia who had hexed Pier with her evil black eyes.

He sighed. Life was full of the pitting of oneself against the bad.

And never had it been more true than the first years of his life in Siouxland. Ae. Those first days.

Those days had been full of disasters and despairs, of calamitous rumors, of storms and cyclones and hails, of prairie floods and fire. Once, small brown Colorado locusts, a fearful vermin with the letter W on the forehead, had rained upon the land in floods, devouring the crops and pasturage, terrifying the women and children. The W no doubt had been the mark of Wrâlda. One year it became so cold that frost reached down from the north to grip the land every month of the summer. Great, week-long snowstorms in October of 1880, in January of 1888, in February of 1909, in January of 1912, blinded the land. And tornadoes in 1890 and 1895 wrote strange scripts on the prairie surface.

And yet the new land had seemed wonderful to him too. When he drove his wagon across it at the head of a tiny caravan of Frisians, he found the rivers and streams crystal-clear. Pike and sunfish and trout sparkled in the rapids. The low places were sloughs, full of moving life, full of frogs who croaked the night long through, "Worrk! Worrk! Worrk!"

He sighed. Those were the days. Men and women, children and dogs, horses and cows, and the young things, trampling in the tall reed grass, became creatures bewitched. There were yellow lilies in the watery bogs and green saw grass on the hills. And flowers everywhere: wild roses, cornflowers, wild black-eyed Susans, fire lilies, pink oxalis, and violets at the foot of tall bluestem grass. And living things: quail, mourning doves, pelicans, song sparrows streaming through the evening dusk, bobolinks, curlews, angry red-and-yellow-winged blackbirds protecting their nests in the slurky sloughs, meadow larks, swallows chasing dragonflies, killdeer calling "Killdeer! Killdeer!", fat plovers mating in the early mornings. And monarch butterflies with wings like the white sailtops of covered wagons.

Ae, bewitched they had been, bewitched; and blind fools not to have seen the trouble ahead. They should have seen the signs in the myriads of mosquitoes that flew up from the soggy swales. They should nave observed the ways of Chief Yellow Smoke and his Sioux Indian bands, who killed only enough for the day's needs and then roved on. They should have seen that the shadows were full of portents of evil days to come. Werewolves and elves and gnomes flitted through the dreams of children. Nightmares troubled the women. One winter, after they had settled snug and warm into their sod dugouts, Âlde Folkwâlda's wife, Nala, she of gypsy blood, had been appointed devil banisher to combat the weird lights at the window, the quick footsteps and derisive laughters in the dark. Âlde Romke nodded. They had been brave.

And they had gone ahead. They unloaded their silver teapots from the covered wagons, their Edammer cheeses, smoked beeves, rye breads, rusks, currants, Sint Nicolas cookies, their beers and whiskies, their anisette that the young boys used at courting time. Before the men could get the plow out of the wagon, the women planted lettuce and radish seeds in the soft gopher mounds.

In the winter they lived on side pork and rye coffee. They shivered with their

horses and Frisian-Holsteins and dogs and Berkshire hogs in the dust and lice
and bedbugs of the sod huts. They burrowed into the earth like gophers. And
they survived it.

Men sometimes got lost on the oceanic country even in the daylight. So they
cut single furrows from farm to farm.

For meat the men shot deer and elk, for fruit the children picked rosy wild
strawberries from the floor of the prairie, for sweets the women poured bumblebee honey from stubby combs.

They shot rustlers on sight, whether the culprits were church elders or not.
To combat claim jumpers, they elected fence-viewers.

Avidly they opened up the land to the sun; they believed that broken land
drew heavy rains more quickly than did virgin.

They felt the need of God. They built a church, called a domeny. And
worshiped.

But not even the domeny had been able to avert trouble. And after a while,
the Frisian settlers, who came from a tribe last to be christianized in Europe,
went each their way, so that the present-day church elders could collect only
enough money to hold two services a month, one every other Sunday. Domeny
Beckstrom, Old White Wings Himself, charged a good price for his sermons.

Ae, the country had been full of evil. It had not made men prosperous or
happy. Âlde Romke nodded. Even good men like himself had lived a doomed
life on it. The land was a woman, treacherous, touched, bewitched; it was like
Kaia, it was like Âlde Folkwâlda's wife; ae, like Ma Lysbeth.

Âlde Romke's feet slowed. He stopped. He had come to the banks of the
Big Sioux. He had walked down the slope from the plateau without knowing it.

The heart-shaped leaves of the tall, curving willows flickered and turned and
glinted in the sun. Below, at his feet, waters twisted and eddied, and washed the
sand bars at the turn, and lapped at the sunburned roots of an undermined
ash. Shadows from the red elm and the towering snake-smooth bass spread um-
brellas of cool and scented air.

Tears streamed down his weather-seamed face. His heart cried. He tugged
at his arrow-sharp beard. His anguish became an ecstasy.

By a river in Siouxland he stood weeping. He could not forget Âld Fryslân.
On fallen willow leaves he rained his tears. His old knees trembled. The weight
of his sorrows was heavy.

His soan had said to him, "Sing, for this is a good land, sing and be happy!"
Ae, how could he have mirth, have song, in a strange land?

"Lân fan myn âldfaers," he cried, "if I ever forget thee, let my bones ache in
agelong misery after I die. Strike me dead if I love not Âld Starum more than
this Gomorrah."

By a river in the Siouxland he stood weeping. He was cast forth by his soan.
He was but a dog in the eyes of his soan.

Lonesome he was for old carnival times, for the merke, for wild music and
anisette and wild fammen.

Lonesome he was for It Âlde Lân where canals were sweet with water lilies, where storks built nests on high.

Gladly would he have given up some prized treasure, or his beloved curve-stem pipe, to see again the purple herons stalking on the dikes like guards, to hear once more the sandpipers and starlings calling.

He remembered the old houses with their alcoves in the walls and their Norman doors to the north, the cows and horses and pigs who lived under the same roof with them and who were kept clean as children. He tasted once more milk sweet with the smell of aniseed. He smelled anew the abele tree white with blossoms.

A fish splashed in the water at his feet. He watched it snap through the curling waters, saw it vanish into the dark beneath the overhanging wild brush on the bank. He peered at the moving stream, wondered how many fish and strange water-breathing creatures were swerveling in its secret deeps.

And an old memory splashed in his mind. He recalled that his grandmother's people had been fisherfolk, a wild, sea-roving people, pagans, woaste Friezen, quick to lust, quick to fight, quick to sing, quick to challenge authority, quick to defend the helpless.

He studied the river speculatively. Maybe he could relive the old days by fishing this wide stream. Could a man make a living with a good seine? There were plenty of catfish, pickerel, perch, carp in every bend of the river. He watched the waters twist at his feet.

The sun, setting on the western hills, thrust long spears of gold into the river waters.

And the splash of memory fell back again, was reabsorbed. The sorrowing waters churned on.

Wanderlust

Bernlef on the Frisians

NEAL FRIEND INVITED himself over instead that next Sunday night.

Hero didn't get to visit much with Neal. Dad Bernlef discovered that Neal and he had a common origin—the Friends were West Frisians while the Bernlefs were North Frisians—and Dad broke out a fresh box of cigars in celebration of the event. The two men roared happily at each other in a revival of an "aep sitting," the ancient custom of sitting around the fire in the evening drinking mead and telling tales.

Hero sat on the floor by the furnace register, curled up, blue dress drawn over her knees.

"Yes," Dad said, crossing his legs, "yes, I was fifteen when I left Sylt. I remember it well."

"You don't have much of an accent."

"Of course not. We're more English than the English. Even you West Frisians are more English than the English. Your family legends should tell you that."

Neal said, "Well, by the time my people left Fryslan, the Hollanders had pretty well knocked out of their heads any myths about them being related to the Angles and Saxons in England. You know how the Netherlands government has sat on them for centuries, forbidding them the use of the Frisian language except at home. Not even the Bible was printed in Frisian. Nor no sermons given in Frisian."

"Persecution. I know. But still, despite all those hundreds of years of it, the Free Frisians remained Free Frisians, didn't they? Ah, what a people." Dad thrust out his chin and held up a fist. "Free Frisia forever!"

"Dad," Hero said.

"What?" Dad had lately shown signs of becoming a little hard of hearing. "What's wrong now?"

"Not so loud. Mother's trying to rest, you know."

"Oh." A gentle smile came to Dad's lips. "That's right."

Dad talked on, quieter. "We're more English than the English, that's right. The language from which the English is derived is really the language of some sub-tribe Frisians. The Angles and Saxons. While the main language was Frisian." Dad puffed on his cigar until it glowed like a radio tube, and he rolled it between his fingers. "When a Sylt boy enters the English world, he learns to speak the language in a couple of months. But when a German or a Hollander tries it, it takes him years. And even then, the German rarely learns to speak his th correctly. It still comes out a d. We Sylters have always spoken the d well forward in the mouth with a light breath over it, so we have little trouble with th."

Neal said, "Your Sylter Frisian doesn't have much use for the English, does he?"

"I should say not. He thinks them sneaks. Sneaks. And that's what they are. Sneakiness is a characteristic of the Saxon. As well as of the Hollander. Whereas the Frisian is blunt and honest. And there are reasons for this. The Frisian lived along the coast and on the islands and they were trained and bred to be tough as seafarers and dyke-makers, while the Saxon lived inland and developed the ways of trade and barter and so became subtle and sly." Dad rambled a little afield to illustrate his point. "Same as what happened between the Norskies and the Swedes. The Norskies always had a tough time making a living on the west coast of the Scandinavian peninsula. They had to scrabble in the rocks and battle the seas for food. It made them direct honest men." Dad waved his cigar. "You can imagine what would happen if Sailor Per decided he had something more important to do on board ship than listen to Captain Lars's commands, especially in the face of a storm coming up. Huh, horrible. So you may be sure that the next time they went out, Sailor Per was left home with the rest of the chapmen. The Norskies, like the Frisians, as a result of years and years of battling the elements, learned to trust each other in the face of a common enemy."

"Oh, dad, are you sure of that?" Hero mocked her father with a teasing smile, and dimped her eyes at Neal.

"What?" The old man reared up in his chair, face heating. "Of course I'm sure. Just look at your ma's side of the family. All chapmen. And your ma herself. When you talk to her about some new idea or project, the first thing she wonders about is how much money is there in it." The old man tried to smile. "Well, poor woman, I guess she can't help being what she is. A mongrel. Her Holland and Saxon strains all mixed up together. Gray paint."

"Yeh," Hero cried, "Friesland ueber Alles!"

At that Neal let go a loud laugh.

"What? What was that?" Dad demanded.

"Nothing, Dad."

"Hmm." Dad went on. "My family's had nothing but sad experiences with the English. My father, and his father, and his father's father, all were sea captains, all hiring out to the German or the English or the Dutch. And of the three, they hated the English master the most. My father, may God bless him in his grave, once gave up the sea for a couple of years to do some exploring and elephant-tusk hunting in Africa. He and a party of men, after many an adventure, finally got their hands on some wonderful ivory tusks in Italian East Africa, on the Blue Nile side. They decided it would be easier to transport the load down the Nile in native boats and then ship it from Egypt, than to go back over their original trail. Well, they hit the border of Anglo-Egyptian Sudan. What happened? The English slapped a border tax on it for half the ivory's value. My father and party paid. Free again, they continued to sail down the Nile. They got along all right until they hit Khartoum. There all native boats were stopped and the ivory had to be transferred to English—at the price of another twenty percent levy. They paid. Free again, they sailed down until they hit the border of Egypt, at Kurusku. Another tax. Again twenty percent of the total. And then, by the Lord, when they wanted to ship it home out of Alexandria, they found they had to pay a ten percent export tax. Well, Pa told them where they could stick it. Which was exactly what the English wanted him to say in the first place."

"Now, Dad," Hero said, "those percentages, are you sure about them?"

"What?" Dad snapped. It was with difficulty that he kept his temper. "Hero, my girl, there are times when I'm sure you're more your mother's daughter than mine."

Hero and Neal both laughed.

Dad went on. "My grandfather Old Landric—I was named after him—had an even worse experience. He was captain of a Danish ship at the time, sailing the Indian Ocean. A ship came over the horizon. As was the custom, Old Landric ordered his flags hoisted, first the flag of the country he was sailing for, Denmark, and then the flag of his ship. The other ship didn't answer. Instead, when it got up close, it fired a shot across the bow. Old Landric lowered sail. And only then did the captain of the other ship let him know who they were. An English man-of-war. Camouflaged as a merchant vessel. The Englishman megaphoned, 'Don't you know these sea lanes belong to the English? Get off!' Old Landric called back to say he would be more than glad to get over to where he belonged if they would tell him where that was. Without a word more, the English shot down his masts and filled his ship full of holes. Then the damage done, the English sailed away, leaving Old Landric helplessly adrift. To make matters worse, the wind died down. They hit a calm. And rations got low. Water was almost gone. The men got the scurvy and became terribly sick. After many days, they drifted onto the coast of Africa. Old Landric ordered the mate and two men to lower a boat and go ashore for water and provisions. He told the mate that neither he nor his men were to take a drink until they got the water aboard. The mate went up a little stream, got fresh water, got some fruit, and came aboard again. Old Landric rationed out the water sip by sip, he himself taking a drink only after all the others had been refreshed. You see, if the water hadn't been rationed out carefully the men would have made hogs of themselves and become sick. It was months before he and all his hands were well again. Yes, that's the English for you."

Neal lipped his cigar. "How come you didn't go down to the sea and become captain if it was in the family tradition?"

Dad's face saddened over. "My older brother was lost out to sea. Washed overboard. And my mother made my father promise never to let me go."

"Oh."

"Yes, it's too bad. Up until that happened, I had a great life with my father. And he taught me many things too besides sailing. One time, some other boys and I were chasing a Chinaman down the streets of Hamburg, taking turns pulling his pigtail." Dad permitted himself a smile. "My father caught me and grabbed me hard by the shoulder and said, 'Look, boy, some day you're going to take a ship to China. How would you like it if the Chinese boys ran after you through the streets of Hong Kong pulling your red beard?"

Neal and Hero laughed.

"O, I tell you, my father's people were strict." Dad's eyes narrowed in memory. "Especially when it came to their children. You never heard of a Frisian boy having a girl in every port. A Frisian sailor always had one girl. And that girl was home, on the Island of Sylt." Dad caught a look of disbelief in Neal's eye. "Just to show you. Once a Jewish peddler by the name of Joseph Stein came from the Danish mainland to do some selling. Stein had to stay over for the night. Bored sitting around in his room alone in the evening, he went down to a local dance in the village. One girl there caught his eye, a lass by the name of Gundel. Stein danced most of the night with her and afterwards took her home. Just to show that he appreciated the good time she had given him, he kissed her goodnight. Well sir, the next day he finished selling and went down to the dock to cross over to the main land. But the captain of the ferry said, 'Oh no, not you. Not until Gundel's father says you can. You're engaged to her.' 'Engaged?' 'That's what I hear, young man.' Young Stein raised a big commotion but the captain was firm. So at last Stein had to go ask Gundel's father if he could go. Gundel's father said, 'Well, we'll have to ask Gundel. Gundel!' And Gundel came blushing out of the kitchen where she was working, and her pa says, 'Gundel, is this the man that kissed you?' 'Ya, Pa.' 'Is he engaged to you then?' 'Ya, Pa.' End result: young Mr. Stein had to marry her. He's still on the island, an old bird now, with many grandchildren. He now spells his S-t-e-y-n-e instead of S-t-e-i-n. He's become a good Sylter."

Neal asked, "Are you sorry you didn't become a captain?"

"No," the old man said emphatically.

"Oh?"

"No, and I tell you why. In the old days it was a challenge to be a captain of a ship. A man had only a few tools to work with to conquer the waves. Sails, a strong heart, the sextant. But nowadays, with all these modern improvements, a captain isn't much more than a taxi-driver. He docks up, unloads, gets his pay, loads up again, gets his instructions, and goes. 'Be in London at two tomorrow afternoon, pier 4.' On the way over he can sit in a nice room and smoke cigars while a university science department runs his ship for him. In the old days, with the old three-master. . . ah, then men were men, let me tell you."

"It's a little easier on the passengers these days though," Neal said.

Hero laughed.

The old man fired up. "Maybe so, maybe so, but you had to be a man to run a ship in the old days."

Neal looked down, smiling to himself.

"Manhood, yes. That's why you found so many Frisian captains on the seas. They learned manhood as part of being Free Frisians. For hundreds of years the Frisians fought to remain free. Time and time again the invader tried to subdue them. Make them slaves. But always they got from under. And it made them tough." Dad dabbed at the ashtray with the end of his cigar. "Ever hear the story of Pedher Lundt? No? This was in the days when some of the Junkers of Germany tried to take over the island of Sylt. One evening a Junker and some soldiers came ashore. First place they hit was Pedher Lundt's cottage. Pedher was just sitting down to supper, he and his family all ringed around a big pot of steaming pea soup. The Junker burst into the door, dressed in armor and waving a big sword. 'You swine,' he said, 'what's your name?' 'Pedher Lundt, a Free Frisian!' 'Free Frisian, you say? Well, from this time on you're Pedher Lundt the servant of Baron Heinrich von Klanx!' Pedher didn't say anything. He just sat. And his family sat as calm as stones, too, Ma and the boys. The calm infuriated the Junker, and suddenly he leaned forward and spat into the soup. That was too much for Pedher. He got up and all of a sudden grabbed the baron by the neck and dumped him headfirst into the steaming pea soup. Then, telling his boys to run out and warn the rest of the islanders, Pedher grabbed the baron's sword and shouted"—Dad pointed at the knitted tapestry over the bookcase with its strange words—"'Nian boven ys; nian önner ys; lewer duad üs slaav!' Which means, 'No one above us; no one under us; rather dead than slave!' And with that he cut off the baron's head and then went out and annihilated the rest of the invaders."

Neal laughed respectfully, one eye on Hero.

The old man simmered down; and after a moment smiled some, winking. "And riddles. Did your folks like to tell riddles too?"

"That's all we heard at the table as kids."

The old man looked up, pawing the air for one. "Ah, here's one: What goes over the threshold, head down: Shh, Hero, quiet now, let him guess it."

"A shoenail." Neal flicked his ashes in a tray. "And now it's my turn. What is it that's white when you throw it up and yellow when it comes down?"

"An egg." Dad beamed. "You're a true Frisian, all right. Hero, mark it well." The old man puffed. "And proverbs, did your folk like them too?"

"Yes, especially in time of trouble."

"Yes, yes. I suppose you remember this one: Everything has one end, but a sausage has two?"

"Ha. Yes. And this one: Where the money is, there the devil is; and where there is none, there he is twice over."

Hero broke in with one she remembered. "God cuts down the tree before it grows to heaven."

"Good girl," Dad said. "And this one: Friends would be dogs if they only had tails."

Neal grinned. "Beer in the man and wit in the can."

"The cow will not admit that it has been a calf."

"He who has a foul mouth must have a strong back."

Dad laughed until there were tears in his eyes. "It's too bad the Frisians were decimated by floods and invasions and pestilence. Yes, and also by their peace-ful method of sending away a tenth of all the people, chosen by lot, every time the land become overpopulated. What a great nation we might have become."

"Oh, now, I don't know now," Neal said, "we could very well have become like the English and oppressed colonies."

"Never. It isn't in us."

Arrow of Love

*I worked for a guy named Lou Van Leeuwen. That means Lou of the Lion
... He was a strong powerful character and didn't think much of college bums
and all that stuff. I worked for him one summer ... He had a very pretty
daughter named Marie who was kind of a tomboy. The only child they had
... wherever I was, she would be tagging along and I didn't mind it. I was a
sophomore in college, about 20 years old. One time she pushed me in a tank
when I was watering the horses and my back was turned, and so on ... Then
she did marry an older guy who had his eye on her, too. About 25 or 30 years
older. She broke the old man's heart when he learned that they were sleeping together. He was wild ... He was a powerhouse. Boy you didn't dare con-
tradict him. But his daughter just did anything she wanted. She was the apple
of his eye. That's why I wrote this story. It caught my eye. There were little
hidden wells sitting underneath there.*

Lew and Luanne
a comedy

To Robert Penn Warren

1

LEW LYONS SAW that his down alfalfa, fourteen acres of it, was ready to be
put up. So Lew clapped on his straw hat and stumped up the road to tell his
neighbor, Rolf Freyling, that he should come in the morning and pay back some
of the help he owed, two men for a day, one to run the bucker and the other to
pitch up. He himself would stack.

"In the morning?" Rolf said, leaning against the houseyard gate. "Tomorrow?" Rolf had a throwback face and bristle hair like the black mane of a mus-
tang. "Mmm," Rolf muttered, "and here I was thinkin' a fillin' the old privy hole
behind the house in the morning. S'long as I had me a giant hand for a week."

"Giant hand?" Lew asked, surprised. "Who's working for you now?" Lew
stood a good two hands under Rolf's burly height.

"The big boy. Thurs."

"Who?" Lew said. "Not that overgrown camel from the orphanage across the river?" Lew lifted his straw hat just enough so he could scratch his bald pate with a finger. Resettling his hat, he next gave his thick brown sideburns a good scratching. "What are you doing with him, starting a sideshow?"

"I borrowed him for a week from Old Lady Brothers. They was slack work there and I needed him. I got way behind on the odd jobs this summer."

How much you paying the big boy?"

"Four-bits a day."

"You're throwing your money away," Lew said.

Rolf laughed. His little animal eyes glinted as if he thought that a good one. "I have to give him board and room too of course." A bead of spit let go down the middle crack of his thick lower lip and slowly it spun down, a long silken thread following after. "Tell you something though, Lew. That big feller does work I couldn't begin to think to do."

"Like filling privy holes?"

Rolf laughed.

"Ain't he the lummox what started college last year?" Lew asked sharply.

Rolf hunched up his shoulders. For all his brutish face and huge shoulders, he had the slim deft fingers of a fiddler. Where the skin showed under his rolled up sleeves and inside his open collar it was fair, almost like a woman's. He said, "He's goin' on bein' a sophtmore next year."

"A what?" Lew said. Lew liked to pretend ignorance when it came to schooling. He read newspapers and agricultural bulletins and listened to radio commentators but he did it, he said, for the sole and simple reason of proving them all humbug. He had a way of backing into his learning. He was the most determined againer in Leonhard County. "A sophtmore, you say? What's that?"

Heavy Rolf stood blinking. "That means he's goin' on his second year."

Lew stood still, thinking hard. "What you really mean is, he's gonna be a year softer'n he was last year, don't you?"

"Ha!" Rolf exploded, spraying spit onto Lew's straw hat. "Lew, you may not believe this, but this morning the big boy scythed down the whole hog pasture this side of the crick for me. All them watermelon weeds, yellow flowers and all." Rolf smiled. "A full-sized man's job, I'd say. And all of it for two-bits. A half-day's work."

Lew quick turned on his stumpy legs and looked out to where a tall lad in blue shirt and blue overall was swinging a crook-handled scythe back and forth beyond the creek draw. The big fellow was bareheaded and the sun shining on his rusty hair gave it a curious burnished edge, almost as if he were wearing a halo. "What's the matter with your mower?"

"Nothing. But the pasture is full a rocks and I don't dare run a sickle in it. A scythe blade you can always quick sharpen. Or buy a new one."

"The big boy always run around bareheaded like that?"

"Mostly."

"Better tell the lummox to wear a lid or he'll scramble his brains for sure in the hot sun." Lew hacked up a scornful laugh. "But then, that's them durn college bums for you. Got no sense when it comes to conditions."

"He was born and raised out here like the rest of us."

"Yeh, but the trouble is he's read a book."

"Ain't you?"

"Ain't I what?" Lew snapped.

"Ain't you read a book?"

"I ain't always liked it."

"And he has, hey?"

"Hain't he?"

"I can't say as to that."

"See? I told you," Lew said. "Farmin' and books don't go together. Not anymore'n blood and gas."

Rolf reached a deft finger in under his collar; scratched; said nothing.

Still looking out to where the giant hand was scything away, Lew suddenly stiffened. "What's he doin' now?"

"Probably throwin' a few boulders in the gully there."

"Them stones we tried movin' with a horse last spring?"

"That's it. For a joke I told him this morning he could throw them in the gully if they got in his way. And if he found the time. And if he thought he was up to it. Rolf's animal eyes gleamed. "Told him I ain't been able to use that piece of land for anything but pasture. Can't touch it with a plow."

Lew stood stock-still for a while.

"Yeh, for four-bits a day, I'd say I got me quite a man onct."

Lew grunted. "Hum." Then he made a little hitching motion with his hand as if he were cranking up an engine to his legs, and, getting it going, started down the lane. "Be there at seven in the mornin' then," Lew threw over his shoulder. "With two men if possible. And if one of them's a freak, God help us, and maybe I can talk my Luanne into driving the bucker."

"Luanne drive the bucker?" Rolf hollered after him. "I thought I was to drive that."

"I'll need you to pitch to me on the stack," Lew shouted from the turn in the lane. "I'm stacking this time, and that college bum'll long have give out by noon-time."

Right on the dot at seven, bald head glowing raw in the morning sun Lew stumped down off the stoop just as Rolf and Thurs pulled up to the gate.

"Mornin'," Lew said. "I see you're on time."

"We're ready to roll," Rolf said. Rolf got out of the car and hoisted up the suspenders of his faded overall. Thurs got out on the other side.

"Fine." Lew leaned back from the hips to look up at Thurs. "How about you, Big Boy?"

"Whenever you say."

"Think you can pitch up?"

"I'll put it where all you'll have to do is step on it."

"Hum," Lew said. "we'll see."

A slim lithe girl of about fourteen stepped out of the kitchen and came down the stoop. She had on blue jeans and a blue shirt open at the throat. In her right hand she carried a wide straw hat. She had just-budded breasts the size of a halved Duchess apple and auburntouched hair and a light sprinkling of freckles. Her lips smiled a child's twinning smile, while slow mischief smoked in her blue eyes.

"Luanne," Lew said, turning, "I guess we won't need you afterall. At least not at first. Big Boy says he's ready to pitch up."

"Aw, shucks, Paw, and I counted on it," Luanne said.

"No, you go back and help the Missus. Come to think of it, I've already let you grow up too much a tomboy as it is." Lew picked up his straw hat from the gate post where he'd hung it going in to breakfast and clapped it on his head. "Rolf," he said, starting for the barn, "the two whites are ready and harnessed, so I suppose we better get at that first."

They got out the dappled whites and watered them at the wooden tank under the windmill and then went behind the red barn and through a windbreak of young trees and opened a gate into the alfalfa field. A bucker stood near the gate. Its long teeth looked like the lower jaw of a whale.

They hitched a horse to either side of the jaw and presently Rolf was moving out into the field, going down a long green windrow. The bucker's teeth slid along the ground and shortly a great mound of dry green hay piled up between the two white horses, mounding higher even than their ears. Then Rolf broke out of the windrow and came in.

"We'll put the stack right here along the fence," Lew said, nervously pacing off a piece of ground beside the barbwires. "So I can throw it to the cattle come winter."

Rolf swung the load onto the spot, stopped the horses, dumped, backed the horses, and went out after another load.

Lew watched Thurs as they spread out the hay for the bottom layer. Lew saw right away that Big Boy worked easy. His shiny fork handle slid back and forth in his hands like a smooth working piston.

Rolf brought in six more dumps of dry tough hay before Lew was satisfied he had enough for the outer edge of his stack, some fourteen feet by forty.

Thurs asked, "Think you'll get it all on here?"

Lew looked out over the rolling field with its winding windrows. The field had the look of a labyrinth puzzle in Wallace's Farmer. "I will if you can pitch it up to me."

"I can."

"The butt will set out some, you know. Two feet all around."

"I've allowed for that."

Rolf and his white horses humped in the spring hay, huge jawfulls first for the far end of the stack and then for the middle and then for the near end. Thurs heaved up forkful after forkful just where they were wanted. Lew spread the hay out to its proper place on the stack patting off a little here and padding on a little there.

Eight o'clock came. The sun began to warm them. Not a word was said.

Nine o'clock came. The sun began to heat them. Still no word was said.

Finally, after bringing in what was really a mighty buckerful, Rolf had to say it. "Hey, Big Boy, slow it up a little, will you? You won't last the forenoon pitching up like that."

Thurs smiled. With a finger he snapped sweat off the end of his nose "What are you worrying about, Rolf? The horses are doing your end of it."

"Big Boy, I was hoping to change-about bringing in the hay, first a wad from close by and then a wad from the far end there. But this way, trying to keep up with you, it's going to get longer in between dumps."

Thurs threw a look at Lew. With his hand he combed alfalfa leaves the size of mice ears out of his rusty hair. "Well, maybe you can catch up along about noon when I give out."

"Ha," Rolf exploded.

"Hey, goddurn," Lew growled, "what's this, a bunch a women having a coffee clatch?" Lew stumped around on the stack butt, fork lifting a wisp of hay from one edge and placing it deftly on another. "This ain't a basket social."

Rolf's eyes gleamed. Alfalfa dust lay over his wide shoulders. "Want to make a small bet, Lew?"

"No, I don't want to make a bet," Lew said, at last leaning disgusted on his fork, "but I would like to make a little hay while the sun shines."

"Ha," Rolf exploded once more. Then he gave each of his sweating white horses a slap on the rump with a line, and was off to buck up another load.

Thurs pitched up smaller bites. He threw each one up with an easy slinging motion, letting it slide off the gleaming tines at just the right moment.

When Rolf came in with the next buckerful, Thurs had a small pile left. Rolf looked at the small pile, then at Thurs, then dumped the new load further down and turned the panting horses toward the hayfield again, this time going to the far back to fill up. When Thurs had another small pile left as Rolf came in, it was Lew's turn to give Thurs an odd look and explode. "Ha."

"Whoa," Rolf said. The horses stopped dead. "What was that, Lew?"

"Too bad I don't believe in betting," Lew said grimly.

"You name it and I'll take it," Rolf said.

Lew growled and fussed with the edge of the stack.

There was a sound at the wooden gate leading into the hayfield, then, and looking up, Lew saw Luanne striding toward them with an easy limber motion, carrying a basket.

"Lunchtime, men," Lew said and he jumped off the stack, hitting the hard ground with a thump and a little bounce. "And time for the horses to catch their breath."

The three men sat against the butt of the stack. It was just big enough to cast a little shade for Lew and Rolf, but not for Thurs. Even sitting down Thurs's rusty head stuck out in the sun a little.

Luanne sat crosslegged in the sun facing them. She took dried-beef sandwiches out of the reed basket and spread them on a clean linen towel. Lew poured creamed hot coffee out of a gallon pail into a set of flashing tin cups.

All the while they ate, Luanne waved her hand, brushing flies off the sandwiches and cake. Under her wide straw hat her freckles looked like specks of rust. Luanne's smiling smoky eyes kept looking up at where Thurs's rusty head stuck out above the stack butt.

Between bites, Lew asked, "Think we got a fourth of it up yet, Rolf?"

"A forkful more or less, yeh." Lew looked at Thurs's faded shirt. "Goddurn if you ain't wet. You ain't overheated, are you, Big Boy?"

"No."

Luanne smiled her twinning child smile at Thurs.

"Sure now? Because I'd hate to have to call Odie Lakewood's renderin' works to haul you off the place."

"It'll be time enough to worry when I quit sweating," Thurs said.

"Ha," Rolf exploded again, bits of bread spraying into the open coffee pail.

Lew said, "Luanne, you helping the Missus?"

"Sure."

"Good. Well, boys, it's time to pitch in again, ain't it?"

"What's the rush?" Rolf said. "I say let's finish lunch first and set a spell. Besides, the horses ain't finished blowin' yet."

Lew gave his foam-flecked horses a look. "Yeh. Guess you're right."

Smiling to himself, Rolf helped himself to a second piece of cake, a rich cut of chocolate topped with nut-flecked white frosting. He also helped himself to a third cup of coffee. The warm coffee made him break out in a heavy sweat.

Lew said, "Luanne, when you bring out the lunch this afternoon, put in cold tea, will you? And no cream neither."

Luanne smiled. "We was plannin' to do that."

Lew said, "Goddurn, nobody smokes, does they?"

"No," Rolf said, "my wife didn't like it so I quit."

"No," Thurs said, "and I play basketball."

"You what?" Lew demanded, ready to argue.

"Nothing."

Luanne smiled. "You go to college, don't you?"

Thurs nodded.

Rolf said, "Then you're figuring Big Boy will last the day afterall?"

Lew ignored Rolf. "And Luanne, tell the Missus to have some homebrew cold for dinner this noon."

"We was plannin' to do that."

Lew bounded to his feet. "Goddurn, boys, the horses has finished blowin'. Let's go."

And letting Luanne gather up the lunch things, they went at it: Rolf bucking, Thurs pitching, Lew stacking.

The stack rose as the sun warmed. It widened. Lew set out the butt carefully,
anchoring down each outer forkful with an inner forkful. He kept the middle
high and the edge out until it hung over a good two feet. The bottom of the stack
began to look like the wide part of an egg.

Every now and then Thurs stopped to comb chaff out of his hair.

Lew said, "This noon you better wear one of my old lids, you hear?"

"I'm afraid it won't be big enough," Thurs said. "And a tight hat'll give me
more of a headache than the open sun."

"What size do you wear?"

"Eight."

Lew gave Thurs's head a queer look; finally said, "You win this time, Big
Boy."

Around eleven o'clock, Lew said, "Big Boy, walk around the stack once more
and see how she looks."

Thurs made the survey. Leaning on his fork, looking up, he said, "You got
her slidin' out on the yard side some."

"No!"

"Probably because the ground throws it a little that way."

Lew looked down off the edge. It was a good eight feet above the ground.
"Big Boy, go get the ladder from across the granary there. I didn't figure we'd
have to use it before dinner.

With a hand on a post, Thurs vaulted over the fence and got the ladder. He
set it up against the south end of the stack and held it in place while Lew climbed
down.

Lew made a tour around the stack then, too. "Goddurn, Big Boy, you're
right." Lew lifted his hat and scratched his steaming bald pate. "I didn't allow
enough for that slope like you said. But it ain't too late to correct it."

The rest of the forenoon, with Thurs every now and then making a survey,
they worked at getting the stack level again. And exactly at noon, just as Luanne halloed from the kitchen stoop, Lew finally pronounced the stack in hand
again.

Lew pumped water for his calves and swilled his hogs and had a look at the
self-feeder in the chickenyard, while Rolf and Thurs watered and fed the horses.
Then they all went in to dinner.

They washed up near the houseyard gate, where Luanne had set out a gray
enamel pan, some tar soap and rain water, a coarse linen towel, and a broken mirror. It was out in the open and they could splash all they pleased. They soaped up
thoroughly, in the ears, under the collar, blowing and snorting. When they finished,
they grabbed out blindly for the towel on the fence and dried themselves.

Of the three, Rolf made the least fuss. His gestures, as he scrubbed away on
the white portions of his arms and down into the feminine whiteness of his neck-
line, were those of a neat man.

When Rolf and Thurs finally climbed the stoop all cleaned up and hair combed, Lew met them with a small jug of homebrew. "How about a snort of wild mule?"

"It ain't poison?" Rolf said with a laugh, knowing it was a good drink.

"Sure it's poison," Lew said. "It's the raisins added that gives it that kick."

"Good," Rolf said, "then I'll take a double dose."

"Here you are." Lew handed out a shotglass of brown syrupy liquor.

Rolf took a sip, then another, then finished it off. He smacked his lips. "Powerful stuff," he said, tears coming in his eyes.

"One of them raisins soaked like that has got enough gas in it to run you all day," Lew admitted. "Wouldn't have to eat except it's a habit."

"Powerful," Rolf said again.

Lew said, "How about it, Big Boy, think you can stand one?"

"Try me."

Lew poured Thurs a snort too.

Thurs sipped slowly. "Good appetizer all right." Thurs finished it off. "But I don't think Mrs. Brothers would approve of it."

Lew bristled up "You let that old witch run you?"

Thurs shrugged. "I have to live with her. Besides, she's paying my way through college."

"Then quit college. Tain't wuth it."

Thurs fell silent.

"Never let a woman run you, boy. I don't. Not even Rolf don't."

Luanne came to the screen door. "Chuck's on," she said. She smiled up at Thurs.

After a heavy meal, the men went out and stretched out on the grass on the shady side of the house. Covering his face with his hat to keep off the flies, Rolf fell asleep almost immediately. Lew, however, had some trouble finding sleep. He heard Thurs stirring around. From under the stained sweatband of his hat, Lew watched Thurs lean back against the house and look around the yard a bit. Then he saw him take a small green book with limp covers from his hip pocket and begin reading.

When Luanne finished washing dishes for her mother, she came out in the shade too. She smiled at Thurs for a while, then rolled over on her belly and fell into a sound slumber. Her seat rose and fell a little as she breathed.

Lew watched Thurs take turns looking at her and at his green book. Lew considered this glumly. And then, smelling the old straw in his hat, he fell asleep.

Some twenty minutes later, one of his own sighs woke Lew. He sat up with a snort. "What?" Looking around, he saw Thurs still reading. He became grim. He reached out and gave Rolf a light kick. "C'mon, let's roll."

"Huh?" Rolf sat up. "What?" Rolf stretched and blinked. "What?"

"Let's roll. The sun's gained on us a little."

Rolf saw Thurs with the book. "Didn't you catch one?"

"Catch what?"

"A cat nap."

Thurs slid the limp green book into a back pocket and got up. "People waste too much time sleeping. You only get seventy years if you're lucky, you know."

Lew snapped, "You'll take what the Good Lord gives you."

The loud talk woke Luanne and she sat up. "What?" She slimmed herself in a long lazy stretch.

"C'mon, let's make hay while the sun shines, you bums."

It didn't take but a half hour before all three men and the two white horses were wringing wet with sweat again. It became fiercely hot. Birds vanished from the brass-flecked sky. Gant field mice and puffing gophers burrowed deep in dark holes. The corn west of the alfalfa parched a little and its leaves curled defensively. The south pasture fried on the high sand hills. The streaming Big Rock vapored in the valley below.

The alfalfa Rolf brought in got so dry at last the men had to handle it carefully to keep the leaves from dropping off. Soon a fluffy mound of chaff formed along the base of the stack. The sun bleached some of the leaves a seared white.

Lew stuck his fork down into the stack and leaned on it. He puffed. He held his straw hat off his head an inch to give his steaming pate some air. He looked up at the sun, then out over the hayfield, then down at Thurs. It burned him some that Big Boy stood leaning easily on his fork, shock of rusty hair only partially wet with sweat.

"Getting tired?"

"No."

"Goddurn college show-off," Lew muttered to himself.

Thurs heard him. Thurs's white teeth flashed in the sun. "Maybe it helps to get your mind off your work sometimes."

"With what?"

"Well, like with what I was reading this noon."

Lew couldn't help but bite. "And what was that?"

"Green Mansions. It's about a green valley running with water."

With an angry grunt, Lew dropped his hat in place again and went back to work.

Around two-thirty Lew began to draw in the sides of the stack. "Goddurn hope we can get it all on here," Lew said, looking out over the field to see how much still lay in windrows. "We must have about two-thirds up by now. At least."

"Don't forget we haven't cleaned off the sides yet," Thurs said.

"Right you are. Let's get at that right away."

Lew climbed down the ladder and the two of them, using their three-tined forks in a combing motion, raked down the sides of the stack until it began to resemble a loaf of bread.

"Good," Lew said. "Now we're gettin' her."

"Yes, it does begin to look good."

"Hum."

At afternoon lunch, Lew asked Rolf anxiously, "Think we got her three-fourths up?" By this time there was plenty of shade on the east side of the stack and all three men and Luanne could sit in shadow comfortably.

Rolf had just gotten his thick tube lips around a big bite of dried beef sandwich and he had to chew and swallow a couple of times before he could answer. "I'd say so. A forkful either way."

"Think I got enough to top her right?"

"Well, if you ain't, you can always finish her off with a little straw." Rolf slid a finger in under his shirt collar and gently pried out an itching leaf of alfalfa.

Lew poured himself a second cup of chilled tea. "That's right, I could. But supposin', taking the other hand, supposin' I got too much."

Rolf poured himself a second cup too. "In that case, dry as it is, you can always throw a few slings of it up in the haymow."

"Yeh. That's right. That I can."

Thurs wiped his sweaty nose on his sleeve. "Don't worry. We'll make it. To the forkful."

"Hum." With a big swallow Lew finished his tea and put his tin cup away.

Luanne eyed Thurs archly. She had her hat off and her brown hair lay flat and slightly damp. Her lips were parted in a child's wondering smile.

Lew looked sourly around at the cloudless sky, looked sourly at where the horses stood puffing, heads down, white hides streaked with sweat and chaff; looked sourly at Luanne smiling at Thurs.

Then Lew's eyes lit on a disk standing on the other side of the fence. "That hired hand I had last year, what a sack of paff he was. I told him to put in a gate there for me, into the oatsfield there, and make it wide enough so's I could drive in and out with the disk without having to take it down. But look at that gate." Lew pointed. "So narrow a team of horses almost has to go through it single file."

"He was a dumb nut," Luanne said.

"I'll say he was," Lew growled. "I'm gone one whole day, mind you, one whole day helping the sheriff round up some chicken thieves t'Bonnie, and all he's got done when I get home is this little eightfooter of a gate." Lew spat in the stubbles to his left. "It'll take a wagon, but not a disk." Lew spat in the stubbles to his right. "As it is now, I still gotta take the disk apart to get it through. And get a horse to help me. A lot of work for one man. Lose a whole hour or so all because the gate ain't wide enough. That's why that disk is still standing there rusted some."

"So that's it," Thurs said. "And here I was thinking you maybe junked it."

Lew was outraged. "Junk a new disk?"

"Though I did notice you had all your other machinery under the roof."

"You goddurn right I have."

Thurs looked at the rusting disk some more. A smile worked on his lips.

Lew glared at Thurs. "I suppose you got an idea about what I should do about that gate."

At that Thurs looked down at the ground and began pulling up a few stubbles.

Luanne reached out a coy toe and gave the sole of Thurs's big shoe a light push. "Mr. Foxy got something up his sleeve?"

"Who? Me?" Thurs said. "No."

"You better not have," Lew grunted.

They went back to work. The sun owled down. Warmth vapored out of the earth. The shadow east of the stack lengthened until at last it reached across into the nightyard.

The men tired. They had to drive themselves to get the work done. Sometimes right in the middle of a stride, like overheated laboring engines that had at last had too much, the white horses stopped pulling.

The higher the stack rose the more Lew fussed. He padded and trimmed, laid and relaid strands of straggly alfalfa. He combed the edge of the stack as far down as he could reach. His fork flicked and sparkled in the light. He kept peering out at the hayfield where only a few more windrows were left.

At last Rolf announced there were just two more buckersful left. Lew prepared the cap. He started at the far north end, laying down neat flat forkfuls on the teetering rocking top, working back toward the ladder.

When Rolf brought in the last buckerful, Lew was exactly halfway across the top.

"Think I'll make it?" Lew called down.

"It's beginning to look like it," Rolf said, looking up with open mouth.

"To the forkful," Thurs said.

Lew scowled down. "Shut up, Big Boy. Don't hex it now."

"I still say to the forkful," Thurs said, pausing to lean on his fork.

"Goddurn," Lew cried, jabbing his fork down at Thurs. "Shut up, will you?"

Luanne came up from the barnyard. She had seen they were about done and wanted to be in on the finish. She stood just inside the shade of the stack, leaning easily against a fence post, wide hat pushed back from her brow. She told Lew all the chores were done except getting the eggs and doing the milking. She smiled at Thurs.

Lew growled. "All right, Big Boy, let's have that last buckerful now."

Thurs parted the hay carefully; threw it up in neat flat bunches.

Lew caught them deftly; kept his balance; put the hay down and patted it in place.

Thurs gathered up the last forkful.

"That it?" Lew called down.

"That's it."

"Well, throw it up here and let's see if it fits."

ARROW OF LOVE 217

Thurs heaved it; Lew caught it; and the last forkful fit to perfection.

"Goddurn. Goddurn."

Lew climbed down, pulled the ladder away from the stack, let it fall to the ground. He walked all around the stack, looking it over with critical eye. Finally he said, "Well, it could have been worse, I suppose. Anyway, it's the best I can do today." Lew took off his hat and scratched his bald head.

"Looks pretty good to me," Rolf said.

"Well, I have done better."

A smile began to work on Thurs's lips again. "You sure you're done now?"

Lew bristled. "Sure I'm sure." Lew saw the smile and cocked back his head. "Something wrong with the stack?"

"No, nothing wrong with the stack." Thurs looked over to where the disk stood rusting in the oatsfield. "But I was thinking about your disk there."

"Disk? What about it?"

"Would you really like that disk in out of the weather?"

"Sure I'd like it in out of the weather, you dummed fool."

"Good. I think I maybe can arrange it for you then."

Lew looked up at him scornfully. "Don't tell me you mean to build me a big gate quick a minute."

"No, not quite that. That's for another time." Smiling, stabbing his fork into the ground, Thurs vaulted over the fence. Next he opened up the small lazy-man gate. He studied the disk a moment, nodded to himself, and went over and pulled back the levers so the two sections came together in a narrow V. Then he set himself in the midst of the angle irons and levers and blades, took hold of the opposing crossbeams with a powerful grip, and, making his thighs do the work, heaved up. And up came the whole works, the two rusting disk sections, the frame, the two little yellow wheels in front, and the folded tongue.

Lew almost fell down he was so surprised.

Stepping slowly, heavily, neck tendons taut from chin to chest, Thurs turned the whole works a quarterturn and carried it sideways through the narrow gate.

"Goddurn," Lew said softly.

"Where do you want it?" Thurs grunted.

"Anywhere that side of the fence. There. That's good enough. Now I can pull it the rest of the way with a horse sometime."

Thurs let the disk down. He staggered a little as he straightened up. For the first time that day he was puffing. Bloodless marks lay white across the palms of his hands and he rubbed them a little to restore the circulation.

"Ha!" Rolf exploded. "I was throwing my money away, hah?"

Luanne laughed the laugh of a young girl. "Paw, why don't we get him for our hired hand?"

"Hum."

While Rolf went to the house for a fresh drink of rain water, and Luanne went to get the eggs, Lew and Thurs unhitched the horses. They removed the bridles and hung them over the hames and with a slap on the rump sent the team to the watertank.

Lew stood on one side of the horses and Thurs on the other while they drank. Lew scratched their necks. He held their hot collars off their sweat-sopped hides. The horses drank slowly and leisurely, with little ipping sounds. Little moss islands on the surface of the water gradually sailed away to the other side of the tank.

Luanne came up from gathering eggs. She stood across from Thurs. When she saw him looking idly at a couple of dark bullheads swimming around in the bottom of the tank she looked down at them too.

Then, mischief smoking in her eyes again, she said, "So you think you foxed Paw some, huh?" And abruptly she leaned down with both hands and cupped up some water and threw it in Thurs's face.

"Hey you," Thurs laughed, "you little dickens you."

"That's enough now," Lew said. "Luanne!"

"So you think you foxed Paw some, huh?" Luanne said again and once more she cupped both hands full and splashed Thurs with water. This time the horses jerked up, the bridles on the hames gingling a little.

"Luanne!" Lew growled.

"Once more," Thurs warned, still laughing, "once more, and somebody's gonna get a ducking."

"You wouldn't dare," Luanne said, splashing him yet again.

"Well I'll be—" Thurs started to say; then, with a swift leap, was around the tank and on top of her. He caught her under the seat and around the shoulders, and whirling once, twice, let go, heaving her bottom-first into the tank. She disappeared under whelming water for a second; then the next second rose out of it, gasping, mouth open, water streaming down her face.

"Here, you two!" Lew said.

"You son of a gun you!" Luanne cried. She climbed out, jeans soaked tight to her body. "Now it's your turn, you foxy college bum." She leaped on him, fastened her slim tough arms around his waist and tried to tug him around and toward the tank. Compared to him she was a terrier worrying a bear.

They wrestled around the rim of the wooden tank. They laughed and laughed as they pushed and hauled.

She probably would never have dumped Thurs if his foot hadn't sunk in a sucky waterhole beside the tank. And in Thurs went, falling backwards, with Luanne on top. This time both came up gasping mouth open, face streaming, soused from head to foot. Thurs laughed so hard he had trouble climbing out of the tank.

Lew couldn't help but smile himself. He looked at Luanne's wet body, then looked at Thurs's dripping body.

The horses, alarmed for a second, went back to sipping water.

And still laughing, covered with pancake blobs of green moss, the two of them went at it again, wrestling around the tank.

Lew watched them for a few seconds, then finally said, "All right, you two, that's enough."

They were so absorbed in each other they didn't hear him.

"I said, that's enough now!"

The two parted, breathing hard.

"What's the matter, Paw?" Luanne asked. "We was just having a little fun teasing."

"Go on, Big Boy," Lew said. "You better go get in Rolf's car."

"What about the horses?" Thurs said.

"I can put them away. Like I always done."

The big smile on Thurs's face slowly faded away. He gave Luanne a look and then slouched off. His wet clothes made a whistling sound. From his back pocket he got out his slim green book and began flipping the pages to dry them.

"Don't you like him, Paw," Luanne asked. "I thought he was fun."

"Hum."

"He'd make a wonderful hired hand. You better hire him away from Rolf."

"Naa. He'll never be any good. He reads books. And goes to college."

"But he's strong, Paw. And he knows how to work." Luanne wiped moss from her brow.

"Huh. One of them one-day show-offs. Go get the milk buckets and we'll pail them cows."

"First, I'm gonna change jeans," Luanne said. Then she added, giving Lew a smile, "I still think you should hire him. He might change his mind about goin' to college, I betcha."

"Go get them buckets. There's plenty of time for that later."

2

Luanne almost always went along with Lew and the Missus when they went to town Saturdays. While the Missus shopped in Rexroth's Department Store, Luanne went with Lew as he popped in and out of stores down Bonnie's main street.

Lew's first stop was invariably at Young's Produce, where he sold the week's eggs and cream. From there he went to Forsythe's Feed & Seed, where he got the latest crop reports and prices. The next stop was at Chauncey Mack's 1st National Bank, where he had things to say about the new high usury rates. Then came Jake's Implement Shop, where he inspected with cynical eye the latest in farm equipment. And finally he went either to the Corner Cafe or to Swaim's Cafe where he and Luanne had their weekly malted milk. Everywhere that Lew went, Luanne's twinned child smile was sure to follow.

What was bound to happen finally did. Luanne caught the eye of young Art Donkers, a clerk who worked in Forsythe's Feed & Seed. Donk liked girls with a touch of the tomboy in them and Luanne in tight blue jeans was made to order.

Donk had always liked girls on the bold side. When he was five years old, he and Forsythe's only girl were sweethearts together. They used to hug and kiss each other in plain sight of everybody. At that time Donk was still a fair child with long hair and Sweetie a bold thing dressed in boy's clothes. Mothers in Bonnie thought it so sweet to see them kissing on the street. "They make such cute little lovers don't they?" the mothers used to say with a nostalgic smile. The fathers, however, didn't say much. They just looked, mostly. And the young couples became self-conscious, the girls turning pink behind raised fur collars and the boys laughing nervously. And the grammas wondered a little behind their blinking spectacles, remembering a time long ago when another pair of little kissing bugs had grown up and come to no good. "Remember when Johnnie Brewer and his wife was sweet on each other as kids?" While the grampas said behind their beards, "That boy is gonna be a wild rip someday. Just you watch. They'll be shivareein' them two before they're sixteen."

Donk and Sweetie probably would have kept it up until sweet sixteen if it hadn't been for a rumor in town that Donk's pa, the local justice of the peace, got mixed up in some kind of bad trouble with a boy named Littlejohn. That made Dad Forsythe put a stop to it. He told Donk to stay away from his kid and ordered Sweetie to stay home and keep house for him.

This like to broke Donk's heart—until he remembered that Sweetie had to get fuel from the woodshed now and then. The thought of the woodshed gave him an idea. By creeping along the west side of the Old Omaha railroad tracks, then sneaking under a culvert, then through a patch of long bunchgrass, and then in through the back door of the Forsythe woodshed, he could still go on seeing her. No sooner thought of than done. Except that pretty soon the kissing and hugging went beyond just innocent play.

Naturally Forsythe was bound to catch them sooner or later. When he did, there was only one thing left to do. That was to hire Donk as his clerk in the store after school and on Saturday. That way throughout the day either the teachers or he had their eyes on one or the other or both of them.

There were also a couple of other reasons why Forsythe hired Donk. One was, Forsythe was slowly dying of cancer in the gut and needed cheap help. The other, Forsythe thought it unjust the way the town of Bonnie had cut Donk. The boy couldn't help it that his father, the deposed justice of the peace, had got into trouble with that Littlejohn boy.

Right after graduation from the Bonnie high school, Donk began to work fulltime in Forsythe's Feed & Seed. Donk was, most times, a good clerk. He was honest; he knew the business; and he kept the place clean, the rough wooden floor, the painted cement block walls, the ornamented tin ceiling. With Donk working full time business improved for a while.

Yet folks wondered why Forsythe kept him on. Because Donk the fair child had grown into Donk the muttface. Grown-up, Donk had skin the texture of rough cheesecloth, with strange black freckles. His gray eyes had dark shadows under them. And his ashen hair was already beginning to thin at nineteen. He

had no lips to speak of, only a pair of edges like knife scars, and his chin fell away
into a wedgelike point. There were times, in the right light, when he looked like
a fish. Folks who knew the family said it was hardly a wonder. His father and
mother were full cousins and it wasn't good for cousins to marry, especially
when both had the same kind of bad markings.

There were other things about Donk too. He talked funny. Even as a kid he'd
talked funny. It probably went back to his grampa, Old Doc, the village healer.
Old Doc had filled Donk full of fish stories. Folks said it was all right for mothers to fill the heads of kids with book fables, because kids would know how to
take it. But when grampas did it, serious, then trouble was bound to come of it.
One week the boy Donk would come to school calling himself King Arthur
and calling his chums the Knights of the Round Table. The next week he was
Robin Hood out to help the poor. The week after he was Jesse James.

Donk also acted funny. He never made a guess but what he rapped on wood.
He believed devoutly that Friday the 13th was hoodoo. He never stepped on a
crack in the sidewalk because that would be desecrating his mother's back. When
he walked past the hitching posts behind Highmire's Hardware he made it a
point to tap every third one. To his own satisfaction he once proved that a
drop of toad sweat caused warts, and later, again to his own satisfaction, proved
that a drop of grasshopper spit took it away. Donk also had considerable talent
as a predictor. He once foretold the exact result of a baseball game between Bonnie and Hello, even giving beforehand the series of plays that would win for Bonnie in the ninth. He also predicted correctly that two certain married couples
would get divorced before the year was out and remarry, the couples changing
partners. He was always so uncannily right that two poolroom bums once placed
bets based on his predictions—and to the astonishment of the village won enough
money to take it easy for a whole winter in Florida. Donk even told Forsythe one
day he'd talked with his dead mother, and proved it when he dug out a glass fruit
jar full of quarters in the front yard. She'd told him where to dig.

Folks tried to laugh his notions away. But the more they laughed the
more he fabled and predicted. To add to their uneasiness, he next developed
the odd custom of giving older folk odd nicknames such as Eric the Redhead,
and Hugh Glass the Grizzly-killer, and Kit Carson the Swift, and Balder the
Goodheart, and Jim Bridger the Gabber. Farmers laughed self-consciously at
the nicknames given them, and clumsily tried to use them on each other, but
after a while quit. Meantime the folks around hung a moniker on Donk too.
They called him Donk the Lady-killer. And it stuck. Because he believed it.
He'd had Sweetie.

It was in April and around four-thirty Saturday afternoon. A couple of farmers were still standing talking just inside the door. A couple of town loafers were
seated beside the potbelly stove—it was out but they sat by it from long winter
habit—and were talking with sallow Forsythe about that damned Jack Skinner
who'd been caught by the game warden with three hundred canned pheasants

in his cellar. Donk was busy behind the dusty main counter where he was carefully weighing out various sized packets of seed.

The front door opened and in stumped hardmouth Lew. Behind him came Luanne dressed in tight blue jeans.

"Hi, Lew," a farmer by the door said.

"Hum," Lew said.

Donk looked up from pouring honeydew melon seed, and it wasn't long before he'd spilled a pound of seed into what was supposed to be a two-ounce packet.

Luanne saw him looking and looked right back, interestedly, possibly even a little kindly as was her way when she saw something new. She followed her father all the way across the store, smiling, lolling along in an easy limber stroll.

Forsythe watched the seeds pouring onto the counter off the scale for a second or two, and then, bemused, said dryly, "Donk, since when did we begin selling honeydew seed by the bushel?"

"Oop!" Donk exclaimed, turning red, at last managing to tear his eyes off Luanne.

"Watch it, Donk," Forsythe added mildly.

Lew stopped in front of Donk. "Luanne, what was them special garden seeds again the Missus wanted?"

"Eggplant and honeydew."

"Hum," Lew said. "Kid, some eggplant and honeydew. About an ounce of each. And hurry up. The cows are waitin' to be pailed."

Donk recovered. "We've got the honeydew all right." He smiled his fish smile. "Plenty of it, as you can see. But don't you think it's a little late for eggplant?"

Luanne smiled. She said from behind Lew, "I think Ma'll want 'em anyway. She plans to put them in the bay window and with the stove still on in the parlor nights they'll catch up. I think."

"I dunno," Donk said, looking past Lew at Luanne's tight jeans, "I'm afraid it's too late in the year already."

"Luanne," Lew said over his shoulder, "Luanne, go round up the Missus while I wait for this seven-day wonder to make up his mind. The cows are waitin'."

"Comin' up," Donk said, quickly pouring out an ounce of each and licking the flaps and closing the packets. He handed them to Lew. He shivered a little when his hand touched Lew's. Then Donk began to hinny. And he hinnied all the while that Luanne smiled at him over her shoulder as she followed her father out of the door.

Neither Lew nor Luanne showed up the next Saturday. Donk figured Lew was probably too busy getting in the crops to come to town.

They didn't show up the following Saturday either.

When they didn't show the third Saturday, Donk knew what was the matter. He'd scared them off by the way he'd looked at Luanne. Lew the old man didn't like it and was taking his business to some other town, maybe Rock

Falls, which already as the county seat drew off a lot of Bonnie's business. A lonesome look came over Donk's face deepening the black of his freckles and the shadows under his eyes.

Forsythe saw the shadows and wondered. Was Donk seeing Sweetie again, this time maybe shinning up the rainspout to her bedroom? Or was she maybe climbing down the porch vines? One thing was sure. The shadows meant Donk wasn't getting his sleep regular.

The truth was Donk had taken to walking out to Lew's place every night, kittycorner across the country along the Old Omaha tracks five miles out and five miles back. Donk was spending most of what was supposed to be his sleeping time lying in the roadside weeds across from the Lyons house, mooning up at where he thought Luanne's room was, hoping to catch sight of her, just the least glimpse of her, and, except for one time, always failing. That one time he saw her she'd gone out to shut down the windmill for the night. He thought of making his presence known to her, like he'd always done with Sweetie when she took her innocent strolls to the woodshed, but Lew's new dog, a police hound bought to scare off chicken thieves, had come out with Luanne, and Donk was afraid the dog might raise a commotion and so raise Lew from his rocker by the radio.

When Luanne and her father didn't show in the store the fourth Saturday, despite the fact Donk had heard they were in town, Donk knew for sure Lew had put the kibosh on her seeing him again.

Donk set down what little chin he had. He made up his mind. There'd be no more mooning around in the dark outside her house reciting poems Gramp had taught him, whispering them into the soft night air of April, hoping she'd catch the magic of them if not the actual sense of them. No. Instead Mr. Arthur Donkers would call on Miss Luanne Lyons in broad daylight. Afterall, hadn't he had Sweetie once? Knowing a woman was more than most Bonnie lads could brag about.

Donk did some sleuthing and found out that Luanne almost always stayed home alone Sunday mornings to watch the place while her father and mother went to church. "Ha," he thought, "that's the time to see her. Come next Sunday morning I'm gonna call on her. If I know smiles atall, that smile she give me back in early April means I'm welcome any time."

Sunday morning came. Donk got up from his cot, made breakfast for himself and his shamed father and sad grandfather, dressed in his Sunday best, a powderblue suit and red tie, told his father he was going to church, and began hiking out along the Old Omaha tracks toward Lew's place.

He arrived behind the barn at ten o'clock, the exact time services commenced in Lew's church. Chickens scattered as Donk made a cautious approach across the barnyard. A few black-and-white cows, lingering beside the watertank, with strings of spittle pearling from their gristle lips, looked up at him wonderingly.

Donk peered past the corner of the barn, carefully sizing up the place. Yes, the door to the red granary was open. Lew and the Missus were gone in the car all right. There was even some smoke coming out of the kitchen chimney. That meant Luanne probably had something simmering on the back of the stove for dinner.

He saw her. She was in tight jeans again and sitting on her heels, digging in the garden behind the house. He guessed she was planting the very seeds he'd sold them, the honeydew ones. It was just about the right time for them.

Then he got an idea. He'd sneak out of sight down below the barn and then go around behind the chickenhouse, climb the fence by the road, and then come walking up the lane as if he'd only happened by, and seeing her, had turned in to pass the time of day with her.

He did exactly that. And, as planned, she didn't see him until he'd turned into the lane and Lew's dog, lying in the path behind her, jumped up and began to bark.

"Hi," Donk called.

Still riding her heels, Luanne looked across at him.

He came along a few steps more and then called again. "Good morning."

"Mor'n," she said shortly. She didn't smile.

He vaulted the houseyard fence, stepped across the flower plot, and walked across the lawn toward her. "I was out for a walk, heh. The next thing I knew, heh, there you was."

"Hum," Luanne said. "A walk? All the way from Bonnie?"

"Sure. I like walking. I like rambling around in the country. You've probably heard of me doing things like that."

"I've heard," she said.

"You planting them honeydew seeds?"

"Hum."

She still didn't smile, and that slowed him. Something was wrong. His cut mouth opened and he sucked for breath. Maybe she wasn't alone afterall. Maybe the Missus had stayed home this particular Sunday.

He forced a laugh. "Nice weather for planting, I'll say that."

She sat staring at him.

"Say," he said suddenly, "say, how did them eggplant seeds turn out?"

"Which?"

"You know, them seeds I said you were a little late getting? You know, the ones you was to put in the bay window with the stove on yet in the parlor?"

"Oh. Them. They grew. We're gonna put them out next week if the warm weather holds."

"I didn't think they'd make it anymore."

She stood up. She looked at him steadily.

Donk pried a finger in his collar; wyed his head around; swallowed noisily. He looked toward the bay window. "That them growing there?"

"No. Them's geraniums."

"Oh. Heh. That's right. Eggplants hardly ever has red flowers."

"Hardly."

A shiver shook his skinny body. He didn't know what to do. Go or stay. "Welll," he said finally, "I was just going by, heh, and I thought maybe I'd, heh . . . Well, so long, be seein' you around. At the store."

"Hum."

He left.

He cursed all the way back to Bonnie. He shuddered every time he thought of the more searing embarrassing details of the visit. What a little devil she was— smiling at him when with her father but scowling at him when alone. Fervently he hoped she wouldn't mention his visit to Lew or the Missus.

But Luanne did mention it. Not on purpose exactly. But casually as part of the rambling account the Lyonses gave each other about their doings when they hadn't seen each other for a half a day. She mentioned it during dinner.

"What?" Lew snapped. He dropped his fork in his gravied potatoes. "What was that?"

Luanne began to laugh. "I said that muttface Donk called on me this morning."

"When we was to church?" Lew cried. His neck thickened, his chest bulged tight in his vest, his ruddy face turned a deep red.

"Yes."

"The goddurn fool. The guts a him."

The Missus stirred in her chair. Her blue eyes, normally benign and ex- pressionless, slowly, by degrees, became two dark intent lookouts. Her big soft body gradually hardened into a dark formidable bulk. Of the two, Lew was less to be feared in a crisis than the Missus. Lew in duress blew his stack, and roared around, and sometimes even shot off a gun. But the Missus in duress sank back in her fleshes, became watchful, and in that very act of watchfulness turned her flab into solid force. Neighbors knew her as a prize-winning baker of buns, a pin-neat homemaker, and a good wife always fitting herself to Lew's needs. But they didn't know the other side of her, when, struck in the quick, hit in the palpitating depths of her being, her Old Eve came up, slowly, by de- grees, ruthless.

The Missus said, "What else did he do?"

Luanne's blue eyes opened. "Why, nothing, Maw."

"No?"

"No."

"Hem," the Missus said.

Luanne had to laugh. "The silly muttface."

Lew broke in. "He better not'uf. Or I'll ring his goddurn neck."

The Missus blinked.

When they finished peach dessert, the Missus got up and poured the tea. Calm again, serene, she moved around the table. For all her size she still had young legs. Lew often said that if the both of them, the Missus and Luanne, was to stand behind a blanket with just their legs showing, he couldn't've told them apart. So now, moving around the table, Lew's eyes happened to light on the

Missus's girlish legs, and that led from one thing to another, and after a while Lew forgot about the muttface's visit.

But the Missus didn't forget. She was waiting.

Two weeks later Donk was back at his post, hiding in the weeds across from the Lyons house, spying on Luanne, hoping to catch sight of her.

He kept it up until one night in June, with the wind east, Lew's police dog got scent of him in the weeds. The dog began to bark with great ruffed-neck fury, bringing Lew out of the house on the run, in his drawers, gun in hand. Encouraged by Lew's presence, the dog then ran to the edge of the ditch where Donk lay and really let go.

When Donk saw Lew approaching, gun cocked, light from the house making his bald head blaze like a red halo, Donk trembled for his life. He was surely caught at last.

Suddenly Donk broke, flushing out of the ditch in full flight. Donk had lean swift legs and was a good runner, but even a ten-second man could hardly have outrun or outdodged shotgun BB's, especially when aimed by Lew Lyons, the sometimes deputy sheriff of Leonhard County. Luckily, Lew stumbled just as he pulled the trigger and the BB's whistled harmlessly by overhead.

Later, on his cot in the privacy of the lonesome Donkers house, Donk decided it hadn't been so bad afterall, that Lew'd probably only meant to scare him some with that close shot. Otherwise Lew would have surely let him have it. Lew might've remembered when he himself was young.

Exactly a week later Donk was back, lurking in the shadows, spying on Luanne whenever he could, sometimes even getting close enough to catch a whiff of her perfume.

Lew and Luanne didn't see him, but they sensed him. Sometimes they knew he was around by the way the animals behaved, the horses, the cows, the chickens, and sometimes they knew it by the way the dog barked.

One Sunday evening, while milking, Lew suddenly said, "Luanne, what the dickens is going on in that calfpen there tonight?"

Luanne looked up from where she was musing. Her auburn hair lay bunched against the black-and-white hide of her cow. "I dunno, Paw."

"There's something going on in there or I'm a monkey's uncle."

"Maybe the door's slammed shut and the calves can't get out."

Lew peered past the side of his cow out through the stanchion. "Naw, the little door is open. By the dust I can see the wind is blowing, in and out."

Luanne let go a short laugh. "Maybe its that muttface again."

"Goddurn, it better not be. Or I'll blast a hole through his head big enough for an eagle to fly through."

When Luanne finished with her cow, she set her foaming pail to one side and went over and had a look.

After a minute she came back.

"Well?" Lew demanded, looking up from where his bald head rested against the flank of his cow.

Luanne gave him a bland look. "Nothin' there now."

"Now?"

"He might've been there. But he ain't there now."

"Didn't you see any tracks in the dust?"

"No."

"Goddurn."

Luanne let go a short laugh. "The funny muttface."

"Dang him anyway." Lew spat into the gutter. "If he had a decent paw I'd go and have a talk with him. Check him up a notch or two."

Donk had been in the calfpen all right. And it was a pair of white slacks he'd worn the day before that gave him away. They had become saturated with a certain feed smell and the smell had attracted the nose of a purebred Frisian-Holstein heifer calf. The smell came from a new mixture Forsythe had invented that year, a mixture of ground corn, powdered clover leaves, linseed oil meal, and the crushed root of mint. It was the mint that got the black heifer calf. She began to suck on a fold of the slacks, and Donk, startled, tried to shove her away. The scuffling between the two was just loud enough to catch Lew's ear. When Donk saw Luanne coming down the alley toward him, there was only one thing to do. That was to scoot. But he wasn't quite quick enough. Luanne saw the seat of his pants going out through the little door just as she stepped up.

Late in June the Lyons got a letter. Kate Damm, a sister of the Missus who lived in the Twin Cities, and who'd been born on a Siouxland farm too, suggested that her boy Peter stay with the Lyons that summer. Aunt Kate wanted her son to get some country into his blood.

"It'll do him a world of good to stay with you folks," Aunt Kate wrote. "Boy gets into so much trouble in town here. He drives me nuts sometimes. If it isn't stealing raisins from our own pantry, it's apples from the corner grocer. I think it's them street corner hoodlum kids he runs around with who've ruined him. I hope Lew can straighten him out and put some manhood into him by setting him to work on the yard. There's always lots of things a boy can do on a farm for his board and room."

When Lew heard the letter read at supper table, he cursed. "Goddurn, now that too yet." And when Boy showed up a week later, Lew took one look at his delicate brown eyes and his lily white fingers and really let go. "Lots a things he can do on a farm, ha! He'll be lucky to make it to the privy alone."

Luanne felt different about Boy. She liked his looks and took him in hand. She'd always wanted a brother. Now at last she had one, at least for the summer. She took Boy with her when she got the cows, when she looked for eggs in secret places, and when she started up the engine to pump water.

She took him swimming too in the old swimming hole in the turn of the river, and caught crabs with him in the mud bottom under the bridge, and dug for mud turtle eggs with him in the sandy turn just south of the farm.

Boy enjoyed it all. He soon thought of himself as more a farm boy than a city boy.

But the naughty streaks that Kate complained about didn't disappear altogether. Boy still had sly fingers. Raisins vanished in the Lyons household just like they did back home. So did peppermints bought for Sunday. So did oatmeal cookies.

"It's them goddurn big city poolhalls," Lew said to Luanne one day.

"Oh, Paw, come now. You know the small town boys pull the same kind of tricks."

"But not as bad," Lew said.

"Aw, Paw, it's just bein' a boy that makes Boy what he is."

"How do you know them things?"

"Because I always wanted to be a boy. Instead of a girl. And then too, I watch boys."

Lew didn't quite catch what Luanne meant by watch. Lew hadn't given much thought to the fact that Boy slept nights with Luanne. The Lyons had but three beds, one for Lew and the Missus in their bedroom downstairs, one for Luanne in her room upstairs, and one in the guest room. The first week Boy slept in the immaculate guest room. But letting him sleep there was soon found to be a bad mistake. Because Boy made a shambles of it. With his scout knife he carved his initials on the door jamb, on the dresser top, on the window sill, everywhere. He also had a baseball and liked to bounce it on the wallpaper before he went to sleep. Viewing the wreckage, Luanne finally said, "Put him in with me, Maw. Then I can watch him."

Boy went along with the family to town on Saturdays too. He mostly followed Lew around. While Luanne took to shopping with the Missus.

With just Boy along, Lew went back to his old custom of dropping in on Forsythe. Lew liked the slowly dying Forsythe. Forsythe had sound market tips. Also, from where he sat, Forsythe liked to look back on life and make sage remarks about it.

Lew still had nothing but disdain for Donk, of course, and gave him the best of his hardmouth manner whenever he saw him.

It wasn't long before Donk and Boy struck up an acquaintance. This ripened into a quick friendship when Donk learned that Boy slept with Luanne nights. The thought of it almost drove Donk crazy.

Boy smirked a little at Donk's black freckles and his wedge-pointed face, but he was intrigued by all the Old West tales Donk knew. Stories about gangsters were pretty pale compared to stories about mountain men. It wasn't long before Boy was giving farmers and townsfolk Old West nicknames too: Old Gabe, Yellow Hair, Broken Hand, Wild Bill.

After a while, though, Donk decided the indirect approach through Boy wasn't going to work. Too slow. If he didn't hurry some other Siouxland lad would beat his time with Luanne. So Donk too settled back in his fleshes and let his Old Adam take over.

Donk's Old Adam took him all the way back to his grandfather, the one-time village healer. Old Doc had an ear for the past. He believed in gramma's herbs. Also, he had an open mind when it came to witchcraft. He could cite cases of where heathen charms had worked a healing. He could even cite an instance of where a spell cast by a certain village widow had enabled him to perform a difficult operation.

Donk remembered in particular a story his grandfather told about a certain farmer living near Chokecherry Corner. The farmer wanted to marry a certain rich city girl from Sioux Falls, so he used hokus-pokus on her. And got her. A heathen charm.

Donk was so crazy nuts about Luanne he was ready to try anything, even charms. And the thought of Boy sleeping with Luanne gave him an idea.

Donk's first move was to get Boy indebted to him. He fed Boy banana splits, sundaes, candy bars; he gave him Wild West magazines, a new bowie knife, a fancy cowboy hat, a trapper's knife. Boy took them gladly. Donk's next move was to try a few local witch tales on the lad. Boy listened to them wonderingly. Donk's next move was to initiate the lad into the secrets of manhood. Boy's eyes opened appreciatively.

Then Donk set the hook. He told Boy of his love for Luanne. He told Boy of his plan to win her. Boy's eyes opened astonished.

"You'll do it?" Donk asked, eyes feverish. They were leaning over the feed counter, facing each other, heads together, Donk's eyes flicking now and again at Lew and Forsythe talking in the back of the store.

"What's there in it for me?" Boy asked, sly.

"My .22 rifle," Donk urged. "The one I showed you last week."

Boy's eyes became feverish.

"Will you?"

"I get that rifle then? For sure?"

"Yes. Will you?"

"I'll try. I'll see."

That very same night there was a mild scream in the Lyons house. Upstairs.

The Missus heard it, and the next morning, after Lew and Boy had gone to the field, she questioned Luanne about it while they washed the breakfast dishes.

"What was going on there last night?"

"Where?"

"Up in your room?"

"In my room?"

"That yell I heard last night. What was going on?" The Missus stood stolid in front of Luanne, blue eyes so far back under her brows they looked black.

"Oh, that," Luanne said, smiling. "Boy tried to tickle me. The nut."

"In the ribs?"

At that Luanne had to laugh. "No. Somewheres else. The nut."

"Hem," the Missus said.

That afternoon she got hold of Boy alone. She questioned him.

At first Boy denied everything. But when the Missus threatened to send him back to Aunt Kate in the Twin Cities, he made a full confession. He was very shamefaced about it.

"Ah," the Missus said, "ah, so that Donk wants three curly hairs from Luanne to put in a magic paper, does he? Gonna work his magic on her, is he? Ahh."

The Missus knew of a counter charm. She made Boy go pick three curly hairs from the back of the black heifer calf in the barn; told Boy to give those to Donk instead.

Her next move was an odd one. It astounded Lew and Luanne.

"What?" Lew cried. "Here for supper? Have you gone nuts?"

"Oh no, Maw," Luanne said, suddenly upset. "Not that."

The Missus smiled, serene. "Yes. I want Luanne to invite him over."

"I suppose you'll serve him some of your prize buns then too?" Lew said.

"I want Luanne to invite him over. And I promise you we'll never be bothered with him again."

"Goddurn," Lew said.

"Let him come here for dinner. Once."

"Please no, Maw," Luanne said.

"Once," Maw said. "That's all I ask."

Donk was equally astounded when Luanne called him on the phone. His brows almost took off. Ahh, the charm. That exorcising he'd done up in his lonely room over three curly hairs had worked afterall.

It was a hot day and Donk decided against wearing his powderblue suit. He chose instead his white slacks and a clean white sport shirt. Carefully he put the charm in his watch pocket.

He arrived at six o'clock, just in time for supper. He came walking alone down the Old Omaha right-of-way.

Before Donk arrived the Missus further insisted on something that completely puzzled both Lew and Luanne. She asked that the black heifer calf be allowed to run free on the yard.

"What? and let her get in the flowers?" Luanne said. "Let alone the garden? We've never had such nice honeydews growing."

"Just set her free a few minutes before he comes. That's all I ask."

The moment Donk showed his muttface around the corner of the barn, the heifer calf spotted him. And it was the black heifer calf, not Luanne who greeted him enthusiastically for supper. Tail high, springing, the heifer calf frolicked around Donk as he stilted embarrassed toward the house. Donk tried to shoo it away, but the more he waved his arms, the more excited the heifer calf became. She fawned on him; tried to suck his white slacks.

Lew and Luanne, still wondering why the Missus had asked to let the heifer calf run free, but seeing what they saw, couldn't help but sit down on the stoop and laugh and laugh. Boy, sitting beside them, and knowing what he knew, couldn't help but laugh too.

The Old Eve in the Missus, knowing what she knew, smiled grimly.

While the Old Adam in Donk, knowing what he knew, was stumped. Something had gone wrong with the Donkers magic.

Donk left on the run, with the heifer calf bellering after him all the way to the old Omaha tracks, still trying to get at that crushed root of mint in his pants.

3

What started it all off was a postscript written in the margin of an accident report:

"Bob, the worst of it is, Luanne's father, Lew Lyons, has let it be known he'll take a potshot at the first insurance agent to show up on his yard. I got this firsthand from Jim Wells, a neighbor of his. Jim came specially to town to warn me. As this report shows, Lyons didn't carry any insurance on the car Marie was driving. He doesn't believe in insurance. So if you don't mind, I'd just as soon handle this case by mail and be done with it. Please advise."

The man who wrote the postscript was lanky Harvey Pierce, an insurance agent in Rock Falls, while the man who finally read it was stubby Bob Vincent, an insurance adjuster in the Twin Cities.

The first time Bob Vincent read the postscript, he could hardly believe his eyes. He held the crackly paper up to the light to see it better. As he reread it his face slowly reddened.

"What! Some hardmouth is going to take a potshot at an insurance man?" Bob reared back in his swivel chair. "Well! here's something I'm going to have to look into myself. Personally."

Bob next reread the last paragraph of Harvey's report, the one with the meat in it: "There is no doubt in my mind that our insured, Ernie Johnson, hired hand, was clearly in the wrong, while the other driver, Luanne Lyons, a farmer's pretty daughter, was clearly in the right. Johnson was not only driving down the wrong side of the road, but he was also soused to the gills. Which of course means we'll be liable in case the old man changes his mind someday about insurance."

Bob glowered. "That Harvey. What a fish. From the way he acts you'd think Siouxland was still full of Indians." Bob's hair shone milky in the morning sun. Bob stretched in his chair, stretched until his shirt came out part way. "If it ain't young punks," he muttered to himself, "it's hired hand drunks."

Behind him Bob heard the office typewriters tapping steadily and the filing cabinets clicking gently and the ventilator fan fluffing slowly. The offices of the Northome Insurance Company were on the top floor of the Rand Tower and from his window Bob could see most of the south half of the Twin Cities. A morning haze lay over everything and far out it was difficult to make out just where green roof line became green trees. Immediately below, along Marquette, where a thousand dangers lurked for the unwary pedestrian, the morning traffic honked and brawled.

"Forty or fifty or sixty, it doesn't matter what the speed is, it's always just fast enough to ruin a pretty Luanne's face. What else can you expect but hash when you ram a face through a windshield?" Bob made a quick violent gesture with his right hand as if he were about to throw something. "And it's never pretty Luanne's elbow or knee that makes the first contact with glass. Oh no. It's always her pretty face, damn her. One look at her and the jury socks us for all the traffic will bear, no matter what the right or the wrong of the case is. The other guy's insurance company is always fair game when it comes to such lawsuits."

Bob stretched again, and this time his white shirt came out the rest of the way. With an irritated gesture, Bob stuffed the shirt back in.

The stretching and the stuffing back were an old habit. Bob had a squarish vigorous body, a body that had been an asset to him when he'd been a star quarterback for the Golden Gopher eleven, but which now at forty was an endless worry to him. It was only by severe dieting and strenuous exercise that he managed to keep a decent waistline at all.

Bob Vincent was a famous quarterback in his day. Twice he led the Gophers to national championships. He'd been famous partly for his quick thinking and all-around generalship, partly for his vicious headlong blocking, and partly for his easily singled out features, milky hair and pale almost blue-white skin, features he helped imprint on the public mind by his habit of taking off his helmet between plays. People recognized him on the street immediately. And because he had a good face, people also stopped to have a word with him. It didn't take Bob long to figure out that he should go into the insurance game to capitalize on his natural assets.

Seven years after graduation Bob hit the top as an insurance writer. He not only wrote the most policies for his company but he wrote the fattest. His name gave him open sesame into the office of every bigshot in town. Doors opened to him as if he were the Duke of Windsor. His commissions were fabulous. And with them he bought a fine home in Edina for his wife and children, and joined the Athletic Club downtown, and took a couple of trips to Acapulco. He had it made, the boys at the Club said.

But the truth was that fat commissions, the hard belly laughs with the bigshots, the endless do-you-remembers at the Athletic Club, bored Bob. Bob wanted bigger game, something he could really sink his teeth into.

It wasn't long before his insurance company's adjusting department caught his eye. A first-rate adjuster had to have special skills. Among other things an adjuster had to be an amateur detective as well as an amateur doctor, a psychologist as well as a criminologist, a highway engineer as well as a metallurgist—in a word a high class jack-of-all trades. And above all an insurance adjuster had to have a rich and sympathetic personality, had to be one who could adjust himself quickly to any and all situations—the kind of fellow who on Monday could win the confidence of a brittle old aunt and on Tuesday could talk pigs with a farmer and on Wednesday could talk working conditions with a union man and on Thursday could talk about the rollback with a manufacturer and on Friday could talk with gramp about the plight of the younger generation—and not only just talk with each and every one, but talk as if he meant it, as if he were genuinely and sincerely interested in hearing the other fellow's story. He had to put on as many faces as there were people to meet. This side of the insurance game appealed to Bob. And not too surprisingly, once Bob learned the ropes, he did very well at it.

Bob usually got the jump on the other fellow. He got the jump because he was a realist. The moment he saw an opening, he plunged in and ruthlessly exploited it to the full. But when he couldn't get the jump on the other fellow, when he saw that the facts were against him, that the opposition was pouring through the line at him, then Bob gave in, or seemingly gave in, and faded back. And when he had the enemy sucked in, had them thoroughly committed, he then reversed his field.

Bob snorted to himself. "So this Lyons character thinks he's tough, does he? Well, we'll see about that. With some fifty G's involved a city boy can get tough too."

Bob slid the report into a tan folder and slid the tan folder into his briefcase. "And that Harvey. He couldn't whittle down a dab of butter on a hot day."

Bob locked up his steel desk and snapped off the light and stood up and put on his blue suit coat. "Poor Harvey. One of these days we'll have to remind ourselves to fire him."

Harvey Pierce was a flap-armed fellow with a low pot. He had gray hair and gray brows, and the grays gave the blue in his eyes a washed out look. He was a sniffer. Those who knew him well understood the sniffing. He was the victim of endless browbeating by an embittered wife named Marah.

Harvey's eyes lost their faded quality when Bob told him he intended to see Luanne in person. "I don't advise it, Bob."

"Why not? There's no law against seeing people you're going to give a small fortune to, is there?" Bob put on his straw hat and started for the door. "You coming with?"

Harvey pinkened over. The pink almost made him look healthy. "Guess I didn't fill you in very well about him." Fingers trembling, Harvey lit up a cigar. "Listen, Bob, I'm not kidding you about Lyons. He will take a potshot at us. He really is a tough redneck. Otherwise why do you think Jim Wells his neighbor would bother to drive into town specially to warn me? Lyons means business."

"So do I," Bob said.

"I'm not going," Harvey said. "I'm scared of him and I don't mind saying so."

"Oh, come off it, Harvey. He can't be that rough. If he was he'd've long ago been in jail." Bob opened the door. "Coming?"

"Wait a second." Harvey filled the small plywood office with clouds of smoke. "Let me tell you a little something else about this redneck. Once, he and his wife and daughter went away on a visit to some relations in Sioux Falls. They'd gone but a few miles when Lew remembered he'd forgotten to shut off the windmill. Lew doesn't have much moisture in those sand hills of his, so he drove back to shut it off to save on the water. When he drove on the yard, they saw him about the same time he saw them. Chicken thieves. They'd moved in the minute he'd left the yard." Heartbeat pulsed in Harvey's gobbler neck. "Lew took one look, slammed on the brakes, ordered the Missus and Luanne out of the car on the house side, ran into milkshed for his double-barreled shotgun, loaded it on the run as he came out of door. The thieves, meantime, piled into their car and didn't bother about going off the place up the lane. They just busted right through a grove of young trees and a barbwire fence straight for the highway and made it. The chicken stealing was bad enough, but when they broke down his trees, Lew's pride and joy, that really made him burn. He hopped into his car and went after them." Harvey worked his cigar. "Then things really popped. He roared after them down the pike, footfeed flat to the floor, doing seventy miles an hour. Those two cars raced down the road like bullets, the boys trying to get into Sioux County before he caught up with them and Lew trying to catch them before they got there. Well, Lew caught them all right. Caught them in Sioux County where he had no jurisdiction. Driving onehanded he shot and blew out the tires of their car on his side, and they rolled over."

"Dead?" Bob asked, still standing in the open door, waiting.

"No, not dead. Just banged up some. No, not dead. They're serving time now." Harvey's cigar went out and he threw it away. "Another time this Lyons fellow—"

"Nevermind any more stories about him," Bob cut in. "I know what you're trying to tell me. That Lew Lyons is tough."

Harvey didn't like being interrupted. His wife Marah was always breaking in on him too. Harvey raised his voice. "In fact, Lew Lyons is so tough that whenever Sheriff Rexwinkel—"

"Rexwinkel? Is he the one they call Old Tubs?"

"Blast it! I don't like it when people take the words out of my mouth. Yes, Old Tubs. Whenever Old Tubs gets into a tight, say when there's some hoodlums from the Cities hanging around he calls on Lyons and deputizes him and lets him—"

"A sort of local Napoleon, then."

Harvey sighed, and gave up protesting the interruptions. "Yes. Except that this Napoleon ain't ambitious. He just sits tight on that little quarter section of his and tries to live out his life quiet. Don't bother me and I won't bother you, is his motto."

"How come?"

"What do you mean how come?"

"How come he isn't ambitious? What's his pitch?"

"I dunno. He's deacon in the church."

"Ah."

"And he's happy living with his wife and daughter on the farm there." Harvey's eyes fell on an inward thought.

"Ah."

"At least until this accident came along and ruined the face of his Luanne."

"This Jim Wells you mentioned, what's he like?"

"An easy going sort. Almost lazy, you might say."

"Mmm. For a lazy lout to get agitated enough to drive into town to tell you you're going to get your head blown off . . . Well, I guess that is something at that."

"What do you think I've been trying to tell you?" Harvey cried. "That's why I suggested we deal with his daughter by mail."

Bob opened the door even wider. "Coming?"

Harvey gaped from his chair. "You're still going?"

"Of course."

"I don't advise it."

"Look. I want to see the girl. Also, I like to know where our money is going. And he can do no more than order me off the yard."

"Yeh, that, or shoot you down like a chicken thief."

"I've never yet been shot at. At least not with a peace offering in my hand big enough to choke a horse."

They took U.S. 75 straight south over rolling land. It was June, and morning, and the land was tender green and the skies were a high blue. Everywhere the grain and corn looked good, even on the yellowhead hills.

When they reached the Lyons place, Bob turned into the lane and shut off the motor. As was usual with him, Bob gave the place a careful going over. On his left was a wooden housegate weighted with a wheel to keep it closed. Flowers grew along the fence on the inside. Onion sets behind the house stood in neat trembling rows. In front of him the main yard sloped off toward a red granary and a long low pioneer-style red barn. On his right roosters crowed in the sun while hens fluffed themselves in dust holes. And down the pasture toward the river a bunch of black-and-white cattle grazed slowly along.

"Well, I haven't been shot at yet," Bob said.

Harvey craned his head around nervously. "Lyons is probably out in the field."

"And I haven't seen a curtain move in the kitchen," Bob said. "Don't tell me they're all gone today."

"The car is home." Harvey nodded toward the red granary where a shiny black car stood parked. "That's the new one he bought to replace the one wrecked by our Ernie Johnson."

"And no dog has come out to challenge us."

"The dog sticks by the old man, I hear. So he'll be out in the field too."

Bob smiled. He tightened his belt a notch. "Well, what are we waiting for?"
They got out and went through the gate and up the wooden stoop.
Bob knocked.

A white curtain whisked to one side in the kitchen window, a pair of blue eyes in a middle-aged woman's round face peered out at them, then the curtain fell back. A second later the door opened and a heavy-set woman with girlish legs stood before them. It was the Missus and there was a slow odd smile on her face.

Bob smiled back. "This where Luanne Lyons lives?"

"Yes."

"Could I see her a moment?"

Still with the slow odd smile, the Missus called over her shoulder, "Luanne?"

Luanne came to the door. Two partly bloodshot eyes peered out at Bob from behind a mask of white bandages. Luanne was dressed in a blue dress; was barelegged; and had on a pair of blue house slippers each decorated with a white puffball.

"Luanne Lyons?"

"Yes."

Bob right away liked her low pleasant voice. She was another case, Bob thought, of where a man could throw a sack over the head and be more than willing to accept the rest. She had a wonderful body, wonderful, and Bob began to feel sorry for her. He wondered how much damage had been done to her face; vaguely hoped she would have some luck in the healing up. Some people did have such luck. And in the back of his head Bob decided he would do the decent thing by her—help her find the best plastic surgeon money could buy.

"Miss Lyons, I'm Robert Vincent, adjuster for the Northome Insurance Company. And this is Harvey Pierce, our representative here at Rock Falls."

"I had a letter from him," she said, with a look at Harvey. "Won't you step in?"

They filed in and were led into the parlor where each took a soft gray plush chair. Luanne took a chair beside the round oak table in the middle of the room. The Missus stayed in the kitchen.

They talked about the weather, the rain last night and the tornado last week up at Ellsworth; about the price of eggs; what the butterfat was on the market; about everything except the one thing that had given Luanne her mask of white bandages.

Finally Bob got around to it. "Miss Lyons, I've come along with Mr. Pierce here to assure you that Northome is more than willing to do what is right by you. We're willing to admit that our man, Ernie Johnson, was clearly in the wrong. There's no need to argue about it, or go to court about it. You have it coming to you." Bob watched her bloodshot eyes for some reaction. "Now this is what we'd like to have you do. Make out a list of all the expenses connected with the accident. Damage to the car. Doctor bills. Plus specialist bills. And so on." Bob paused; then asked. "You've seen a plastic surgeon of course?"

Luanne touched her bandages. "That's what this is."

"Ah. Who did it?"

"Dr. Steven in Sioux Falls."

Bob nodded. "Well, he's all right, I guess. But have you thought of seeing one of the Mayo Clinic specialists at Rochester?"

Luanne laughed easy under her bandages. "Oh, this will turn out all right. I wasn't much to look at to begin with. Covered with freckles."

"I can hardly believe that." Bob smiled too. "But I want you to be sure you're happy with this job Dr. Steven did for you. Just let us know if it isn't up to snuff."

"I will." Luanne curled up a slim leg and sat on it.

"And when you've had everything done the way you want it, don't forget to add a little for shock and pain suffered and so on."

"There wasn't much," Luanne said. "On the farm a girl gets used to pret'near everything."

Bob saw Harvey trying to catch his eye. Bob thought it was to warn him not to be too generous. Bob ignored Harvey. "I want you to be sure you're satisfied, Luanne."

There was a quick low voice in the kitchen behind them, and then Bob knew what Harvey had really been after. He'd been trying to warn him that the old man was home.

Bob sat up. The muscles on the back of his legs tensed for the play coming up.

The Missus was explaining who the company was, and then Lew himself came through the door.

Both Bob and Harvey got to their feet.

"Hello," Lew gruffed. "Don't get up." Lew stumped over to a black rocker by the bay window overlooking the farm. A dark radio stood beside the rocker. Bob had a quick vision of Lew sitting of an evening listening to market reports while admiring his crops outdoors. "Sit down," Lew said. "I am."

They sat down again, Harvey with an involuntary sigh, Bob warily.

Luanne explained what the two men had come for. All the while she talked her bloodshot eyes behind the white mask rested lovingly on her father's red bristly face. Her fingers picked at the edge of the crocheted centerpiece on the table.

When Luanne finished, Lew grunted and rocked his chair, once. Lew Lyons was quite a man all right, that Bob could see. But Lew wasn't such a man one had to be in mortal fear of him. Luanne, for example, seemed to have taken the hardmouth in stride, though of course as his beloved daughter she probably knew how to play up to his soft side. As for the Missus, well, she didn't seem to be in any particular fear of him either, though she did keep to her kitchen. Stern Lew was probably just an old-style family papa. Tough, but not so tough he wasn't human.

Bob combed back his milky pompadour with slow fingers. Out on a foot-ball field Lew would have been a terror. With that quick stumpy body of his he would have been hard to bring down.

A silence fell in the parlor. The wall clock tocked slowly above the radio. Lew's black chair cracked every time he rocked; one of the runners was dry and had popped loose. A yellow canary in a white cage looked for lice under its wings. A maidenhair fern trembled green to one side of the window. In the kitchen the Missus began to play drummer with pots and pans. Presently the sweet smell of fresh buns came in through the door.

Bob said, "I hope you understand that we've come to do right by her."

Again Lew grunted and rocked, once.

Harvey at this point remembered he'd come armed with a quiver of cigars and got up from his chair and went over and offered Lew one.

Lew gave them a glance. "I don't smoke but three times a day. After meals."

Harvey turned pink. In his confusion he offered Bob one even though he knew Bob never smoked. Harvey's bony hand shook. The cigars rattled around in the little packet.

"No thanks," Bob said, smiling.

Harvey sat down and put his cigars away.

Luanne said, "Was Blackie's calf all right, Paw?"

"Belly full and kickin'."

"That's good. Heifer?"

"Yeh."

"Black like Blackie herself?"

"Her deadringer."

"We can keep it then."

A mite of a smile drew down one corner of Lew's grim mouth. But only for a second. "Sure we can keep her, kit."

Another silence.

Bob saw Lew look toward the kitchen, and looking himself saw the Missus beaming at them from the doorway.

"You can come now," the Missus said.

Lew got up. He looked briefly at Bob, then at Harvey. "You had chuck yet?"

"No," Bob said. "Though really we shouldn't stay for dinner. Thanks just the same."

"Whatt!" The word was like a pistol shot. Harvey in his weakness almost sat down again.

Bob smiled. "No, really, we're due back in—"

"My Missus made a special batch of homemade buns and you're not going to stay?" Lew stood but a foot away from Bob and his eyes, though level with him, seemed to look down at him. "I'll take it personal if you don't eat with us."

The Missus in the doorway said, "I just churned some fresh butter too."

"Wait'll you taste the two together," Lew snapped. "My wife's buns melt in your mouth. Before you can even swallow them. C'mon."

"Well . . ."

"Sit down to a good farm meal once. Goddurn, nobody turns down my wife's meals." Lew waved his arm in a peremptory all-enclosing circle. "C'mon."

The meal was first-rate: steaming mashed potatoes with dried beef gravy, warm red beets, buttered yellow carrots, sliced pot roast, strong coffee, crisp cinnamon-sprinkled applepie. But the best was the hot brown buns running with fresh butter.

Nobody said a word except to pass things around. It was kind of eerie to Bob. Back home at mealtime his wife and kids chattered like a cageful of monkeys. But here it was all business. Shut up and eat.

Finished, all three men went outdoors and stood on the stoop and stretched in the sun. Harvey passed his cigars again and this time Lew took one and lit up.

Bob saw Lew's cows coming up from the pasture for a drink. Bob watched them gather around the tank under the windmill.

"Nice herd a Frisian-Holsteins you got there," Bob said.

Lew grunted, then looked at the ash end of his cigar.

"Mind if I walk over for a look?"

"Help yourself."

Bob said over his shoulder, "Coming with, Harvey?"

Harvey took his cigar out of his mouth. "No. Go ahead. I've got another account in my briefcase I want to look at before we go back."

Bob nodded and headed for the black-and-white cattle. Lew walked with him, chewing on his cigar with a dour look. They walked to the wooden fence beside the tank overlooking the barnyard. Bob picked a blade of grass and stuck it in the corner of his mouth and put his foot up on the fence. After a moment Lew put his foot up on the fence too, still chewing on his cigar with an odd look.

The barnyard was dusty from all the stomping feet. The sour smell of manure hovered over everything. The cows and steers took turns drinking. They were orderly, almost mannered. They drank slowly at length. Little ipping sounds escaped their lips as they swallowed. Islands of green moss floated away to the far side.

Bob said, "See you keep a couple of bullheads in the tank."

Lew suddenly tossed his cigar away into the dusty barnyard. "Goddurn. Tastes like rotten rope. Cheap." Lew threw a look of contempt back at Harvey in the car.

"The bullheads haven't kept down the green stuff much though."

"I just put this batch in last week. They've been gaining ever since. The other batch I had in there got too fat to move. So we ate 'em."

Bob watched a heavy cow undulate toward the shade of the barn. "I bet there's a real milker. Four gallons to a sitting."

"She gives ten a day."

Bob whistled softly. "A man can tell, all right."

"Some can, yeh."

Bob chewed on his blade of grass. It began to taste bitter. After a while he said casually, "You've got papers for them, I suppose?"

"Most of 'em."

"In Europe they're just called Frisians, I hear."

"That they are." Lew threw Bob a close look.

"Your American papers recognized there?"

"So far as I know."

Bob chewed some more on the bitter blade. "They're prize Frisian-Holsteins all right. You should enter some in the county fair."

Lew picked off a blade of grass too; began chewing on it. He looked at the cattle; said nothing.

"In fact I'd be willing to bet they'd win a couple of ribbons for you at the state fair even."

"I don't bet."

"Mmm."

Then Lew took his foot off the wooden fence and turned around as if itching to get back to work.

Bob took the hint. He held out his hand, firm. "Well, take it easy. And don't worry about Luanne. We'll do right by her."

As he turned north out of Lew's lane, Bob said, "Well, I haven't been shot at yet."

Harvey chewed glumly on his bitter cigar.

Bob laughed. "Well, Harvey, you were right about one thing though. He's a tough one all right. A Lyons that is a lion."

"Hrmm."

Bob saw a mailbox coming up on the right and he slowed to read the name on it. "J. Wells. Hey, isn't that the Wells who told you Lew would shoot the first insurance man to show up on his yard?"

"That's the guy."

"Ah. Let's drop in on this Jim Wells a minute. I want to hear more about Lew. He intrigues me."

Jim Wells turned out to be just as Harvey had described him: a lazy lank of a fellow. Jim's milk-spotted overall was loose and unbuttoned on both sides and his dark shirt was torn over the shoulder. If it weren't for the pegs that his nose and ears made, the skin on his face would have slid all in a heap under his chin. Jim's yard was no better. A dead stinking half-defeathered chicken lay near the house gate, a broken wheel lay beside the corncrib, a mower stood rusting by the machine shed, and ragweeds were tall in all the corners.

Jim was a pig man where Lew was a cow man. And it wasn't long before Bob and Jim were looking at Jim's pigs, each with a foot up on the wooden fence and a blade of grass between the teeth. Red pigs boiled in the yard beneath them.

Presently they got around to Lew. Bob said, "I suppose as a neighbor he's not too easy to get along with."

"Not atall," Jim said. Jim had a loose wet voice. "Them that know Lew like I do get along fine with him. When Lew borries anything, he brings it back the minute he's done with it. When Lew says he'll be here in the morning at seven on the dot he's here seven on the dot." Jim threw his blade of grass away and got out a chew of tobacco instead. He offered Bob a bite; was refused; crunched off a good hunk for himself. "Course that makes it tough on a easy going joker like me. I'm always a little slow about bringing things back. But we get along. We get along."

"Has Lew always been a hardmouth like this?"

"Not atall. I mind me of the day when he was plenty jolly. That was afore his Missus got the cancer."

"What? Cancer? She's the picture of health!"

"Oh, she had the cancer all right all right. But they cut it awayf'n her. That was just as Luanne was born." Jim spat and hit a red pig exactly in one of its earholes. The pig flicked its ear as if an ant had crawled into it. "That's why they can't have any more kits. Yeh, and why the Missus named the only one they had Luanne. That cancer was a hard one."

Bob's eyes opened a moment; then narrowed.

"Yep, Lew took it hard. He wanted sons. A lot of 'em. But all he got was Luanne. And that from a wife he still hankers after." Jim spat again. "You know, he once told me"—Jim chuckled and his watery blue eyes rolled—"he once told me how he come to marry his Missus. He was one of them gandy dandies, you know, one of them who thought he was too smart to get caught by a woman." Jim chuckled again, loose and gravelly. "Lew was a stepper, see, and when he saw this girl at a basket social, husky, cheeks like apples, healthy as a heifer in spring clover, he thought, 'How come I missed his one?' Well, she really was there in Rock Falls right along. Only she belonged to another church. Well, Lew tries to date her and she says no. A week later he tries to date her again, and again she says no. She says no six straight times. Finally on the seventh try, this time after church Sunday evening, she says yes. He drives her home with his fancy buggy and frisky steppin' chestnut trotter. By this time he's all adither. He hain't met a woman yet that hasn't gone for him the first time. They get alone somewhere. He tries to put his arm around her. She pulls away. And then this is what she tells him. At least so Lew tells me. She says to him, 'Lew, before we're married it's no to that stuff. But after we're married, anything you want.' Lew said he was so floogled by that he married her before the month was out. She was the first to handle him like that and he liked it."

Jim hit another red pig with a spurt of tobacco juice, this time on the tip of its curlicue tail. The curlicue tail first unscrewed itself and then screwed itself up again to get rid of the clinging tobacco. "Yep, Lew took it hard when the Lord closed the gate on them." Jim grimaced and his slack face raised itself a little on its nose and ears. "And then this kit Luanne had to have this terrible car acci-dent." Jim raised his dirty cap and with a finger scratched his dark wild uncombed hair. "It was like gettin' burnt where he'd already had a blister."

"What's this business about you driving into town special to tell Harvey that Lew was going to shoot the first insurance man to show up on his yard?"

Jim's slack face drew itself up on its pegs in surprise. "I didn't drive into town special for that. I just happened to bump into Harvey one day"—Jim gave Bob a wrinkling wink—"and I was just trying to be sociable. Harvey comes from the Cities, you know, and I was only trying to help him understand the folks here'bouts."

Three months later, happening to be in the vicinity of Rock Falls, Bob dropped in on Harvey to see how the Luanne Lyons case was getting along.

"You must be a mind reader," Harvey said, as he leaned back in his swivel chair. "I was just about to mail you a letter about her."

Bob tipped back his hat and scratched his milky hair. "You don't say. How much did she finally decide to ask for?"

Harvey tossed a big brown envelope over to Bob. "Here, read it for yourself."

Bob read. Behind him the agency secretary, a farmbred blond, pecked slowly and laboriously at the typing of a letter. An electric clock on the wall hummed as its red second hand circled swiftly. The smell of heated plywood was strong in the tight little office. Outside a farmer trundled by on a tractor.

Bob looked up. "Is she kiddin'?"

Harvey smiled. "That's the kind of people I sometimes have to deal with out here."

"Really!"

"Yes. She's dead serious. She means every word of it."

"Only ten thousand! Including even that new job done by my specialist at the Mayo Clinic."

"That's right."

"I better get the heck out there with a release paper and a check then. But quick. If I can settle this case for ten thousand, Northome can give everybody including the doorman a month's vacation with pay. We actually did expect to shell out fifty G's on this one."

Bob quickly made out a check for ten thousand and fished up a release paper and alone set off for the Lyons farm.

Both Luanne and the Missus greeted him at the door with a smile. Luanne showed him to a plush chair in the parlor. Luanne took her perch as before at the round oak table while the Missus began to play drummer in the kitchen again with her pots and pans. This time Bob didn't wonder what the Missus was up to.

Sitting there, with the morning sun coming in through the east windows past the yellow canary in the white cage and the green maidenhair fern with its trembling fronds, Bob at last got a good look at Luanne. The white mask of bandages was gone. But in its place was another mask, scarred pink waxlike flesh. And looking at it, Bob began to wonder if it was right for him to quick close the case before she or the old man changed their minds. If the face lifting specialist at the Mayo Clinic had done his best, what a mess her face must have been after the Sioux Falls specialist finished with it. Let alone what it looked like after the accident. The bone structure underneath had healed fairly well. But the grafted skin and the remolded flesh had not. The skin shone pinkly transparent; the flesh underneath was uneven. No amount of surgery and no amount of make-up would ever hide the fact that she'd been all cut up by slicing glass.

Yet, somehow, part of Luanne's old smile had been salvaged. And coming through that patched up flesh it was enough to give a man the mortal shivers.

Bob got out the check and the release paper. "You're sure now, Luanne, that you want it this way?"

"Yes."

"Remember"—Bob wetted his lips with the tip of his tongue—"remember, when you sign this release, it's all over. Done. You have no more claim on us as far as this particular action is concerned."

"I know."

Bob hesitated. The poor girl really deserved more. At least twenty G's. She was too simple for her own good. And he was a quick-working no-good city slicker.

Bob thought: "But a man has to figure the easy cases make up for the tough ones. Simple-hearted people always balance off the greedy ones. Northome has to consider all claimants impartially, without exception, has to keep sentiment down to a minimum. If Northome doesn't, Northome is doomed. Some other insurance outfit'll eventually shove us to the wall."

Bob got up and handed Luanne the check and the release paper. He also handed her his fountain pen.

Luanne glanced briefly at the check, and modestly, almost casually, pushed it to one side. Then she looked at the release. "Where do I sign?"

Bob pointed at the dotted line.

There was a gruff low voice in the kitchen behind them.

"Ah," Bob thought, "the old man's come home." The muscles over the back of Bob's legs tensed for the new play coming up.

The Missus again explained who the company was, and then bald Lew came in though the door.

Smiling, Bob got to his feet.

"What's going on around here?" Lew demanded. Then Lew saw Luanne with pen in hand. "What's that you're signing?"

"The release, Paw."

"And what's that, the check?" And not waiting for a reply, Lew snatched up the check.

Bob came forward a step.

Lew looked at the check; then looked at Luanne. "I thought I told you a check for costs was plenty. The price of the new family car we got and all them fancy operations."

"I know, Paw, but—"

"Then why don't the check just read four thousand seven hundred and ninety-five dollar?"

"Well, Maw and I figured I had a little extra coming for the working time lost."

"What working time lost? The work got done, didn't it?"

"Yes, but Maw and I—"

"I don't care what you and Maw thought. The work got done. Goddurn."

Luanne kept holding up her end. "But Maw and I figured I had a little pride money coming."

Lew reared back. "Pride money? Since when has a Lyons growed a pride that can be traded for money?"

"Well, we thought it wasn't going to be easy . . ." Then Luanne flushed, her scarred face turning an especially deep red. Lew glared at her. "Ah, so that too, huh?" Lew let out a snort. "Women!"

"Well, Paw, it was my accident."

"Women! Thinking that money can always buy a man." Lew snapped the check back and forth as if it were a whip. "Listen, if you was to buy yourself a husband I'd never talk to you again." Lew continued to snap the check. "Listen, could you live with a man who let himself be bought?"

"No, but Maw and I thought I should have something for the time when I'm an old maid."

"What? Then you don't expect me to provide for you in my will? You, my onliest child?" Lew stared at Luanne for a moment; then with a growl tore up the check. "What do you want Mr. Vincent to think, that we're so hard up we have to bloodsucker him for a living? Not with them prize-winning Frisian-Holsteins around we don't."

"But, Paw, it was my accident."

"Hrrr." Then Lew turned to Bob. "Write a check for costs. Four thousand seven hundred ninety-five dollar."

Bob blinked. It took a moment to come to. "I don't quite understand."

"Write out a check for four thousand seven hundred ninety-five dollar."

"Now wait a minute. We at Northome want to be sure Luanne is satisfied. Northome is more than willing to double the amount."

"She's satisfied," Lew said.

"Well, now, but Luanne's been very honest about this all. And we're willing to pay more."

"Four thousand seven hundred ninety-five dollar is plenty."

"Now, Mr. Lyons—"

"Why, it wouldn't be right to ask for more. We don't believe in making a profit on what the Lord wills. Goddurn it."

"Well, all right, if that's your mind. And if you're sure of it."

"I am."

Then, as the full meaning of Lyons's remarks sank in, Bob flushed.

After the new check had been written, and the new release finally signed, Lew mellowed some. He gave Bob a scowl that wasn't quite as grim as before. "Followed your advice, Mr. Vincent. Entered some of my best calves and cows in the county fair. And then entered a couple in the state fair too. Won the top ribbon every time." Lew smiled. "You ought to see the prices I get for my stock now." Lew gave Luanne a big wink. "Yep, you can always tell when a man's been farm-raised as a kit." Then Lew saw the Missus in the doorway. "Well, Maw, is chuck ready?"

"It is."

"Good. With company come that means fresh hot buns again." Lew once more waved his arm in a peremptory all-enclosing gesture. "C'mon, we eat."

4

The minute Lew hung up the receiver he knew he was in for a wild day. Speed Swazy, not Arie Bolen, was coming out to pick up the bull.

Lew sat down hard on the pad seat of his armchair. The thump of it resounded like a small boom of thunder in the big country kitchen. "Of all the truckers we got around here it has to be Speed." Lew jerked up a suspender. "Not Arie, who's already half in jail the way he chases. But Speed, who's got enough blab to run for town crier for the whole of Sioux Falls. How he ever talked that poor rail of a wife of his into marrying him, let alone bearing him nine kids in eight years, is one of the miracles of this age."

The Missus looked up mildly from her second cup of coffee. An old smile beamed out of her round sweaty face. The smile was one she'd always worn for Lew. She'd loved him in the beginning, and she loved him now in the middle years of their married life.

"Speed," Lew said again. "And my bull Barney already so full of whatever it is that's the matter with him. Why, you just stick your pinky through a crack in the bullpen and he charges you. And charges you silent. Like he's already past the bellerin' mad stage."

"Why don't you just shoot the bull?" Luanne said with a laugh. The laugh made a wide crack across her stiff pink face. "And then call the rendering works and be done with it?"

"I never did understand what you thought was wrong with our Barney," the Missus said. "Just what is wrong with him? I always liked our Barney."

Lew glared first at Luanne, then at the Missus. "Shoot the bull? Ha. When the price for even old bull is what it is? Wrong with Barney? And you already married a quarter century?" With quick hooked fingers Lew combed smooth the ring of brown curly hair circling his bald head. "Besides, I've got a better purebred ordered, and I don't want him to catch whatever it is that Barney's got." Lew resettled himself in his armchair. "No, the old bull's gotta go."

Speed Swazy showed up an hour later with a roaring exhaust and a burst of dust. He leaped from the door of his manure-spotted cattle truck even before its braked wheels finished skating across the sandy yard.

"Hi, Lew," Speed called out, on the run. "Well, I hear you've got a little bull for me today."

"Hum." Lew stepped down off the stoop and slowly walked toward the gate.

Speed was dressed in a tan shirt and moleskin pants and shiny laced leather boots. A license button gleamed on his cocked trucker cap. Speed was short, had a face the hue of just-rendered lard, and his eyes hardly had bluing enough to make color. The feature that caught the eye most was his mouth. It was thick-lipped and presented the picture of a boy trying to say "but" and stammering "bbb" instead.

Speed stood directly in front of Lew, toes out, legs spread. "Sure's a fine morning this morning, ain't it? This morning."

Lew glared coldly at him.

"And how's Luanne? Coming along just fine now, I hear, huh?"

Lew grunted.

"She still havin' some pain? Coming along fine on that too, I hear."

"Hum."

"Have you collected her blood money yet? Bet you folks sure socked that insurance company, huh? Well, they can afford it, them bloodsuckerin' devils."

"Mm."

"And how's the Missus? She still bake the best buns in captivity?"

Lew shoved a balled fist into his pocket.

"And the oats? Ready to cut yet?"

Lew finally had enough. "Speed, don't you ever start the day in low gear?"

"Huh?" Speed stared at Lew a second; then laughed. Speed had a laugh like an engine with little or no compression. "No, not on the downgrade I don't."

"It'd be easier on your gaskets if you did."

Speed abruptly switched faces; said brusquely, "Well, where's the bull? To make up my load I've still got four other calls to make this morning. And I've got to be in Sioux Falls before the buyers knock off at noon. You get the best prices before lunch."

"I'm ready if you are. Have been ever since you came." Just then the horn in the truck began to howl. It startled them both, made them whirl half-around.

Lew smiled grimly. "Truck must a heard us. Told you you should start the day in low once."

Speed's eyes whirled; then he became a ball of action. With a run he jumped on the runningboard and began to bang on the horn button. "Danged thing's stuck again," he yelled. "Does that every now and again when the weather's going to change. Like a bad leg acting up."

Despite all Speed's pounding the horn continued to blow. It blew with such a piercing howl that teeth hurt in the bite. Chickens on the yard scattered. The cows watering at the tank backed away, and, tail up and wild, ran for the pasture. The blurred moonfaces of Luanne and the Missus appeared in the green panes of the pantry window.

Speed next opened the hood of the motor and with a wrench banged on the black bugle of the horn itself. Speed yelled, "Was stuck a whole night once. Constable finally made me cut the wires. Cost me five bucks to get it fixed."

"Hum." Lew glanced at the red barn where Barney was waiting in the bullpen. The howling wasn't going to help the old boy's nerves much either. The day was sure starting off in fine style all right.

Speed continued to pop in and out of the truck, out from under the hood and into the cab, out of the cab and in under the hood. He banged; hammered; pounded.

Big lips set wide, Speed finally yelled, "Got a plier?"

"What for?" Lew yelled back. "You don't need that. Try jerking the steering wheel back and forth a couple of times."

"Oh. Yeh. Forgot about that." Speed leaned into the cab and gave the steeringwheel several vicious jerks, this way, that way.

"Bigger ones," Lew yelled.

Speed wrestled the wheel around in huge swinging lunges.

Then, as mysteriously as it began, the horn abruptly fell silent. The ensuing silence was such a relief it hurt.

Speed looked up with a pleased surprised laugh. "Great bulls a Bashan! What a racket that horn makes. Enough to make stones grow ears."

Lew said grimly, "Can't say as I blame the horn any. Hard as you're on that poor truck most times."

Speed bubbered protest. "B-b-but I ain't hard on her. I give her the best gas and oil money can buy."

"How old is that truck?"

"Goin' on four year."

"Hum. If that truck could have had kids, you'd a had you five runabouts by her by now."

"Yeh, and if she'd a throwed twins each time I'd a had ten by now. I know." Speed jumped to the ground. The morning sun shone on his polished boots. "Well, how about slingin' a little bull, huh? I'm late already."

They went to the barn to size things up. Barney the Frisian-Holstein bull waited huge and dark and strangely silent in his bullpen near the loading door. Barney had white markings over the shoulder and a tiny white star on the face. Oddly enough a streak as thin as a string ran down from the star to the nostrils, where it broadened out into a perpetual white sneer. Barney's hump loomed a good foot above the highest board of the pen. A couple dozen flies sat on the hump, just out of reach of both his white nose and his short tail. He stood utterly silent, gazing at them.

Cobwebbed windows muted the morning light. Dawn still hung dark in the corners of the barn. At the sight of the two men some calves in the back of the barn got up from their straw nest and, with tails lifted, began sucking the top board of their pen where milk had been spilled. The cow stanchions hung open and deserted. The smell of old dried manure mingled peculiarly with the aroma of fresh alfalfa. For some reason the combined smell made Lew think of a loose woman.

Speed stood sizing up Barney. "For an old bull he's sure fat."

"That's it," Lew said, low, quiet. "When with thirty wives around he should be more of a skinny runt like me." "Not very active then." Lew smiled some. "Them calves you see there ain't even his. Sired by Jim Wells's wild tom. Jumped a fence and come over."

"Wasn't there a fight?"

"Barney fight? Guess again."

"Tame, huh?"

"Around other bulls, yes. But around humans, no." Lew put up a foot on the feedbunk. He added, voice almost down to a whisper, "You'll notice I got his pen braced with three-by-twelve bridge planks all around. And I had him dehorned. He took out after me and Luanne every chance he got."

"Maybe he wasn't meant for married life. Some men ain't, you know."

"Hum."

"Maybe instead he was meant for one of them whatch-ma-call-its. Bullfights."

"No, I think it's mostly a case of nerves."

"Well, anyway, he don't look so tough to me." Speed reached between two boards and gave the old boy a pat.

Lew grabbed Speed's arm and jerked it back. He jerked so hard he turned Speed half around. "Cut it out, you jackass! Get him riled up and he's liable to bust out of them bridge planks even."

Speed flushed. "Bulls a Bashan, Lew, you act like this was my first load of bull flesh. Heck, I've been around some, man." Speed reached in again.

Barney turned slightly. He focused an eye as big as a black plum on Speed.

Speed jumped back, hand still stretched out in an unfinished pat.

"I'm telling you he's a bad devil when he gets his blood up."

"Godsakes, Lew, I've handled tough bulls before." Speed tipped back his trucker cap. "You know Tom Keith living just south a Bonnie there? Well, he had a mad bull once . . ." Speed spun out a long tale about how it was only he, Speed Swazy, who'd finally got Keith's bull up the chute and into the truck. "And the critter didn't even have a ring in the nose. While yours has. Heck, Lew—"

"Shh. Shut up. Have your size-up and let's get out of here and your truck backed to the door."

Speed said, short, "I notice I ain't the only one talkin'."

They backed the truck to the big loading door, tight, and slid the ramp down, siding it with partitions from the calf pen.

All the while they worked, Speed kept right on blabbing about all the animals he'd subdued and hauled away to Sioux Falls. "Why down t'Alvord only last week I had me a real picnic. And I mean it was a real picnic. Yessiree. Six wild steers straight out of the Badlands. Never seen a fence till they hit Siouxland. Let alone seen a human. Spooked quicker'n antelope. And with them bayonet horns, a whole dozen of 'em, I thought I was back in the Big War again, bein' charged by a division a Huns—"

"Speed. Listen. I'm warning you. If you don't shut up you'll be halfway to your reward in a minute."

"I notice I ain't the only one talkin'."

"Shut up anyway," Lew said, low, quiet. "At least Barney's used to my voice."

"Used to your whisper, you mean." Speed snorted. "I say, talk up like a man, in a good round voice, then maybe—"

"Dang it, Speed, shut up or you can load him on alone."

"All right, all right."

They pulled the gate to the bullpen and stood back.

But Barney ignored the opening. Instead, standing in his straw bed, he turned his great triangular head around and rolled a black plum eye at Speed.

"Shh," Lew said. "Let him get used to seein' the gate open before we move in on him. Maybe he'll walk right up the chute alone. I've seen it to happen."

Speed waited a few seconds; then, impatient to be getting on, took matters in his own hands. He reached for a hay fork and poked its three gleaming tines between the heavy bridge planks and gave Barney a prick in the rump. "Suh baas! Suh! Get!"

The sharp tines had barely touched hair when Barney was around like a revolving hill and rammed the planks with the big shield front of his skull. The planks cracked with a boom. And Speed jumped back, his fork flying to a far corner.

"Bulls a Bashan!' Speed said, bubber face paling.

"Told you."

"He has got a case a nerves."

"Yep."

"What a temper. Whew! What're you doin' with a bull like that around anyway?"

"What do you think I called you for?"'

Slowly, warily, Speed leaned a trembling hand on the top bridge plank. And the second his hand touched the plank, Barney rammed the side of the bullpen again. A moment later he peered out at Speed between the planks with his big black eye.

"How about that ring in his nose? Can't you lead him up with that?"

"If we could snap a lead rope to it, yes."

After a wait of some ten minutes, the dust having settled, Lew finally climbed the partition on his side and waved his hat at Barney. Hi yuh! Get, you black devil you! Suh baas! Suh! Get!" In the mellow gloom of the barn Lew's bald head glowed like a pumpkin. "Get, you old devil you! Suh! Up the chute with you! Yah!"

Impassively, solemnly, silently, Barney turned, backed a step, and then, like a steam engine, rammed the plank directly under Lew. The bull hit it with such force Lew almost toppled over into the pen with Barney.

"Hold it," Speed yelled, "hold it. Shooin' him in ain't gonna work, I can see that." Speed wiped sweat from his brow. "Whew! What an ornery cuss."

"Hum." Lew lifted his hat and scratched his bald head. "Say. Hum. I just now got me a idee. We'll fix a snap to a long fishpole and catch the ring in his nose that way. Goddurn, now why didn't I think of that before."

But the snap on the end of a fishpole didn't work either. Trying to catch the ring in Barney's nose was like trying to spear a wise old pike through a narrow cut in river ice. At each thrust Barney merely moved his white sneering nose a little to one side or another. Finally, when Barney had enough of it, he simply charged the side of the bullpen again with a clap of thunder.

Speed cursed. "Lew, we're never going to get that black devil loaded. By cripety, and me with still four more stops to make this morning."

"Patience," Lew said. "Patience."

"Wild devils like that should be shot, then hauled off to the rendering works. Instead of to the market. Holy jumping Peter! Good God in heaven! Man oh man oh man oh man oh man—"

"Hey!"

"—what a wild devil he is! What?"

"Your horn is stuck. Better give your steeringwheel a jerk or two."

"What?"

"Your horn is stuck."

"Oh. Yeh." Speed suddenly laughed. Again his laugh had the sound of an engine with little or no compression. "Yeh. My horn. I forgot." Speed absentmindedly leaned a hand on the top plank.

Barney charged again. Wham!

Speed's eyes abruptly filled with tears. He got a little wild then and began to jump up and down, the chaff in the alley puffing up around his shiny boots. "That did it. I've had enough. The boss can fire me if he wants to, but I'm not hauling your bull. Barney don't like cows. He don't fight with other bulls. He don't beller. He don't even switch his tail at flies. All he does is stare at you and buck them boards if you so much as smile at him. I say that's onnatural. Onnatural."

"Hum."

"How did you ever get him penned up in the first place?"

"Why, I put some green alfalfa in his feedbunk. He fancies it." Lew stopped short. Then he snapped his stub fingers. "Goddurn. That gives me a idee again."

Speed paused. "What does?"

Lew gave the gate to the bullpen a jerk. It fell back into place locking the bull up again.

"I don't get you, Lew."

"Speed, get that truck of yours out of here. And back it up in front of that big haymow door there. Not under it. Just back it in front of it."

"No, Lew," Speed said then. "No. That ain't gonna work."

"I lifted our car motor into place that way once."

"No, Lew, not that. Instead, why not throw a little fresh alfalfa up in the truck, if he fancies it so? He might go in by hisself that way."

"No. Don't you see? He knows what that truck is here for. He's got that figured out. And he's smart enough for that too."

"Well, we can try my idea once, can't we? Fresh alfalfa in the truck?"

"No. I say it won't work. He's got that truck figured out. No we'll try my new idee."

"Well, in that case, Lew, I think I better pull out now. Before it gets any worse."

"It won't hurt to try my new idee once."

"No, Lew."

"Goddurn, Speed, I say to try it. I want that big black devil off my yard by sundown. Now get your truck awayf'n that bullpen door."

Reluctantly Speed got into his truck and pulled it over to where Lew wanted it.

Lew called Luanne out of the house and together they harnessed up Lew's dappled whites and hitched them to the haymow draw rope on the other side of the barn. The haymow door under the peak was already open, so it took but a moment to pull the hay carrier to the end of the rail in the overhang and lock it in its slot and haul the dangling hay-sling down and finally spread it out on the ground.

Speed watched from the door of his truck, motor purring softly underfoot. "No, Lew. It ain't gonna work. I'm tellin' you. That bull"— Speed's eyes flicked over to where Luanne stood—"that gentleman cow ain't gonna like that."

"We'll see," Lew said. "I'm bound and determined to get that black devil off the yard by sundown. Today."

Lew got a forkful of fresh-cut alfalfa, hay Barney fancied, and scattered a trail of green wisps from the gate of the bullpen to the haysling. He placed the biggest part of the forkful a little to the far side of the sling. "Now. One whiff of that and we'll have him."

Speed snorted. "One step out of that pen and he'll be off with the birds, you mean."

"Now that's mighty curious of you to say that," Lew said. "Because Barney's never run away yet. No, I trust Barney to fancy that fresh alfalfa. Won't he, Luanne?"

Luanne nodded. Her eyes twinkled behind the scarred pink mask. She had on tight blue jeans and eased back on a leg.

Lew said, grim, "Just you sit tight in that truck, Speed, until I give the signal."

Speed cackled. "Ha. You bet your sweet life I'm gonna sit tight in my truck."

Lew said, "Now here's the idee. We'll open the gate to the bullpen again and let Barney gobble up that trail of green alfalfa. Then, as soon as he walks on top of the sling to get at that biggest pile there, I'll give Luanne the signal to start the horses so the sling'll come up around the bull, and, hist! up the bull will go. Then, soon's he's high enough to clear that rack of yours, I'll give Luanne another signal to stop. That's when you get your signal to quick back under him. Then Luanne can let the horses ease back a little, and whango! there the bull'll be. In the truck. Goddurn."

Speed stared. "I got one question."

"What's that?"

"How'll you get that sling out from under him once he's in the truck?"

"What do you think I got the end of this trip rope in my hand for, to skip rope with or something? A jerk on this and the sling parts in two, right out from under whatever is in it."

Speed stared at the ground "I don't believe it. Something's bound to go wrong with that scheme."

"Just the same we're gonna try it. I want that big black devil off the yard by sundown. Just you watch for your signal, is all I ask."

"I'll watch for the signal, all right. But don't be surprised if you see me and the truck take off in high when you give it. And not in reverse."

"Hum." Lew turned on his stumpy legs and opened the gate to the bullpen.

Barney's white lip lifted. He savored the air. And then, solemnly, silently, a dark hill moving on fat stub legs, he stepped out of the pen and began to eat up the trail of hay wisps.

Everybody watched.

A couple of swinging steps on each move, and taking his time Barney approached the sling, munching away like a deacon slyly chewing on a plug of tobacco in church.

The closer Barney came to the sling, the tighter Lew held the trip rope.

When Barney finally did reach the sling, he paused, sniffed the air with a knowing white leer, then moved hugely into the exact center of it. Big black eyes closing in bovine ecstasy, he began munching on the biggest pile of alfalfa.

Lew leaned over a little at the hips, made sure all was set—then gave Luanne her signal.

Luanne clucked softly, flipped the reins once. The white horses leaned into their traces.

The ropes of the sling rose up off the ground like cobra heads, and gradually, inevitably, closed around the bull. When the ropes first touched Barney, he turned his head mildly, wonderingly. But when the ropes closed around Barney for good, catching him under the belly and neck, one of the sling ropes even catching him precisely under the chin, a different look came into Barney's black plum eyes. He made as if to lunge at something.

But it was too late. His lunge only gave his huge boiler of a body a little swinging motion just as the sling lifted his hooves clear of the ground.

The dappled whites dug in. The ropes whistled in the pulleys. The sling cut deep into the tenderest parts of Barney's underbelly—and in an instant there was a tremendous scream. It was a shriek to scare a man half out of his wits. Lew stiffened in his tracks, Speed almost fell out of his truck, and Luanne dropped the reins.

What it did to the white horses was even worse. Their heads came up out of the pull, they reared wildly for a moment, even fantastically, and then, front hooves hitting earth again, leather traces slapping, they dug in enmaddened. The draw rope sped through the pulleys. The carrier clanged in its slot on the rail. And the bull, big black Barney, wondrously, unbelievably, shot up in the air, tail switching madly around and around, still screaming in horrible pain, great triangular head twisted around and up in torture like a contralto trying to get out that last high final note.

Of course, with Luanne having dropped the reins, the horses were free to run. And they did. They galloped. And the next thing everybody knew Barney the bull was being rapidly delivered to the rear of the haymow, tail first. Still screaming.

The sight of the bull rapidly disappearing into the gloom of the haymow, and the sound of the trip rope untwisting out of its coil at his feet with a hissing noise, finally woke Lew to what was going on. "Great Gasper!" he cried. And recovering, Lew got a firm grip on the trip rope and jerked.

He jerked just in time. The sling parted just as Barney's rear hit the back of the haymow. Barney dropped into the hay below. And the screaming stopped.

"Holy sufferin' bulls a Bashan!" Speed said, eyes as big as white onions.

"Great Gasper!" Lew said again.

"My—good—ness!" Luanne said, expression of a sort showing through the scars on her face.

"Catch them horses!" Lew cried "Or they'll take the barn with 'em!"

Then Luanne woke to what was going on too, and she ran after the dappled whites and caught them.

"Holy sufferin' bulls!" Speed said once more. Then Speed's eyes came together. "That did it!" he cried. "I've finally had enough of this!" And he slammed shut his door, shifted gears with a crash, and with a roar was off the yard.

Silence.

Lew looked at Luanne; Luanne looked at Lew. Abruptly both burst out laughing.

Lew laughed so hard he finally fell down. He lay beating the ground with his fists, ruddy face so tortured with laughter he looked like an idiot.

About then the Missus poked her head out of the pantry window. "I see Speed drove off. Did you finally get rid of Barney?"

Hardmouth still tortured with laughter, Lew said "Luanne, get the gun. you were right in the first place. Shootin' the bull is a whole lot better than haulin' the bull. Let alone slingin' the bull." Then Lew hollered at the Missus, "Yeh, we got rid of Barney all right. And how."

Late that afternoon, Odie Lakewood came around with his stinking truck. He quartered Barney in the back of the haymow where Lew had shot him, and loaded him into the truck, quarter for quarter, and hauled him away to his rendering works.

5

Luanne wouldn't help Lew on the yard anymore, wouldn't wear jeans even on cold days. She took to wearing dresses on all occasions, and sat with her knees prim together, and wore her hair done up in tight beauty parlor curls, and scented her person with various luring perfumes ordered from a mail order catalogue, and took up sewing and cooking with patient determination.

The Missus noted the change and shook her head. The poor girl. The blue jeans and the limber tomboy walk and familiarity with yard work stood her in better stead in landing a husband than all the homemaker airs. The Missus knew. The first years of married life a man wanted the sporting gal more than he wanted the homemaker. Of course, later on, after a man's blood had cooled some, a man wanted a nestmaker again, like he had when he was a boy and at home with ma. But the first while he wanted his tomboy sister. The Missus had often noticed how Siouxland couples took their honeymoons and their first vacations in the Black Hills where they went on climbing expeditions. Sisters in jeans could still climb; pregnant women couldn't.

The Missus knew a woman usually got but one chance at a man and that was when she was in bloom, just as there was but one time for the apple blossom to catch its bee. There had to be honey in the pistil or the bee wouldn't plant pollen grains in it. Once the flower was gone, it was too late. So the Missus, knowing, schemed of ways in which she might help Luanne nab a man.

Lew had his private thoughts about Luanne getting a husband too. Years before, right after Luanne was born, Lew had taken in stride the news that his Missus would never bear him another child. That had meant no son and heir. Lew consoled himself with Luanne's tomboy ways and with the thought that someday she'd marry and present him with a batch of grandsons. The name wouldn't be Lyons, which was too bad, but at least each grandson would have a piece of Old Lew in him.

Lew began to cuss himself nights for having butted in that time when Thurs the big boy showed interest in Luanne. Lew remembered that Luanne had liked Thurs too. She'd talked about him for days after the tank dunking incident. Lew saw now that it had been a mistake to nip that in the bud. What giant grandsons they might have had from Big Boy and Luanne by now, big bodies with maybe big brains. Man, yes.

Lew also regretted somewhat that the Missus had chased muttface Donk away. It was just possible that the Lyons blood might have been strong enough to make up for the bad parts of the Donkers blood, maybe even put together the best parts of both, the sturdy Lyons chassis with the sharp brains of the old grampa Doc.

Lew lamented the accident most of all. After that there hadn't been a ghost of a chance that a lad might come driving on the yard to spark Luanne.

So the time finally came, on Luanne's twenty-third birthday, when Lew said, "Even a shotgun wedding would be welcome now."

The Missus thought of it first.

They were in bed. It was dark. Overhead they could hear Luanne getting ready for bed. Outside the elms were threshing in the cold February wind. The hardcoal burner in the parlor just outside the bedroom door flickered pinkly blue. Under their woolen blankets the two of them lay folded snugly into each other, the Missus's bulky S curved around Lew's banty s.

Lew groaned.

"Lew?"

"Hum."

"That your back acting up again?"

"Hum."

"Then you worked too hard again today."

"I guess so."

"You're getting on in years, Lew, to be doing all that yard work and field work. Alone."

Lew slowly turned his head on his pillow to hear the better. "You ain't getting ready to bury me now, are you, Maw?"

"It's too much for you." The Missus drew her cold feet up inside her flannel nightgown. "Yes, it's too much for you."

"Maybe if Luanne was to help me on the yard a little, like in the old days, I could get by yet for a while."

"That's just it."

"What's just it?"

"Lew, I think it's time you got yourself a hired hand. A quarter section of land is just too much for you alone." The Missus put her cold feet against Lew's thighs.

"Hey," Lew said with a start, "warm your feet on your own legs."

"But you're always so hot in bed, Lew. I thought I'd just borrow a little of it."

"I won't be hot for very long with all those icebergs ag'in me."

The Missus drew her cold feet back inside her flannel nightgown. "I still say, you need a hired hand. Steady. The whole year round. Not just now and then during the busy seasons."

Lew fell silent. He lay blinking in the dark. What was the old woman up to now?

The Missus continued to rummage around on her side of the bed, trying to find a warm spot for her cold feet. "Yes, it's too much."

"Hum. What can't be cured will have to be 'dured."

"Too much," the Missus repeated.

Lew hardened up to it then. "Well, Maw, s'matter of fact, I've been thinking of getting me a tractor."

The Missus fairly lashed her big body around in bed. She moved so huge so fast she pulled the covers off Lew. "What?"

"I said, I'm thinking of getting me a tractor."

"Why, Lew Lyons, I'm surprised at you. You get a tractor? After all you've said against modern inventions?"

"Well, the neighbors've all got one. Jim Wells. Rolf Freyling. Even old Tunis Freyling, Rolf's pa, he's got one. All of 'em. I'm the last in the valley to get one."

"Hem." The Missus slowly rolled back into her own place. With heavy arms, in a billowing motion, she respread the bedcovers over them both. The two nestled snugly together again, her big S curved around his little s.

Lew said, "Course, like you say, I could hire me a man. And that way work out the full value of them horses before I buy the tractor. Might as well wear them down to the nub and be that much ahead."

"Ahh," the Missus said, lifting her head off her pillow. "Now you're talking like the Lew I know."

"Except that the hayland'll have to stay hayland a little while longer. Instead of raising a crop of corn or grain off it."

"Hem."

"And, a course, there's Luanne to think of too."

"Luanne?"

"Sure. You see, I figure it this way. The right kind of hired man, a steady man, instead of, say, one of them shortcut poolroom bums, maybe such a feller, seeing Luanne every day, seeing how steady she was, maybe he'd take a shine to her. Marry a steady goodhearted woman instead of one of them fake-tit Hollywood floozies."

"Ahh," the Missus breathed up into the dark.

"Because Luanne grows on you. You know that. Even after the accident she grows on you. It takes time for good to show."

"Ahhh," the Missus whispered.

"As it is now, that poor face of hers scares 'em off before they get to know her. They never take that second look to see both the character and the chassis."

"Mmm."

"Yep, maybe a hired hand ud do it. The right kind, of course."

"Of course."

"And if that don't work, we can always go back to inviting that muttface Donk back."

"Oh, it's too late for that," the Missus said. "Donk just last week married one of them Wayne twins."

"No! Them two pretty girls that always sit together in church by the door there?"

"Yes."

"Hum."

Lew's new black car turned out to be a lemon. There was always something the matter with it. Sometimes it was the motor; sometimes it was the chassis.

Lew and Luanne and the Missus were having afternoon tea, talking about it.

"Cheap iron and cheaper tin," Lew said. "The old car had twice the work built into it and it only cost half as much."

Luanne said, "But the new one has more style."

"Pah!" Lew said. "Your stylish horse may win the style show but she won't last once the races start."

"Oh, I don't know," Luanne said. "Who wants to win all the races?"

Lew said, "That goddurn Ernie Johnson, he sure threw a monkey wrench—"

"What's done is done," the Missus quick broke in. "No use crying over spilt milk. The Lord giveth, the Lord taketh away, blessed be the name of the Lord. We've got to look to the future. To tomorrow."

"Hum," Lew said. "Tomorrow I've got to take this new tin lizzie in to town and let Roy Wickett fix her again. I know I can't."

Luanne said, "What's wrong with her this time?"

"The timing gear is out of kilter. She ain't firing right. Won't pull."

The Missus said, "She took us to town all right last Sunday to church."

"Ha," Lew said, "in low gear up every rise and in second on the level. As she stands now, one of our Leghorn hens kin outscratch her in a pulling contest. Even with the chains on."

The next afternoon Lew and Luanne took the car to the best mechanic for miles around, Leroy Wickett, the Bonnie garageman. Roy had standing offers from big shops in both Sioux City and Sioux Falls to take over their repair business on his own terms. But Roy was a bachelor and wasn't in a rush. He liked the slow pace in Bonnie. Aside from being a target of juicy gossip by the local matchmakers, he considered bachelor life in a small town the perfect life.

Lew didn't care for Roy's easy going ways. Life was hard; life was grim; and to act as if it wasn't was a sin. Lew always had to swallow twice, and circle the block an extra time, before he could drive up to the big double doors of Wickett's Garage.

When he finally did pull up in front of the big gray doors, Lew blasted the horn long and loud.

"Why so loud, Paw?" Luanne said. "He ain't deaf."

"I still say it ain't right he ain't married yet. The good Lord meant for natural man to have an helpmate. I got married, and I liked my freedom too. So why can't he?"

Luanne's eyes sparkled behind her mask of pink scars. "Maybe he married a car."

"Ha!" Lew blew the horn again. "I suppose he expects to get twowheelers for kids? motorcycles?"

Luanne laughed. "Don't worry about Roy. He don't lack for girls. And one of these days one of them will nab him."

"What do you know about it?"

"Oh, I have ways of finding out."

"Hum. Maybe he's the one that keeps the orphanage going across the river."

The big gray doors finally lifted up, revealing Roy Wickett standing to one side of the doorway. Roy had a round face and a large warm smile and big white teeth. Roy was about Lew's size, and almost Lew's age, yet he looked like a young man. Behind Roy in the dusky interior stood cars in various stages of repair. A new demonstrator model sparkled behind a big glass display window. Two mechanics with greasy caps and blackened coveralls, their faces streaked and eyes vivid, were working over the motor of a school bus.

Roy had a brother named Crimp who didn't help him any either in Lew's eyes. Crimp was a Siouxland fiddler and square dance caller who made his living playing the various Saturday night dances around. Crimp had fallen off a ladder as a boy, cracking his neck, leaving him with a permanent humpneck. The humpneck or crimp seemed to give his fiddling a special quality and depth, and in time Crimp became quite popular in Siouxland, and made a fair living. But in Lew's eyes, Crimp, for all his house and wife and half-dozen kids, was a lazy poolhall bum who'd used a short fall off a ladder as an excuse not to do a day's work. Any man who could make his living sawing a fiddle one night a week and then lay around the rest of the time plinking scales was a no-good bum.

Still smiling, and looking more at Luanne than at Lew, Roy pointed to where Lew should put the car.

"What's wrong this time?" Roy asked.

Lew said, "Timing gear, I guess. Won't pull."

"Start her up again," Roy said, "and let's let her purr some."

Lew punched the starter button. The car motor came alive in a low roar.

"Let her idle," Roy said, face serious a moment.

The motor idled irregularly.

"It's the timing," Lew said.

Roy nodded slowly. "Yeh. That and the valves."

"Valves too?"

"Yeh." Roy took off his cap to scratch hair no longer there. Like Lew he was as bald as a moon. His fingers traced two smudges across the top of his pate. "Yeh. They ain't closing right. There's at least two cylinders with little or no compression."

"Great Gasper!" Lew said. "This goddurn lemon is going to ruin me yet."

"Why don't you trade her in for another model?" Roy nodded toward the shiny demonstrator behind the display window. "I'll give you a good trade-in allowance." Roy looked at Luanne and gave her a large warm smile. "Can't let the Missus and your girl here run around with a car that'll break down any minute."

Lew looked glumly down at the oil-spotted cement floor.

Roy said, "There's a ninety day guarantee on the other model too."

Lew snorted. "What's ninety days? Make it ninety weeks and I'll buy." Lew shook his head. "No. I'm going to make this one run or know the reason why. Goddurn."

"Okay. You're the doctor."

"When can you have her ready?"

Roy looked around in his shop. "Got to have that school bus ready by to-morrow morning. And there's two other cars ahead of you. Still, what with Dode to help—" Roy interrupted himself. "Care if I let Dode work on it? I'm going to be too busy to do it myself for a couple of days."

"Who's Dode?"

"My nephew. Dode Wickett. In from Whitebone. Out of work, so I took him on for odd jobs for his board and room."

"Is he any good?"

"First class. That's him there. Coming in through the back door."

Both Lew and Luanne looked.

A grave youth in neat gray coveralls with a flat almost lifeless face walked slowly across the garage. His neat dull-blond hair was combed severely back. He stopped in front of a car up on a hoist that had just been brought in.

Roy said. "I only wish I had enough work to keep him the year round ."

Lew said abruptly, "Year round, huh? Has he ever worked on a farm?"

"That's where he came from," Roy said. "A Whitebone farm. He and his brother ran it for their widow mother. But now with tractors there ain't enough work for them both."

"Married?" Lew snapped.

"Paw," Luanne said softly.

Roy smiled, gave Luanne another large warm look. "No, I'm afraid Dode takes after me. Likes to go it alone." Roy chuckled. "We're hard to catch, I guess."

"Hum." Lew watched Dode pick up a wrench and a long screwdriver, watched him dismantle the front wheel assembly of the car in knowing fashion. Dode's motions were sure, fluid, with no waste motion. The front wheel, its rods, its brake drums, came apart like the wings and legs of an overdone goose separating under an expert knife.

"Slow but steady," Roy said. "He'll have your car ready by tomorrow noon."

Lew said, "All right. And tell the kid if he does a good job of it, I'll have him for my hired man. At his own price. Plus room and board."

"I'll tell him," Roy said, with a large slow smile for Luanne.

Dode came to work for Lew in April.

Dode wasn't much of a wizard around the animals, but he was around the engines on the yard. He kept Lew's car in tiptop shape, kept the water pump running without so much as a missed explosion in the coldest weather, kept the Missus's washing machine waggling vigorously even when the heavy rag rugs were in. In fact, Dode kept things running so smoothly Lew began to joke that he needed Dode more as a hired hand than Luanne needed him as a husband.

The Missus was delighted with Dode. With him around there was little if any extra fuss. Dode was quiet. He kept his room neat. He wasn't hard on his clothes. He didn't smoke and stink up the curtains. He ate what was set before him without question. A perfect match for Luanne if there ever was one, she thought. The Missus made it a point to give Dode the biggest cuts of steaks and pies.

And Luanne behaved just right too. She dressed in freshly ironed clothes every day. Mornings she combed her curly brown hair until it shone like corn-silk. Quietly, in her own way, she did her best to show Dode the steady good-hearted side of herself.

Lew was finally so pleased with Dode he made up his mind Dode deserved a good-looking wife. He told Luanne to go get herself a new face. He'd read about some plastic surgeons at the University of Minnesota Medical School who had devised a brand new way of skin grafting and who had become famous for the number of successful operations they had performed.

Luanne went off to the Twin Cities late in June and came back early in August.

She came back a changed woman. When she got off the bus at the head of the lane and walked in, Lew and the Missus were sitting in the kitchen having a mid-morning cup of coffee. Both stared at her. They recognized her voice and her chassis, but they hardly recognized her face. Gone were the rough pink scars. Her cheeks were once again marvels of delicate texture. The only telltale mark to show there'd ever been an operation was a very narrow white ridge running down from her temples past her ears and around under her chin. The white line resembled a white hat-string to keep a hat in place.

"Like it?" Luanne asked.

Lew and the Missus stared some more.

Luanne smiled. "Like it?"

The Missus saw it then. The old smile, the twinning smile of the little girl, was gone. Luanne'd had a little of it left after the last facelifting job, but now it was completely gone. The University surgeons had managed, at last, delicately, to cut it away.

"Like it?"

Lew finally found his tongue. "Like it? Why, girlie, you look wonderful." Lew fumblingly put his pipe to one side and got up from his armchair, and then rushed up and put his stocky cumbering arms around her and gave her a great big kiss. "Luanne."

Luanne kissed him back.

It was Lew's turn to notice something. Her lips were stiff in the kiss.

They had more coffee, then, and Luanne told a little about it. How the docs did it. First they examined every inch of her body for the most suitable skin. They couldn't very well take it off her legs because then she'd have boy fuzz on her face. They didn't like to take it off her arms because there she'd often had a tendency to break out with a rash in the spring. "So they finally settled," Luanne said with a rough and a laugh, "so they finally settled, of all places, on my back. Here."

"Ahh," the Missus said, eyes becoming two dark holes.

"I lay with my head turned around, facing backwards, for all of seven weeks while they gradually shifted the skin from there to my face. First one, then the other." Luanne looked at Lew. "I know what you're thinking, Paw, so wipe that look off your face or I'll never talk to you again. It wasn't quite where you think."

"Oh no, Luanne," Lew said. "I'm too glad for that."

Luanne laughed. "Well, it's all right, Paw. And you're right too. When you spend a good two months looking backwards day and night like you had eyes in your . . . well, all I can say is, you learn things. You see life in a new light."

"Luanne," the Missus said.

Luanne humphed. "Paw works in the barnyard too, Maw. He has eyes."

Later Dode came in for his coffee. He came in quietly, gravely, shoes clean, dull-blond hair brushed severely back. He drew up a chair to the table.

"Hello, Dode," Luanne said.

With a sliding throw of eyes at her, he said, "Hello."

"That all you got to say after two months?" Luanne said.

Dode took a sip of hot coffee.

Luanne said, "Well, I can see I wasn't missed much around here."

Dode took another sip of coffee.

Lew couldn't stand it. "Goddurn, Dode, hain't you noticed nothing about her?"

Slowly Dode lifted his grave eyes from his steaming cup. "I can't say as I have."

The Missus blinked a look at Lew to shut him up.

But Lew wasn't to be stopped now. "You must be as blind as a fence post."

Dode set his cup in his saucer and looked around. "Was I supposed to have noticed something?"

"Great Gasper," Lew said.

Dode's glance finally fell on Luanne's face. "Oh," he said. "So that's what you went away for."

"Yes," Luanne said. Her blue eyes sparkled expectantly. "Do you like it?"

"Well," Dode said, cocking his head to one side and looking at her face like it might be the repaired grillwork of a car, "well, I can't say as to that."

Luanne's eyes opened. "You don't like it?"

"Not so very."

"Oh," Luanne said.

Dode went on. "Well, maybe at that it's pretty good. I didn't see the chassis before it got all bunged up."

"What!" Lew cried.

After Dode had gone out on the yard again, Lew had a few choice remarks to make. "That deadhead. If you stuck a lily under his nose he'd look for a place to oil it." Lew cursed. "I can't say as to that didn't see the chassis before it got all bunged up. Man alive!"

The Missus had a word too. But she spoke up for Dode. "Oh, Paw, Dode was nervous. When a boy's in love like that he's bound to say the wrong things."

"He's bound to say things like that about the face of a girl he's supposed to be in love with?"

"It's all a blur to him," the Missus said.

"I'll say it's a—" Lew caught himself. His eyes became great round staring onions. "Listen, Maw, when I was sparkin' you back in the good old days, believe you me I always knew when you had your veil on or not." Lew cursed. "If I myself didn't hold Luanne so high, I'd say it was money thrown away, her going to that University Medical School."

"What about me?" Luanne said. "It's me that has to look in the mirror when I look for the part in my hair."

Lew's face underwent a swift change. "Sure, girlie, I know that." His voice almost broke. "I know that, girlie. You're right."

Luanne's new face didn't take to the sun too well. It burned easily. Sometimes it even pimpled over. And when Luanne wore a sunbonnet, her grandmother's on Lew's side, her face became as pale as egg-peel, so that she looked like one dying of consumption.

Meanwhile, for all the goodhearted side of herself she showed, and for all the money they'd spent, Dode never once gave her a tumble. Not once. He went on being his flat efficient self, servicing the machines on the place.

"Favor him a little more when you get a chance," the Missus urged in a low whisper when she and Luanne were alone. "You know. On the stoop in the sunset there. Let him know you're at least cheerful."

"I have," Luanne said.

"Or else, ask him to take you places. To them dances his uncle Crimp Wickett plays for. You've got to do something."

"I have," Luanne said.

"You have?"

"Yes."

"What does he say?"

"Nothing. He just looks at you. And when I ask him, 'Don't you like to dance?' he just says, 'I can't say as to that'."

"Ohh!" the Missus said with a quick hunching motion of her solid body. "If only he had half, yes, even a tenth, of what that nervy Donk had."

Luanne laughed. "Yes, that muttface was at least a little fun." She sighed. "But I hear he's happily married to that Wayne twin."

Lew urged her on too when he had a chance. "Don't be afraid to jolly him a little when you're alone."

"Like how?"

"Well, when he's working on something, on his watch or so on the table in the evening there, when he's got it all apart . . . well, you know, how girls do. Lean on his shoulder. Touch him now and then here and there. A little. You know how girls do."

"I have."

"And he don't do anything?"

"No." Luanne paused. "Well, yes, once he did. That was when he brushed me off his shoulder like I was a speck of rust."

"That deadhead. That fence post. Goddurn."

Luanne laughed. "I suppose next you'll be wanting to patch him up at the University Medical School too."

Lew fired Dode just before Thanksgiving.

Soon after, things began to happen. First, the various engines on Lew's yard went on the blink: the Missus's washing-machine wouldn't start, the waterpump began to miss, the big four-horse with which Lew ground corn blew a gasket, and Lew's lemon of a car once more wouldn't pull much in high.

Next, Luanne's failure to nab Dode, for whom the Missus had a soft side, precipitated the Missus into a change of life.

But the worst was, Luanne began to go out alone and stay out all hours of the night. She also began to put on powder in clouds, and lipstick like blood-lettings, and flashy clothes like a cheap city girl.

Both Lew and the Missus protested: Lew with the offended dignity of a patriarch used to running things; the Missus erratically.

"May I kindly know where you're going tonight?" Lew asked.

"Paw," the Missus said warningly.

Luanne said, "Around. Maybe in town. Why?"

"Why? Well, ain't we your folks anymore?"

"I'm free, white, and twenty-one," Luanne said with a city girl smile. "And I guess that lets me do what I want when I want to."

Lew almost choked. "Well, all right, girl. Drive careful. Watch out for drunks. And don't stay out too late."

"I'll try not to."

Face turning red and white by turns, the Missus said, "And who is it with this time? ah?"

"You'll find out soon enough."

"With Dode?"

Luanne laughed. "Him? That's more dead than Dode?"

One evening Lew and the Missus dropped in on Rolf and Greta Greyling for a sociable visit. There they heard something that made them sick to their stomach. In fact they couldn't believe it at first.

The next morning, when Luanne came down sleepy-eyed for breakfast, Lew asked her about it.

"What's this I hear about you riding around in the country with Roy Wickett?"

Luanne's blue eyes sparkled "The car was on the blink again, Paw. So Roy drove it around a little to see what was the matter with it."

"Well," Lew said, biting back bitter thoughts, "well, I guess you're old enough to know your own mind."

"Ain't it about time, Paw?"

Next, rumor had it she'd been seen out riding with Roy's brother Crimp, the Siouxland fiddler and square dance caller.

"I suppose this time you'll tell me you were out helping him tune up his fiddle?"

Luanne laughed. A curious odd wriggling expression worked on her pale moon face. "If that's what you want to think."

"Ahh," the Missus said, low, first flushing, then turning white.

Then in the spring Luanne was gone for three days.

When she came back, she wasn't alone. She was married.

She came up the front stoop and into the kitchen with her husband. Lew and the Missus were having their usual mid-morning cup of coffee.

"Him?" Lew said, staring hard. "Him? So it was Roy Wickett afterall."

"Him," Luanne said. "Roy. Ain't you gonna congratulate us?"

The Missus said, "You eloped?"

"Eloped," Luanne said "We took our honeymoon in the Black Hills. Ain't you gonna congratulate us?"

Roy smiled his large warm smile. Roy looked dapper in his blue suit, and would have looked every bit as young as Luanne if it hadn't been for his moon head.

Lew glared at Roy.

"Ain't you gonna congratulate us?" Luanne asked.

"No, I ain't," Lew said.

"Lew," the Missus said.

"Well, I ain't and be damned to you all."

Then the Missus said, "Luanne," and she got up and put her arms around her. After she'd kissed both the bride and the groom, she sat down again and covered her face with her apron and began to cry.

Later, when the Missus and Lew were alone with Luanne, the Missus said, "How come with him, Luanne? When you knew Paw was against him so much?"

"I dunno. Maybe because I felt Roy and me were meant for each other."

"You two meant for each other?"

"Well, take a good close look once. Weren't we? Me with my bald face and Roy with his bald head?"

Lew exploded. "Bald head is right. He's balder'n me."

"But what you forget, Paw, is he ain't related."

"Luanne," the Missus said, "don't blaspheme. Remember what happened to them children in the Bible who blasphemed Elisha the baldheaded one."

Lew looked at the Missus, looked at Luanne, then shook his head slowly, sadly. "My own little girl," he murmured.

Through Lew's mind lashed pictures of Luanne back when she was a little tyke, how in the old times after supper, while he sat in his rocker beside the warm hardcoal burner, snug inside the house against the winter, how little Luanne would put her dollie beside him in the rocker, the dollie on one side and she on the other, and she would ask him to kiss the dollie, and then would ask him to kiss her, Luanne, to see how it felt for the dollie to get kissed, and how after she would get up and go tizzying around in the room like she was a dancer going up to Jerusalem before King David, how she—

"Is this what I grew old for?" Lew cried. "And him, that Roy, yet to begin?"

The Missus meanwhile took to wearing red.

Afterwards, of course, Lew and the Missus got used to it. Roy smiled his big smile, and Luanne spoke with her blue eyes, and the little tots, the grandchildren, a boy named Lewis and a girl nicknamed Missy, trusted Grampa Lew with their teddy bears and dollies.

It was like seeing double. They had Luanne's twinning child smile all over again—only the smiles were larger and warmer than ever.

Fathers and Sons

I think it is more of a problem to be a father, more difficult to be a good father, than to be a good mother. I think a woman can be a good mother no matter what happens to her . . . But to become a father, that's something that is difficult to learn . . . Natural instinct and nature are against it. I remember as a boy seeing a boar go on a killing rampage. He killed over half a crop of pigs. . . And in the horse world, look at what the old leading stallion does. He gets rid of all the males. All he wants is mares and little colts. He doesn't want any grown males around. And for a male to learn to be a loving father is the most difficult of all steps. A woman naturally loves her children because she carries them for nine months and then has to feed them for three or four more months closely and intimately. So that it is utterly natural for a woman to be a mother. She just can't help it. She is it. But to be a father, this is something you learn.

FROM

Green Earth

New Pa

THE LITTLE PIGS didn't need their mothers any more. They could drink Pa's skim milk. As soon as the sow mothers got lazy fat, Pa had them loaded on the Cannonball freight. Pa went along with the sows to the Sioux City stockyards to get the money.

For two days Free and Ma did the chores for Pa. Everett got the cobs for the stove. Everybody worked except Albert, the new baby.

The third day about noon Old Horsberg drove onto the yard in his new copper-trim Ford. When Old Horsberg stepped on the brake, the new Ford stopped and stood shaking.

A tall man stepped out. The tall man had on a new gray hat with a black band and a new overcoat with a small velvet collar. He also had on new black gloves and black shoes.

Free didn't know why but he was afraid to say hello.

Old Horsberg goosed the motor and the copper-trim Ford shook and then it slowly turned short and rattled off the yard.

"Wal," the tall man said, "ain't you kids gonna greet your pa with a tight hug?" The tall man had a smile like Pa's.

Everett walked up and gave the tall man's leg a tight hug.

Free smiled a little but hung back.

266

Ma came to the doorway. The doorway was around her like a picture frame. "Why, Alfred, you're all feathered out like a new rooster."

"Yip," the tall man with Pa's smile said. "How do you like your new husband?"

It was a new Pa then.

Ma had to laugh. "As brother John would say, you're all dressed up like a sore toe."

The new Pa's smile became bigger, like a half-moon. He was carrying two packages. The new Pa walked into the house. "I thought it was about time I looked the part of the husband of the queen of Leonhard County."

"I'm no queen."

"You are to me." The new Pa set down the packages and threw his arms around Ma and gave her a squeeze so hard she groaned. "And how did all my loveys get along while I was gone?"

"Just fine," Ma said.

"I got the cobs," Everett said.

Free didn't know if he dared to brag to the new Pa. Everett sure was free with the new Pa. But then Everett never knew any better.

Ma said, "We had no bad weather. Nothing but sun every day. And the boys were both so busy they didn't have time to get into trouble."

The new Pa paraded up and down in the kitchen in his new clothes. "Wal, it looks like you were all good peoples while I was gone. Come, let's see you open this package once. This one here."

"I hope you didn't buy us anything foolish now," Ma said.

"Open it up," the new Pa said.

Ma felt of the new Pa's coat sleeve first. "That's good material. I'll bet it cost you a pretty penny."

"Seventeen dollars on sale. Gray kersey."

"I like that Chesterfield collar. It becomes you, Alfred. But weren't you afraid it'd get covered with soot on the train?"

"Truth to tell, I had all these new things of mine in this other package here until I hit Bonnie. Then I just had to put 'em on so I could show off a little when I hit the yard."

Ma untied the strings of her new package. "Did the sows bring a good price?"

"I got the top market. The right weight on the right day."

Ma lifted a new purple dress out of the package. "Alfred, you shouldn't have."

"Why not? If I can wear a Chesterfield overcoat, you can surely wear a queen's dress."

Ma was smiling as big and as wide as the new Pa.

"Try it on. See if it fits."

"How would you know my size?"

"Now wouldn't that be a pretty how-do-you-do if I didn't know that. When I hold your middle in my arms every night."

It really was their Pa then except that he was also a little new.

Ma looked at her boys. "You do not."

"Put it on."

Ma went to their bedroom to try it on.

Free asked, "Did you bring us a present too?"

"You betcha life I did. Here." Pa opened the package deeper and lifted out some new leather mittens, one pair for Free, one for Everett. They were lamb-lined. "For next fall. I got 'em cheap on a sale."

"We can't wear them now then?"

"No. They're for when you start school next fall. When it gets cold. Won't that be nice? You can carry your lunch bucket without getting your hands cold. They're much warmer than just wool-lined mittens."

Free and Everett put them on to see if they fit. They were a little big.

"Just right," Pa said, "by next winter you'll have grown into 'em."

Ma came back in, wearing her purple dress. She'd piled her gold hair on top of her head.

"Wow!" Pa said. "Now I'm glad I did come back." He put his arm around Ma's middle and made her bow to the kitchen stove with him. "Your majesty," he said to the black stove, "the Duke and Duchess of Siouxland."

Ma and Pa looked better than a picture in a book.

Pa made Ma take a couple of fancy dancing steps with him and then he gave her a little airplane ride.

"Eee! Alfred, put me down."

Free liked the new part of Pa. Maybe this new part of Pa would let him have two spoons of sugar on his oatmeal for breakfast. Maybe he'd even let him have some raisins and some shredded coconut on his rice for dinner.

That noon, after they'd all had meat and potatoes and vegetables, Ma set a big bowl of steaming rice on the table. The rice kernels were so swelled up they looked like hailstones. Pa gave the boys each a good plate plumb full. Pa sprinkled on a spoon of sugar.

Free touched Pa on the elbow. "Can I have two spoonsful, please? And some raisins and coconut on the top?"

Pa almost fell out of his swivel chair. "What!" Pa looked over at Ma. "If that don't put the cap on it. Have you been spoilin' my boys while I was gone?"

"No."

Pa looked down at Free. "Where'd you ever get the idee that you could have double the usual amount of sugar? Including raisins and coconut?"

"I thought maybe the new part of you would let me."

It hurt Pa to hear that. "No, son, your Pa hain't got a new part to him. It was just the clothes that was new." Pa tried to smile like Uncle John. "I'm your same old Pa. I hope that's all right by you."

Free looked down at where the one spoon of sugar had been sprinkled on his rice. `

He watched the little islands of sugar slowly sink away. Finally he picked up his spoon and began eating before all the sugar had disappeared. It was the same old Pa all right.

Prime Fathers

Ninety is Enough: Portrait of my Father

MY FATHER WAS BORN in the small village of Tzum, near Franeker, Friesland, in the Netherlands, March 31, 1886. He was baptized Feike Feikes Feikema
VI, though he later was known as Frank Feikema.

The first Feike back in the 1750's had been a man of property, owning a big
farm called Groot Lankum near Franeker, but he'd lost it due to a pestilence
which wiped out his herd of Frisian-Holstein cattle. The once proud Feikemas
fell into the labor market.

Feike V, my grampa, still had some of that old pride left in him. He refused
to be a laborer, and instead sailed before the mast. He talked a lovely Frisian
girl named Ytje Andringa, who came from a rich family, into eloping with him.
When she was disinherited for doing so, Grampa Feike V decided he had enough
of the Old Country, and with his wife and his just-born son, my father, left for
the United States.

Several years ago, when I visited Tzum, I discovered that Grampa's house
had been razed, along with others, and had become part of the property owned
by an old people's home. I did find my father's name registered in the Doop
Boek (birth book) in the beautiful old Tzum church and saw my grandfather's
signature. I saw the font where my father was baptized. I tried to imagine what
that baby might have looked like before it was whisked off to America.

When Grampa landed at Ellis Island, the immigration officer had trouble
pronouncing his name, Feike F. Feikema. Finally the officer told Grampa that
he'd better have at least a first name people could pronounce. He asked Grampa
what town he came from, and when Grampa answered, first Frjentsjer, the Frisian
version, and then Franeker, the Dutch version, the man said, "We'll put you
down as Frank and whatever that last name of yours is." So Frank it was after
that, and in time my father was called Frank too. That was a strange naming; the
Frisians and the Franks had been enemies for centuries. Actually Frederick would
have been a better translation. Frederick and Feike come from the same Indo-
European root of pri-tu meaning "love, free, friend." And ma means "man of"
or "son of."

Grampa and wife and child first headed for Orange City, Iowa, a Dutch set-
tlement. Restless, still full of pride, Grampa next moved the family to Grand
Rapids, Michigan, also a Dutch settlement and where some relatives of his wife
lived; then to Perkins Corner, Iowa, where he farmed a quarter section; then to
Lebanon, Missouri, where he worked on a railroad; then to Doon, in Northwest
Iowa, where he became a stone mason; then to what later became known as the

Bad Lands of South Dakota; and finally to Doon again, where he built storm cellars and cement block houses and worked part time on the railroad as a section hand in the wintertime. Five more children were born to Grampa and Gramma during all that wandering, Kathryn, Jennie, Nick, Abben, and Gertrude. All were raised as Americans, not as Frisians or Hollanders. Grampa swore when he landed in America that he would never speak either Frisian or Dutch again, but only what he called "American." He made only one exception and that was to speak Frisian to his mother, my great-grandmother, who came to America shortly after he did and lived in Sioux Center, Iowa. My memory of Grampa is that he spoke good English, with no trace of a foreign accent. Frisians are related to the Angles and Saxons and have little trouble learning to speak English.

Shortly after Gertrude was born, Gramma Ytje died and the family was broken up. My father was farmed out to various American families living out in the country, the Pohlmans, the Harmings, the Reynolds, all of them originally coming from New England by way of the Western Reserve. Aunt Kathryn went to live with a wealthy family in town named Holmes. Thus at a very early age my father was taken out of school and such learning as he had soon vanished. It had also become apparent that he had some trouble learning in school, unlike Aunt Kathryn who was very good at it. He was good at figures but never letters. When he signed his name he had to stop and think each time he wrote a letter, as though he had trouble remembering their right order, which later on suggested to me that he may very well have had some form of dyslexia.

In the 1890s people got around by horseback or by horse and buggy. There still were many wild prairies left, especially along the rivers and where it was hilly. My father told me that he remembered riding a horse once for some ten miles without hitting a fence. Some homes were still being built of sod. There were no groves or trees about except along the rivers. There were of course no radios or telephones. There was a local newspaper, The Doon Press, but gossip moved slowly from home to home. And moving slowly, it was thoroughly digested, until various kinds of usable wisdom emerged.

Pa soon found out that he had a good ear for music and learned to play the harmonica, the accordion, and the fiddle. Presently he was in demand to play at as well as call square dances. The church he went to, the Congregational, didn't frown on dancing or singing. He also developed into a pretty fair country baseball pitcher.

He apparently was a doughty fellow. Once he accidentally jabbed a hayfork into his knee in the dead of winter. He was a long ways from the yard at the time but had the presence of mind to first make a tourniquet with his handkerchief before jerking the hayfork out of the bone. On another occasion, while shingling the cupola on the locally famous Reynolds round barn, the cleat on which his foot rested gave way, and he began sliding. He fell off the cupola and hit the main roof. Despite desperate clawing and scratching, he kept on sliding. When he knew there was no way of stopping the slide, he figured out where the fresh cow manure pile lay below and, deliberately rolling himself over and over as he slid, managed to aim himself for it. He shot out over the edge of the roof, and miracle of miracles, landed in six feet of loose green slush. The cupola was seventy feet above the ground. He came out of it covered with manure but otherwise "without a scratch."

Pa met my mother, Alice Van Engen, tall and golden blond, when he was twenty-three. There is no evidence that he had a girl friend before he met her, though I did hear from some old timers that the girls of his day considered him a catch. He was handsome with black hair, light gray piercing eyes, and a powerful six-foot-four frame. He liked to say that he was just as tall as Abraham Lincoln. He had fair skin and always had a sweet smell about him. Even when he sweat he had a good manly aroma about him. He danced with girls but didn't date them. He met my mother at her cousins' house on a farm near Doon. She'd had a sad romance with a fellow in Orange City, Iowa (my mother wouldn't let him kiss her much and the fellow, not being able to wait, knocked up the hired girl where he worked), and her father, my grampa Frederick Van Engen, sent her to her Van Engen cousins near Doon to get over it. While she was there, Pa happened to drive onto the Van Engen yard and the two fell for each other. From what my mother told me, and from what Pa has said, they were innocents, virgins, when they got married. My father often remarked to us boys, as though to instruct us, "When I got married I could look any woman in the world in the eye. And I still can."

Ma was devoutly religious, though not of the fanatic kind. She was gentle, quietly determined, and very bright. (I go into all this in great detail in my novel *Green Earth*, which is in part autobiographical.) She quietly got Pa to leave his church and to join hers, the Dutch Christian Reformed Church. She also persuaded him to quit playing and calling at square dances, though she didn't mind if he played his jolly tunes on the harmonica and the accordion at home. She herself was highly musical and they often played together, he on harmonica and she on the parlor organ. Sometimes she sang (she was a good soprano) while he played. She also urged him to quit playing baseball, "a little boy's game," but that he wouldn't do. He no longer played for the town team but did play for the church team. I remember only two arguments or tiffs between the two, and one of them had to do with baseball. It was the Fourth of July and Doon was playing Sioux Center at a church picnic. Pa was to play third base. Ma wanted him to listen to a famous Navajo missionary instead. Ma worked on him all the way to the picnic grove and all Pa did was smile his sideways smile. When they got there, Ma discovered the missionary had moved his talk up an hour so he could watch the game. Pa would never admit it but I think he knew that the missionary loved baseball.

Pa and Ma got married January 22, 1911. They had only a couple hundred dollars to begin farming and only a few possessions. They bought a team of horses (Pa already owned a wonderfully swift and willful trotter named Daise, a pretty roan), a cow, a heifer with calf, a few chickens, and a few pigs. They also bought a few implements at farm sales, a walking plow, a walking cultivator, a disk, a drag, a cornplanter. At the end of the first year they'd paid off all debts and bought more horses and cattle.

I was born January 6, 1912, during a fierce blizzard. It was 24° below. My grandmother, Jennie Van Engen, was there and she helped Ma have me while Pa was gone to fetch the doctor with a team and bobsled. When after a great struggle Pa and the doctor finally made it through the storm, I was already lustily bawling away. Earlier Pa had found a full bottle of whiskey in the haymow and he promptly asked Ma for permission to break it open and celebrate with the doctor.

My mother, who was death on drinking, reluctantly agreed. Later she took the bottle and put it in the bottom of her wardrobe. When my mother died in 1929 there actually was some whiskey left in that bottle. Uncle Hank, my mother's brother, gave her a slug of it to revive her for a time when she was dying of rheumatic fever.

My father insisted that I be named Frederick, and not either Feike or Frank. He had come to love my mother's father, Frederick Van Engen. Furthermore he was a little tired of all that Feike the Fifth and Feike the Sixth stuff. He stuck to his guns too when his father's brothers, my great uncles, drove great distances to protest my being named Frederick. "He is the Feike," the great uncles proclaimed, faces livid, "the stamhâlder, the son and heir, the seventh in a row since the first Feike!"

Pa's insistence on naming me Frederick helps explain why he didn't object when I changed my name from Frederick Feikema to Frederick Feikema Manfred in 1952. I'd found out from a linguist that Feike and Frederick had the same Indo-European root at about the same time that I had enough of having to spell out my name to long distance telephone operators as well as having to explain that as a Frisian-Saxon I really was about as Anglo-Saxon as anyone could be in the English-speaking world. Pa knew the problems of having a "funny name" in America.

My first memory of my father was the day he caught a ride to town with a neighbor and later in the afternoon, to our surprise, came rolling onto the yard driving a new car, a chain-drive Overland, beeping the bulb horn, scaring the dog into hiding under the corncrib, making the cattle bawl out in the barnyard, causing the horses out in the night yard to pop their tails, and chasing the chickens back into their coops. My mother appeared at the screen door to the kitchen, drying her hands in her green apron and wondering what all the racket was about. My father invited her to get in and he'd take us all for a spin around the section. My brother Edward and I quickly climbed in back, our usual seat in the carriage, breaths short for joy, eyes as wild as cock-eyed roosters. My mother got in very reluctantly. She didn't like "the automobile" as she always called it. Pa bugled the horn again and we were off. The sun was shining and all the neighbors' chickens were working the ditches for grasshoppers. When Pa blew the horn, the chickens sprayed in all directions. The front of the Overland went through them like the prow of a boat pushing through white water. When the ride was over, my mother got out of the car, not saying a word, and with a sick smile went directly back to her kitchen. Ma never did get to like "the automobile" and so long as she was alive she never permitted Pa to drive over 30 miles an hour. "Or I jump out."

Pa continued to surprise us when he came back from trips. One day he went to Sioux City with a shipment of hogs, taking the Great Northern from Doon. A day later he arrived home catching a ride with a neighbor. Eddie and I ran out to the gate to see who it was. When Pa stepped out of the car we didn't recognize him right away. Pa had bought himself a complete set of new clothes, a new gray overcoat with a black velvet collar, a new gray hat with a black band, a new gray suit, and a pair of black gloves. The face looked familiar but all those new clothes threw us off. Also this strange man with Pa's face didn't act like Pa. This man acted like a high monkey-monk from the city with fancy dude manners. He had a package with him which he carried into the kitchen and proceeded to open. It turned out to be a special dress, floor length, for my mother. It was when Pa took off his hat and bowed to Ma and then kissed her that I finally made out for sure who it really was.

One day I heard some coughing in the barn and when I looked I found Pa's favorite horse Daise down. I'd known he'd kept her in the barn that day for some reason, but I was shocked to see Daise lying on the floor. One never caught a horse down. I ran to get my father in the house. Pa was smoking his pipe, feet up on the reservoir of the stove. When I told him what I'd seen, Pa clapped out his pipe in the range, and hurried out to the barn. Pa took one look and knew the worst. He got down on his knees beside her and held her head.

After a while Daise coughed in his lap. That ignited Pa. He gently laid her head down in the straw and ran to the house to call the veterinarian. When my mother wondered a little about the cost of the long distance call, my father whirled on her and cried, "My God, woman, that's Daise that's sick! My Daise! You know, the pretty roan what's been with me all these years. Who even took me to Orange City to see you."

When he couldn't raise the vet, Pa asked Ma if she had some liniment around. She didn't. So next he asked her for the whiskey bottle lying in the bottom of her wardrobe. She gave it to him reluctantly. He ran to the barn with the whiskey to give Daise a slug of it. But Daise only coughed when he opened her lips and poured some into her mouth. The whiskey spilled out into the straw.

Daise was dead within the hour.

My father cried. I'd never before seen him cry and I was too petrified to move. I didn't want to see it but at the same time I couldn't move either. Pa dug a huge hole for Daise in the pasture and buried her. He refused to call the rendering plant.

I was about nine when my father awakened me in the middle of the night one March. He was full of tender concern, which surprised me. What was up? I soon learned. After I'd dressed we went to the hog barn. There he explained to me what he wanted. He had purebred Poland China sows, with papers, and they had one fault. Because of special breeding they often had difficulty giving birth. What was needed was a long slim arm to reach inside the sow to help the little piglets down the birth canal. Somewhat numb, and curiously also liking what I was doing, I helped most of those sows have their pigs that spring.

Later that year hog cholera hit. The vet came too late to give the little pigs serum and they all died. My father once again cried, and then retired to his favorite spot beside the kitchen stove, feet up on the reservoir, pipe clamped tight in his mouth. He refused to move. Ma didn't know what to do with him. Finally I took it upon myself to get out the old walking plow and open up a long deep furrow in the hog pasture and bury all the little pigs. They'd begun to stink and were covered with green flies. Gone was Pa's dream that by selling purebred hogs he could finally make a killing and then buy himself a farm. He and mother dreamed every spring that someday they'd own a farm and be independent. Both hated being renters. Pa with his brother Nick and his three sisters Kathryn and Jennie and Gertrude owned Grampa Feikema's cement block house in town, but that was not the same thing as owning a real farm.

It was about the same time that an investment man heard that Pa and Ma had managed over the years to build up a savings account of some fifteen hundred dollars. The man persuaded them to invest half of it, seven hundred fifty dollars, in the Northwest Harness Company. It happened that Pa liked the Northwest harness for farm work. Pa thought them the sure thing. The man told Pa and Ma they were bound to double, if not triple, their money in a year's time. The company was new and was sure to grow. With fifteen hundred, possibly even two thousand two hundred fifty dollars, they would finally have enough to buy the farm they had their eye on. It would help make up for the loss of all those purebred Poland China pigs. But in 1922, during a recession, the Northwest Harness Company filed for bankruptcy.

That same summer Pa and Ma invested the remaining seven hundred fifty dollars in their savings account in a general store that a friend of theirs built in Lakewood, halfway between Doon and Rock Rapids, Iowa, for the convenience of nearby farmers. On stormy days, rain or snow, both Doon and Rock Rapids were pretty far away for quick shopping. Lakewood, unincorporated, had a grain elevator, a depot, a lumberyard, and a blacksmith. There were five houses.

One afternoon, no one knows how, a fire started in the storekeeper's house and then jumped across to the general store. There was no fire-fighting equipment in town. Ma learned about it via the country telephone when Central gave the alarm with a general ring. Pa with the whole family drove like mad to the final hill. When he saw how far along the fire was, he pulled up. Pa and Ma watched it all burn down from the hilltop. I remember staring down at the two great pillars of flames and smoke with a boy's deep sick feeling in my stomach. There went another seven hundred fifty dollars.

When there was nothing but ashes left, Pa turned the car around and drove home. All he said was, "Couldn't even get close enough to light my pipe with it."

At the Doon Christian Grammar School, which my mother decided I should attend instead of the country public school, there were two boys much older than the rest of us. The law was that you had to go to school until you were sixteen. One noon when I went to the church horse barn where I kept my mare, Tip, I caught the two fellows tormenting her. They had climbed onto the rafter above her and with long sticks were jabbing her in the ass just under the tail, and laughing loudly when she bucked and eenked up in the air.

It happened that about a month before I'd complained to my father that these two fellows were bullies. My father listened a while and then gave me some father-son advice. "Look, what do you want me to do, take off work and go to school and punish those boys for you? Their parents would be in an uproar if I did that. No, son, that's a battle you've got to fight yourself. Even if they're much bigger than you, go after them. Let them know you're a fierce critter if they push in too far. Go after them even if you know you're going to lose. They'll remember your teeth the next time." He paused; then went on. "Course I don't ever want to hear that you started the fight. Or that you're a bully. Then you're going to have to deal with me. But otherwise, if you know you're in the right, fight!"

Seeing those two bozos tormenting my horse enraged me. I lost complete control of myself. I never once gave it a thought that both of them were twice as strong as I was. I grabbed Tip's bridle which was hanging on a nail behind her and went after them. They made one mistake. They dropped down off the rafter and, still laughing at the great joke of it all, started to run for the rear of the barn thinking to "escape" that way. But the rear door had been nailed shut and they couldn't get out. I had them cornered. Tip's bridle had a heavy breaker bit in it because she had too strong a mouth for me. The bit was a good inch thick, and heavy, and every time I came around with it over their backs as they tried to scrunch down as small as possible in the corner of the stall, they yelped twice as loud as Tip ever did. Finally an image of my mother popped into my head, and she asked, "Boy, boy, is this what I raised you to be? A killer? Alice's boy?" I let up. But I swear that if her image hadn't spoken up, I would have killed them. It's the only time in my life I ever thought of killing anyone.

My father was soon called before the church consistory. The minister told him what the problem was. His boy, Freddie Feikema, had beat up on two boys, members of the church, and what did he have to say about it. My father got to his feet and said he'd like to ask one question of each of the parents of the two boys.

He asked the first parent, "Nuh, and how old is your boy?"

"Well, yah, he is going on sixteen."

He asked the second parent, "And your boy?"

"Well, yah, Frank, you know, he's going on sixteen too."

Pa then turned to the minister. "Domeny, my boy is only ten years old. Why, even the horse they was tormenting is younger than them." And left.

I was in high school, going to Western Academy in Hull, Iowa, some seven miles away, when one weekend in late November, running all the way home, bursting into the kitchen, I found my father sitting beside the stove again, feet up on the reservoir. This time, instead of smoking his pipe, he was holding a hand over his nose. Something wild had happened. His nose was as purple as a plum and as big as an Idaho potato. There was still some blood on his upper lip.

Mother was ironing workshirts nearby. "Yes," she said, pointing her iron at Pa, "there sits a man who's now taken to jumping off windmills. Instead of just barns. And worse yet, there sits a man who won't go to see a doctor when he might he mortal hurt." My mother rarely indulged in irony, but when she did angels revolted in heaven.

I asked what had happened.

Pa didn't say a word.

Ma said, "Like I just said, he jumped off the windmill."

Pa finally said, voice nasal and gravelly, "Naw, not that. Like I said before, one of them rungs on the ladder broke and I fell off."

"You said you jumped the last ways."

"Well, yeh, after I saw I was gonna fall."

"You could have at least called the doctor." Ma went on to explain what Pa had done instead of going to the doctor. He'd whittled out two pieces of soft willow twigs, doped them with horse salve, then slowly stuck them up his broken nose and molded the nose into shape around the twigs.

I winced.

Pa saw my look. "Nah, you better get your yard duds on and do the chores. You still know what to do, don't you? Schooling still ain't chased that out of your head yet, has it?"

I hurried into my clothes. Without Pa, I'd have my hands full getting everything done on time, the feeding of the hogs and cattle and chickens and horses, milking and separating, feeding the calves. Eddie was a help but he was slow. But before I began, I had to know what had happened. I hurried down the hog pasture to the old wooden mill with its huge wooden fan. The fan was stuck; it was half-turned around, facing the wind when it should have been going with the wind. I climbed up the wooden ladder until I found the broken rungs just at the entrance to the platform on top. There were three of them. They'd become rotted at the nail holes and parts of the rungs were still caught in the three nails. I climbed down carefully, noting as I did so there were other near-rotted rungs I next worked out where he'd fallen. The ground was frozen some two inches deep, and I found where his heels had hit and dug a hole some three inches deep through the layer of frost and the softer earth beneath. The next thing I saw was a gouge in the earth some fifteen feet farther along. There was blood in the gouge. It must have been the place where his nose had hit. I looked up at the mill platform above me and figured Pa must have dropped a good fifty feet.

I had trouble understanding it all, and was trying to imagine how it happened, when I heard some neighing behind me. Looking around, I saw Pa's team of grays, Pollie and Nell, still hitched to the cornfield fence. The wagon was half-full of picked corn. Pa was almost finished picking corn; there were still two rows left. When he came to the end of the field he must have noticed that the mill was stuck and had climbed up it to turn the head around.

Pa back at the house hadn't mentioned the horses and the wagon out in the field. It meant he'd really banged his head, so hard he'd forgotten that he'd been picking corn. I climbed the fence, untied the horses, and drove them home. The sun was just setting, shooting great strokes of amber across the rolling fields.

Later on I got Pa to tell me how it really happened. I had to know. Just as I'd guessed he'd decided to turn the mill head around before picking the last two rows of the year. The mill head had somehow gotten stuck. The windmill could be pumping water while he picked. Just as he took hold of the top rung into the opening of the platform, it broke in his hands. "I quick grabbed for the next one," he said. "But it too broke in my hands. I made one more grab for the next one, and when that broke, I knew I was gonna go. When I looked down, I saw how the old mill was all spraddled out as it went down and I knew that if I didn't jump outwards, I'd fall into those cross bars and really wreck myself. So I jumped for all I was worth. Then, as I fell, I knew that if I didn't do something special, I'd spill my guts all over the hog pasture. I then remembered how grasshoppers lit after they'd jumped, their legs all scissored up like so, so I pulled my feet up into a half-crouch. By that time I was hitting the earth. And by dab, if I didn't land like a grasshopper and then bounce ahead. I couldn't quite get my hands out ahead of me in time, so that's why my nose took such an awful wallop. It knocked me out for a little bit too."

I kept thinking that he could have broken a leg or a hip joint. But he never complained about any aching bones or joints.

"Just that fetchsticking nose, which I had to remodel to look a little like I use to."

It was also about that time that Pa realized he was losing me. As long as I was a little boy I'm sure he always believed I'd become his right hand man on the farm. He rejoiced in the way I caught on how to do things: milking, driving horses, starting engines on cold mornings. But as the weeks and years went by it became pretty obvious that I was going to be a lover of books. Whenever we went to visit the neighbors, I always checked the neighbors' parlor first to see if they had any books before I went outside to play with their children under the trees.

"You've always either got your head in a book or in a cloud," Pa would say. "And when you walk across the yard, even with you staring down at the ground, you don't see what's underfoot. Pick up that loose piece of butcher paper there and put it somewhere. There's nothing so unsightly as a littered yard. Pick up, pick up, pick up."

Yet in a curious way, ambivalent, he gloried in my ability to read important documents for him. I started high school at the age of twelve, far too young really, but for his boy he thought it nothing unusual. When I told him stories about happenings at the academy, he'd follow my telling with a high light in his gray eyes, lips imitating my lip movement, waiting for the punch line so he could burst out laughing.

Except for one year, when I ran the seven and a half miles to and from school every day, he always took time off from work and brought me to school on Monday mornings. When it was raining he took the horse and buggy and when it was dry he took the old Buick.

In 1928, right after I'd graduated from the academy, we began to get little signals that Ma wasn't feeling too well. She spoke of fainting spells, of her heart beating funny. None of us children (by this time Mother had six sons and no daughters) believed that it was serious. Fathers and mothers just never died. They were always there. Just like God was always there.

But Pa took it seriously. They tried various doctors. By the time Ma arrived at the doctor's office she usually looked like she was in the bloom of health. She'd had a rest on the way over. Finally one doctor said it was her teeth and told her to have them all pulled. It was while she was having her lowers removed that she fainted dead away. It took some desperate action on the part of the dentist, Dr. Maloney, to get her back. From that day on she began to go downhill.

When she died on April 19, 1929, my father took it hard. (I was home at the time; my mother had asked me not to start college until I was eighteen.) Pa looked like a tall cottonwood with the upper branches blasted white by lightning. He was one of those who'd turned gray early, but on her death he rapidly turned white. We had no housekeeper, couldn't get one in those days, and the days were dark in that country farmhouse east of the Doon water tower. Pa never struck us, or cursed us, just went about in whitehaired smoldering sorrow. But he kept us neat. He did most of the housework (cooking, washing clothes, ironing) plus doing his share of the yard work. He got us to church in time on Sundays. When company dropped by, he was polite, and set out the coffee and cake just as Ma would have done it.

In the middle of that dark sorrowing time, my brother Ed almost got killed. It was in November and very cold. The month before there'd been a powerful south wind for several days, sometimes almost eighty miles an hour, and it had ripped a lot of corn ears from the stalks, at least a good third of them. With Pa up on the cornpicking machine, Ed and I followed him, bent over as we ran along picking up the fallen ears and tossing them into the open section of a small elevator in the back of the machine. That running and gathering on the run just about killed us.

Pa felt sorry for us and gave us a lot of rests at the end of the field. Once we stopped on the far side of the north seventy. We were about a half mile from the house.

Our breaths caught, Pa climbed back up on the machine. He unloosened the lines to the five horses and shook them, saying, "Giddap. Time to get going again."

The horses didn't move. The bitter north wind was on their tail and they had it cozy for the moment.

Again Pa called out his resonant, "Giddap!"

Still they didn't move.

"Ed, pick up a clod there and toss it onto Old Nell's tail. That'll wake her up." Nell was in the lead team and was the most dependable horse we had.

Ed picked up a clod and deftly hit Nell in the tail with it. She didn't even switch her tail at it.

"By gorry now," Pa exclaimed. "Ed, pick up another clod, this time a big one, and let her have it harder."

Ed had to kick around in the frozen ground to find a clod. Finally he found one in front of the snout of the cornpicker. He chunked the big frozen clod hard on Nell's tail. That woke her up, and she leaned into her traces. The other four horses woke up then too.

The picker was always heavy-ended on the snout or left side, and the paired snouts swung left and grabbed Ed's right leg. He didn't have a chance to get out of the way in time. The snapping rollers began to chew into his leg. Ed was too startled to cry out.

Pa saw it all in a glance, and he hauled back on all five lines with all his might and let go with a great chilling, "WHOA!" His voice, always powerful, so pierced the consciousness of those five horses they all froze in their tracks.

Holding tight onto the lines, Pa barked, "Fred, unhitch those horses one at a time. Queen first, since she's the friskiest. And let's hope she don't smell the blood." He leaned back to shut off the machine.

I unhitched Queen and Pa let go of her line. I led her to the fence and tied her to it. Then I peeled off the rest of the four horses, with Pa all the while sitting up on the picker seat eyes alert for the least motion in the machine. If those snapping rollers made one more revolution Ed's leg was gone. Ed meanwhile stood absolutely still, as though a wrestler had him by the leg and the best policy was just to stand still.

The moment I started to lead the last horse away, Pa scrambled down off the machine and had a look at Ed's leg. I joined him. The snapping rollers had just begun to grind into the bone about a half foot above the ankle.

"Ed, Ed," was all Pa said; and then, all business, he told me what wrenches to get from the toolbox on the back of the picker. Working carefully, silently, Pa and I managed to take off enough nuts to loosen the snapping rollers and open up the metal snout a little. Ed stood silent above, an occasional tear dropping off his wind-red cheeks and falling on our hands. Finally, thinking he had enough room, Pa began to extricate the mashed leg. I got to my feet and held Ed up.

When we finally got the leg out, we discovered that Ed could still stand on it. And it was then, everything finally safe, that Pa let go. He simply bowed over and cried, grinding his teeth.

The crying lasted about thirty seconds. Then, having had enough of that,

Pa got hold of himself and half-carrying Ed helped him home and took him to
the doctor. It took several months for Ed's leg to heal.

The incident added gloom to the household.

Worse yet, Pa got undulant fever that winter. He'd be his usual self for about
an hour in the morning, and then was done for the day and had to go to bed.
That left a lot of the yard work in my hands. In a way it was lucky it was winter;
there was no field work to do.

When pigging time came around, Pa called me into the bedroom. "Son, according to my calendar, those sows will be coming in any day. Now you know
what I've been doing the last couple of years. Trading young boars with a fellow from Edgerton, Minnesota, so's not to get inbreeding."

"I know," I said.

"Well, now when those pigs start coming in, I want you to watch for the pep-
piest and orneriest little boar pig in each litter. Make a mark in your mind about
him. Do that with each litter. And when all the pigs are in, we'll trade our pep-
piest little boar for a peppy boar from that fellow in Edgerton. That little boar
will be the one to wake up first after he's born, be the first to crawl between his
mother's legs to get to titty, be so ornery about it he'll want all those tits to
himself until he's had enough. You know, make a real hog of himself."

I wasn't sure I liked hearing all that.

"There may be one or two others that'll be just about as good, and if our first
one dies, they'll make pretty good replacements."

"Yes, Pa."

"The rest of the males we'll nut. They won't be much good for anything but
fattening."

"How about the gilts, must I watch them too to see which ones will make
good breeding stock?"

"Naw. Cripes, where've you been raised? Naw, most all of them will make
good sows. And you know, that's a funny thing. Let's say we get a hundred little pigs. About fifty-four of them will be males, and forty-six females. Some ten
of those males will be stumperts, peewees, and will die no matter what you do
for them. And there will be at the most only two females that'll die. All the rest
of the females will make good breeding stock. All of them. Sometimes of those
forty-four that are left I have a hard time picking the twenty I want to keep for
breeding sows next year."

A thought shot through my head. "Is that true of human beings too, Pa?
Where only one or two of the men are any good and the rest peewees? And where
most of the women are good?"

A big smile grew sideways across Pa's grizzled chin. "I wouldn't want to
say. Besides, I dassent ask around of my friends."

Some twenty years later I happened to tell this story to Dr. Starke Hathaway,
psychologist at the University of Minnesota, the man who invented the Minnesota Multi-phasic Personality Inventory test. He let out a hoot and started to
laugh. "Why, there's a fellow down at Indiana University who's been making a

survey of human beings on that very subject. A guy by the name of Alfred C. Kinsey."

That summer, undulant fever gone, Pa managed to get a housekeeper named Hattie. She had eight daughters and one son. Three of the youngest daughters began living with us. All the rest were married. With all that femininity around us, things changed drastically in our home.

Later Pa married Hattie. They didn't always get along, which was a grief to Pa, since he hated all dissension. He'd only had two disagreements with our own mother, mentioned above, and he didn't know how to handle it. But as time went on, as he put it, "We managed to bang it out together until we got along better."

In the fall of 1935, a year after I'd graduated from college, I hitchhiked home to visit my father. I still didn't have a steady job. I helped him get out the last of the corn and then went over to a neighbor to help him finish picking his corn by hand. It had been a bad year for farmers. The corn was mostly nubbins, short stubby ears, hard to jerk out of the husk, and the pay was poor.

When there were no more odd jobs to do, I found myself at loose ends. I loved my father and my five brothers and liked living with them again for a while. But it was uneasy living under the same roof with a stepmother who quarreled with my father a lot and who in addition considered me a college bum because I didn't actively seek a teaching job, for which I was qualified with a Life Certificate from the state of Michigan. But what I'd seen of practice teaching, and of teachers, I knew it wasn't for me, especially if I wanted to write.

Then my stepmother got an idea. Why didn't we go to Los Angeles and visit two of her daughters. As long as I didn't have anything to do, I could drive for them. Pa had just traded in the old Chevy for a new Dodge so we could ride in style. After some talk it was agreed that we'd go. We took with us a farm boy named Bill DeBoer who wanted to try his luck milking cows in Artesia near Los Angeles.

We started very early one morning from Doon, in the northwest corner of Iowa, and headed down 75 past Sioux City, and at Freeman, Nebraska, picked up Highway 30 and headed went across Nebraska. We drove steadily all day. It got dark while we were still in Nebraska. And it was around ten when we got a cabin in Cheyenne. There were no motels in those days. All day long all we'd seen was flat land, sometimes gently rolling land, not unlike the land around Doon. During those hours when we drove in darkness, the gathering hills of Wyoming couldn't be made out.

We woke to a deep fog in the morning. Visibility was almost zero. We had breakfast, and then slowly, lights on, we started out. As usual I drove, with the farm boy Bill sitting next to me in front, with Pa and Hattie in back, Pa sitting on the right side. From the sound of the motor I could tell after a while we were climbing. But from what we could see, a few feet on either side of us, and for all we knew, we were still traveling across flat land.

We came around a slow curve, going left, when abruptly the fog lifted, and below us on the right lay a vast long valley. We were traveling along the top of a mountain. Pa popped bolt upright on his side, staring down at the valley. He exclaimed in Frisian, his mother tongue, "Gotske, hwet gatten!" He pronounced the last two words as, "Hwat gawten!" It means in English, "God, what holes!" I hadn't heard him speak Frisian for years. What with his father dead and most of his uncles gone, he rarely spoke it any more. Then, as the road dipped down and the mountain side rose on our left, he said, "Why, these things (the mountains) are upsidedown holes!"

I've laughed about that many times. For a true expression of awe I've never heard it beat. It could have been Jim Bridger saying it the first time he saw the mountains.

It was on that same trip that Pa stunned me with his talent for music. One evening as Hattie and her two daughters were having a good time gossiping, Pa said to me, "Ain't there anything going on in this town that you and I could see?" I told him that I thought maybe there was and looked through the amusement section of the Los Angeles Times. I spotted a little story about the operetta *The Countess Maritza* being given in a theatre downtown.

"Hey," Pa said, "I'd like to see that. We had an opery house in old Doon once and I saw a good one there."

We got there early and took one of the cheaper seats. I told Pa how I and my friends in college used to get cheap seats and then watched to see what seats weren't sold up front and, after the first intermission, stole down and took them. Pa thought that a great idea.

We never got around to it. A few minutes into the singing, I heard a sound next to me. I looked. It was my father, crying. Tears were streaming down his cheeks, he thought the lyrics so beautiful. We didn't get up during either intermission. Afterwards, as I drove home, he still didn't say anything. He was too choked up with all the lovely music. When we got to the house the first thing he did was to ask his stepdaughter if she had a harmonica or an accordion in the house. She had an accordion, which her boy friend owned. Pa got it out and then, before my astonished eyes, proceeded to play most of the operetta The Countess Maritza back from memory.

My passionate strong-willed father was basically a musician who'd never had a chance to develop his talent.

A couple of years later Hattie decided she wanted to see her California daughters again. But she was puzzled as to how they'd make it safely without a driver to read maps.

Pa said, "Oh, well, if that's where you want to go I'll get you there. We don't need any map readers."

Sure enough, Pa talked her into going without a map reader. They took the exact same route that I drove. Pa remembered all the corners where you had to turn. Hattie told me afterwards that she was as astonished as anyone when Pa pulled up in front of her daughter's door without once having to ask for directions. His head was full of landscapes, one flowing into another.

Restless, Pa quit farming in the fall of 1935 and ran a filling station at Perkins Corner, Iowa, for a year in 1936. That wasn't the right thing for him either, so he quit that and came back to Doon and ran a dairy for a few years. It still wasn't right, so he sold the dairy and ran a cafe in Sibley, Iowa. That too turned sour on him and he took up carpentering. It developed that he was an excellent woodworker.

It was about that time that I came down with tuberculosis. I took the rest cure at the Glen Lake Sanatorium near Minneapolis. Pa came to see me at least once a month. While some of my other relatives might come to gloat over me, thinking, as I lay in my white bed, that's what Fred got for dreaming of becoming a big shot, a writer, Pa sat quietly by. All I can remember of those visits of his are four words, "Hello, son," and, "Good-bye, son." In betweentimes he tried to smile. Several times he'd take my hand and hold it a while. He was so gentle about it that at the time I completely forgot the few lickings he'd given me.

I didn't see much of him after I left the sanatorium. I got married and had part-time jobs and starting writing books. My wife Maryanna was never sure she liked him. She spoke of the piercing quality of his light-gray eyes. The way he looked at women always made her feel uncomfortable.

When I did see him he was always curious about my work. He couldn't read my books, but he was always interested to know about their success. He carried newspaper clippings about them in his pocket book.

When the Second World War came along, Pa heard the Navy needed woodworkers in California. The pay was very good, better than anything offered for carpenter work in Sibley, Iowa. He decided to give it a try and got a job doing the woodwork in the captain's cabin in Liberty ships. Hattie soon followed with the children and Pa became a Californian.

I wasn't there when Hattie died. From what my brothers John and Abben, who'd also gone to live in California, told me, it was pretty rough on him. He didn't like living alone. His stepchildren, all of Hattie's eight girls and their children, had come to love him as their own father and spent a lot of time visiting him. But at night when he went to bed he was still alone.

One day his milkman told him, "Frank, it ain't good for you to live alone like this. I can see it's getting you down."

"That's old news," Pa said.

"Tell you, Frank. I got a lady on my route who lost her sidekick a year ago and she too mopes around feeling sorry for herself. Why don't I have you two come over for dinner next Sunday so you can look each other over."

"Nah, it's too late."

"When you're both so lonesome? I tell you, you two were made for each other. I'll expect you next Sunday for dinner. Two bells."

"I'll think about it."

So the two met, Pa and Beatrice, in the milkman's house for dinner. And after the dinner they went their separate ways.

Pa thought about it for a week, then called Beatrice up and asked if he could come over for a cup of coffee the next Sunday. She thought it a fine idea.

She had him sit at her kitchen table while she set out the coffee and cake. They talked about the weather and how California was a fine place for people with old bones.

Pa had picked up his cup of coffee, and was about to take a sip, when he set the cup down again. "Say, Bea, before we go any further, you got to agree to one thing. It's something we better get straight right from the start."

"What's that, Frank?"

Pa had found out that she was Catholic and what he was about to ask her was a tough thing. He was still Christian Reformed (the word Dutch had been dropped by his church by then). "Well, Bea, you got to agree to join my church or it's all over between us."

Bea was startled, but she had come to like Pa's forthrightness. Furthermore, as Beatrice Roxanna Torrey before she got married to her Catholic husband, she'd originally been a Protestant in Haverhill, Massachusetts. "All right, Frank. If that's what you want, that's what it'll be."

So in a strange way my father's life had come full circle. He'd started out as a young boy living with Protestants who'd originally come from New England and he was now going to marry a Protestant who'd come from there.

One of my brothers was a little shocked that Pa wanted to get married again. The brother called me long distance.

"But, Fred, he's been married twice before. He should start thinking about the next life. Why should he want to get married again at his age? He's seventy-one. And then too, this Bea is so much younger than him. Much younger."

"So what? If they love each other that's all that counts. Age has nothing to do with it. She might just pep him up enough to give him another twenty years of life. No, I'm all for it."

"But she smokes cigarettes! It's funny that Pa would want to tolerate that. You know how he always was about bobbed hair women smoking in public. He's acting silly in his old age."

"Maybe he loves her."

They did love each other. Whenever we visited them and were about to take them out to dinner, we could never get them to sit separate, whether it was riding over in the car or at the table. Several times we tried to get one of my brothers to sit between them but that didn't work.

"Hyar, not on your life," Pa would exclaim. "Bea sits with me or we don't go out."

Once we did manage to get him in the front seat and Bea in the back. All the way over to the steakhouse she leaned forward and put her hand on his shoulder while he reached back with a hand and placed it on hers.

I stayed with them many times. Lying on the couch which had been opened out to make a bed for me, I used to listen to them talk in their bedroom, door open. They had a light teasing game going at all times. Nothing rough, or mean.

Tender. About whose turn it was to get up and make the coffee. Both loved that coffee spout. About who had the most pep. Both bragged to beat the band about that. About who scratched the worst with their toenails during sleep. It made me cry listening to them. It was the happiest chatter I'd ever heard be-tween two people, especially between a man and a woman.

Bea once confessed to me, "Fred, that father of yours is almost too much for me. Heh. Such a sweet pest. But I wouldn't want to have him any different."

One day Pa came to me with a request. "Fred, one of these days it'll be time for me to go on. As well as for Bea."

"Naturally, Pa."

"You're my oldest son and so I'm telling you. You know how I loved your mother Alice. She was a fine woman. A good mother to all you boys. And you know how I got along with Hattie. But, Fred, I tell you, Bea is the best yet. She surely is a good woman. I'm really sweet on her and I want to be buried with her. And she wants that too. She says I'm her best man. I hope that's all right with you."

"Pa, I can't legislate your love affairs. We'll do what you ask of us."

Everybody had expected Pa to go first, he was so much older, twenty years. In fact when Pa and Bea first got married some of her friends thought it terri-bly unfair to Bea. She'd only have him a couple of years and then she'd once more be alone. She'd be much better off marrying someone her own age.

But Bea died first, of lung cancer. She'd never given up her smoking, espe-cially not since Pa always enjoyed his pipe.

My youngest brother Henry saw Bea during her last days. "It was something to see when Pa went to visit her in the hospital. She'd be almost comatose until we'd enter her room. Then, the moment she'd hear Pa's voice, she'd light all up again. And when he said good-bye, he'd pick her up, she was so shrunken by then, and give her a hug and a kiss. It shook me up something terrible to watch that."

Once again at eighty-eight he was alone. It was decided by my two Califor-nia brothers, John and Abben, that he should be moved to a home for the el-derly. He was given a good room, had his favorite chair and television set, his box of pictures and other mementos.

He took it hard for a while. Then, picking up what he would call his gump-tion, he decided to learn to read. It was about time. He'd watch programs on public television showing the text of certain books and plays. By following the words shown with the voice reading them he managed to build up a reading vocabulary.

John learned about it one day when he dropped by to ask if Pa had got any mail he wanted read to him.

"Yeh, I got mail all right. A letter from Fred."

"Well, here, let me read it to you."

"I already read it."

"What?"

With a smile. "Yeh, I learned to read a little." Then Pa explained how he'd done it.

I visited him in October of 1976. He was eighty-nine. I was astonished to see how sharp his mind was. His memory of the old days was very keen. I didn't tell him at the time that I was writing *Green Earth*, a novel about our family, about his and my mother's life before I was born, all the way to her death when I was seventeen. I needed to know some details about the time when our new Reo threw a piston. I first told him what I remembered. He shook his head. "That ain't the way it went." Then he proceeded to go into such exact detail that I knew right away that his version was right and mine was slightly off. But I kept my version in the novel; it made for a better story.

The second day I was there visiting him, someone asked me a question about something I'd talked about when I'd first arrived. When I finished, Pa gave me a raised brow look. "That ain't the way you told it yesterday." I was stunned. He not only could remember things accurately from the distant past, but he could remember in detail what had happened the day before.

His hearing remained keen until the very end. He had good eyes and used glasses only for what he called close work. He had a little trouble walking the last couple of years because a young doctor had removed a thick callus from his foot. The callus should have been soaked off. When the scar finally healed he got around quite well again and walked as straight as ever. He prided himself in walking straight even though he was very tall. Three of his sons grew to be taller than his six foot four. I became six nine, Edward John became six eight, and Floyd became six six. Henry, the youngest, at six four became as tall as Pa. The other two, John and Abben, weren't quite as tall. He got after every one of us to stand straight and walk straight. He had to get after me the most because I had trouble with six-foot-eight doorways.

The last time I saw him I noticed how steady his long fingers were.

Then the next August, 1976, he'd had enough. He told my brother John that he was ready to go. There was nothing more for him to do. He'd pretty much done it all. There was nobody around he knew any more.

John tried to talk him out of the mood. "But you got us. And then there's all your grandchildren and great grandchildren."

"You boys are great, of course. But you're related to me and that ain't the same as being friends. We didn't choose each other."

Several times he was heard to say strange things. One of them was, "Where is everybody? Nobody around I can talk old times with any more. When I start telling my children about that baseball game at Alvord, where they tagged that guy out at home plate with a potato, they say, 'But Pa, you told us that yesterday already.' Well, I want to talk to somebody who'd like to hear that story again because they saw it too. Because it was a funny thing to see."

Again and again John would try to divert his attention to all his wonderful grandchildren, who loved him.

Pa hardly heard him. "Everybody in my bunch is gone. And if there is one left, he won't know from nothing no more. No, I've outlived all other memo-ries but my own. Kids my own age, kids ten years younger, kids twenty years younger, are all gone. Why, I've even outlived my young wife and her bunch, so I can't talk about even their old stories. I'm forsaken, that's what I am. Left behind."

The nurses would sometimes try to pep him up. It didn't help much. Not even the nurse he sometimes had an eye for could get him out of his mood.

"No, I think I'll go now," he said. "I've had just about everything earth has to offer. I've finished all my jobs. I miss Bea. I want to go jolly her up." He'd shake his hoary old head on which the white hair had become so old it'd turned yellow. "Bea surely was a good wife. We always had a joke going. She was neat too, with the house, with her body. That's important for a woman to do. She always smelled like cinnamon and wild roses."

"Oh, c'mon now, Pa, there's a lot left yet for you to do."

"For the first time I feel as old on the inside as I look on the outside. Ninety is enough. Be good to my grandchildren. Maybe they can do it. Live forever."

Over the next month his vital signs slowly went down. His doctor put him under an oxygen tent.

"What's that thing doing here? I want to go. Get it out of here."

It was removed. His doctor next gave him heavier doses of vitamin pills and had special foods served him.

"I don't want those things. I liked the old grub."

Then on the morning of September 30th, 1976, Pa rang for the nurse. He had to go to the bathroom and he'd promised that if he got out of bed he'd always call the nurse. He refused to use a urinal. The nurse helped him to the bathroom and back to his bed.

Pa sat down on the edge of his bed. With a little smile he said, "Well. I feel pretty good. Now I'm ready for a good breakfast."

"I'll get it for you," the nurse said.

Pa lay down then to wait for the breakfast. The moment his head touched the pillow he was gone.

We buried him with Bea. In California.

This Is the Year

Not to be modest about it, for my own purpose, I find the language and technique to hand often short of words and idioms, so that, to express my problems and my findings, I have to coin new words, new word arrangements, or take them up, still raw and bloody from birth, from the talk of relatives, friends, and neighbors. As a matter of fact, to write This Is the Year, *in addition to a new language, I had to work out a new strategy, a new frame, a whole new throw, to get said what was said in it.*

Glossary of Unusual Words and Phrases
(most of them Frisian) which appear in the text

ÂLDE HAN: *Old Hand, or Old Hired Hand. A mischievous, playful devil or evil Spirit whom men blame for their hard luck. A convenient scapegoat.*

ÂLDEN: *Elders*

BIDIMJE: *To calm, to smooth down*

DE ÂLDE HAN SIL DY SLAEN: *The Old Hand shall slay thee.*

IT JONKJE HAT N WJIRM YN IT BREIN: *The youth has a worm in the brain.*

KERMIS: *According to Webster: "An annual outdoor festival . . . characterized by feasting, dancing, clownish processions, and other forms of amusement."*

PATICLE WORK: *Frisian-Americanism for "particular work." Pronounced pa-tee´-cle.*

IT DEL!: *Sit down!*

SOAN: *Son*

Eviction

PIER SAID, as soon as Âlde Romke had gotten to his feet, "That settles it. Come with me." He tugged angrily at the leather sleeve of the old man's jerkin.

"Ae, but I couldn't help it. He broke loose from me," Âlde Romke protested, his light blue eyes rolling.

"Yeh, an' that smile broke loose from you too. C'mon to the house. We're settlin' this right now."

Pier led the way, stomping into the kitchen. Both women looked up surprised: Nertha with a rising flush, Ma Lysbeth with chilling mien.

Ma Lysbeth stood up. "What now?"

"Ma, we've all got a bone to pick together." He pointed to the armchair for Âlde Romke. "An' it ain't gonna be a fresh one either."

"Now, now, bidimje." Ma Lysbeth moved imperially toward the stove and picked up her own teapot. "Some tea?"

"Uh . . . ain't Nertha set the coffee?" Pier asked. "It's coffee time. I've been waitin' for one of y'u to bring it to the field."

Ma Lysbeth tightened.

"Besides, this ain't gonna be no polite jawin' match," Pier growled.

Âlde Romke stood up. "Soan, I deman' respect."

Ma Lysbeth pointed. "Sit del!"

Âlde Romke plopped down. He turned his favorite armchair toward the door ready to spring.

Pier reddened. He remembered that Âlde Romke was so in fear of Ma Lysbeth that he kept a change of clothing in the barn against the day of one of her rampages. "Ma, you sit down too." Pier pointed.

She remained stiffly by the stove.

Pier made a threatening step toward her.

Slowly, reluctantly, only partially cowed, she bent her body and sat down. She clasped her hands over her windbelly.

"There. Now." Pier sat down too. "Ma, I'll come to the point. I think it's best you old people retire and get yerselves a house in town. Ye're sixty-seven an' Pa's seventy-two. It's high time y'u did."

"What?"

"Yeh, that's right. You heard me."

"But why?"

"Ma, God gives some people the brain of a human being, but when he came to our pa here, he gave him the brain of a bumblebee. He don't know beans from buttons."

"Soan!"

"But it's true."

"Soan, he is your father. Respect, soan!"

"Respect, my ass. He's always bulloxin' things up. Here I am, trying my level best to make a go a things here, trying to make things hum, runnin' mysel' down to a breath an' a bone, hitchin' an' hoppin' an' runnin', figurin' an' thinkin' an' calculatin', an' then this Pa here a mine comes along to bullox the business up."

"Soan," Ma Lysbeth said severely, drawing herself up, pinching in her wind-belly, "soan, I must ask you to hold your tongue."

"Ask me to hold mine? Lissen, Ma, ain't you got it through yer thick wood-head yit that I'm runnin' this place? That it's fer me to say who's to shut up?"

Âlde Romke jumped up. "An' where did you get this place, I ask?"

"I got it from you, what's left of it. An' mighty little too."

"Soan!"

Pier ignored him. "An' another thing, Ma. When I come into the house, I expect Nertha to answer me first, not you. You're livin' with us, not we with you."

Nertha, flushed, got slowly to her feet. "If I'm causin' trouble, I—"

Pier reached forward, gripping her arm. "Now don't act like a pussyfoot. Talk up to the old folks like you been a doin'. Remember, you an' I's took over. You're my wife an' what we say goes."

Ma Lysbeth paled. "Do you mean, soan, that you've put Nertha ahead of me?"

"Yes."

Ma Lysbeth stood up. She held her long arms tight over her breast as if she were afraid someone were going to strip her.

"Now, Ma, sit down." Pier took a deep breath. "Let me tell you two a thing or two. I know it's you people who's given me this farm to run. An' I know it was good a you to make the deed over into my name, so that, if I want to, I kin kick you off. But kickin' you off ain't what I'm aimin' to do. It's that I'm askin' you, fer godsakes, please try to understand Nertha an' me. We're young. We're full of vim an' vinegar. An', if we're let alone, we're gonna get someplace. If." Pier found himself out of breath. "Two famblies in one house don't work. We just get into each other's way. So, I say, go to town an' retire. Take a rest. Please. Because we wanna get while the gettin's good."

Âlde Romke bounced up again. "Soan, are you forgetting you'll need a hired hand on this place? One hand needs another to wash itself clean, you know."

"Pa, I can do it all better alone."

"Is that so? Do you think you kin milk better than me? Huh? Ae. That's paticle work."

It was true. Âlde Romke was a miracle around cows. If one of the tits gave out, it was the old man who brought it back to normal again. He had a touch that calmed cows, relaxed them. No one could get more milk out of them than he. "Just the same, Pa, I want to do it alone."

Ma Lysbeth drew her gray shawl around her neck. She lifted a long needle-thin finger. "Soan, you're telling us to go?"

"Yes." He looked directly into her eyes. "Yes. I simply just can't stand this kermis no longer."

She shook her head. "My own soan. My own soan. He says that to me." She shivered. "Soan, you've got a heart as cold as ice an' as hard as stone." She shook her head again. "Nertha, well may you pray God to have mercy on your soul. This wild one is going to boss you right into your grave."

"Ma, I just know what's best fer us, is all."

Âlde Romke waggled a prophetic finger. "Soan, I predict a terrible day ahead for you, belittling your âlden so. De Âlde Han sil dy slaen."

"Maybe so. Maybe so. But if he does, it'll be my doin', not yers."

"A terrible day."

"Look, you people goin' or not?"

No one moved.

"I'll even pay yer rent an' grocery bill."

"We can pay our own way," Ma Lysbeth said, lifting her head superiorly. "We ain't helpless yet. Before we take charity from our children, we'll go to the poor farm first."

"Now, that ain't necessary. An' you know it."

"A terrible day," Âlde Romke continued to murmur. "A terrible day. It jonkje hat 'n wjirm yn it brein. Ae. De Âlde Han sil him slaen."

Pier rolled his shoulders.

"'N wjirm."

"Shut up."

Softly but distinctly the old man continued to mumble in his redgray beard. "'N wjirm yn it brein."

But a worm had also crawled into Âlde Romke's brain.

Quarrels with God

Green Earth

If I have any religion at all it is that I don't mind being a human being, and that I like other human beings, and that I think that to himself he is all important, that only knowledge that is man's subjectively has much value with the rest interesting but mostly guesswork.

"You should know better," is often thrown at me. Do I? Because of my early training? Well, here is a fact not too well known by my Calvinistic brethren, that I had a wonderful grandfather who was both a socialist and an atheist. Actually, he said he was an agnostic. He died when I was a boy, but he left a tremendous imprint on my mind, despite the fact that all the relatives tried to bury him, literally and physically, in an obscure place. He was ahead of his time. He came to this country for religious freedom. . . And moreover, there was another powerful agent at work in my growing up: my mother's determined wish that we live what we were. She was a glowing Christian, wonderful, but she was so great a Christian that she could say to me, on her deathbed, "Fred, my boy, I can see that your path is going to be different from what mine was. I'd like to see you in heaven with Jesus and me, but don't act the Christian if you don't feel it."

Ma's Church

MA DECIDED TO HOLD CHURCH ANYWAY. It would be with just their own family and they'd have it in the parlor. The parlor was for Sundays and what better time than now what with everybody all dressed up.

Ma went out to where Grampa sat on the cistern head. "We should be very pleased if you'd join us in worship, Pa." Ma gave Grampa one of those smiles that was hard to turn down.

Grampa shook his head. "Enter your parlor in these duds?"

"I'm sure the Lord won't mind your clothes if I don't Pa."

"Now, Ada, you know I don't hold much with that autocratic institution, the church, where one man does all the ordering around and the rest of us have to just sit there and take it."

"I know you don't. But this will be a family service in which all members of the family can participate."

"I can't stand hypocrite sin-busters."

Pa just stood in the doorway with a funny smile.

Grampa gave his pipe a great suck. "Daughter, I'm a socialist. The exact opposite of what your minister believes in."

"Why don't we discuss this in our service in the parlor?"

Grampa slashed his short right arm this way and that way. "Your church believes in a government run by ministers who act on what they suppose are God's instructions . . . were He there. And that kind of government can lead to a tyranny worse even than Bismarck's. Or Cromwell's. Or that goddam John Calvin's in Switzerland."

"Careful what you say there about John Calvin there," Pa said.

Ma said. "Don't you believe there is a God?"

Grampa clapped out his pipe and slipped it into his bib pocket. "All right. daughter, I'll give in a little, seeing it's Sunday. Let's go into your parlor if talk religion we must."

"Good," Ma said. She smiled to herself as she led the way inside.

Grampa took off his shoes on the porch and went into the parlor in his socks. He took a high-back chair next to the maidenhair fern. He hooked his engineer's cap over his knee.

Ma let up the shades and everybody could finally see what there was in the parlor. The shaded room suddenly became a gold room.

Ma sat on the round organ stool, Bible in hand, while Pa took the big oak rocker and Free and Everett and Albert sat down in a row on the leather seat chairs along the wall. Jonathan the baby was placed on his belly on the floor. The rug under him was brown with a picture of a gold lion in it.

"Now," Ma said, "it happens I believe that the man should conduct the service, but since Alfred has trouble reading I think that in this case the woman can be forgiven for reading a short passage from the Bible." Ma opened the good book and lay the blue silk marker to one side. "I shall read Psalm 100, one of my favorites. 'Make a joyful noise unto the Lord all ye lands. Know ye that the Lord He is God. It is He that hath made us and not we ourselves. We are His people and the sheep of His pasture. Be thankful unto Him and bless His name. For the Lord is good. His mercy is everlasting, and His truth endureth to all generations.'"

By the time Ma finished, the parlor was very silent. Pa was studying his crossed legs and Grampa's lip was stuck out like he was trying to pry a piece of food from between his teeth with his tongue.

"What was the last word read, Free?"

"Generations."

Everett gave Albert a sly pinch in the sitter. Albert cried.

Ma looked severe at the little kids. "Still, you. This is church." Ma then gave Pa a look that meant he should lead in prayer.

Pa folded his hands over his crossed knees. He closed his eyes slowly. "Forgiving Father in heaven, we come to Thee at the midpoint—"

Ma broke in, eyes closed. "This is not at the table, Alfred."

"—of this day in humble family worship out in the country instead of church in town. We are sorry we can not foregather with Thy beloved congregation. Our old Reo went on the blink—"

"Alfred," Ma whispered sharply.

"—but maybe in the long run it'll be for the best, since I can get a better guarantee on a new Buick—"

"Alfred."

Free snuck a look at Pa.

Pa opened his eyes a second. "But, wife, Domeny goes into pa'ticulars in his long prayers on Sunday. He talks to God personal, about the weather, the crops, about the rowdy boys in the back seats, the laggards not paying their share of his salary, and all such like other things no different from our brokedown Reo."

"Alfred, I fear the head of this church in this parlor here serves without salary."

Grampa hadn't closed his eyes. He was smiling.

"Yeh, well . . ." Pa closed his eyes again. "Bless the Word read and may it touch our hearts and minds so that we'll be better citizens of Thy kingdom."

Everett gave Albert another pinch.

Albert was going to bawl. He opened his mouth for it, but when he saw that neither Pa nor Ma had seen Everett do it, he decided it was no use to bawl. So instead he gave Everett an elbow in the belly.

Pa finished up the long prayer with a brand-new ending. "And lastly, we have a scoffer in our midst who is also a loved one. In Thy infinite mercy, an it please Thee, show him the right way. Let him know that him being stubborn will get him nowhere. Also, being that all pots have ears, his being that way sets a bad example for the little ones, one of whom already shows signs of being another Bolshevik."

Free quick closed his eyes tight. Bolshevik meant him.

"In His name we ask it. Amen."

Ma wasn't sure she liked that Bolshevik part. There was the start of a black look around her eyes. But at last she decided not to pick at Pa about it and instead got up a sweet church smile. "Let's all sing a psalm together." She swiveled around on her stool and opened up a songbook on the music rack of the organ. "Psalm 84." Ma pumped up the organ and played the prelude. The red silk in the sound holes vibrated. Ma sang the first few notes alone. "How amiable are Thy tabernacles, O Lord of Hosts." Then Pa joined in, and then Everett. Pa sang a little behind like he didn't know the words quite and had to wait for Ma to mouth them first. "The sparrow hath found an house, and the swallow a nest for herself, where she may lay her young."

Grampa didn't sing. He just stared at the sleeping lion in the rug. He was still smiling.

Ma sang clear above them all. "Showers passing through the valley make it a well." Sunbeams shining through the colored glass above the bay window picked up some motes and made them fly around like fireflies. "A day in Thy court is better than a thousand in a desert. Rather would I be a doorkeeper in the house of God than a dweller in the tent of wickedness."

When the song was done, Ma thought to herself a second. "Who would like to expound on the word read?" Ma fixed on Pa.

Pa thought hard. Pa liked for the domeny to pound on the pulpit a little, to make the dust fly out of the big brown Bible. Free thought that was what Ma meant by expound. Too bad Pa wasn't a preacher. If Pa was to pound the Bible, he'd surely make those sleepers in the back of the church sit up and take notice.

"Nothing?" Ma said.

Pa didn't have a single idea.

"Grampa?"

Grampa harumphed. The last couple of days he sounded like he had a bit of a cold. "Daughter, I have no comment to make on Psalm 100. The way you read it, its meaning is perfectly clear." Grampa looked Ma in the eye. "But I wonder if you'd read my favorite psalm?"

"Of course. Which one?"

"Psalm 137."

Ma looked up the psalm. She gave the children each a look to make sure they'd keep quiet, then read it aloud. "By the rivers of Babylon, there we sat down. Yea, we wept when we remembered Zion. We hanged our harps upon the willows in the midst thereof. For there they that carried us away required of us a song, and they that wasted us required of us mirth, saying, Sing us one of the songs of Zion. How shall we sing the Lord's song in a strange land? If I forget thee, O Jerusalem, let my right hand forget her cunning. If I do not remember thee let my tongue cleave to the roof of my mouth; if I prefer not Jerusalem above my chief joy. Remember, O Lord, the children of Edom in the day of Jerusalem, who said, Raze it, raze it, even to the foundations thereof. O daughter of Babylon, who are to be destroyed, happy shall he be that rewardeth thee as thou hast served us. Happy shall he be that taketh and dasheth thy little ones against the stones."

The motes in the sunbeams slowed down.

"What a strange way for a psalm to end." Ma closed the Bible slowly. "It's almost a hymn of hate."

Grampa was surprised. "You never read it before?"

"It really belongs in the Devil's Bible."

"Now there's a thought," Grampa said. "if God would allow the Devil to have a Bible of his own. To give his side of it."

Ma's blue eyes opened wide. "Well, true. Since God is supposed to love all creatures, that must also include the Devil."

Grampa's eyes shone at Ma like he thought her an angel.

Ma said, "Yes, I wonder if anybody ever speaks up for the Devil."

Pa said, "Say, you two better remember who's on our side."

Ma said, "Grampa, tell us why you like that psalm?"

Grampa made a motion as if he still had a pipe in his mouth, then when he saw he didn't, stuffed his hand in his pocket. "The older I get the more I remember the days when I was young. In the Old Country. And those memories have absolutely nothing to do with what I see around me here. As if I am utterly cut off and alone. And the more I live the more lonesome I feel."

Ma sat up straight. "Why, Grampa, you're with us. You know that. We all love you."

"Yes, my daughter, I know you do. And I love you for it too." Some yellow tears ran out from under Grampa's dark glasses. "But you didn't have your youth with me. We have no memories together of the Old Country that we might share."

Free couldn't stand to see older people cry.

Pa couldn't stand to look at his dad crying either.

Ma's face became all worked up. "I didn't realize. . ."

Grampa wiped his tears on his shirt sleeve. He tried to smile. "But I have to say one thing for America. I've gradually come to learn it's a place where you just naturally look ahead to the future. Everything's done here with an eye on what it's going to be like tomorrow. While in the Old Country they're always looking back over their shoulder."

The sun moved across the carpet. It shone on the lion's tail and then on the shiny buttons of Albert's new black shoes.

"Well," Ma said, "this has turned out to be quite a rewarding service after all. We all learned something about each other, something we didn't know before. The Lord is right when He says that it's good for the soul to bring private thoughts out into the open. There's nothing like confession."

The sun next reached the golden oak floor. It reflected up at Ma, making the beads on her purple dress shine like the eyes of ladybugs. Each time she breathed the chatelaine ladies' watch pinned on the bosom of her dress shone like a little gold sun.

Wanderlust

The harness of the Christian faith inflicted many a gall and shoulder sore but I'll be a bastard before I admit that it killed me off. On the contrary, having survived it, I have a knowledge and a power that few have.

A New Light

TO FORGET HERO, Thurs turned to other matters.

He had a paper to write for Prexy on "Proofs for the Existence of God." He got a stack of source books from the library and piled them on this desk. He tackled them with a will. He decided it was time to get to the bottom of something that had been bothering him for some time—his lack of faith.

He studied St. Augustine, Erasmus, Luther, Zwingli, Menno, Calvin, Abelard, Aquinas. He read the confessions as well as the more formal statements.

After he had read around in them all, it struck him one day that there actually were no proofs for the existence of God. For a fact. The most that any of the great Christian minds had to offer as to His existence was but an elaborate guess. Not a single one of them had dared to claim that he had seen, face to face, the full glory and power of a God. It was true that a few of them did suggest that they had caught a vague intimation of His presence. A close reading of their lives, however, indicated that a good share of them were highly emotional, as well as overly conscious of the sins of their youth.

As for the elaborate guesses, they all hung or fell on the original premise that the Bible was the Word of God. Literally. That actually it was the hand of God that had written the Bible because it had guided the hand of man as he trace out the words. The Christian accepted this premise without question. He did not even ask the very simple, even childlike, question: had anyone actually seen the hand of God guiding the hand of man? Literally?

Once Thurs got himself positioned on the other side of the "original premise," he suddenly saw the Bible in a new light. It was a human document, a poetic history of a people. This explained much. Among other things, it explained why the so-called Word of God could present such an ambivalent world. A hell and a heaven. A jungle and a garden. On the one hand there were such things as incest, fornication, adultery, beast-man cohabitation, seed-spilling, persecution, torture, fratricide, slaughter, murder, crucifixion. On the other hand there were such things as love, charity, kindness, ideals, hopes, dreams, faith, prayer, tithing, sacrifice, self abnegation. It was hardly a wonder that men read it so avidly. It described him down to his last miserable dropping at the same time that it praised him. It condemned him at the same time that it offered him hope.

What problems there were to explain away if one accepted the Bible as actually "the word of God." If the sons of Adam had souls why not the apes of God? If the seventh day was the Lord's along the equator, what day was his on the north pole where, before man invented the sun dial and the clock, there were no "days"? Where were "the four corners of the earth" when the earth was a sphere? And where was "up in heaven" and "down in hell" when astronomy taught that, in any direction away from the earth, there was only circumambient space with dust and stars and galaxies of stars riding through endless empty places?

Furthermore, what kind of faith was it that encouraged men to snoop around in each other's lives for God's sake? That made the orthodox fear-of-God boys always have it in for the radical God-is-love boys? That made the Christian, when he traveled in a strange country, look for his own kind rather than seek new faces and new experiences? That made the Christian ask, does Einstein belong to the Church, is he one of us, before he was willing to examine what Einstein might have to say? That made the Christian brag that he knew for a fact that the great of the land were members of the Church (secretly, of course, so all was safe for God's side), when at the same time he was always setting himself apart from the "worldly" world? That made the Christian so arrogant he regarded men of another faith as doomed to everlasting destruction? That made the Christian a terrible despot once he got state power, as witness Cromwell?

Having got this far with such questions, Thurs decided to weigh the pros and cons of the Christian faith. He made two lists. Beliefs that looked like fable or fiction, such as virgin birth, Adam as the father of all men, resurrection of the dead, belief in a personal God, these he tossed aside as useless baggage. Beliefs that had a practical aspect, such as honest trading, use of intelligence, the expression of brotherly love, the worship of beauty for its own sake, the search for truth for its own sake, these he kept. He made a real housecleaning.

But, aha, what about the term paper meanwhile? Suppose he were to put in all his findings? Would Prexy give him a passing mark? Afterall a flunk was a flunk. And a flunk, should Mrs. Brothers see it on his report card, would mean a cutting off of income.

The same day that these thoughts squirmed in his skull like angleworms caught on a hot griddle, he got a long letter from Mrs. Brothers, a letter in which she wondered if he wouldn't reconsider his plan to teach instead of preach. He read part of the letter aloud: "It is my earnest wish and my constant prayer that you will change your mind. God wants his followers in every walk of life, but really, Thurs, the minister is his chosen child, his choicest. Remember, you are a covenant child."

Thurs wrestled.

And then, tired of it all, eager to be at solid things again, he dashed off a five-page paper, liberally sprinkling it with texts from the Bible (argumentum ad authority, God existed afterall), and handed it in.

But he did gain one thing from all the stewing, He no longer felt guilty about staying away from church services. He had freed himself from a boring and an intolerable custom. Fellowship with fellow Christians in a stuffy edifice was one thing; fellowship with fellow man in life was another.

Learning to Breathe Air

SOME MONTHS PREVIOUS Howard got Thurs elected to the Plato Club. This was a thrill for Thurs. At last he was one of those broad-browed Olympians he had worshipped as a freshman, one of those who went about with a philosophic air, inclined to be ironic, walking with the head bent a little to one side.

The first meetings were somewhat upsetting to Thurs, especially when he saw how ruthless the logic-chopping could sometimes become. Once, the boys pushed blustery Erasmus Dannen into making a wild statement of a skeptical nature and then promptly cornered him into admitting that if he were to be truly consistent he should shut up for the rest of the night. Another time, they jumped so hard on Howard for his near-atheistic learnings that he was moved to rare anger. "Listen, you smug pharisees, I believe that an atheist is every bit as religious as a Christian. Probably more. To get where he does, in defiance of friends and relatives, he has to go through some desperate self-probings and heart-searchings. And the least you can say for him is that he has searched religion and searched his heart, that he has become an active searcher for truth. Can you say as much for the Christian?"

Thurs was glad his paper was not due until March. It gave him a chance to learn the club lingo as well as work out the area in which he might make a decent contribution. His first plan was to make a report on Plato's theory of art. But on investigation this proved to be vague and shadowy. So at the last moment he switched to Plato's notion of justice. The subject, he thought, concerned him directly. As an overgrown man he might someday do something abnormal—in fact already had the night of the wassail. He was very much concerned with what the attitude of the law might be to misfits.

Finally his big night came. The club met in the back of the Dorm dining hall: Thurs, Howard, Neal, Ben, Erasmus, and a half-dozen other young platos. The group was about evenly divided between the liberal lads and the pre-seminarian boys. Most were dressed in vest and pipe and slippers. Last to come, just as he was in class, was Mr. Hobbs, smiling, underslung pipe spuming smoke.

They sat in a circle around a low table. On the table stood a half dozen ashtrays and various cans of tobacco.

Clearing his throat, Thurs read slowly through two closely packed pages of manuscript, the others following from mimeographed copies:

"Plato believed that 'to do one's own business in some shape or other is justice.' This short statement is more profound than might appear at first glance. Plato believed that each individual should have a certain job to do in the state and that that job should be the one to which his natural capacities are best adapted. To mind one's own business and not be meddlesome meant for the Guardians that they should be wise, for the Soldiers that they should be courageous, and for the Workers that they should be temperate. Just as the wisdom of the state resides in the Guardians, and the course of the state in the Soldiers, and the self-control of the state in the Workers, so each man in his private and individual life must be wise, courageous, and temperate. When the three classes of society function harmoniously we have justice. When the individual strikes a balance in his life between wisdom, courage, and temperance, we have the same justice. . .

"Modern notions of justice, however, have become pretty heavily legalistic in nature. Modern man does not tackle a social problem form the point of view of a system of justice but from the point of view of 'what does the law say?' Legal codes and procedures stand in the way of justice, and lawyers often engage in battles of matching wits. It was an attempt to dispense justice in the real sense of the word that caused Judge Ben Lindsay some years ago to humanize his juvenile court in Denver. . .

"Which brings us squarely before this problem: do we impose sentence to punish or do we impose sentence to correct. The usual view is: punish. The human view is: correct. The first is often the Christian position; the second the rational. The Christian and the Totalitarian believe that the dignity of the state demands punishment. The Humanist and the Liberal believe that the dignity of the individual demands understanding and charity."

Thurs finished. There was a momentary silence. All members solemnly filled their pipes and lighted up. Coiling clouds of smoke rose to the ceiling, slowly forming nebulae, planets, Milky Ways.

Erasmus was the first to speak up. He questioned Thurs at length, and somewhat noisily, about the notion that the Christian believed in punishment more than he did in correction. Was Thurs hinting that God was not a God of love?

"I was only reporting the fact," Thurs said, "that people known as Christians generally do not put much faith in correction."

"Oh." A sly look came in Erasmus's eyes. "What about President Cooper's letting you off so easy after that drunk of yours? Or that time he overlooked your stealing all that fruit from the fruit cellar? Wasn't that charity?"

"Hey, hey," Howard growled, "let's keep the personal out of this."

"Nevermind, Howard," Thurs said, neck thickening, "it's all right. There's nothing like bringing a theory down to earth. Hitting home. And now I'd like to ask Erasmus a question. This love you mention, what do you mean by it, Erasmus?"

"I use it as it is explained in the New Testament."

"As Christ preached it?"

"Yes."

"And lived it?"

"Yes."

"Ah, maybe we should dig into that a little. Christ preached love, yes. But from what wellspring in his personality did that idea of love come from?"

"I don't understand your question."

"I mean, certain psychologists have suggested that Christ was not a whole man, that he might have been homosexually inclined."

"What!!" The whole dining hall rang with it. Those who had been sitting on two chair legs now came down on all four. Faces paled.

"Well, hasn't it ever occurred to you that it was rather odd that Christ never got married? That he had twelve men friends? Men friends who themselves never got married or had girl friends that we know of? That as far as we know Christ never had sexual relations with any woman? That he never kissed a woman except his mother? That he had considerable pity for those who had broken sex laws and tabus?"

"What!"

Thurs didn't dare look anyone in the eye. What he was saying sounded horrible even to himself. Nevertheless, his mouth went on. "I'm not saying he was a queer, you understand. I'm only saying that we should examine the possibility. That we should examine all the evidence. Because I think it is important that we know a little about the people who contribute such terms as 'love' and 'comrade' to our language. Comrade was a term that Whitman was fond of using. And he was a man scholars now suggest was not normal either."

Again a sly look came into Erasmus's eyes. "Are you suggesting that we accept ideas only from the normal?"

"Welll . . ."

"Don't you want us to accept your ideas?"

Thurs thought, "Hey, that's right. I'm a misfit myself."

Mr. Hobbs broke in at that point. He placed his pipe carefully on the table. "Going back to your paper, Thurs, what you are trying to say with respect to legal justice, is it not, is that to the ego of the murderer the line that marks the difference between not having killed and having killed is a thin one?"

"Yes."

"But, oho, young man, it happens that that ego isn't alone here on earth. There are some two billion other egos. And to them it's a very important difference. Especially as it concerns the life of any one of them."

"Well, what about Christ and his parable of the lost sheep?"

"True enough. Except that the parable implies that the lost sheep admits his lostness, his sinning. Which only a saving Christ can forgive."

Thurs became aroused at last. The argument with Erasmus, the argument about the manhood of Jesus, and now finally the argument about legal justice with the great Mr. Hobbs himself, had gotten his waters to rolling again. Eyes wild, forelock flashing white, long arms waving, he let go another horrendous proposition. "Saving Christ, uh, that's assuming Christ was truly the son of God."

"Yes. Don't you believe that?"

"No. I have my doubts. Who's to prove he was? The Bible? Haven't you

ever thought it odd that only the Bible says the Bible is the Bible? That we have
no other proof? You see, in the final analysis, as far as we know, it is only in the
mind of man that there are any thoughts at all about anything. They occur only
in man's world. We cannot get outside of man."

"But Thurs, the idea is, as I've so often said before, that we can't question
our being in God's world. Just as a fish is born in water and must live in it, so
we are born in God's world and must live in it. Religion is a fact in the field of
the spiritual just as respiration is a fact in the field of the physical. God is sov-
ereign. All is subsumed in Him."

"I doubt it!"

Mr. Hobbs smiled. He looked at the others. "We have now arrived at an old
classic difference of points of view. And that is this. The Christian starts from
the top down. God is, and the Christian works from there. He interprets all experience in that light, which not only helps him explain life but gives him an
ever clearer view of God Himself. The non-Christian, however, starts from the
bottom up. There is no thing except the non-Christian himself, and the non-
Christian works from there. He proceeds to have experience. He picks up facts.
After a considerable number of facts have been accumulated, he begins to make
a few observations. The first position is theologic; the second scientific. The first
is mostly deductive; the second inductive. But note this: both assume certain
things. Both assume that the mind, if it works at all, can find some kinds of truth.
And both assume that a truth can be found. And both start somewhere. Both
the Christian and the non-Christian, if they have faith in their respective sys-
tems, can be happy about it. But the Christian will most likely be the happiest
because he knows he will also get life in the hereafter." Mr. Hobbs picked up
his pipe again. "You see, the Christian posits the incarnation. Christianity is
the affirmation that God reveals Himself by and in Christ as his prophet, priest,
and king; who is portrayed in the Scriptures; who was incarnated in Jesus; and
who is the living validity in the Christian Church. Incarnation means more than
just the mere fact of incarnation. It means that into one being there is gathered
all that is possible: nature, man, God. The sovereignty of God. Thus, summing
it all up again, the Christian believes that we are all born in God's world and
must live in it. All is subsumed in him."

Thurs was irritated by the long monologue and the moment Mr. Hobbs
stopped to give his pipe a puff he broke in with one of his own. "Poppycock!
With equal validity I can say we are born into a situation of chaos. Both terms,
God, chaos, are equally all-inclusive and equally vague. No, I say again: Poppycock! A lovely dream! A lovely dream that stands or falls on one thing—whether
Christ was the result of a union between Mary's ovum and God's spermatozoon
or the result of a union between Mary's egg and a Hebrew lad's seed. And I say
it's common sense to think that Mary was but a low-class Palestinian girl who
got caught by a lad, and who, to hoodwink an impotent old husband by the
name of Joseph, invented the fable of virgin birth. Or rather used the fable, since
at that time folklore was full of fables about virgin birth." Thurs paused for

breath. "In fact, in those days women didn't know that intercourse with men was necessary before there could be conception. They believed that it was spirits who were responsible, woodland spirits, water spirits, moonlight spirits." Thurs waved his hand. "A likely story indeed. Maybe that's why the expression 'son of a bitch' is such an anathema to you Christians—it strikes a glancing blow at that truth."

Hands hid ashamed eyes all around the table.

But Mr. Hobbs merely behaved as if he had been told that eggs were selling for thirty cents a dozen on Wealthy Street. He said, "Christianity is not narrowly concerned about the problem of Virgin birth. Christianity—"

"But Christianity has to be. The whole thing started out of that lie!"

There it was. It was out at last. All had heard what Thurs really thought. The young platos in Christ sat as if clubbed.

It was a full hour before the members recovered—aided no little by coffee and doughnuts and Mr. Hobbs's gentle and urbane manner.

The very next day Thurs was called into President Cooper's office.

"Young man. I heard that you have publicly denied Christ!"

Thurs thought: "Should I admit it? I've still got two months to go before I graduate."

"Young man, we can tolerate your fruit cellar raids, and your wanderings away from the campus for a few days, but we cannot tolerate your spurning our precious Savior Jesus Christ. For when our dear Christ is attacked, we Christians are duty bound to stamp out the blasphemer. To survive, we have to be ruthless with radicals and non-conformists in our midst."

"You and Cromwell."

"What!"

Thurs thought: "It takes a long time and a lot of guts before a man can cut himself free of his own umbilical cord—especially when his only friends are still more or less a part of Mother Religion. It takes a long time for a fish to learn to breathe air." Thurs got up to go.

"Just a moment, young man"

"Yes?"

"Young man, tell me, who or what has led you astray?"

"I don't know."

"Was it Howard? Or Neal? Or Ben? The Brain Trust?"

"No."

"Was it Mr. Hobbs?"

"No."

"Mr. Maynard?"

"Never him."

"Are you sure?"

"Yes."

"But it must have been someone or something."

"Maybe it was my own nose. Lately I've been following that around."

"Young man, I'm afraid the trouble with you is that you are too proud. You question too much."

"But what am I to do? God gave me this ability to question, should I bury it in the ground? God is against that too."

"Tell me, Thurs, have you committed some heinous crime lately that you've suddenly become so wild?"

Thurs thought of self-abuse. This he was too ashamed to mention. So he lied. "Not that I know of."

"Tell me, does Howard ever discuss his private beliefs with you?"

"I'm not a child, Mr. Cooper, that I tattletale."

"What does he talk about?"

"All right. I'll tell you. Poetry. Life. Women."

"Life?"

"Yes."

"Be careful of him, Thurs. Associate too much with a rotten apple and you may become contaminated yourself."

"You can't compare an apple with a human being. I had logic and that I know."

"Ah, Mr. Hobbs again, eh?"

"Don't blame Mr. Hobbs. If anything, he teaches us that logic helps us find God."

Prexy leaned forward, flushed, dark in mien. "Thurs, I'm afraid Howard was a crooked branch to begin with. And you can't straighten a crooked branch, you know."

"Are there ever any straight branches to begin with? Isn't it precisely this prone-to-sin business that you always talk about that argues against there being any?"

Prexy looked at Thurs's whitelock. "Be careful that that does not become your mark-of-Cain."

"What!"

"Don't let your questioning mind run away with you. Remember, you are as nothing in God's eyes. And besides, why desert one uncertainty for an even greater uncertainty?"

"And in the meantime continue to support the present one?"

Prexy shook his head. "You are too proud."

But Thurs hardly heard. It wasn't pride at all.

I was accused of being a man who was filled with freewill and I was just in college yet.

Green Earth

Preface

I VISITED MY UNCLE AND AUNT on the farm shortly after my first novel was published. It was on a Sunday, and I went to church with them. After the service, their minister stopped me as he shook hands with departing parishioners and asked me how it felt to have written a best seller.

"Best seller?" I exclaimed. "Where'd you get that idea?"

The minister said, "With all that filth and dirty sex in it, it's bound to sell, isn't it?"

"Not any more than all that filth in the Bible might sell it."

"Oh, but the Bible is God's word."

"Did you buy a copy of my book?"

"No. Your uncle let me read his copy."

"Domeny, a friend of mine once advised me that I should never pay attention to criticism unless it came from someone who'd bought my book."

Later that evening at supper, as everything was going along smoothly, food being passed around the table, mean gossip kept to a minimum, proper thanks given for the good summer just passed . . . Aunt suddenly said, "Yes, I read your book too."

Silence.

"Domeny's right. That scene there by the crick, what that Maury done there to that Kirsten, that's awful. It's pure filth. How can you, Alice's boy, write about such things?"

"And I'm not my father's son?"

All eyes down the long table fixed on me for a second, then went back to concentrating on the food.

Aunt sat up very straight at her end of the table. Her blue eyes flashed. "Are you ashamed of your mother?"

"I loved her."

"Well then?"

"She would want me to tell the truth according to my own lights. Rather than be a hypocrite. Pretend to be something I am not."

"I still think you didn't have to write that stuff about them two there by the crick."

Uncle raised his graying head. Held it partly sideways as if trimming his sails to the solar wind coming from Aunt's burning eyes. His blue eyes just barely dared to look into mine for a moment. "That's right, Fred. You didn't have to write that stuff. It's not Christian Reformed."

I decided not to raise a fuss. My cousins around the table were too young to understand what I was up to. I said instead, "Tante, you always make the most wonderful pies. Better than my mother even. This lemon meringue is num num."

After a bit Aunt had to smile a little. "Now you're buttering me up, Fred." Aunt had often been jealous of the way her husband's older sister could cook.

"But this pie is good, Tante. It almost evaporates in your mouth."

"Well, I try my best," Aunt said.

At six o'clock the menfolks went to the barn. Uncle milked some twenty cows six on six, six o'clock in the morning and six o'clock at night. The cows gave more if milked every twelve hours right on the dot. Uncle and his tall slim son attached the milking machines while I stood well back of the gutter and watched.

Once the milking machines were going, Uncle had time for talk. "Say," he said, shaking his head gravely in admiration, looking me directly in the eye, "some of those passages there in your book, man, they surely was good. About how the dust blew around. And how the earth was cracked. And yet how the people hung on. How they wouldn't give up. That surely was good. Just the way it was. Yes, everything was good in it. Even that passage by the crick there, where you tell about what that boy done to that girl, that was all just the way it was."

I was surprised, and showed it. "Hey, Uncle, where were you at the supper table when Aunt jumped me about that crick passage?"

He waved that off. "Oh, I just said that to quiet her down. Womenfolks and ministers all think alike about them things and there ain't much you can do about it. But we here in the barn now, we menfolks, we can speak plain. Now you take that passage where . . . ."

In the country, in small towns and farms, there are actually two societies living side by side. One is the barnyard and what the males do out there and the way they look at sex. The other is the women in the house, the women who have never had fun in sex—and ministers. They're on the other side. And there are two languages. The language in the barnyard gets very vivid and tremendous, and then there's the polite, sort of hidden kind of dialogue that goes on between ministers and old ladies—two different sexes going on and two different languages. When you get over there to the ministers' and women's side, then you object somewhat to my vivid language and my lively language. Then, over on the males' side, you object once in a while when I write about some of them, like in Eden Prairie, *where they pray so much.*

Sex and Longing

Did you read "Dinkytown"? The last line in there, I say, "I was a virgin till I was twenty-five." Which is true. I tried to make up for it in a big hurry afterwards.

Well, the race would vanish if there wouldn't be sex. And raised on the farm, I saw boars breeding sows, and stallions breeding mares, and bulls mounting cows, roosters mounting chickens. So it was around me all over the place.

Culture is a little bit of whitewash on a powerful animal. That's just all it is really, just a little whitewash . . . A tincture of the neo-cortex. And I think as time went on I had to recognize that brains and genius sit very uneasily on top of the animal. And that the animal really runs things, the lizard really runs things. Not even the mammal mind, but the lizard mind runs things. And they don't care about morals, the lizards don't. They don't give a rip about it.

FROM
Green Earth

Tess

ONE FRIDAY HE BROUGHT HOME *Tess of the D'Urbervilles.* In paging through it he'd spotted a reference to an English dairy farm. He'd also spotted a passage about Tess feeling sad about something. The description of Tess reminded him of beautiful Winifred Bonner.

That night right after supper, he plunged into the book. He sat with his back to the gas lamp and with his stocking feet up on the sewing machine in the corner.

After about an hour he vaguely heard Ma say, "I wonder what that boy is reading there. I've called him three times and he hasn't heard me."

"Free!" Pa called sharply.

Free broke away from his book. "Yes?"

"Pay attention to your mother once when she asks you a question."

"Yes, Ma?" The gaslight in their farm kitchen was much sharper than the lamplight in Tess's house.

"What are you reading there that's so interesting?"

Free had got far enough into the book to know that that dirty Alec D'Uberville had just ruined Tess. That Ma had better not know about. "Oh, just some schoolwork," he lied.

"What's it about?"

"Oh, about some farm people in England." To make up for his lie, Free read a few lines from the paragraph he'd just finished. "After Tess had settled down to her cow there was for a time no talk in the barton and not a sound interfered with the purr of the milk-jets into the numerous pails."

Ma was amazed. "Since when have you become so interested in milking that you get lost in reading about it? Especially English milking? When we can hardly get you to help with our American milking?"

"It's just a story, Ma."

Pa said, "You mean to tell me we're paying good hard-earned money to send you to school to learn how they milk cows in England?"

"It's the story of it, Pa, that makes it important. And what it means."

"Ha," Pa said, "a cow's swift tail in your eyes will tell you what it means a whole lot better. Especially if it's a little damp."

Ma shook her head. "Shakespeare, yes. But reading about Tess milking a cow in England, no."

Pa mulled it over some more. "Though I have to say that that purr of the milk-jets into all those pails sounds pretty good."

Ma shook her head some more. "They sure must be backward in England that they still require young girls to milk. I wouldn't milk here in America for love nor money, even if I was starving to death."

Pa filled his pipe and lit it. "Wal, as to that, wife, young girls in the Old Country, Fryslan, they still milk."

Free said, "You still haven't told me what you wanted, Ma."

"Oh. That. Yes. Could you go down cellar for me a minute and bring up some jelly for breakfast tomorrow morning?"

"Sure thing."

The next Sunday, Ma decided to stay home from church for once.

When they got back from church Free right away spotted an offish look in Ma's eyes. He soon found out why. When he looked around for *Tess of the D'Urbervilles* he couldn't find it. He still had about fifty pages to go. When he asked Ma if she'd seen it, she had an answer for him.

"I put Tess away." Ma set the steaming rice cooker on the table. "Imagine, you reading that kind of stuff."

He liked warm rice with butter and sugar on it, along with a sprinkling of cinnamon, but that noon it didn't taste very good.

The next morning off to school he went as usual.

To his surprise, right after chapel, he spotted Pa and Ma being ushered into Principal Hedges's office. Ma was carrying the book *Tess of the D'Urbervilles*. The door closed behind them. Through the rippled glass in the door Free could see vague shadows moving about as the three people inside turned their chairs a little and sat down. For Pa to take off half a day from fall work, and Ma to go along with him, meant his folks were really upset.

He was working on his Latin II lesson during study hour right after school lunch, when someone tapped him on the shoulder. Looking up, he saw Principal Hedges and his little square mustache. Principal Hedges crooked a finger at him to come along with him. Free got up and quietly followed him into his office.

"Have a chair, Free."

"Yessir."

"You already know what this is all about no doubt?"

"I think so."

"What did you get out of that tale of Tess?"

"Well, I learned a lot about the way the English run their dairy farms."

Principal Hedges bent a quizzical smile upon him. "And?"

"I learned that adultery does not pay. Though that poor Tess, she couldn't help it. That devil Alec caught her sleeping in the woods and before she knew it he'd ruined her."

"Is that what you got out of it?"

"Well, but, adultery is wrong, isn't it?"

"Yes. I guess it is." Principal Hedges looked down at the wide gold ring on his left hand. "Do you think you understood, fully what you were reading?"

"Hardy is hard to read. He writes awkward."

Principal Hedges laughed. "Now there is a bit of pretty good literary criticism. Those are exactly my sentiments about him, son. I much prefer Mark Twain." Principal Hedges often took on Mark Twain's imperial stance when he was aroused. "Well, Free, of course you know that your mother loves you. She's a fine woman. But she feels you are too young to read about sex. So she's asked me to work out an agreement with you. That you must first get my approval for any novel you want to take out of the library. Okay?"

Free looked black. Slowly he nodded.

Principal Hedges folded his hands and then formed a church steeple out of his forefingers. "For myself, I don't see any harm in your reading about poor Tess. You seem to have handled reading about her in a mature way. But you want to remember that your mother is not used to that kind of reading matter."

"Ma's pretty smart though, prof."

"I know she is. It's just that she hasn't read many novels." Principal Hedges smiled. His little black moustache thinned out. "I admire her for coming here. And I admire you for your loyalty." He got to his feet. "Now, just remember that before you can take out a novel you've got to get my approval. Okay?"

"Okay."

A couple of days later, Principal Hedges found Free in the library browsing through the fiction section. Principal Hedges seemed irritated to find him there so soon after their talk. "Got your studies done?"

"Mostly."

Some of the kids lounging under the tall windows snickered.

Principal Hedges whirled around and blazed black eyes at them. "And that question goes for you mockers too, you know."

The kids got up and moved into the study hall.

Principal Hedges turned back to Free. His eyes fell on the length of Free's shanks showing beneath his knickers. "You're beginning to shoot up, aren't you? Well, so it goes. Sometimes nature goes in for brains and sometimes for brawn."

"And sometimes she goes in for both," Free retorted.

A look of genuine surprise, even pleasure, bloomed on Principal Hedges's face. "Atty old comeback, boy. Now I know you've got something upstairs there. Good."

FROM

The Chokecherry Tree

First thing I knew I had a character who insisted on more work. His name is Elof Lofbloom. He is a college graduate who has no specific training and so can't get the job that fits his notion of what a hero should have. He bums around, and finally returns home where his father greets him roughly. He carries with him Peregrine Pickle, *which all through the book . . . he is trying to finish, and also carries a few lessons in Accounting by Correspondence which he thinks will get him into a well-paying job . . . Gradually, despite struggles, and protests, he sinks slowly away into the common mass of people. And becomes the village queer duck.*

I am always writing with a little smile on my face. . . People talk about the brooding in my books. And they speak of me being naive. But they never mention that little smile. And it is true I am naive. And in a sense I make it a point to cultivate it . . . I want to keep that attitude. Among other things I like to think of myself as a person who likes touching and who is always smiling a little.

The Dancing Schoolteacher
with the Broken Balance Wheel

. . . Maybe we wisenoses work ourselves into a lather over nothing. Maybe we read into Elof our own frets and worries when we consider the problem of: "Why am I here?" Maybe Elof doesn't worry about it at all. Maybe he just lives. Exists. Actually, we cannot be absolutely, categorically finally, and at last sure that animals do not enjoy their lives. Just try once grappling barehanded with weasels, minks, skunks, bobcats, tigers, lions with intent to kill. Even sheep will surprise you . . .

BRIGHT AND EARLY THE NEXT DAY Elof and Fats dressed and shaved—Fats trying to hide the turgid flush on his face with a couple of pats of baby-buttock powder—and broke fast and roosted wholesomely on the can and packed their clothes and then were ready to go.

They drove downtown and parked and went up to Van Dam's office to get their assignment.

Fats knocked on the door of the sixth-floor Kingsfood office.

"C'mon in."

Fats entered, cleared his throat, a smile on his masklike face, Elof following after.

"Well, well." Van Dam hopped up from his armchair and out a box of huge cigars. "Well, well. How are my soft singers today?"

Both declined the proffer of long smokes.

Fats took a chair and caught his breath. "Don't want to take your time, boss, but where do we go?"

Van Dam waved Elof to a seat. "Sit down, sit down."

Elof found himself a chair near the door.

The mood of the room almost shushed what little enthusiasm Elof had awakened with that morning. The plastered walls were painted a cloudy-day gray, the ceiling a muted gray. The floor was covered with a tufted white-gray carpet. The office equipment was scant: two visitors' chairs, a huge map with red and white and blue pins, an armchair, and a gray steel desk. Outside of an ink pad and ash tray, the top of the desk was as empty as a twister-swept prairie. Elof had the distinct impression he had suddenly and willfully stepped into an iron jail; had gone into see a bald-headed miser living in a steel vault. Elof moved his chair still closer to the door.

Fats repeated his question. "Where do we go?"

Van Dam sucked on his big cigar, chewed it, squinted his glinting black-brown eyes at Fats, and then waved a hand. "Well, let's take a look at the map." He strode to the wall, planted his feet well apart before it. The map was a huge one, six by eight feet, and it spread out the geography of Siouxland and its neighboring territory: the southeast corner of North Dakota, the eastern half of South Dakota, the upper northwest section of Nebraska, the northwest corner of Iowa, and the southwest region of Minnesota. "Well, boys, this is our territory. Lots of it still virgin as far as Kingsfood is concerned. Now what I'd like to do is to send you two into fresh territory."

"Good," Fats put in from his chair.

"—so you—Huh?" The oversize cigar almost fell from Van Dam's mouth. He looked queerly at Fats a moment, brushed a hand over the fly of his pants, recovered, laughed, said, "Fats, no wonder you're a hot-shot salesman. You—well, never mind." Van Dam walked around in a circle, as if the idea he was nurturing were almost too big for the three of them to consider. "I tell you. There's an area here"—he waved his hand at the belly of what was to be seen of South Dakota—"an area right through here which always beats down the tail of my best men. Beats 'em down to a frazzle. Whips 'em. It's as tough to crack as a petrified nut. Can't seem to make inroads a-tall. And I thought maybe, since you did such a hot-shot job over at Passage, a tough territory too, full of them tight suspicious Hollanders—"

"What's the biggest town there?" Fats asked, pointing at South Dakota.

"Huh? Town? Heh, heh. Now Fats, you know there ain't no towns out there. Just names for gopher holes."

"Well, what's the name then?"

"Iota."

Fats nodded.

Again Van Dam buzzed around in a circle. "Yessir, Iota, South Dakota. Hardest nut to crack in the Union."

Elof got up from his chair and studied the map while they talked. It occurred to him that the recent droughts, especially the blasting heat of August just gone, might have cleaned it out. "Maybe they ain't got no money, Van Dam."

"Hoch. Poch. Don't tell me that."

"They've had some pretty bad days in that part of the country. Some's been burnt and dusted out."

"Aw, don't tell me. Farmers are always complainin'. Always. And all along they've got a sockful of dough hidden on the place somewhere. Or buried in some old pisspot someplace. Or up the old lady's garter. Plenty a money."

Fats said, "Iota, is it?"

"Yeh."

"Let's get goin' then, Elof." Fats got up with an effort and stepped to the door. He offered Elof and himself a cigarette, and lit them, and said, "So long, boss," and stepped out into the hall with Elof.

"Huh? What?" Van Dam exclaimed. "Wait."

The door closed after them slowly, leaving Van Dam standing alone and flabbergasted in the middle of his empty office.

Fats went down the hall to the elevator door, pushed the Down button.

After a moment Fats said, "Trouble with Van Dam is that he smokes too many big cigars. Gives him a blown-up notion about himself. Gives him the bighead. Gives him the diarrhea of the jawbone."

Elof nodded. They went down the elevator and out into the street and a bright September sun. Fats got into his parked coupé.

Fats said, "Well, let's get goin'."

"Wait," Elof said, holding back. "One thing before we go. I'm down to two bucks. How soon before I get my first check?"

"Forget it."

"No, c'mon now, I—"

"Forget it."

"But —"

"Skip it. The car runs jut as cheap with two in it as one. A room with a double bed don't cost much more than one with a single. An' if we get real hungry, we'll dip into some of the sample groceries we got along with us. If we have to."

"But —"

"Forget it. I'll carry you till you get on your feet."

"Well—okay. But remember. I'm gonna pay you back."

"You goddamn right you are. Now shut up an' get into the car."

They were out on the road, riding west, going into the desolate country, following the narrow white ribbon of Highway 16 sliding past enormous rectangular farms and ranches. They saw corduroy-ribbed fields of green and yellow-drying corn, saw purple plowed stubble fields, saw gray sun-dried pastures. And every mile they went west, the land became drier, the air more burning and rasping, the country more lonely and empty. But it was wonderful land, Elof thought, wonderful. It fit what he felt in his heart.

They drove on; sometimes Fats driving the old black coupé, sometimes Elof.

A figment of an argument Elof had had with Fats earlier in the morning came back to him. He had been packing his accounting-course lessons and *Peregrine Pickle* into his suitcase when Fats had interrupted with a sarcastic remark. "Guys readin' books're wastin' their time. An' wastin' the time of others."

Elof turned to Fats at the wheel. "That wisecrack you made this morning about reading books—how can a smart fellow like you make a statement like that? You know well enough that most ideas come from books. If it wasn't for books you wouldn't be driving this car right now today."

"Crap," Fats said, "crap. Books, goin' to college, all that guff, it's a big waste a time. Take me, f'rinstance. I've been sellin' six years and I'm makin' more money today than any guy in my high school class that went on to college."

"Sour grapes."

Fats turned slowly from his driving and drilled Elof with a cold gray eye. "You and Van Dam. You blab too much."

"I was only suggesting."

"Uh-huh."

But Elof couldn't resist bucking the other's belligerence. "Still and all, I think college, reading, education, ideas, books, they do something for you."

"What?"

"Well, they open up your mind. It's like flying like a butterfly instead of grubbing like a grubworm. Like living by a hundredwatt bulb instead of a ten. More light."

"Light for what?" Fats asked, coughing a little. "I take it you went to college?"

"Some. Yeh."

"Well, boy, I'll bet my light will lead me faster to more money than your light any day of the week. Includin' Sundays."

"But there's more to life than money."

"What?"

"Sure there is. I tell—"

"Look, bo. There's one thing I've learned from my short life. That's this. You see, I was born and raised on a farm, then went to high school, later worked in a packin' plant—and from that I learned one thing. That life's a fight. That the first law is to fill that belly. No matter what. If somebody gets in the way, you get rid of 'im. In such a way, of course, so that you don't land in jail. Because if your belly don't get filled reg'lar, your body dies. And if your body dies, where's your ideas then?"

Elof said nothing. Fats was right.

And, Fats was wrong. There was more to it than that. Just what, Elof couldn't say. He felt he should say something about the value of dreams and hopes, of being a hero, but against Fats's brilliant mink logic he had no matching argument.

They got to Iota about noon.

As Van Dam had suggested, it was little more than a gopher hole. The little village lay north of a railroad track: a depot, an elevator, a grocery store, a filling station, a town hall, a couple dozen scattered homes. And the sun was so bright in it, so white with heat, that the reflection from the cement sidewalks and streets had given the inhabitants all a sunburn under the chin.

The country around was as dry and as dusty as a street. And as barren of live growth. It was grazing country, and on the vast rolling terrain within the circle of the entire horizon only a half-dozen ranches could be seen.

Fats parked in front of an eat shop. "Well, no use hurrying out right away. Best time to hit is between two-thirty and five, just in between naptime and supper-making time. Babies are all awake by then, and hard-boiled hubbies still ain't home from work. So we might as well lunch. An' take a nap ourselves."

At two-thirty the boys drove down a short residential street. Clapboard frame houses predominated: some gray, some brown, some white. Only a banker and a preacher had been able to afford brick homes—just like in Hello.

"It won't take us long to work these," Elof said.

"I'll say not. That's what Van Dam meant when he said Iota. The son of a bitch."

Fats parked at the end of the street. With foxy eyes he studied the houses on both sides and at last said, "Well, those on the right look the easiest. I'll let you learn on them."

"Now, none of that. I can—"

"Take 'em. An' I mean take 'em."

They got out. Elof's bared gold hair tingled in the stinging heat of the sun.

Fats opened up the back of the old black coupé, broke into a box, and handed a giveaway mixing bowl to Elof. "Well, bo, here's your leader, the little item that's bound to put the bead in the little old lady's eye."

Elof took it gingerly.

"Well, bo, good luck. Hit it hard an' get behind it."

Elof nodded, swallowed, tried to quiet his leapfrogging heart.

He started up the street, carrying the bowl under his stubby arm. A sales pad jugged up and down inside the jacket pocket of his gray suit. Out of the corner of his eye he watched Fats approach a house, saw him knock nonchalantly.

"T'hell with it," Elof muttered to himself. "If he can, I can."

Whistling bravely, he went up a sidewalk. He sized up the house carefully, just as he had seen Fats size up the block.

The trees in front of the house were as bare of leaves as a doglicked bone. The grass was brown and as brittle as flakes of ashes. Orts and shards littered the yard. The paint on the house had weathered off. The shades were all drawn. A dust dune behind the house rose to half the height of the first-story windows. Two black-eyed children played on a wind-ribbed side of it.

Elof knocked on the door.

After a moment he noticed a window shade moving. A face peered out onto the yard; saw him. The shade flapped to. There was a moment of silence. Then the door gave a little.

A life-weathered housewife looked at him. She was taller than he.

"Good afternoon, ma'am," Elof rattled hastily, "good afternoon. I've got something here that I'm sure you'll like." He held up the shining yellow mixing bowl. "Did you ever see anything like this?"

The woman stared. Her hands picked up her gray apron and slowly began to wring it and then wiped the sweat from her brow with it.

"No? Well, ma'am, it's all yours. Yes, yours. All you got to do is . . ." Elof singsonged off a series of phrases. Vaguely he realized it was an aping of Van Dam's demonstrators. In the background, across the street, he could hear the murmur of Fats's voice and a customer's warm response.

Elof went on, tried to hit it hard. "Ma'am, this mixing bowl's put out by one of the finest kiln manufacturers in America. And I'm here to tell you . . ."

The woman still stared.

Elof caught himself scowling—instantly forced a happy grimace to his lips.

The woman loosened a little.

"Sure," Elof said. "And now I want to tell you something. This swell mixing bowl can be used for— "

"Step inside," the woman said, interrupting, "you're lettin' the heat in."

"—used for—Huh?"

"Step in. You're lettin' the heat in."

"Oh." Elof popped inside.

She closed the door.

She said, "I keep the doors and windows closed and the shades down. I got a theory it keeps the house cool that way. It does." She pointed to a chair. "Take a seat."

For a moment the house seemed dark, but, forcing his eyes, Elof managed to make out the form of a chair by a window. He sat down.

"Now, what was it you said again?" the woman asked.

"Well—I've got a free mixing bowl here for you that—"

"No hooks or crooks to it?" The woman asked sharply.

"No. You just—"

Abruptly the brightening look of a cunning and a hungry shopper came into her eye. "I've crazed for one a them fer years. Let me see it."

The woman took it and loved it fumblingly in her callused redveined hands. She smiled to herself in the artificial dusk. "It's nice. Real nice."

Elof's heart melted. Her sudden longing was so pathetic, so endearing, that he had half a notion to give it to her with no strings attached. Had there been no mink-eyed, cocksure Fats to face later on, he would have. He looked away from her, looked at the shades casting buff twilight in the parlor, smelled the noseclogging odor of summer house-sweat, and remembered his mother, remembered how she, too, had craved the best that a master potter's wheel might offer.

"What do I do to get it?" the woman asked.

"Well—give me an order for Kingsfood groceries, sign a receipt for it, and a bowl like this—not this one but one like it—is yours. Our follow-up man will give it to you when he delivers your order two days from now. And then, after you've bought about forty dollars' worth altogether, it's yours for good."

"You mean, I can't have this right away?"

"No, not this particular one. But one like it."

"When did you say I was to get it then?"

Poor people, Elof thought, poor people. Surprises were so rare in their songless lives that their minds had lost all one-time child elasticity. He started over. "You give me an order for groceries. You sign for it. I turn it in. Two days later a truck delivers it. And delivers you a shining yellow bowl."

"Oh."

"Sure." Elof sighed massively. He handed her an illustrated booklet.

She took it. "These the groceries?"

"That's right." Elof got out his pad and pencil, waited. She paged through the book, looking at the colored pictures in what little light the shade-drawn windows allowed her. "Sure's nice groceries, all right. Sure would like to have some."

"Well, you know how to get 'em. All you got to do is to give me an order."

"We ain't got the money."

"You've got some kind of income though, haven't you?"

"Some. Relief checks. An' what my old man kin steal from the railroad."

Elof started. "But you get groceries somewhere, don't you?"

"Sure. What our one store will allow us on our relief checks." She looked at the booklet again. "Pretty high, ain't they?"

"But look at the quality you're getting."

The woman paused. She turned herself so that more of the dim light from the windows could fall on the glossy page. She looked off to one side, considering. A sly look came into her eyes; and vanished. "Well, I'll take some oatmeal. An' a bottle a vanilla. An' some flour. Five pounds."

"And the money?"

"I tell you. We got a little cash comin' in beside the relief check."

Elof scribbled. "Anything else?"

"I guess that's all."

"Now, will you sign right here?"

"Sign?"

"Yeh." Elof smiled at her, leaned off the edge of his chair toward her. "Right here." He held out the pencil.

She shook her head. "I don't sign things. Can't. My old man'd kill me."

"Well, now . . ."

"Nope. Don't like to sign things. Scared of it."

Elof swallowed, considered, retreated a little. "Well, I suppose I tell you what. I don't see why your word ain't as good as your signature. Mine is." He got to his feet. "I'll send this in, and in two days at the most you can expect our Kingsfood followup man here to deliver your order. And your mixing bowl."

"Fine." She stood up too.

"Good-by, Mrs. . . . ? Mrs. . . . ?" Elof hinted.

"Good-by."

Elof opened the door. Again he tried to get it out of her. "By the way, who shall I say this order is to be delivered to? Mrs. . . . ?"

"Mrs. Aasland."

"Mrs. Aasland? Henry Aasland?"

"No. Anders Aasland."

"Good. Well, Mrs. Aasland, I hope you like the mixing bowl."

"I hope so too." She shut the door.

Elof stumbled out into the sun. He was soaked with sweat. He pulled his shirt gingerly from his wet body, fluffed his suit jacket open like a bird preparing to take wing.

Fats was coming down the steps of the second house, saw him, stepped slowly across toward him, puffing. They met in the middle of the dusty street. The sun owled down on them.

"Well, did you get her?" Fats asked.

"Yeh."

Fats's eyes opened. "You did?"

"Yeh. It was as easy as eating lemon pie a la mode. All I had to do was smile."

Fats nodded. He eyed Elof. "Yeh, I think maybe you'll make a salesman after all. But one thing. Don't let them visit with you. Cut 'em short. Smile, but cut 'em short. Drive it home an' get. Because, you see, while you were doing one, I did two."

"But a man's got to be polite."

"Drive it in an' cut it short."

Elof shook his head. It didn't sound very civilized.

"Well, go get number two."

"Yeh."

Elof worked the street, going up each walk, knocking, talking, blushing, smiling desperately, watching himself learning the mechanical patter, inwardly noting that the faces he met began to blur into each other—also inwardly noting that he wasn't warming up to the game very much.

At five o'clock Fats called a halt. "No use buttin' in on their meals. Especially not when it's time for your own."

Elof let out a huge sigh. And discovered that his shoulders and back had been hunched up from the tension. He rolled his short arms and shrugged his shoulders to get rid of it.

"Well, bo, how many?"

"Seven," Elof said. He spoke uncertainly, not sure that unsigned orders counted.

"No!" Fats was stirred into giving him a white-toothed grin. "Huh. And I only got six myself."

Elof said nothing.

"Well, bo, you're on your way. You just earned yourself seven bucks in a little less than three hours. Easy work, ain't it?"

"Yeh," Elof said sourly.

They had reached the black coupé at the end of the block, and Elof opened the trunk and put away the bowl in its box.

Fats took him by the arm. "You act like you lost seven bucks."

"I lost more than that."

"What?"

Elof let it slip out. "My self-respect."

"Crap," Fats puffed, his light blue face turning purple.

"I did. There's something wrong with a guy who likes sellin'. It's too pushy."

"Got to fill that belly."

"There should be a better way of doing it." Elof waited until Fats had put away his sample mixing bowl, too, and then closed the trunk door. He got into the car. He rolled down a window and began fanning himself with a handkerchief.

Fats got in on the other side.

Elof said, "It's all so false, false. Babbittry. You go up to a door, and you smile, and you say, 'Ah, hello there, Mrs. Grizzle, how are you this fine bright sunny day? Ah, come now, give me a fine nice smile, Mrs. Grizzle, because in about ten minutes, after a nice heart-to-heart talk as old bosom friends, you're going to give me a hundred dollars for twenty dollars' worth of goods—the other eighty representing fast and friggy talk.'"

"You're gettin' your tail over the line again, bo."

"And, by God, she falls for it. She falls for it so hard she even puckers up for you."

Fats took a cigarette and offered Elof one.

"Thanks," Elof said shortly, "but not this time. I've been sponging off you too much as it is."

Fats lighted up for himself. He smoked quietly for a while.

At last Fats asked, "Got any more to say?"

"No."

"Good, now let me get in my two bits' worth," he drawled slowly. "Bo, what you need is a little success."

"Huh."

"Grow yourself a pair a horns."

Elof said nothing. He looked out of the window and with a fingernail picked at the gray striped cloth on the door.

Fats started up the old coupé and drove slowly down the street. "Well, bo, you'll get used to it."

"If I do, I'll never look myself in the face again."

"You'll get used to it. You got the makin's. An' in the meantime, what you need is a little fun."

"What do you mean, 'fun'?"

Fats pointed. "See that sign?"

Elof looked. A crude placard hung in the show window of an empty false-front store. It read:

BIG DANCE AND JAMBOREE

FREE

BUD RUDD'S ORCHESTRA

TOWN HALL

BIG RALLY

AUSPICES THE PEOPLE'S PARTY

(SILVER COLLECTION)

"There's your fun," Fats said. "Come to think of it, I'm in the need of fun myself. Look, we'll get ourselves a quart a gin, load up, an' walk in. An' you just follow me around. Because, bo, me, I'm a politician of the puss."

Night came on, and the majestic bow of the heavens, the Milky Way, shimmered. From out of the wide outspread reaches of the short-grass or great plains country, came dozens of cars full of young people primed for the dance. The number amazed both Elof and Fats.

Elof said, "Van Dam was right. They do live in gopher holes. There just ain't that many houses around."

Fats said, "Just look at 'em. Every one means a buck. Bo, you an' I are goin' to spend the rest of the week rootin' 'em out a their holes."

Elof made a move to get out of the coupé.

Fats held him up. "Wait. Let's kill the bottle first, an' then go in. I want you all likkered up. Put out some a that light a yours. Cut your wolf loose. Because tonight your hoot owl's goin' to hoot."

Elof laughed. A whole evening ahead, and no selling until tomorrow. He swigged heartily.

Fats swigged.

They smoked awhile.

They swigged again.

"Funny," Elof said, "I don't feel nothing."

"Take some more."

Elof did.

"Now how do you feel?"

"All right. Don't feel nothing yet."

"Christ, you must put it away in your big toe. Don't you feel no yen to politic a puss yet?"

Elof listened to himself, shook his head. "No."

"For such a sawed-off runt, you sure got resistance to alky."

Elof grinned.

"Cripes, I could take on two right now myself."

Elof moved uneasily.

Fats said suddenly, a lusty wise gleam in his eyes, "Say, don't tell me you ain't had a woman yet."

Elof pawed for time. "Well . . . I . . ."

"Cripes, so that's it. Bo, there's two legs life stands on. One is fill that belly. The other is pussin'."

"Think so?"

"I know so. Now look, bo. Tonight I want you to pick yourself out a woman and then we'll take a long ride in the country and you do it, see? That'll make a man out a yuh. Give you horns. Give you such zip that tomorrow you'll sell Kingsfood in Iota like St. Peter workin' hell with popsicles."

"I hope so." Fats handed him the bottle again.

Elof drank.

"Finish it."

Elof did.

"All right. Now you're primed. Get'n a woman'll be a wrap-up for you. Let's go." Solicitously, smiling a little, Fats opened the door and shoved Elof out. They started up the sidewalk toward the light of the unpainted hall.

Elof said, "I still don't feel nothing."

"Not a thing?"

"Nope."

"You're too high strung. But it'll hit you pretty soon."

Elof said, "Women. How do you find out when they want it?"

Fats laughed. He coughed, puffed shortly. "You'll learn that fast enough once you've had it. I was once green too. But then I had a couple an' now"—he snapped his thick-ended fingers— "now I kin spot 'em a mile off. Like once in Jerusalem last week. You know, that Hollander town near Anxious? Saw a girl walkin' along slow. It was sundown. After supper. I saw she was a christian, an' I was afraid she'd turn out to be a prune if I popped her the question the first night. I looked at her again, closer, an' then saw that she was moonin' to herself. You know. So I went around the block an' drove past her again. Stopped casual-like. Asked her if she wanted to go out in the country for a ride. Well, she acted like she didn't wanna. But she got in. So I drove around. Easy. Gassin' a little about this an' that. Then I sort a accidentally parked by a pasture." Fats stopped talking, puffed a moment, held still until a young couple had passed out of earshot. "Necked her awhile, an' then climbed her through a fence an' led her into the pasture a piece. On a blanket."

"She must a been a praying whore."

Fats coughed a laugh. "Naw. She was a virgin. I know. I can tell. But she was old enough an' her body was ready. An' I just happened to be the right guy around at just the exact right moment. Well, then I took her home. Got by the door. All of a sudden she wanted to again. Made me take her out to the pasture again."

Really?"

Fats chuckled, coughed softly, stroked his lantern jaw. "Yeh." His eyes half closed in memory.

Elof said, excited, "That won't be my luck, though."

"You'll see," Fats said.

They approached the single light. The sound of a noisy but very rhythmic band came out of the hall. Squeals. Talk. And the sussing of scuffling feet.

Fats stepped inside, held open for Elof.

Both dropped dimes into a collection plate on a wooden table in the hall. Guarding the plate were three old roosters, chukking happily, chewing cigars, rolling eyes, leching after girls, rattling red wattles.

Elof and Fats stepped through another door.

And before them, on a poorly lighted waxed oak floor, swirled dozens of couples. The floor was almost clogged with them. Along the sides were two rows of folding chairs. The hall was of paneled pine knots, weathered. It had far too few windows. Dull gray shades hung down to the sill. Overhead leaped rusty-brown rafters. A chimney came down from the ceiling in the northwest corner, and beneath it, taken down for the summer, stood a tincovered wood-burning stove.

On the far end, on the stage, gesticulated the band. A glaring conical spotlight held them pinned to their chairs. The maestro, Bud Rudd, dressed in white slacks and blue shirt, waved a baton. In contrast, the band members were dressed in blue pants and white shirts. Rudd, a chubby fellow, beat out a steady, clear-cut drum. Though Elof hadn't danced much, didn't have much sense of rhythm in his toes, he could feel this beat. Music pulsed up his legs.

Ten years ago, Elof thought, ten years ago there would have been kerosene lamps, accordions, fiddles, jugs. And ballads. But now there are the new fads: furtive hip flasks, pocketbook condoms, douches, and mad rides in fragile autos. And brittle music.

He listened a moment:

> *Who's afraid of the big bad wolf,*
> *the big bad wolf,*
> *the big bad wolf,*
> *Who's afraid of the big bad wolf,*
> *tra la la la la.*

Fats smiled to himself and, nodding to Elof, winking, picked himself a couple and tapped the man's shoulder, and gracefully, lightly, very slim, eased himself into the arms of the man's girl. Instantly Fats hobbled her fast tempo, led her into a slow one. He was masterful.

Elof envied him.

Elof studied the girls sitting around on the wall benches, saw none that appealed to him. Many had lined faces. All were as dark as walnuts from the burning sun. The country was hard on its people.

Young men stood around talking in clusters, laughing, stinking of strong raw alcohol spike, brown faces flushed almost black.

A tall, very plump young woman got up from a seat and approached a farmer standing alone. Her face was wreathed in smiles, as if she were a perpetually happy woman. She was wearing a wine-red dress, modestly long enough to hide her knees. She had a huge bosom, a strong and well-arched back. Her legs were huge, too, but they had the tapering of a vase and suggested form. She had the shape, all right, Elof saw, but she was just plain big.

In a moment she jogged past him in the arms of the farmer.

Elof studied her some more. And decided that, despite her size, she was the most likely candidate on the floor. A big plump jolly woman was his only chance.

When she came around again and the number had ended, Elof stepped out on the floor and touched her partner's shoulder.

The farmer stepped back, almost as if relieved he had been cut in on, and bowed, and nodded, and walked away.

"Can I have this dance?" Elof asked, remembering to smile.

"Why, I don't think I'd mind," she said. "Surely."

The band began to slam-bang into a new number:

Brother, can you spare a dime?

Elof took her free hand and arched it up. The judgment that she was big was confirmed the moment he put his arm around her. She not only stood almost a foot taller than he, but his finger tips just barely reached her deeply embedded spine. A big mare of a woman. Elof wondered what it was in him that impelled him into the bosoms of tall women. Ma; then Gert; and now this one. Even Marge Berg.

He closed his eyes to catch the strong beat, got it, and miraculously found himself in step with it. He drew the woman close to get her into it too.

At first she was with him. And Elof congratulated himself.

He turned her slowly around the side of the hall. The crowd jostled them, but she was too solid to be bumped out of rhythm.

After a few turns he became aware that she had horrible armpit odor. He sniffed a little to make sure it was she and not the sawdust on the floor. To help in the identification, he opened his eyes a little as he did so. Yes, it was she and not the floor. Then, remembering that he should be considerate, he closed his eyes. They circled the floor.

The number was over. They stepped back out of each other's embrace.

Fats was standing near. He winked at Elof.

The plump woman said to Elof, "You're a stranger around here, aren't you?"

Elof fumbled for a word. "How'd you guess?"

"I go to all the dances. And I never saw you around here before."

"Well, I guess you're right at that."

"What do you do?"

Elof remembered what Fats had once replied in answer to that question; "Why," Elof said softly, "why, I sell."

Oh.

"And what do you do?"

"I?" She waggled her big mare's head. "Oh, I teach."

"Country school?"

"That's right."

"Uh-huh."

"Not very romantic, is it?"

"Oh, I wouldn't say that."

She laughed and winked broadly at him.

The band started up again; feet scuffled up around them.

Elof took her in his arms once more.

This time the number was a fast one, and, to his dismay, his partner started to hop. She didn't seem to make sense, she wasn't hopping in tune as far as he could see, so he took a firm grip on her and held her down and forced her to keep step with him and then fitted them both in the beat of the music.

> *You push the middle valve down*
> *and the music goes round and round—*
> *Oh-oh-oh, oh-oh-oh,*
> *And it comes out here.*

Dancing was wonderful, Elof thought. Wonderful. A great invention. Happily, cozily, he pressed his rosy cheeks between her breasts.

> *You push another valve down*
> *and the music goes round and round—*
> *Oh-oh-oh, oh-oh-oh,*
> *And it comes out here.*

But it wasn't long before she started hopping again, like a dancing mare in heat. And the next thing Elof knew she had galloped them both into a wild, jangling, banging run. A crashing of body against body.

Elof lifted his face a little to catch her eye. He glared at her.

But she was galloping with her eyes closed, a beatific smile on her fleshy lips, her arms tight about him, irresistibly taking him with her, taking the lead.

Elof glanced around wildly, saw brown faces flying past, saw the room spinning.

The mare schoolteacher hurtled him round and round. She rammed his narrow hard buttocks crashing into the stage on which the band was playing, rammed her own broad beam into it, whirled off, rammed him into the tin-covered wood stove, thundering, rammed herself into it, buckling clanging tin, skipped on, heaving him around, knocking down couples, bursting couples apart, skimming, high-jumping, tromping.

"My God!" Elof muttered under his breath, "she's like a clock that's lost its balance wheel. Cripity, she's gonna kill me and her both!"

Then the number ended. Out of sheer momentum she gyrated on for a few moments, vulsed once or twice more, slowly came to a stop.

Her eyes opened. "Awh," she breathed, "that was wonderful."

Breathing hard, Elof grunted, "Yeh."

"Well," she said, "let's sit the next one out. I always sweat so."

They walked to a wall bench and sat down.

After a while, his breath caught, Elof turned to her and asked, "Did you say you was a schoolteacher?"

"Yes. Marthea Dix of District Six."

"Oh."

"And your name?" she asked brightly.

"Perry Pickle."

"Glad to meet you," she said gaily, curtsying a little, fluttering her eyelids.

Elof lowered his eyes. No wonder she was interested in strangers. They were the only ones she could get. "Where's this school of yours?"

"Fifteen miles north of here."

Elof whistled. "You drive in?"

"Caught a bus."

"Bus? You staying overnight?"

"Oh no. I've got to get back by morning. Teach. But I usually catch a ride." She trilled a knowing laugh.

Elof heard himself saying, and it told him the gin was working on him at last, "Why, then maybe I can see you home."

Marthea beamed. "See?" she said. "I always manage to get that ride home." She chittered. "Oh, that'll be just wonderful. Just wonderful."

Fats came up, smirking. He led a slim brunette. She had a simpering, bean-narrow mouth. "Like to have you meet a friend a mine, Teena," he said to her. "Elof Lofblom. Teena Metchouck. An' visa versa."

Elof got to his feet. "Glad t'meetcha."

"Meetcha."

Getting to her feet, too, Marthea gasped, "And I thought you just told me you were Perry Pickle?"

"I am. The other's my traveling name." Elof was astounded to hear the words ease out of his mouth.

Marthea's eyes cleared. She laughed and nudged him with a wise look. "You men. You know, I thought Pickle was an odd name."

"Oh, but Pickle is a real name. There's even a book by that name."

"Oh?"

Fats butted in, puffing, "How about tradin' wives?"

"Well . . ." Elof was reluctant. He found himself liking his woman despite her scenty armpits and her bulky domination on the dance floor.

"An' introducin' us?"

"Oh, excuse me," Elof said. "This is Marthea Dix. Morton Pott. Fats. And . . . ?"

"Teena Metchouck."

"Pleased to meetcha."

"Meetcha."

"Meetcha."

"Well, what about it?" Fats pressed.

"Well—all right." The band struck up again, drumming it out:

Dancing cheek to cheek . . .

And then Elof found himself suddenly in the arms of the most willing and elastic body he had ever touched. For the first minute, because his sense of timing had been thrown out of gear by Marthea's hopping, he had trouble finding the step. But simpering Teena helped him. She nestled against him, her head coming even with his eyes—an odd sensation for him—and she soothed him, and gently suggested where the step was, and in a moment, to Elof's delighted surprise, they were undulating smoothly down the floor, in and out, up four steps, back two, and two to one side, on and on.

When the number was over, Fats came up, rasping for breath, wiping his face, and looking at Elof with a desperate eye.

Marthea was happily flushed.

Elof grinned.

Fats said, "You girls mind"—gasp—"if we step outside a minute?"

"Oh no."

"Go right ahead."

"Thanks," Fats said dryly.

The moment they were out in the cool night, Fats gripped Elof by the arm. "God! Where did you pick up that pickle?"

"Cucumber, you mean. I'm Pickle."

Fats chuckled, coughed, panted. "Cucumber is right. By God, not only is she bigger than a hippopotamus, but she's got more agitation to her than a trotter with a cocklebur under her tail. Why, she goes down the pike like a wild hog-headed boxcar."

Elof spilled guttering laughter; held his sides. He said, between bursts, "Anyway, she'll wear well."

Fats said, "Cripity. Such a critter."

"Yeh. And I'm stuck with her too. For the rest of the night."

"What?"

"Yeh. Like a damn fool with a loose Adam's apple I made a date with her."

Fats stared.

"Yeh, and she lives fifteen miles out."

"Which way?"

"District Six."

"Where the hell's that?"

"I dunno. But I'm stuck with her."

Fats said, "You better ditch her. An' quick."

Elof sobered. "Well, that wouldn't be fair. I asked her and now I've got to go through with it."

"You don't owe her nothin'. When they come that big, etiquette is out."

"Well—but when I give my word I mean it. She's my gal tonight."

Fats stood a moment, puffing. "Well, maybe at that it's all right. Maybe at that the good Lord picked her for the job of makin' a man of you. Yeh." Fats coughed. "Yeh. She looks a little hard up an' she'll probably go out of her way to help you."

They were parked on the yard of a rancher where Teena worked for two bucks a week and room and board. All four had crowded onto the single seat of the coupé. Fats was holding Teena on his lap under the steering wheel; Elof was submerged beneath Marthea on the passenger side.

From the noisy wet sound of mingling fleshes, it was apparent that Fats was going to town with his girl. But Elof himself was having a devil of a time surviving a tondrous crushing. Marthea had enveloped him like some huge amoeba gone cellulation crazy. Her big legs and rump literally folded halfway around him.

After a little he heard Fats whispering, heard him get out with Teena.

Wanting to see what Fats might be up to, Elof, with a terrific effort, pushed Marthea up. But by the time he had managed to get her perched up forward on his stubby knee points, Fats had already disappeared (into the barn?) with Teena. Elof saw nothing but moonlight glittering on a dusty yellow land.

Elof suggested that Marthea sit on the seat beside him.

"Aw gee," she trilled, "and I was having so much fun up here."

A half-hour later Fats appeared again, his breath short, licking his lips.

He coughed as he came near the car. "You folks about ready to go home?"

"Sure," Elof said. "Where's Teena?"

"She's gone in. T'bed."

Fats came around and got in.

Marthea moved over to make room. She sat between the two of them.

"Which way?" Fats asked her.

Marthea sighed. She pointed north.

Fats drove, following the country road, the headlights weaving through the moonglow. The moon was a full round burning orange.

At last Fats found her home. It was another ranch, this time tucked in between a fold of low hills like a clustering of child blocks caught in the hollow of a pillow. Fats parked in front of the weathered ranch house.

Marthea sighed again.

Fats licked his upper lip. "What's the matter, honey, ain't you been taken care of?"

She sighed once more.

The unusual charm and tenderness in Fats's voice made Elof cock up an ear. So that was how it was done.

Fats murmured, "Well, honey, maybe we better take care a that then, huh?"

The next thing Elof knew Fats had an arm around her. Elof followed suit.

Presently Fats had a hand over one of her muskmelon breasts. Again Elof copycatted. Fingers pinched and pressed and played.

Marthea giggled. She snuggled between them.

When they were driving back to Iota, skimming over the moonsilvered plains, Fats turned to Elof and grinned and said, "Kind a on the big side, wasn't she?"

"Well, judging from the area assigned to me, I'd say so."

Of Lizards and Angels

God wouldn't have made sex so pleasant if it were just for procreation. Sex drive and creativity seem to go together into a great flowering of energy.

Honeymoon

AT FIRST THEIR HONEYMOON in the Black Hills was lovely, much better than Tressa had expected. Wallie was bossy, but he was kind. The first night he didn't bother her, just held her close all night, and in the morning he let her sleep while he made breakfast. The second night he touched her but did not make her his own. The same for the third night.

The fourth night was to be their last night. Tressa hoped that Wallie was thinking of saving the best for last. By the fourth night Tressa was ready and welling with desire. To her great surprise, that last night, instead of holding her in his arms as a beginning, he plopped his pillow upright against the head of the bed, and sitting high, announced he had something to say about their married life.

"Yes, my husband?"

"You know how I believe in Christ?"

"Yes, my husband."

"And in the Biblical injunction to be fruitful and multiply?"

"Yes, my husband."

"How with that injunction goes another Christian law?"

Tressa waited, wondering what in the world he had in mind.

"That there shall be no sex unless we have children in mind when we couple."

Tressa's head slowly came up off the pillow. "What?"

"Since I don't think it's a good idea to have a baby before the year is up, until June next year, we shouldn't couple during our honeymoon."

"But, husband, what after all is a honeymoon for but a time to make love."

"No! It's a sin if we do it not intending to have children."

"Ohh."

"So. All we're going to do is hold each other warmly in Christian love, cuddling and kissing, but no more. That way nobody can point the finger at us that we did it before we got married."

"Oh."

"I hope this is all right with you."

Tressa sat up then too. "Well, I'm surprised! Especially after the way you courted me! Hot breath. Hands everywhere on me like an octopus in Lover's Lane. Panting and gasping. I respected you nevertheless for holding back always at the last minute. But this! I never expected this from you."

"I could neck you hot and heavy so long as we weren't married because I knew you'd stop me, being the noble girl you are. But now that we're married, and we're alone in this bed here, far from home and church, the temptation is almost too much. Nobody to watch us. So we have to watch ourselves all the more. And I pray God that he may give you even more strength to resist temptation. We must not have flesh fun for fun's sake."

Tressa continued to have trouble believing what she was hearing. After the thrilling flush of love she'd once had. . . was she now going to have an old man's tormentive kind of love with an overly pious groom? It was enough to make even Mother Mary laugh out loud exasperated.

"What do you say to that, wife?"

Tressa couldn't resist a Dirk stinger. "In the eyes of God, there is no marriage until after it is consummated. So I'm still not your wife."

That stumped Wallie Starnes.

A little laugh escaped Tressa. "If I told this to Dirk, he'd laugh his head off."

Wallie cleared his throat. "Maybe he'd be glad."

"I don't understand."

"That his sister hadn't been violated yet."

"Then in your eyes the act of love is a violation?"

"Isn't it to you if it isn't done with children in mind?"

"No. I think it is a gift of God to enjoy as we decide."

Wallie shook his head, so vigorously the bed shook. "Ho! Have you got a lot to learn yet about being a partner in Christ with me."

Tressa groaned. "You're all wet about that." Then she laughed softly to herself. The truth was she was all wet expecting love. Aloud she said, "The girls in your church told me you were a good catch. And that they were real jealous."

"Who?"

"That'd be telling."

Wallie Starnes sniffed to himself, still sitting up in a tight bundle at the head of the bed.

To herself Tressa whispered, "Please, God, this is not happening to me. Please, God, don't let this be true."

Wallie finally spoke up. "I suppose you're mad at me now."

Tressa whispered some more to herself. "That's what I get for being impatient about getting married. Almost thirty years old and worrying I was going to wind up an old maid. So that I went out to trap Wallie. Making a tender trap of myself. Oh, how I wish now I'd led him on when he was hot to have me in Lover's Lane."

"Aren't you?"

"No, Wallie. Not mad. Just a little sad."

"Hmpf. The way some people's kids are brought up."

"Your father and mother, with all those children, do you think they always waited to do it until they thought it was time to make another baby?"

Wallie seized her by the shoulders and shook her, so violently her head snapped back and forth like a rag doll in the mouth of an angry dog. "Don't you talk like that about my father and mother!"

"Wallie," she whimpered, hurt.

"My father and mother are noble Christians! They don't do a thing but what they don't first pray to the Lord for guidance. You hear? You hear?"

"Please, you're hurting me, Wallie, your own wife."

He let her go. "Oh." He was still so taken with wrath he shook as though he had a bad case of the chills. "Just leave my parents out of it. I love them very much. They're great Christians. None better."

"Then you can leave my brother Dirk out of it too."

"Hmpf."

She lay in silence. Her neck hurt.

He sat crouched up, sullen.

Slowly she turned away from him, nestled her head in her pillow, and rolled her under shoulder back and forth until she found a comfortable spot in the bed.

Wallie slowly simmered down. He sniffed several times through his big nose. "Well," he said finally, "I suppose we should try to sleep. But first, I've got to take this up with my Lord. I've sinned in getting angry with you. And I must ask for His forgiveness."

Tressa thought: "And not ask me for mine?"

"Prayer helps me an awful lot when I lose my temper. Christ always helps me handle it." Wallie slid out of the sheets and kneeled beside their honeymoon bed. He folded his hands and in the dark presented his face to the heavens. "Father in heaven, look down upon this thy humble servant kneeling here in this strange place, about to go to sleep in innocence with his chosen bride. Forgive him for having touched this bride in wrath. I am sorry. I am asking her for her forgiveness too with this prayer as well as asking for Thy forgiveness. Be with us in the night to come. Keep us from evil. Bless our hearts together. May we live in peace and love all our lives. In Jesus' name we ask it, Amen."

Tressa felt torn inside. She wanted to believe in Wallie's God but she wasn't sure she wanted to live in the peace and love he wanted for all their lives.

Wallie crept into bed, drew up the sheets to his chin, nuzzled his head down on his pillow, and let out a huge sigh of satisfaction. He had done his duty as a God-fearing husband.

Tressa rolled over on her back. She stared up at the log ceiling in the dark. After a while she whispered, more to herself than to her husband, "I wonder why we ever came here in the first place on what's supposed to be a honeymoon."

"Why, Tressa," Wallie said, "to get acquainted with each other while we're far away from our families. Get a chance to know each other."

"I'm not sure I wanted to know what I've just learned."

"Pray, Tressa, pray and it'll be given to you. I'm sure the Lord will do this for you. Otherwise I wouldn't have chosen you for a wife."

"Hehht!" Tressa almost spat on the bed covers, she was suddenly so out of patience with what she'd done—marry the pious clod lying beside her. . . .

The next morning Tressa persuaded Wallie they should end the charade of a honeymoon. "We both better get back to our jobs. Especially since we still have to pay off the mortgage on the old Trigg house."

FROM
Sons of Adam

Jen and Uncle Red

. . . UNCLE RED WAS A FAVORITE of the family. When Uncle Red came over for a visit, Dad would quit being mean and would get along wonderful with Ma. Ma always welcomed Uncle Red too. During supper Uncle Red would tell a lot of funny stories. Uncle Red was in real estate and had come across a lot of comical clients. Later on in her bed, Jen could hear Dad and Ma laughing in their bedroom about the stories.

But while Dad and Ma were laughing in their bed, Jen was trembling in her bed. Pretty soon, after Dad and Ma had fallen asleep, Uncle Red would come tiptoeing into her room and get into bed with her.

Jen was thirteen the first time he came into her room. She'd just had her first period and had been pretty frightened about that. Ma hadn't been of much help about the period either, except to say it came because Eve had once sinned. "And now you be neat about yourself, you hear?" So in a way Jen was kind of glad to see Uncle Red come smiling through the door in the moonlight and seat him-self at the foot of her bed. She loved him because he liked to play little tricks on her when she sat on his lap by the table, like pinch her on one side and then pretend Dad had done it, or pull a single hair on her head and pretend Ma had done it. He was so jokey. She liked his green eyes. There was a look about them which seemed to say "You and I have a secret, don't we?" She liked secrets. So that fist time Uncle Red came into her room she brightened and raised up on her pillow and got ready for some fun.

"Jennie, you're getting to be such a big girl. . . just how old are you?"

"You know. You sent me a birthday card."

"You're almost too heavy to sit on my lap."

"Oh, you. I'm not either."

The moon was shining bright into her room. All he had on was his shorts. He had a hairy chest. It was almost as red as the hair on his head. It made her shiver. She looked at his green eyes instead.

"I don't think Ma would like your being here."

He picked up her hand and played with her fingers. "I bet you've got a lot of boyfriends in school, haven't you?"

"I'm not old enough. You know that."

"You're big enough. What is it the boys say? A real hot tomato."

"Now you're teasing me."

"No, I'm not." He moved up on the bed and then slipped his legs under the covers with her. "Come, put your head on Uncle Red's shoulder." When she didn't move right away, he slipped an arm around her. "There. That's better. Now we can have a real heart-to-heart talk. You and I have never had one of those, have we? And here you're a great big grown girl already."

"You shouldn't be here, Uncle Red."

"Come, let's have a kiss."

"I don't think we should, Uncle Red."

"You've kissed me before."

"Yes, but that was in front of company."

Slowly Uncle Red slid his arm farther around her. His hand moved to her breast. "Why, Jennie, you're a grown girl already."

The moonlight in the room began to bounce funny. What was happening was wrong, but she didn't dare cry out either. She didn't want her father and mother to think bad of Uncle Red. She liked Uncle Red too, and that made it all the harder.

Uncle Red began to breathe hard. His hand began to hold her breast harder. He began to kiss her hair and then her ear and then her brow.

She could feel her eyes cross.

"Jennie, Jennie," Uncle Red whispered winningly in her ear, "what a sweetheart you are. It's so nice to be holding you in my arms. I wish you were older, because then I'd marry you."

"But we're related," she said out loud.

"Shh, not so loud. You don't want your dad and ma to find us like this, do you?"

She'd let her nightgown slide up and her belly was exposed.

Uncle Red's hand moved down there. He began to rub her belly up and down. He began to breathe hard again.

Something was going to happen.

Uncle Red parted her legs with his hand and held her in that place where she'd never let anybody touch her before. He really began to breathe hard. "You're big enough." Then Uncle Red pushed down his shorts and got on top of her and that place began to sting something awful. Her eyes hurt in the corners. Pretty soon he was done. He lay beside her awhile and slowly his breathing went back to normal.

It really stung her inside. It hurt like that time when she had her tonsils removed.

Pretty soon Uncle Red sighed, and he patted her shoulder, and said, "You're a good girl, Jennie," and pulling up his shorts got out of bed and went on tiptoe to his room.

She lay a long time feeling the stinging in her belly and the tickle of his hairy chest on her breasts.

Uncle Red came quite often after that, about a dozen times. Both Dad and Ma were surprised, and pleased, that he suddenly wanted to visit them so much.

Jen always smiled at Uncle Red at the table, a little, guardedly. But she was in terror that her father and mother would discover them some night. Worse yet, it was a bad sin.

She didn't know what to do. She thought of killing herself. The worst was that she was afraid she was going to like what he was doing to her. She also thought of getting a scissors and stabbing Uncle Red.

She began to wonder if the way Uncle Red treated her wasn't the reason why Dad and Ma fought so much when they first went to bed. Maybe Dad wanted the same thing from Ma. Men were certainly beasts.

One Saturday night Jen decided she'd had enough. She was going to fix him.

At supper table she asked him why he didn't have a date that night with some girl. "Most other guys are out with their girl on a Saturday night, ain't they?"

Uncle Red winked at her, on her side of his face so Dad and Ma couldn't see it. "Well, you're my girl, ain't you?"

"Uncles don't marry nieces."

"Well, I wasn't thinking of marrying you." Again he winked sidelong at her.

"Oh, so you were going to throw me aside like some old dishrag, were you?"

Uncle Red warned her with another look to be careful around her father and mother. "Honey, Jennie, I was only joking. You know that."

Dad asked, "Why, Jennie, what's got into you?"

"I know what he wants. And no, I don't love him anymore." It was like a balky cat had got into her throat and it wasn't going to behave.

Uncle Red was scared. He began to squirm in his chair.

Ma woke up at her end of the bale. "Whatever has happened between the two of you? Jennie?"

"Well, Uncle Red can just quit coming into my room at night when he thinks you people are asleep."

"What!" Dad jumped straight up out of his chair. He upset his cup of steaming coffee.

Ma almost fell off her chair. "Jennie," she whispered.

Uncle Red put down his fork and knife very carefully.

Now that it was out, Jen decided to ease things a little. At least Uncle Red wouldn't be visiting her room anymore. "Well, I just don't like it that he wakes me up to talk to me. I like my sleep just like anybody else."

Dad sat down very slowly. He ran a jumpy hand through his curly brown hair. His eyes glowed as though they were burners on an electric stove. He drilled a look into Jen for a moment and then like a slow-turning spotlight on a police car looked at Uncle Red. "Is what she just said true, Red?"

Uncle Red picked up his fork and knife again. He cut his meat in his usual fancy city way and with his fork still in his left hand lifted the meat into his mouth. Between chews he said, "I heard her coughing one night and I went to see what was the matter. If she had a cold."

Dad turned his spotlight eyes on Jen. "Is that true, Jen?"

Ma broke in. She was afraid of what Jen was going to say. "You're not going to call your brother a liar, are you now, George Haron?"

Dad said, "Well, no, I guess not."

After that Uncle Red didn't come very often.

Jen often wondered if her life would have been different if her baby sister Veloura hadn't died. Jen was four and Veloura was two when they both got the croup. They were very sick. But finally Jen pulled through and Veloura didn't.

Jen was glad Veloura was gone. Jen had hated to share her playthings with Veloura, she hated to share Dad and Ma with her.

Had Veloura lived, though, and had Veloura slept in the same room with her, Uncle Red wouldn't have dared to come into her room.

When Jen was a little girl Dad wasn't home much. They lived in the town of Brokenhoe and Dad was a drummer for a nail and wire company out of Minneapolis. He sold nails, staples, barbwire, and woven-wire fencing all over Minnesota and the Dakotas. When he'd come home once a month, he and Ma would right away get into one of their awful rows about a husband's rights.

The nail and wire company finally went broke. Dad next barbered in South St. Paul near the stockyards for a year. For a while he was a lot of fun again. He'd gotten over Veloura's being gone and didn't drink much.

Sometimes barbering was slow, especially for the second chair. The first barber did well, but not Dad, and pretty soon Dad began to drink. Dad got to thinking about his dead Veloura again.

Ma took to visiting spiritualists. She wanted to get a message that Veloura was in heaven. Ma thought that if she could get such a message in a seance she could then take Dad down some night and have Veloura tell him. If Dad could just hear Veloura once, talking to him from the other side, it might cure his drinking.

The medium never convinced Ma that she'd heard Veloura from the other side, and so Dad continued to mourn the loss of Veloura. Jen hated Veloura.

Jen went to the Brokenhoe High School. She was a scared kid all the way through. She was too shy to recite well in class. She always had the feeling that, behind her somewhere, a cloud was following her around. She refused all dates, wouldn't go to the junior-senior prom, didn't join any clubs.

The first year out of high school she moped around home, helping Ma with the housework, sometimes helping Dad clean out the cellar and the garage. She learned to start the mower and pushed that around in the summertime.

No matter how much Dad and Ma urged her to go to church socials and mingle with people, Jen wouldn't go. Jen said she was cured of men. Uncle Red never came anymore, and that was the end of that. She heard he'd gotten married and had two little girls. She often wondered what Uncle Red's thoughts were when he looked at his girls.

> I haven't been too surprised with these stories that I'm reading about incest because I think there's a whole lot of it going on. Having taught those kids in my class for 18 years, I ran across hints of it everywhere. . . I ran across it four or five times in my classes.

FROM
This Is the Year

Who Was Nertha?

PIER LAY ON THE HORSEHAIR SOFA in the living room. Supper lay warmly in his stomach. The gas-lamp light was white and sharp on the cream-and-silver wallpaper.

He rubbed his back on the hard leather, pushing himself up and twisting his head deep into a pillow. His muscles ached sweetly. The day had been a hard one.

It was a good life. He sighed happily when he thought of the dark earth and the juicy seedling potatoes he had planted in it. His sharp hoe had cut it easily. He could still feel the rhythm of the work in his arms and legs: drop one, kick one, and cover over with a half twist of toe. He stretched and yawned. And sighed again.

Nertha sat beyond his feet, slowly creaking a brown wood rocker. She was patching one of his overalls. He looked at her and wondered what thoughts were buzzing in her head. A faint smile turned on her lips. Her eyelids were slightly flared, as if she were staring into a dream and smiling at what she saw in it. The gaslight cast a path of light across her crown of silver-blond hair. It was like a flash of moonlight on water.

Pier watched her, and wondered. It was four weeks since the ceremony but he still didn't know what it meant to be married. He forced his thoughts to the fore part of his brain. Just what was a wife?

He could not get the feel of her in his fingers. He could not call up a live and flesh-warm image of her when he closed his eyes.

He looked at her face. He noted the few pale freckles climbing the slope of her nose. He examined her thin flared nostrils, the vague blue shadows under her eyes, her white forehead, her green eyes, her silver hair.

He looked at her breasts. Had they trembled beneath his fingers last night? He had barely touched them then, fearing too much of a good thing, turning away from her, drifting away into a restless sleep.

And what was a bosom? Wal, it was soft rising bread dough. It was a soft hill fuzzy with grain. Yes, and for the suckling, it was the cup of life that mysteriously ever refilled itself.

He resisted an impulse to reach and touch them, to have them real, this moment, in his fingers.

Or her thighs? What were they? They were two falling slopes, with a slough. Ah, the woman of her was sweet and moist.

He forced his thoughts to one point in his brain. Who was Nertha? He wrinkled his brow. He knew more about her sitting off to one side, studying her, than he did touching her.

That first night. The room had been mellow with lamplight and wedding gown. He had moved, and his head had filled with a roaring, had filled with the bursting spume of blood-red mist. A long breath later, and he had awakened to the shining of the morning sun upon them. And he had found himself lying startled and frightened beside a woman, a real woman, with gently sloping breasts tossing as she lay sussing in her sleep.

Every morning he had awakened thus and yet, every day, he had been unable to fix her solidly in his memory. She was a dream, a mist. He was sure of it.

And something strange, a way of living, was growing up between them. She was at once more his and at the same time less his. He could possess her body and yet not possess her spirit.

Sometimes she could be so far away from him that even her body seemed not there. He detected it in the sly smile on her lips, as if she had a knowledge of him that he did not have. He felt it in the slightly exasperated "Good morning, Pier." Oddly enough the sly smile, the exasperation, always appeared the morning after he had taken her.

He pondered.

What a Young Man of Twenty-Eight Would Say

previously unpublished

Memories are not enough for me.
I need the feel of mammae against my chest,
To feel the bone of her hip in my hand,
Feel the urgent thrusts of her love full-fleshed.

Nor are the primal throes enough for me.
What I long for is an emerging chthonian wife,
A kissing out of a dark mystery underwoman,
Skin absorbing skin, become the other's life.

Memories are better than nothing though.
In fantasy a man can have the ultimate groan.
In fantasy a man can dream of being received,
Hear the loving duet of bone on bone.

Becoming an Artist

Without the artist we'd all still be pigs. Without the artist there'd be no language, no tool, no face-to-face lovemaking, no wheel, no books, no spaceships. Without the artist such minds as C.G. Jung, Otto Rank, Harry Stack Sullivan would never have had the chance to elaborate on the concept that the ideal man has a beautiful soul in a beautiful body.

FROM
Green Earth

Watching the Ants

AUNT KAREN VISITED IN AUGUST. She was going to teach school on the corner. She arrived early to clean up the school before the pupils came. Later she was going to room and board with the neighbors.

Ma didn't feel well about then, and to get Free out of the house Aunt Karen took him with her to the big cottonwood on the northwest corner of the grove. It was cool under the high green leaves.

Aunt Karen found a nice spot of short grass by the fence. Like Rover sometimes did, she turned around twice before settling down. She got out her tatting and began to make doilies.

Free walked around the cottonwood a couple of times. He measured it with his arms. It wasn't nearly as big as Grampa's giant tree. He examined it on the north side to see if it had the rot cancer. He even poked in between the cracks in the rough bark with a piece of rusty barbed wire. But so far as he could tell the cottonwood was all right. Good.

Free spotted some red ants running up the cottonwood trunk. He watched where they ran. They went out of sight up into the green leaves. He wondered what they were looking for up there. Pretty soon he spotted some of the red ants coming down again. They were all carrying what looked like a tiny drop of white syrup. Free wondered if it was sweet. But he didn't dare rob the red ants because of their stingers. Free followed the ants carrying their white drops into the grass. They ran along a kind of a road. The road went through some tall grass and then across a bare spot of dirt and then over some twigs and finally, there near the fence post, right behind Aunt Karen's sitter, was a heaved-up piece of ground

340

that was full of boil holes. The red ants went in and out of the holes. Some of the ants in the anthill came out to help the other ants carry in their little drops of white syrup.

"What are you doing there?"

Free had forgotten all about Aunt Karen. She was looking at him over her tatting. "Nothing."

"Crawling around on your hands and knees like that. It's no wonder your overalls are always worn out at the knee." Aunt Karen held her head over to one side so that her red hair hung down a little. Her eyes were like green glass and blinked a couple of times. "What were you following there in the grass?"

"Just a red ant."

Aunt Karen began to smile pretty. "What was the ant doing?"

"He came down out of that tree carrying a drop of white syrup."

"Tree sap. Gathered from a tree tip. Food for next winter."

"You mean he got that from way up there at the tippy top of the tree?" Free leaned back in the grass and stared up at the top of the tree. "That high up?"

"Yes, Free. The ant is a wise creature. It knows enough to get in its food when the weather's warm. Because when it gets cold it can't move on the snow. In the winter it lives deep in its home there under that anthill, where it's warm, and lives off the food it has stored in its underground pantries."

Free stared at the anthill a while. So that was it. They lived like people did.

Still smiling pretty, Aunt Karen went back to her tatting.

Free lay on his back in the grass looking up at the tree. He lay with his head cupped in his hands, legs crossed at the knee. The treetop moved back and forth in the light breeze. The leaves rattled against each other like a lot of little leather mittens. The top leaves were so high they were almost blue. "Aunt Karen, if I was to climb that cottonwood way to the top, like Jack did that beanstalk, could I see the angel country?"

Aunt Karen breathed funny. "Why, whatever made you think of that?"

"Well, Ma says Grampa is up in heaven now with the angels, and I'd like to see what he's doing there."

Aunt Karen didn't say anything for a while. She just sat there in the grass and tatted.

Free dreamed that he could easy fly up there. There had to be some way of doing it like he sometimes flew around in his dreams.

"What a strange boy you are."

Free crossed his legs the other way.

"Whatever is to become of you Free?"

"I dunno."

"Farmer like your father? Teacher like me? Or a preacher like your domeny?"

"Pa says he wants to be the best there is."

Aunt Karen tatted a while. "Well, me, I wish I could have been a really good poet. Not just a rhymer of pretty words." Aunt Karen had written a little green book full of poems. Free had heard her read some of them to Pa and Ma one evening. Ma thought the green poems were sweet. Pa didn't have much to say, except that once, when Aunt Karen read about Grampa Alfredson in one of the poems, he took his pipe out of his mouth and said, "Pah." Aunt Karen tatted some more. She waved a fly away. "Yes, like Elizabeth Barrett."

"What's the best thing to be?"

"Why, a poet, of course."

"Better than being a general?"

"Yes. Nobler even than being a President."

"Then that's what I'll be someday. A poet. Because I want to be like my pa. Be the best there is."

Love Poet

GRETCH ASKED FREE to get her some pork chops from the butcher shop. It was after school and Free was reading an article in a sports magazine about Babe Ruth's having hit sixty home runs the past summer. Babe had broken his old record of fifty-nine made six years earlier in 1921. Free hated to let go of the article, but felt he owed Gretch a favor. Frowning, he took the dollar bill she gave him and without a word left to get the meat.

Just for the heck of it, and to be taking a different route downtown, he crossed the street and cut through several backyards until he came out on the street Ada Shutter lived on. Ada and Margaret Newinghouse boarded in the last house on the south side of the street. Margaret was a sister of the Josie Newinghouse who'd once come to visit Ma on the farm. Margaret always had a warm smile for Free. Free kind of liked Margaret, and sometimes did smile back at her. But he preferred Ada. The only trouble was Ada didn't even bother to give him a part interested look when he tried to meet eyes with her in school.

Ada wore her brown hair in a bob that hooded her face, with bangs that curved down to her brows. With her head tipped forward it gave her a very modest appearance. Yet she walked with a vigorous stride. She was a star forward on the girls' basketball team. She could run. She'd once raced Tony Streetman from downtown to the Academy on a dare and had won going away. She strode directly off the hips like a man. She had lovely muscular legs and a fine bosom. But the hooded look puzzled Free.

Headed for the butcher shop, deep in thought, eyes on the ground, Free scuffed along.

He passed under a double row of tall young cottonwoods. They formed a precise corridor, with the sidewalk going exactly down the center of it. Their tough leaves had just turned yellow. The sun was almost down at the far end of the street ahead and its light bloomed on the undersides of the cottonwood leaves. The yellowed light fell upon him in little rains of gold. It even made the sidewalk gold. There was also a vague tint of pink in the yellow light and it gave his swinging hands a healthy glow. The sound of the cliddering leaves in the easy evening breeze was like the accidental chords of leather wind chimes. He was aware of walking down an avenue of beauty. It was as if he'd walked in on a sonnet of Shakespeare. "That time of year thou mayst in me behold/ When yellow leaves, or none, or few, do hang/ Upon those boughs which shake against the cold,/ Bare, ruined choirs, where late the sweet birds sang." He sauntered slowly along. He seemed to be wading into a golden moment of some kind. A judgment day was flowering around him. Some glorious revelation was about to dawn upon him. Wondering, in a daze, he looked up to see what was about to happen.

There she was. Ada Shutter. With her modest hooded look. She was coming home from downtown, entering at the other end of the corridor of yellow cottonwood leaves. There were just the two of them in the golden avenue. Her gray eyes were looking straight at him. There was a little smile on her pink lips. It made her lips look like a pair of cherries. Luscious. She was wearing a dark blue dress and a light blue blouse. She had on brown loafing sandals. Her smile was a smile showing she was for once having pleasant thoughts about him. Her teeth showed ever so little. She too was sauntering along. Her limbs, especially her plump calves, were swinging along resilient and muscular on every step. Sunlight glancing off the undersides of the tough yellow leaves touched her brown hair. It made her brown hair look as if it had been burned blond by the summer sun.

Ada.

Saying her name was like saying a first baby word.

He scratched around in his head for something to say, desperately, anything, to make that tiny bud of a smile grow. But the only thing to pop into his mind were some words from *The Taming of the Shrew*. He'd finished reading all the books in the school library and had lately taken to reading Shakespeare. "I never yet beheld that special face which I did fancy more than any other." But those words weren't quite right.

He prayed: "Let me say something that'll be just right. I want to touch her."

His legs kept carrying him forward. He could feel the gold of the cottonwood leaves lighting up his face.

Her shapely legs kept carrying her forward too. Her eyes filled with bluing. Her little smile of interest widened. It invited him to enter her with some kind of hello. The good word.

He shaped his lips to say something.

They were only a dozen steps apart. Her head came up. Her hair swung back from her pink cheeks. She looked directly into his eyes; then shifted her look to his lips.

He knew he looked like a fool with his lips all bubbed out and no words coming forth. He bit on his lips.

She saw his teeth sink into his lips. Her bud of a smile abruptly vanished. Her head tipped forward, her hair slid around her cheeks, and the hooded impenetrable look came back into her gray eyes again.

They walked past each other.

The heels of her brown sandals made light clicking sounds.

The sun set.

A shadow rushed under the double row of yellow cottonwoods. The golden moment vanished.

He wanted to turn around and look back and call out her name. But he didn't dare.

Yet despite the shadow racing past him he was oddly, crazily, happy. He was breathing marvelous air. Now he knew what life was all about.

As he continued on to the butcher shop, he saw her again in his mind's eye, sauntering toward him, gold-touched hair thrown back, eyes very blue, calves muscling out on each step. If he'd only given back the same smile she'd given him.

Ada.

A wonderful name for a girl. Even if it was the same as his mother's. And maybe for that reason all the more so.

He got the meat from the butcher shop and started back. He took the same street. He walked down the avenue of beautiful cottonwoods. Darkness had settled a clear rust brown over the world and the yellow leaves of the cottonwoods hung a subdued gold. The evening breeze had also died down and only occasional bunches of leaves, here and there, cliddered lightly overhead.

He looked at her boarding house. It was a one-story bungalow, painted a soft yellow, with white trim windows. The roof was blue. The blinds on the street side were drawn.

Rhymed words rose to mind as he continued on to his own house: "That special face in a new place. Blue eyes, cottonwood leaves. Blue skies, oat sheaves. Ada of old Atlantis, Ada come to hant us." The words didn't make much sense, but they belled in his head like a lovely set of wind chimes.

He floated into the house. He gave Gretch her meat.

"Say. What's the matter with you? You look like you've just had the fits."

He felt sorry for Gretch Van Arkle. Compared to Ada she stank.

"Did you see a ghost or something?"

"No." He hurried up to his room. He found his roommate Lew sitting foursquare at his desk, a palm to either temple, elbows akimbo on the blotter of his desk. Lew didn't look up from his fat Modern History book.

Free settled in front of his own desk. He snapped on the desk lamp. Swiftly he wrote down the wind-chime words before he forgot them.

Free stared at the words. A second thing had happened to him that day. He was a poet. A young boy had found his girl and so had become a poet.

Free looked across at where Lew burned at his desk. Lew was no doubt dreaming of the day when he'd conquer the world. Well, Lew wasn't the only crazy dreamer in the house. While Lew in his imagination was conquering the world with a sword, he, Alfred Alfredson VII, was going to conquer the world with words.

Wanderlust

With the trilogy Wanderlust, *for its original version I had over a hundred and twenty, maybe a hundred thirty, pages of real fine note-taking for the plot. Where everything went. This is to lead to that, and this is to follow that, and this means this, and this movement here is eventually going to end up being reactivated over here. I was quite profoundly struck by music, how a symphony is built . . . I tried to work that scheme all the way through that book . . . .*

Mentor

THE NEXT NOON, restless, Thurs got up from his lunch of cheese sandwiches and cold water and began roaming through Old Main. The music room drew him and he wandered in. He looked at the lectern where Mr. Maynard usually stood. He glanced at the seat in back where he always sat. He sniffed the air and imagined he could still get a whiff of eau de Cologne a middle-aged woman student had worn the past semester. He looked at the portraits on the wall: brooding Beethoven, gentle Mendelssohn, solemn Sibelius.

The white keys of the upright piano near the lectern caught his eye. Some one had forgotten to close the piano. He went over and touched a few of the keys, lightly. He noted that despite its ancient style the piano still had good tone. He sat down and sounded a few more notes. He fumbled with a fourth, then a fifth, then spread his hand for a fourteenth. The last sound caught his ear. Not many were capable of such a spread. He tinkled some more, finding consonant bass notes with his left hand.

Grubbing around, he found three quick related notes, then a pause, then three slow rising notes set upon a heavy bass chord. Struck by it, he set himself directly before the keyboard and played the phrase again. Then he hit each note separately, letting the sound ring in his ears. Then he put the notes together once more, noting how each helped the other, how they built into columns of sound, how the columns resembled glinting prisms.

He probed around, idly, as he might have on his harmonica, but found his fingers considerably more ignorant than his tongue. They would not go on, and, exasperated, he gave up on the musical musing, crashing his hands any which-way on the keys. And got up and joined Ben for the afternoon labors.

But the next noon he was back again, grubbing around on the keys, finding the chords he had come upon the day before and adding a few more. Just as then, the first discoveries thrilled him. And also like them, he found he couldn't go on. The same thing happened the third and fourth day. It was like trying to write a poem in a language that one did not know too well.

The fifth day, early in the forenoon, he heard a bird sing in a basswood, four notes, the first one long, the next three shorter and falling away. He whistled them, committing them to memory.

At noon he ran down to the music room. Unerringly he found the bird's notes on the keyboard. He decided the first note was four beats long, the second, three, and the last, one. The third note was troublesome. It wasn't quite two beats. He toyed with the sequence awhile, letting it soak in. He worked out a few bass chords to harmonize with it.

Presently he found that the four notes led easily to another phrase despite the stiffness of the third note. He linked the new phrase with the first one. He played the combination over and over, finding that this time he did not tire of them, that the notes seemed to awaken some tuning fork deep within him. It satisfied some need.

"Where's that from? I don't ever recall having heard that before," a grave voice said.

Thurs whirled around, and saw ascetic silver-haired Mr. Maynard standing in the door. He made as if to get up, and in so doing hit the corner of the piano with his knee.

"No no. Please remain seated," Mr. Maynard said.

"I was only just—"

"Please." Mr. Maynard held up a hand. He came forward slowly, looking at Thurs kindly. "Tell me, where's that from?"

"I heard a bird sing it this morning."

"Ahh. What bird?"

"I don't know. I didn't see it. It could have been an oriole."

"But you heard it clearly enough so you could come down here and translate it into music on the piano?"

"Well, I tried to."

"No one helped you pick out the notes?"

"No."

"Take your hand away from your mouth so I can hear you." Mr. Maynard looked down at him intently. "You've had piano lessons then?"

"No."

"Not? No music at all besides my History of Music class?"

"I play the mouth organ by ear."

Mr. Maynard brushed a piece of lint from is gray summer suit. He said, murmuring to himself, "So, he has an instinct for music too."

With a quick motion of his hand, Thurs threw back his whitelock. He looked at Mr. Maynard. "I hear tunes all the time. Some I can't get out of my head."

"Such as?"

Thurs told him about cutting peonten to the rhythm of The Shadow Waltz.

"Do you like poetry?"

"Some. But I'm not taken over by it. I mean, it's like admiring a lovely girl. She's nice but you're not really in love with her."

After a second or so of silence, Mr. Maynard asked, "Tell me, when you were a boy, did you like music?"

"I always liked listening to the psalms in church. And of course always the birds."

"Did you play anything when you were a boy?"

"A violin once. It was an old one and it soon cracked. Then I got the harmonica."

"How did you happen to come into the music room here?"

"I don't know. Unless it's because I like listening to the ringing sounds a piano gives off."

"Ringing sounds? Just what do you mean by that?"

"Well, sounds that sting you inside."

"Sting?"

"Yes. Not like when you scrape a spoon across the bottom of a pan, of course, but like when something vibrates and it makes you feel good."

"Mmm."

"And I mean something more too. I've had it happen already that I thought I was going crazy listening to certain vibrating sounds."

"When did this happen?"

"At a concert. And once at a house where someone was playing."

"Mmm."

"It was like my spine was on fire. I could feel every nerve in my body burn, down to the toe tips even. I felt like jumping up and running along the tops of the bench knobs all the way to where the pianist was playing on the stage."

Mr. Maynard looked at him oddly. "You have just now described the reaction of a sensitive primitive to music."

"Oh." Thurs felt slapped down. He thought he had been describing ecstasy, true aesthetic experience.

"Yes, a sensitive primitive. Later, should you go further into music, you probably won't have these sensations again. A trained mind will enjoy the music, not just a highly excited nervous system."

"That'll be a loss then."

"Perhaps so. But the other will give you more."

"Oh."

"How old are you?"

"Twenty."

"Mmm. Almost too late."

"You mean, too late to learn to play the piano?"

"Yes."

"A man of twenty can't make up for lost time and become a real pianist?"

"No."

"Not even if he worked? Slaved?"

"No."

"Well, could he learn it well enough to teach it?"

"Possibly." Mr. Maynard snorted. "My dear boy, that first basket you made for Coach Williams, did that make you a basketball star?"

"Nooo, I guess it didn't."

"Well then."

"Was there anything in that fumbling around though to indicate I might be able to teach it?"

"A little."

"What, for example?"

"Oh, that you have a feeling for relative pitch. That you have some touch."

Thurs thought: "Something's going on here. Old Maynard wouldn't be wasting all this time with me if he didn't think I had something."

His heart began to pound. Maybe sound was his forte, not words. Music not English. Could be. And maybe that was why he hadn't made a better showing with Hero. Only part of him was getting through to her. From where she sat he probably didn't look like much of a man to her. Women were knowing about such things.

Then the image of Mrs. Brothers crossed his mind, and his young brows came together. "Well, actually, I'm wasting your time talking like this. I forgot about Mrs. Brothers."

Mr. Maynard stiffened visibly. "What's she got to do with it?"

"Well, she's my foster mother and she's got say over me until I'm of age. She's paying most of my way through college."

Mr. Maynard stood very still.

Thurs said, "You see, if I change my course, I'll have to tell her about it. I did change it once already, from pre-sem to maybe teaching English, and she raised hel. . . I mean raised heck about it. And you know how those religious people back in Siouxland are. At least some of them. Preaching God's word, that's all right, but anything else, that's probably of the devil."

Mr. Maynard suddenly had the look of a bachelor who hated women.

Thurs went on. "If I switch to teaching music I'll have to tell her."

"If you think you have to, well, then you have to, yes." Mr. Maynard coughed. "But before you write her, let's see what you can do first."

"You mean explore the idea of my taking music in my spare time this summer?"

"Why not? You say you aren't particularly in love with Miss Poetry."

"Do you really mean that?"

"My dear boy, we professors are always happy to get new students for our classes."

"I see."

"Are you willing to try it?"

"Yes."

"Good." Mr. Maynard looked at the backs of his old veined hands. "It just happens I'm working on a manual for adults. Teaching you piano would fit in perfectly. I can test it out on you." Mr. Maynard smiled thinly. "You see, young man, I too started music late in life, and I always thought I should do something about it. Help other adults so that they can brighten their lives with music. As I have mine."

So that was why Mr. Maynard had shown such an interest in him. The old gentleman had been looking for a guinea pig.

"Teaching you may help me recall some of my old difficulties and so help me find the shortcuts."

"I see."

Mr. Maynard went to his desk and sat down. He looked tired. "When can you start?"

"Right away."

"When are you through work in the afternoon?"

"Five."

"I'll meet you here every Tuesday and Thursday at five then."

Suddenly Thurs felt very happy and he couldn't help but show it. He cried out, "That's wonderful, wonderful. Man!"

At that Mr. Maynard gave him an odd chilling look. "Good afternoon, Mr. Wraldson. I'll see you this coming Thursday after five."

Thurs got to his feet. "All right," he said, and left.

[MONTHS LATER]

Mr. Maynard lived in a duplex on Alexander Street just off Franklin Park and it took Thurs but five minutes to get there. He mounted the stone steps of the brick house and punched the doorbell on the left.

The door opened. Red cap tight on silver hair, bony legs showing beneath red dressing gown, silver belt tassels dangling, eyes supported from below by tiny pouches, Mr. Maynard lowered at him.

"Good evening, Mr. Maynard. Can I quick see you a minute?"

Mr. Maynard grimaced. "Quick, eh? I suppose you've just composed some fifty pages or so of a new sonata."

Thurs drew back a step. "What?"

"Yes, yes. I know all about you young geniuses."

"But I thought—"

"—that a professor always has a little time to spare? For his students?"

"Yes."

"Ha. Yes." Mr. Maynard mimicked Thurs's voice. "Professor! Professor! Could you please spare me a minute and tell me what you think of a great new work of art I've just now finished composing?"

"Well, if you're too busy, Mr. Maynard—"

"No, no. Step in. I'm never too busy to listen to a great work of art."

"No, really, if you're too busy—"

"Please step in. You're letting in the night."

Thurs followed Mr. Maynard down a hall and then into a long parlor. A grand piano stood near the far window. A neat pile of oak logs lay beside a red brick fireplace.

Mr. Maynard pointed to one of the fireplace armchairs. "Have a seat."

Thurs sat down.

Mr. Maynard sat down too. He coughed. Then he politely brightened. "Well well. Now, and what have we here?"

"Welll, I was sitting in the Dorm lobby, when I heard a train—"

"Don't describe how it came to you. Don't bring in literature. Remember, we musicians have our language too." Mr. Maynard pointed to the grand piano. Play it. Don't say it."

Thurs reddened. Meekly he got up and spread his sheets on the music rack. He sat down. He turned on a light. The pages shone chalk-white in the glare of the blue bulb. He stammered, "I'm not really—"

"Play!"

Thurs looked down at his hands, closing his eyes.

The instant he closed his eyes, he saw it all again. He swung into it. He built it up powerfully—and then, just as at the Dorm, he ran stuck. His fingers fell idle.

"Go on. Go on."

"That's all there is to it."

"And you came all the way over here to bother me with an unfinished piece of music?"

"That's just why I came to see you."

"Ah. Then you come as a student and not as a composer?"

Again Thurs blushed. "Isn't it any good?"

"Good? Good? Does an apple tree grow half an apple?"

"What about Schubert's *Unfinished Symphony?*"

"Is Schubert's defection your model?"

"But Mr. Maynard, what I came over to tell you was that. . ." Then Thurs got angry and he jumped up from the piano and gathered up the sheets in one swoop and crumpled them up in a ball.

"Temper, temper."

"Well, why not?"

For the first time Mr. Maynard smiled some. "Well now. So." He got to his feet and came over and stood beside Thurs. "Sit down again, boy. I didn't mean to discourage you, really. It's only that you young people give up too soon. And usually just when the hard work begins. Now you know you should have pushed on with that." Gently Mr. Maynard took the crumpled sheets from Thurs. "Should have pushed on until you had it finished."

"But I did try. I did."

"All right, boy. Sit down now."

Thurs continued to stand. "Mr. Maynard, you don't know how hard I tried. I sat there and worked and willed. . . I willed until I almost killed."

"What sort of nonsense is that now?"

"But that's what I almost did. I was playing and trying to break through when my friend Howard came up and touched me on the shoulder and in my concentration I throw my hand out, so, and knocked—"

"Careful! don't hit me now!"

"I'm sorry."

"It's all right. Go on."

"Well, I knocked him down." Thurs shivered as he thought of it again. "And I hurt him."

Mr. Maynard reached out a hand, not quite touching Thurs. "Come. Let's go sit by the fireplace. Please. Here in this armchair here."

Thurs took the chair.

Mr. Maynard sat down across from him. He flattened out the crumpled sheets of music on the arm of his chair. "You say you hurt your friend?"

"Yes. And that's another reason why I came over. I wanted to have a talk with you about that too." Leaning forward, Thurs rubbed his big hands together harshly. "I'm all mixed up. When I'm at the piano, then everything is wonderful, wonderful. It all seems so free and good. Tonight with this piece, this fugue or whatever it is, I felt I was worse off than before. Howard was hurt and I was still stopped up."

Mr. Maynard hid his face with an old veined hand. "Go on."

"And I've noticed that whenever I begin to enjoy myself I always get into trouble."

"Such as?"

"Welll, for example when I kiss girls. When I let go, I hurt them. When I don't I hurt myself."

"Go on."

"Well, it seems to me that's all wrong."

Mr. Maynard smiled slowly. "My boy, you are at last learning at first hand that no advance is ever made without some cost."

"But Mr. Maynard, I don't want to hurt people. I like people."

"I know you like people." Mr. Maynard coughed hoarsely. "But to get good things done people sometimes have to suffer."

"You make it sound as if I'm supposed to think of myself as a special privilege person. And, Mr. Maynard, I don't want to be thought of as a queer. I want to be accepted as a regular guy."

"Why?"

"Well, I stick out enough as it is."

Mr. Maynard shook his head. "It's too late. Too late."

"What do you mean, too late?"

"Boy, haven't you seen yet that once a human being sees the light, he never can go back to a condition of non-light? Even more so when he is the origin of such light? Boy, you are a composer." Mr. Maynard rubbed his hands together. "Let me repeat it. You have in you the movements of the true composer. And that makes you a wanderer forever. A walker of the world. 'A world's wanderer,' as Doughty so aptly put it. A nephew of atmosphere even. Once your brain is awakened and has become the mouthpiece of a powerful spirit, it is too late to go back."

"You mean, you like it then? The piece?"

Mr. Maynard got up and set aside the fireplace screen. He put on paper and some kindling and a few oak logs, then took a match and scratched it on a floor brick and held the flame to the paper. In a quickly rising series of red flashes the hearth became a tiny inferno.

Mr. Maynard waited a second or two. Then, sitting down again and holding out his thin old hands to the warmth, he said quietly, "What there was of it, yes." Mr. Maynard's ascetic brows came together in a frown. "It's sensual. But the main thing is, it's no longer dependent on literary content. Like that doleful song of yours was."

Thurs drew back. "You mean Melancholy? I never showed you that."

"Miss Bernlef sang it for me."

"She. . ." Thurs got to his feet. "She did?"

Mr. Maynard gave him an owl's wise look. "She admired the composer in it."

"Oh."

"Sit down, boy."

Thurs slowly sat down again, face flushed, eyes on the fire.

"Sensual, erotic, yes. And I guess that's all right. There are some who believe that music is demoniac, that in the erotic sensual genius music has its absolute object."

"Whatever that means."

Mr. Maynard picked up the manuscript again. Reading it, he began to hum to himself, cocking his head this way, that way. "Ah, yes. Fine new coinage. New." He hummed some more, this time shaking his head. "Now here's a trite bit. Trite." He hummed on. "Ah, here it's good again. New Modern. But in a way as to suggest that it may be music for all time." Humming and whistling, the old man worked through the manuscript, phrase by phrase. And at last, stacking up the pages in a neat pile on his knee, he said, "Yes, it is good. The rhythm is the old beat that the skops used in the old days to work up the warriors for battle. It asks the old questions in today's language. A little weak here and there, but nonetheless there are some very very fine things in it."

Thurs sat stunned and thrilled both.

Mr. Maynard asked, "Have you given it a title?"

"No."

"Perhaps that's just as well. Sometimes a title helps one focus the main thought, sometimes not. Sometimes it even brings in a non-musical idea. The programmatic."

"Offhand, the only title I can think of is Opus I ."

Mr. Maynard smiled. "Unfinished Fugue, Opus I, by Thurs Maynard . . . Thurs Wraldson."

"Don't worry. I'll finish it."

"I know you will." Mr. Maynard handed back the manuscript. "Here you are. And now, my boy, how about a fresh brew of coffee?"

"That'd be fine."

"Good. Come with me."

Mr. Maynard got up, set a screen before the fire, then led the way into a small kitchen in back. He set the water to boil on a gas burner, put four tablespoons of coffee leveled with a knife into the top of percolator, set a tin on another burner and put two cups upside down on it.

Thurs pointed to the cups. "What's that for?"

"You've had coffee in a restaurant?"

"Sure."

"And you've had it turn cold on you by the third sip?"

"I get it."

Mr. Maynard next got out a tray and set out spoons and a blue porcelain sugar and creamer. "My boy, when you get to be an old bachelor like me, you'll develop testy habits too. Preheated cups, food just so, no noises, no interruptions."

Thurs smiled. Sitting in the kitchen with its blue range and white refrigerator and blue pantry shelves and white enamel table and clean blue linoleum floor, he felt suddenly as if he were at home with a father, as if with mother gone the two of them were having a comfort cup of coffee before they went to bed.

"Have you decided yet what you're going to do next year?"

Thurs picked at the tablecloth. "No, I haven't."

"Isn't it about time you decided?"

"You're right. All my friends are finding themselves jobs. Applications here, applications there."

"Remember, we have a responsibility, you and I. When we. . .when you cut yourself free from Mrs. Brothers, it meant you had to make a go of it on your own."

"What shall I do, teach English as we planned?"

"How about trying for a musical scholarship in New York?"

"Think I can qualify?"

"You can always try."

"Well, I better do that then."

The water began to boil and Mr. Maynard measured off two and a half cups into the coffeepot. "Yes, you better."

"Now that I think about it, right now, I don't think I want to teach."

"Oh?"

"From what I have seen, teaching tends to dry up creative impulses."

"But teaching can also be very rewarding. Teachers and librarians, you know, and certain mothers, are the custodians of our cultural heritage."

Thurs shook his head. "That's all right for people who don't want to do something new, but—"

"You're not afraid of sticking out then?"

Thurs fell silent.

"Of course, you're mostly right. In many cases teaching has become commercial. You crank out so much information in your lectures for so much pay, and never worry about the boss's, society's, actual satisfaction." His voice slowly worsening, Mr. Maynard suddenly pitched into a hoarse coughing spell.

Throat cleared, Mr. Maynard went on, only now on a slightly different topic, as if a needle had skipped a few notches on a record. "Yes, there may be drawbacks to teaching in a small college like Christian. Narrowness. Bigotry. So forth. But compared to the huge factories that the state universities have become, it is some better. At least the student here learns he belongs to a family of dedicated people. He learns to become a moral citizen, to take a moral stand. I don't happen to agree with the Christian stand, but a stand it is—"

"You don't agree with the Christian stand?"

"Not altogether. But that's another story." Mr. Maynard felt the cups gingerly. They were at last warm enough and he turned off the low fire under them. He went on, his voice seeming to pick up strength again. "As I was saying, at Christian here we teach them to take some kind of moral stand. But I'm afraid that at most of our universities and at many of our secondary colleges we do not. That in fact we turn out far too many students who are interested in nothing but power. Sheer raw power. And these power-minded students have pretty much taken over the running of our country. They fit in very well with what went before. So that we as a people today are more of a danger to the world than a blessing. What else can you expect of a system that doesn't make it a point to nurture a moral intelligence to go along with that power? You see, these days you have only to touch a button and a mountain moves. Mountain ranges, in fact. And whole valleys fill up." Mr. Maynard cleared his throat. "And I think it is very important to the future of the world that moral intelligence shall have something to say about which hand shall do the touching."

Thurs went back to his question. "This about your not agreeing with the Christian stand—are you an atheist then?"

"Detective Thurs."

"Well, I'd like to know. Because I'm troubled about that too."

"Go see Mr. Hobbs then. That's his department. Or President Cooper. He handles the God problem."

Thurs felt the sarcasm. "I have seen them."

"And?"

"Ha. President Cooper tells me to pray and read the Scriptures. Mr. Hobbs tells me I'm already a fish and that I'd darn well better learn to breathe in water."

"Ha!"

Thurs laughed too. "You know, that Mr. Hobbs, he overwhelms you with his knowledge. Arguing with him is like arguing with a library."

"But do his arguments convince you?"

"Not always."

"Oh? What do you mean by that?" The coffee began to percolate. Mr. Maynard glanced at the clock over the sink.

"Well, that my points are just as cogent as his are but that I only lack the experience to make them seem so."

"Ah."

"Really, I'd like to know what you think about all this. I'm almost to the point where I'm going to turn atheist."

"Foolish."

"But you said yourself—"

"Agnostic is better. To argue that God does not exist is ridiculous. You can't argue about something you know nothing about."

Mr. Maynard glanced at the clock over the sink again and then nodded to himself. The coffee had perked exactly long enough. He turned off the flame and with a potholder lifted the coffee neatly onto the tray. Then he set the cups on the tray too and, gesturing for Thurs to turn out the light, led the way back to the fireplace. He drew up a small coffee table between the chairs and set the tray on it. He took down the screen from the fire again and once more beckoned for Thurs to take a chair.

Folding his robe over his bony legs, Mr. Maynard poured coffee for them both. Then, holding his warm cup between his hands, he said, "Yes, I suppose I should tell you a little about how I came to reconcile myself to Christian here and all the while have a private ethic of my own." He sipped, his old blue eyes half closing. "Many are the events that have made me what I am. Loss of a loved one. Then a bitter experience with a woman. Then a wandering alone and aimlessly. Then study in Germany. Then finally a complete change of interests." Mr. Maynard sipped some more. "I'm afraid though, Thurs, that all this would bore you very much if I went into it. Besides, it would not be very instructive. Your case, thank God, is different."

Thurs sipped his coffee too. He found it perfect. All the old man's fussing and special attention had resulted in a master brew. "I don't mean to be disrespectful, but maybe you should've got married. At least you're not a monstrosity."

Mr. Maynard winced.

"Whereas I am."

"What of it?"

"What woman would want to marry me? Women like to show off their catches."

Mr. Maynard looked down at his coffee.

"For odd guys like me women have no time."

"Maybe that's a good thing in this case."

"What?"

"Yes. For the average dolt who has nothing to give society but unimaginative labor, marrying a woman who'll make him conform is perhaps a good thing. But for the creative mind that's murder."

Thurs fumbled his pipe out of his pants pocket.

"Don't light that." Mr. Maynard set down his cup and reached for a box of cigars on a side table. "Have one of these."

Thurs looked in the box. There were a dozen or so long brown beauties left. They had the aroma of sweet beer. "Mmm. They smell good. Havanas?"

"Yes."

Thurs bit off one end and lighted up. "Ah."

"Ah is the only word for it." Mr. Maynard lighted up too.

They smoked in silence a while. Thurs looked at the fire. Mr. Maynard occasionally sipped at his coffee.

Thurs said, "Well, since I'm doomed to be a freak all my life, it's probably just as well I don't marry then. Besides, for a long time to come, I wouldn't be able to support a woman anyway. I might just as well resign myself to being a bachelor like you."

Mr. Maynard coughed.

"And if I don't get a music scholarship somewhere, well, maybe I can go out and play in a nightclub. Help some guy play sex on a sax."

"Hmm."

"Or, if worst comes to worst, go back to Siouxland and become my true self, a musical mule braying in the fields."

Mr. Maynard chuckled.

An hour later, feeling for once ennobled for having opened his hand in the presence of an older and perhaps wiser intelligence, Thurs went home and to bed.

Milk of Wolves

Done in Stone

JUHL ALMOST DIDN'T FINISH HIGH SCHOOL. Father Ancher was killed in the Meuse-Argonne battle in France in the first World War. Mother hadn't wanted Pa to enlist, but Ancher, who hated Germans with a passion, felt he had to go. Pa'd hardly been gone, it'd seemed, when the news came he was dead. Ancher's death had made Juhl the male head of the family. Widow Naemi Melander thought of turning the blacksmith shop over to Juhl despite the poor trade. But Juhl rebelled at the thought. "I'm not sticking around this old burg," he told his mother. "So there's no use in asking me to take the business over. I'm gonna finish high school first and then I'm striking out on my own, out in the world somewhere."

"But you're so handy with your hands," Mother Naemi said. "You'd be perfect for the blacksmith shop. The way you can make things. Even whittling you make wonderful things."

"No, Ma, I'm not staying around here, not in Hackberry Run nor in Whitebone."

"Where will you go?"

"I like to work with stones. When I see a good stone my hands just itch to carve it up into something. And for that I'll probably have to go to the city somewhere."

"Son, you'd please me very much if you'd take over Pa's shop. Stay here in Hackberry Run so I can have somebody in the family near me in my old age."

"Ma, if you force me to run your blacksmith shop, I'll run away before I finish high school."

In the end, Naemi Melander sold the old dark blacksmith shop. Juhl was allowed to keep certain of Ancher's favorite chisels and drills and hammers. Phyllis by this time had a job teaching kindergarten in Whitebone and she sent home half her earnings to keep her mother going. Phyllis hated teaching but she agreed that for one year at least she would help the family while Juhl finished high school. Phyllis was meant for better things. She had her mind set on becoming a personal secretary to some great man somewhere, in Sioux Falls or so, or maybe even in the Twin Cities, and then later on marrying him.

The three of them were home for the summer and already after a couple of weeks had gotten on each other's nerves. That very morning right after church they'd fallen into a wrangle. As they crabbed away, rehearsing each other's worst faults, Juhl got madder and madder, especially at Phyllis, until finally he found himself ready to hit her. But he managed to quick slam out of the house before he did and went for a walk out to the river to cool off. Dinner wouldn't be ready for an hour anyway.

The screen door slammed again.

Juhl looked across the rising blue pasture to the north end of town. Sure enough, there was Phyllis again standing in the doorway of their white house, waving at him to hurry home. What a boss she was. He waved back to let her know he'd seen her.

He stood up and stretched. His shadow fell on the rippling light-green water, big and ballooning on top, slimming to almost nothing at the bottom. The shadow looked more like the shade of a genie than that of a man. The odd shadow made him pause for a moment, sobered him. That outline on the water there, was that a sign of some kind?

About to step down off the pink boulder, his eye next lighted on one of the stepping stones farther ahead. It also was pinkish and it resembled a human head. The way it lay in the water, moss tendrils trailing off one end like green human hair, with only an inch of its surface showing, like some human being with just enough of its pink face out of the water to be able to breathe, it almost seemed alive for a moment. But what should have been its face was a blank, no eyes, no lips, no nose. Nobody after all. Only one among many stones for someone to step on.

"Just a little work, though, with a handpoint, and I'd have me a pretty good head," he mused. "And a feller could make it look like anybody. A good guy or a bad guy."

The smooth eyeless stone reminded him of something, something he'd promised himself to do a long time ago when he was a boy. Go have a look at that stone thing up on Buffalo Ridge northeast of Pipestone. Old Peters the stone-cutter at the Whitebone Monument Works had often talked about that stone thing lying in the grass there. Old Peter's guess was that it had been made by Indians. Because it was on a high place of worship, like in the Bible, Old Peters said. Juhl wanted to see it for himself. Anything done in stone intrigued him.

And while he was at it up there, he ought to also go search out the source of the Big Rock River. He'd often wondered just where their river did start, just what spring flowed first and from under what rock or bush. And what did that first spring look like? And what did the country around the spring look like? Did the river start in some farmer's slough somewhere? Or in a patch of willows alongside a road? It'd be something to know. Every man should have a picture in his head of what his whole river looked like.

"Juhl!"

Juhl again waved his hand to let Phyllis know he was coming. Then, still in a thoughtful mood, he stepped on the eyeless stone and all the other stepping stones to the bank, and ascended the shelf of the prairie land above.

They were well into the meal when Phyllis at last broke the silence. Her eyes came at Juhl like the frosted ends of bolts. "When will you be leaving for your new job?"

A cramp grabbed Juhl in the stomach. "Oh, one of these days. When I get into the mood."

"Well, you better get into the mood pretty quick."

"And when I run into a job I like."

"Beggars can't be choosers."

"Boy, you sure can be original sometimes, can't you?"

"Because a beggar is what you're going to be if I decide not to give Ma any more money. The little she has left of the inheritance isn't going to be enough to keep you two going for very long."

Juhl cut what was left of his sausage into small dollars. He placed his knife precisely across the top of his blue plate. "Who says I ever intended to live off you?"

"Well, you act like it, the way you've been laying around here lately."

"I'm thinking."

"Well, get on with your thinking and do something."

"And I've also decided that I'm not going to take just any old job that comes along."

"It's not going to be easy picking what you want, buster, now that the war is over."

Juhl chewed his sausage thoroughly, thoughtfully. He could feel his cheeks reddening. It made him mad that she should spoil the eating of Ma's wonderful home-made sausage. "I think I know what I want and I'm not going to make the mistake of not going for it."

Phyllis placed her knife precisely across the top of her plate, too. "What do you want?"

"Learn to make heads of stone. I'm tired of just trying to whittle 'em out of wood with a jackknife."

Phyllis stared at him. "You mean you want to become a sculptor?"

"If that's what it is, yes."

Phyllis erupted. "Hah! You a sculptor? Where did you ever get such a crazy wild idea? You dreamer."

"That's why I was kind 'f thinking I might even go to college first."

"You? With the marks you got in high school?"

"I was still the smartest in my class. I had to work my way through, remember?"

"Where will you get the money to go to college? Besides, you never made a habit of reading. And you've got to read in college. My one year in normal school taught me that."

"Never found anything worthwhile to read around here."

Ma spoke up. "Maybe I sold the blacksmith shop too soon."

Juhl gave his mother a son's soft look. "Not at all, Ma. You're lucky you got rid of it when you did."

Ma looked to one side. The sun blooming through the bay window lit up the deep hollow in her right cheek. "Still, maybe blacksmithing here would've been better for you than this other."

"No, Ma. Never. Not here. In Sioux Falls, yes. But not here."

Phyllis thought she caught a hint of what he had in mind.

"You're not thinking of blacksmithing in a big city?"

Juhl glared at his sister. "I want to make heads, I said. So what's blacksmithing got to do with that?"

Phyllis finished the last of her potatoes. "Well, all I will say is this—whatever it's going to be, hurry up and get at it."

Juhl thought it a little strange that Phyllis had hit so close to the truth. Because he had been thinking of getting a temporary job blacksmithing, not in Sioux Falls exactly, but in Fort Sod a few miles northeast of Sioux Falls, where the Blair Quarries were still active. From Old Peters the stonemason at the Whitebone Monument Works he had heard the Blair Quarries needed as many as six blacksmiths at a time to keep all the drills and chisels sharp. Old Peters said they paid good wages too. Juhl had it in mind that if he could do good work as a blacksmith, he could talk the bosses there into letting him switch to working with stone after a while. He needed the money and he wanted the experience of working with stone. Old Peters had no room for a full-time worker, so all the stone work left in the area was at Fort Sod.

Juhl shied away from using the word "sculptor." There was something about the word that bothered him. To call oneself a worker in stone, a stonecutter or a stonemason yes. To call oneself a sculptor, no. Too high-toned. It was like someone calling himself an author instead of a writer.

That business about going to college he'd tossed out to give Phyllis the fits. He had no intention of going to college. He couldn't stand teachers. Teachers spoke of him as being a wisenose, and they were right. But he didn't give a damn. He knew what he wanted to do and he was going to go after it in his own way and in his own time. Someday. "Just watch my smoke."

I suppose it's true that being raised as stubborn Frisian with all that background, and having to overcome the objections of my relatives that I wanted to become a writer or an artist, and that then as the years went by I started ignoring all those prescriptions, I just went on my own . . . I don't know what they are going to make of me, I don't fit in any categories and I don't worry about that.

Judgment

FROM
Riders of Judgment

As a boy I remember reading Westerns occasionally in the drugstore on Sat-urday afternoon. It occurred to me at that time that I would like to do one that was true. I always had the feeling that there was something false about them. Or invented. Usually invented by people living in Brooklyn who had never been west of the Hudson. And also I had the dream as a young boy that I wanted to become a cowboy for a couple of years. . . It was always my feel-ing that the real story hadn't been told.

What I meant to do a little bit in Riders of Judgment *was to [take] peo-ple . . . that I know back home in Siouxland and I put them in Wyoming. The hero and his family all came out of Siouxland and I had an intention for that in this sense, that people, if they're unhappy in Siouxland, they're a little on the roisterous side or the community is a little too tight for them or close, where people are living as too close neighbors.*

The Killing Bee

WITH MITCH BESIDE HIM on the democrat, Jesse led the way. Behind them trailed a dozen tough punchers on horseback.

It was just noon. Though the sun was out, bright, it was biting cold. It was November and all shadows leaned long to the north. Each shadow glinted with night's lingering hoarfrost. The gray ground rang like a great stone bell under the iron horseshoes and iron rims of the wheels. Every man was bundled up in winter clothes: overcoats with fur collars, heavy gloves, and hats tied down over the ears with varicolored silk bandannas.

They breasted the final hill. Jesse held up a gloved hand. "Whoa!" Mitch hauled back on the lines and the spanking pair of bays stopped. The horsebackers behind stopped too. Horses puffed. Men breathed deep. Bridle bits and spurs gingled gently.

Below and to the left of the trail lay Avery Jimson's Hog Ranch; to the right lay Cattle Queen's spread. Rust Creek under the little wooden bridge sparkled in the noon sun. There were no birds. Wolves and coyotes lay hidden. West of them loomed the Big Stonies, high and pure and white, with new snowfall reaching far down the slopes, into the near canyons and low passes. The white peaks glinted against the sky like icicles against a vast silk bedspread, blue, fine-spun.

Jesse stroked his game leg. He was careful to stay well away from a big bandage covering a pussing pulpy wound. "Well, there she lays." Jesse's face was beetling red in the cold. "Now, boys, I want you to get this straight. No killing bee today. We can't afford it. Lord Peter is ready to back out and bolt as it is now. A killin' would queer him sure. Hangin' or shootin', one."

Mitch glowered beside him. Mitch was for the killing bee. His wife had been eating him out for tolerating a whore in the valley.

Jesse turned in his seat and looked up at wizened soureyed Stalker on horseback. "All we're going to do is go in and scare the daylights out of 'em. So they'll pack up and leave. Got it?"

Stalker spat. "Got it."

Jesse looked at the rest of the boys one by one: Hog, Ringbone, Spade, Beavertooth, Peakhead. Dried Apple Bill, Stuttering Dick, Four-eye Irish. "You boys got it too?"

"Got it, boss."

Again Jesse examined the valley below. Gray smoke rose in slow and wafting spirals from the chimneys of both buildings. Whiteface cattle browsed on rusty bunch grass in Queenie's pasture. A solitary cowboy's pony waited at the hitching rail outside Avery's place. Jesse snorted, high-headed. "Take her pay in my calves, will she? Write letters to the paper about me being a crook, will he? The blinkin' buzzards."

The boys sat quiet. Their horses chafed under them.

Jesse smiled some under his dark mustache. There wasn't a waddy in his bunch who hadn't contributed at least one calf to Queenie's herd. Even Mitch who was now all for killing her. Silently Jesse thanked his lucky star that he hadn't got around to asking her for a private viewing of her famous breasts. He was the only one free to do what had to be done.

"Sorry, boys," Jesse said at last. "But I'm afraid our Queenie's got in the way of progress."

Stalker spat. "Will her little herd be enough to fill out the tally for the earl?"

Jesse's smile held. "It'll help."

"How many you figure she's got in there?"

"Mitch, how many? You had them counted last week."

"About a thousand."

Jesse whistled. "She and Solomon would have made quite a pair." At that all the boys smiled, even Stalker.

"Remember now. No killin'," Jesse warned again. "Just a durn good scaring bee is all we want."

"Hell, boss," Spade said, "if it was to be the other bee, you wouldn't a got us with. You know that."

Jesse nodded. "I know, boys. And I appreciate it. I almost took titty there myself. But you know she's been putting on a style we just can't tolerate in this valley. It's got to be done."

Yes, it had to be done. From somewhere he had to pick up a thousand head or the deal was off. Lord Peter would go elsewhere for a buyer. Jesse felt he was right in taking Queenie's calves away from her. Hadn't they all originally been the earl's? Besides, wasn't it high time somebody did something to put a chill into all them homesteaders coming into the valley? Let alone them goldurn over-bold rustlers Harry Hammett and Timberline? And especially that king rebel of them all, Cain Hammett? Yes, getting rid of Queenie and Avery would be just the thing to start the ball arolling.

Jesse rubbed his bad leg slowly. "All right, you saddlestiffs. Mitch and I'll drive up to Queenie's cabin. While Mitch holds the horses, I'll shoot down that goldurn big black monster she's got for a dog. Then you boys cut the pasture wire and drive off her beef. Head them for the hills under the Horn where we'll vent her Hanging RH and put on the Derby brand. Got it?"

"Got it."

Jesse waved his arm again. Mitch slapped the reins over the rumps of the bays. Off they went. Wheels cracked on stones. Green spokes shone whizzing in the sun. Throwing hooves kicked up sparks. The two men rolled with each lurch of the green democrat as it careened down the irregular roadbed. The cowboys racked after them. Hoarfrost held down the dust.

Slope-shouldered in his heavy black winter coat, Mitch held the bays firm in hand. A smile worked his wily Mongoloid face. He laughed short, once.

Jesse saw the smile, and he yelled over the noise, "What you chokin' on?"

Mitch shrugged. He yelled back, "Heard tell that if you can't find no weapon on Queenie, look for a derringer hid on her somewheres."

"What!"

"They make them tomtit guns mighty small these days. No bigger than a thumb."

"What?"

"I wouldn't put it past her to hide it there. A woman will do anything when she gets in a tight."

Jesse grunted. "We'll make her keep her hands high."

Mitch pulled slightly on the right rein and they whirled into her lane on two wheels. Small red rocks shot out from under the twisting spinning wheels. Behind them trotted the pack of tough punchers.

Jesse saw the big black dog rise to its feet in front of Queenie's door. Even from where he sat on the tossing democrat, Jesse could see the big black devil blink its cold evil eyes. Jesse picked up the Winchester from the floor of the democrat; levered a shell into the firing chamber.

When they got to within fifty feet, Jesse commanded, "Hold up."

Mitch drew back on the lines, hard. The bays reared up, forefeet pawing the air; then stopped so sudden both Jesse and Mitch slid forward off their seat some.

Jesse took off his right glove. He stood up and brought the carbine to his shoulder. He caught the center of the dog's head, just above the blue nose, in the sights of his gun. He pulled the trigger. There was a roar; the bays reared again; the dog dropped to the ground.

Almost the same instant the cabin door opened and out stepped Queenie. As usual Queenie wore a light green dress, narrow at the waist and bosom enormous. Her hair, the color of a lion's tail, was done up in a bun on the top of her head. She'd apparently been napping and had quick slipped on a pair of beaded moccasins. She burned hell's own light green eyes at Jesse. "What goes on here?"

Jesse waved an arm. From behind him swept the cowboys. One of them stepped down off his horse and got out a pair of blue nippers and cut the barbwire pasture fence. The next thing the horsemen were all in the pasture, spreading out on circle drive.

Queenie looked down at her dead dog. A final wink closed its eyes. A trickle of scarlet blood ran down its blue muzzle. It stiffened slowly in the cold. Queenie looked over to where the pasture fence was cut. The ends of the barbwire had been ripped off the fence posts and dragged back a good hundred feet. Queenie's face convulsed a moment, showing wrinkles and age; then smoothed over. She made as if to dart back into the cabin.

"No, you don't!" Jesse yelled, throwing down on her from the green democrat, aiming the Winchester straight for her big breasts. "Reach for the sky! Reach!"

Queenie glared at him. Slowly she raised her small white hands as high as her face, palms out.

Jesse said, "I've heard tell you been expectin' me on a private visit for some time."

"Go to grass."

"Well, I finally have come for a private look-see at them wonders of yours." Jesse looked at her bosom while at the same time he nodded toward her cattle. "Steers that use the multiplication tables like them do should go under the name of mule-eared rabbits."

She turned slightly and stared out to where the punchers had just finished rounding up the herd. They had them bunched for the opening. Little triggering movements jerked at the corners of her eyes. "Them sonsa! So this is what I get for being goodhearted to poor lonesome cowboys."

All of a sudden the bays on the democrat smelled blood. They snorted; shied away from the dead black dog.

"Whoa, boys," Mitch growled, "easy now." Mitch held them steady.

Jesse stepped down off the democrat, careful to keep his carbine trained on her bosom. "All right, Queenie, step right up."

She shivered, dress rippling all the way down to her moccasined feet. "Won't you at least let me get a coat and shawl?" She looked down at her feet. "And something warm for them?"

"Get aboard!"

"But, my God, Jesse, I can't ride this way, wherever it is you're taking me. I'll freeze to death."

"It'll be plenty warm where you're going."

Calves and young steers bellered behind them and in a moment all of Queenie's wealth began to chouse past, around both sides of the democrat and the brown cabin. Jesse looked at them admiringly. Choice whitefaces. Chunky. Almost all of even weight. Lord Peter couldn't kick on them.

Queenie watched them go, one by ten by hundred, and she cried. Tears in her lashes gave her light green eyes the look of just fallen hailstones. "Them sonsa!"

Despite heavy hoarfrost, hooves slowly began to kick up red dust. The boys in the drag soon had to cover their noses with silk kerchiefs.

Jesse waved for Stalker and Ringbone and Spade to come over. They came at a gallop and pulled up almost on top of him and Queenie.

"Yeh, boss?" Stalker said, leaning on the pommel of his saddle, face sour, hard. He ignored Queenie.

"Get over to the Hog Ranch and corral Avery before he gets wise. And whoever else that waddy is with that lone horse at the hitching rail there."

Spade held a hand over a frost-pinched ear. "What if the lone waddy is one of our boys, Jesse?"

Ringbone broke in. "It's Harry Hammett."

Jesse's eyebrows raised. "No!"

"It's his hoss. Star."

"Well, well. Now we will really have us a necktie party. We'll string him up too."

"Why, you strangling sons-a-bitches," Queenie said, low. "So that's your game."

Stalker and Ringbone and Spade gave her a sliding look; then galloped toward the Hog Ranch. They were afoot and had gun in hand before their horses had stopped. They popped into the front door, one right after the other. But they had hardly vanished inside when out of the back door darted Harry in his flashy rigging. With a run and a flying leap, Harry forked his bay and was off, heading for the hills. As he disappeared over the rise, he stood up in his stirrups and thumbed his nose at them. Then he fired his gun at them, once. The bullet skipped across the ground in front of the bay team. Once again Mitch had to steady the horses with a sharp haul on the lines.

"Hah! Good!" Queenie said, "Now he'll bring his Red Sash boys on the run."

"Won't do you much good, Queenie. The party'll be over by then." Jesse gestured with his Winchester. "Get aboard!"

"You won't let me get a coat and shawl? Or some shoes for my feet?"

"Get aboard!"

"Jesse, my God, where are you taking me? You're not really going to hang me?"

Jesse smiled, mean. "Well, if you really want to know, we're running you out of the country on a rail, hive you back to where you came from. To Old Cheyenne and your old biscuit-shooting job in that U. P. restaurant."

"If that's where I'm going, please let me change clothes first, Jesse. As a woman I have a right to show up in my best."

"No."

"Haven't you any respect for a woman atall? I look a fright in all this dust."

Jesse considered a moment. "All right, where's your coat hanging?"

"Just behind the door."

"Mitch, hold down on her."

Mitch put the reins in one hand and with the other held down on her. His blue gun glinted in the sharp sunlight. "Up," Mitch said, "and no reaching under the dress on the way up either. I know your puncture tricks."

Queenie swore. "Mitch, you Judas you. I knew I should've had at least one good talk with that poor wife of yours."

Mitch's round face reddened. He held steady on her.

Jesse went in and got her coat, a long black affair, velvet, voluminous. He also got her a shawl, a light blue woolen one.

"And my overshoes, Jesse. And a muff, if you please. And oh, yes, my diamond earrings."

Jesse said, "Goldurn, no. I've already been enough of a gentleman as 'tis." Jesse glanced across the road. "Ah! I see they got Avery ready for us at the Hog Ranch. C'mon, get aboard."

Queenie still balked. "I won't feel dressed unless I have my diamonds."

"Durn you, Queenie, get in or by the Lord I'll rope you and drag you out of the country. Instead of just ride you out. All the way to Cheyenne."

Queenie got in.

"Sit down on the floor just back of the seat. Facing me. Hands up."

Queenie got down on the floor.

Jesse climbed in. He sat facing her, back to the horses, Winchester still aimed for her bosom. "Let 'er rip, Mitch, across the road and we'll pick up Avery next."

Humped Avery stood waiting for them. Avery showed fight. His bulbous brown eyes were burning mad. He looked up at Jesse. He had on his overcoat and hat, but still looked cold. The wattlelike goiter under his chin was purple with it. "Stalker says you got a warrant for my arrest, Jacklin."

"I have," Jesse said. "Climb aboard, you blinkin' wedger-in."

"Let's see it," Avery said. "I want to see with my own eyes just who signed a complaint against me." Avery gave Queenie the merest flick of a glance.

Mitch drew his gun again. "That's warrant enough, I reckon. Straight from Judge Colt hisself."

Avery looked into Mitch's gun barrel. "You going to dry gulch us in the hills, Jacklin?"

"Might. Climb aboard."

"You don't have the warrant then, Jacklin."

"Get in. I didn't come here to have a chin with you, Avery."

"You don't have the warrant then, Jacklin."

A new rope of pain tightened around Jesse's bad leg. It was almost a doubling of the usual searing twinge. It gripped his whole leg, down into each toe, up into his groin. Jesse already resented the way in which Avery used his last name and the sudden increase of pain in his leg didn't help any. It was Avery who had given him the bad leg in the first place, whacking him in the shin with his stool the night he fought Harry Hammett. He took dead aim with his Winchester on Avery's brow. "By the Lord, Avery, we can end it right here, if that's your mind. I'll put this carbine to your head and scatter your college-warped brains all over the ground."

Queenie spoke up from the floor of the democrat. "Better get in, Avery, dearie. They're giving us a free ride to Cheyenne, is all."

"Free ride to hell, you mean," Jesse roared, high-headed.

Queenie added, "We can look up the law later, Avery. Climb in."

Avery thought it over a moment; finally climbed in beside her.

Jesse pointed with the barrel of his gun. "Mitch, follow Rust Creek up the gully a ways."

Mitch drove. Stalker, Ringbone, Spade followed on horseback. The trail became rough with red stones. Iron hooves and iron rims rang loud in the bitter cold.

Jesse watched the two narrowly for signs of weakening. Except for that one moment back at the cabin, Queenie was taking it calm. She seemed to have guessed it was only going to be a scaring bee. Avery meanwhile sat nodding over his purple wattle. His thin humped body rolled with each pitch of the democrat. Avery was burning but he had dampered it down some.

Jesse hated them and their guts. It always made him as mad as the devil when people dared stand up to him, and especially so when they did it after he'd got the drop on them. He cursed them silently to himself. They'd upset the smooth and orderly flow of what had been the first real paradise on earth—big-time ranching in Bitterness valley. Life had gone along as merry as a marriage bell for him and his family and his friends until these two satans had crept into his Garden of Eden. It enraged him that a smart painted cat like Queenie and a smart ornery cuss like Avery could get his very own boys to play the game of grab against him. A settler or two he could have tolerated. But not an out-and-out calf-stealing whore and a college-warped letterwriting saloon-keeper both of whom went out of their way to encourage his boys to traitor him.

They rode in silence. The stone-pocked gully deepened into a rocky red canyon. They followed a crude dugway along the cliff edge. Junipers, then stunted pine, appeared along the upper edges of the crimson canyon cliffs. With every twist and jolt the wheels of the green democrat cracked like they might dish and collapse. Sometimes the twisting jolts were so violent Jesse had to hang on with one hand while with the other he held the carbine. Queenie and Avery rolled away from each other; rolled against each other. Once they cracked heads. Mitch had the advantage of hanging onto the lines. The three horsebackers followed along slowly behind.

Queenie finally had enough. "Jesse, if this is your idea of a shortcut to Cheyenne, you can stop."

"Blast it, if that ain't just what we will do. Hold up, Mitch, this is far enough."

They stopped on a narrow ledge. There was just enough room for the bays and the democrat to pass along the dugway. Above them on the left climbed the south wall of the canyon, straight up, overhanging them, red, tipping, with gray-green mahogany brush sticking out of an occasional crevice. Below them, on the right, some twenty feet down, ran Rust Creek. The mountain stream gurgled like the sound of someone faintly choking. A single tree, a sturdy mountain ash, grew at the edge of the ledge, rising some twenty feet above them. The sun had begun to fall and in the shadow of the south wall the wind seemed a bit more cold and bitter. Teeth chattered. Jesse was jumpy from both the cold and the tension. High and far to the west rode the pure white blunt icicle peaks of the Big Stonies. The Old Man and the Throne were just barely in view.

Jesse looked up and around and down. He gestured with his gun. "Get out."

"Jesse—" Queenie began.

"Get down." Jesse prodded them both with the barrel of his gun.

Slowly they rolled to their knees; then rose to their feet. They were stiff from the jolting ride. They shivered. They looked around at the sky and then down below at the canyon. A wonder turned in their eyes. Their eyes seemed to say: "Is this it? Is this the place?"

They climbed down slowly. Queenie winced once when her moccasined foot touched on sharp rock.

Jesse climbed down with them. "All right, you mullygrubs. Here's what we'll do. If you'll promise to leave the country, and stay out, we'll let you loose. But if you don't, so help me God, I'll have you drowned in that stream there like you was rats in a sack."

Queenie glanced down at the thin but noisy stream. She shivered. Then she laughed, short. "Why, Jesse, there ain't enough water in there to give me a decent bath even if you was to dam it up for a week."

Jesse boiled over. He realized he'd been a jackass to mention the water at all. He should have set himself to kill them in the first place. Then they would have caught from the tone of his voice that he wasn't bluffing. Jesse said, "Climb down there and we'll see if there's enough water or not. We might just want to hold your heads under until you've drowned. Like a calf in a bucket of milk."

Avery looked up. "You got a warrant for our arrest, Jacklin?"

"Oh, I got warrants for you two all right, which I'll serve on you, hot, from this muzzle, if you don't get down on your knees by that stream."

Queenie said, "Jesse, be careful how you joke us."

Avery shivered from the cold. "You can't start your lead pump any too soon to suit me, Jacklin."

Jesse shook his head like a baffled bull. Tarnation, they sure were the cool ones, wasn't they?

Mitch couldn't stand the palaver any more. Again taking out his .45 he said, "Shall I cut the dirty buzzards in two, Jesse?"

For the first time Avery showed a trace of fear. The thin lids to his bulb eyes flickered some; his head sank a little. Queenie still wore a pinched smile, though she too showed that Mitch's move had given her check. She looked back at the boys on horseback.

"Stalker," she said, appealingly, "Stalker, you ain't going to be a party to my murder, are you? I know I was sometimes cold to you, but I sometimes wasn't feeling overgood."

Stalker couldn't hold up to her. Neither could Spade or Ringbone.

"Boys, I'm surprised at ye. After all the favors I've done for you too."

Stalker said, "Aw, now, boss, hain't this gone far enough? They ain't really hurting anyone in the valley."

Ringbone said, "Yeh, boss. What's a few measly calves for fun? And as for the homesteads . . . I see Queenie and Avery ain't got any kids or kin to pass it on to."

Jesse reared back. His red face blackened. "This brigazee has gone far enough. Stalker, Spade, toss down your ropes."

Stalker and Spade said nothing. Neither moved.

Queenie's warm smile came back. "Jesse, you really wouldn't joke us now, would you?"

"Boys, get them ropes down here. Pronto!"

Two coils of rope whirled down into the democrat.

"Mitch, keep holding down on them while I set the knots."

Mitch held down on them. Jesse built a noose for each of them and then with thirteen wrap-arounds built the knots. He kicked around under the seat and dug up a pail of grease. He grabbed a handful of it for each noose and slicked the rope up and down. "This should slip like a heel in fresh prairie mustard." Jesse dropped one of the nooses around Avery's neck. Avery stood very still. He quit shivering from the cold. Avery's fat goiter kept the noose from fitting snug. Jesse got it up as tight as he could under Avery's chin. He threw the other noose over Queenie's neck. Her smile once more went back to being pinched. Yet she helped him by holding out her head some. Then Jesse threw the ends of the two ropes high up over a limb in the mountain ash and tied them to the base of the tree. The ropes hung with some slack in them, with the crude knots lying on the shoulder blades of the two. Both Avery and Queenie could breathe with ease, could even take a step or two.

A gun boomed on the canyon wall opposite. Everybody jumped. Jesse swore. "I'll bet it's that thievin' Harry Hammett!" Jesse saw a bright spot move on the opposite wall, behind a red boulder. Jesse raised his carbine to his shoulder and sighted carefully and fired. Mitch fired then too. Stalker, Spade, and Ringbone held. They looked on. Bullets whistled back across the canyon, the canyon quickly filling with loud echoes. The echoes jangled together; then boomed up and out. After a moment the bright spot behind the boulder moved; rose; became a man; and then became Harry leaping around a corner out of sight.

Queenie smiled. "I knew my Red Sash boys would come to the rescue."

Jesse got desperate. "Durn you, Queenie, Avery, play the game. If you'll just promise to leave the country, and stay out, I'll let you loose."

Even with the rope snug around her neck, Queenie laughed him bold in the face. "I know you now, Jesse. You really don't dare."

Avery asked quiet, "Have you got a warrant for our arrest, Jacklin?"

Jesse stomped around, black, almost beside himself. This wasn't going right atall. "Queenie, if you don't promise to leave the country, balls of fire, I'll just have to kill you. I hate to do it but I must."

Again Queenie laughed bold. "I know you, Jesse." She toddled her bosom at him. There wasn't the least trace of fear in her eyes or in her face.

It was finally too much for Mitch. He let go of the lines and jumped down to the ground. In a single leaning motion, with his sloping shoulders hunched high, he gave first Queenie a shove, then Avery.

Both lost their balance; twisted half-around. Then, with faces suddenly drawn taut in surprise, eyes shuttering wide, mouths sucking air, they fell backwards off the ledge; and down. The ropes snapped tight; two cries were suddenly choked off; two separate neck-popping sounds followed as of giant cracking his knuckles.

"Holy suffering Jehoshaphat!" Jesse exclaimed.

The two bodies momentumed back and forth, slowly, above the gurgling stream. Both heads hung crooked, as if both Queenie and Avery were craning around to get a good look at something that could only be seen with the head bent to one side. Queenie's light green eyes and Avery's dark bulbous eyes slowly closed, dulled over sleepily.

"Holy snakes, Mitch, now you've gone and done it!" Jesse cried out. "You goddam fool you—that wasn't in the plan atall!"

Stalker and Spade and Ringbone cried out too. "Goddam!" All three dropped hands to their guns. But they didn't quite draw.

Mitch laughed, shrill. "Last time I saw Queenie she complained about how she'd got off on the wrong foot in life." Mitch laughed some more. "Haw. Look at her now. She ain't got no footing atall."

That very moment both of Queenie's moccasins slipped off her small feet and fell into the flowing water below. The moccasins floated down the tossing stream like toy canoes, unmanned, whirling around and around.

This Is the Year

BULT: *A word used in both the Frisian and Dutch languages. In Frisian it is a very common word for pile, heap, swell, knob. In Dutch it is used almost exclusively for the hump of a hunchback. Bult so caught the feel of the prairie knob that I decided to use it.*

The Everlasting Weird

PIER'S YARD WAS BLACK with blue-clad farmers.

From the southwest came gentle veils of red-brown dust. They trailed over and among the men. A gray-brown sky cast an ashen light upon all things. It graved the weathered shingles on the barn and the woodshed.

The sheriff's sale was almost over. Two horses, and the cows, were all that was left.

Baskets of clothes, furniture that still shone from Nertha's care, the phonograph and radio, barrels of nails and staples, boxes of wrenches and bolts, tubs, chickens in crates, cultivators and plows, cleaners, the sheller and shredder and corn picker, a white chamber pot, all these, had already been knocked down by Sheriff Rexwinkel's auctioneer's cane. Everything was going, everything except a team of horses, a plow, a few personal belongings which the law allowed Pier to keep.

Pier trotted out the grays, Betts and Belle. A circle of shrewd-eyed bidders surveyed them.

It was cold and the men in the circle drew down their flap-eared caps. They pressed closer.

Pier drove the grays around once more.

Someone raised a finger.

Sheriff Rexwinkel roared, "Sold. Sold to Otto Grimovich there for a hundred and fifty dollars." The barrel-heavy sheriff waved his cane, stopped to wipe his beer-red face. He stepped down from the box and started for the barn.

The swarm of bidders broke up. They followed the sheriff. The descendants of Âlde Romke's black-and-whites were next.

As Pier turned to follow them, he saw Ma Lysbeth hobbling toward him from the house. Herman Brackx had brought her. Except for her grotesquely protruding windbelly she was very thin. Wrinkled skin lay in folds over her long bony frame. Her two legs were almost as spindling as the cane she used, and one followed the other as she crept along: first the cane, then the right leg, then the left. She was three sticks walking through dust.

371

Pier's impulse was to snap at her. But he took hold of himself. "Hi, Ma."

"Soan." The old lady's voice was barely a breath. It was harsh. "Soan, them thieves, they stole my jar of yeast."

Pier remembered it. "Oh, now, Ma, you must be mistaken. They wouldn't do that."

She tapped her cane in the dust. "It ain't there, soan. An' as sure as I'm standing here, I know they stole it." Her vague, milky eyes searched his face. "Thieves."

"What would you want with it now anyway, huh?"

"Why, soan, you're to come home an' live with me. An' I'm to keep house for you. Like I once did."

Pier shook his head. "No, Ma. That's all done now. No."

"Soan, you're to come with me."

"No, Ma. That wouldn't work atall."

"Where are you going then?"

"Me? I don't know. Somewhere. Certainly not with you. Never get along. It'd never work. No."

"You're going to let me die alone then? With no kin aroun'?"

"Wal, Ma . . . Oh, now, Ma, you've got a long life ahead yit. Besides, ain't Âlde Folkwâlda there to take care a you?"

She bowed her head, wrote in the dust with her cane.

"An' then too, Ma, I'm through with wimmen for a while. With land. I don't wanna be around where anything reminds me of 'em."

"Oh."

"I'm sorry, Ma." Pier turned away.

He followed the last of the men into the barn.

Pederson tugged at his jacket sleeve. He was thin, bent.

Pier forced a watery smile into his eyes. "Hi, Pederson."

"How are you, Pier?"

"Fine. Good."

"I'm sorry to see this, Pier."

"Huh. Ye're about the only one who feels that way."

Pederson shook his head. "I wouldn't say that, Pier."

"Not? Just look at them buzzards then. Look at 'em crowding into the pie plate. Just like a bunch a botflies crawlin' in a fresh shoulder sore. Only this time the horse ain't got no tail to switch 'em off."

Pederson's gray eyes tightened with troubled thought. He said, "Maybe you've heard this from me before, but don't you think you had some of it coming?"

"Me?"

Pederson looked down at the ground and scuffed the dirt. He coughed and wiped his lips. "You yourself sowed the seed of the rod that's now beating you, Pier."

Pier stared at him.

"You wouldn't take advice, Pier. You were too proud."

"Huh."

"Just like Jim Hill. He wouldn't listen either. When he wanted something, and wanted it bad enough, he'd just close those ears of his to everything except what he wanted to hear." Pederson tugged at his tan cap. "A long time ago I told him, I told him that some of this country wasn't to be farmed. There wasn't enough water. But he knew better. He said, 'I'll send Professor Shaw down there and he'll show you.' Sure. And this Shaw came and he told us and this is what we got. No, you can guess at dry weather, but you can't finance it."

Pier tried to pull away.

Pederson was right after him. "Pier, tell me. Why do you close your ears to good advice? Tell me."

"I dunno."

"Take vaccination. You'll vaccinate pigs, but not kids. Why?"

Pier shrugged.

Pederson pointed through a window. Beyond in the dusty gloom stood the house. "See that? A good frost bulge and the south wing of that house'll tip into the gully. Or even just a good jerking wind. Pier, I saw it coming years ago, when you started plowing your furrows up and down the hill instead of along it. I told you about it, Pier. But you wouldn't listen. Oh no. No, you thought we fellows"—and Pederson's voice became edged with irony—"we guv'ment fellows was buttinskys. We had too long a nose. We was dictating to you farmers. Huh."

Pier looked down. He pulled his cap over his white hair. In the background he could hear the farmers talking, hear the sheriff get ready to auction off the cattle.

Pederson took a deep breath, became abruptly gentle. "Pier, I shouldn't go on like this. But you're my friend. Tell me, Pier, what are you going to do after this?"

"Hit the road, I guess. Live in a ditch somewheres. I dunno." Shep the dog, excited by all the attention he was getting, came up and licked Pier's hand. Pier petted him for a moment.

"I hate to see a good man turn bum. There should be some place for a man like you. A hard worker."

"It's a cinch it ain't in this neck of the woods." Pier wiped his nose. A blob of wetted dust hung in it. Holding his fingers alternately over each nostril, he blew vigorously through both passages. "No, I guess I just don't fit here. At least not as the owner of my own piece a land." Pier looked sneeringly at the other farmers milling around. Most of them were renters; the rest guv'ment pail-feds.

"Oh yes you do, Pier. With just a little more sense you'd make a perfect fit. It takes a hero to live out here and that's what you are. A hero."

"Or a fool."

"No. Not a fool. Hero. Pier, where have you ever seen country with bigger ups and downs than this here God's country? Why, when it rains, it floods. When it shines, it burns. When it blows, it raises hell to high heaven. When it snows, it blizzards. Why, just take this dust blowing right here right now. In two hours, with a Nebraska hurricane blowing behind it, we could be right in the middle of a first-class black roller, piling up dust so thick you'd think it was the devil's snow coming out of hell itself. Man, it takes a hero to survive such stuff. A hero who thinks. Thinks."

The talk made Pier nervous. He coughed and looked through his pockets for his pipe. He found it and lit it and said, "Aw hell, don't waste yer breath on me. I'm done. Go talk to the kids growing up."

Pederson blinked. His eyes opened. "Oh say. That reminds me. I saw your boy Teo last week. In Sioux Falls."

Pier's eyes lighted. "You did?"

"Sure. You got a nice boy there, Pier."

"Don't I know it. Tell me, what was he doin'?" Pier didn't mention that there were two letters from Teo in the house, that he had been too proud to ask a stranger to read them to him.

"He was working in a machine shop nights, going to school days."

"That's wonderful. Good."

"Yes, Pier. There's a good head screwed to that boy's shoulders."

"Wal now, wal now . . ." Pier flushed. "Wal now . . ."

Pederson looked respectfully off to one side. He pulled his gray cap deep over his old eyes. He pulled his coat up close around his bone-thin hips.

"It's sure good to hear that," Pier murmured. "Sure good."

Pederson coughed, and said, "Well, Pier, you still haven't told me what you're going to do."

"Wal, it's a dead cinch I ain't stayin' around Starum here. It ain't no fun livin' near a dyin' town, where everybody you see is eighty years old or more, an' the graveyard's lost in dust drifts, an' the stuff you buy in the stores is all dried up because everybody buys in the big towns now. No, Siouxland, she ain't for me no more. I'm pullin' out."

"Pier, you ain't running away from her? Deserting her?"

"If you want to call it that, yeh, I am. I'm sick a seein' her. I hope I never see her again."

"Oh, now, Pier, that's foolish talk. You know you can't run away from her."

"Oh yes I can."

"No, Pier, no. You can never escape her. You see, someday you'll die, and there's only one place you can be buried in. And that's the earth. In her."

A drum of laughter beat up around them. Glancing over, Pier saw that belly-heavy Sheriff Rexwinkel had rolled off a box. Deputy Ain'it, his crow-black eyes wrinkling with mirth, was helping the fat man to his feet again and brushing fresh cow dung from his clothes.

Pier broke away from Pederson. He leaned against a dusty, cobwebbed upright. He blinked his eyes. He smelled the sweet earthy straw, the warm hides of the cows. He glanced at his friends. They were greedily eying his possessions. There was Otto Grimovich, silent, quiet, much older, no longer the rebel, still spitting sunflower seeds; the Brandt boys, caps tipped back on their necks, long-stemmed pipes dangling from half-opened lips; noisy Ol' Spit Triggs chewing a stalk of straw; Blacktail, neat, nervous, mustached, and taking down the sale on his pad; and Red Joe, whose eyes were furtive with shame. Again Pier blinked.

Sheriff Rexwinkel was merry today, and he waved his cane, and the words flowed from his mouth like straw from the blower of a thresher. "Well, men, here we are. You know these cows, men. Some of the best in the county. An' you all know why. Because they've been raised by one of the best cattlemen this country's ever seen. Just look at 'em. I don't need to spend a lot of time telling you about 'em. You kin see for yourself. There ain't a cutback in the lot. Not a buzzard bait. Not a hatrack, stripper, three-tit. They're all either wet stuff or good sound springers."

Pier smiled tiredly to himself. It amused him to hear this pompous blowhard bragging about his very own work, his breeding skills.

"Just look at them Frisian-Holstein prize winners. Them spots. Them critters is all good grassers. And them snip-nosed steers back there, why, they're the best hamburger on the hoof you ever saw. Fine good long-eared beefsteak."

Eyes became crafty with speculation.

"All right, Pier, lead out yer duke. Your rip-gut bull."

"I ain't got no bull, Rex. I got rid of him. Look at yer list there an' you'll see."

"Oh, that's right. Well, lead out something else then. Anything atall."

Pier led a haltered steer before the crowding farmers. He held tightly onto the halter. The animal gave off a little heat.

"Ha, there he is, boys. Now, what am I bid for this critter? Who'll give me a bid to start 'er off? What? Fifty dollars? Fifty I got. Fifty, fifty, fifty, who'll give a hundred? Hundred, hundred, hundred? How, how, how? Ho, ho, ho? Fifty I got and a hundred I want. FiftyIgotandahundredIwant." Sheriff Rexwinkel caught a gurgling breath. His purpling lips bubbled. "Well, then, try seventy-five. Seventy-five, five, five? Fifty I got, and five I'll take. Five, five, five? How, how, how? Ho, ho, ho?"

Someone raised a finger.

"Seventy-five I got. Who'll give a hundred?'Dred, 'dred, 'dred? How, how, how?"

Pier mused to himself, studying the slow roll of eyes in the stilled heads of the men around him. Dot-centered, white eyeballs swung back and forth as the creature strolled in a circle before them.

"Ninety, ninety, ninety? Who'll give me ninety? Going at seventyfive. Going once. Going twice. Going three times. Gone. Sold to that gentleman over there with a"—Sheriff Rexwinkel waved his cane at a face for Blacktail—"sold to that man there with a wart on his ear."

Pier brought out another steer.

"An' now what'll you give me for this snip-nosed critter?" Sheriff Rexwinkel pointed his cane.

There was a bid. Two bids. Three. And, in a moment, it too was sold.

When the steers were gone, Pier brought out the calves.

"Now, fellers, you kin see what we got here. Fine good half fats. Pail-fed skim-mies. Fine good slick-ears. All good feeder stuff in time. What am I bid? Ho, ho, ho? How, how, how?"

Then came the cows. Pier watched them hammered off, saw strangers lead his good, stupid, cud-chewing cows away. Shred by shred Pier felt himself being torn apart.

At last Pier led forth Young Lysbeth, sister to Young Maybelle.

"One hundred? I got a hundred. Hundred I got an' twenty-five I want. Twenty-five for this fine good springer. Look at her, boys. Look at her. There's proba-bly twins kicking around in her belly right now."

Slow, speculative faces moved amongst the clothes-stiff men. Massive ham-hands bulged in pockets.

"A hundred and twenty-five? How, how, how? Ho, ho, ho? C'mon, men, let's finish off this job with a whing-ding whing-dang sale. I got a hundred, who'll give twenty-five? Twenty-five? Twenty-five? Twenty-five? Not? All right. Going once, going twice, going . . . sold to Red Joe Faber."

Pier handed the halter to Red Joe. He looked at his stubby neighbor briefly; then pushed through the crowding farmers.

Blacktail came fluttering after him. "Pier, if you'll sign this, we'll call it all square."

Pier turned. He glanced at the other, said nothing. With Blacktail's pen he traced out the little row of hen tracks he had learned to scratch as his name.

"Thanks."

Pier paused, held up his hand. "By the way, Blacktail, you might as well sell the rest of my stuff too. The team a horses, plow . . you know, what the law al-lows me."

"What?"

"Sure."

"You leavin'?"

"Wal, what else is there?" Pier brushed his face. "Go on. Sell the rest. An' put the check on the top a the telephone."

"Where you goin'?"

"I dunno. I just don't know."

Pier stepped away from the snettering neighbors into the flying red-brown dust.

To himself he muttered, "Blown out, by God."

He was a torn blade of grass, wind-blown, flying over the land, one moment soaring, the next caught on a stone.

He found himself entering the the moment ahead without thought or plan. Where to now?

On an impulse he decided to take a last walk over the farm, to torture him-self for the last time with scenes where he had ached and dreamed, where he had sweat blood.

He swung past the old straw-pile butt, now a frozen mass of brown vinegary manure. He stepped through the willow windbreak west of the barn, and, back creaking, crawling through a barbedwire fence, started across the hog pasture. He skirted the lizard wriggling edges of the gulch.

The southwest wind was bone-chilling. He could feel by the touch of the cold on his skin just where his patched overall was wearing thin.

Dust rose. It stung his eyes. He narrowed his eyelids to razor-thin slits.

He climbed a fence, entered the cow pasture. With dimming eyes he looked at the rugged breaks beyond the Big Sioux. He had once worshiped those massive Hills of the Lord. A streaming red-brown wind almost obscured the bare, gaunt oaks on their crests.

With the worn toe of his leather shoe he scuffed the earth, kicking up a blister of stones: a crystal pebble, a bright bit of pink-purple quartzite, a gleaming green. He looked up, sniffed the air, held his aching back.

He pressed on, pushing his rugged, wind-scoured, wind-bitten face into the cold. He drew his cap down deep over his white old head.

Tiny bubbles of energy puffed up within him. Little wisps of song, like smoke rings, floated upward in his mind. But before the impulses became full-grown, the clefs rived, and vanished, as if ripped by a savage hand.

He strode on. He was a wanderer, a captain without a ship or port.

He came to the west fence of the pasture; turned north. He strolled along the edge of the valley. Below lay tossing bults and bosses.

He looked down the trail of the afternoon when he and little Teo had gone grape hunting in the hills of Gitchie Manitou. He remembered that soil-wise Old Dreamer Pederson had called it the land where the Great Spirit dwelt. Pier smiled at the fable.

He fronted a low hill, climbed it, fronted another tall rising slope, reached its crest too.

At the north-line fence Pier stopped to catch his breath. One of the new hollow steel posts he had bought the year before moaned in the wind. He crossed his arms over the top of a wooden post, leaned and looked into the valley.

Below, a long way down, lay the burrowing Blood Run Creek and the tableland where the mounds of the Mound Builders lay. He saw where Pederson lived on a headlong cliff.

He studied the mounds. Pederson had once told him that somewhere east in Iowa the strange ancients had built a mound resembling a sleeping woman. She lay flat on her back on the land. She lay as high as a haystack and as long as a prairie swell. Pier's eyes ran over the curving sweep of the mounds below, saw how each mound became a dot in a serpentine row. No wonder Âlde Romke had believed that ancient peoples had once worshiped there, facing the Hills of the Lord to the west. This was holy land! The footprints of religion were in it.

He mused. Âlde Romke was probably right. A person could sense such things. It was like coming upon an abandoned house. There was always evidence in it that it had once been full to bursting with family life, that the teakettle had once sizzled on the stove. And if one looked closely enough one usually found that the walls of the kitchen had been soaked with the vapors of many cookings.

Âlde Romke had always claimed that the Frisians had sailed all the seas, the great and the small, before even the Wylde Wytsingen, the Vikings, had dared to venture forth, that they had settled in Chile, Mexico, India, Greece, Norway, Britain. Even America before the time of Columbus. And maybe they had. The old mounds down there did look a lot like the Frisian terps of Europe, those bults built to give safety should the North or Frisian Sea come rushing in. Maybe the mounds were the remaining evidences of a lost tribe of Frisians. Through the ages, after Atlantis had fallen into the sea, many Frisians had been lost in the wallowing reaches of the earth. It could be.

Pier studied the mounds, tried to push back the mists of time, tried to see the ancients face to face. But the vision would not come clear. The ancients were gone forever.

He nodded his head. Gone forever. Ae. Just as he too would soon be gone, soon be out of the mind of man.

A bitter thought possessed him. The fiery Frisians had given England its law and language, had given her many of its legends and myths, had given her its heroes Hengist and Horsa, but had never been given credit for it. And now he too here in America, having given his work and his dreams, would never be honored for it. Ae, injustice was still afoot in the world. The Âlde Han was still at work. The old song and dance.

Wal, such was life. So it went. Grass grew, grass withered.

How long, how long had the grass been blowing?

Pier's old face chilled to gray stone. He stared at the moving soil, at the restless land, at the flying loess. He winked. He took off his mitten and, with a rough red knuckle, dug a speck of stinging dirt out of his eye.

Why hadn't he and the land been able to get along? Why? Pier lifted the massive question in his mind and turned the long bole of it over. Why?

He had loved Siouxland. He had wanted it. He had tried to tie himself to an alien past, to the old Mound Builders, to the Sioux, to the heroes Jesse James and Buckskin Teddy. To Cyclops and Ulysses even. What was wrong?

Ae, he had tried to catch his anchor into the soils, had tried to get his roots down so deep that neither the wind nor flood, heat nor cold, could ever tear him out again . . . and had failed.

Did a man have to die before he became a part of the old lady earth? Did a man's land work easier after it had been sweetened with the dust of his blood and brains?

Pier stood up and shivered. Life was a double task here on the new prairies. A man had to fight the Âlde Han, the elements; a man had to get his roots into the soil, earn his birthright. A double task. Ae.

He turned on his chilled toes, started for Red Bluff. He sluffed through a shallow swale that was gray with shrieking weeds. He went past Ol' Spit Triggs's rendering works. Its retching smells were strong even against the wind.

He started up the slope of Red Bluff.

On the peak of the hill he stooped over and picked up a red stone and hurled it far out. He was a blinded Cyclops hurling a stone at an invisible enemy.

He watched the stone hurtling away from him. It traveled in a long arch. It went upward, slow; held steady; then, descending, fell ever more swiftly to the ground. The arch was life.

He looked north, saw the slow swells of the land waving away toward Squaw Tit and Dell Valley, toward the ripped wounds of the red Palisades and Devil's Gulch, toward Nertha's land. He looked west, saw the bluffs the ancients had worshiped. He looked south, saw the land falling away toward Canton. He looked east, saw the land smoothing away into an expanse of horizon—so far that it was like looking into the very ends of the world itself. With the sandsharp, glint-bright wind beating on his back, he leaned forward. Rags of dust, like leg-long cranes, flew past him. He stared ahead into the grayish white-blue band where earth and sky were blended. He wondered if out there, out there where eternity began, he would find peace someday.

He stepped down the hill toward the road. His eye happened to see a splash of green beneath the fence. Curious, he kicked at it, wondered how grass so green could be growing in so arid a country. He knelt. He took off his mittens, tore up the sod to search out its secret. What had kept these few spears of cord grass alive? The sod parted reluctantly. When he lifted it up, he found the ground frost-wet. He flupped it a few times in his hand, gave it another toss, dropped it. He stood up. Shading his eyes against the wind, he peered down the fence. Sure enough, there were traces of green all along it. He remembered now that oats or corn accidentally spilled under the fence had always seemed taller to him than crops in the field, that the sun had never seemed to burn the spilled grain like it had the planted. He shook his head. He couldn't understand it. Land needed stirring up, needed plowing to make it grow . . . and yet, here beneath the fence, where the sod was as hard as rocks, the grain and the grass grew best.

He stepped past Kaia's place, looked at the gray house half obscured by the twigs of the lilac and chokecherry bushes, looked at the barn and wondered how Stephan was making it now.

He came to the southeast corner of his farm. He paused for breath.

The wind began to die down.

Rested, he started for home, climbing the slow rise west. Cars brommed up the highway past him. The last of the buzzard flies were leaving his sale.

He scuffed down the hill, walking alongside the gulch. He entered the dead orchard. He walked up to the house. The wind had almost stopped. The yard was stealthy-quiet.

He looked around. Ae, the moment the sale was over the buzzards had left. Not one had remained behind to commiserate with him. Not one. They hadn't even bothered to wish him good luck for tomorrow.

He entered the kitchen. On the phone lay the check from Blacktail. Below it stood his brown cowhide suitcase.

He folded the check into a neat square, dropped it into his scabbed leather purse. He opened the suitcase, took a few clothes off the hooks behind the door, balled them up, stuffed them in. "Might as well fill the chuck bag with all the duds I can." He took off his patched, faded overall, stuffed that in too. He put on a clean one.

He made one last survey of the house to see if he might have left anything. He stepped through the living room, through the parlor, through the bedroom where Nertha had died and where he and Kaia had lusted. All the rooms were empty, dusty.

He climbed the stairs, passed through Teo's room. It was empty. He remembered how, on the morning of his wedding day, he had awakened in it eighteen years ago.

He glanced in the bedroom where Âlde Romke and Ma Lysbeth had lived for a while. It was empty.

He opened the door to the south room, the guest room where he and Nertha had loved one white winter day. Noticing an old, redtrimmed trunk on the far side of the room, he stepped toward it. He flipped back the lid of the trunk. Pier caught sight of silver lettering. In the dim light Pier could not see the wall Bible sayings distinctly but he knew that one of them said, GOD IS THE HEAD OF THIS HOUSE; the other, THE EARTH IS THE LORD'S AND THE FULLNESS THEREOF.

He picked both up. "Never kin tell, might have some use for them someday."

As he turned to leave, the floor sank away. There was a cracking, a splintering of wood. Nails screeched. Earthquake? The great cave-in at last? Pier hoarsed in a sudden breath.

The floor sank a bit more, then steadied.

A quick glance, and he saw that the ceiling and the roof had parted above the door, that the floor had opened at his feet. The subsoil beneath the south wing of the house had given way. The weight of his body had been just enough to start it.

Pier's eyes opened momentarily; then half closed. Now he had seen everything.

He went downstairs, stuffed the placards in the suitcase, closed it, stepped outdoors.

Shep the dog ran up to him, sat down, whined. Pier touched the animal. Shep licked his hands, got to his feet, rubbed Pier's leg.

Dusk was falling rapidly. The dust flowing over the land was the rising mist of a vast sea.

He started up the lane, carrying his suitcase, Shep following. He glanced back for a last look. Like a great gray whale, the old house Âlde Romke had built lay cleavered beneath the skies.

His feet did not track well.

He crossed the culvert.

Where to now? Where?

To Ma Lysbeth?

No.

To Teo? Theodor?

"Wal," he said to himself, "wal, why not? I might as well. It won't hurt none to go see the boy. See what he's up to. An' then go on. Somewheres. Shucks, after all, I'm a young buck yit. My heart's still green."

He climbed the hill, the dog pattering in the dust behind him. Night as black as chimney soot fell around upon him.

Blacktail's whistle in Starum blew up. It screamed in his ears. Eerie, piercing.

Lifting his hoar head defiantly, Pier roared back at it, sang loud, trying to drown it out:

> "Oh, braid her a crown of clover,
> Braid it pink and green and silver.
> Oh, cover her over with clover,
> Ae, crown her the queen forever."

Actually, he is a hero. He survives. And the earth is still there too. And he can say at the end that he has learned some things and that he still has a green heart. He has lost one battle, but he is still alive. And you remember a tragic figure longer than you do a happy figure.

To me, somehow, Pier and Hugh Glass are somewhat similar men except that one lived at a time when there were no farms—not many farms around— and when Pier lived he had to fight his bear in the land.

FROM

The Man Who Looked Like the Prince of Wales

Confrontations

DEACON ABT HELD THE DOOR OPEN for them and they entered a small hallway. There was an instant smell of cigars and chewing tobacco. There was also a very faint aroma of peppermints about.

Deacon Abt glowered at them from under a throw of blond hair. It was plain to see he considered them the lowest of all congregational worms. He opened the consistory door next and ushered them inside. A single electric light burned in a smoke-filled room.

Much scraping of chairs followed, and both Reverend Tiller and the entire consistory turned to face the guilty pair. Deacon Abt sat Garrett and Laura at the near end of the table. Reverend Tiller sat at the head of the table. Six elders sat in a line down one side and six deacons on the other. Elder August Highmire, father of the four Highmire old maids, sat on the reverend's right, and Deacon Abt, ranking deacon, sat on the reverend's left. Elder Big John Engleking sat at the end of the line of elders, next to Garrett. The consistory was meant to be an exact reproduction of the Lord Jesus Christ and his twelve disciples. On the long pine table lay three books: a Bible, a church concordance, and a psalm book open at the form for the confession of fornication.

Thirteen pairs of consistory eyes sat in silence, examining the guilty couple hair for hair.

"Nuh," Reverend Tiller said from the head of the table. He put aside his cigar and folded his hands.

All eyes swung to the head of the table.

"We understand you two have something to announce that involves church discipline."

Garrett swallowed loudly. The sound of it was like the click of a hiccup. "Yes."

Reverend Tiller wiggled the tips of his folded fingers. The good reverend was a stocky man of some forty summers. He had a fine head of brown hair that had just begun to gray over the ears. His eyes were blue, his face round, his lips full and pink. He enjoyed being alive. Yet he had a duty to do and he had put on a formal air. "Is there anything in what you have to tell us that might stand in the way of your remaining a Christian Church man and woman?"

Garrett's throat pumped again. "There is."

"Can you tell us about it?"

"Well, you see, Reverend . . . Well, we're going to have a baby and we ain't married yet."

"In other words, you wish to confess fornication?"

"I guess. Yes."

"Nuh."

Garrett flushed a bluish red. Laura bit her lip.

"You freely admit to this?"

"Yes."

"You are both members of the church?"

"Yes."

"And you now wish to stand up in church and confess your sin before the assembled congregation? After the child is born, God willing?"

"Yes."

"And you do this having also in mind that you wish to have your child baptized into the church?"

"Yes."

"Do your parents know? Both of them?"

"Yes."

"You have your license to wed?"

"Yes."

"When do you plan to wed?"

"Next Saturday. If you will, Reverend."

"Nuh." Reverend Tiller looked from face to face around the pine table. "Is there anyone else here who wishes to ask the penitents a question?"

Deacon Abt cleared his throat. He lowered a leonine lood at Laura. "When do you expect the baby? Exactly?"

Garrett looked sidelong at Laura.

Laura blinked, then looked Deacon Abt in the eye. "Late in September."

"I see."

Elder Highmire across the table next cleared his throat. Elder Highmire had a great head of hair too, shock white, with thick white brows. "How did this thing happen? Garrett, here, we already know about, what kind of a mess he can get into. He's got a weakness for them kind of things. He can't let it alone. But you, young lady, a nice Christian girl like you, how could you do a thing like that? Didn't you feel guilty doing it?"

"It just happened, is all," Laura said in a small voice.

"You didn't stop to think?"

"No. We was in love."

"Love, pah!"

"Well, we were."

"You know, of course, don't you, that it is only the married people who can do these things? That you're not supposed to be doing these things unless you intend to have children?"

"We did intend to have children."

"What? Before marriage?"

Laura looked down at her hands.

Eleven pairs of consistory eyes looked at Laura's swollen belly. Elder Engleking didn't look at Laura. He instead was looking at his folded hands. He sat very quietly inside his huge blue-clad bulk. His eyes, half-closed, were full of inward reverie. Reverend Tiller, meanwhile, was studying the ceiling in the dark above the lampshade.

Garrett volunteered, "It was really all my fault, not hers."

Elder Highmire's thick white brows rose as he swung his full attention on Garrett. "You forced yourself on her?"

Garrett swallowed. He was afraid the consistory could read in his eyes what he was hearing in his head. "Garrett," Laura had said, "be a devil for once."

Deacon Abt had further questions. "How did it happen? I mean, where were you? Out riding in your buggy?"

"Now, now," Reverend Tiller warned. "The questions need not be that particular, you know."

Deacon Abt said, "Reverend, I think we should know if it happened in a buggy. You yourself once preached on the evils of buggy riding out in the country for our young people."

"Yes, yes, I know." Reverend Tiller stared at the ceiling some more. "But in this case we don't need to be any further particular. These two have already freely confessed what many people never confess. And that is enough for now. If they had not it would be a different matter."

"I still think we should know if it happened in a buggy or not."

"And if it did?"

"Then you should preach another sermon on it. And we should make a ruling against letting our young folks ride around so free in the country."

Garrett broke in. "Well, if you really want to know, we did it in a bed. Between clean white sheets. In Sam Young's house."

Stiff silence.

Reverend Tiller's eyes came back to the table. "I think this has gone far enough." A mischievous look played at the corners of his eyes. He cleared his throat. "All this pick pick pick at these poor children. Remember, it is the lost sheep that is at last found that the Lord loves most."

Elder Highmire suddenly had red roses in his cheeks. "Yes, the ninety-and-nine who behave themselves, they're never given any credit for self-control and right living."

Reverend Tiller leaned back in his chair. "It reminds me of an experience I once had in my parish at Pella. Every Sunday there was this middle-aged couple sitting up front, almost under the pulpit. The woman was somewhat of a pusher. Ambitious. She had it in her heart that her husband should become a leading pillar in the church. She was always after him be prompt this, be neat that. She always put on a good front for the Lord. Which was probably all right. Poor soul. But she was especially picky when it came to clothes. This one Sunday in particular I'm thinking about, I happened to catch her looking at her husband's collar. As I began to develop my sermon and entered into a discussion of my second point, I saw her secretly sneak over a hand and pick at a white thread sticking out of his shirt collar. She gave it a quick little jerk, like so, and snapped it off, and then, pretending she was paying extra close attention to me, she casually let the snip of thread fall to the floor under her bench. After a little while, her eyes ran over her husband's shirt collar again. Well, well. There was still some of that white thread sticking out. Again she secretly reached out a hand and gave the white thread a jerk, and after a bit let it fall to the floor. Pretty soon, looking yet again, she saw it was still there, a tiny piece of it. I tell you, all through that sermon she kept picking and picking at that endless snip of a thread. And all the while her poor husband sat quietly enduring it all. Never once did he blink his eyes. Well! the upshot of it all was that by the time I ended the sermon she had completely unraveled her husband's underwear off him out from under his blue suit. It all lay in a pile of white snips on the floor under her bench."

Laughter burst from every face around the pine table, including even Deacon Abt and Elder Highmire. And Garrett and Laura.

"So you see what happens if you look too close. And I don't think any of us here wants to pick pick pick at these fine honest young folk so that we finally unravel their underwear off them."

Deacon Abt raised a hand.

"Yes?"

"I have one final question though, Reverend, and then I'll let them go."

"Shoot."

Deacon Abt directed a bull's goring look at Garrett. "Brother Engleking, these awful things now, they just don't happen. It's true we're all born in sin, worms miserable in the sight of God, but yet, sometime, somewhere, the idea to do it has got to come from somebody. The Devil must have told you to do this, didn't he, ah?"

Garrett stared at Deacon Abt.

"Tell us, Brother Engleking, really, where did you learn about fornication? It was from the Devil, wasn't it? He whispered it into your ear."

Garrett turned white around the edges of his nostrils. He began to tremble. His mind flashed with all sorts of ideas. Then a certain thought came to him and he let fly. "I learned it form the Bible."

"The Bible?"

"Yes. Where it says in Genesis how Onan knew the seed would not be his, and it came to pass when he went in unto his brother's wife that he spilled it on the ground lest that he should give seed to his brother."

In the following silence fourteen watches ticked very loudly.

Garrett thought: "Now let just one of those pious bastards tell me I should've spilled it on the ground. Or on the white sheets."

Reverend Tiller harumphed. "Well, now, son, you know of course that the various events recorded in the Bible were not intended to be used as examples to live by so much as they are examples to be used for instruction. As warnings from God what not to do."

"Deacon Abt brought up the subject, Reverend. I didn't."

"Mmm."

"You know how it is: tell the truth and shame the Devil. If you must."

Laura flicked Garrett a look. She whispered under her hand, "Ask the deacon when his oldest daughter's birthday is. And then ask him the date when he got married."

Garrett nodded. He leaned with both elbows on the pine table. "Reverend?"

"Yes, my son."

"We came here of our own free will and told you what we done, didn't we?"

"Yes."

"When we could just as easy've gone away somewhere?"

"Yes."

"Or had the baby thrown? By that dirty old doctor over in Last Chance?"

"Yes."

"We just let it all fly out, didn't we? Freely confessed?"

"Yes."

"Reverend, since we wasn't at all sneaky about it, or small about it, why can't certain members of your consistory here be equally high-minded about it all?"

"Son, are you about to make an accusation?"

"Reverend, let's put it this way. Laura and I will accept the discipline of the church in this matter. Yes. Because we got it coming. We're big enough to be small enough for this one time. But are the members of this consistory big enough?"

"What do you mean, son?"

"Let me ask every one of you here this question." Garrett looked them all in the eye, one by one, up and down the table, thirteen of them. "Which one of you can honestly say you didn't do it with your wife before you got married?"

The bulb in the single lamp glimmered momentarily.

"Wasn't every single one of you just plain lucky you didn't get caught?" Garrett pointed the finger from face to face around the table. He wound up holding his finger in his father's face the longest. "In the old days, according to the Law of Moses, they used to stone people taken in adultery. What we should really do, Laura and me, is say unto you this: He that is without sin in this matter among you, let him be the first to cast a stone upon us. And this includes you too, Reverend."

Reverend Tiller relit his cigar and puffed a tremendous puff of smoke. As he did so his sharp blue eyes watched the confrontation between Big John the father and Garrett the son. Finally he said, "Nuh. Enough of this. What we want to know is this: Do you, Garrett Engleking, and do you, Laura Pipp, freely confess your sin in this matter up for our consideration?"

"We do. Not, Laura?"

Laura nodded.

"That is all we really need to know. You can go. You will be told later what our decision is. Thank you. And goodnight."

Garrett and Laura pushed back their chairs and got their feet.

Laura said steadily, "Thank you, Reverend. Thank you for your time."

"Not at all. Not at all."

About an hour later, Garrett and his father met again, in the dark out on the street. Garrett and Laura were heading for the north road out of Bonnie and Big John for the south road. Smart Ears Alfred, Garrett's younger brother, as usual sat in the driver's seat of his father's carriage. Big John and Mem rode regally in back.

"Hold up," Big John called.

Alfred drew the trotters up close. The carriage wheels stilled.

Garrett stopped on his side of the road.

Three vague white faces in the black carriage faced two vague white faces in the black buggy.

Mem spoke testily from her place. "Pa told me what you done in front of the minister. Have you no respect?"

"For you and Pa?"

"For the church, that's what."

"For the church, yes. So far. That's why we came at all."

"But not for us?"

"Do you deserve it?"

Mem swished her white fan across her long dark dress. She turned to her driver son. "Alfred, home! Right now, right away."

"Wait," Big John grumped from his big belly. He held up his hand. An Old Country ring on his finger sparkled in the starlight. "Garrett, ain't you wondering what the consistory decided?"

"Sure I'm wondering. But I'll be darned if I ask you. I'll wait until the minister tells me."

Mem said, "Alfred, drive home. I see that one of your father's sons wants to be stubborn in his sin."

Laura threw Mem a glittering, almost venomous look across the buggy wheels.

Big John chewed on one of the tufts of his heavy mustache. "Well, I might as well tell you. Reverend asked me to. The consistory decided to accept your confession."

"Good. Not, Laura?"

"Yes. Good." Laura snuggled closer to Garrett.

"You're to stand up and confess it before the congregation when it comes time to baptize the baby."

"All right."

"And if the baby should not live at birth, you're to confess anyway."

"Whatever the Lord gives."

"Scandalous!" Mem hissed. "And my own son yet!"

"Be honest now, Mem. Isn't it true that you and Pa were just plain lucky?"

"Alfred, drive home! One of my own sons has become too proud to be humble in his sin. Repentant."

Garrett couldn't help but smile a bit devilishly. "Mem, we'll be over for coffee after church when the baby is finally baptized."

"Hnrff."

Big John asked, "Where will you two live?"

Garrett could sense from the sound of the old man's voice that Big John was also smiling to himself a little. "We've rented the lower floor of that redstone house on the corner. Opposite the Congregational Church."

"Alf got himself a new hired hand yet?"

"Alf thinks he can make it alone for the rest of the year with his oldest boy Free. Except for maybe corn picking."

"How'll you make a living?"

"I'm opening my store again."

"With what?"

"Laura's pa settled some money on us."

"Hmm." Big John folded his hands over his belly. "Well, all I can say then is: Son, this time give no credit. Not even to anybody from our church. You've got to be tougher."

"Thanks."

"Goodnight."

"'Night."

"At last!" Mem cried.

～

Laura's baby was born dead.

Garrett asked the doctor how come.

Dr. Fairlamb scowled. His black hair came up in a ridge as firm as the bristles of a new hairbrush.

The three of them were sitting in Dr. Fairlamb's office where Garrett had taken Laura for a final checkup.

Dr. Fairlamb said, "There's no accounting for it. It just happens. In the best of families."

"Maybe if we'd've done something different..."

"No, no. In fact, you're probably lucky it was born dead."

"How so?"

"It would have probably been a bad baby had it lived. Malformed."

"I see."

"Let's just say that the good Lord never really meant for it to be born."

"I see."

"Now don't worry about it, you two. Try again." Dr. Fairlamb pulled at a heavy Waldemar chain hanging across his vest and took out his watch. "Well, I've got to be going."

Laura was as pale as a sunburned turnip. "Was it alive long enough to have a soul, doctor?"

"How should I know? Certainly not on this side of the womb."

"I mean, in me."

"It had to be alive at first."

"I mean, until how late was it alive?"

"It was probably alive until a couple of weeks ago."

"Ahh," Laura said. "Then we better bury it in that plot we bought, Garrett."

"All right," Garrett said.

"Well, you two, better luck next time," Dr. Fairlamb said.

"Thanks."

Garrett thought: "Another of my seed born dead. And this one blue." Garrett cried inwardly. "My darling June Memling, she died of the green gangrene." Then Garrett thought: "But at least this time we saved the mother."

Out in their buggy again, Garrett put his arms around Laura and hugged her.

Laura suffered him. "I suppose we still got to stand up in church."

"I'm afraid so."

"We'll do it. We did it and we'll do it."

The confession before all the congregation went off smoothly. The church was full for once, which made Garrett grumble some, but nobody pointed the finger at them with their eyes. Most of the congregation felt sorry for them. Especially for Garrett.

Garrett and Laura were the last to step out of the side door into the bright sunlight. For a few seconds the people stood apart from them. Then tall Ada Alfredson moved out of the crowd and came up and said, "I hope nobody's asked you over for coffee yet."

Laura pulled down her corset. Laura had of late put on weight. "No, nobody has."

"Good. Then you two can stop by."

Garrett gave Ada a grudging smile. "Thanks, Ade, old girl. If worst comes to worst you're still always a friend, I see."

Ada smiled gravely. "If the Lord can forgive, I surely can."

> *They get me mad once in a while. Privately I'm quite religious in my own being, but I'm religious as a literary man, in that I like all life and it's a miracle we're here. That kind of religion is sitting in me.*

FROM

Green Earth

A Good Stomp

FREE WAS BY NOW FIFTEEN and some of the older boys in his class had taken a liking to him. What helped win them over was the way he'd handled Sam Ruffman.

One noon hour, during a pickup game of basketball in the gym, Free startled everybody by twice breaking up Sam's dribble and stealing the ball from him. Sam fancied himself as quite a dribbler. And he especially liked to show off when a certain Mabel James was present. Mabel didn't care a rip for Sam. Instead Mabel liked Free. Sam had grown into a powerful six-footer, with heavy calves and huge sloping shoulders. Except for slightly bowed legs and a low brow, he was a handsome physical specimen. Free was almost as tall, but was mostly a long stretch of bones.

Sam was so mad at being made a fool of that later on, when they were all showering together, he struck Free in the jaw. Free happened to be standing in the far corner of the marble shower stall. It was like getting cracked on three sides of his head at the same time. Free dropped to the cement floor. For a second he was only vaguely aware that Sam was standing over him like some victorious bull, and then that Sam, suddenly scared at what he'd done, had turned and left Free lie there.

Water spraying down out of the nozzle helped Free come to. It also helped him get mad in a hurry. He jumped to his feet, and skinny-limbed, shot out of the shower for Sam, yelling, "You goddam coward!" Sam with a red-faced smile had stopped at his clothes locker. But when Free came at him enraged with his clanking skinny bones, Sam bolted. He ducked out into the hall, yelling, "But Free, I ain't dressed yet!" Free kept going after him and Sam kept running. To the consternation of the girls standing on the sidelines in the gym, including Mabel James, the two raced around the basketball court stark baby naked, pintles bobbing, one mad bull chasing another red-faced bull around and around.

Sam finally took refuge in the boys' room, where he locked himself up in a toilet.

Wild laughter broke out everywhere. The boys especially went into hysterics when Sam begged somebody to please for godsakes bring him his underwear at least.

Free let Sam beller a while in his locked toilet. Later, cooling off, and seeing the humor of it all, Free relented and finally let Sam out.

Tony Streetman and Johnny Ralph were especially gleeful to see Sam humiliated, and they invited Free to join them after supper and bat around town looking for fun. Johnny was the young brother of Professor Ralph. The three of them checked on a deserted house where rumor had it Del and Jo and Flop and Nellie went screwing every night. They checked on a certain upstairs window where the blind was never drawn and a widow could be seen undressing at ten o'clock.

The boys usually wound up their prowling about at Jansen's Cafe. Tony and John took turns buying each other treats—a candy bar or a malted milk—and they always included Free.

Free had no spending money. He knew he'd lose his new friends if he didn't soon stand them to treats once in a while.

One day Free learned from two other boys, Arthur Cage and Bert Whiffler, that it was an easy thing to swipe Eskimo Pies from an ice-cream freezer Jansen had standing out in back of his cafe.

Free went along with Art and Bert a couple of times and stood watch to make sure Mr. Jansen wasn't coming while they snuck up the alley and raided the freezer. The best time to raid was when Jansen left his kitchen in back and went out front to take an order. Afterwards, running off into the dark of the public school grounds, under the same fire escape in which Art Cruellen had done it to Angie, they shared their spoils, two Eskimo Pies each.

It was kind of a lark to raid an outdoor freezer and get away with it. It wasn't much different from raiding Ma's pantry for raisins, or swiping a watermelon from Sam Young's melon patch. It was a little like young Indian braves raiding another Indian village for their horses. Yet Free felt guilty about it.

One night Tony and Johnny didn't ask him to join them. Free knew right away why. It was not very nice of him that he never treated them back. Well, too bad. But he'd be damned first before he'd tell them how poor his folks were.

Walking the streets alone, Free wondered if he shouldn't steal some candy bars and then go around and treat his friends Tony and Johnny with them. Art and Bert sometimes bragged that they'd also stolen candy bars inside Jansen's Cafe, right under Jansen's nose. And if a man thought about it, you know, there really wasn't much difference between swiping an Eskimo Pie out back and stealing a candy bar out front. Both were done on a dare. And it would be for a good cause. He wanted to be nice to his friends. He'd been a lone wolf most of the way through Western so far. Since the days of Larry Grey at Rock No. 4 county school, he'd had no real chum to share secrets with. He hadn't even told anyone yet about that sweet fit he'd accidentally had with Fredrika in her glider. Or about the times he'd shook hands with his third leg when all by himself.

Jansen took the Sioux City *Journal* and usually had it on hand for his customers to read with their coffees. Free sometimes asked Jansen if he couldn't read it too. He wanted to keep an eye on the Cubs, Free said, to see how they were doing during spring training. Jansen told him to go ahead.

The guys liked Jansen. He was a blond fellow with graying hair, about forty, slightly bent, steady, with a kindly tolerance for any kind of story, clean or dirty. He sometimes treated a hungry student to a malted milk. It happened several times that Free was among those he treated to a candy bar. Jansen kept a very neat shop and was known to have quite a good memory for names and prices.

Free finally hit on a scheme on how to steal, no, borrow the few candy bars from Jansen, which he'd pay back later when he had the money.

Jansen usually kept his candy bars in a glass case on the left as one entered the cafe. The sliding door on the back side of the case was mostly left open. Free selected a *Journal* that was still fairly fresh and stiff. First he spread the sports page out over the candy case and pretended to be reading it as just someplace, anyplace, to be leaning on. Young fellows were always leaning over things, or against them. Presently, as though tiring of that stance, he propped the paper up on the left side by holding it up stiff from the right side with his right hand. It didn't surprise him to find that his face and his left hand were completely hidden from Jansen out in back or from anybody else in the cafe. Sure he had it arranged perfect, Free with his left hand reached over the edge of the candy case and selected two O'Henrys and pocketed them. For a couple of minutes more he pretended to be absorbed in the sports section, and then, apparently finished, folded up the paper and went over and placed it on the counter near the cash register where Jansen usually kept it. And walked out.

Overjoyed, at the same time stunned by his own daring, trembling, he began looking for his two chums Tony and Johnny. Young Indian braves must have felt the same way after they'd crept into the enemy camp and had counted coup on a sleeping chief or had stolen a chief's favorite war pony.

Free found Tony and Johnny checking out the deserted house where Del and Flop were busy polishing their canes with Jo and Nellie.

"Hi, been looking all over for you," Free said.

"Hi."

"Say, ain't it about my turn to treat?"

"No. Not really."

"Yes it is. Here." Free handed them each an O'Henry.

"Thanks." They unwrapped one end of the bar and bit off a chunk. "Where's yours?"

"I already had mine."

Tony and Johnny gave him veiled looks. But they said nothing.

Free managed to treat Tony and Johnny two more times. And they treated him to candy bars in turn. He felt he was back in their good graces again.

One Thursday evening, after Young People's Meeting, Tony and Johnny went their way while Free drifted off to Jansen's Cafe.

A dozen or so young fellows from his church were having malted milks at the main counter. They were joshing each other, and ribbing Jansen, and trying to top each other's stories.

Free said hi and after a moment went over and selected the stiffest *Journal* there. It turned out that even the freshest-looking paper was pretty limp. He was going to have trouble making it stand up on one side. He was about to spread the *Journal* out over the candy case when he was startled to see that a new advertising display had been set out on top of the candy case. Free stared at it a moment. It showed a rosy-cheeked boy eating a dish of Hello Creamery ice cream. The Hello Creamery ice cream was the best around, as rich as gold almost. After some hesitation Free decided to use what was left of the top of the candy case for his operation. He folded over a corner of the sports page and hooked it over the top of the display. It worked. It helped hold up the limp paper on that side. He stared down at the paper, making his eyes move back and forth as though reading hard about the Cub prospects for the coming year, while with his left hand he reached around the side of the candy case and dipped in and borrowed two O'Henrys and then dropped them into the near pocket of his leather jacket.

"What are you doing there?"

Free's left hand turned to stone. Instinctively, like a child that'd been caught, he said, "Nothing." Then he wished he hadn't said it. He'd been caught flat out.

Jansen was standing on the other side of the candy case and was staring at the pocket into which Free'd dropped the candy bars. "What did you just do there?"

A nervous silence spread through the cafe.

Jansen continued to stare down at Free's pocket. His blue eyes slowly turned sad.

Free decided to pretend that he was buying the candy bars. He folded up the newspaper and brought it over to the cash register. He pulled out the two candy bars and placed them on the rubber pay mat. Then he began to search through his pockets for the money. His fingers turned damp.

Jansen followed him and took up his position behind the cash register. He watched Free looking through his pockets a moment. Then he said, "You haven't got the money, have you?"

Free could feel the eyes of the young folk bombarding his left cheek. He was surprised to hear himself, his own voice, say quite firmly, "No, I haven't I see."

Jansen stared at him. After some thought, with a flick of a look at all the eyes watching them, he said, "Well, in that case we better put them candy bars back where they came from." Jansen picked them up and went around to the other counter and put them back in the candy case.

Free shrugged. "Okay."

At that the boys along the counter went back to their joshing around.

As Jansen came back past Free, heading for the back of the cafe, Jansen whispered, low and quick, "Go outside and I'll meet you around in back."

"All right."

"Do it. Now." Jansen then sauntered toward the kitchen.

Free lingered around a moment longer. He thought: "What will Ma say?

Worse yet, what will Pa do? And even worse than that, what will all my cousins back home say?"

Free left then and went around in back. He had to walk past the very freezer from which Arthur Cage and Bert Whiffler had swiped their Eskimo Pies.

Jansen let him in through the back door. Jansen was careful to lead Free to the far corner of the kitchen, well out of sight of the boys out front. Jansen looked Free in the eye, then placed both hands on his shoulders. "Just how many candy bars have you taken so far from that case?"

Free knew exactly. Six.

"You know I can call the constable and have you put in jail for this, don't you?"

"Yes."

"Well, then?"

"Six."

"Are you sure?"

"Yes."

"Why did you take them?"

Free was ashamed to tell Jansen that his folks couldn't afford to give him spending money. "I didn't eat any of those six myself, you know."

Jansen could hardly believe that.

"Yes, I gave them away. To my friends."

Jansen stared at him.

"You see, my two friends, Tony and Johnny, they're always treating me. But I couldn't treat them back. I almost lost them as friends once, until I took those six bars and gave them to 'em."

"My God." Jansen's eyes became very big and blue.

Free had the feeling that all this was happening to some other fellow. While the real Free, Alfred Alfredson VII, had departed his body and was riding in the air above it, about a dozen feet off the ground. "I'll be glad to pay you for those six. Somehow. I meant to pay you for them anyway sometime. And would've. When I got the money."

Jansen chewed to himself. "Well, all right. I'll let you work out those candy bars. You come around after school tomorrow and I'll fix you up with something to do. Six times five is thirty cents. What I'll do is give you fifteen cents an hour."

"But I can't tomorrow. Tomorrow is Friday and right after school I always run home for the weekend."

"Run? Home?"

"Yes. I did that most of last year. Seven miles up and seven miles back." Free allowed himself a smile. It was only a little smile of pride though. "I had to. It was the only way I could go to school. Pa said it was that or nothing."

"I didn't know that." With his thumb and forefinger Jansen tugged at his lower lip, then doubled it up in thought. "Maybe I'm being too hard on you."

"No no. Actually, I really should work more for you than thirty cents' worth."

"You mean, you took more than six bars?"

"No no. I mean, I should also get punished a little for having borrowed them from you without your permission."

"Oh."

"I want to do double the work for you. But please, for godsakes, don't tell my folks."

Jansen gave his lower lip such a pinch it turned white over the edge of the fold. "About that now . . . Well, son, that's what I meant when I said maybe I'm being too hard on you. You see, I've already told your folks."

Free almost passed out. "You have? Oh my God."

"Yes. You see, I always know exactly what I've got in each showcase. So I keep accurate tab on how much each display makes. You're right you only took six. That's all I've missed out of that case. And I actually saw you taking them the second time you tried. And God, kid, I didn't know what to do. You, of all the kids to come in here, I never expected you to be the one. You're one of the nicest-looking kids I know. So I didn't know what to do. For one thing if I let you go on, you could very well drift into becoming a thief. Anyone can drift into thievery. Even Jesus Christ. That's why He had such patience with thieves. Even whores. So I had to figure out a way to stop you before it became too late. That's why I finally called your folks long distance."

"Long distance!"

"Yes. Your mother answered. The first thing she said was, 'Thank you very much for calling us instead of the constable.' Then she said, 'But the boy must be punished. He must be given a good stomp to get him back on the true path. So this is what I want you to do. Catch him in the act. In front of his friends even, if it can't be avoided. And then I want you to have a good heart-to-heart talk with him.' I told her I thought that a little strong, that it might drive you into being worse. Get revenge. But she said, 'No, I want him to have that stomp so as to scare him back into his senses. Meanwhile, on my end of it, I'll get down on my knees and pray to God.'"

On her knees.

"Yes, son, you've got a good mother."

"Ma knows then."

"Face up to it. And next Monday when you come back to town, drop by after school and we'll work something out."

Free ran home Friday after school. He ran hard to punish himself.

He entered the kitchen puffing. He was so pooped out he hardly had it in him to act sheepish. "Hi, Ma."

"Hello, son." Ma was leaning over the ironing board. She gave him a steady blue look. Then with a glance at the clock, she said, "I think Pa's expecting you to do the chores alone tonight. That'll give him a chance to finish the west forty and so catch up a little."

"All right, Ma."

Ma tipped up her iron a moment. "Your father doesn't know. I thought it best for now that he didn't."

Free whitened. "Thanks, Ma."

"Yes." She went back to her ironing.

Free changed clothes in a rush. He was almost wild. Pa didn't know yet. That meant his brothers didn't know either. Nor his many cousins. Nor the domeny or the people in church. Maybe it was not going to be so bad after all. He hurried to do the chores and the milking.

"Man, from now on I'm never even going to look at something that ain't mine," he whispered to the real Alfred Alfredson VII still riding in the air some dozen feet above him. "Not even if it means taking no more raisins from Ma's pantry."

The next day Ma asked him to hitch up Tip. Everett and Flip had to go to catechism and she had to get groceries.

After Ma had finished buying the groceries at Tillman's Mercantile, she went over to the millinery a minute. Free lingered behind in Tillman's Mercantile.

After a moment Tillman came around from behind his counter. His usual smiling face was strangely grave. "Free, can I talk to you a minute?"

"Sure." Free knew what that meant. Ma had talked it over with Tillman. Ma respected Tillman's judgment.

"Come with me in back then."

Free followed Tillman into a little storage room.

Tillman put his foot up on a store box. "First off, Free, let me tell you that there are only four of us who know about this. You, your mother, Mr. Jansen, and myself. I was brought into this thing by your mother. She was afraid of your dad's wrath, that he might order you to stay home and work on the farm no matter what kind of a talent you might have."

Tillman looked through the door to make sure no one had entered out front. "Also, she wanted to know if I'd ever caught you stealing a candy bar from me. Or ever suspected that you might have. I told her, never. Not once. I told her I was as shocked as she was to learn of your taking candy bars in Hello. Now tell me, honestly, just why did you take them?" Tillman reached out as though to lift up Free's chin; then, at the last second, seeing that Free was going to stubborn up against it, changed it to the friendly gesture of roughing up his shoulder a little. Tillman had wide heavy hands.

That Tillman, whom he admired so much as a great man in church, should know about this bad thing about him was almost too much to bear. Free looked down at the floor. The smell of the oiled floor mingled with the odor of ripe bananas. The real Alfred Alfredson VII rose a couple of feet higher in the air above him. Alfred Alfredson VII was watching him with an air as if he was about to disown him.

"I understand if you don't want to talk about it, Free. In fact, I sort of like that in you. It means you have pride. Which in turn means you are, fundamentally, an honest boy. Which means further there must've been something special eating at you to make you take those candy bars."

Special, yes. All of a sudden the real Alfred Alfredson VII came down and snapped back inside the skin that was him. And he broke down and cried.

Tillman was careful not to touch him.

After a bit Free told Tillman what he'd told Jansen, that he felt he should treat his friends if they treated him.

"So that's it." Tillman whacked his right hand off his left hand. The gesture made a loud report, like someone popping a paper bag. "I knew it had to be something like that."

Free could just barely make out Tillman through his tears. What a wonderful fellow. Free wished Pa was in on this thing then too. It would have been wonderful if Pa, knowing, had said something like Tillman to show he understood too.

About then Ma came back. She didn't look at Tillman to see if he'd had a chance to talk to Free. She just simply said, "I don't like those new flapper styles at all. That Jazz Age. It's as if some nutsy street dandy created those hats. So I guess I'll just have to make do with the old one." She raised a hand to the hat she had on. It was her old blue Gainsborough. She shook her head a little at her sad lot when it came to hats. The imitation pink poppies on her hat rattled like old dried rose hips.

Tillman shook his head too and smiled. He turned to Free. "Would you do me a favor? I promised Old Lady Kolder I'd bring her groceries over this afternoon. Poor soul, she's got the rheumatism pretty bad this spring."

"Sure." Free knew Tillman wanted a word in private with Ma. "Where are they?"

Tillman picked up a heavy cardboard box from behind the counter. "You know where she lives?"

"Sure. Down the block across from Tante Engleking."

While Free delivered the groceries Ma and Tillman had their talk.

On their way home, Ma said, "Boy, boy, if I'd only known."

"I'm sorry, Ma."

"And at the same time I don't want you to feel ashamed about how poor we are."

"I'm sorry."

"All right, son, I accept that. But remember, from now on sorry is as sorry does. For all of us."

On Monday morning early, while Pa was out in the barn harnessing the horses and the kids were dressing upstairs for school, Ma said, "Free, before you go, come here with me a minute."

Free knew what she wanted. A breakfast of cornbread and syrup lay heavy on his stomach. "Aw, Ma."

"Come." She knelt by the chair under the north window. She reached back a flour dusty hand. "Come. Kneel with me a minute."

Abashed, he set his pack of books aside and knelt beside her. Ma placed her elbows on the seat of the chair and closed her eyes. Folding her hands, she lifted her gold face to God. The smell of Pa's coffee was strong in the kitchen. Just as he was about to close his eyes Free saw how wonderfully blue the sky was over the grove to the north.

"Father," Ma prayed, "a troubled mother comes to you this morning. She asks, where did she go wrong? Was she wrong to send her boy to the Academy? Would she have been wiser to have kept him home away from the temptations of a strange town? Or should she and his father have gone to the bank and borrowed some money for him to go to school with, for proper clothes and spending money? What should we have done?" Ma let go with a deep sigh. "Well, Lord, now that the worst has happened, what will become of my boy?" Ma shifted on her knees. She often complained of sore knees while polishing the kitchen floor. "Father, in his strange misguided way, this boy of ours appears to have meant well. But stealing for whatever purpose is still stealing. Father, now that he has seen the right way, and has said he is sorry, I am sure he will never do it again. Forgive him, Father, and guide him in the path of right living. We ask it in Jesus' name. Amen."

By the time the prayer ended, Free was quivering.

Ma stood up. She sighed profoundly. Then with a hand to his shoulder she raised him to his feet. "Go, son. Let's look ahead and think of tomorrow."

Free ran hard to school, punishing himself all the way.

I took my first notes for this book while I was in college. I was 18. My mother died the previous summer, and I was lonesome for her, because I thought she, more than any other person, would have understood what I was trying to do.

FROM

Wanderlust

Everything but the Heart

IT WAS AN EVENING IN AUGUST. Howard stepped off the bus on the corner and, tired, walked down the street toward Butler Hall. He saw a light on upstairs. Slowly he climbed the narrow stairs and pushed into the apartment. Looking around, he saw that both boys for once were home: Ben sitting bare-chested in shorts and smoking. Thurs sitting in shorts and reading.

Ben put his pipe aside. "What's the matter, Howard, you look like you might've heard bad news?"

"I have."

"Don't tell me the city sewer system blew up?"

"It has," Howard said grimly.

"Or did you get fired?"

Howard began to pace slowly back and forth. "By God, sometimes I wish they would fire me. Then I wouldn't have to report on all the asininities I hear at our Christian Church synod meetings."

"Asininities? Oh, come now."

"You don't think it an asininity for them to be thinking of giving Hobbs the gate?"

"What!"

That's what I said. Prexy Cooper and his gang are on the warpath again. Because of a report they made about him harboring certain Satanic beliefs, Hobbs has been called on the carpet by the Board of Trustees."

"That can't be. Did they give any specific cause?"

"Cause? Ha. They made a survey. And the survey showed that far too many of Christian's graduates became dissenters for it to be accidental. In almost every case the defection was traceable to Hobbs. You know. It's that old charge we have been hearing about for years."

Ben looked sick.

"Of course the highest percentage of dissenters went to Hobbs's class," Howard said, fleeringly. "Why shouldn't they? Good brains usually get around to dissenting sometime or other and good brains also get around to attending his classes. You could say the same thing for some of the other profs."

Ben picked up his pipe again and slowly refilled it. "Where's Peters in this mix-up?"

Howard laughed. "Christine's father is sitting silent on the sidelines, waiting to see which way the frogs are going to jump."

"That's slander," Ben burst out, "that's slander. It just happens that Hobbs's best friend is Peters."

"Just wait. We'll see." Howard shook his head. "When a fanatic religion really gets hold of you, it'll make you betray even your own brother. Let alone your children, if you have children."

Ben lit his pipe slowly.

Howard took off his coat and shirt and tie and shoes and one by one heaved them all through the bedroom door onto his cot. "Yessir, and the best part of the story is this. The Board of Trustees had already decided to kick him out last winter. But they waited until now to announce it to the synod. You know why? Because they were afraid of a student demonstration. They waited until everybody was safely off the campus." Howard picked up his pipe; dropped it in his excitement; picked it up again and stuck it empty into his mouth.

Thurs spoke up then. "That's what we boys get for playing at being a Brain Trust. Plus questioning the idea of virgin birth in Plato Club."

Howard whirled around. "Jumping Jupiter, Thurs, you've hit on it. That's what triggered it off all right."

Ben said, "Well, in a way you can't blame them, can you, from their point of view?"

Howard next whirled on Ben. "You sellout you! Bah." And with that Howard stomped into the kitchen. "I don't know about you guys," he muttered, "but me, I'm going to have me a cup of coffee."

～

The very next day, as Thurs was spading up some dead bushes behind the girls' room, Howard came swiftly around the corner. "Thurs?"

"Yes?"

"Come along with me a minute. Hurry."

"I can't. Old Noland will give me the devil if he catches me loafing on the job."

"But this is important. You've got to come. Hurry."

"What prof is getting it in the neck now?"

"Just come with me."

"But my clothes. I'm all sweaty. No shirt. Mud on my shoes. I can't sit in there with all those slicked up ministers."

"Slide into a back seat with me then. I want you to hear this. Hurry."

They entered Old Main through a back door, went upstairs, and quietly took seats in the back of chapel.

Cigar smoke rose blue to the ceiling above. Most of the church dignitaries were sitting down toward the front. All were well-dressed, in either dark blues or blacks. A few had the warm red face of the jolly soul. But the rest had the pale drawn lineaments of the fury-driven ascetic.

Up on the rostrum President Albertus Bogardus Cooper was reading a statement in a solemn Judgment Day voice: "Because the brother has consistently refused to admit his error in Christ, because he has exhibited a stubborn attitude that is not becoming to the Christian, because he teaches in his classes that his particular interest is the most noble of the sister sciences when we all know that theology is the noblest, because he approaches all matters from an historical attitude and inculcates that attitude in his students, because he refuses to discuss discrepancies in his original application for professorship at Christian College, and because finally he has refused to discuss with the Committee and the Board of Trustees the sins herein listed, and thereby refuses to admit his grievous sins, yea, heinous crimes before God, therefore it is with the heaviest of hearts that we recommend to our brethren congregated here in holy synod that Mr. Brad Maynard be dismissed from the faculty of the Christian College and Theological Seminary at Zion, Michigan. Further, the Board of Trustees recommends that the synod send a resolution to the pastor of the church at which Mr. Maynard attends religious services to the effect that he be re-examined as to his fitness to be a member of the Christian Church. God be with us. Amen."

White-faced, Thurs turned to Howard. "But not Mr. Maynard!"

"Yes!" Howard said, brown eyes burning. "Yes! That's what I mean."

"But not that dear old man!"

"They couldn't trap Hobbs. So, to show some kind of result for all the snooping they did, they got Mr. Maynard."

Thurs got up, stood uncertainly a moment, then walked out into the hall, Howard following.

Thurs murmured, "That does it. Now it comes to me. Everything is sin with them. Everything. And the result is, they chase love away. They have organization, they have edifices, but they have no natural love. Neither of brotherhood nor of sex. They have everything but the heart."

Howard looked oddly at him.

Thurs said, "That does it."

"Does what?"

"I'm writing a letter of resignation to my church at Eastern Avenue. I've got to have love."

"Resign? Ha! What good'll that do? You can't resign from the Christian Church."

"I'll write it anyway. I live with me."

"They'll ignore it. And'll cut you off instead. Read you out. In a big public ceremony like they did that Saul Onanson. Remember? And remember his poor crying mother?"

"I remember."

"That's the way they hold people in line. By threatening to make public examples of them. So the people'll be afraid because of friends and relatives."

"I know."

"They'll make a big spectacle out of you."

"Make a spectacle out of me? I am one already."

~

Thurs stood in the doorway to Mr. Maynard's apartment on Alexander.
"Mr. Maynard?"

"Yes?" Mr. Maynard stood blocking the way.

"I came here to say how terribly sorry I am about what the Board of Trustees did."

"Oh. So you've heard."

"Yes."

"Well. It's good of you to come, Thurs."

"What will you do?"

Mr. Maynard permitted himself a slow smile. "Oh, I have means."

"Teach somewhere else?"

It was hot out and Mr. Maynard opened his smoking jacket and wiped sweat from his brow. "Oh, I think I've had enough of teaching. I'm quite an old man, you know."

"But how will you live?"

"Well, thanks to you, Thurs, I have my *Music for Adults Manual* coming out, you know. My publisher tells me there may be quite a sale. Quite a sale."

Thurs scuffed the rubber mat underfoot. "You're going to keep on living here then? In Zion?"

"Why not? It's as good a place as any, isn't it?"

Thurs's face began to work. His voice faltered. "I don't need to tell you that, Mr. Maynard. You know why."

At that Mr. Maynard's lips abruptly thinned. "Is that all you wanted to see me about?"

"I—guess—so."

"Thank you for your concern, Thurs, thank you. And now I must get back to my work. Good afternoon." Then the old man's voice gave way and he pitched into a violent cough. And still coughing he closed the door in Thurs's face.

Mr. Maynard . . . I don't know where he came from. He is literally . . . he is a figment of my imagination if ever there was one. I had a fine philosophy teacher in college, the only good teacher really I had there. A Dr. Jellema. But Mr. Maynard doesn't resemble Dr. Jellema. And Joseph Warren Beach, a poet, teacher and critic at the University of Minnesota. I always liked him in many ways, and Mr. Maynard does possibly resemble him just a little bit. I think that Mr. Maynard is somebody that I think maybe I'll grow to be.

FROM
Boy Almighty

I had tuberculosis once, almost died of it. In fact, I saw my file one time when I was recovering. I was on a gurney, and the doctor brought me to his office downstairs, at the Glen Lake Sanatorium. And then he went out of the office for a minute and I reached over and picked up my file and looked at it, and it said 'Terminal.'

Anyway, I wrote Boy Almighty *within a year or two of being dismissed from the sanatorium, mostly because I noticed that I couldn't remember the names of the doctors that were there in my room, and some other people, and slowly but surely I could see that my brain was freezing over.*

How do you make it interesting for a guy laying in bed for three hundred pages? Well, that's because my memory was keen and I finally unravelled the whole thing and got it all in there.

Moreover, I am convinced I first worked at Boy *not for the purpose of art (though it became that perhaps later) but for the secondary purpose of getting rid of an obsession. It was a catharsis. A blood-letting. A public confession. An open psychoanalytic purging. It's obvious too when you read it. None of [the] detachment that Thomas Mann got into his* Magic Mountain. *Were I to write it today it would be quite a different story, and in a different mood . . . .*

The Whipper Recognized

TUBERCLE BACILLI. Bacilli. A treacherous sounding name. Tuber. Like a pickle or a cucumber. Watermelon. Tuber.

How much of a flame had a live Tuber in its brain? Or in its seat of life? Its center? Its nucleus? Was it an illumination? Actually a perceptible nimbus? Did it think? Did it feel? Did it cognate? How long was the night? He wished he had a radio. Or a friend. The friends outside the San had faded slowly away. They came occasionally, but the visiting hours were too narrow to keep the touch alive. Talk was always too hurried. Their worlds and his veered away from each other.

Where was sleep? Had he come to the time Dr. Abraham had described, the time when he would feel better than he had ever felt in his life, the restless year

403

of bed-curing before he could move around again? Or was he still slipping? Was this the one last burst before collapse?

Lovely Old Lady Poplar. Dear Old Mother.

Sleep, O soul. Obey. Sleep. Sleep. Time to sleep. Obey my command.

But his being rebelled. It wanted action. It wanted to run. It wanted to see; just as years ago when the animal glow within young Eric had been too daring, too curious too hungry, and he had wanted to grab at the apple hanging out of his reach. It had not learned from the whipping.

. . . Young Eric had seen his Ma Memme go into the fuel shed near the house with a tub and a pail of water.

"Whatcha gonna do, Ma Memme?" He longed to lay his head between her pillow-breasts.

"Nothin'. None of your beeswax, sonny. Run along now an' play with Ronnie." Her voice was tired. She was suffering from shock too: the pigs had died of hog cholera, the grasshoppers had come three days later. For a week she had been in fear of what Pa might do.

"Whatcha gonna do, Ma Memme?" He loved to say her name. It was also his name for milk. And he had tied Ma and Memme together the day he had seen creamy memme dripping from her breasts as she was about to give suck to little Ronnie.

"Nothin', I said. Go. Go play with Ronald." With a tired shove she had sent him on into a grove of ash where Ronnie was climbing trees in hunt of birds' nests.

But after he had played a while, he wondered what Ma Memme looked like in the dark toolshed. He ran into the cornfield behind the grove and stealthily worked his way up close to the shed. He studied the small shanty. He listened. Water splashed within. He studied the red wall before him. He spotted a knot-hole just a foot above the ground. Cautiously he crawled out of the cornfield, crept over the grass, through the weeds near the shed. Cautiously he lifted his head. He peered. It was dark inside. Black. But soon the darkness became purple, then gray, then . . . he saw her: white skin, bowl-large breasts, blonde pubic hair, blue eyes sad, washing hands.

And suddenly the Universe convulsed. There was a roar. A shattering thunder of words. A mighty *swissshh* of the whip. A whipper had come.

Agonized, little Eric whirled catlike over on his back to face his foe, his feet and hands clawing the air. Through fumes of fear, he saw Pa with a horsewhip, flailing him, and wailing over him with a strange chant: You dirty little sneakin' brat, tryin' to see your mother naked. You dirty little devil." *Whang! Whiiip!* "I'll teach you." *Whing! Whiiip!* "You ain't no born son a mine, nor no child a God no more." *Wheng! Whiiip!*

With Pa no longer a friend Eric had searched for a new pal, a kindly uncle or aunt. He never found one. And by the time that Pa had become loving and kindly again, it was too late. The magic and the laughter of their early love had vanished forever . . .

Thinking about the incident now as he lay on his bed, he was almost tempted to believe there was a vengeful God or a Pa-like Satan, a Whipper.

What was there about him that invited hurt? Disaster? Had he not good impulses? And did he not have a natural longing for joy? It wasn't as if he expected grief and therefore got it. No. By inclination he was a happy lad; and a good Lord could have made anything of him. A long nose should have been a blessing. Eric nodded. Malevolent beings always resented curiosity.

He considered his father. Lately Pa had become a gentle old man. But there had been a time when Pa had looked like a Jehovah, a terrible Whipper.

Holy Moses, come to think of it, there had been a Whipper in the religious academy too. The English teacher there had been tall like Pa, had been frustrated like Pa, had taken a savage delight in destroying Eric's dreams. Every theme day, with glittering eyes, the teacher had read Eric's effort to a guffawing class of fools, emphasizing his grammatical mistakes and ridiculing his imagination.

And in the south Minnesota college too, by God, a Whipper had hounded him. There it had been no single person, but a foreboding air; and a few black-coated crows, professors, ready to croak their caws at him should he wander off the straight-and-narrow into the fragrant pastures of fancy.

Yes, it was easy to figure it out now. He had been too curious for a Whipper. Eric re-examined the three greatest shocks of his life, devastating shocks, all coming within the last couple of years; three quakes coming so close one upon the other that they had knocked him into this invalid's bed. When it had come time for him to explore the world of love, a Whipper had presented him with Martha. When it had come time for him to seek a way of earning his own livelihood, a Whipper had clapped him into poverty. When he had felt it was time to try his hand at creation as a way of compensating for his failures, a Whipper had sent him that January letter. Every time his nose had quivered the least bit to the scent of a new adventure or search, a Whipper had been right there with his whip. *Wheng! Whiiip!*

Even after he had been out of work for a year and a month, had worn his last pair of shoes down to the fake-leather insole, even after his hungry body had almost given him up, a Whipper had bothered to toy with him once more. And the Whipper had been clever with the way he had laid his bait.

Life and Death

Boy Almighty

*I quite deliberately tried to portray the doctor as he was. Dr. Abraham. The
actual doctor's name was Sumner Cohen. . . When I got through writing the
book I had him read it carefully to check everything out. When he got all done,
he said two things. He was quite curt about it. He said, one he had never really known how a patient felt, he had never really seen this whole problem
from the point of view of the patient. . . Two, everything was plausible in the
book. Nothing was overdrawn or too realistic or raw or anything. Except that
he thought the operation was atypical. . . I said to him about the operation,
"But it has happened." "Yes." "Well," I said, "sometimes a writer to make
his point has to take an atypical case or an atypical scene to point something
up."*

from The Whipper Described

ERIC PUSHED HIS MIND ahead to understand. He looked down at the papers
again:

*Sometimes I think that the universe is a chaos of parts, pieces, fluids, into which
organizations are working their way, making a living off the countryside as they go,
and dying after an effort. Measured against the strongest concept of duration that
we have, what is a life? A civilization? Both, as with organizations and organs, collapse, and the parts, once hitched to each other, separate, and break up, and com-
mingle again with the gray immensity of waste . . . until another temporal organization arises.*

Eric looked at Fawkes, narrowing his eyes. "Heck, aren't you loading the
same old gun with the same old powder and shot?"

"How so?" Fawkes smiled, as if he already knew what Eric was after.

"Well, take your words 'parts,' 'pieces,' 'fluids,' here. Aren't they the same
old cookies, units, stamped out of the same old mass of dough?"

"Yes. Of course. And that's the trouble. Science has not yet been able to work out a language, a set of tools that will come to grips with chaos. The evanescent organisms have a voice, but chaos does not. The only way we'll ever be able to describe chaos is to jump our world. Leave it."

"Chaos, huh. Well, that means that the Whipper wins again."

"Who?"

"The Whipper. The whip of the universe."

"Oh, that bird again. You've got Him on your mind, haven't you?"

"Well, sometimes I really believe He exists. I mean . . . He's like a person to me."

"Maybe so. Such persons make good scapegoats."

"Oh, but I'm not rationalizing."

"Oh, but you are."

"But I'm not."

"Sorry. I'm saying what I see."

Eric pondered. "Don't you believe the universe hates you?"

"No."

"You don't fear the universe?"

"No. Why should I? In fact, it's just possible that the universe, or the Whipper, fears me."

"Huh."

"Sure. Because I'm trying to be a scientist. And I look at Him as impersonally as He supposedly looks at me."

"Oh."

Fawkes' eyes became smoky with thought. "You see, the true Whipper is neither concerned nor unconcerned about us. He is a universe that has no knowledge of us. He can't have. Because he neither feels, nor hears, nor sees . . . nor probably knows."

Eric nodded. He looked vaguely into the dark corner of the room where once Huck had lain. An idea occurred to him. "You know, Fawkes, reading this, a man'd almost think you were writing your swan-song."

Fawkes grunted and sat up and reached for the papers and pulled them from Eric's unwilling hands. "Maybe I am."

Eric crossed his legs. "By the way, what has your temp been lately?"

"Oh. All right. Up a little." Fawkes dropped the notes into the bedstand drawer.

Eric grunted. Empty questions begot empty answers. He studied Fawkes, wondering what was going on in his mind. The light on Fawkes' bed shone angularly across his thin face, accentuating the out-thrusting forehead and nose and mustached upper lip. Eric was startled to see how bony-thin his remaining roommate was. Could Fawkes have slipped so much in one week? Or had the seven-day absence allowed him a fresh impression of his roommate?

"Fawkes, don't you feel well?"

Fawkes' eyes clouded. "Oh, I feel all right." He shifted the book from his chest to his raised knees.

"You look good." Eric recalled the smell of decayed excreta he had noticed as he came in from the fresh outdoors.

"I better look good. I'm going to have an operation tomorrow."

Eric gripped the edge of his bed. "Serious?"

"Extra-pleura pneumonolysis. Nothing really. When they get done, I'll be able to take treatments something like those you were getting. Your doctor was trying to collapse your lung there by injecting air between it and the pleura. In this deal, after the operation, they'll inject air between the pleura and the ribs."

"Why no pneumo for you?"

"Adhesions." Fawkes paused. "Yes, it's too bad, all right. But, we've got to hurry. My left lung is developing cavitation."

"Is your father coming?"

"No. It's not that important."

Eric nodded. He understood. This man, who had never irritated him, who had been a perfect roommate, who had been tolerant of every tantrum and idea of his, was a wonderful man to say that. And even now, dying perhaps, he had bothered to soothe a child. Eric remembered too that Fawkes had been willing to risk his precious lungs when Huck died. Eric thinned his lips to keep from blurting something sentimental. "What about a rib-sectioning for you?"

Fawkes gestured. "Too late for that. Bad heart. Just like father."

Tears circled Eric's eyes and gradually filmed them. He felt ashamed. Here he was floundering and roaring and crying around in this ward, thinking he was getting a pretty bad lashing from the Whipper, when all the while he had a roommate who, deathly ill, was not raising a hundredth as much fuss as he was. The Whipper was evoking from Fawkes no more than gentle comments. Eric looked down at his feet. "Tell me, how does this operation go?"

"Oh, it's really quite simple. Butcher Boy Stein'll cut off pieces of two ribs to make a hole just big enough for him to get his paw into my chest. Then he'll pull the pleura away from the ribs just like you would pull out a rubber inner tube that's stuck to the insides of an old tire casing. Then he'll fill the sack he's made with air and sew it up. When the wound's healed, you got a little pocket of air there, pushing the lung down."

"Say. I wonder. Why didn't Doc try that on me?"

"It's the last acey-deucey the doctor plays."

"Oh." He took a deep breath. "By God, Fawkes, I wish you a lot of luck."

"Luck won't do it. I've either got enough energy, or . . . I haven't."

"Man, you . . ." Eric turned to hide his face. He look into the dark corner where Huck had died.

"Well, Eric, it's all right. I learned long ago to expect changes." He sighed. "And some of them are good. Like getting new roommates."

Eric caught at a word. "Say, that's right. We'll soon be having a new roommate, won't we?"

"You will, you mean. And two of 'em. I'm going up on Critical tomorrow. For two months."

"But Moses, man, I'd like to keep you."

Fawkes did not reply.

Eric stood up and went to his stand and poured out a glass of water from his water-bottle and drank a little. After the country water on Mary's farm, the chemically treated fluid was bitter.

He got back into bed and settled into his pillow, thinking. He worked at cleaning his wick. Presently his flame steadied and lifted, and his vision opened. What if Fawkes should die? Should never come down from Critical again? He wished he were a surgeon, skilled. He looked out of the window. Long ago September sundown had flown. Purples at the western horizon had deepened to black. Just above the rim of earth the planet of love burned whitely.

He nodded to himself. This flame of Fawkes should be saved and burned in an American Athens. Fawkes should have offspring. Children. Two boys. A girl. Cups to catch his fuels.

Yet a child could never be Fawkes. The moment Fawkes died he would be gone. Just as one could not move a piece of flame from one place to another without moving the wood that burned, or the oil, or whatever the fuel might be, so no one could move a piece of a man's spirit without moving too, a piece of his flesh.

Besides, it would be terrible punishment for the child. One soul is burden enough for any temple, crumbling or gleaming in the sun. Two souls in one body would double the tears. The child would become twice as desperate to avoid a death. He would be twice as anxious to foist his spirits upon his children.

No, when a temple fell, the spirit in it should vanish too. It was best that a man returned to the universe the dust he had borrowed to live in and the ideas he had learned to live by.

Eternity. Eternity. Who knew the word? The idea? For each man, forever lasts from the moment he is born until the moment he dies.

He moved his head to look at Fawkes. Why, the man had returned to his reading. That Fawkes. Imperturbable orb of fire. And the book? Doughty's *Travels In Arabia Deserta*. That scripture cut from basalt by the fragile fingers of a poet equipped with the brain of a Zeus.

Eric stirred and sat up. He made up his mind that the flame of Fawkes should not vanish. His knowledges, his gifts, his spirit, had to be saved. They had to be captured into imperishable cantos. If Fawkes were but a man who had merely discovered a specific cure for tuberculosis, mankind could let him die with only a few tears trembled. But Fawkes was more. He was the hardy flame up front taking the first leap into the darkness ahead. It was he who really met the Whipper face to face.

Eric sat stilled for a moment.

Then an anguished flame leaped to the roof of his skull. It could not be. It could not. If Fawkes should die on the table tomorrow, he would live on. He had to.

Eric swore an oath to himself. He swore that he would get Fawkes down on paper and pass on to others the prevailing attitude of this man's noble wonder at life, his gently critical spirit, his unprejudiced curiosity, his roving mind quietly asearch for pure truth, little caring what the Whipper might say or do. Fawkes was the silver-brained Poet that had been wrestling for expression in the fleshes of mankind. Fawkes was the evidence that Chaos, the Whipper, could be encroached upon.

"Fawkes, man, can I see your operation tomorrow?"

"Why, I dunno. It's against the rules, I think."

"But, I . . . Look. If you request it, I can see it. You know that. You're a doctor too. And I want to see it."

There was a long silence.

Then Fawkes moved in his bed and put aside the book that he had been waiting to read and turned off his bedlight and said, "I understand. Of course you can."

The Whipper Strikes Again

MAN IS A SEALED LAMP.

At birth an infant is given a certain measure of oil, a certain length of wick, and a spark. The oil is energy, the wick hunger, and the spark enjoyment.

The father and mother and the uncles and aunts of the little infant fan the spark into the flame of manhood.

The flame burns, varyingly, for a lifetime.

When the oil has burned, or the wick shortened, the old flame fluts. It dwindles to the infant's spark again. Presently it dies.

Sometimes, when the flame is fading, a lamp-trimmer with a cunning hand will come. He will remove a little of the carbon. He will jostle the last few drops of oil against the wick. He will stretch the wick. And the flame will live a moment.

But after the extra drops have burned, the flame will die.

In each man there is only a certain measure to burn.

The walls and the floor of the operating room were of green tile. Indirect lighting came from the north window. Except for the sliding doors that opened upon an observers' gallery, it was the same room where Eric had been given his pneumothorax, and where the negro in his wrath had flicked a razor at Dr. Abraham.

When Eric slipped into the gallery above the table, he found two young University interns, cynical Dr. Sauer and hearty Dr. Hansen, watching the operation, which had already begun. Eric sat down quietly. He straightened the long white smock that a nurse had given him to wear. He adjusted the germ-collector mask.

Stiffened by a local anesthesia, Fawkes lay nervelessly on a table. It was tipped so that the left side of his chest lay four inches higher than his right. He lay with his head toward Eric. Eric could barely catch the vivid dart and flash of his eyes past the prominent brow.

To Fawkes' left stood the butcher-big Dr. Stein; to his right, gentle narrow-lipped Dr. Price. Both were clothed in white from their eyes to their elbows and ankles. Both wore opera-long rubber gloves. Nearby hovered Dr. Abraham, his face wrinkled, his brow bubbled with sweat. There were three nurses.

Dr. Stein wielded the scalpel, and talked. "Ted, you got the skin of a toad. Gray, and rotted t'hell."

Fawkes grinned a little.

Dr. Stein swore on. He cursed his luck. He wondered, aloud, when he would once again have the pleasure of cutting up the gentle flesh of a woman or of a sixteen-year-old lad. He cursed. He swore he was tired of cutting into the gray, dead, tubercular flesh of Phoenix patients. Christalmightygodtohellanyway.

For a little while, Eric inwardly condemned the braying, ass-eared Dr. Stein. But presently, as the operation progressed, and after he had studied Dr. Stein's orange pumpkin face, he began to understand that behind those craggy molds of flesh lived a kindly man who was continually being shocked by new hurts.

Peach-faced Dr. Price, in the meanwhile, stood by, blandly smiling.

Dr. Abraham leaned near, alert, silent.

No one else moved or spoke.

Eric watched so intently that his fisted hands soon pained him and he exercised them to ease the strain.

As Dr. Stein plowed on, he did not wait to hand the attending nurse his fouled instruments. Finished with a knife, he tossed it over his shoulder as if it were a corn ear and he an old-time cornshocker, and snatched at fresh gleaming one.

Soon Dr. Stein picked up an instrument resembling a pair of wire nippers. He gritted his teeth into a ferocious square as he tried to snap off the first rib. He growled "Fawkes, your ribs are as tough as oak roots."

Fawkes barely flinched. His brown eyes were alight with interest.

Aawwwrrrk.

"There. What a tough son of a bitch you are, Fawkes. Well, let's try the other end of it." He set the pincers and gripped.

Aawwwrrrk.

The bloody rib snapped over Dr. Stein's shoulder. It clattered to the floor, where a darting nurse jumped on it with a white napkin and covered it and covertly dropped it into a waste can.

Aawwwrrrk.

"Damn good thing we're not cannibals. How we'd cuss you if we were. Imagine having these god-damned ribs for supper."

Dr. Price laughed for the first time. "You know, the patients kid about that. When they're served spare-ribs, they always say, 'Yep, somebody's had a rib-clippin' today.'"

Dr. Abraham grinned momentarily.

Fawkes made a move as if he were about to say something.

Dr. Stein lifted his bloody nipper menacingly, and roared, "Accc! Shut up, damn you. Save your breath."

After a silence, Dr. Price chuckled, and mused, "You know, Stein, it's a good thing you're not in private practice, cussing the way you do. After a month of it, you probably wouldn't have a patient left."

"Oh yeh? I suppose you want me to operate like that suck-hole Dr. Sittaroni? What a racket he's got."

"Well, at least he makes a good living."

"Yeh. And how."

"Takes care of a lot of people. Averages a dozen an hour."

"Huh. And how. Look. Let's suppose you're a patient. All right. You come in. Okay. Sittaroni throws you up on a table. He rams a rubber glove up your sport, twirls it around a couple of times, says, 'Ten bucks. Come back Thursday. Next?'"

Everybody laughed.

"Sure he does!"

Aawwwrrrk.

"There. There's the son of a bitch." Dr. Stein heaved the second rib to one side. Like a foetal rabbit, it hopped around on the floor until a quick nurse caught it. Fawkes moved a little.

"What's up?" Dr. Stein leaned over him.

"Right lung. Short there."

All three doctors moved forward. The nurses moved nearer. Silent.

"Better?"

"No. It's a . . . spontaneous." Fawkes gasped. "It's tight!" He sucked wildly for breath. He wrestled like an infant being choked in its blankets.

"Catheter," snapped Dr. Stein.

Quickly Dr. Abraham pulled up a stand to the operating table near Fawkes' head. He plunged a catheter through the ribs and the pleura of the right chest. He pressed down firmly, drew air as rapidly as he dared.

The surgeons waited. Dr. Stein's brow wrinkled. Dr. Price remained bland.

"Better?"

"Much."

"All right. Now," said Dr. Stein, moving in again. "Now." He cut through the opening he had made in the chest barrel; then started his hand up underneath the uncut ribs.

Fawkes moved.

They stopped again.

"Hurry," whispered Fawkes.

"Adrenalin," ordered Dr. Stein.

This time Dr. Price moved in.

After a long moment, Fawkes whispered, "That's better." Shifting his body a little, he whispered, "God. Now I know how a patient feels. Now I know. I can use that."

Eric became conscious of a movement somewhere above Fawkes. He looked up. He was startled to see a reflection of Fawkes in a mirror above the table. Fawkes was looking into it, and at him, smiling.

Eric sat, stilled.

The men were silent. They hurried. There was a tenseness in the room, a tautness.

Again Fawkes gasped, "Spontaneous."

Dr. Abraham leaped forward to the right chest.

"Acccc . . . No. The other . . ."

Dr. Stein jerked away. "No!"

Eric stared. He had an impulse to jump up and tear the doctors away from Fawkes. He knew now why doctors were loath to let husbands see their wives in the act of giving birth to bloody babies.

Fawkes lay motionless.

In a calm voice Dr. Stein called out directions to the doctors as one calamity after another hit Fawkes. The doctors were servants to a king. "Adrenalin." Yes. Yes. "Left lung now." Yes. "Vomiting." Yes. "Adrenalin." Yes. How cool they all were. How calm Fawkes was. Eric almost gurgled with talk, with irrepressible excitement.

There was a sound of a door gently opening, of someone silently entering, of a faintly chuckling whisper.

Eric looked up at the mirror. Slowly Fawkes' bright, brown eyes became smoky, as if he had a thought and were searching for words to explain it. Then the smoke vanished and the eyes were blank.

Dr. Stein turned away. Slowly, almost casually, he drew the rubber gloves off his arms and hands and fingers, and took off the germ-collector mask, and walked heavily out of the room. A moment, and Dr. Price followed, mincing out on stiff thin legs.

Dr. Abraham glanced up, wild-eyed.

Eric closed his eyes and saw, a little to the right, and in a front row seat, the Whipper.

The Great Cat of the universe, stupid in its blinking and timeless repose, had opened its Pa-cold eyes, thrown out a paw, and slapped to death a tiny inquisitive ant.

I felt "Look buddy, you should have died but you didn't." I came out of that a raging bull.

Apples of Paradise

Footsteps in the Alfalfa

to Uncle Hank

WHEN THE SUN WARMS THE EARTH in early spring, seeds and roots stir with life, and sprouts come up tender and green and buds thicken the silhouettes of trees.

Wild life stirs too: muskrats poke rusty noses out of mud huts in the river bottoms, gophers emerge from their holes, male rabbits thump after female rabbits, bullsnakes catch their first field mice, and foxes come out and play on the hills.

Tame life becomes restless too: cows reach between barbwires for the first faint greens, brood hens cluck up their chicks, young sows stand patiently beneath impetuous boars, and geldings whinny lonesomely.

And human life stirs. Men get up in the morning, and yawn and stretch, and do the chores, and eat breakfast, and over a second cup of coffee muse out of the window at the countryside. Eyes half closed, muscles easy, men slowly formulate plans for the coming year, work out ways on how to make nature serve them, while the women behind the men clear off the table, and do their spring-cleaning, and get out the seeds for the garden.

It was after breakfast, and Frank Bramsted, a renter, was on edge. He was on his way back to an all-weather shed behind the barn where he had been up most of the night with Spot his favorite Shorthorn cow. Frank was afraid he was going to lose her. For two days running she'd been in labor. She was a red cow with white markings on her forehead and right front leg. She lay alone.

As Frank stepped through the door of the shed, Spot looked at him over her shoulder. The cow's soft doe eyes were dulled over. The wrack of birthing had thinned her to staves.

Frank stood over her. He took off his leather mittens. He next took off his cap and ran a hand through his milkweed hair. He saw that if she didn't deliver in the next few hours he'd have a dead cow as well as a dead calf on his hands.

He sighed. He stood on one leg and thought a while. He sighed again. He put his cap and mittens back on, then picked up a fork and went out to get some fresh bedding.

Straw whiskered against his face as he pulled at the sides of the strawpile. A few oat kernels trickled over his wrists. He imagined he could still smell last summer's harvest season in the straw, the dust and grime of the separator, the sandwiches and coffee his wife brought out to the men, the smoke of the old steamer engine. For a moment, as the warmth off the strawpile breathed over him, cold late March seemed but a dream.

Coming back to the shed with a good forkful, he found the rest of the milk cows staring silently at the door, alert to the sounds within. Like true mothers they'd come to sympathize with the laboring mother within. He choused them away before kicking open the door with his rubber boot.

He spread the straw around on the cold dirt floor. He pushed some under her. He wanted her to feel she was in a deep warm nest.

He set the fork against the wall and took off his mittens again and shoved them into a back pocket. He squatted down on his heels and patted her back. He stroked the hide over her jutting hip, stroked it hard enough to stir up skin dust. Red hairs caught in the rough corners of his fingernails.

The swollen cow moaned, stirred; then abruptly jerked.

Frank bent over her quickly, face wincing each time she struggled.

Again she convulsed; and groaned dolorously.

The groan was so human, so agonized, Frank couldn't stand it any longer. He jumped up and forearmed his way through the door, in his haste losing his mittens out of his back pocket. He strode rapidly across the yard toward the house.

He burst into the kitchen, found his tall wife Laura putting a few cobs in the flaming mouth of the kitchen range. "Say, Laura."

"What's up now?"

"Laura, I need some hot water . . . Oh, I see you got some ready on the back of the stove. Good." Frank tromped over, rubber boots squinching on the yellow-and-blue linoleum floor. He picked up the steaming kettle. "Good girl. Now. Will you do the old man a favor? Quick call Jack Matly. He's kind of a half-baked vet and should be able to help. Besides, he owes me a half day's work."

"Say!" Laura exclaimed, brushing back a curl of brown hair, blue eyes sharp, "say, what's the big idea? I had in mind usin' that water myself. To rinse out some clothes. And those dirty boots!"

Frank's jaw set. "No. I need it worse." And with that he rushed outdoors, striding stringy-legged across the yard.

When he got near the barn he remembered he needed some Lysol, so he detoured through the horse stalls to pick up a bottle of it from a medicine cabinet on the wall.

Back in the shed, he had just settled to his heels when Laura came in behind him. She had quick slipped on one of his jackets and his new blue cap.

She said, "Ah, a new mother, is it?"

"You dumright." Frank noticed that in his jacket and cap she looked a little like a girl playing grown-up in Dad's clothes.

"You sometimes get so worked up over almost nothing I thought I'd better come out and see."

"Did you phone Matly?"

"I did."

"Good. Well, now that you're here you might as well do some work. Here, mix some of this Lysol in the hot water there. While I go get me a broomhandle and a leather strap."

"All right."

He was back in a moment, shouldering through the door, breathing heavily.

"Frank, don't take on so," she said reprovingly. "Spot'll be all right. Shucks, womenfolk sometimes wrestle around three days before they're ready. And still have it born natural."

"I know, I know," Frank growled. He stared down at Spot a moment, studying her, then whipped off his faded blue jacket, slipped off his overall suspenders, took off his gray shirt, and peeled down the upper part of his underwear. His slim muscled body was so white and hairless it took on a luminous hue. He shivered. He sniffed. He stuck a long prying finger in his ear, twisted it around, and wiped it on his overall. "I dunno, but that danged ear's been ringing all morning for some reason."

"Frank, you'll catch your death of cold, all bare like that."

"Nah."

"Frank, really, you will."

Frank shrugged. "I should worry about that now."

Laura stirred the Lysol-treated water with a stick. Steam rose from the pail. "Besides, why don't you call the veterinarian?"

"Have you got the money?"

"Health first, debts after."

"Huh. Words are cheap." Frank soaked his hands in the astringent. "Jiminy whiskers! That Lysol bites t'beat the band."

"That's because you always got sores on your hands, Frank. If you wasn't always so much in a rush to do your work, you wouldn't get them sores. Just look at them hands now. They look like poor potatoes with all them scabs."

Frank knelt beside the cow, mumbling to himself. That woman. She could find fault with perfection itself. Aloud, he said, "You know, it could be that we got a breech here. It just could be." He explored from an awkward position. "By golly, that's just what it is. A breech."

"You'll have to get the vet then, won't you?"

"No."

He washed his entire arm in the mixture. When he finished, he said, "Laura, you get down on your knees there, and hold her head close so she can't get a look at me. If there's one thing I can't stand it's an animal looking at me in pain while I'm trying to help it."

"Me? On my knees in this dirt?"

"Sure. Might as well make yourself useful. And when she raises a fuss, twist her nose some. Hard, even, if you have to. Get her 'tention off me."

He waited until Laura had settled into the straw and had Spot's eyes hidden from him. Then he once more explored where the calf lay in numb sleep. He swore softly to himself. "A case of a goose egg in a thimble again."

The cow twitched.

"Whoa, bossy. Take it easy, girl."

"How is it?" Laura asked. Her voice was pitched higher than usual.

"Nothing yet."

He stood up slowly. "Well, like you say, no use rushing things." He rinsed his arm. Goose pimples stood out on the skin of his arms and back. Quickly he slipped into his upper clothes again. "Whoof. That was hard work." He bent over and patted Spot on the back. "Well, old girl, it's up to you now. I've done all I could for you. Get to work."

They waited.

It was quiet in the cattleshed. Shafts of sunlight daggered the dusty air. Sometimes a low wind moaned in the loose shingles over head. The door swung a little and creaked on its rusty hinges.

Frank liked such quiet moments with his wife. Except that this time he found his mind latching onto something he hated to think about. Why was Laura barren? Ten years married and still no kids. There hadn't even been a miscarriage. Was God punishing them for some sin they'd done?

There was the sound of a car out on the yard then, of a motor being gassed to a high pitch, and then the choking cough of pistons stilling.

"Jack," Frank said.

"Probably."

In a few moments Jack Matly's broad shoulders filled the low door. Jack hadn't shaved and his black beard looked like a matted brush. Jack had thin narrow lips and wide heavy jowls. Where Frank was long, Jack was stout.

Jack smiled. "Trouble?"

"Trouble?" Frank suddenly felt better. "I'll say. This cow's gonna have a calf the size of a horse."

Laura smiled up at Jack. "Hello," she said. She pulled her dress down over her knees.

"Hi, Laura."

Frank said, "Well, how does she look to you?"

Jack studied Spot. "You fussed with her much?"

"Some."

Jack bit his lip reflectively. "Hmm. You're always gonna have trouble with her." Jack took off his cap and brushed back his hair. His hair was bristly black and it lashed over his hands. He scratched his scalp a few times and then captured his wild hair under his cap again. "How long's she been quiet like that?"

"Say, that's right," Frank said. "She's been stone-still for quite a spell now."

"You probably did wrong," Laura said.

Frank shot her a look.

A grin slowly spread over Jack's hard bristly face. He said good-naturedly, "Frank, you make more fuss over that cow than most men do over their wives."

"Well, why not? Spot's out of Old Beaut, one of the best cows that ever saw the light of day. Her line goes back as far as the Bramsted line itself. Why, Old Beaut was so good we could milk her from both sides at the same time. A reg'lar river of milk."

"I still don't see why that makes Spot such an all-killin' matter."

Suddenly Spot moved. She struggled a moment; then lay still again.

"Hey!" Frank said.

Jack said matter-of-fact, "Hmm. It'll take a couple of hours yet."

"Jack, you sound a little like you think Spot's gonna die."

"I'm only sayin'."

Frank dipped the leather strap in the treated water.

"You going to help her anyway?" Jack asked.

"That's the gen'ral idee."

"She ain't ready."

Frank's lips thinned. "And I say she's gotta be." He reached gently inside and fastened the strap in a loop around the numb calf's slippery feet and tied the other end of the strap midway on the broomhandle. He settled into a pulling position.

"Well, if you're bent on helping her contrary, easy does it then," Jack said. "Don't hurry it along too fast."

"That's what I'm aimin' to do."

"I was just sayin'."

Laura said, "Gosh, I wish she'd hurry. I've got so much to do in the house this morning. Spring cleaning. Washing clothes."

Frank tilted his head to one side and burned a look at her.

"Well, who's holding you back?"

"What?"

"Go on. We don't need you here now."

Laura flushed. She got up from where she was sitting beside Spot's head. "Of all the . . . First he steals my hot water. Then when I come out here of my own accord, offering to help him, he tells me—"

"Go on, I said. Go. Get out of here."

Laura whirled and left, slamming the heavy door.

"Darn wimmen," Frank muttered.

Jack sat down in Laura's place beside the cow's head. He got out his makin's and began rolling himself a cigarette. "Frank, you shouldn't take it out on your wife. It's none of my business, but—"

"She has it comin'."

Jack licked his cigarette carefully and then smoothed it between his fingers. "I know a lot of fellers here'bouts who'd give their right arm to have married Laura. She's a queen if I ever saw one."

"They don't know the half of it."

Jack scratched a match across his taut pantleg. Instantly a flame flared up bright and very scarlet in the dusky shed. "From where I sit, Frank, it's hard to see that." Jack held the flame to his cigarette. He puffed. A fine mellow smell filled the shed. "I'd trade wives with you at the drop of a hat."

"Your kids thrown in?"

"Welll, not them of course." Jack chuckled. "I guess not."

Frank's lips twisted some. "That's why you don't know the half of it."

Jack spat out a crumb of tobacco. He rubbed his black beard. The rubbing of it sounded like sandpaper being stroked across a rough board. "Frank, changing the subject, how come a bright feller like you still monkeys around with tight cows? Why don't you get yourself an easy breed once?"

"There's nothing wrong with Spot. She's just temperamental, is all. When she's ready, she'll give."

Again Spot's belly humped up. This time Frank pulled with her. The purple feet of the calf appeared. She relaxed. Frank eased up.

"Easy does it," Jack said.

"Give me a drag of that smoke."

Jack held the cigarette to Frank's lips.

Frank took a deep puff and exhaled. Smoke streamed from his nostrils. "Thanks." He spat over the cow.

Jack took a last puff and then crushed out the cigarette beneath his workshoe. "Frank, really, you ought to get rid of these tight cows."

"I know what I'm doin'."

Another spasm gripped Spot. With Frank helping, the wrinkled nose of the calf appeared.

Frank threw Jack a wild look. "Say, quick dip your hands in that Lysol there and help her a little."

Jack wetted his hands in the pail and quick slipped his fingers around the calf's head.

Spot's effort broke, and she sagged.

Puffing, shaking his head, Frank said, "Whew! What a fuss it is to get born."

Thick body hunched over spread thighs, Jack breathed heavily too. "You can say that again."

"Here she comes again!"

Suddenly the calf emerged, sliding into Frank's lap, the bag-of-waters breaking over the straw.

Jack smiled, still hunched over.

"Ah," Jack said.

Frank said, "Quick. Clean off its nose."

Jack brushed the film off the calf's soft nose; then whacked the calf over the belly. A shiver stirred through the helpless tumble of bones and fur.

"Again!"

Jack did.

The little creature coughed. Blew. And was alive.

"Ah," Frank said.

Jack smiled, still hunched over.

Frank let down his shoulders. "What a battle that was."

Jack picked up a short twine string lying loose in the straw and tied the umbilical cord close to the calf. He tied another string on Spot's end of it. Then he got out his jackknife, dipped it in the treated water, and severed the purple cord.

"Whoof," Frank said, getting to his feet, brushing off his overalls. "What a relief. I'm glad that's over."

Jack stood up too.

Still lying in the straw, the young cow turned her head, and lowed, and with a rough pink tongue began cleaning off her firstling.

After a while the calf got the notion, and with a crude lunge, first on its front feet and then on its rear, got up. It staggered around in the straw, gasping some.

The men chuckled.

Soon the calf found the cow's white satiny udder. It nosed it, bumped it, at last found a teat. It suckled eagerly. The other three teats began to drip pink milk.

"Say, I forgot to look," Frank said. "Why, it's a girl calf! A fine little spotted girl calf just like her ma. White ring on the right foreleg and a star on its forehead. A deadringer."

Jack tipped back his cap. "Girl, huh? Probably another one of them blamed tight cows of yours."

"It's gonna have a nice red color too." Frank stood looking down at the calf, resting on one foot, hands hanging.

Jack cleaned his knife by sticking it into the earth several times.

He wiped his hands in a clutch of straw.

At last, knowing he was already late with the morning chores, Frank turned to Jack and said, "Well, neighbor, much obliged."

"Don't mention it."

"Don't know what I'd done without you."

"Easy does it." Jack waved a hand, and left.

Then Frank picked up his fork and went out to get some fresh straw. As he stooped through the door he spotted his mittens. He picked them up.

But the next morning, when Frank hustled out to have a look at mother and child, he found Spot dead on the straw-strewn floor.

Stunned, Frank slowly settled on his heels and hid his face. His wide shoulders sagged and his back humped over.

After a while, recovering, looking up, he picked up a straw from the floor and began chewing it.

Yes, what was the use? There were so many things cutting away at his hopes and dreams. Drouth, grasshoppers, floods, hails, rats, low prices, hog cholera. And now a cow dying in calf-birth.

He chewed viciously on the straw. Farming was the biggest gamble this side of heaven. In no other walk of life did a man put out so much in the form of sweat and money, and expect to get so little, with so slim a chance of getting it, as in farming. There was no two ways about it—farming was for the dumbheads.

A dead cow. While outdoors it was springtime. That time of year when the earth was beginning to warm and seeds itched to get going. When a man began to think of the future.

A dead cow. His favorite at that. What a sign that was for the coming year.

Frank chewed the straw to shreds. He remembered how the signs of previous springs had been different, had in fact fired them up. Once it was pigs that had come in, tens in the night, a hundred in two days, a great birthing of little wriggling baloneys from the bellies of grumpy sows. Another time it was a surprise batch of chicks that had made themselves known in the haymow. Fluttering, wings trembling, safe and warm beside the chute funneling warmth from the cows below, they'd survived an early spring frost. Yes, other years the signs had been good ones.

But not this year.

Frank ruminated. In a way, a man was foolish to hang all his hopes on one sign. Such things were old-wiver superstitions. The real thing to do was to work hard, to do one's best, and then to just sit back and wait—and wonder if it would be the earth's pleasure to come up with a crop. And like as not, the less a man expected, the more likely he was to get that bumper crop, that one big year that all men dreamed of.

Looking up, Frank saw that the morning sun had come out and was trying to pry through the perpendicular cracks of the shed. He sat quietly on his heels for a few minutes more, and then, hearing a little rustle, turned on his boot toes in the straw. Spot's little heifer calf. He had completely forgotten about it. The calf had awakened from its first night's sleep and now stood head down, bumping its nose into the prostrate mother's cold stiff udder.

Frank stood up. "Well, I know what Laura's gonna think when I tell her that Spot's dead. Having babies has its dark side too."

Grimly Frank lifted the fresh calf in his arms. The smell of birth in the matted hide was like the smell of smoke from a reviving wood fire. He kicked open the door and strode across the thawing barnyard and then, jostling the lively calf up to free a hand, opened the door of the calf barn. He kicked the door closed behind him. Like a bachelor bringing an illegitimate child to an orphanage, he dropped the calf in with a bunch of older calves.

The older ones stared at the newcomer, tails lifted; the little calf stared at them, tail lifted. Abruptly the new calf bellered. Startled, both Frank and the older calves jumped back. Then a slow grimace twisted Frank's lips. Poor little jigger, he thought. It'll have to drink the milk of a strange mother.

Spot, the beauty, was dead. And all the feed and all the care he'd put into her was gone, thrown away. It would take months before he could bring up her calf to the point where it would be come as valuable. And it might take years to fill that big hole in his heart.

Frank caught himself. He rubbed his nose. There was no use crying over spilled milk. What was done was done. A good man always worked from where he was.

Stepping outdoors, he stopped a moment to collect himself. He had a look around at his farm to reassure himself it was still worth while. He didn't own the place, since he rented it from a boyhood chum named Tom Reilly who was now the local banker, but he had lived on it for so many years, and had dreamed of owning it for so long, that he considered it to be as good as his.

Wind-whipped maples screened the buildings on the west and north sides. Inside their protective spread, a shrunken strawpile tottered like an undermined mushroom. A few head of red-and white Shorthorn cattle, some steers, just now feeding from it, had rubbed their backs and necks around the base of it, chasing each other sometimes like children playing tag around a house. Their chasing had worn a deep groove around it. Brown-winged sparrows spurted from the old strawpile butt and then congregated in a bare armed maple for a complaint against the steers. Nearer the barn, and away from the trees, a windmill clanked. Echoes from it spanged off the sides of the farm buildings. The vane on the red barn nosed back and forth in the rising southwest breeze. Where the manure pile caught the sun on the south side of the barn, flies were festering.

Spring had come. Time to pull in the belt a little, a few notches. Time to roll up the pantleg, out of the mud. Time to get the pig pens ready for the brood sows, to clean out the coops and brooders for the setting hens.

Looking within, looking out, intent, he could feel the slumbering earth slowly opening its ears and eyes, sleepily stirring. Soon rain would come. And sunshine. And warm nights.

She was like a fickle woman. Old Dad Bramsted, who with Ma lay buried beneath a cottonwood beside the Big Sioux River, sitting in his rocking chair on the front porch, used to say, "To get some thing out of her I always had to be ready to take advantage of her goodhearted streaks. I had to be sure it wasn't my fault that my grain didn't catch the big rains. Because as sure as shootin', some years when I hadn't worked hard enough, she'd get liberal, and I'd miss my big year. The one we all lay back for."

Frank got out his corncob pipe and lit it. He nodded to himself. Yes, all in all, when everything was said and done, you had to hand it to the women. Even without kids, Laura'd made him a good working partner. How many wives offered to do the milking when things went wrong on the yard? Not many.

He began to look forward to the evening, after supper. It had been on just such a spring day last year that she had shown sudden want for him. As long as a woman felt that way there still was a chance.

Her warm desire sometimes made him wonder a little. He knew her passion was a bit unusual. Stories he'd heard from neighbors told him that. Once he'd asked Jack Matly pointblank if his wife, too, ever showed hunger for him. And Jack, eyes suddenly narrowing with dark envy, had said, "Not my wife. She's the old-fashioned kind."

Frank looked over the yard again, puffing on his corncob. There was no doubt about it. Laura was a fine helpmate. A fine good woman. And it was his duty, as a good husband, to overlook those times when she got mad because she still didn't have a baby. Laura wasn't much different from the earth. Sometimes the earth got mad too. The earth had been known too to strike out at anything in sight, when something bothered her in crop time. Just hit out and whatever was there got hit. The earth, for just some reason like that, had struck Spot and had taken her back. The earth was a great deal like Job said the Lord God was: the earth gives and the earth takes away, blessed be the name of the earth.

What fools men were to live in the city. Even in such a small town as Wodan. Tom Reilly his boyhood chum and now his land lord had a good home. But did Tom enjoy the bloodless gold in his bank vaults like he, Frank, enjoyed the foxy earth? Or friend Hans the barkeep who slopped out barley suds in Al's Cafe, who kept saying to each and every customer the same thing over and over, "Between me and you and the fence post, how's every little thing, huh?"—was he happy? There was nothing like good hard work in black dirt. Nosiree.

Frank knocked the ashes out of his pipe. "Well, I guess I better call up the rendering works." Muttering, he added, "And Laura will have something to say about that, too. Well, she's right. I should've called the vet."

He put through a call to the rendering plant on the old style wall telephone in the kitchen. Next he filled the range with dried corn cobs, building a fire that would last until either he or Laura returned from the milking.

Stepping outdoors, as he went out through the yard gate, he happened to glance up—and saw above the kitchen chimney a wisp of smoke thickening into a little cloud. Still another sign, this time a good one? Maybe lots of rain this year?

At that very moment he heard the moan of a cow in trouble. He jumped. It couldn't be Spot. Because Spot was as cold as a stone in Siberia.

He stood alert in the middle of the yard, ears going all over the farm. In his mind he ticked off each of the milk cows, wondering which one of them could possibly be calving. He'd marked the breeding dates on the calendar behind the stanchions and there was not a single cow due.

Unless it was Old Kicker. Ah. Now he remembered. Old Kicker had jumped the fence some nine months ago, had gone over to visit Jack Matly's bull. He'd made no record of that, of course, except to burn a batch of cuss words at her for being a whore cow.

He heard the dolorous moan again. Deep.

At that he broke into a run, going around the side of the barn, then across the barnyard to the other side of the mushroom straw pile.

There she was. Old Kicker. And man, had she strayed. Had she run off the reservation. Because there suckling her was as fresh and lively a bullcalf as ever a cow had throwed. And with Jack Matly's tombull markings too.

Frank slapped his thigh. Yessiree. Another calf. And this one an easy-come. Spot was maybe dead but the other cows kept right on bringing in their young.

Frank went over and sat down on his heels beside the calf. He patted it on the back. Ahh. Now this was something a man didn't mind telling the wife about.

Just then their collie Rover came running out of the barn and leaped on him. Before he could put up his hands, the dog licked his face. Gently he pushed the gold-haired dog away and stood up. Rover sat down on his haunches, soft eyes attentive and affectionate, tail wagging. Frank rubbed the dog's head. Rover jumped up then and licked his hand.

There was an angry bellow. A rushing hurtling body loomed up. Frank turned on his toes, ready to jump. He caught sight of Old Kicker's bold white face coming on him, horns low. Rover let out a yelp, sprang away on quick springy feet, yipping out a string of frightened barks. Old Kicker veered after the dog, leaving Frank standing safe in the straw.

Frank quick whistled at the dog, and then, with a sharp command, sent it on into the barn. Old Kicker stopped, lowed after the dog a second, and then, slowly turning, stalked back to her calf, kicking up loose straw as she went.

Frank laughed again. What a mother she made. In her old eyes Rover was just another wolf hungry for a little fresh calf meat.

Frank waited until the calf found the udder, then went to the barn to help Laura finish the milking.

Stepping through the door, he heard the sound of a filled pail banging lightly against the side of the alley. Looking up, he found Laura eyeing him.

"Oh. Hi. How far are you?"

"Done."

"Already?" He quirked up a blond brow.

"Sure. I even milked the bull."

He grinned. "You must've gone right smart," he said. "Fine."

He picked up a pail and a five-gallon can of milk. Laura picked up two other pails. They walked out through the door after each other and Frank closed it behind them with a soft kick of his rubber boot.

As they stepped across the yard, Frank surveyed the contents of the three pails and the can, and observed, "The cows could use a little of that green stuff again."

"Huh, so could I," Laura said. "I'm sick and tired of winter. All that dirt and mess of melting time."

"Hmm."

"It's always so dirty at the end of the winter. Dirty. But then when things turn green, the houseyard and the pastures and the grainfields, why, then everything seems to perk up again. Even the house picks up."

"That it does."

They entered the milkshed. Frank removed the cheesecloth cover on the separator tank and then poured in the milk. The flat oval tank just held the morning's milking.

When Frank turned around from the pouring, he found Laura standing in the doorway, her back to him, looking out over the yard and its morning quiet.

Early sunlight shone in her hair, lighting up its deep brown to an auburn halo. Frank looked past her. Hens fluttered and peeked in the sunyard. Beyond them the maples shone with spring's wetness. He could hear Spot's new calf bawling in the calf barn.

Then, his eyes coming back to Laura, he saw her smiling, saw little wrinkles form in the flesh under her blue eyes. And watching her, he couldn't help but look at her with pleasure. Except for the crow's-feet she looked almost exactly like the girl he'd married ten years ago.

He remembered their first year of married life. Ah. How happy they'd been. So happy. They went to sleep laughing. They awakened laughing. That first summer life was an endless unrolling of quips and kisses and pranks. While underneath burned an almost livid passion. Sometimes they couldn't wait till nightfall. They tumbled into each other's arms in the tall grain. They became warm together under the clittering cottonwoods. They made rough love on the musky hay in the mow. And always they came away smiling, wide-eyed with love, alert to living.

Why, in those days they'd been ready for everything, could do anything. They were sure they could clear up the few debts they had, buy the farm they rented from childhood chum Tom Reilly, start a good breed of cattle, and fill the houseyard with playing tots.

Frank choked as he thought about it. The real fact was though that they hadn't cleared up their debts. They hadn't bought the land from Tom. They hadn't filled the houseyard with children. All they had to show for their ten years' work was a few good cows. And that special calf of Spot's.

He looked around at the milkshed. How neat Laura kept it. There was the brush she used to wipe the separator spouts with, so clean the bristles showed pale. There was the copper oilcan, shiny. There were the towels, neat and in order. How could a woman who was so handy in so many things, how could she fail to bear him children?

Thinking about Old Kicker again, it abruptly occurred to him that, actually, sign had come. Good sign, that is. The thing to fire their hearts. He'd just been too thick-headed to realize it. Even though he'd looked right at it.

Frank scraped out his corncob with his jackknife and filled it afresh with a few shakes of tobacco from his leather pouch. He lighted up. Puffing, he looked out at the shelved land on the bluffs where soft clouds were drifting eastward. Then, smelling the creamy milk cooling in the tank behind him, he stirred and reached out a hand and touched Laura's arm. "We're gonna do her, ain't we, Laura?"

She turned to face him, surprised. "Why, what makes you ask that?"

"Nothing. Nothing. Except that all that time you thought I was fixing up Spot and her calf snug and warm, I was just sitting there looking at her and wondering where I was going to get the gumption to tell you I found Spot dead this morning. And wondering if it was worth going on with us still having no—"

She tightened. "Spot dead?"

"Yes."

"Dead?" Her eyes widened very blue and big. "My God, another cow dead." She leaned against the doorjamb. "I told you we should've got the vet."

"I know."

"I told you."

"Yes. Well, we'll just have to make it up somewheres else now."

"Another mother dead." Her eyes filled with quick tears. "I thought it was funny it took you so long."

"Though we did save her calf."

It took Laura a moment to get out the next words. "Saved the calf? Well, at least that's something."

Frank puffed on his corncob. "But what I was gonna say was that at the same time I saw our sign this morning too."

"Oh?" Laura winked the tears out of the corners of her eyes.

Frank laughed softly. "Old Kicker."

"Her?"

"Yes. She just now calved in the strawpile. Remember that time I cussed her up and down for jumping the fence and running over to Jack Matly's place?"

Laura nodded.

"Well, that's when it must've happened."

Laura said nothing. She still seemed somewhat stunned. More tears appeared in her eyes.

He patted her shoulder. "Come," he said, "let's look at it this way. Spot is dead, yes. But at the same time Little Spot's come. Along with Little Kicker."

He liked the warm feel of Laura beneath his hand, liked the submissive, the sad quality in her bearing, and it occurred to him that if he was willing to plant seeds in the earth on the gamble that it would produce him a crop each year, he could take the same gamble with his wife.

Rain did not fall in June. Frank, cutting alfalfa west of the house, remembering last year's bitter drouth, kept scanning the skies for rain clouds.

Though things weren't too bad yet. The grain across the fence was still luxuriant, nodding with heavy heads. The cornfields farther on sparkled green with morning dew. And the pasture grass was still ankle-high in the draws.

Dew also lay deep in the green alfalfa. In some places it weighted down the straggly stems. Fresh heady scents came wafting off the waving purple blossoms.

Corncob lit and going well, Frank worked on, driving his team of bays along, sometimes sniffing the perfumed air, sometimes puffing on his bone pipestem. He watched the long scissoring arm of the mower, wet with the sop of cut alfalfa, move stealthily into the root world where it scared up crickets and grasshoppers. Sometimes the tiny fear-crazed creatures hit so hard against his stiff overall pantlegs they stunned themselves and fell into the mown stalks like tiny pebbles.

He kept looking up. Vaguely he sensed an ominous quality in the air. He had the odd feeling that something was about to happen. Sniffing, rolling his high shoulders, drawing his lips into a thin defensive grimace, he waited and watched.

Coming to the end of a round, putting his pipe away, he stopped to grease the machine. Though he loved the old mower, he wasn't too sure of it. Many of its moving parts were badly worn. The sickle-driver rattled and pounded, and the grease cup riding it was always hungry. The boxing which held the flywheel ball bearings had threatened to burn out all morning. It sucked oil like a tornado. Patiently, like a veterinarian fixing up an aching old horse with salve and rubdowns, he doctored the old machine along. Finished with the greasing, Frank wiped his fingers on his grimy overall.

He'd settled into his seat again, and had just clucked up the horses Nellie and Kelley, when he remembered that this was the day the rent was due. Tom Reilly was coming out that very morning to see him about it. Frank sucked in a breath. God, yes. That was it. That was why he'd felt offish all morning. Because, dad nab it, the truth was he didn't have the money to meet the rent. Besides which he still owed some on last year's installments.

He drove along feeling whitish around the gills. He'd been putting off seeing Tom for days, hoping that something would come up so he could have good news for Tom. But it hadn't, and now he was in for it.

Out of the corner of his eye he saw Rover come running across the fallen alfalfa. The sight of the golden collie made him feel better. He reached back and patted Rover on the head. Rover ran panting, red tongue long, behind him.

Tying the lines on a lever, letting the bays follow the edge of the standing alfalfa by themselves, he pulled out his corncob again and filled it thoughtfully. He lighted it equally thoughtful. He puffed deeply, hardly noting the taste of the smoke. He shifted in his seat, scratched himself, then, absently, took up the lines again.

He watched the stalks of alfalfa fall in staggering columns across the moving sickle. The stalks were like soldiers who, though always courageously advancing, could never quite get to him because of the deadly gunfire of his sickle.

Tireless swallows swooped past the horses, looking for flies and insects. A flock of redwing blackbirds chattered in a gnarled maple nearby. Three tall cottonwoods near the west end of the field sparkled in the sun. Farther west, the trees hid the Big Sioux River and the rising folds of Dakota land. Overhead, a thin wisp of a white cloud curled ceaselessly against a blue sky.

Frank shivered. He wished Laura were around. He glanced at his dollar watch. Ah. It was time for her to bring him lunch. Any minute now.

The day warmed. Sweat trickled down his face and along his neck. Wet stains spread across his faded blue shirt.

Soon he became conscious of another kind of warmth. His first thought was of Laura, but after a few seconds, when the thought of her barrenness came to mind, the secret vagary switched images, and he saw instead Bertha Matly, Jack's oldest daughter, supple and budding, especially that time he found her milking in the barn and smiling up at him from behind the flank of a cow. Sweet slim Bertha. What a cuddlesome sagehen she would be.

Then he missed Rover. He quick glanced around the field. When he couldn't spot the dog, he stood up on the moving rocking mower, trying to sight it in the tall green legumes. He cursed. That dummed dog was probably sitting somewhere in the unmown alfalfa. First thing a man knew the dog would wind up cut in half. Like the time the sickle had accidentally cut through a nest of soft young bunnies. He remembered how their mother had so lost her wits on the appearance of the strange snaking sickle she'd deserted the nest in a single tremendous bound.

He stopped the horses. He called the dog, whistling sharply. Again. Again. Then he called it by name. "Here, Rover. Here, boy. Here." Finally, yes, the stalks of the alfalfa began to flow toward him on the other side of the horses. And then in a moment the golden dog emerged, red tongue drooling, leaping lightly over the sickle.

Shocked to see how close the dog came to the deadly sickle, that the dog had shown no fear of it, Frank looked down at the dog severely. "Say there, old fellow, if you can't be more careful around that thing you'll have to go home."

Rover wagged his tail. Tongue lolling, smiling, he looked up at Frank full of love.

"Hmm, maybe at that you better go home. You ain't doing much good out here."

Rover's mouth snapped to. He looked up puzzled at Frank.

"Yes, you better go home. Go on. Go. Get."

Rover turned, slowly, and slinked off a ways.

"Go on!"

Rover sat down, alternately dropping and wagging his long gold brown tail.

"Go on. Go home. Go on!"

Again the dog ran a ways, cowering; then turned, wagging its tail, looking at him hopefully.

"Go on! March!"

The dog continued to slink away, every now and then looking over its shoulder to see if Frank hadn't changed his mind.

Frank shifted in his seat. Rover meant no harm. He watched Rover step slowly through the fallen alfalfa until he reached the houseyard where he turned and sat beside a fence post, looking mournfully out to him.

Frank sat smoking his pipe awhile. Now he was sure something was up. Something beyond just that the rent was due. Luckily, this time, he had wondered where the dog had run off to. But the next time something worse might pop up. Narrowing his eyes, he looked back at the yard again. Yes, the dog was still there.

The minute he'd got up that morning things had been off. There was that broken sickle he'd found in the mower. He'd been lucky to spot it. Suppose he'd gone to the field with it broken? Starting up, one of the blades could have easy flown in his face, or hit a horse, setting off a runaway. Or worse still, the broken sickle might have jammed the old mower and wrecked it. Funny, too, how the sickle seemed freshly broken, as if some intruder had come in the night with a hammer and had deliberately cracked it.

Then he grimaced. Ha. He was getting spooky. He had goblins in the head.

He clucked up the horses. He watched the sickle closely. Sniffing, he threw quick glances over his shoulder all the while that he kept one eye on the rattling driver under him. He filled the oil holes as he bumped along.

There was a sudden squeal. He jerked on his seat. "Whoa!" he yelled, and hauled back on the lines. The horses stopped short.

He threw the mower out of gear and jumped down to the sickle. A bronze pheasant cock, bright, glinting, belly cut open, gasped up at him, eyes fierce, vindictive.

Frank heaved a sigh. Thank God. It was only a bird.

He stared down at the bright feathers, still trembling a little. Then all of a sudden he cursed. What in the blazes was up any way? Angry, he picked up the flopping pheasant, caught its head between his fingers, and with a flip of the wrist snapped off its head. Searching through the toolbox he found a piece of baling wire and hung the bird from the seat of the mower. He and Laura would have fresh fowl for supper.

Before getting on the seat again, he kicked through the standing alfalfa to chase up the cock's mate. Pheasants often went about in pairs. He found nothing. The hen had probably run for its life into the deep grass under the fence. Grumbling, he started up the mower again.

It was when he was oiling and greasing the machine the next time around that his eyes happened to light on an odd design in the mown alfalfa. It was as if someone had scuffed through the fallen stalks and had kicked them into little mounds. He could even follow the trail of the stranger's footsteps. Seven feet apart they were, and they stretched in from the east side of the field, from the houseyard, and came toward him. He tightened inside. The stranger, or whatever it was, was right on top of him.

Then footsteps did sound nearby and he bounded up. "My God! Oh. Laura. You!"

Laura laughed. "Why, Frank Bramsted, you're white! You look like you've seen the devil himself."

Frank looked down, sheepish. "Well, maybe I have."

"Oh, Frank, come now."

"Lady, it ain't no laughing matter. All morning long I've been having a funny feeling that something's up." He looked up at the sky, quick, then at his hands. "I dunno."

"Piffle. Come, you better sit down here and drink your lemonade before it gets warm. I just now took it out of the cooler."

Groaning, he settled in the cut green hay. "Cold lemonade sounds good at that."

She sat beside him. "Frank, are you having one of your funny spells again?"

"No. This is different."

She gave him a friendly push. "Aw, Frank, you've just got a guilty conscience about something, that's all."

He wondered if she'd read his mind about Jack Matly's oldest daughter Bertha. "Maybe it's that Tom Reilly has been on my mind. He's coming out for the rent today, you know." He cocked his head, thinking. "No, it's more than that."

She opened the lunch basket and laid out dried-beef sandwiches and raisin cake. She got out two cups and from a small sweating pail poured some pale lemonade. "Here, this'll make you feel better."

He took a bite; then sipped some lemonade.

She looked around at the blue sky, eating and drinking at the same time. "I haven't noticed anything odd. Seems like a fine day to me."

Frank mumbled something with his mouth full of bread and dried beef.

"What?"

Frank swallowed and cleared his throat. "Take that broken sickle I found this morning. Last night I put it in, new sharpened. Came by right after breakfast and there it was, broke."

"Aw, you probably broke it yourself when you put it in."

"No. Fact is, I ran the mower by hand a little last night just as I was about to leave and it worked swell. That's the last thing I did.

"Man, man, what a nestful of worries you are."

"And that reminds me, there was something else funny this morning. When I went to do the chores I found five dead chickens in the coop."

"Oh?"

"Sure. And it wasn't weasels, either. There wasn't a mark on them broilers. Why, they didn't even look sick. Just dead. For no reason at all."

Her mouth hung open. Small bits of chewed food lay plain on her tongue. Then her mouth snapped to. "Oh, Frank, now you're trying to scare me."

"No, I'm not."

"Aw, it's just your guilty conscience, is all."

"Noo."

Abruptly her manner changed, and she said quietly, "Speaking of the devil, here he comes now."

"What?" Frank jerked around. "Where? Oh." He saw a car turn into their lane. "Tom Reilly."

"Yes. Him."

Frank's manner changed then too. He said sourly, "Good old Tom. Always johnny-on-the-spot for his money."

Laura got up, bread crumbs rolling down her blue dress. "The old pinch-penny. You'd never think he once was your chum. The old Judas."

"Well, actually, it's not him so much. It's his old man."

Laura quickly drank the rest of her lemonade. "Finished?"

"Guess so." Frank got to his feet too. "What's the hurry?"

"I don't like Tom. I'm going back to the house, if you don't mind."

"Now wait a minute. Take it easy. I'd kind of like to have you around. It might keep him from telling me to get off the farm. Move."

Laura hesitated; then said, "No. I'm going. Really. I can't stand the man. He always reminds me of them white-faced grain rats."

"Well, then at least take this pheasant with you." Frank unhooked the bird from under the mower seat. "It should be bled by now."

She took it. "Ohh. It got caught in the sickle."

"Yes. That was another one of them funny things to happen to me this morning."

"Oh, Frank, come now. Really."

And with that she left.

Frank watched her go. He saw Reilly get out of the car in the yard and start for the field. He saw Reilly slow for a word with Laura. But she hardly nodded to him.

There was a roar behind Frank. He whirled around. "Rover! You devil you. What are you doing here?"

The dog quit barking. It slunk up, wagging its tail.

"Didn't I tell you to get out of this dummed field before some thing happened to you? Now go. Go on. Git."

Slowly the dog started for the house again.

"Git!"

By this time curly-haired Reilly had come near, and he called out, "Oh, the dog's all right, Frank. He won't hurt me. I like dogs." With an easy laugh Reilly reached down to pat the dog.

Snarling, Rover snapped at him.

"Hey! He's mean!" Reilly exclaimed, jumping back and rubbing his fingers. "Lord, Frank, do you need to keep a mean dog?"

"He ain't mean," Frank said, short. "Really. That's the first time I ever seen him like that. Must be something wrong with him today." Then Frank recalled Reilly's mission. "Hello, Tom."

"Hello, Frank." Reilly continued to rub his fingers.

"Dog didn't actually bite you, did he?" Frank asked.

"Just about."

Turning on Rover, Frank snapped, "Git home you. Git!"

Reilly said with a short laugh, "If it's true what they say about dogs being like their masters, you're in a bad mood today."

"Maybe I am."

"Got a nice crop of alfalfa here, Frank."

"Yeh. Ain't bad."

Reilly picked up a few stems. He fingered them, smelled them. "Real good alfalfa. Should go about ten tons to the acre."

"About eight, I figger."

"Well, that's not bad."

"Yeh. But the price of butterfat being what it is, it don't pay to have a lot of it."

Reilly got out a pack of cigarettes from a shirt pocket. "Smoke?"

"Don't mind if I do." Frank scratched a match on an overall button and then, with nervous fingers, held up the lighted match for both Reilly and himself.

Puffing, blowing out smoke, Reilly said, "Oh, say, Frank, by the way, you've got the rent money ready today, haven't you?"

"Well, the fact is, no."

"Not?"

Frank kicked at the mown alfalfa. Then he faced Reilly. "Tom, the fact is, I ain't got a red cent to my name."

"Oh."

"You know how it was last year. That terrible drought. I had to borrow against this year to get my start again this spring. That's why I didn't finish paying you last year and why I can't pay you this year yet."

Reilly's brows came together. "But, Frank, we can't do business this way. Suppose . . . Look, Frank, I didn't cause the drought."

"No, I guess you didn't. But I didn't either."

"Anyway, the point is, legally, you owe the bank the rent."

"I know that."

"Well?"

Frank puffed on his cigarette. "I suppose now you think me a poor farmer?"

"No. In fact, I think you're as good as any in the valley. No, it ain't that. It's that business is business. An honest debt is an honest debt. We got to keep things straight."

Frank dared him another direct look. "For who?"

"Why, Frank, you know we've all got to pay our debts or else everything'll go to pot."

"What will?"

"Well, you know," Reilly said, "everything. Society, churches, banks."

"Banks, yeh."

"Oh, now, Frank, we don't want to get aboard that merry-go round now, do we?"

Frank suddenly laughed, looking off to one side. "Heck, Tom, you know it's really your old man who chased you out here to sweat me for my last red cent. Sitting there as chairman of the board and putting the screws to you."

"Oh no. Not at all. He had nothing to do with it. It was just routine bank procedure. Business is business."

"Even if it is with the devil himself?"

"Yes."

"Tom, what are you trying to tell me?" Frank then asked, sharp.

Reilly flushed. "Frank, I'm afraid the bank wants you to pull up stakes. The bank can't renew the lease under the present conditions."

"You mean, you're gonna rent this fine farm to some other . . . to somebody else next year?"

"Yes."

Frank turned and looked over the fields, fields he'd once dreamt of buying from Reilly. As he looked, it occurred to him that Reilly's last "yes" hadn't been too emphatic, that there'd been a hint in Reilly's voice that personally he hadn't really been in favor of his leaving the place either. Slowly swinging around again, getting up his guts, Frank faced Tom and said, "Tom, I got a question to ask you."

"Shoot."

"How can you be agin me when me and you once was chums?"

"Welll, in the grown-up world, business is business. You know."

"Tom, did it ever pop into that curly head of yours that you're on the wrong side? You're choosing your old man's side. And he belongs to another time. Another generation. Not to yours and mine."

"Well . . ."

"Why, you and me are really closer to each other than you and him. We belong to today's family."

"That's—true—enough," Reilly said slowly.

"Sure. We should stick together. Your old man, and mine, they're the ones who let this old world get into the mess it's in. And now they're turning on us and working us for their mistakes. Making us pay for their sins. No, Tom, I can't help but think you're a traitor, kind of, joining up with him."

Welll . . ." Reilly kicked at a bunching of alfalfa.

"Heck, Tom . . ." Frank's voice cracked a bit. He waited for Reilly to pick up the ball.

Reilly stood still.

"Tom, I once dreamt of buying this farm from you. Just like I once bought marbles from you. Or that jackknife. You know. Because this is wonderful good land. Wonderful. You always did have wonderful good marbles, glassy and green."

Reilly kicked once more at the mown hay and then, lower lip thick, said, "Well, I'll see what the old man has to say. If you're sure you can pay later."

Frank cleared his throat and looked away.

"I'll see what he says. But I warn you, I'll have to sweat blood to change his mind."

"Well, what do you think I'm doing out here, sweating sweat?"

Reilly was gone. Still stunned by Tom's unexpected backdown, Frank stood silent and tall in the alfalfa.

Across the field, Laura appeared in the doorway of the house. Faintly he heard her shout.

He roused himself. He cupped his hands to his mouth and yelled, "He says we can stay."

Again, faintly, her "what" came to him.

"He says we can stay!"

He saw her listen, saw her tip her head to one side to catch the words. Then she nodded and went inside.

He went back to his mowing. He looked back a couple of times at the house-yard. When he saw Rover looking out toward him longingly, still sadly sitting beside the fence post, he relented. The dog was usually quite careful. It was cruel to deny the dog the pleasure of being near him. He whistled sharply. In long joyous leaps the dog came bounding across the field and ran up behind him. Frank reached back and patted Rover on the head.

But in a few moments he forgot the dog. He couldn't keep his mind off what Tom had come for and what had happened. He wondered what Tom would tell his old tightwad dad. He twisted in his seat as he scorched Tom's old man in an imaginary conversation.

Then Frank's eyes opened in horror. He saw it coming. Rover had gone off to prey in the alfalfa. Now suddenly the golden dog was in front of the sickle. Before Frank could haul back on the lines and stop the horses, there was a muffled snap. The mower hawed; hesitated; rolled on. For a second, Rover ran on too as if he hadn't been hurt—then toppled forward on his nose. The dog's eyes filled with surprise.

"Whoa!"

Frank had leaped off the seat even before the machine stopped rolling. He lifted the dog in his arms. Both its golden forefeet were sliced off just above the knees Frank grabbed the paws, tried to fit them, then jam them, back on again. Blood spurted over his hands and spilled on the freshly cut alfalfa. The blood was sharply crimson on the green oval leaves.

Crying, cursing, Frank ripped his red handkerchief into strips and tried to stop the flow. But the severed veins and arteries bled terribly.

After a while Frank realized it was no use. A dog's life was a running one, and without its legs, it would suffer endless misery. Even if he stopped the flow of the blood, Rover would die of inactivity.

Frank looked at the golden rover. Strangely, the dog's brown eyes were full of love, not pain. The dog licked his hands. It gazed trustingly at him with gentle eyes.

Frank jumped to his feet and reached for a heavy wrench from the toolbox and swung it. Hard. There was a crunch of bone, and Rover slumped. Reluctantly the gentle faithful eyes closed over. Frank swung again, this time with more precision, more power.

Then the horses, who had been snorting at the smell of fresh blood, jumped and started ahead. Frank dropped the wrench and the dog, and caught the team before it got a good start. He drove the horses to one side of the field and hitched them securely to the gnarled maple.

He went back to the dog and carried it across the field, crawled through a fence and threw it into a large eroded black-mouthed gully. He tromped on the edge of the gully and buried the dog with a small avalanche of black humus. "Dust unto dust," he murmured, wiping his eyes.

Just before he started up the mower again, he remembered he had dropped the wrench in the alfalfa somewhere. He got off, searched, found it, picked it up, wiped it with a handful of alfalfa, and laid it carefully away in the toolbox.

I would have like to have had about 12 [children]. . . It could be the drought years that I lived through. It could be that I didn't get married until I was 30 years old. Time was going by, some of my best seed wasn't being used . . . Who knows what was going on in my mind . . . And that happened to me when I was mowing alfalfa for my uncle Herman. I kept sending that dog home and he didn't want to go home. But the dog liked me. Everywhere I went around the yard, he was everywhere I went. The damn fool one time jumped in front of that sickle and cut his leg off.

Eden Prairie

Plumming

. . . THE MOST WONDERFUL TIMES WERE IN THE SUMMERS.

Once after supper Pa had sent the two younger boys out to the cornfield north of the grove to go weed out some cockleburs.

Brant and Kon found the cockleburs without much trouble. The cockleburs were a foot high to the corn's three feet and their leaves were a light green to the corn's dark green. Also they already had seed with stiff hooked spines while the corn still hadn't put out either tassel or silk.

As Brant and Kon pulled out the weeds by the roots one by one, they gradually drifted apart a dozen rows or so. The sun was setting. Where the sun's light hit on the top surfaces of the green corn, the blade leaves shone as if varnished white underneath in the shadows the stalks took on a horehound-green hue.

The boys stood in the rippling greens up to their chests.

The freshly cultivated earth, a rich chocolate brown, was full of wonderful clods. It was Brant who first thought of it. After pulling up a cocklebur, he also stealthily picked up a clod the size of an egg and when Kon wasn't looking threw it high over Kon's head so that it dropped on the other side of him.

"Hey," Kon said, looking up. The setting sun lay like a flash of lightning over his blond hair. His eyes opened, surprised, full of light-blue wonder.

Brant feigned innocence. "What's the matter?"

"Something almost hit me out of the sky." Kon stared up at the yellow stripes of light arching across the heavens.

"What makes you think that?"

"Something just fell over there."

"Maybe it was a meteor or something."

"You think so?"

"Did it make a kind of sizzling noise?"

"No."

"Maybe it's a hex witch then."

"You mean it's one of them bad hex teasers?" Kon's boy eyes opened very wide and filled to the brim with sunset. "Like Mother used to talk about?"

"Could be." Brant had to work hard to keep a straight face. "You remember them Oorts living by Starum there? In Outlaw Country?"

"No."

"Well, I guess you was too young then to remember. Well, every time you went by Oort cornfields by Blood Run Creek there, where them old Indians used to have their mounds, clods would suddenly fly out of the corn and hit you."

"They would?"

"They once even had the sheriff out there. And then the sheriff called up a college professor and asked him to dig up one of them mounds. Called him long distance too yet."

"Did they find anything?"

"A couple of skulls and a whole lot of bones."

"Then it was maybe them Indian ghosts what was throwing them clods."

"That's what they think."

"G-o-s-h."

"Maybe we got one of them mounds in the field here, a little low one that's been all plowed flat, and them Indian wizard ghosts are trying to chase us out of here. Maybe even trying to hex us. Because this land really belongs to them."

The sun set. The rim of the earth was scissored free of the sky for a moment.

Brant was touched by the grave look on Kon's boy face and couldn't go on with it. He said instead, "Well, I guess we better get to work or Pa'll be after us."

"Maybe we better tell Pa about them wizards throwin' things at us."

"Aw, maybe it was only a meteor after all. A little one."

"I'm kind of scairt, Brant."

"Oh, don't be scared. C'mon, or we'll have Pa on our tail." Brant began picking cockleburs again.

Still puzzled, somewhat stiffly, Kon also went back to pulling up cockleburs.

They worked awhile in silence. Sometimes the cockleburs had deep roots and it took all their boy strength to yank them out. The boys had to grunt on occasion.

The dark east came on. Overhead the sky turned a green purple. A glowing brilliant rust lay all along the western horizon. Each cornstalk, and both their boy bodies, took on a separate atmosphere of amber light. It was so clear out, so pure, that to breathe was to drink air.

Ten minutes later Brant found another hand-sized clod. He couldn't resist it. Choosing a moment when Kon wasn't looking, Brant hurled it high over Kon's head so that it landed well beyond him. This time Brant accompanied the clod's falling with a low sizzing sound. Then Brant quickly stooped over and began to tug at another cocklebur.

Kon jerked erect. "There it was again."

Brant looked up, nether lip hanging a little, moist. "Say. I heard that too."

The expression on Kon's face slowly changed. His keen ears had caught an odd nuance in Brant's voice. "Brant."

"What?"

"It was you."

"Me?"

"You did that."

"What?"

"It was you making that sizzing noise. I heard you."

"You couldn't've. It wasn't me."

"Why, you. . . ." Then with a laugh, and pretended ferocious anger, Kon leaped across the rows and jumped on Brant.

They fell to the ground, wrestling, laughing. They rolled over and over, first the one on top, then the other. They flattened several cornstalks. Ground and dust worked into the sides of their overalls and in at the necks of their shirts. They laughed until their bellies hurt, until they had terrible stomachaches. And it got worse and worse. When one would start to get over it, the other would start up again. One look and they'd fall into a fit of it again. They laughed until they almost couldn't get their breaths anymore. Their throats hurt deep in back. Even their sitters hurt. They completely emptied themselves out, they laughed so long and hard.

Oh what fun oh what joy oh what heaven.

But all for nothing.

And then there was the time when once after breakfast Mother wondered if the two younger boys shouldn't go plumming in the Wasteland. The Wasteland lay along the Big Rock River north of Bonnie. It was the last Saturday of summer vacation, before school was to start, and the wild plums there just might be ripe.

"Oh, boy," Brant cried, "can we really?"

"To the wasteland," Kon cried, "really?"

"Well, why not?" Mother said. "I'm sure Pa will let you have a horse. Anse?"

Pa smiled at their cries of joy, his lip hanging a little, moist.

"Oh, boy."

Pa helped them hitch up Whitetail to the stripped-down running gear of the old family carriage, and Mother gave them a couple of pails and the old washtub to pick the wild plums in, plus some sandwiches, and off they went.

They arrived at the black iron bridge around eleven. Brant opened the gate to the Faber pasture on the near side of the river and Kon drove the horse and running gear through. A quarter of a mile farther on, they tied old Whitetail to an ash tree. Then, each with a pail, and the tub and the bag of sandwiches between them, they pushed into the Wasteland.

They followed an old buffalo trail. White man's cattle had kept it up, well marked. They stepped across rotting trunks of fallen trees. They ducked beneath broken branches. They skip-roped through hanging loops of grapevines. Fifty yards in, the foliage high overhead became so dense it was as if the sun had gone into an eclipse. Occasional plum trees appeared in the green dusk but they had only sparse leaves and tiny pale-green plums. Green moss coated the trunk of every standing tree on the south side as well as the north side, so that in the prevailing gloom directions were impossible to make out.

There was a riot of bird cries overhead: scolding crows, mourning turtle-doves, chipping song sparrows. Once a flicker rapped on a hollow tree, trying to chase out the beetles, so loudly that both Brant and Kon jumped.

Raccoons with the manners of monkeys peered down at the passing boys.

Kon finally stopped. "I don't see any ripe plums here."

Brant stopped with him. "Oh, they're here all right. Otherwise Mother wouldn't remember it."

"Well, I don't see any."

"They'll be mostly yellow when you finally spot them. With a little red on them. Like a Chinaman with a touch of rouge on his cheeks."

"This place is scary."

"It's not either. It's just that we're not used to it. C'mon, somewhere in here we'll find them plums."

They pushed on. Vaguely off on their left they could hear the river rippling over a sandy shallows. The path into the dense underbrush almost vanished. They had to work their way through. Their pails banged; their big tub boomed.

A dozen tough steps more, and they exploded into sunlight. Before them opened a glade. The river ran rippling through the middle of it. And there, on both banks of the river, stood a scattering of little prickly trees laced with pendent rows of yellow drops.

"Plums!" Kon cried. "Look at all the plums."

"I told you."

"Millions of 'em."

"Trillions."

They looked into each other's eyes full of delight. They'd found the plums together.

They dropped their pails and tub. They rushed up to the first little prickly tree and reached up and picked themselves each a plum. Each took a tasting bite.

"Ripe," Kon said. "Mmm. And sweet."

"Mmm," Brant said. "That first little clear drop is the best. Like pure syrup."

"Like nectar."

Brant threw his arms around Kon and kissed him on his silverblond hair. "Boy, this is fun."

Kon smiled shyly.

"Boy," Brant cried in joy, "am I glad Mother sent us."

Kon looked at the myriad plums again. "Now Mother can make a lot of plum preserve and jelly."

Brant sampled plum after plum. "Nicest wild plums I ever saw. Not a worm in the bunch."

They drifted from tree to tree like bees.

The outer plums tasted warm. The sun was in them.

Presently Kon went back and got his pail. "I guess we better start picking."

Brant got his pail too. "Boy, will these taste good on warm fresh bread. Buttered."

"Don't eat too many now," Kon warned. "Or you'll get a bad stomachache."

"Not when they're so ripe like this you won't."

"Well, maybe you won't."

Brant held up a handful of plums. "See, I told you they'd be yellow with a little red on their cheeks."

"Mmm, they're good," Kon said. "Just like nectar all right."

They felt safe inside the clearing. There wasn't a breath of wind. The sun shone warm on their bare heads, the one a fine bleaching blond and the other a somber walnut brown. Being alone together was like being tickled all over.

There were so many plums within easy reach, their pails filled rapidly.

Brant was first to empty his pail, gently, into the tub. "It's like it ain't true."

Kon emptied his pail too.

"What're you thinkin', Kon?"

"Nothing."

Brant wished he could jump like a grasshopper, straight up into the air. "If only we had us a big mirror."

Kon's eyes opened in blue wonder. "What for?"

"Well, then I'd hold mine up to you so that when you looked at me you'd see you in me. And I'd see me in you."

Kon didn't catch on.

"Sometimes I get the funny feeling you and me wasn't supposed to be two people. That we've really got one me together but that somehow we got split up. Like I'm only half there without you."

Kon still looked puzzled.

"I once even dreamt that."

"You didn't."

"Kon, I just bet you that if you was to take our blood, yours and mine, you couldn't tell the difference between us."

"Our hair and eyes are different."

"Sometimes I don't even feel I'm me. But that I'm you, Kon."

"Maybe that's what it means to be brothers."

"Yeh."

"But then there's Charlie."

A shiver ran down Brant's spine. "Now why did you have to mention him? That spoils it all."

Kon studied to himself a moment. "Let's pick plums."

"That's right. Mother's expecting us with lots of plums."

They moved from tree to tree, picking the outside plums, the best and easiest to reach.

When the tub was half full they stopped to rest awhile. They got out their bag of sandwiches and, finding a soft grassy spot, sat down and had lunch. They chewed solemnly together. After the plums, the dried beef sandwiches tasted salty sweet. The thick butter made the bread easy to eat.

Finished, Brant rolled up the empty bag into a ball and threw it into the shining water in front of them. Both watched the ball bob down the river.

A yellow-green apple dropped into the water, landing with a light splash immediately behind the floating ball of paper.

Kon looked up and spotted the tree from which the apple had fallen. Part of the apple tree hung over the water. "Say, there's a real wild apple tree."

Brant's dark eyes lighted up too. "Just the thing for dessert."

They jumped to their feet and went over for a closer look. The tree was a good fifteen feet high, slender, with stiff spiny branches. It had been neatly trimmed underneath by cropping cattle. It wasn't nearly as thick with fruit as the wild plums were.

Kon said, "The thing about a wild apple is, it's a prairie crab apple really."

"Where'd you learn that?"

"Read it in my nature book. The one Teacher gave me."

"Wisht I could read fast like you."

Kon jumped for one of the little yellow-green apples; missed.

Then Brant jumped for one; and got two. He gave one to Kon.

They each took a good bite. They chewed, gravely savoring.

Kon nodded. "Tarty but sweet."

"Real sweet."

Kon took a deep sniff of the open bite in his little apple. "If you smell it slow like, you can catch a whiff of perfume in it."

"Yeh. Like mothers put on for church."

Kon finished his apple, threw the core of it into the river at their feet. He studied the apple tree some more. He spotted bigger apples near the top. "I'll bet those up there ain't so tarty. They've had the most sun."

"They look riper."

"I'll go get us some." Kon began to climb the little tree.

Brant looked down at the river. It had the dark-green look of depth. "Don't fall into the river now."

"I won't."

"But those big apples hang over the edge of the bank."

"Brant, sometimes you act like an old woman."

Kon climbed swiftly. Soon he was at the very top of the little apple tree, riding on a willowy branch. He snatched at one of the top apples; got it. He threw the apple down to Brant. Then Kon made a grab for another big apple; missed it. The other big apple was just out of reach. Kon placed his foot in a slightly higher crotch, set himself to make another grab for it.

"I wouldn't do that if I was you," Brant warned.

"Are you being afraid for me?"

"But you can't swim if you fall in."

"I don't aim to fall in."

"That water is awful deep." There was a shivery catch in Brant's voice.

Kon tested the higher crotch. He decided it would hold him. He gave himself a heave and up he went. He got the apple. But when he came down, the crotch parted under his foot, and the lower half broke off, and Kon lost his hold, and Kon came tumbling down through the tree on the river side. One of the bottom limbs, a sturdy one, caught him for a moment. It first gave a little under his weight; then, springing up again, boosted him outward. Kon somersaulted once in the air and then fell like a broken frog into the deep green water. Under he went. First water splashed out; then water fell in. Rippling rings widened out from the spot.

"Kon."

More rings widened out.

Brant stood stunned. "Kon!"

The yellow-green apple Kon had just picked bobbed to the surface. After a moment it began to drift downstream with the current.

"*Kon!*" The knuckles of a white hand appeared on the surface. The knuckles vanished.

Brant stared great dark eyes at the water. For a deep moment. Then, throwing his apple away, he scrambled down the bank. Black earth broke off ahead of him. He slid to a stop just at the water's edge where gravel showed.

There was some boiling action in the water directly in front of him. After a second Kon's head popped to the surface, eyes pinched shut, mouth drawn back as if trying to shout. Then down again Kon went.

"Kon!"

Brant spotted a thin polelike branch sticking out over the edge of the brown bank above him. He ran to get it.

A dozen feet downstream there was more boiling motion under the surface of the water.

Brant followed it along the edge of the water. He held his long pole out toward the spot, hoping that when Kon's hand came to the surface again he would grab hold when he felt it.

The back of Kon's head washed to view. His blond hair lay parted like the mane of a horse in a wind.

Brant reached as far as he could with his pole. Too short by far. Kon was drifting toward the center of the current.

"Kon!" Brant threw the pole away.

Kon slowly sank from sight.

"One more time and he's a goner. God."

Too bad the both of them hadn't learned to swim.

"Got to save him before the third time. Somehow."

No sign of Kon.

"We both might as well be dead if one of us is to be dead."

Then Brant took a deep breath and sprang into the river. He hit with a big whacking splash. He went under; came to the surface; went under. He remembered to flail his arms, gasped and choked and gasped.

It came over him that his flailing and struggling were keeping him afloat. He was swimming. God, he was actually swimming. For the first time in his life.

He opened his eyes. Sure enough. His head was out of the water and above him hung the brown riverbank and ahead stood all the trees of the farther wall of the Wasteland. God.

He kept flailing and pounding and kicking. Of a sudden, directly ahead of him, Kon's fine white hair washed to the surface once more. Brant grabbed for the white hair with his left hand. And got hold of it. Then with a second effort he got hold of a bigger handful of Kon's hair. Then, brain and eyes crackling with terror, he began pounding for the shore with his right hand. His breath came in erratic gasps. Shivers of wildest terror shot up and down his spine.

Slowly he gained on the shore. He was keeping both afloat. God.

Kon felt dead under that hair, dragging so heavy in the water. Maybe he was dead already.

Brant's elbow hit solid earth. He scrabbled out of the water on all fours. He tugged Kon with him. A dozen feet ahead there was a crack in the riverbank. It was a place where cattle came down to drink. Brant crawled toward it, still dragging Kon with him. When he got to where he could get some leverage, he heaved Kon up on dry ground. Then he carried him up the cattle path to a flat place above.

He rolled Kon over on his belly. He slapped him on the side of his head. "Kon!" He whacked Kon on his back. He lifted Kon up and let him drop. Whoosh.

He couldn't get Kon to come out of it.

He rolled Kon over the other way. He opened one of Kon's eyes with a fingertip and yelled down into it, crying, "Kon!" He shook Kon.

Kon lay as limp as a dead herring.

"God in heaven, now what?" Anguish came out of Brant with a hinnied sound. "What am I going to do? Pa! Mother!"

Kon lay on the hoof-pocked ground like a broken sack of oats.

"Mother's got a dead son now."

A trickle of water ran out of Kon's left nostril.

Brant shook Kon one more time. Hard. Wild. Desperate. He slapped Kon's cheeks with loud cracking sounds. He called his name with a great loud call. "Kon!"

Kon's mouth sagged open and a gush of water spilled out.

Brant stared. "Kon?" Quickly he put an ear to Kon's chest.

Something faint.

"Kon?"

A mourning dove called, "Ooah—koooo-kooo-koo."

Brant pressed his ear closer.

Heartbeat. Kon was still alive.

Brant picked Kon up again and shook him ferociously. Then he deliberately dropped him hard on his belly on the rough cattle path.

Kon's neck cracked. There was a sigh. "Huhh-ahhh."

"Kon! You're alive. Oh, thank God." Brant bawled. "Thank God, thank God."

Another sigh.

Brant kneeled beside Kon and rolled him over, face up. "Kon? Kon? Can you hear me?"

The wonderful blue eyes opened.

"Kon?"

Kon broke into a wet choked cough. Deep. He coughed and coughed. The coughing grabbed hold of him so deeply it brought him up to a sitting position.

"Kon, oh, God, I thought sure you were a goner. Dead."

Kon finally got on top of his coughing. When he could talk again, he asked, voice hoarse, "Where's my apple?"

"Your apple?"

"Yes. I wanted it. I gave you one."

Brant stared in disbelief. "You crazy nut, you blame near drowned and yet you're still worried about them apples?"

Kon looked down at his soppy overalls, at his dripping shoes, then at Brant's wet clothes and shoes. "What happened?"

"You fell in the river. And I fished you out."

"You did?"

"I sure did. I swum and hauled you in."

"You can't swim."

"Well, I sure as the devil learnt how getting you out."

Kon's blue eyes softened. "Then you saved my life."

"Well, somebody had to."

"You saved my life."

"How do you feel now?"

"Fine."

Brant got to his feet. "C'mon, we better take off our wet clothes." He reached down a hand to help Kon up. "Before we catch something."

They sludged to their tub and pails. They undressed back to back and spread out their wet clothes over a fallen log. They poured the water out of their shoes and opened the sides wide so that the sun could get into them.

The sun shone warm on them. Dry air made their white backs itch.

Brant looked at the half-filled tub. "Suppose we might as well keep on picking while our clothes dry."

"Might as well."

They avoided looking at each other. They moved apart from tree to tree. The grass gave underfoot. The plums still came easy and fast. Soon the tub was full.

Kon spotted a strange green tube of grass. "Look." He kneeled and parted the grass around the green tube, the better to see.

Brant came over. He recognized it. "Snake grass."

"Ma calls it scouring grass. She used to use it to clean pans with in the old days."

Brant kneeled beside Kon. "You can take and pull them apart real easy. Like toy stick sets." Brant pulled the green tube apart. The several sections let go with easy releasing sounds.

"Don't do that!"

"Why not?"

"They're precious."

"It won't die. You can stick 'em back together again." Brant gently pushed the sections back into place. "See?"

"I bet it'll die now."

"No it won't. I've done it many times."

"Are you sure?"

"Of course."

They mused on the striped tube of grass. It had the sinister look of something one might see in a nightmare. Even in the Wasteland it seemed out of place.

Brant wondered aloud to himself. "Wouldn't it be something if we could grow trees like that? If you wanted a log for the stove, all you'd need to do would be just to take out what section you wanted, the right thickness, the right length, then stick together what was left again and let it grow some more. You wouldn't even have to plant new trees and yet you'd have all the firewood you wanted."

Kon smiled. "Or take out the size you wanted for fence posts. You'd never need to buy them."

"Say, wouldn't that be something? Maybe someday the world will grow trees like that."

"That'd take millions of years."

They smiled together. Under the warmth of the sun, they felt a glow coming from each other's naked bodies. The clear air in the middle of the Wasteland was sweet with the scent of the ripe plums and wild apples.

"I'm glad we came plumming," Brant said.

"The Wasteland is fun," Kon said. He continued to look down at the sinister tube of scouring grass.

"Kon, sometimes I get funny ideas."

"We all get funny ideas sometimes."

Brant looked away as he spoke. "Like I wish we could try standing back to back close together once and at the same time I could throw my arms around you."

Kon had a shy smile. "That'd be a funny sight."

"Maybe someday in a dream we can do that, huh, Kon?"

Kon got to his feet. "Let's see if our clothes are dry. We can't stay here all day."

"Yeh. I guess we better mosey on home at that."

The clothes weren't quite dry.

Brant said, "Maybe we ought to fill the pails too in the meantime. Keep busy."

Kon nodded. "By that time the shirts should for sure be dry."

They went back to picking.

When they finished filling the pails, Brant found a long stick and went over to the wild apple tree and poked down a half dozen of the top yellow apples. He gave Kon half of them. He went over to his wet overalls and got out his jackknife and cut one of the apples into thin slices and popped the slices one by one into his mouth.

Kon got out his jackknife too. "I should've thought of poking 'em down in the first place."

"They fall and bruise easy that way though."

Kon was first to finish eating his three apples. He went over to test his shirt. "Let's head for home. They're dry enough now."

Back to back again, they got into their clothes and shoes.

Brant was sorry it was all over.

They returned home heroes. Mother just couldn't get over it that they'd picked so many plums.

Pa thought they'd done pretty well too. "Maybe we should give them a medal. They didn't wreck a single solitary thing. And they even look cleaner somehow."

"Well, if not a medal," Mother said, "surely all the plum jam they want all winter long."

Neither Brant nor Kon ever told about the near drowning. All they ever talked about was the best most wonderful time they had. . . .

> *I was hardly 16 years old, when Aunt Katherine and Uncle Clarence . . . showed up on the yard one day, and my mother loved Uncle Clarence, because he was kind of a Jesus type. He was never going to make a pass at her. He was going to be warm towards her, but he was never going to make a sexual suggestion . . . And I heard him shoo the kids off and close the door. Before he could do that, I heard him say, "My brother committed suicide."*

> *Later on, when I looked that family up, I found out they were twins, and the wife of this man who committed suicide was sitting with her mother in law, doing some needlework, when all of a sudden she says, "Oh, I've got to go home." And she grabs the kids, and gets on her coat and drove in the yard, and she's just too late. He's already taken strychnine, and when he sees her coming in the yard, he then goes and runs and gets his double-barrelled shotgun and blows his brains out.*

> *She was beautiful, German, dark type, wonderful breasts, a real earth mother, warm and really sweet. And it hit me just like a flash that he married her because it was his only chance to be a man. And he really was in love with Clarence. . . Aunt Kathryn . . . just let go floods and floods and floods of information I knew nothing about . . . So, there's where I got the idea that there was a tremendously deep attachment. He'd hardly had any intercourse at all with Aunt Kathryn, nor did the other boy with his wife. Because the brothers were deeply in love with each other. Maybe not incestuous, but the two were so attached, that they couldn't break out of it to get into a woman . . . That's the duty of the artist. When you run across something like that, you've got to explore it. And it has depth that no one knows is in there.*

The Manly-Hearted Woman

As a very little boy I was somewhat of an Indian in the sense that I felt that all things were talking to me. That's why it was relatively easy for me to write Conquering Horse, *in which I said that stones and various things talk, and even move a little. We had a big grove on one farm, I remember, and my mother used to wonder what in the world I was doing in it, because I would go over to a tree, put my arms around it and my ear against it and listen, and go down along all the trees, up and down in the grove, to check their sounds. I still do that today. Each tree has a different sound. What you hear, if the wind's blowing, are the various fibers rustling against each other, the bark rustling against the cambium, and of course the leaves, and here and there if there's a branch about to break off, you can almost hear it about to break. But each tree has a sound of its own. It is a form of music.*

The Death of Flat Warclub

BITTEN NOSE COULDN'T STOP his pellmell berserk rush. He piled on top of Flat Warclub. He too was aiming his blow for the top of Weaseltail's skull. But because Flat Warclub happened to stop directly in the path of Bitten Nose's downward swing . . . crackkk!

Flat Warclub fell. A great lightning had struck him in the brain. Stars scattered.

Flat Warclub rolled over several times, finally fell off the narrow path down a slope. His body flopped into a little glade of grass. His clamshell fell off. His little medicine bundle of the seven clovers and the one clover spilled open.

The end was near. There would be just time to sing his death song:

> *"Yelo, here am I crying my life away,*
> > *soon the long long sleep.*
> *Yelo, here all is dark,*
> > *the light of my eyes is wiped out.*
> *Yelo, I am very alone,*
> > *no father, no uncle, no brothers to help me.*
> *Yelo, I must give my life back,*
> > *I am finished using it.*
> *Pity me."*

He sang in a weak tremulous voice. He was almost thrown away:

> *"The juices! The juices!*
>   *will they never run again?*
> *Pity me.*
>   *What is life without the sweet juices?*
> *He-nala yelo.*
>   *It is all over."*

Yet a little light was given him. His eyes rolled in his head and their rolling around parted his eyelids.

He saw Bitten Nose standing over him. For a moment he couldn't understand the look on Bitten Nose's face. Bitten Nose was weeping.

Flat Warclub whispered, "How goes the battle?"

Bitten Nose wept hot yellow drops of salt on him. "The enemy flies. The Buffalo Jump On The Blue Mounds will now be ours forever."

Flat Warclub let his eyes fold shut.

He remembered two last things.

First, he was walking along the sandy shore of Talking Water. His mother Cornmilk was calling him home to come and get mama, it was ready and warm. But he didn't want to come right away. The beach was full of little glowing stones fallen from the clouds and each one was telling him something. The points from the clouds were singing in unison like cicadas in a grove of cottonwoods. The air was very clear. The sky was as blue as the paint of peace. The air smelled of lapped water. His favorite giant cottonwood cliddered its wax-green leaves over him. It was all very clear. It all had a sweet wonderful dizzy edge to it, dizzier than he remembered it being as a boy.

Suddenly he saw his life coming full circle. In a moment he would start the circle a second time around. The circle always brought the sun, and the sun always brought life and power. It was going to be doubly sweet the second time.

Second, he was sitting in Manly Heart's tepee. He saw her weeping. He saw she'd put away her manly clothes. She wept that he hadn't talked to her to give her a baby. He felt sorry for her. At that moment he liked her better than he'd ever liked any other woman. He wished now that he had talked to her. It would have been a good thing to do. Not even his mother had been as kind to him. Manly Heart had taken him in as a guest when no one else would. Wife Prettyhead wouldn't have invited him in if left to herself. Manly Heart had the big heart. Compared to her, Prettyhead was but an ornament. Manly Heart should have been made the mother, not Prettyhead. Had Manly Heart not provided him with a hearth, he would not have had a place from which to make his offer to throw his life away. Now that he had got to that place where he now lay floating, he knew Manly Heart had perhaps loved him best of all.

Six white spirit lance bearers came with a white buffalo robe. They lifted him onto the white robe and carried him away. He himself was the seventh white spirit.

Work

Of Lizards and Angels

What I finally saw in all those notes was history of Siouxland from 1880 on . . . Every deed in the area has an English name on it in the beginning. Then the Dutch came in and they just out-worked and out-bred everybody around them. And the Germans. East Frisian Germans. Then they slowly pushed the English out. Some English go back and some intermarry, and that caught my eye and I thought I ought to follow a nuclear family for at least four generations.

When you start, Tunis is twenty-some years old in 1880 . . .

Sodbusting

THE NEXT MORNING, right after breakfast, Clara got out the new rake and new hoe and leveled the blacker dirt Tunis had thrown up out of the well. The soil was wonderfully crumbly and worked well. She made two neat square plots, five feet by five feet, and raked and reraked it all until the dirt was as fine as flour. Then she got a couple of packets from her trunk she'd been saving. One was lettuce seed and the other radish. She sowed the seed evenly and then got down on hands and knees and patted the soil firmly down over the seed. From her mother she'd learned that if one packed it down firmly one got quick results.

From her mother she also learned about using fresh-turned soil. When her father and mother first arrived on their virgin prairie home in Welton one hot August, it was too late in the year to break virgin prairie and to plant crops. But an old Fox Indian had come by and showed them that if they were to throw radish seeds into the mounds freshly heaved up by pocket gophers they still could have fresh vegetables before frost time.

The weather couldn't have been better for Tunis's spring work. Usually April brought showers. But a quirk in the weather brought them nothing but a series of sunny days. There was to be no wasting of those God-given planting days. Tunis decided that the first virgin sod he'd break would be just west of the cabin.

449

There was just enough room, he said, for a plot of twenty acres between the cabin and the river.

But first he had to get rid of the tall grass to make for easier plowing. The dry weather was perfect for burning off the prairie. With no wind out it was easy to keep the fire under control. He first backfired around the cabin. Once he had that done, he let the fire burn as it would toward the river. It took a whole day for the twenty acres to turn an ashen black. Burning slowly, it also gave the animals, mice and rabbits and gophers, time to escape to either side.

As Tunis plowed the next day, Clara sometimes heard him talking to his horses Fred and Bill and Gyp. From the tone of his voice, she could make out that he was barely able to keep his temper. And it wasn't because of what the horses were doing either.

She decided to bring him some food for his lunch break. She fixed some tea and a dried-beef sandwich and carried it out to him. "I hope you're not mad at me."

"You? No. It's just this turf. It's as tough as a leather belt six inches thick. Man! One minute I'm too deep in, and the next minute I'm skimming over the surface." He pointed to a single strip a dozen rods long of very uneven plowing. "I'm strong enough but I'm not heavy enough."

Clara looked down at the long gleaming share of the breaking plow. "Maybe it's not sharp enough."

"Hoo, it's sharp enough all right. I could shave with it if I had to."

Clara knelt down to look at the thick turf. There were so many intertwined roots the turf looked like a thickly woven house carpet. Some of the roots were as thick as rat tails. Dozens of pink angle worms were already at work sucking out tunnels toward the surface.

Tunis coughed. "How busy are you there in the house?"

"Why?"

"Maybe you won't like this, but how about you riding me piggyback? That way there'll be enough weight to hold the walking plow down."

Clara didn't know whether she liked that or not. Her valuables would be right up against his neck.

"Look, I'll show you." He rehooked the knotted lines over one shoulder behind his hack. "Fred! Bill! Gyp! Giddap."

The three horses groaned and leaned into their collars. Tunis quick aimed the point of the huge heavy plow down to catch into the woven turf. The point caught and dug in, and then, as the horses really began to pull, it suddenly went straight down, hurling Tunis for all his two hundred pounds of broad stubby weight up in the air and dropping him between Fred and Bill. The startled horses stopped dead.

"Oh! Tunis! Are you hurt?" she cried.

"No!" Tunis cursed, then got to his feet. Rubbing his shoulder he walked back around behind the plow.

"I see what you mean," she said.

"Well?"

"Oh, but you can't hold me up and drive at the same time."

"Try me."

She felt a giggle coming on and quick made it into a laugh. She hated gigglers. He was a powerful man, that she knew. She'd several times had a glimpse of his body as he undressed for bed. She hadn't meant to peek; it had happened accidentally as she tried to find the right soft valley in her pillow.

"Well?" Tunis wasn't laughing. "All right. How do I climb aboard?"

"Like this." He settled on his heels. "Okay, swing your legs around my neck."

She drew up her long gray dress to her hips and one leg at a time climbed onto his broad shoulders.

"Sit up closer. That's it. Now catch your toes under my arms and back around behind me. Good. Here's the lines and you drive. I'll be too busy holding down this wild bronco of a plow to drive."

"Like a stagecoach driver."

"You bet. Now. Slap those lines and yell at the horses. Let's go."

Laughing, trying to be serious, Clara slapped the reins up and down. "Giddap. Fred. Bill. Gyp."

The three horses didn't move.

"Put the growl of a bear into it, woman."

She tried again. Still the horses didn't move.

Tunis under her let go with a strong command. "Get!"

The horses got and the plow dipped in, then dug in, and when it wanted to head for China, Tunis powerfully clutched the long handles and, aided with Clara's weight, held them firmly fixed at a certain angle and kept the great plow exactly level. There were tearing anguished sounds in the turf. A strip of sod some eight inches thick and sixteen inches wide rose up and, getting caught on the long moldboard, slowly curled over and fell, grass down. The long strip of sod jostled around like some long live black python. And it kept writhing after Tunis and plow passed by.

Clara could feel Tunis's power with every step. And with every step her valuables snuggled closer in toward the back of his neck. She wondered if he was aware of how intimate it all was. Probably not. Too busy holding down the plow. She thought it all rather homey.

At the end of the round he'd marked out, he tipped the plow on its side and it popped out of the ground. "All right there, lady above, turn the horses left, tight, and we'll start the back round. That's it. Now. Once more." He lifted the plow a little and then jabbed it down. Again the plow wanted to dig itself down out of sight, but Tunis powerfully held it at the right angle, muscles thickening over his back and neck and shoulders, giving Clara a vigorous rolling ride.

Clara could feel herself first softening toward Tunis, then swelling in love for him. She feared she would dampen his neck. She worked herself back an inch. When the round was completed, he shouted, "Whoa."

The three horses stopped dead. They had begun to breathe heavily. Each horse stood on three legs, resting the fourth leg.

"How you doing up there?" he said, muffled under her.

"Fine."

"Enjoying the ride?"

She tried not to laugh. "Sure am."

"Well, down here I'm slowly turning into a nigger. All that burnt grass."

"I can smell it up here."

"By the time we get done we'll both look like we came out of darkest Egypt. Even the horses' legs are black."

She smiled. "We'll just have to get out the tub and scrubbing brush."

"Will you scrub my back?"

"Maybe."

He wriggled his neck around. "Lady, you got scratchy underwear, you know that?"

"Maybe I should go put on my flannel ones."

"Well. No. I got you up there now and we can wait until noon." He looked ahead at the horses. "I sure wisht I had another horse. With a four-horse hitch instead of three, we'd move through this stuff as easy as pushing a paring knife around a potato." He inhaled a deep breath, tossing Clara about a little. "Well, let's go. Get!"

They plowed until noon, making twenty full rounds, all of it some fifty feet wide. When Tunis settled to his heels to let Clara to the ground, he estimated they'd turned over about two acres of sod.

"Not at all bad. At this rate within a week we'll have turned over enough for a start this year." He hardly puffed after all the work of holding down the plow and carrying Clara. "I figure I'll put ten acres to wheat and ten to corn. After I get the crops in, I'll turn over another twenty. And that second twenty I'll let set through the next winter. There's nothing like letting frost act on fresh-plowed prairie soil. It cures it of alkaline at the same time that it softens and sweetens it. Besides getting that turf to rot into soft mulch."

It took them seven days to turn over the first twenty acres. The three horses became gant from all the hard pulling. Tunis too seemed leaner and Clara was hard put to keep him satisfied at the table.

A two-day rain set in. It turned the burnt black to earth black. Tunis welcomed the rain. But with Tunis underfoot all day in the tight cabin, Clara became nervous. After all the intimacy of her riding on his shoulders and of their scrubbing each other's backs each night to get rid of the black ash, she was sure he had ideas.

But Tunis didn't make a move toward her. He was content just to fatten up a little again.

The moment the rain ended and the birds were singing once more, meadowlarks and redwings and robins, Tunis got the hoe and went out to the plowed ground.

"Too bad I don't have a harrow. So the hoe will have to do. I've got to loosen up the dirt on the black side of the turned sod so the wheat kernels can catch in." He chopped away furiously. "It's only ten acres. When we do the ten acres for the corn we'll use the spade every few feet."

Clara saw that Tunis was going to wear himself to a frazzle if he hoed the whole ten acres alone, so she dug through an old storebox, where she found an ancient hoe. She joined him. Between the two of them they managed to scratch the black soil loose in a couple of days.

She watched him sowing the grain. It was a sight she would never forget. He'd made a sling for the sack of wheat and carried it on his left side. The sun shone on his rusty hair and his pink hands and his glowing tanned cheeks. First one hand dipped into the sack and came up with wheat and made a sideways spraying motion, and then the other hand dipped in and sprayed. It was like he was stepping to music and was waving his arms to either side like a child lost in a dreamy waltz.

Finished with the sowing, he got out the garden rake and swiftly began covering the wheat. He had to hurry because the blackbirds had begun to help themselves. Clara quickly made a scarecrow out of an old pair of pants and a shirt of his, and then she too dug out an extra rake and helped him.

In April the days became longer and green shoots began to show at the base of old dead stalks of last year's grass. Fuzzy purple mayflowers popped out over the hills to the east. The rounded slopes appeared to have been decked out with a series of silken coverlets. In some low spots the rain had rotted fallen bluestem along with trailing wild roses and the smell of fermenting gave the air a heady bouquet.

Green Earth

I remember when I used to plow that I would hide a book inside my shirt and pants and pull the belt up tight and pull my stomach in and take the horses out to the field, hitch them up, and when I was over the hill I'd hook the lines up on the plow (I had a good lead team), and then I would read to the end, turn around and read until I got to the top of the hill and then hide the book again. This I had to do. I think that resistance is good. I wanted this and they said no to me and this made me feel as if I were an outlander or outsider of the group.

Pitching Manure

FREE LAY ON THE GRASS on his favorite hill in the pasture. He took to watching cumulus clouds drift in from the west. They were sky ships from another world.

As he often did, Free fell into an old daydream of his, in which he'd set out to conquer the world. He and the neighbor boys would first conquer their own township, then conquer the neighboring townships, then hit the county seat, Rock Falls. Once they had a county in control, they would go on to conquer the state of Iowa county by county, until finally they'd march on the state capital, Des Moines. Man oh man, wouldn't the governor of Iowa be surprised one morning to see two wings of a country boy army standing on the capital steps demanding his surrender. The governor would stare and stare at Emperor Alfredson VII. The corners of his eyes would wibble a little and it would be seen that he was trying to think of some way yet to let the President of our country know about the new threat—

"So here you are. Son, son, I've been looking all over for you."

Free put up a hand and looked past it. There was Pa standing between him and the sun. Pa looked like a monument. "Something the matter?"

"Matter? A lot of manure needs to be hauled out of the calf pen. And you're just the man to do it."

Free remembered some talk that morning about him cleaning out the calf pen. It made him sick to think about it.

"Son, son, I can't be having a big fellow like you lollygagging on his back all day looking up at the sky doing nothing. You're twelve years old now, and it's time for you to pull your share of the load."

Free slowly sat up. He hugged his knees.

"When I was your age, boy, I was practically managing a farm alone for Charlie Pullman."

"That was them days, Pa."

"Get to your feet and let's go. I've got your horses all hitched up to the manure spreader. All you have to do is pick up the fork and start pitching."

"Why can't you do it?"

Pa shivered a little in his tracks. "What!"

Free got to his feet.

"Son, if you was born in Fat John's family, you'd be putting in ten-twelve hours a day of real hard work. Those boys of his are already first-class hired hands. You know darn well he'd never've let you lay in the grass dreaming the whole day away like this."

Free lowered his head.

"And you better dig out your work shoes. That calf manure comes pretty sharp. It'll chew up your bare feet worse than battery acid."

Free started walking home.

Pa followed a few steps behind. "Man, man. I had a time finding you. What were you doing there all alone in the grass?" Pa asked the question as if he expected to catch him at some kind of sorry deed.

"Well, if you must know, I was out conquering the whole world."

"On your back?"

"Yes."

"Wal. You and your grampa with your crazy wild notions."

"Grampa Alfredson was a great man."

"And not your father?"

Free fell silent. He lowered his head a little more as he trudged up ahead of Pa. He hugged his chest.

The calf manure was tough to pull apart. Hay in the calf manger usually spilled over into the pen, and when the manure was allowed to build up and get tromped on by the calves all winter long, it became as tough as old wine leather.

Free first used a four-tine fork. He jabbed at the yellow matted stuff, tugged at it, tore at it, but couldn't dig up much. All he managed to pry loose were several strands of stinky straw along the edges of the pen. After a half hour he still only had the manure spreader about a fourth full. He was wringing wet with sweat.

Meanwhile, the grays Polly and Nell, stood outside switching at flies.

He next tried the potato fork with its knife-sharp points. It did cut the matted mess a little better, but at the same time it made lumps almost too heavy for him to throw into the spreader. He had to shag the lumps along the floor and then, with all his might, heave them in. It was back-breaking.

He shagged six big lumps into the spreader and then had enough. He threw the potato fork into the alley.

He got Pa's hay knife next. But it didn't work good either. The point of the hay knife was too round.

"Goddammit, I'm gonna go and get me the axe. Even if it means chopping off my toes and so never play baseball again. Let alone conquer all of Iowa."

The axe helped in cutting the matted manure into sections. But he still had to pry each section loose from the cement floor, and that was like trying to scrape burnt gravy off a frying pan.

After an hour of grunting and struggling, he still had only half of a load on. "Goddammit, this is worse than what the jailbirds have to do in the state pen."

"Is it really all that hard?" Pa said suddenly beside him.

Free almost jumped a foot.

Pa picked up the four-tine fork and tried it. Pa did pretty well with the sections Free had already cut with the axe. But when Pa tackled the uncut part, he didn't do much better than Free. After a couple of minutes Pa began to sweat and then to cuss. "By dab, I plumb forgot how tough it was."

Free wanted to say, "Yeh," but didn't quite dare.

Pa grunted and struggled. He tore at the calf manure like a mad bulldog pulling at an old cowhide. He managed to separate several hunks of it and heaved them onto the spreader.

Free stood watching. Soaked with sweat, he still puffed a little.

Finally Pa threw the four-tine aside and went at it with the potato fork. "This calf manure is going to be removed or my name ain't Great Pier."

Pa did better with the potato fork. Pa was powerful enough to make it work. It took a strong back and mighty arms. Pa managed to throw out a dozen forkfuls in short order. Soon the spreader was full.

Free was grateful for the help.

"There, dagnab it," Pa said. "Haul it away. And when you get back, call me, and I'll help you with the next load. I can see that this is too tough for you. Not even Johnny Engleking could've loaded this stuff." Pa wiped sweat from his face with a red handkerchief. "And pee-uu. What a smell. In all the world there ain't no smell as awful as old calfshit."

Grunting and cutting, and tearing at it, Free and Pa finished cleaning out the calf pen by three o'clock.

They had some dried-beef sandwiches and cool lemonade together.

Then right after that Ma had a job for Free. It was time to churn again, Ma said, and if Pa could use their oldest boy for barn work, she could use him for some housework.

The Chokecherry Tree

Wanted: Aggressive Young Man

> *... Cuts and bruises, stings and pains, heartaches, yes, even executions—*
> *and still the Elofs go on. Why are they always "going on"? Perhaps it is be-*
> *cause consciousness, mind, light, once you have it, turns out to be a possession*
> *worth having—at least until something better comes along. Just see how few*
> *people commit suicide. Just one in millions ...*

THE FOLLOWING WEEK, after Fats had left him to go selling in The Bench country, the southeast point of South Dakota, Elof hustled around to find himself another job.

Each evening he went through the Men Wanted section of the Sioux Falls *Free Thought*, found a few promising opportunities, and the next morning called on them. He first hit for solid jobs, for sweat pay. But by the time he arrived to apply, he invariably found the street in front of the shop, or factory, or store, or whatever it was that had advertised, full of job hunters. Gradually it broke over him that Sioux Falls swarmed with unemployed.

Once Elof was the first man there. The job was to scatter horse manure over a rich man's lawn. He was about ready to start work when another appli-cant arrived. Elof heard the other tell of his need, that he had a large family, four children and wife, that he hadn't had steady work in five years, that two of his children had rickets, that almost all of the family's teeth had cavities. The story smote Elof in the quick, hit him where he lived. Wordlessly he handed over the fork and wheel barrow. Six mouths outvoted one.

At last, reluctantly, he probed the idea of selling once more. An advertise-ment read:

WANTED:

AGGRESSIVE YOUNG MAN.

SPLENDID OPPORTUNITY LIMITED ONLY BY YOUR ABILITY.

COMMISSION AND EXPENSES.

ROOM 406. REDSTONE HOTEL.

Elof went down to the Redstone, met two beady-eyed young blades. They were throwing money and clothes around the room with saturnalian abandon. One was on the phone murmuring honeyed words into the earpiece, the other was ordering up drinks. At last they found time for him. When they explained that they were selling glossy national magazine subscriptions, singly or in clubs, using candy as a come-on, Elof recognized old surroundings—he was back in the vague queasy world of Kingsfood again. But he decided to give it a try, and the next day he was on the road with the boys. Grub, South Dakota, was the first town on the itinerary. And once again Elof tried to be a combination browbeater and lover, this time to get three-month trial subscriptions. What astounded Elof most was to see the boys list subscriptions on one pad, seductions (with details and phone number) on another. They were not selling to make a living; they were selling to make bivulve conquests. After three days of it Elof quit. He had sold only two subscriptions. But the wandering stallions, meanwhile, had made a killing. Such a killing, in fact, that upon arriving at the Redstone they began to whoop with joy, and showered, and heaved soiled laundry and sale slips all over the place; and, naked, laid plans for another frontal attack upon Dakota virginity.

It was after breakfast and Elof was sitting on the burgundy plush davenport in Sis's parlor. Through the bay window Elof could see the neighbor children playing in the street. Though his eyes followed their movements, his mind was busy with his troubles.

Sis, who had been rustling in the kitchen, came out and asked, "Will you be home for noon lunch?"

Elof sat up and reddened a little. Another charged meal? And pregnant, flustered Sis even more worried that she wouldn't make ends meet? "No. No, I'm going downtown in a minute. Got an appointment."

Sis looked at him a second; dropped her eyes. She drew her pink housecoat over her swollen belly. "You'll be home for supper then?"

"I don't know. Depends. This new job may take me out of town. Like the other one. I'll let you know."

"All right then." Clumsily turning, she re-entered the kitchen. Elof picked up last night's paper, desperately paged through the Want Ads again. He looked for honest jobs under Men Wanted; found none. He looked under Grand Opportunity; saw dozens listed.

He found the magazine-selling ad again; hurriedly jumped to the next paragraph.

He ran his finger down until he came to a promise set in heavy type:

MAKE $100 A WEEK SELLING RELIABLE LINE.
NEED ENTERPRISING, ALERT YOUNG MAN TO BRING
REAL SERVICE TO COMMUNITY.
ROOM 709 CODY BUILDING.

Elof stared at the advertisement for a while, at last decided to give it a try. And if this one didn't work—he would head for home.

The new opportunity to make millions involved selling Whingding cleaners. It was a blue-white aluminum all-purpose tank cleaner complete with attachments. The main section was made up of a one-foot-by-two cylinder with a long hose. To it the housewife attached various appliances, ranging all the way from suction lips to a round screened funnel. A housewife could clean rugs, floors, furniture, shades, walls, ceilings; could demoth clothes, blankets, plush chairs; could spray paint. The housewife paid down twenty-five dollars (the salesman's commission) (twenty-five dollars! sell two a week and be on easy street!); paid the rest on time. The production cost of the machine was fifteen dollars; the selling price, ninety-eight dollars. The whole thing fit into a little black satchel, so little a child could carry it.

Elof saw there was no point calling on the poor with such a remarkable invention. Only the rich would have the dough to buy it.

Carrying a sample unit, Elof hunted up the Park Avenue of Sioux Falls. Finding it, he selected a mansion suggesting fatty opulence. He adjusted his quiet green tie, combed back his gold hair with stubby fingers, brushed off his gray suede shoes, and stepped boldly up to the front door. He rang. The name on the bronze doorplate was *Phineas Flattard*.

A maid, wearing blue with white trim, came to the door. A fringed hood cowled her face. "Yes?"

"Could I speak to the lady of the house?"

"Well—what is it you want?"

Since the maid was elaborately formal, Elof fell in with the mood. "I have a matter of grave importance to discuss with her."

The maid looked at Elof's satchel, frisked his clothes with suspicious eyes, at last decided he was all right. She left.

After a moment a middle-aged lady, wearing her hair in a gray pompadour, and dressed in striped blue silk, came to the door. She leaned forward from her hips. "Yes?"

"Could I interest you in a matter of health?"

"Why . . . Yes, of course. Come in, won't you?"

Elof stepped in.

"Have a chair," she said, pointing to a blue lounging chair before an empty fireplace. A matching ottoman stood nearby.

Elof sat down.

Unbuttoning his suit jacket, he glanced around the room before beginning his song.

The place unsettled him. He had never seen such magnificence. This, without a doubt, was the home of a hero. Deep wine-red drapes hung from ceiling to floor. Walls were of oak paneling. Cathedralic arches soared across the ceiling. The blue rug underfoot was an inch deep—the kind which, when walked on, generated electricity in body and reaching hand. Two huge sofas and a collection of incidental chairs were tastefully scattered around. Before one davenport stood a yellow coffee table, Chinese, with a glass top.

Elof looked at the huge window again. Its panes were so clean, so clear, so free of smelting defects, it was as if the outdoors and the indoors were of the same heaven light.

"Yes?" Mrs. Flattard had perched herself on the edge of a couch.

Elof collected himself. "Oh yes. Well, Mrs. Flattard, I'm Elof Lofblom. What I have here has been mildly described at one time or another as a revolution in the housewife's life."

"Oh yes?"

Elof opened up his little black satchel, lifted out the cleaner. "A revolution, yes. Now this, this is the Whingding cleaner. It cleans everything from soup to"—Elof caught himself, quickly righted—"from curtains to floors to sofas." He saw Mrs. Flattard's face first wrinkle with surprise, then tighten with anger. Elof hurried to keep her from interrupting him. "And it does it more thoroughly, more efficiently, more economically, with less fuss and dust, with less disturbed, and therefore with cleaner air, than any machine on the market today. Here. I'll show you. Your maid's cleaned here today, I presume?"

"Why—I think so."

"Sure. Now watch." Elof opened up the cylinder. "Empty, see?" Closing the cylinder, he fastened the swivel rug nozzle neatly onto the hose of the cylinder, then plugged the cord into a wall socket behind a chair. There was a soft melodious hum. "Now." He ran the nozzle over an apparently clean place on the rug. He ran it back and forth twice; then shut off the machine. Again he opened the cylinder and held it up for her to see. A mound of dust and debris two inches high lay piled on its bottom. Mrs. Flattard, who had been about to get up, now slowed. Elof, quite surprised himself, lifted a handful and declared,

"That's what we call cleaning, Mrs. Flattard. Not that your maid doesn't clean good. But that she doesn't use the right kind of machine."

"Yes, I know. But—"

"Now, now, Mrs. Flattard"—Elof saw he was losing her, so leaped to the attack—"Now, Mrs. Flattard, you see these extra attachments?" He pointed to a pile of bright aluminum.

"That's all very well, but—"

"That's what makes this a special machine. This thing"—and he put the machine together again and fitted on another snout—"this thing cleans your curtains and shades." He walked over to the big window and, holding up the long rubber hose, expertly ran the snout over the fixtures. "See?"

"But you see, young man—"

Next, Elof fitted on an anteater nozzle and pounced again. "And this you use to clean out the furniture. Like so." He shoved the nozzle into a corner of the couch she was sitting on. There was a buzzing; some puffs of dust. "See? Did you know there was dirt there?"

"No, but you see—"

"I tell you, Mrs. Flattard, there isn't a thing this machine can't do."

Mrs. Flattard began to look ill.

Seeing her face, disgust at what he was doing suddenly overwhelmed Elof like an October fog smothering a bush. His voice trailed off. "You see, a woman . . . any woman . . ."

How foolish. How foolish and insane this was. He didn't care a snap for the lady, had really no sympathy for the rich, yet here he was, trying desperately to sell her something she didn't want and which he himself wasn't sold on—except that he needed the twenty-five-dollar commission.

The pause in his harangue was fatal. Popping up from her seat as if chains had fallen from her limbs, Mrs. Flattard said crisply, "No, really, young man, the cleaner we are using will suffice for the present. Thank you just the same." Mrs. Flattard hurried to the door, held it open for him.

Elof picked up the parts of his machine, packed them into the little black satchel. As he walked out he said, "Thank you, Mrs. Flattard. Thank you. You've been most kind to have listened at all."

"Oh, that's all right." The door closed firmly behind him.

His blocky shoulders slumped.

FROM

Milk of Wolves

Star Drills

ROUNDY WAS A WELCOMING COMMITTEE of one all right. Juhl observed
how the smith next to him, a lefthanded man, had a drill caught in the jaws of
his vise. He followed suit. It didn't take him long to see that it was his job to
deepen the star-shaped grooves in the business end of the drill. Grabbing hold
of a heavy gray file he immediately set to work. On the very first stroke steel filings began to sprinkle onto the pink floor of the quarry. The rasping sound of
steel on steel was of such penetrating sharpness it was as though someone were
poking around in his ear with a matchstick.

Roundy beat on his anvil some ten minutes, then suddenly snarled around
on Juhl. "That ain't no way. Goddam. You a blacksmith? Hell."

Juhl began to hate the big sorenose. But he needed the work so he made up
his mind to take abuse for a while. "You tell me then."

"Hrrh. You're making the ridges on the star too sharp. They'll bust off that
way. And if you make them too blunt they won't cut. They gotta be blunt sharp-
like. Both."

"All right."

"No, it ain't all right. You better go over and see how they use a drill so you'll
know what I mean. Because this way we're going backwards. Losin' ground."
Roundy pointed up at the far pink wall where four pairs of men were working
on a narrow ledge. "See them drillers up there? Go up and watch them a while.
Tell 'em Roundy sent you for a looksee."

Juhl lay his file to one side. "I'm already on my way."

"Ah ha. So. A hotshot I see. Get your tail up pretty high, eh? Well, young
fella, before we get through with you here we'll have that tail of yours down
where it belongs, between your legs."

Juhl said nothing. He started off for the far pink wall.

He clambered up a jumble of fallen rock and shattered seams hand over
hand. Close up the freshly broken rock was even more beautiful. The rock looked
so fleshlike in both texture and color it appeared to need only the prick of a needle to make it bleed. A little out of breath he at last reached the ledge where the
drillers were at work.

He stood watching the four pairs of workers as they worked their drills down
into the hard rock. A boy helper held the drill in place while a heavy-armed man
pounded it down with a sledge hammer. After each stroke the boy helper reset
the drill a quarter turn, always to the right.

Juhl could see by watching a mark on the drill that the drill was going down a fraction of a fraction of an inch on each stroke. That rock really was hard. It took muscle and elbow grease and bone-stinging jolts to make even the tiniest dent in it. One of the men was pounding on his drill so hard that on each stroke his blue cap gradually became dislodged, the back of it rising over his brown curls while the bill of it settled down over his nose, until at last, between swings, he had to reset his cap with a swift swipe of his hand.

One of the star drills was two-thirds of the way down. The man on the sledge paused and the boy helper pulled the drill out of the hole. The boy picked up a small bellows and blew most of the powdered rock out of the hole, pink dust flying up around his face. The boy helper got rid of the rest of the dust by sticking a gob of wet clay to the end of a slender rod and probing the bottom of the hole. After each probe he cleared off such clay as was studded with pink bits until it came up clean. The boy picked up a fresh star drill and dropped it into the hole. It fell to the bottom of the hole with a clean ringing sound.

Juhl picked up the used star drill to see what the wear on it had been. The semi-sharp edges were almost blunted off.

He studied it closely; ran his finger over it; nodded to himself; and turned to go.

At the far end of the same ledge he saw four other drillers and their boys retreat from their spot. Immediately two blasters went to work. They dropped a length of cord fuse into each hole, carefully poured in a small sack of black coarse blasting powder, and packed each hole down with mud. They tied the various fuses together, and then one of them, kneeling, lighting a match between his knees inside his cupped hands, set off the fuses. Crackling smoke raced down each fuse. Both men ran for safety behind boulders, calling out, "Heads up! Blasting!"

Just to be on the safe side even where he stood, Juhl ducked behind a boulder too. The four men behind him and their helpers also jumped behind places of safety. Juhl had barely got hunkered down in a squat, an arm over his head and face, when the whole rock fundament quivered under him like a dried lake bed. Then he heard the sound. Nearby it wasn't too loud, but where it echoed off the far wall it made an awful resounding clap. Immediately a pink haze smoked up over them all. It made Juhl cough.

"Learn anything?" Roundy asked with a sneer when Juhl returned to his vise.

Juhl nodded curtly. He picked up his file and went to work.

Juhl took his time for a while, making sure he was filing exactly like Leary, the man working next to him. Juhl made up his mind that he was going to get Roundy to admit his work was as good as anybody's, even if he had to ram it down his throat.

Roundy kept squinting around at Juhl. Every little while he stepped over to run his finger over Juhl's newly sharpened star drills. About every third one he rejected and told Juhl to do it over.

Juhl got sick of seeing all the rejects. He took one of them and sighted the edge of it against the high horizon to see what he was doing wrong. For the life of him he couldn't tell the difference between those Roundy accepted and those he rejected.

Juhl asked finally, "What's wrong with these rejects?"

"Use your eyes. And show a little speed, hotshot. We're falling behind."

Juhl burned. He would show that big tub of mud.

Juhl filed and filed, as accurately as he could, as swiftly as he could. His strokes peeled off sparkling sprays of iron filings. An ache awoke in his shoulder blades.

Towards noon, when Roundy still continued to reject occasional sharpened drills of his, which Juhl was deadsure were perfectly all right, and which he was sure his father would have approved of, Juhl decided to fix Roundy. Once, when Roundy's back was turned for a moment, Juhl with a wink at his neighbor Leary took two of his neighbor's finished star drills and replaced them with two of his own.

Sure enough, Roundy found fault with one of those Leary had sharpened, which before he'd accepted.

Leary cast Juhl an underdog's glittering look of sly satisfaction.

It made Juhl all the madder. Juhl lay aside his file and promptly reached over and put the rejected star drill back on the good pile.

A roar erupted from Roundy. "Hyarr!" He shouldered Juhl out of the way and with a grabbing motion threw the star drill back on the reject pile. "I'll decide what's good around here. Not you, punk."

Leary's face closed over.

Juhl said, "That's the trouble. Because Leary filed the one you rejected."

"What? How could he have."

"Because I exchanged a couple of his with mine when you weren't looking."

Roundy stuck his nose into Juhl's face. "So now it's tricks, is it? For that I can have you fired."

Juhl didn't budge. "Not with the old man short of blacksmiths, you ain't."

"Are you standing up to me?"

"What does it look like?"

Sons of Adam

Families are large out here, but the farms no longer require large families. Therefore, a goodly share of the seventeen year-olds leave for the cities, for the west and east coasts. They leave, however, after their ways of thinking, talking, living are pretty well set.

Pig-Butchering

. . . AS THEY GOT UP from the breakfast table Dad said "Red, you're helpin' me butcher today."

"But I was gonna—"

"But me no buts." Dad clapped on his blue woolen cap. "In fact you're gonna stick the pig today."

"But Dad—"

"Yeh I've noticed it already, that when it's time to butcher you always find some kind of excuse. It's always Albert that has to help me. Well, this time you're gonna do the sticking or my name ain't Fat John Engleking."

Red began to shake.

"You'll be getting married pretty soon and then you'll have to do your own butchering." Dad pulled open a cabinet drawer and got out his sticking knife and his flensing knife. "C'mon, let's agitate them rear legs of yours."

Dad led the way across the yard, waddling along with his great belly swinging on each step. They put up a pulley in the corncrib alley and then went out to the feedlot.

Dad called up the barrows. "Suu-boy! Suu-boy!" When the barrows didn't right away come running, Dad called again. "Pee-eg! Pee-eg!"

When all the barrows had piled into the feedlot, hairy ears and round rubbery snouts raised up, Dad pointed out the one he wanted, the very fattest barrow, a red one.

Red thought: "What a dirty trick. Calling up the pigs for food when he really means to kill one of them."

Dad climbed over the wooden fence, rope in hand. He pretended to be just walking through. When Dad got close to the barrow he wanted, he nimbly flipped a slipknot around its right rear leg and shagged it out through the gate and then pulled it toward the corncrib.

Red closed the feedlot gate behind them.

465

The red barrow squealed and ran on three legs as far as the rope would allow to the right, and squealed and ran on three legs as far as it could to the left.

Dad's big teeth were set tight together. "Go get the sticking knife. I put it there over on the wheelbarrow."

The newly honed edge of the knife glittered in the morning sun. Red picked it up by its wooden handle. He was so clumsy at it he almost let it slip out of his hand.

"Get over here now."

Red came over.

"Reach around under the pig and jerk his opposite leg out from under him. C'mon."

"Dad, I can't."

"What?"

"I can't do it. I just can't kill animals."

"Well! by God, then you are a sissy after all. Like I was suspecting all along. A momma's boy."

Tears began to film Red's eyes. The knife shimmered. It almost fell out of his hand again.

"Lord God in heaven. You're about as much use to me as a fifth tit on a cow."

"But Dad. You know I can't even kill a chicken."

"For catsake. Here I was hoping I'd raised me a man."

Red quivered. He loved his father and he had hoped that by working hard he could help his father pay off the mortgage on the farm. He'd even been a little slow about dating girls thinking that so long as he didn't get married he could stay home and work.

"Your younger brother Bert is twice the man you are. He don't flinch when it comes to sticking or cutting a pig."

"Bert and me are two different people."

"Grab that pig by the leg and tip'm over on his back!"

"I can't."

All of a sudden Dad dropped the rope and dove for the barrow. Dad's wide right hand shot under the barrow grabbed the off leg and quickly as if it were only a bundle of oats flipped the barrow over on its back. Dad held the barrow's front feet apart. Between set teeth Dad growled "Stick him!"

"Dad."

"Gott dammit, stick him!"

Red stared down at the underside of the barrow's chin. It was the only white spot on him. The barrow squealed so loud its tongue vibrated like a garter snake's. Red couldn't bear its utterly helpless look.

Dad grabbed the hand in which Red held the knife. "You're gonna stick that pig even if I have to take your hand and make you do it!" Dad's grip was powerful on Red's fingers over the knife. Dad's great bulk was so balled up with anger Dad almost rode up off the ground. "Now!" Dad guided Red's hand and knife for the white spot below the barrow's jaw. Stick him just ahead of where the

breast bone joins. Where it looks like he's talking. Stick it in. Deep!" The curved
point of the flashing knife went down. It made a crisping noise as it cut through
the white bristles. Then it sank in easy. Still between set teeth Dad snarled, "Now
twist the knife up and around a little to catch the aorta . . . ah! There."

Blood geysered up out of the barrow's slit throat. It gushed over Dad's
hand and Red's hand.

Dad let go of Red's hand. "All right. That's it. Now let him up so he can bleed
out while up on his feet."

With a twisting roll the red barrow struggled to its feet. It ran a few steps;
stopped. Blood spilled over its forefeet. It screamed wetly; lolled its head, finally
had to stand all straddled out on four feet to keep from falling. Blood spilled in
pulses from the rent in its throat. As the stream of blood slowly thinned the pig's
head lolled. It fought to keep from fainting. It coughed. Coughed. And collapsed.

Red went to wipe his nose with the back of his hand and then stopped. He
smelled the strange swamp stink of stiff bristles on his bloody hand. . . . The knife
dropped from Red's hand and clattered to the frozen ground.

Red hated Dad.

Dad let his big shoulders down. "Well. So. You've finally stuck your first
pig."

Red vomited his breakfast on the ground.

"Good. The next time it'll be easier for you."

Red wiped his mouth with the back of his clean left hand. "I hope you're
satisfied. That I'm a man now."

"Not quite. We still have to scald it in a barrel. And then scrape the hair off."

Two weeks later, after they'd butchered again with Red doing the sticking
and all the cutting Red looked up from his cup of coffee at breakfast. "Dad. I've
decided something. I'm getting to be too old to stay at home."

Dad held his cup halfway to his thick red lips. Dad's little pinky was lifted
like it was too good for the other fingers. Dad had on his little straw hat, something Ma had never been able to get him to remove in the house until he went
to bed. "So?"

Red Said, "So I thought I'd go get me a job somewhere and help you pay off
the mortgage on the farm."

Dad lowered his cup and set it in its saucer. Slowly he raised his blue eyes.
"Well now, that might not be such a bad idea. You're the oldest and'll probably inherit the place."

Red felt a funny gush of love for his father. If he could earn a couple of thousand dollars, and if Dad could have one good crop, together they could pay off
the debt on the quarter section. Then he'd have Dad won over at last. "You and
Bert can handle the farm, can't you?"

Ma's blue eyes were full of soft warmth. "Albert wants to buy that butcher
shop in town." Ma glanced at Bert sitting beside her. Ma favored Bert too. "Ha,
Albert?"

Bert had very white hair, already thinning at twenty-one, and he had a nose like the plucked tail of a chicken, a regular pope's nose. His white brows moved up his forehead. "Well, not right away, Ma. I can wait a year or two for that. It would be nice for you and Pa to own this place for a while without anything against it."

Dad threw Red a look. "Where will you go?"

Red tried to act like he knew exactly what he was doing. "I thought maybe I'd try the cities. They pay a dollar an hour in some places. There ain't a farmer around who can match that."

Dad's eyes opened wide and blue. "Where'd you ever get such a crazy idea, for catsake?"

"Been reading about it in the Sioux Falls paper."

Dad had himself a sip of coffee. The sun had just popped over the horizon, and it filled the wide kitchen with a sleepy pink glow. "Well, I guess you can easy catch a ride with some trucker to Sioux Falls."

Ma's eyes began to tear over. "My oldest boy John to leave the nest for the city."

Red said, "I'll be the same no matter where I live, Ma."

Dad nodded. "Working hard in some factory might just be the finishing off you need."

> *My dream was to write a history of Siouxland and environs from the year 1800 on to the day I die. Two hundred years. And there would be a long hallway of panels of all kinds: long novels, short novels, novellas, and poems and sketches and essays. So if you read the whole business you'd have a wonderful picture of the epic of the white man overrunning this land. That's really what it is. It's one book really that I'm writing, one huge, long book . . .*

> *Not only must the history be fairly accurate, and the description of the flora and fauna fairly precise, and the use of the language of the place and time beautiful, but the delineation of the people by way of characterization living and illuminating. It has long been my thought that a "place" finally selects the people who best reflect it, give it voice, and allow it to make a cultural contribution to the sum of all world culture under the sun. In fact, it is the sun beating on a certain place in a certain time that at last causes that place to flower into literature, the highest expression of intelligence (and not necessarily human intelligence).*

> *This is what I think [people] should find in the* Manfred Reader . . . *glimpses of this long hallway that I've been working on.*

SECTION FOUR
Leaves

FROM
No Fun on Sunday

I've thought about baseball a lot. It's a typical American game. In any given moment, one player . . . it's up to him whether the game's gonna be won or lost—short stop, or center field, or the pitcher, or the catcher, and so on. It's a highly individual game at that moment, but it's still a community effort together—unlike football and some of the other games. Football is in masses, moving here and there. But in baseball it's very individual, yet it's still a group effort at the same time. . . It's real invention. . . . And there's so many subtle things going on there. To be good, you have to not only have natural talent, but you have to be, what I call. . . not sneaky brains, but clever brains—how to outwit the other guy.

Home Field Rules

FINALLY SATURDAY THE FOURTEENTH of July came around.

All the farmers had finished cultivating their corn and their oat-fields still weren't quite ripe. Sweeps of gold had begun to show over the grain on the hills but down in the draws dark stippled green still prevailed.

John and family, and Sherm, left at twelve sharp. The game was to start at one o'clock at the fairgrounds, where a diamond had been laid out inside the race track oval. When the Bonnie team arrived, the Rock Falls team was already out taking infield practice and a fat tub of a man was hitting fungoes to the outfielders. Some fans had settled in the stands at the race track finish line.

As the Bonnie team sat on their plank bench, putting on their spiked shoes, they studied the other team. Sherm and Garrett in particular watched pitcher Dink Scholler warm up. Dink was one of those smiling fellows with a lazy sweeping motion.

Just before the game started, both John and Sherm were shocked to learn that Wild Bill Alfredson, who'd shown up late, was going to umpire the bases.

Garrett spotted it too. He walked over to talk to the manager of the Rock Falls team, Jim Albers. "I thought you told me you'd get two out-of-town umpires. That Wild Bill is a member of your Little Church, not?"

"Well, ya, he is." Jim Albers had a heavy red wattle. "But we couldn't get anybody else. So we had to take him. He was willing to do it for free."

John overheard what was said. "Ha," he snorted. "Wild Bill would, the minute he learned I was going to play. And the worst is, he'll be standing near the first base bag most of the game, right behind me, breathing fire and brimstone down my neck."

Lanky Alfred, Wild Bill's cousin, didn't like it either. "None of us Alfredsons have ever been able to get along with Wild Bill. When he gets his head fixed on something, it sets in as hard as cement."

Sherm had a question. "What about that umpire at home plate? He ain't an out-of-towner, is he?"

Garrett said, "That's Doc Maloney the dentist. He's okay. He gets more trade from Bonnie than he does from Rock Falls. He has a way of saying things that rub people the wrong way, but I like it."

Four of the Rock Falls church team were wearing baseball uniforms; the rest new blue overalls. All the Bonnie boys were wearing overalls, some of them not so new.

"Play ball!" Doc Maloney bawled from homeplate. "Battery for Rock Falls, Scholler and Albers; battery for Bonnie, Van Driel and Engleking! May the best team win!"

The couple dozen fans in the stands let go with a weak cheer. Two women fluttered lace-edged handkerchiefs.

For three innings there were no runners. Both pitchers were sharp.

Sherm struck out his first time up. He'd never run into a pitcher who threw slip pitches. The arm came around fast, but the ball seemed to dally on its way to the plate. The first time Sherm saw it he swung too early. When Sherm set himself to time the slower pitch, Dink Scholler fired a fast ball by him for the third strike.

The next three innings both sides got runners on base but couldn't drive them in. On his second time at bat Sherm punched out a single over first base on a fast ball.

Neither John nor Sherm could complain about a single one of Wild Bill Alfredson's calls. Wild Bill wore a light gray summer cap tipped back, revealing a high sloping forehead. His tight smile slit back into his cheeks, giving his chin the same slope as his forehead.

In the top of the ninth, with the score tied one to one, Sherm was first up. He decided to look for the slip pitch instead of the fast ball. Dink was bound to show it somewhere along the line. Sure enough, with the count one ball and one strike, there it was. Sherm held himself back as long as he could, then lashed into it. He lined a screamer just inside the third base line. The ball bounded all the way to the race track fence on the east end of the oval. Sherm ran with long elastic strides, and slid into third just head of the throw. Nobody out and a runner in scoring position.

Catcher Albers called time. He strolled out to the mound for a conference with Dink. The first baseman and the shortstop joined the two. There appeared to be some fumbling around with the baseball. The catcher gave the ball to the pitcher, and the pitcher shook his head and gave it back to the catcher, but after some vigorous talk the catcher gave it back to the pitcher. They'd only had one good ball to play with during the game so far, and by that time, the ninth inning, it was pretty well scuffed up and stained a tannish brown.

The catcher and the pitcher and the other two men finished their conference. All four returned to their position. Dink, who'd been smiling through the whole game, was now frowning, and had an uneasy air about him. He stared in for a sign. And stared in. Garrett, up to bat, waggled his bat menacingly. Sherm took a short lead off third. Dink slowly wound up, came to a complete stop, then suddenly fired at third. Wild throw. The ball sailed high over the third baseman's head.

Lanky Alfredson was coaching at third. He yelled, "Run, Sherm, run!"

Sherm ran.

As Sherm approached home plate, Albers the catcher threw off his mask. Albers smiled at Sherm, and extracted a baseball from his back pocket. He tagged Sherm. "Out!" everybody on the Rock Falls team cried. "Hurray!"

Albers pretended to be sorry. "You're out, Sherm. Because this is the real ball."

Garrett erupted in the batter's box. He whipped off his cap and slammed it to the ground. His bold pompadour hair seemed to lift. "What! Then what your pitcher Dink threw at your third baseman was not the ball in play. You can't win on a trick like that."

Within seconds, both teams were milling around home plate. Shouts. Curses. Roars. Waving fists.

"He's out!"

"He's safe!"

"He can't be!"

"He is!"

Finally Umpire Maloney stepped on home plate and waved his arms up and down. "All right, everybody, shut up!"

It quieted down.

At that point Wild Bill strolled over from where he'd been standing near first base.

Umpire Maloney pursed up his mobile lips, rolled his brown eyes heavenward as if he were giving it all one more review, and then rendered his decision. "I'm calling a balk on the pitcher. The runner is safe."

The faces of the Bonnie boys opened, and then they cheered loudly. And Sherm quickly tagged home plate to make sure he'd scored.

The Rock Falls boys groaned.

Wild Bill turned to confront Umpire Maloney. "What did you say?"

"Runner is safe. The pitcher committed a balk."

Wild Bill's slit smile cut back even deeper, sharpening the point of his chin and his nose. "How do you figger that?"

"The object thrown wild over the third baseman's head was not the ball in play. It was a potato. And a potato can never be a legitimate part of a baseball game. So the pitcher made a false move towards third."

Wild Bill turned white with rage. "You really are calling it a balk then?"

"Yes, I am. I'm the head umpire here and what I say is final."

"That's what you think." And before Umpire Maloney could defend himself, Wild Bill lifted a haymaker from his hips and caught Umpire Maloney with four farm knuckles on the chin. Umpire Maloney tumbled to the ground.

Wild Bill stared down at Umpire Maloney. "Now, that sure should've shook up your piles."

Umpire Maloney lay perfectly still.

"But what's more important," Wild Bill continued, "is that I say, the runner is out on the grounds of . . . let the buyer beware."

John moved in a step. "'Let the buyer beware?' What's that got to do with baseball?"

Words seethed out from between the teeth of Wild Bill. "Maloney may be the head umpire, but I'm the strongest umpire. So what I say goes."

Umpire Maloney came to. Slowly he got to his feet. Umpire Maloney looked around at the wild flushed faces circling him. "I want all of you to go back to your positions. Or to your bench, if that's where you belong. I want a private word with my fellow umpire. Okay?"

Gradually the players from both sides retreated a dozen steps.

Then speaking in a low voice which neither side could make out, Umpire Maloney whispered fiercely in Wild Bill's ear. The satanic smile cutting back into Wild Bill's cheeks didn't leave, but Wild Bill's feet turned him around, and slowly he headed back to his spot just off first base.

Sherm said low to John. "Wow! I wonder what he told him?"

Garrett snorted. "Probably reminded him of the big dentist bill he owed. That if he didn't shut up, he'd sic the sheriff after him to collect the bill." Garrett also had a private grudge against Wild Bill. It went back to the time when Wild Bill used to brag uptown how he'd seduced Garrett's sister up in the haymow while the rest of the family was in church.

"Whatever it was," Sherm said, "it sure worked."

"For now," Garrett said.

Loose-lipped Pete Haber with his thick sly eyes quietly slipped away from the Bonnie bunch and going around behind the backstop all the way beyond third base, retrieved the potato where it had rolled into deep grass. When Pete came back he gave it to John. John, with a smile, dropped it into his back pocket.

In the bottom of the ninth, two out, with a man on first, the Rock Falls cleanup man, Buster Broene, came to bat. Buster was a left-handed hitter and had the nickname of Wagontongue because of the huge homemade bat he swung. It looked like it might be forty inches long and in the meat part was as thick as a car piston.

Wild Bill couldn't resist making a comment. "If Wagontongue ever connects, pulls it low, look out. He'll take your head off, John."

John backed up a couple of steps. "I'm ready."

Garrett called time and strolled out to the mound for a conference. John, lanky Alfred, and Sherm gathered around Garrett and Van Driel.

Garrett said, "Van, old boy, think you can hold 'em?"

Van Driel flashed his rectangular smile and rolled his right arm around. "I think I got a couple more good pitches left in the old soupbone."

"I'd put Big Alfred here in. But I think Buster will have more trouble with your underhand rising ball on his fists than Alfred's soft curve."

"Hey," Alfred said, "I like that. If you need a hard curve from me, I can give you one." Alfred rolled his right arm around too. "That old I ain't."

Garrett said, "Slim, what do you say?"

John said, "Nope. You're the manager. One Alfredson mad at me is enough."

Garrett rolled the old scuffed-up brown ball around in his hand. Finally he placed the ball in Van Driel's hand. "All right, here goes nothing. We'll take a chance on you. Now remember. The strike zone is the width of the plate from the kneecap to the shoulders. So get that pitch in close to his Adam's apple."

Van Driel gritted his big white teeth. "He'll feel the wind of it under his chin."

"All right, let's get 'em."

Van Driel looked in for the signal; then, with a glance at the runner on first, wound up quickly, and snapped the ball towards home. To the horror of catcher Garrett, Van Driel's toe had slipped a little off the pitching rubber, and the ball headed straight for the center of the strike zone.

Buster Broene blinked, surprised to see the fat pitch coming where it was; recovered; swung mightily. There was a sickening sound. Out of the swing came a screaming line drive. And it almost did decapitate John. Then it climbed towards right field, rising, rising, where Pete Haber started to yell, "I got it, I got it." Of course Pete Haber wasn't within a mile of it.

The runner on first started to streak around the bases, second, third, and headed for home. Buster Broene followed close behind. The two men would be the tying and winning runs.

John woke up to the coming disaster. He stiffened. He absolutely couldn't have his brother-in-law Wild Bill crow over him. A mischievous smile broke across John's lips. He reached back into his handkerchief pocket and extracted the hot potato and yelled, "Garrett! Garrett! Here's the ball." And threw it.

Garrett, mask off, was already standing on home plate. His blue eyes widened; then he caught on. A grimace of sorts set on his lips. He hunched down, set himself for the catch. Then, potato caught and clutching it, he whirled and dove for the incoming sliding runner and tagged him on his shoes. In so doing he managed to block the plate.

Everyone expected Umpire Maloney to make a call. But Umpire Maloney didn't. He stood smiling, looking down at Garrett holding the potato, and at the runner.

Meanwhile the real baseball fell to earth. By chance it hit one of the fence posts in the railing around the race track and bounced back toward Pete Haber. Pete Haber slid to a stop, picked up the ball, whirled, and hurled it with all his might toward John. John leaped up and caught it; then he in turn hurled it towards home plate. Again Garrett set himself, all the while blocking the plate. The ball landed in Garrett's pud with a flat whacking sound. Then Garrett tagged the runner a second time.

Umpire Maloney rose on his toes, jerked his right thumb upward, roared, "The runner is out!"

"Hurray! We win! Two to one. Hurray hurrah!" The Bonnie boys jumped up and down in glee.

Men from the Rock Falls bench converged on Umpire Maloney, roaring, swearing, pushing, "What!! What!!"

Again Wild Bill advanced on Umpire Maloney.

Silence.

The Bonnie players ran up to see what was going to happen next.

Wild Bill's thin lips foamed over. His lips were drawn back so tight they'd turned white. Eyes slitted in rage, chin and brows more pointed, he looked more satanic than ever. "Did you call him out?"

"I did."

"But their catcher tagged him with a potato."

"I know. But he also tagged him with the ball."

"How come you didn't call this a balk too?"

"I couldn't. The pitcher threw the ball the way he was supposed to. And the batter hit it the way he was supposed to."

"But you can't tag a man out with a potato."

"I know."

"Well then?"

"He also tagged him out with the ball."

"But it was a trick again."

"I know. But the runner just lay there after he was tagged with the potato. He should have kept on trying to touch the plate. With his foot. Or with a hand. But since he didn't, and since the catcher has a right to protect the plate, and since the real ball finally showed up, he was tagged out."

"Tain't fair!"

"Besides, I've called him out. And an umpire never changes his mind. A call is a call."

"Well, we'll see about that. Because I'm gonna help you change your mind." Wild Bill cocked his hand near his hip.

Before Wild Bill could swing, John couldn't resist taunting him. "Well, Bill, how do you like them potatoes?"

"Why you! . . . Wild Bill turned and went after John instead. Again he cocked his hand near his belt.

Sherm couldn't let Wild Bill hit his brother. He dove for Wild Bill's ankles.

Wild Bill tried to step forward; couldn't; cursed, trying to step out of Sherm's hobbling embrace.

The Bonnie boys woke up, and first Garrett, then Van Driel, then hunching Pete Haber jumped on Wild Bill, bringing him down with a loud thump. Garrett settled on Wild Bill's right fist, Van Driel on his left fist, and Pete Haber squatted on his broad back. Wild Bill kicked up with his heels several times, but Sherm hung on. Wild Bill kept squirming and cursing and wriggling under the four bodies.

Umpire Maloney stood over them. Finally he said to Manager Albers of Rock Falls, "Maybe we better call the sheriff after all." He said it more down at Wild Bill than at Albers.

"Maybe we better."

After a moment, Wild Bill quit squirming.

Garrett said, "You had enough, Bill? Because if we have to, we can sit here on you all night."

Wild Bill muttered something into the chalky dust.

"Did you say yes?"

Silence.

Umpire Maloney said, "Let him up. And we can all go home." Wild Bill got up slowly, brushed off his clothes, cast those nearest him a glittering silverish look of hate, then stalked off to his car.

On the way home, John asked Sherm, "Where'd you ever get the idea of grabbing him around the ankles?"

"I learnt that at the Academy. I went out for football there, for one day, before Ma told me she wouldn't let me go out for sports."

"Well, at least that wasn't wasted on you. Besides your *amo, amas, amat.*"

Sherm laughed. "It's a case of where if love doesn't conquer all, a good tackle can do the job."

The Chokecherry Tree

The Carnival at No Place

ELOF STARTED TO PACK AGAIN.

Fats lay quietly smoking for a time. When Elof was almost finished Fats said, "Look, bo, I want to make a proposition."

"Talk on. But it won't do you any good."

"Okay. Look. I wasn't due in from The Bench till next Tuesday. But I finished up fast an' came on in because I wanted a little extra cash. A little extra cash for a little extra-special fun. That's where you come in."

"Go on."

"Well, there's a three-day carnival goin' on right now t'No Place, South Dakota. A carnival I ain't missed for years. It's in its third day an' it should really be wild by now. A whorin' hell of a time. Gamblin', car races, horse races, baseball tournaments, wild wimmen, circus, drinkin', fightin', bettin'—a hell of a whorin' time." Fats cleared his throat. " 'By God,' I says to myself down on The Bench there, 'by God, Fats ol' boy, there ain't no good reason why you should skip the carnival this year, is there?'"

Elof said nothing.

"You follow me, bo?"

"Go on."

"Well, that's where you an' me are goin'. I've got my check from Van Dam, an' we're ready to go."

"Huh. But where's my check?"

"You don't need it. I'm poppin' for it. It's all on me."

"Oh no, you're not."

"Oh yes, I am."

"You've popped for it too often for me."

"Look, bo, this is something I do every year. It's part a my blood. I was born near there. On the other side of No Place, between Avon and Dante, out Bon Homme way. So it's part a my life. An' invitin' you down there is like invitin' you home for supper. An', bo, you ain't aimin' to turn down a supper invite, are you?"

"Well . . ."

"C'mon, get your hair combed an' let's move." Fats got up and kicked Elof's suitcase under the bed. "Let's move. We've got a long ways to go before we get there."

Reluctantly Elof got up too. He asked, to get from where he was to where he could feel somewhat at ease accepting still another gift from Fats, "Where's this No Place of yours?"

"As the crow goes, about seventy miles southwest a here."

Elof stepped up to the mirror on the dresser, began combing his gold thatch. He pulled out yet another question to cover the awkward space. "Was selling down on The Bench easier'n out to Iota?"

"Some."

"By the way, how was the schoolteachers out that way, just as big?"

Fats chuckled. "I dunno. I didn't need any educatin' the past week."

Elof juggled his tie up tight, adjusted his white collar. "Now me, me, I needed some."

"Boy, you opened your mouth an' really said it." Fats goosed him sharply, and Elof jumped. "Now maybe we can promote you out of the kindergarten class."

As they were going down the stairs Elof said, putting on the belt-in-back gray jacket of his suit, "Now remember, Fats, I'm making this up to you someday."

"Forget it."

~

After a bit Elof began to warm up to the idea that fun was just ahead and, re- membering they might date some girls, decided to get out his pocketknife to pare his nails. In hunting around on his person for it, he found a dollar bill.

He stared at it a little while; then realized where it had come from.

He turned angrily on Fats. "You son of a seacook! Now why did you have to do that?"

Fats said nothing; drove on; swigged; drove on.

"You son of a gun. I knew there was something odd about the way you stum- bled against me back there."

Fats wheeled on.

"Look. I'm not going to take it." Elof tried to shove it into one of Fats's pockets.

Fats jabbed him with an elbow; then, freeing a hand from his driving, stuffed the bill into Elof's clothes again. "Bo, you're gettin' your tail over the line again."

"But why? Don't you understand people might not want to be given things?"

"I like the way you part your hair."

"Oh hell."

They swooped through the palm-up valley of Menno.

Another five miles, and Fats said, slowing the coupé, "Bo, I got high water. How about you?"

"Man, you hit it. My teeth are floating."

Fats stopped the car, and they got out on the same side and stood looking a moment at the open country, with the nearest farm home a mile away. Then turned away from each other, and stood buttock cheek to buttock cheek.

Elof trickled quietly. Weed pollen tickled his nose and he sneezed. He heard the faint brittle champing of insect claws in the undergrowth. In the striding forenoon sunlight, the shadows in the roots of the ironweeds were green-black.

An uneasy thought stung him: It ain't how big you are, it's what you do with yourself.

Behind him Fats hawked; spat.

Across the ditch spread a stubble field. Through it wriggled wheel tracks where hay racks had gone laden with grain. The wriggles reminded him of worm trails under long-lain boards.

Two pheasants, a multicolored male and a gray female, whooshed out of the stubbles across the fence, wing-wapping powerfully into the air, the male *uck-uck-ucking* angrily. They rose to a height of about ten feet, then stiffened their wings and became streaking monoplanes. In a moment they vanished beyond a knoll.

Elof jerked at the explosion of their flushing, and the usual gesture with which he finished his watering, a careful retreat into his trousers, was foregone this time. "Damned pheasants scared the hell out a me," he exclaimed.

"By God, me too," Fats said, turning around and, like Elof, buttoning up. "In fact, I think I wet my pants a little." Fats coughed. "Oh well, it'll be dry by the time we get there."

Elof laughed and got into the coupé.

Fats, puffing, got into the other side.

In a moment they were rolling again, tooling on, and sipping spiked coke.

On they went west. They cruised slowly through Olivet, through Tripp, and on.

They followed a dirt road.

Presently the road became heavy with traffic, mostly family cars filled with cheering children.

They came to a deep, tree-lined, dry-creek draw. They coasted into it in second gear; climbed out of it in low. Dust from the passing of previous cars hung high in the coulee.

Then the country began to change. It was bleaker. Except around the pastures, there were no fences. It was open to wind and man. There were scatterings of stones, of boulders, sometimes on the knolls, sometimes in the meadows.

The country rolled a little, rocking, just enough to break up the monotony of tableland, and on the tops of each swell, the horizons extended so far away into the haze of the muggy day that the earth and sky seemed continuous.

There were sudden tufted valleys, unseeable until Elof and Fats were upon them—the vacated beds of vanished and departed rivers.

"Where the heck is this No Place?" Elof asked finally, coughing in the dust stiving up behind the car ahead. "All we see is traffic, but no town."

"Bo, it's just a mile away."

Elof sat up. "That close? I don't see no steeples. No water towers."

"You won't either."

They rose on a prairie boss, and there, ahead and a little below, on a flat plain, where dust was rising to the sun, were herds of cars, and clusters of brown tents— some two stories high, one almost as big as a red butte—and two race tracks, and a diamond with a baseball game going on, and a joy-ride airplane warming up in a nearby grazestead.

"Is that the town?"

"Yeh." Fats laughed. "Yeh. Like I said, no steeples, no buildin's. An', no city fathers to bullox up the works with rules an' regulations. No curfew, no constables. Everything wide open."

"God."

"Yeh, bo. There's no stoppin' the human bein' when he wants fun. So every year they set up this town for three days, tents an' pasture streets, have their fun, an' then, flewt! it's all gone, an' everybody goes back home to work an' pray again."

"I'll be darned."

They stepped out, stretching stiff legs, putting away bottles, straightening clothes and ties, and looked around.

All about was merry sound. Children—naughty-eyed boys in overalls and proud slips of girls in pigtails and cotton prints—were whisking around cars, and licking ice-cream cones, and nibbling crackerjack. Farm and small-town wives were standing in bunches, and pulling corsets over burly buttocks, and sighing, and shrilling occasional laughter with breast pressed to breast in gossip, and waving autumn flies away with scented handkerchiefs. Older men, a philosophic foot to one side, calmly, some chewing tobacco and some snuss, heads down, eyes peering at eyes from underneath sunburnt brows, were talking bulls and boars and next year's mighty crops.

"Looks like an oversized threshers' picnic," Elof said.

"Yeh."

"But where are the frills you talked about? And the hot-shots juning them?"

"You'll see 'em," Fats said shortly, combing his sparse hair, wiping sweat from his flushed face with a snow-white kerchief. "You'll see 'em. They're down by the Midway tents there."

Elof and Fats picked their way through the mass of cars. Some of the cars were old and some new, some were black and some green, some were rain-rusted and some wax-shiny.

They walked at last into an open space filled with gangs of young folk heading for fun. Some of the gangs had stopped in to watch a baseball game: the All Nations nine—Sioux Indian and Negro and Chinee and Caucasian—against the Tennessee Rats—soft-spoken losers of syllables. Some had dropped in on an auto race: small streaking beetles brattling noisily on a smoking oval track.

Elof and Fats at last came to the entrance to the temporary Midway. They paid a dollar (Elof using the one Fats had thrust on him in Free Men) and strolled inside.

And then Elof saw the gay ones, girls exactly like the chickens he and Cor and Wilbur had chased in Amen, and youths like himself. Light tripping bird-talk tweeted all around, and sometimes a girl shrilled protest and flounced a dress. Color rioted in the agitated swarm: cherry red and orange dawn, and sunburnt brown and reindeer brown and water blue.

Fats said, nudging Elof, "Pretty nice, huh?"

"'S wunnerful."

They legged it slowly down a fifty-foot-wide improvised street. To either side concession boys had set up stands, and barkers and hawkers were singing and howling and waving the people in to see the human freaks, and to spend pennies in the arcades, and to gallop on the mounts in the merry-go-rounds, and to take the airplane spins, and to try their luck in the shooting galleries, and to spike their mixes in the drinking lean-tos—everything to excite the human blood.

They passed a funhouse. Two girls in blue voile and shoulderlength bobs, twins, with thick lips stretched in violent screaming joy, came flying out of an exit. Air holes beneath their feet had blown up fierce blusts under their dresses; had prettily exposed naked thigh and tufted pubic triangle.

Elof and Fats saw two couples lightly loving in an open space.

Fats stopped. "Look at the bums them gals got. I'm of half a mind to bust it up an' give them gals a break."

Elof studied a moment. "The gals are nice, but I'm afraid them bums got a little too much muscle."

Fats continued to stare and to growl disapprovingly. "Bums!" He shook his head. "Them poor gals."

They ambled on.

Dust swirled, hanging lazily in the air, glinting.

Fats puffed; mopped his face. Elof took off his coat; hung it over an arm.

Fats drew Elof over to a beer-and-burger stand. Fats said, "Two both ways."

Elof demurred a little again.

Fats said, "Shut up."

A flushed hand-over-fist proprietor shouted at a cook in white who was over a sizzling open-air stove, "Two beer burgs!"

They ate, wolfing noisily, gulping. They looked; listened.

As they stepped away, Fats paying, Elof saw something glint in the trampled grass. He reached down, brushed away a broken tuft half covering it, thinking the glint but a tinfoil cigar band. It was a dime.

"Hey, look," Elof said. "Look what I found."

Fats stopped. "Huh. Bo, that's a sign. This is gonna be yer lucky day." He handed Elof a cigarette, took one himself, lighted up both.

"Could be." Elof stared at the shining silver in the palm of his square hand; then reached it out to Fats. "Here's part payment for that beer and burg I just had."

"Don't be a dumb bastard."

"What do you want me to do then, save it for a rainy day?"

"You're still talkin' dumb."

"Well, suppose you was in my boots, what would you do with it?"

"I'd take a chance on it. Gamble it."

"Where?"

Fats's eyes half closed. "Bo, I just got me an idea. Follow me."

Fats led him to a lot fronted by a huge sign:

THE TEMPLE OF POWER!

TEST YOUR STRENGTH!!

BING THE BINGER!!!

A DIME WILL GET YOU A DOLLAR!!!

Behind the sign, the lot was filled with big-armed young bucks, with admiring ladies-for-the-day on their arms, all milling about a contraption that looked like an oversized scale. It was a bell binger.

"Here," Fats said. "Here, let's try this."

They pushed into the crowd, got to the front line. Some protested the sudden shoving.

Fats said, "An' watch close. There's a reason why they lose a dime. Or make a dollar."

Elof gave the machine a quick frisking look. It stood about fourteen feet tall. At its top was a nickel bell. Below, at its base, was a platform, a two-by-two affair, which, if hit with a sledge hammer, kicked a metal object up a groove. If the platform was hit exactly right, the metal went high enough to bing the bell. A dime gave you three tries at the bell. One hit returned you the dime, two gave you a quarter, and three brought you a full round silver dollar. What particularly caught Elof's eye were the names printed along the groove, each marking a level of attainment. At the bottom was Morgan, next came du Pont, then Ford, then Capone, and, going up, near the top, where the goods were more good than bad, were Sinclair Lewis, Thomas Benton, Gershwin, and Henry Wallace, with Einstein at the very top. But the bell itself had no grade marked on it.

Elof asked—there was a lull for the moment in the business—

"What's it when you hit the bell?"

The snuss-chewing harkee-proprietor leaned a long sly look into Elof. "Brother, then you're in a world by yourself."

Guffaws burbled up around in the crowd. One silly tittered.

The harkee said, "You want to give it a try?"

"No."

The harkee said, "Oh, a wise guy, huh? Well, back up there then. An' let another man try it. Back. Back."

Elof let himself be pushed a little.

But Fats held against the shoving. "Just a minute, bo," Fats whispered in Elof's ear. "When the next bo steps up, watch how he does it. There's a trick to it."

Presently a buffalo-heavy farmer decided to give it a try. He spat in his hands.

Self-conscious, blushing a bit, he swung with a great sweat-flying effort. But it was no go. He failed to raise the binger more than a foot or two from its resting place.

Fats said, jolting Elof with an elbow, "See how it's done now?"

"No."

"Look, bo, give a good look. See how low that platform's built? See? When a guy hits it, he hits it with the edge of the sledge, not with its flat. Like so." Illustrating, Fats pounded a fist into the flat of his hand.

Elof said, "If you know so much about it, why don't you risk your dime?"

Fats hardened. "Bo, bo, who's needin' the money?"

"Well, yeh."

"Get on it then, bo."

Elof watched the buffalo swing again, saw instantly that Fats might be right. The man's power was too high off the ground.

"Get on it, bo. Get on it."

Elof held for a moment; then let go. "Okay. What the hell. It's only ten cents." He paged through his pockets; found the dime.

Elof stepped forward. "Here. I'll give it a try."

The man's chewing jaw stopped; his hard blue gimlet eyes flickered. He glanced at Elof's strong stubby body. He took the dime.

Elof tried a half-dozen sledges for weight; found one he liked; stepped up.

"Ready?"

"Ready."

Elof planted his feet far apart. He lifted the sledge slowly above his head, to a full long stretch. Then, with muscle-gathering power, he came down with a crouching stroke. The sledge landed with a flat solid smack. And miraculously, the binger shot to the top. *Bing!* The clustering crowd cheered. The harkee shouted, waving an arm, "There's his dime!" Again Elof swung. Again the miracle. *Bing!* "There's his two bits!" Once more. Whish. *Bing!* This time the harkee was a little sick. But he made a quick recovery. "You see, ladies an' gents? See how it's done? Three bings an' you get a big round silver dollar. Even the little squirts can do it."

Elof took the dollar.

Fats chuckled. "Bo, this is your lucky day all right." He patted Elof. "Now try it again."

"Oh no, he don't," the harkee said, "oh no, he don't. Only one chance for everybody."

They left, with a dozen blowing buffaloes wrestling for the next chance at the bell binger.

Outside the Temple of Power, Elof reached out the dollar to Fats.

"Keep it."

"But no. I owe it you."

"Let's first see if it'll double itself. Then you can pay me an' still be ahead."

They idled down the Midway, Fats grading the fillies, Elof fingering his riches.

They came upon a small zoo. A man was shouting. They stopped to listen.

"Everybody this way. Evvv-rybody. Come see the zebra with thirteen stripes around his belly and one around his Peter hand me down that rope."

Roars of coarse mirth boomed up around them.

Then they came upon another golden opportunity.

A sign bugled:

THE TEMPLE OF CHANCE

WHERE DIMES MAKE DOLLARS
WHERE DOLLARS MAKE TENNERS
WHERE TENNERS MAKE MILLIONS

"Ah," Fats said, "ah, here we are."

Elof held back. "Don't you think we've pressed our luck far enough?"

"Bo, I got a hunch. An', bo, when I get hunches, money comes in bunches."

They stepped inside a huge brown tent with a trampled grass floor. There was merriment, and the sound of jerking levers, and the sound of clicking wheels, and, occasionally, the sound of rattling coin.

"Slot machines," Elof said.

"Sure. One-armed bandits."

"Robbery."

"Sure. But sometimes in your favor."

"Nah," Elof said.

"Yeh," Fats said.

They watched a man punching half dollars into a machine, watched him trip the lever, watched him bite a mustached lip, watched him lose.

"Nah," Elof said.

"Yeh," Fats said.

"Well, which one then?"

"Wait. Let's size around a little first."

They mingled with the sweat-smelling crowd: farmers, small town bankers, small-town barbers, and hard-line women. To give it all a happy-go-lucky air, the machines had been given names: Kentucky Derby, World Series, Luck-in-Love, Pot-o'-Gold, At-the-Foot-of-the-Rainbow, Fox-and-Geese. Some had dime, some had half-dollar, some had dollar slots.

Then Fats's hand was firm on Elof's arm. "Look, bo," Fats whispered, "look. I've been watchin' that Marriage Machine there an' I figure its about time."

Elof put in, "My God, what a name for it."

"Yeh, I know. Look, I been watchin' that Marriage Machine there, an' I counted forty bucks goin' in, an' only five comin' out. Bo, that machine is about ripe to poop a jackpot. Get on it with your buck."

"A buck? A whole dollar?"

"Yeh."

"No. I'd rather pay back what I owe you."

"Get on it."

Reluctantly Elof let Fats push him up behind a man playing it.

The man dropped a silver dollar into a slot, shoved it in, jerked a crank. Three narrow drums, a section of their edges appearing in a gaudily colored panel, started whirling side by side. On the drums, at regular intervals, were pictures of fruit: a cherry, a peach, a date, a prune, a lemon, a crab apple. Three cherries brought fifty bucks' three peaches twenty-five, three dates ten. Any combination of the three brought sums all the way down to two dollars. However, any combination in which a prune or a lemon or a crab apple appeared automatically lost the player his dollar.

At last the man, a pool-hall shark, gave up. "Christ Almighty anyway. Stuck seven unlucky devils in there an' didn't raise a twitch."

An attendant, dressed in gray, shook his head in pretended commiseration.

Fats shoved Elof into position.

"Wait," Elof protested, "not so fast. Let me see what I'm gettin' into first."

"Just a lot of luck. Just a lot of luck. That's all."

"You hope."

"Bo, I got that hunch."

"If you say so, okay."

Elof shoved in his dollar; jerked the crank; stepped back; watched the drums.

At first the drums whirled so fast the fruits were all blurred together. Then the one on the left clicked and stopped and showed a date.

"Ah," Fats grunted.

The middle one clicked and showed a date.

"Ah," Fats coughed.

The third one clicked and showed a date.

"Ah hah," Fats chortled. "Three times an' out. Out she comes."

There was a whirl, a sliding of metal on metal, a click, a jangling, and then a little door at the bottom of the Marriage Machine opened up and ejaculated a handful of big round silver dollars. A rattling jackpot.

Dumfounded, Elof picked them up, counted ten.

"Lucky bastard," the man who had just lost seven in it muttered, "an' now I suppose you'll walk away without playin' more.

"Mister," Fats said, "there ain't no point in pushin' luck, is there?"

"But I play these things for fun," the man said, "not to make a lucky stab an' run."

"I suppose you think it ain't fun to pick up ten bucks. C'mon, Elof, let's vamoose."

Stepping out in the hot sticky sun again, with people pressing around, Elof reached out one of the ten silver dollars to Fats. "Here, darn you, this time you've got to take it."

"Keep it."

Elof grabbed Fats roughly and dropped it into Fats's pocket.

Fats made a protesting move.

"No, no," Elof growled, "don't you dare give it back. Or for once I'll slug you."

Fats said, "Oh, I want that buck back from you all right. But I was thinkin' it might earn you another ten."

Elof retreated rapidly. "Now, now," he said, "I've played my luck far enough now."

"Bo, I'm still gettin' them messages. Hunches. Better play 'em." Fats in turn dropped the dollar into Elof's pocket.

"Please."

"Nope. Don't want it."

"Please."

Fats smiled a little and, taking Elof in tow again, stalked down the milling Midway.

They came upon a long tent. A banner read:

LOVE PALACE
DANCING AND DRINKS
BEAUTIFUL GIRLS
MUSIC AND ROMANCE

Elof said, "I suppose you want me to try that?"

"Nope. No money in it. But lots of grief. I wouldn't give you a plugged nickel for your chance a gettin' out a there without catchin' a dose."

Finally they were at the end of the wide Midway and were directly in front of a huge temporary gate. High over the entrance, like an arch of triumph, soared five-foot block lettering:

THE TEMPLE OF SPEED

Below it, a black etching against the bronze-blue sky, was the metal silhouette of a magnificent horse caught at the top of a gallop.

"Ah," Fats said, "a hoss strip. Playin' the ponies should really give you beginner's luck."

"Nah."

"Yeh."

"Nah."

"Big money in it, bo."

"Big sorrow in it too."

"Not if you know how. Look, bo, you kin play the ponies two ways. If you got lots a cash, play the sure-fires. If you got only a little, play the long shots."

"Fats, really, I don't think I—"

Fats placed sudden lean claws on Elof's arm. "Bo, just got another message. A hot hunch. Money in a bunch. Bo, walk in an' grab yourself a hundred."

"What? Again?" Elof wailed.

"Bo, walk in."

Bowing, Elof meekly went in under the arch of hoss triumph.

A temporary grandstand had been built at the stretch end of the bull-ring track. The track was a mile-and-a-quarter run.

Elof sensed instantly that here he was among a different kind of people. There were fewer farmers, more small-town men. And sprinkled among them, like pepper in white batter, were professional racing addicts: jockeys and stable-men and trainers and clockers, tip-slingers and dopesters, blind stabbers and track owls, railbirds, slip snatchers, horse lice, and fixers—all the mink-eyed worshipers of sudden fortune.

Fats led the way through the dust millers; got a racing form; studied it, frown-ing. Elof stood wondering at it all.

A man wearing tan clothes and dung-spattered boots came along.

Fats hailed him. "Got a minute, buddy?"

"Yeh." The man halted. He carried a whip which he cracked playfully against his legs. "What can I do you for?"

Fats held out the racing form. "What race're they in now?"

"They've just finished the tenth."

"Ah. Then the next is the big race of the day."

"Right."

"Who's the favorite?"

"Hamlet will lead the field down the stretch."

"What about Arabia Deserta? Heard a guy say he's a real monarch."

"Naw. That's a Doughty hoss. An' Doughty hosses ain't proved theirsel's yet. Naw, Arabia Deserta's an outside long shot."

"What about Anonymous?"

"A filly. A sprinter. Makes a fast start an' a slow finish."

"Does, huh?"

"Yeh."

"Well, thanks for the tip."

"That's okay."

The man passed on.

Fats studied some more, still frowning.

A little weasel of a man, wearing a burnt-out cigar in the corner of his brown-rimmed mouth, came up, winking, wagging. He held his narrow face to one side, as if the pose helped him get a better look at life. "Who you bettin' on in the eleventh, boys?"

Fats drew back his ear. "Heard Canterb'ry Tales had plenty of run in him."

"Naw."

"What about Tom Jones?"

"Naw. Doesn't quite have it."

Fats glanced at his form. "Faerie Queen?"

"Dead meat."

"Who, then?"

The burnt-out cigar jiggled between the weasel's brown lips.

"Moby Dick. That's the hot hide. That's the well-sugared nose. Bet on him, boys. I got it right from the hoss's mouth hisself."

"Thanks."

"Uh-huh."

The little blinker passed on.

The feverish eyes in the crowd began to work on Elof. He reached for the racing form. "Give me a look."

"Just let me handle this, bo."

"But I—"

"Bo, just got another message. It's Beowulf. Pays ten to one. Bet your ten an' you can go home with a C-note. One hundred fish."

"Or no fish at all."

"Bo, that message was strong. Beowulf, the imported stallion, is a cinch. Post position lucky seven. Man, you can't miss. Give, an' I'll dump your wad at the mute window where it'll do the most good."

Anguished, yet unable to stop himself, Elof lifted the ten silver dollars out of his pockets and dropped them into Fats's lean claws.

"Ah, now you're in the bucks."

Together they shoved through the thousand-elbowed crowd milling in front of the pari-mutuel window. Fats put the ten across through the wicket.

"Now let's get down to the saddlin' barn an' have a look at him. We got a minute or two before they begin."

Arriving in the tent barn, they were directed to Beowulf's stall by a blond stableboy. Elof and Fats stepped up close. Before them, on straw bedding, pranced a bridled and saddled black stallion, sleek, coat shining, alert, with 7 as its marking.

Fats nodded. "Hmmm. Just look at that. A sight for sore eyes. A winner if I ever saw one."

Elof blinked; tried to see what Fats was seeing.

A groom came up. He was a softhearted lank. "Like him?"

Fats coughed. "Like him? Hell, he's just gonna make us rich, is all."

The groom nodded. "He's been a little restless, though. I just came down now to walk him a little."

"What's wrong with him?"

The groom said nothing.

The groom went into the stall cautiously. "Whoa, boy, whoa. Easy, boy, easy. There." The groom took Beowulf by the bridle and led him out. The stallion whinnied.

"Whoa, boy."

Elof and Fats backed up. Other horses, also being saddled and readied for the next race, raised a little stir.

"Whoa, boy."

The groom led Beowulf down a wide clean alley. Just as they passed a filly, also being readied in a stall, with 11 as its marking, Beowulf rumbled out a low whinny. The groom cursed soft, led Beowulf the other way.

"What filly is that?" Fats asked sharply.

"Anonymous." The groom flicked his deer-brown eyes at her bitterly.

"Cripes."

Elof asked, "Now what?"

"Don't you see? We've just bet on a horse that's fallen in love. He just got one whiff of that filly an' he dropped his rod. He ain't got his mind on runnin'."

"That's right," the groom agreed.

"Will he be scratched?" Fats asked.

"No."

"Will the filly?"

"No." The groom looked down sadly. "No, the concession boys need the money."

"Don't they know she's in heat?"

"The concession boys need the money."

"My God in heaven! There goes Elof's little fish."

The groom looked down.

"Cripes." Fats kicked at a mound of wet horse droppings, scattering them into brown bits.

The groom said, "You might have a chance if the jock'll get him started ahead of her. Beowulf here is seven an'll be closer to the rail."

"Has the jock been told?"

"Yes. I told him."

"Good. Because otherwise, once Beowulf gets his nose at her rump, she'll beat him by a length no matter what the other beetles do."

"Yeh."

Then the jockey came to get Beowulf for the parade to the post, and Fats and Elof left.

On the way across the grounds Fats rented a pair of field glasses.

They had taken but a half-dozen steps toward the track when a loud-speaker awakened and an ear-brasting voice announced, "THE HORSES ARE AT THE POST!"

Shouts, roars, whistles went up. Swarms of legs and arms thickened at the rail ahead.

By dint of vigorous wriggling, Elof opening up a hole and Fats following and widening it, they got to the rail. Elof climbed up on the bottom board, raised himself to see.

The horses, fifteen of them, entered in a fairly orderly manner. Only Beowulf moved uneasily. All were mounted by rump-in-the-air jockeys. Red and white and blue, silks and rayons—the array was a colorful mass of pulsing hair and bone.

The crowd hushed. All eyes became tense.

A bell rang. Gates opened.

"THERE THEY GO!" the loud-speaker cheered.

There was a pound of hoofs on soft earth, and sudden rising clouds of dust, and horse legs streaking past, and glossy necks stretching, and jockeys hopping high, and then a tower of dust blurred them and they were gone.

"AROUND THE CLUBHOUSE TURN. IT'S BEOWULF IN FRONT BY A LENGTH. ANONYMOUS IS SECOND. ARABIA DESERTA IS THIRD BY A NECK. DAWN IN BRITAIN IS FOURTH BY HALF A LENGTH."

"Wow!" Elof shouted.

"AT THE QUARTER. BEOWULF BY A LENGTH AND A HALF. ANONY-MOUS IS SECOND. ARABIA DESERTA THIRD. THEN IT'S DAWN IN BRITAIN. CANTERB'RY TALES. HAMLET. LEAVES O' GRASS. TOM JONES. KING LEAR. MOBY DICK. FAERIE QUEEN."

"Wow!" Elof yelled.

Fats, looking through the glasses, frowned. "Wish that damned filly would drop back a little." He handed the glasses to Elof.

"Here, you take a look."

"AT THE HALFWAY MARK. BEOWULF IS IN FRONT BY ONE LENGTH. ANONYMOUS MOVING UP ON THE OUTSIDE. ARABIA DESERTA THIRD. DAWN IN BRITAIN FOURTH."

"Still leading!" Elof shouted, waving his speckled hand wildly, his eyes googling into the glasses, his hair a throw of gold. "Good old Beowulf!"

Fats growled, "She'll bullox it up. Just so that jock keeps Beowulf's nose ahead of her."

Suddenly there was a commotion in the crowd. Exclamations of surprise. Elof, too, gulked. "My God!" Elof gasped.

"What? What?" Fats demanded, grabbing Elof's arm.

"Something screwy . . . I dunno . . . Beowulf, he—"

"Here, let me look," Fats said, grabbing the glasses from Elof.

Fats adjusted the glasses, glared through them. "Holy smokes!" Fats exclaimed. "That goddamned Beowulf's turned around an's swung in behind the filly." Fats gave the adjusting screw on the glasses another slight turn. "Yessir. That's just what he did. An' now he's got his nose stuck up her behind like a hand in a glove."

"AT THE THIRD-QUARTER MARK. ANONYMOUS BY A LENGTH. BE-OWULF SECOND. ARABIA DESERTA AND DAWN IN BRITAIN NECK AND NECK AND MOVING UP. HAMLET. CANTERB'RY TALES. LEAVES O' GRASS. KING LEAR. MOBY DICK. FAERIE QUEEN. TOM JONES."

"That goddamned Beowulf."

"Oh," Elof said.

"That goddamned Beowulf." Fats spat over the rail onto the track. "That filly better not make a sudden stop or he'll have the honor a bein' the first beetle to start a race a cinch winner an' wind up a foal."

"THERE THEY COME INTO THE STRETCH. ARABIA DESERTA AND

DAWN IN BRITAIN NOSING AHEAD AND STILL NECK AND NECK. CAN-
TERB'RY TALES. HAMLET. LEAVES O' GRASS. ANONYMOUS. BEOWULF.
KING LEAR. TOM JONES. MOBY DICK. FAERIE QUEEN."

Sadly Elof watched the thoroughbreds come in. The leaders could be distinctly seen, neck out, ears flicking, eyes bugging. The rest were partially obscured by a rolling mass of bursting dust. But not obscured enough to hide the
strange antics of Anonymous and Beowulf. With his nose still tucked up under
her tail, they came rolling along in a paired gallop, eight hoofs hitting the turf
in unison.

Fats glared at the ground, chewing his teeth.

Screams, screeches, shrills, shouts rilled out above the roar mounting from
the massing crowd.

"IT'S DAWN IN BRITAIN BY A NOSE! THEN ARABIA DESERTA! THEN
CANTERB'RY TALES! AND HERE COMES HAMLET! AND LEAVES O'
GRASS! WITH FAERIE QUEEN MOVING UP STRONG FOR THE NEXT
SPOT! KING LEAR! TOM JONES! MOBY DICK! ANONYMOUS! BEOWULF!"

Then all was swallowed up by the brulling sounds of victory. An unknown
had won. And another unknown had taken second. Long shots. Doughty sta-
blemates. Monarchs.

Elof and Fats were having a bite to eat at the beer-and-burger stand.

Between munches Fats muttered, "It's always a mistake to run fillies in
with stallions. Whether they're in heat or not." Fats cleared his throat. "Unless
you want colts."

Elof said nothing.

"Damned stallion. Those concession boys were absolutely nuts."

Elof took another bite.

"An' what a slowpoke that filly was. Even with Beowulf's nose shoved up her
seat, she still couldn't do better than come in second t'last." Fats bit viciously
into his burger; swigged some beer. "Her jock sure come in with a lapful a horse
that time."

Elof still made no comment.

"Played wink with him all the way."

Elof burrowed silently into his burger.

Fats wiped his pallor-and-purple face with a white kerchief. "That damned
Beowulf. That damned hay-burner. That oatsgrinder. That bangtail. Playin' last-
couple-out with a filly."

Elof cleared his throat, said, "Oh, shut up."

Fats did.

The happy lark was over.

I spent about a year reading Doughty's Travels in Arabia Deserta. *He made his life in Arabia so real to me that often, as I walk around the yard, or wake in the night, I feel profoundly lonesome for Arabia . . . .*

He felt that the English Language had become bitched, that Spenser and Chaucer, not Shakespeare, were the titans, the natural fathers of our litera-ture. He said they wrote and spoke the richer language because they kept close to the original roots of the Angles, Saxons and Frisians. Well, anyway, after you catch onto his charming uses of odd words, and his peculiar rhythms, he is a titan himself.

Green Earth

Kisses

FREE WAS IN BED about an hour when he remembered he hadn't kissed Pa and Ma good night. He flipped back the sheet and in his B.V.D.s went downstairs. Pa had his feet in the open window to cool them off and was having a last cup of coffee, and Ma was darning some socks under the sharp gas lamp. Ma was nearest and Free kissed her first, "Good night, Ma," and then went over and kissed Pa on the whiskers near the corner of his mouth where it was moist, "Good night, Pa."

Free thought they acted kind of strange, but went back upstairs to bed and thought nothing more of it.

He had some trouble finding the right spot to curl up in. He tossed and turned back and forth several times. On one of his turns he bounced a little too hard and the mattress collapsed under him and there was a loud slam on the floor below the bed. Darn. One of the slats had slipped out again. Good thing the pot was under the other bed.

Groaning, he slipped under the bed and pushed the slat back in place.

Albert woke up. "What's going on around here."

"Flip, you guys must've been rousing around when you went to bed. That middle slat slid out again." The kids lately had given Albert the nickname of Flip. He had a funny way of flipping over in sleep sometimes, sudden-like, and still not waking up.

Flip said nothing.

Free climbed back in bed.

Free must've napped. Because for a second he didn't know where he was. He followed his thoughts about for a time, one thing after another, about Fredrika and her bossy ways, about Wilma and her velvet belly, about Johnny and his snow geese.

After a while it came to him he'd forgotten to kiss Pa and Ma when he went to bed that night.

At least he couldn't remember that he had.

He went back over the evening. Nope, he couldn't remember that he had. It was the night before last that he'd gotten out of bed late and had gone down and kissed them.

After a while, sure that he'd forgotten again, he got out of bed and on bare feet went downstairs. Pa had his feet in the open window to cool them off and was having a last cup of coffee and Ma was darning some socks under the sharp light.

Free kissed Ma first. "Good night, Ma."

Ma smiled funny at him. "Good night, boy."

Free next went over and kissed Pa. "Good night, Pa."

And Pa said, "Goodness, son, what have you done? This is the third time you've come downstairs to kiss us good night."

Free was dumbfounded. "Maybe I fell asleep so fast I forgot."

"Three times, son?"

Free blushed. That night at the table he'd read the last half of Chapter 26, from Matthew, where three times Peter had denied he knew Jesus of Galilee. "I know not that man," and immediately the cock had crowed.

"It's all right, boy," Ma said. "You might not have kissed us at all. At least you're not mad at us."

Free looked down at the floor. He wondered what was wrong that he should have forgotten he'd kissed them twice before. It was kind of like denying them all right. "I'm sorry."

Ma smiled. "Kisses from one's own boy a mother can never have enough of."

Free went back to bed.

Apostle Peter had gone outside to weep bitterly. Free himself didn't quite feel the need to go outside to weep, certainly not bitterly. But he sure felt sheepish.

This Is the Year

The Land Sermon

BUT EVEN BEFORE Pier could get halfway across the field, the wind began to brush up swiftly. By the time he reached the foot of Red Bluff, directly cater-corner across the field from the yard, his horses were walking in whirlwinds of dust.

He glanced back. The soil the disk churned up was not as dark with moisture as other years. The earth was drying to its core.

At the end, he turned around, started back. The two halves of the disk, constantly grinding against each other, like two stubborn iron onions, cut and sliced and tossed the earth about. The disk groaned and squealed.

The horses bucked into the tailing wind. Their manes flowed with brown dust. They snorted. They lowered their heads to the ground. They wavered, drifted off from the straight rows.

Glimpsing past the edge of his mackinaw, Pier guided them as best he could. The track of his previous crossing was already erased by the whisseling southwest wind.

Lips burned from the dryness. The nose stung from the uprush of gritty air. Sharp bits of sand ground between the eyelids and eyeball.

Then he saw it; an unbelievable thing.

On from the west came great clouds of dust, rising from the far slopes of the earth. They boiled up like thousands of mountain-high, madly growing mushrooms. The dusky heavens blackened. The whole earth went into an uproar, exploding skyward, throwing chunks of dirt and humus into the air. It rushed toward him. Titanic winds shoved. The mass of brown-black harrowing horror droned toward him.

He stopped on the crest of the rise, stood up against the wind to have a look around. With swelling breath and widened eyes, and stiffened body, he watched the black destruction drive toward his yard. He saw Nertha come out on the walk, look up, look around, run back into the house. A second later the brown deluge of dust enveloped the entire farm.

The end of the world was coming toward him. It rushed up the inclining hill. Toward him came a turmoil that was the unraveling edge of the world. In a moment he would fall off into an endless black void, into the deeps of the universe below. The earth was vanishing. Unraveling.

He stared upward. He looked up so sharply his Adam's apple hurt. The massive wall was rising beyond the heavens. It was sweeping the stars out of the skies. Its height was so overpowering that Pier had impulses to vomit. His misery, his feeling of abysmal insignificance, was turning him inside out.

He swallowed, gripped himself. Quickly he turned the horses around, away from the wind. They whirled readily. They fluttered nostrils, whinnied. They lowered their heads, waited.

Pier drew his mackinaw collar up over his head, waited too. He drew out his red handkerchief, wet it with spit. He tied it around his nose. He cowered inside his clothes, hovering.

Strange bluish-green lights played about the disk. When Pier accidentally touched steel he got a shock. The air became charged with electricity; sparkled as if it were full of flying fireflies.

Warm yet chilling wind rushed up underneath him. In a wink of an eye the levers before him vanished. Streams of black dust poured around him, upon him, into him. It tried to choke him, throttle him. Furies tore at his coat.

He huddled. Miserably he clung to his seat. He feared the gale might even be strong enough to throw the heavy iron disk around. He trembled. Never before had he seen such a horror of whirling chaos.

The mighty storm lashed. It struck him. It smashed at him. It blasted the earth around him. It geysered loess thousands of feet into vanishing heights above. It struck, struck, struck. Once more and again. Ever and anon it beat upon him and blasted him and beat upon him.

He nodded. It was the Âlde Han at last. Ae, and this time He would get him, strangle him. He didn't have a chance to survive. Clinging to his steel seat, holding on, his head down, his face deep in his mackinaw, his mind raced around in his skull. It milled with thoughts. He pondered on life, on what he had done so far.

He had been born, he had grown up. He had eaten, he had dunged.

He had pushed his father off his shoulders. He had bred and raised a son, who, in turn, was getting ready to push him off his shoulders.

Ae, there wasn't much to be proud of. It was a poor accounting.

Ae, life was like grass. It grew in the spring, it greened in the summer, it grayed in the fall, it rotted in the winter; and, the next spring, it made room for the new grass.

Ae, and now he was dying in the middle of a land that had gone crazy, that had lost all reason, that had lost all sense.

The storm brulled; bombommed.

He waited. He was sure he was being buried alive.

He waited an hour.

He waited two hours. He choked. He coughed up muddy spittle. Sometimes, through the tossing lines, he could feel the horses stirring in the brown dark ahead. He dared not open his eyes to look.

Corn leaves cut at his back. Cornstalks swapt him. Weeds whipped him. Bits of flying clods pelted him. An old weathered corn ear hit him.

And then something heavy and big hit him. It bounced against his head, rolled over his shoulder, fell into his huddled lap. It snuggled against his chest. It was as soft as a puppy, as slim as a cat.

Pier opened his eyes cautiously, wonderingly. What strange creature was seeking haven in his arms? He stared. Meek ears long on its neck, bloody eyes blinded, a lonesome wild jack rabbit lay trembling in his cradling arms.

At last, just as Blacktail's modern-day siren shrilled up from Starum, the storm began to abate. The sound of the noon-hour siren was like the scraping of tin on steel.

The wind lay down. Slowly the revolving air stilled. Gradually the air cleared a little.

Pier opened his eyes to mere slits. He saw the levers again. Beyond stood the horses, slouched on two legs. The gray horses shook their heads, snorted.

Pier moved. He rolled his shoulders slowly, loosening the numbness in his arms, his hands, his finger tips. He turned on the steel seat, awakening the muscles in his thighs, his calves, his toe tips. He stirred. Dust spilled off his shoulders. He took off his cap. It showered puffs of dust into his eyes. Dust poured out of his gray-red hair.

Pier looked around. All about lay drifted banks of dust, sand dunes. What had once been a field of dead cornstalks was now a shifting desert. Behind, where two hours before his disk had cut out a crissing pattern in the soil, there was not the faintest trace of his going.

Coughing, he headed the horses home, into the dying wind. He cradled the lonesome jack rabbit.

He drove down the lane, turned past the woodshed.

He saw that the chimney was dead. He sat upright. He stopped the horses, stepped off, gently laid the tamed rabbit in the door of the woodshed, ran into the kitchen. "Nertha!"

No answer.

"Nertha girl!"

Still no answer.

Agonized, he ran through the dust-carpeted rooms. They were empty.

He rushed outside, searching through the brown, eerie, noon-hour dusk.

Dust dunes rippled, billowed everywhere.

He ran around the south side of the house. He stumbled. In the riding dust it was difficult to see just where the floating air began and the rising earth ended. He gasped. A great mounding immane pile of dust reached to the eaves of the house, fully fourteen feet high. Terrified, he ran the other way, past the box elder. Again his feet beat into soft, flour-fine streams of billowing dust drifts. He saw that the privy had vanished, and the pump beneath the windmill, and the fences beside it.

Crying, he stumbled across the yard to the barn.

When he jerked open the door, the cows lowed at him. The aged trotters, Queen and Daise, neighed.

He jumped inside. He stared at the cattle, the calves, the horses. Each had been masked with wet bits of sack. For a second he was sure Teo had stayed home from school to save the animals.

Something rustled in a corner. He looked around, wild-eyed. There, seated against the wall, with a sack serving as a wimple over her face, her green eyes staring, sat Nertha.

He started toward her. "Nertha?"

She looked.

"Woman," he murmured, "girl. Good girl."

Nertha gathered herself to her feet, stood up. Dust cascaded from her shoulders. "Pier?"

He nodded. "Yes, girl."

"I was worried, Pier."

He swallowed. "You're a good girl, Nertha." He waved at the cattle.

She looked down, fumbled with her clothes, stood on one foot. "I dunno. I was thinkin' . . . Maybe instead I should a gone to church like everybody else did. Edna. Gert. An' left everything in the hands a God."

"Church?"

"Yes. But then, I knew you'd be mad if I didn't try to save the animals first."

"Do you mean to say they had church this morning? In town?"

"Sure. I didn't tell you, but yesterday, after all those dry days they decided to have a special prayer day for rain. Domeny Beckstrom said he'd come down an' pray God. Central gave a gen'ral ring on the phone."

Pier cracked a laugh. "Huh. No wonder the Lord was mad today."

Nertha's eyes crossed at the blasphemy.

Pier patted her shoulder. "Never you worry, girl. What you did today was the best prayer ever prayed, church or no church."

He nodded to himself. He could see the church full of solemn, stunned farmers. Beside them would be cowed wives. In the dusky, glowering interior the only thing alive would be the gleam of mothers' fleshy teats as they gave suck to their babies. He patted her again. "They talk about rain making. Wal, if what you did today don't scare up a rain out a the sky, then I don't know the last of it."

She said nothing, looked down, fooled with her clothes.

Pier became aware of a stillness about. He looked up, listened. It was as if an enormous cave were opening, were about to sigh, about to cough.

It became stock-still.

A noise scurried toward them. It grew. It roared. It bellowed.

The barn shook. The beams cracked. The stanchions and the cows jostled each other.

There was a sucking sound; then a crashing upon the earth.

Pier ran to a window. He brushed away the cobwebs. "Why, the old mill's fell down. Why."

Beyond, barely discernible, stood the four horses still hitched to the disk, lonely, heads down, manes drooping, tails to the wind. They had turned around by themselves.

～

The dry, hot spring droned on. Creeks dried. Tarns dried. Weeds in the fenny blew away. Stiving dust billowed up from the chapped soils. Wells filled with dust. Subsurface lakes vanished. Bark peeled from the willows in the slough.

All through April the dust storms rode. For twenty-two consecutive days the skies were inflamed with red, smoke-gray dusts.

Highway maintenance crews, like bugs startled up from overturned logs, scurried out of sheds with their snowplows to clear the roads of dust drifts.

May came; the hottest May ever recorded. Temperatures held steady in the hundreds. Not a film of moisture appeared in the sky. The few clouds born in the Rockies vanished the moment they appeared on the plains. Tough tornadic wind squalls skinned the land of its humus fell.

Disease crept into the scaly skin. Vermin crawled in it. Chinch bugs thrived in the dying carcass of the old lady earth.

The days of June swirled by, puffs of wind, blasts of heat. The sandy soils dried, became loose. The clay soils cracked, became cement. Sandy loams, silt loams, clay loams shriveled beneath the burning skies.

The greens died.

The weeds pumped furiously. They sucked loess for water, found dust instead. Presently they fell slack, grayed.

The trees thrust stalwart arms into the sky, thrust powerful sucking hoses into the earth, deep, down to the subsoils, into the fundament. But they died too. The waters of the old lady had passed away.

The tame animals were helpless. Long ago they had surrendered to man their deed to life. They awaited his wisdom. He would see them through.

The cows waited, chewed air for cud.

The horses whinnied, grew thin, fluttered nostrils.

The pigs rooted deep into the dust for wet roots.

The chickens chased flying specks of soil.

Still the dust came on. Columns of it reached from the very floor of the earth into the ceiling of heaven itself, from the fundament to the nostrils of the sun.

The wind was a sweeper. It stroked a great broom across the wide walk of the prairie earth. When the walk was moist, the skies were glass-clear; when the walk was dry, the sun choked.

People suffered. Colds, whooping cough, pleurisy, dust pneumonia, tuberculosis, milk leg, ravaged them. Coughs bent their bodies into snapping hoops. Fevers wrinkled their brows.

At last July came; came hot, came wet. When it came hot, it killed horses and men. When it came wet, it fried.

The hardy corn that had survived the shriveling dry days burned now too. Pastures blew up. Haylands scabbed.

At last the blinded plainsman had nothing left but a high wind and a bone-dry soil.

Birds flew away.

The bewildered robin hesitated on a gray post east of the woodshed. Stunned, half blinded by the dust, it looked around, hopped down to peck at a wormlike twig. Then, with a fluttering of sandfrayed wings, it drove off for the moist airs of Wisconsin.

The swallow, returning to its mud hut in the hog barn, found it gone. It hovered near where its nest had once clung to an upright. It banked and fluttered over uneasy, rooting pigs. Then suddenly it saw. The mud nest, drying, had fallen off. The swallow screamed, dived down, shot up. The pigs were tearing her nest and her young to shreds.

The sparrow sat stunned in the bare limbs of the orchard. It huddled and drew in its neck and dropped gray dung and flew off.

The crows built nests out of scraps of barbwire.

The hummingbird vanished.

The meadow lark sang with the harsh craking accents of a blackbird.

The redwing cried.

The motherly old soil, bound to the ball of the earth, could not protest at the clumsy love-making. Breasts flung out, arms wide, black nubile thighs bare to the sun, it could do nothing but suffer man his pleasure.

And the wild animals suffered.

The badger, eater of gophers and mice and beetle and snakes, burrowed deeper into the hide of the earth.

The cottontail and jack rabbit, nibbler of the bark of young trees, and of grass and red clover and vegetables, thirsted and starved.

The fox and the coyote, killer of rabbits and poultry, became more crafty.

The mink, devourer of grubs and frogs and lizards and eggs and fish, ran to the north country.

The mole, ravager of roots and worms, dug deep.

The muskrat died when the water plants died.

The weasel was the only one who fattened for a time: chirking crickets and yellow-bellied grasshoppers, hatching by the billions, provided him with an abundance of sweet white meat.

Slowly the rivers of dust unraveled the black skin of the woman. Slowly she paled and sickened. Yellow-head hilltops pimpled her tawny-black hide.

Old Dreamer Pederson, doing his few chores on his five-acre plot overlooking the Mounds near Blood Run Creek to the south, nodded. "Fools! Let them go to a church to hear their soothsayers, let them go to their salvers to close over the mouths of their wounds. They wouldn't listen to the hard-iron facts of a friend. Oh no. Fools."

Pederson went to the woodpile. He hacked at a log until it fell in half, split into quarters, into eighths. Despite the dusk of a dusty evening, and his old age, the old man's keen eyes and sharp-edged ax hit exactly in the center of the wood each time. "Fools. What's one going to do with these children? They won't look around. They won't see what's happened, even if it's right under their noses. How is one to get them to worship the true God in the great cathedral of the outdoors? The fools."

He looked up; he had caught himself talking. He glanced sheepishly around to make sure he was alone, that no one had heard him.

He carried the wood to his one-story farmhouse. He entered, dropped the wood into the fuel box by the stove. He looked at his watch, decided he had time to feed the chickens before he started the stove for supper.

He wiped sweat off his thin forehead. His thin blue shirt was soaked. He pushed back his tan cap, rolled up his sleeves. In the unseasonably warm March, chopping was hot, hard work.

He went outdoors. He scooped up a pail of grain from a feedbin north of the chicken house. He scattered the golden manna over the yard. Fluttering pullets, old gray hens, red-combed cocky roosters, followed after. He was a Joseph feeding his tribe.

"Fools," he thought bitterly, "fools. If they'd only listen. Give an ear to brasstack facts."

He nodded. "But that's the way it goes. The memory of the people is short. As fleeting as a breath."

He nodded. "Well, they got what they deserved. Dug their own grave. They can lay in it too. Poverty. Drought. Disease. Eroded hills. They sucked the land of its riches, gambled madly, gave no heed to the warnings, hardly noticed the first shock in 1911, the second in 1921, the third last year. Well, they got what they had coming. Over forty per cent of them renters now. With most of the rest so heavily mortgaged they're worse off than the renters."

He scattered another handful of grain. Hens followed. "Fools. And so now they have to hire a domeny to pray God for rain. Fools. God isn't that literal. God isn't that cheap that he follows man-made rules and regulations, that he heeds the man-made Laws of Nature. Fools."

Pederson asked, holding aloft his arm, scattering grain to the twolegged creatures, "Huh, if they wanted to hear sermons, why didn't they listen to mine? I talked to them plenty. I gave them beatitudes."

He stood still. "What a sermon I could give them now, if they'd ask me. What a sermon. I'd blister their backsides."

He stood, thinking. "And why not? I feel as ordained to preach on the ways of man on this earth, and his sinning, as any domeny living today. Yessir."

Once more he looked around to make sure he was alone. And then, though he realized he was probably a little senile to be talking alone by himself, he started in. His feelings, his thoughts, his words would out. He had a sermon to say. And he had to say it.

"Well, first, I'd read them a passage out of the scripture as I know it. I would read to them out of the Gospel as lived by the Lion of the Great Alone.

"'And the Lion of the Great Alone, the Almighty Lion of Chaos, blinked, and It looked casually at the earth, and It saw impersonally the miserable evidences of man's handiwork. And seeing, and being revolted thereby, It left man to his fate.'

"Yes, so I would read the text of my sermon.

"And then I'd preach. In parables.

"As follows:

"'After a time, man crossed a mountain and came to a valley. There he found a dusky woman of exceeding beauty and worth. And he fell in love with her, became enamored of her. And he took her, possessed her, and made her his own.

"'And after a time he discovered that the woman he had taken to his breast was a sister, and a wife, and a mother to him.

"'As his sister she played games with him, hunted and swam and fished with him.

"'As his wife, she gave him fruits: corn, wheat, grapes, honey, milk.

"'As his mother, she gave him shelter. In her he built mounds and crept into the womb of them and sheltered his bare limbs from the winter chills. He did this as the Mound Builder of ancient times, as the terp builder in Europe, as the sod-hut maker on the plains of America. And elsewhere.

"'But man, being part fool at heart, a restless wanderer, worked her to death. And she, aging prematurely, and wrinkling, became a creature despised in his eyes, and he sickened of her, and climbed another mountain, going west, and found a new valley. And again he discovered a lovely dusky woman. And her too he made his own.

"'But, once more, this new woman he slaved, worked to death and she aged too soon, and he sickened of her, became tired of woman, and deserted her. He climbed still another mountain, going west, and discovered still another valley and a new woman.

"'Always he found new valleys, and new lovely dusky women. And always he overworked them, and always they aged.

"'And man, the fool, never learned. Never. Always he put the blame on the woman, always he claimed that it wasn't his fault she made a poor mate.'"

Pederson waved his arm, scattering grain.

An old hen at his feet, lifting her red-combed head, and staring at him with beady eyes, craked. "Ae, ae, ae, ae, ae, how it hurts me."

"But actually, the old lady, she's all right. It's only that she's been mistreated.

Treat a woman right and she'll treat you right. Mistreat her and she'll miscarry; even leave you. She is human, palpable, friable. She is made of the same stuff man is.

"Man is born of the earth and the earth is born of man. All the chemicals, all the ingredients, all the parts that are to be found in man's body are to be found in hers.

"The soil breathes. Its nostrils are the plants and the trees and the animals and man.

"The soil digests. It digests even more efficiently than man's alimentary canal. Throw iron into it, or steel, or even radium, and the old lady will decompose it, digest it.

"The soil has blood. As long as she keeps her skin, the waters flowing under it will bring to all plants and trees and man all the nutrients they need.

"Man, the fool, has been reckless with his wife. He has behaved foolishly on her breasts and her thighs. Here in America he is losing her, will lose her, has already lost half of her.

"When he came through the mountain passes of Pennsylvania and Virginia and Georgia, he found an innocent black virgin. He saw convexes and concaves of rich humus flowing endlessly away to the horizon. Grass was blowing in the virgin's sleepy, slumbrous eyes.

"Snorting, excited, nervous, he attacked her with his ax. He ripped her. He tore her up with his plow.

"And she, a true woman, suffered it meekly. She waited for him to learn, to become the lover."

Pederson waved a hand, spread his fingers, threw grain.

The old gray hen, scratching, first with her left yellow leg while balancing on her right, then with her right yellow leg while balancing on her left, ahead, back, craked, "Ae, ae, ae, ae, ae, how it hurts me."

The old man led on, a Jacob wrestling with the Lion of the Great Alone, lifting his voice. "But man never did learn, never at last considered her a mate. Always, and ever on, he ripped her, he raped her; he misused her, he abused her.

"And finally, of course, the woman could stand it no longer. She reacted violently, had convulsions, had hiccups, tossed her fleshes to the skies.

"And she sickened. And her skin peeled from her.

"And then into the bayous, into the deltas, into the bottoms of the seas, flowed her tissues, her skins. Her dark nubile fleshes, once so lovely in the Indian moonlight, were gone forever.

"She was too good. The thousands of years she spent preparing herself for the mating, for the love-making, for the bearing, were spilled away in a few short years. And by an oaf who laughed at her efforts, at her nest-making."

The old man stopped. He gazed through the red evening shadows, at the Hills of the Lord to the southwest. He sorrowed. "O sister, O wife, O mother. How I remember thee. How I recall thy greatnesses, now gone, thy soil swelling when the rains fell, and holding it all in thy breasts against the dry days.

"But he raped thee, and now thy enemy, and his, the impersonal Lion of the Great Alone in the skies, is tearing off thy dark humus robe. The black blizzards rage, the coarse floods roar."

It became dark on the yard. Night came on.

"Fool. Such a fool.

"Man assumes that the soil is eternal.

"It is not.

"The old lady, like man, is only a tiny creature in the vast outspread of chaos. And the endlessly undulating stretches of outspread chaos care not a snap of the fingers, not a whit, for either. Whether she or he thrives does not interest chaos. His dying, her dying, will not disturb it, affect it, will not contort chaos into cosmos, or wreck cosmos into chaos.

"Thus, if man values his life at all, he must learn to love her. If he does not, if he does not replace the clothing he takes from her, if he does not protect her, the eagle-winged winds of the Wild will carry her away.

"The old lady is mortal. Like man, she has been dying ever since birth. Always and ever, in the running out of eternity, she is losing her oceanic pastures to the winds, to the swamps, to the seas, slowly exposing her bones, slowly uncovering her ribs to the rotting airs."

A flock of wild geese, lost, going south, flew over. The whisseling of their whipping wings was near.

"Chilly little laboratory technicians take comfort in the belief that before the rivers and the winds can completely unravel the hills and the fertile valleys, the globe will have contorted itself and have sprung forth new continents from the seas, boosting them out of the swamp waters like dinosaurs rising up dripping.

"Huh. By the time the earth ball gets around to bulging new muscles out of her birth waters, it will have been too late for man. By that time the generations of man will have been unraveled too.

"To save in his own lifetime what is still left of her, what is still good of her, man must hurry. He must haste to cover her with soft green clothes again."

[This Is the Year] *deals exactly with the tragedy of what happens when man tries to love the soil in a wild, chaotic, unreasoning way. Pier did have some elements in him that might have led to a wise love of the land, but he was handicapped by what he had been handed from his father. Knopf thought there was too much horror in it. Exactly. That is the terrible consequence of what happens when the soil and man do not become loving and working partners. (As a matter of fact, I am rather shocked to think that I wrote a 'shocking' book. To me it was a passionate avowal of my love for the land, it was a stirring, eloquent book, full of exalted poetry. That is, to me.)*

Prime Fathers

from In Memoriam: Sinclair Lewis

MUCH HAS BEEN MADE OF the fact that Red Lewis the man and Sinclair Lewis the artist were lonely. Much has also been made of the theory that the American artist is lonely in America.

In the case of Lewis we know he was lonely, incredibly lonely. He was so lonely in the beginning that he left his Minnesota home to seek the fleshpots of the cities in the East and in Europe; he was so lonely in his middle years that he came back to America and bought and sold more homes in various sections of America than is ordinarily permitted even the most privileged of men in this our accidentally most privileged of nations; he was so lonely in his last years that he consciously or unconsciously began to seek out his origins as a child of the Western Civilization by sojourning in its older cultures.

And Lewis *was* lonely. When you met him you instantly felt compassion for him. Not because he lacked vigor or strength or selfhelp, but because he had too much of these things. His eyes, his face, his hands, all seemed to cry for affection, for simple love between men and men. And when you smiled at him, or indicated that you had some sense of his worth to you both as friend and as artist, he almost broke his back, yea, gave the shirt off his back even, to be good to you.

Up to a point. Because it wasn't long before Lewis' natural wary instincts warned him he might be endangering both himself and his livelihood by keeping his hand open too long. He knew history, that it is full of instances of betrayal, where Joseph's brothers turn on Joseph, where Saul turns on David, where Judas turns on Christ, where Sparta turns on Athens, where Brutus turns on Caesar, where Anthony turns on still another Caesar, where, in Lewis's own field, a friend turns on Edgar Allen Poe and forever leaves a blight on Poe's great fair name, where, in the realm of human brotherhood, Englishman and Russian and American and Spaniard and Frenchman and Italian, turn on each other with bared and knifesharp teeth of destruction. Red Lewis knew.

It is the old story of everybody wanting to be the king—except the king. Men create kings. Either passively or actively. We are all brothers, yes. But we are more. Living apart and separate in this fragile sack of skin, we are insecure, both as individuals and as brothers. And, in addition, we are all busy making a living, getting a subsistence at least, keeping the sack of skin hale and hearty if possible. And these two, insecurity and hunger, cause us, first to need, and then to hope, and then to seek a Something or a Someone who will Save Us, as we say, who will Protect Us, who will Love Us. And since there is no more obvious a combination of both Power and Mind known to man than what man finds in himself, man exalts these two aspects of himself and attributes these exalted aspects to some one man and makes him King. Some people choose kings by breeding, some by lot, some by vote. In any case, King someone has to be and King someone is.

Some men, because of the heredity handed down to them, either by their father's hand or by their father's genes, have more energy, or more mental excellence, or more will power, or better organization of their parts—whatever it is— and it is these upon whom the bloodbirth, the lot, the vote falls. The Call to Kingship comes. And off they must go to live beneath the Golden Bough.

It is no accident that Christ was and still is called both the Son of Man and the Son of God. And it is no accident either that we are not afraid of that part of Christ which we call the Son of Man and that we fear that part of him which we call the Son of God. Thus it is that He must be of us as well as apart from us—at the same time.

Men not only need this kingship, they also use it. Because it is power: power to bring food, power to get clothing, power to provide shelter, power to acquire comfort, yes, even power to obtain second-rate kingships. Thus men seek the favor of the King, not so much because they love him as the Son of Man, which they may, but more because they need him as the Son of God.

Now he who has been chosen to be the Son of God as well as the Son of Man, knows this, knows that they seek help from the image that they have read into him. And Sinclair Lewis as the artist king knew this. And Sinclair Lewis as the world artist king, not just the American artist king, knew this.

The American artist isn't the only lonely artist king. Artists, writers, have been lonely the world over, have been lonely in every culture known to man. Can you name one great artist who felt at home in his culture? Homer? Read Plato's notion of what the artist should mean to his society. Virgil? Read his *Georgics.* Dante? Read his homesick laments. Goethe? Read his *Faust.* Cervantes? Read his *Don Quixote.* Camoens? Read his *The Lusiad.* Shakespeare? Read *Hamlet* or *King Lear.* Tolstoi? Read the tracts he wrote after he quit writing novels. Mann? Read *Der Zauberberg.* As artists, as kings, they have all been homesick for a home. And it is with pity that one looks at the Expatriates who think they have to go to the Left Bank in Gay Paree, or to Eternal Rome, to find their home— where they meet Parisian artists or Roman artists who have to go to America now to find their "home."

But, and ah! this is it—is there a home for the Son of Man in man? Possibly. Just possibly. And it is this part of the King, the Son of Man, who should stay, if possible, near the place of his birth, near his fleshly roots. Because then at least a part of the King's ravenous hunger will be appeased. Which may keep him from becoming a despot. Which may give us a chance as neighbors to see that he remains "safe for us."

It is to the eternal credit of the manhood, and of the artist, in Sinclair Lewis that he tried, most of his life, to live in the country he was born in.

We stand here, then, looking down upon the still warm ashes of this brave and once eager warrior, this once powerful greatheart. We speak the words. And as we speak, we know that lofty words will not bring Red Lewis back, nor increase by a whit the height of his stature as a man, nor bring him a step nearer heaven, nor endear him the more in the eyes of a God in heaven. Lofty words will not touch him, nor change him, nor gladden him. He is now insensitive to anything we might do for him, or say of him, or demand of him. Mortal concerns are all out of his hands.

His course is run. His log is written. And it needs only the work of reading the log to know how well or how poorly he captained his craft across life's serene seas and tumultuous oceans.

What we have left, then, is us, and our sense of loss. Thus, really, we are addressing ourselves.

We speak because we must speak to each other. We speak for *our* comfort, not his. Looking down at these his warm ashes it is as if we are reaching ahead to realize our own deaths, What will It be like? now while we are still alive, as if, to make our deaths meaningful to ourselves, we are experiencing it in symbol, in magic identification, while we are still sentient.

We are like them who have seen a great comet, yea, a great star flash across the skies. While it cut its great saffron arc we had little to say, really. Most of us were speechless. Because our thoughts hadn't, couldn't, form, much less rise.

But now the star is gone. And even as the vapor trails are fading from view, vanishing, and its ashes are still warm at our feet, we turn to each other in amazement and begin to speak of the wondrous passing thing, and each of us brings forward his little comment, his little observation of what he thinks he saw.

Some will belittle what they saw. They will compare themselves with what he was and they will see their own shortcomings and they will seek to deny such shortcomings. Some will indulge in excessive eulogy, and forget that the real Red Lewis was mortal and human and as full of error and sin as any man. They will erase the error and fill in so as to make it seem that the whole was errorless—as was done in the case of Dickens and Hawthorne, and many another.

And some will try to forget that he ever lived. Many of them will speak out of hate, or, perhaps, only out of deep hurt. And, perhaps, that is to be expected. Afterall, when you light a hot fire there is always someone who will complain of the warmth. And even someone who will complain of having been burnt because he happened to stand too close. But, ah! for those of us who stood afar off, we speak of the light we saw and how it helped us.

Why did Red Lewis write as he did? Why couldn't he have written more sweetly, more comfortingly? Why? The psychiatrist or the analyst may perhaps tell you that it was some unresolved hurt or some unsatisfied hunger suffered in youth, yea, even in babyhood before the time of remembered consciousness, some lack that festered long enough to have invested his whole personality, which harried and drove him to get psychic justice. The man of God may perhaps say that it was some hidden or inward or deep sense of guilt or sin in his conscience that drove him on. And so on. The critic, the social worker, the lawyer, the doctor, the politician, the relative, the friend, all will have their particular theories. And, in a sense, all may be right.

For myself, since I am a simple man, I have only a simple opinion. I like to think that he wrote what he did because somewhere sometime there leaped into focus in Red two simultaneous visions, or knowledges, or insights: one, of the way things ought to be; two, of the way things were. Red Lewis was an honest man. And a man who loved justice. Thus when he saw the vast, the awful, gulf that lay between the two knowledges, he was outraged, and a fire started in him that never went out, that harried him until he gave in to it and he had to take up pen and paper.

Where these knowledges come from I can't say. Nor to my knowledge and to my satisfaction (and I have attentively searched both the blood in my veins and the ink on pages, both my heart and the scriptures) has any one else been able to explain their origins. So far all we know is that they are there and that a few of us have them consciously enough to exercise ourselves about it. Perhaps, maybe, possibly, we may someday know the mystery of the origin of these knowledges.

It is these knowledges that cause men to take up medicine, the ministry, law, artistry, social work, palmistry, to take up all those many and varied missions which cause us to say of one: he has heard The Call.

Red heard The Call too. Not to preach, or to admonish in particular, or to hurl unctuous maxims and hellfire anathemas at us. But The Call to lift a light, a lamp, so that the rest of us could clear away the lies, the deceit, the sloth, the sins of omission and of commission that beset us as humans. And not only that. But also to lift the light so that we could see what it meant to be human. Red wanted us to be active. Red believed that in action there was humanity. Red held up a flame to illuminate our way a little distance at the same time that he goaded us, even seared some of us, into action. Until we saw.

This is the charge then: do not, while you are admiring the vapor trails fading in the firmament, while you are lamenting these his ashes still warm at our feet, do not forget that Red Lewis was human and mortal and errorful; do not forget that lights eventually burn out; do not forget that someone must leap forward to grab up the torch or else much that was human shall have been lost to darkness. And do not forget that anyone of you, and all of you, are candidate torchbearers.

About the Editor

John Calvin Rezmerski is Writer-in-Residence at Gustavus Adolphus College, St. Peter, Minnesota, where he has taught English since 1967. *Held for Questioning,* his first book of poems, won the Devins Award in 1969. Since then he has published three other collections of poems. His poetry and nonfiction have appeared in many magazines and anthologies, and he has edited several periodicals and anthologies.

Along with Frederick Manfred and several other writers brought together by Robert Bly, he was a founding member of the Minnesota Writers' Publishing House. During the 1970s Rezmerski organized and led Minnesota Poetry Outloud, taking groups of poets (including Frederick Manfred) to small towns for performances of poetry and music. During the 1980s, he expanded his writing activities to include instructional video, radio documentary, dramatic film, journalism and public relations. In 1993, he collaborated with a troupe of performers to present *Chin Music and Dirty Sermons,* three 30-minute programs of poetry, stories and music in live-radio format, issued on cassette tape.

Recipient of a National Endowment for the Arts fellowship, he has also won the Rhysling Award of the Science Fiction Poetry Association. A Minnesota Private College Research Foundation grant underwritten by the Blandin Foundation supported much of the work on *The Frederick Manfred Reader.*

A member of Heartland Storytellers, Rezmerski includes adaptations of several Manfred stories in his storytelling repertoire.